P9-AGU-212

SHANGHAI
Christopher New

BANTAM BOOKS
TORONTO • NEW YORK • LONDON • SYDNEY • AUCKLAND

This low-priced Bantam Book
has been completely reset in a type face
designed for easy reading, and was printed
from new plates. It contains the complete
text of the original hard-cover edition.
NOT ONE WORD HAS BEEN OMITTED.

SHANGHAI

A Bantam Book / published by arrangement with Summit Books

PRINTING HISTORY
Summit edition published May 1985
Bantam edition / June 1986

ISBN 0-553-25781-1

Published simultaneously in the United States and Canada

PRINTED IN THE UNITED STATES OF AMERICA

KR   0 9 8 7 6 5 4 3 2 1

PART ONE

1

It must have been the change in the ship's motion that woke him, the roll of the open sea giving way to calm of the estuary. Propping himself up on his elbow, Denton looked out of the port-hole, through which the scuttle was channelling warm, moist air onto his face. It was dawn. He could see a pink flush in the sky, and across the smooth, still-dark, oily water he could make out the dim shape of land, a low, smudged bar of earth darker and more solid than the sea.

The other passengers in the crowded cabin were still snoring and sighing in their sleep. Dressing quickly and stealthily to avoid waking them, he made his way up to the lower deck. The sun had risen over the horizon already when he reached it, and the banks of the river, clear and distinct now, were closing in on the ship. The pilot was just climbing aboard; his launch, pouring black smoke from its sooty grey funnel, was curling away to a cluster of tumble-down grey stone buildings on the bank. The water was a yellowish muddy colour, its opaque surface glittering under the long slanting rays of the sun.

For more than an hour Denton leant over the stern, watching the level countryside slip placidly past: vivid green squares of paddy fields, tall thick bamboo groves, squat stone and mud villages, little shrines with curled, tiled roofs glistening in the rising heat of the sun. Everywhere there were narrow overgrown ditches lacing the fields, their torpid waters gleaming through the green. The villages looked still and empty, not even a dog barking, but the fields were alive and full, men and women standing knee-deep in the paddy, legs spread, backs bent double, as they groped in the mud for the rice seedlings. They all wore wide straw hats with shallow conical crowns, the browny-yellow brims spreading out over their shoulders. Under each brim, black, braided queues swung down, men and women alike. Occasionally the peasants slowly straightened their backs, looked incuriously up at the liner steaming remotely past, then bowed to their work again.

Now and then Denton saw water buffalo plodding through the mud of the few unplanted fields, or ambling along the banks between them. Grey and slimy from the water, they were prodded on by half-naked children with pointed sticks, who kept shouting out strange shrill cries. Some of the children waved at the boat, grinning or making faces. *So this is China,* he kept thinking, half-awed. *So this is China.*

Then Everett joined him. "We've passed the Woosung forts, then?" he asked, his freckled fists gripping the rail beside Denton.

"Woosung forts?"

"Yes, the pilot gets on there. Bit of a ruin. We shelled them in eighteen forty something or other. When we took Shanghai."

"Oh yes, I saw the pilot coming on board."

Everett nodded, breathing deeply and regularly through his nose, making long hissing sounds in his nostrils. "You'll be seeing them again, I should think. There's a Customs post there, too."

The breakfast gong sounded on the first class deck above them, struck by a dough-faced, spotty youth, insolent in his white P & O steward's uniform. Time for them to eat too, then, in the airless third class saloon with its plain wooden tables and smells of stale cooking.

"Coming?" Everett asked.

"Not just yet," Denton answered awkwardly. "Think I'll just watch a bit more first."

He stayed on deck till it was too late to eat, gazing across the yellowish water that swirled gently past the ship's smooth white hull. He watched wooden junks drift past, their stiff, ribbed sails like patched grey bats' wings, he watched the light and dark green squares of the paddy fields, he listened to the clanging of occasional bells, behind the feathery bamboos that sometimes screened the villages. The sun grew slowly hotter. His cheek began to burn. He moved reluctantly into the shade of one of the lifeboats. But still he watched.

And then, at last, the thing he scarcely knew he'd been waiting for: the city of Shanghai began to emerge from the shimmering haze ahead. First tall black columns of smoke from unseen funnels and chimneys, then the bright shapes of large buildings, windows intermittently sparkling in the sunlight, then the dark rigid fingers of pointing cranes and the masts of ships, bare as leafless trees. While he gazed at

3

the approaching city, he heard the deep throbbing blast of a siren, and almost at once a rust-streaked liner slid round the next bend, heading downstream towards the sea. For a few moments Denton looked at the two raked stacks billowing sooty smoke and at the silent faces of the passengers lining the side, then the ship had passed and he was watching the Russian flag flopping limply at the stern above the muddy foaming wake churned by its propellers. Another liner was making its tortuous way upstream behind them, sailing almost in their wake. As it slowly turned at a buoy in the middle of the channel, he saw the American flag drooping from its mast.

They swung slowly round another bend and all at once they were in the middle of the city. On the starboard side, large stone buildings with colonnaded façades lay back behind a wide green park. On the port side a dirty grey slum of houses, factories and godowns sprawled, all crammed together. The river was dense with ships of all kinds there— liners, cargo ships, coalers, barges, lighters and junks. Between them and the shore, smaller boats dawdled over the smooth, sluggish water, Chinese sampans rowed from the stern with a single oar. From the quays came a continuous hubbub of noise—voices shouting and chanting, wheels grinding, chains squealing, whistles blowing, cargo thudding onto shore or barge. *So this is China,* he thought again half-exhilarated, half-afraid. He went below.

Everyone else in the six-berthed cabin had gone, their trunks and boxes piled outside. Denton quickled folded his few remaining clothes and started packing them into the dented metal trunk his father had bought him from a pawnbroker in London. The cramped cabin was on the lowest deck, hot and stifling now that the ship had stopped moving and the scuttle no longer scooped in any air. He began to sweat, and took off his jacket and tie. His best collar, which he had had starched for threepence in the ship's laundry the day before, was damp and curling already.

As he was closing the lid the stamp of approaching feet sounded outside, then an abrupt, authoritative voice. A large man in a white drill uniform pushed the door open and ducked inside, holding his topee in his hand. He seemed to fill the doorway.

"Denton?" His face was red and perspiring, and he had a bristly ginger moustache. "My name's Mason. Been sent to meet you." He made it sound more a duty than a pleasure.

"Where's your kit? That all?" He sniffed and then, as an afterthought thrust out a meaty red hand that was also perspiring. "Mason's the name," he said again. "How do. Only one trunk?" He shouted over his shoulder in a hectoring voice, and a small crooked-backed Chinese padded in on bare feet, peering deferentially, warily, round the cabin, as if expecting to be cuffed or kicked. Mason gestured to the trunk. "One piecee topside," he ordered curtly.

The Chinese wore faded blue trousers and a shapeless, torn tunic. "Master no more piecee?" he asked in a sing-song voice, shaking his head so that his waist-long queue twitched at his back. His head was shaved in front, giving his face a strangely naked and mask-like appearance.

"One piecee!" Mason repeated impatiently. "Quick, quick top-side! Master later look-see, you blithering idiot." He looked round the cabin distastefully as the Chinese heaved the trunk onto his shoulder and staggered out with it. "Glad to get out of this, I should think, won't you be?"

Before Denton could answer, Mason frowned. "I say, you have got a jacket and tie, haven't you? Better put 'em on, then."

"Yes, I was just going to—"

"Put 'em on if I were you," Mason said again, ignoring Denton's assurance. "The Chief's hot on that sort of thing."

"Yes." Denton obediently adjusted his tie and slipped on his jacket under Mason's watchful, rather peevish gaze.

"You'll be hot in that," Mason said accusingly, brushing the tips of his moustache upwards with his knuckle. "Couldn't you get tropical kit before you left?"

"They said it would be cheaper here?" Denton turned "their" statement into a hesitant, mild inquiry.

"Did they now?" Mason asked indifferently. "Well, they were right about that at least."

The lascar cabin steward appeared in the doorway, a towel over his arm, smiling and nodding at Denton.

Denton gazed at him inquiringly.

"Wants his tip," Mason muttered. "Slip him a quid."

"Oh," He gave the man a pound note. Now he'd only got nine left.

The steward stared down at the note without moving. "You are not liking my service?" he asked in a sullen, injured voice.

5

"What?"

"Only one pound?"

"Isn't that enough?" Denton asked meekly.

" 'Course it is!" Mason answered for him roughly. "More than enough!"

"Other passengers are giving more."

"Other passengers are bloody fools, then." Mason pushed past the lascar. "Come on, let's go. Just leave him to whine and snivel here. He'll soon get fed up with it."

But as he followed Mason out, Denton added five shillings surreptitiously to the pound note. The steward took it ungraciously, still muttering his dissatisfaction.

On deck, Mason made his way through the waiting passengers commandingly, his uniform giving him licence. As they crossed the gangway down to the landing stage, Denton looked down at the beggar boats that had swarmed round the vessel's side. They were bare, dirty sampans rowed by women or children, who held up deformed infants, filthy, naked, covered with sores, while they wailed and clamoured against each other. "Dollar, master! Baby hungry! Baby hungry!"

"Beggars!" Mason glanced at them contemptuously. "I suppose you've seen enough of them on the way out?"

Denton nodded. Malta, Port Said, Suez, Aden, Bombay, Colombo, Singapore, Hong Kong—everywhere there had been beggars, smelly, sore, mutilated, emaciated and importunate. And everywhere they'd made him feel obscurely guilty. "Yes," he answered. "Not so many as here, though. There must be a lot of poverty."

"Brought it to a fine art," Mason sniffed disdainfully. "Don't give 'em a cent, you'll never shake 'em off if you do."

"The children look very sick," Denton protested uneasily, remembering the missionaries' slide shows in the church hall at Enfield, the blurry pictures of starving children that their weekly threepences would feed.

"Sick?" Mason scoffed, either at Denton or at the beggars. "They're probably dead. They steal corpses to beg with. Dead babies their parents have chucked out. Begin to pong by midday, too."

Denton stared at him incredulously, but he had gone on ahead to shout at the Chinese, who was patiently waiting with the battered trunk.

Already gangs of coolies were trotting up and down the gangways to the holds, chanting deep rhythmic cries as

6

they lolloped along, giant loads swaying at each end of the springy bamboo poles they balanced on their shoulders. Denton sniffed the air of the quayside. It was rich and heavy, smelling of the muddy water, of dirt, sweat, greasy smoke, of incense and the food cooking on nearby charcoal braziers. All around him there was the din of shouting coolies, bustling hawkers, grinding cranes and squealing pulleys. Only a few ship's officers and a bearded Sikh policeman were aloof and quiet, surveying the tumult with detached superiority. And another Customs officer, dressed like Mason, whom Mason nodded casually to, brushing his moustache upward with his knuckle again.

A hand touched Denton's shoulder. It was Everett again. "Cheerio," he smiled amiably. "Might run into each other some time, eh?"

"Yes. All the best."

"Friend of yours?" Mason asked, or demanded rather, as if he had a right to know.

"He was in my cabin. He's with the police here."

"Oh, with the slops, eh?" His voice seemed to drop a tone in disparagement. He strode on through the gangs of coolies towards a brick arch with an iron gate, guarded by another Sikh policeman. "We'll take a rickshaw."

"Is it far?"

"Nowhere's far here." He brushed past the policeman. "Customs," he said brusquely.

The policeman saluted.

Mason's puffy, florid face was sweating copiously. He mopped it with a silk handkerchief. Denton noticed dark stains of sweat under his raised arm and round the high collar of his uniform, which his neck bulged over, red and irascible.

"It's very hot," he said peaceably.

"Hot?" Mason gave a short, ill-tempered laugh. "That's not the trouble. It's the humidity that's killing." He turned away to shout something at the man carrying Denton's trunk.

Outside the gate they were surrounded by an insistent mob of rickshaw coolies, all calling out and beckoning, lowering the shafts of their rickshaws invitingly so that the two Englishmen almost tripped over them. Mason kicked out sullenly at several, before he chose one. "Here, this'll do. Hop in. The trunk can go in the one behind. Suppose you've seen these things before, Hong Kong and so on?"

"Yes. And Singapore. But what's that?" Denton point-ed to a large wheelbarrow on which three Chinese women were sitting, chirping noisily, while a single coolie pushed it along. "I haven't seen that before. What is it?"

"That? A wheelbarrow. What's it look like?"

Denton gazed at the coolie's arms, stretched wide to grip the wheelbarrow shafts. A strip of cloth, fastened to each shaft, passed over his shoulders to help him take the weight. It was about three times the size of an English wheelbarrow. "They carry people in them?"

"Unless my eyes deceive me," Mason said with weighty sarcasm. "I've seen the big ones carrying twelve people." He laughed sardonically, derisively. "It's their idea of an omnibus." But then, "After all," he added with a note of sulky concession, "You couldn't run a team of horses through these little streets."

They climbed into the rickshaw, Mason's bulk squashing Denton to the side. The rickshaw coolie was small and stringy, grey hairs glinting among the black in his queue. Surely he was too frail to carry them both? But he lifted the shafts and, leaning against the cross-piece, with a sigh and a grunt tugged them into motion. Denton watched his calves, nothing but skin and corded muscles, jogging along at a trot. The coolie had the cart so finely balanced that his bare, calloused feet seemed scarcely to touch the ground as he lifted himself at each stride.

They jolted down a crowded, unpaved alley, lined on each side by barbers, fruit and vegetable hawkers and sweet-meat sellers, each squatting in the shade of a make-shift awning or large wax-paper parasol. All round them men and women bargained, jostled, shouted, spat and ate. The coolie's feet splashed into a pile of rounded, steaming dung.

"Pooh!" Mason covered his nose. "Filthy devil! Why doesn't he look where he's going? Now we'll have that in our noses all the way! Good mind to get out and take another one." But he didn't move. Indeed, he actually seemed to be growing better-humoured.

The coolie raced up a steep wooden bridge that spanned a stagnant, dirty canal. As the brow approached, he began to lose speed. Watching the man's knobbly back bent almost double as he strained against the shafts, listening to his breath wheezing harsher and harsher, Denton felt that same obscure twinge of guilt that he'd felt

8

throughout the voyage whenever he was approached by beggars. For a giddy moment he thought of—he saw himself—getting out and helping the old man to pull. But Mason's white-shod foot rested so negligently on the shaft and his corpulent body was lolling there in such indolent unconcern, that Denton felt almost ashamed of the impulse, as if it had been a breach of etiquette. He leaned back again with a show of ease and indifference.

At last they cleared the hump and ran down the other side, the coolie taking long, flying strides. Mason called out imperious directions and the coolie grunted, swinging them round into one narrow alley after another. They seemed to be passing through a poorer part of the city now. The alleys were more cramped, the houses smaller and more dingy; the open drains stank with rotting refuse, at which cowering, mangy dogs with rheumy eyes furtively sniffed and nibbled. And every alley teemed with bustling Chinese, on foot, in rickshaws, in those strange, large wheelbarrows. Everywhere they were shouting their wares, bargaining, hawking and spitting, eating, bawling out conversations across the narrow spaces. The rickshaw coolie often had to stop when he met another rickshaw or a wheelbarrow head on, and every time a wheedling cluster of beggars gathered round them, children, women, old men. The coolie hissed at them through his teeth and shooed them away, as if he too regarded them as worthless dross. Mason merely sniffed and surveyed them distantly through half-closed lids.

"We're in the Chinese city now," he said, as they lurched into another festering alley. "Longer way round, but I wanted to show you something." He tilted his topee down over his forehead against the sun.

Shading his own eyes against the heat and glare, Denton gazed passively down at the coolie trotting like a human horse between the shafts. Sweat was running down his creased neck, and his loose, patched tunic was wet with it wherever the faded blue cloth touched his bony body. Under his rolled-up trousers, his legs too were running with sweat. Denton watched the glistening rivulets trickling down between the dried splashes of dung on his protruding ankles.

Some way ahead there seemed to be the dull confused murmur of a crowd. Mason stirred ponderously beside him, taking a gold watch out of his fob. He opened the

9

case and frowned down at it. "Twenty past nine," he muttered. "Should be at it by now." Denton glanced at him questioningly, but he settled back again without explanation, only letting a secretive little smile twitch his small red lips beneath the ginger bristles of his moustache.

The muffled murmuring grew gradually louder and more distinct, then suddenly the alley gave onto a wide open space. It was full of Chinese, all peering towards the centre, laughing and talking excitedly in their shrill, hoarse voices. Women with babies strapped to their backs, men in long gowns, coolies and children—some of them perched on their parents' shoulders. Near the centre, Denton saw a sprinkling of European men in straw hats and topees.

The rickshaw had stopped. "Stand up and you'll see something," Mason said in his loud, peremptory voice. "Get a good view from here. One of the local sports."

The coolie, panting, held the shafts level for him, grinning slyly at Mason as if the two of them were sharing some private joke. Behind, the rickshaw carrying the trunk stopped with a long-drawn-out sigh from the coolie as he lowered the shafts to the ground.

Gingerly Denton stood up, gazing over all the bobbing and turning heads, each of which was also straining to see. The crowd suddenly hushed, so that his voice sounded too loud when he asked "Where?"

"In the middle. Can't you see anything?"

The rickshaw lurched as Mason stood up unsteadily himself, gripping Denton's arm above the elbow. The coolie muttered as he balanced the shafts again. He too was stretching his neck to see. "There, look," Mason pointed. "Over there."

"Where? Oh." Denton saw a Chinese kneeling in a small clearing of the crowd. He was bare to the waist. Another stood behind him, pulling his arms back, while a third seemed to be yanking his head forward by the queue. It was as though they were wrestling. Or, rather, as if the two standing men were using the other as the rope in a tug of war.

"What are they doing?" he turned to Mason uneasily, a vague premonitory fear gathering like a cloud on the blank skies of his mind.

"Watch." Mason's brown button eyes were gleaming slightly. His grip tightened on Denton's arm.

Denton looked back. A fourth man, obscured till now

by the crowd, had appeared. He raised both arms. His hands held a heavy sword. The sun glinted a moment on the blade. The crowd was silent and still, as if frozen. Not even a baby cried. For one paralysed second Denton gazed in disbelief, his heart thudding helplessly, at the two braced men, at the kneeling victim, at the tensed, poised swordsman. Then the swordsman's arms swung and the heavy blade hurtled down in a flashing arc. Denton heard the soft thud as it sliced through the kneeling man's neck. The head dropped off and a dark spurt of blood shot out from the trunk as it collapsed onto the earth. The man holding the queue jerked the dripping head up in the air and swung it round and round like a ball on a chain. The headless body lay there twitching and jerking, like a fish flapping desperately about on the stones of a jetty.

An exultant roar, deep-throated and satisfied, had gone up from the crowd, and now they were surging forward round the body in a sudden powerful tide, men, women and children fighting to dip their hands in the blood that was still pumping from the severed neck.

Denton slumped down suddenly, shuddering. The rickshaw rocked and Mason wobbled dangerously. "Hey!" he exclaimed, "Watch what you're doing, can't you?" Then he eased his own body down carefully. "That was a pirate," he said, the sudden indignation fading from his voice, replaced by a tone at once gloating and indifferent. "You'll see plenty of that before you're through. Still want to join the service?" He chuckled when Denton didn't answer, and called out to the rickshaw coolie, who was still grinning appreciatively, standing on tiptoe to peer over the crowd while he balanced the shafts.

"Chop-chop! Chop-chop!" Mason shouted at him again, clapping his hands impatiently.

With a reluctant shake of his head, the coolie turned them round and pulled them away, leaning against the cross-piece.

"See them putting their hands in the blood?" Mason asked. "They think it's lucky. It's not their hands actually. They were holding cash, see? It makes the cash lucky. They think it'll make them rich." He chuckled again, thickly and chestily. "It may be nineteen hundred and three in England, but it's the Middle Ages out here. Still want to join the service? Hobson's choice, I expect."

Again Denton gave no answer. But Mason didn't seem

to notice. "Of course they do get the blood on their hands as well," he added reflectively. "But it's the money they care about."

A deep, wild, ecstatic roar welled up behind them again. Like the roar of the crowd at the football match his father had taken him to see before he left England. England, how far away!

"There goes another one," Mason nodded over his shoulder. "They'll be at it all morning." He took a cigar out of his breast pocket and cupped his large hand carefully round the match as he lit it. "Want one?" he offered perfunctorily as he buttoned the flap again. "No? Suit yourself. Yes, they stick their heads on poles when they've chopped 'em all off." He glanced round, funnelling a pale blue stream of smoke out between pursed lips. "There's a couple over there, look."

2

"You're lucky to get these quarters." Mason threw his topee onto the bare mattress and strode with a tread that shook the floorboards to the shuttered French windows, through which the sunlight shone in blinding slits. The Chinese servant in white jacket and trousers, who had met them deferentially at the entrance to the mess, let Denton's trunk down carefully with a groaning sigh and stood expectantly, his quiet, slant-lidded eyes glancing respectfully from Mason to Denton.

Mason was unbolting the shutters. He turned, his half-smoked cigar between his teeth. "Must get you some of the local cash," he muttered. He pulled a handful of change grudgingly out of his pocket, selected a tiny coin and with a "Here!", held it out for the servant, who fumblingly caught it as he let it go.

"Give the boys the odd cent or two, it oils the wheels," Mason advised Denton loudly as the servant left the room on slippered feet, pocketing the coin. "Don't overdo it, though. The blighters get greedy in no time. You can change your English money downstairs." The bolt on the shutters moved with a squeak and he swung them back, then unlocked the doors behind them. They opened onto a large veranda which ran the whole length of the room.

"You've got a sitting room next door. View of the harbour from both rooms, look. Bathroom's back there." He seemed better-humoured since the execution, strolling round the room and humming, looking about him appreciatively.

Denton went obediently out onto the veranda and looked numbly out. Two floors below was the street they had come along, teeming with rickshaws, those strange large wheelbarrows, and people hurrying up and down, many of them women with parasols over their heads. Here and there a donkey moved, loaded with heavy panniers, a man leading it or goading it from behind. He saw a sedan chair carried by four bearers on long swaying poles, everyone giving way to it as it passed. He looked up over the roofs of the low houses opposite. There the river glittered in the sunlight, sailing ships, junks, steamers and warships moving silently and slowly over the oil-smooth yellow waters. On the other bank there were long, low buildings—warehouses, he supposed—with the black jibs of cranes rising austerely over them.

"Yes." Mason came and leant over the parapet beside him. "You're lucky to have these quarters." He flicked his cigar butt out into the air, watching it arch slowly, spinning, down into the street. It landed beside a coolie trotting past with two baskets swaying from his springy shoulder pole. "I only had one room when I started." He sounded momentarily resentful on Denton's better fortune. "Old Smithy waited over a year for these quarters, ever since he was a griffin, and then he only lasted three months." He pushed his weight off the parapet and strolled back into the shade of the bedroom. "That's what we call the new chaps by the way, griffins. It's a racing term. Young and green, that's what it means. No offence."

Denton nodded absently. He was recalling the execution, the thud of the blade striking the man's neck, the spouting blood, the helpless flapping limbs. He still felt shaky and weak. He knew that if he spoke, his voice would tremble.

"Yes, old Smithy..." Mason was gazing reflectively round the room. "Silly fool got cholera."

Denton listened now with a new, apprehensive interest. Then a sudden movement on the ceiling by the gas lamp caught his eye. It was a little greenish lizard, like a miniature dragon, flickering along then suddenly freezing. "Er, what's that?" he asked anxiously, imagining it might

13

be poisonous or carrying cholera germs. He was right, his voice *was* trembling.

"What? That? A tjik-tjak. Quite harmless, they catch mosquitoes. Only their damn droppings fall on your sheets sometimes. Seem to like white for some reason, the little brutes... No," Mason resumed his interrupted thread, "Say what you like to him, you could, old Smithy *would not* take precautions. This is your sitting room, by the way. Not much in the way of furniture yet, just a couple of armchairs and a table—you'll have to get curtains and covers and all that sort of stuff yourself. No," he surveyed the bare sitting room, gloomy and musty behind the unopened shutters. "Silly bastard thought he'd be all right if he only wore a stomacher. *Would not* take advice. Ate anything, drank unboiled water, went anywhere." He shrugged, loosening the brass buttons of his tunic. "Marvel he lasted as long as he did, when you come to think of it. Only died last week. Still, he got it in the end, all right." He laughed, a short harsh laugh of retributive satisfaction. "You got a stomacher, by the way?"

"A stomacher?" Denton asked diffidently. "What's that?"

Mason's eyes widened with almost petulant surprise at Denton's ignorance. "A cholera belt! Didn't they tell you that in London? Well, you can get it with your kit later on. I'll show you the tailor's. It keeps the chills out, that's half the battle against cholera. But the thing is, you've got to watch the food and water too. Only old Smithy, he would know best... Still, there you are," he shrugged disclaimingly, his jacket falling apart at last as the lowest, straining, button popped open. "There, that's my stomacher." He gave a proprietary pat to the wide felt band that girdled his swelling paunch. "You can get one when they kit you out, after you've seen the chief. Brown's his name. Deputy assistant commissioner. I'll take you along to see him presently, after you've had a wash and brush up." He reached with two fingers into his fob, hauled his watch out again, and frowned down at it, holding it away from him in the palm of his great red hand. Denton glanced shyly at the stomacher and the vest beneath it, moist with sweat, and at Mason's heavy chest, in the middle of which a little jungle of curly reddish hair grew, spreading right up the base of his bull-like throat.

"Yes, in about an hour." Mason closed his watch with a snap. "Don't know why he couldn't make it later." He turned to leave. "Old Smith's things are being auctioned this afternoon, by the way. You could get his furniture if you want it. It's the usual thing when a fellow dies, auction his stuff off. Help to pay his chits and things. Well, I'll leave you to it. I'm off to have a nap. Night duty last night, see? Need a bit of kip. Give me a knock if I don't turn up by ten-thirty. I'm just next door to you." He took his topee from the mattress, set it rakishly on the side of his head and sauntered out, leaving the door swinging open behind him.

Denton closed the door softly and looked round the room, his hand still clasping the brass handle. The glare from the unshaded veranda dazzled his eyes and the cries from the street rose up strident and raucous. He closed the door, closed the shutters and leant back against them. Above the bed, a greyish-white mosquito net hung, tied in a loose, bunchy knot. On the white-washed ceiling, its cornice garlanded with cobwebs, were several of those little green lizards—what had Mason called them? He eyed them warily. Either they darted rapidly, or else they were immobile, as if glued where they were. They never moved slowly. The very way they turned their heads was swift and jerky, even the way their flanks moved as they watchfully breathed.

Somewhere down the corridor a door banged, and he heard Chinese voices, a man's and a woman's, shrill in argument. Otherwise the building was still and quiet, and the voices died like the chatter of birds round an empty pool. There were several faint rectangular patches on the walls, darker than the surrounding paint, where pictures must have hung. For an instant he saw the twitching, pumping trunk of the pirate framed in one of them. He looked quickly away to his homely, battered tin trunk, focussing his eyes on the large dent in the lid by the handle. There was sticky sweat on his neck, on his wrists, all over his body.

For a moment he wanted to climb onto the bed, pull the mosquito net down round him and hide behind it like a child. He imagined himself lying there with the net like a filmy wall all round him. Then he thought of Smith. Perhaps Smith had died on that mattress, with the screen of the net round him? Death by cholera, death by decapitation—was that China, the land he'd come to? But the mattress was new; Smith couldn't have lain on it.

Probably they'd burnt the old one. He took a deep steadying breath and took off his tie, jacket and waistcoast before bending to unlock and unpack.

He laid his clothes tidily on the mattress, trying not to think of Smith or the pirate. There was a cupboard of bare, yellowish-varnished wood in the corner. When he opened the door, he caught his breath—two large, metallic-brown cockroaches about three inches long scuttled out over his shoe and disappeared behind the back of the cupboard. After a moment he went to wash his hands at the wash-stand in the bathroom, pouring water from the jug into the basin beside it. There was no soap, no towel. He splashed his face and dried himself slowly on his handkerchief. As he glanced at his lean, pallid reflection in the heavy wood-framed mirror, its glass cracked in the top right corner, he glimpsed his Adam's apple above the parting of his loosened collar. He had nicked it whilst shaving that morning. Now there was a clean little scab over the cut. He touched the scab gently and then without warning he was helplessly imagining the executioner's sword slicing through his own neck, just there, where the scab was, slicing through the skin and bones and muscles, through all the veins and arteries, in one savage stroke which seemed for all its speed to go on and on, always cutting and cutting again. He closed his eyes tight and shook his head, only to see the stiffened grimaces of pain and fear on the heads nailed to poles that Mason had pointed out to him as they left the execution ground.

He shuddered and walked back to sit miserably, not on the bed where his clothes were neatly piled, but on his empty trunk. How far away from England he was now! England, where he had packed those same clothes tidily into the trunk! How far from the P & O liner, with its civilised routine and order!

A mosquito was whining monotonously by his ear. He took out his watch and wound it. He had set it to Shanghai time by the ship's clock the night before. Forty-five minutes still to wait.

3

Denton tapped hesitantly on Mason's door at half-past ten, and heard a slurred, morose acknowledgment. Ten minutes later Mason appeared, heavy-lidded and taciturn as he fastened his jacket, and they took another rickshaw, this time by a direct route, to the deputy assistant commissioner's office in the Customs House on the Bund. The Customs House was like the Town Hall at Enfield, Denton thought, with a tall square tower and a clock, its solid Englishness reassuring. Mason led him through an outer office, where Chinese clerks sat watchfully silent at tall wooden desks. "There's the door," he nodded off-handedly. "Got some work to do. Come to my room when you're finished. Number eleven, down the corridor."

Denton tapped on the dark wooden door. After a moment, a calm, abstracted voice called out, "Yes?" He turned the polished brass knob and went in.

A bald, bulbous-browed man with sallow skin sat writing at a large desk by the open window. The thick ring of hair round his head was a woolley grey, and he had a heavy drooping moustache. A punkah swung gently over the desk, creaking like the timbers of a ship. "Yes?" Mr. Brown asked again, stroking his moustache as he wrote.

"I'm Denton, sir."

"Who?" Mr. Brown dipped his pen in the ink well, then looked up inquiringly. "Ah yes, of course. Mr. Denton." He shook the ink off the nib, examined the tip fastidiously, knitting his strangely scanty grey brows together, then laid the pen down, gesturing to the upright chair facing the desk. "I was expecting you fifteen minutes ago," he said precisely, glancing pointedly up at the mahogany-cased clock ticking on the wall beside his desk.

"Mr. Mason brought me," Denton murmured apologetically. "I didn't know what time..."

"Ah yes." Mr. Brown stroked his moustache ruminatively. "Met you off the boat, didn't he? What was it, the *Orcades*?"

"Yes sir."

Mr. Brown tilted back his head, gazing down his nose at Denton's crumpled collar. "Pleasant trip?"

"Oh yes, sir, very pleasant thank you."

"Good," Mr. Brown stroked his moustache again and tilted his head still further back, staring broodingly up at the punkah for more than half a minute, as if he were puzzled by its gentle flapping motion and didn't quite trust it. He seemed to have forgotten Denton was there.

Denton glanced uncomfortably at the topee hanging

on the lowest branch of the hatstand behind the desk, then back at Mr. Brown as he cleared his throat. Despite the heat, his high winged collar and cravat, his linen jacket and the mauve silk handkerchief tucked in his breast pocket were all creaseless and unsullied.

"Mason's shown you your quarters?" Mr. Brown was asking. "Quite satisfactory? Good. You can have tomorrow to get fitted out and settled in. Report for duty on Thursday morning. In the meantime, I..." His voice faded as his eyes narrowed faintly and he glanced up at the punkah again. A crease of annoyance appeared in the loose sallow skin of his forehead. Denton followed his upward gaze with respectful puzzlement. The wide, cloth-covered board had stopped its creaking motion and hung above them like a giant windless palm.

Mr. Brown banged the bell on his desk imperiously three times, and after a few seconds the punkah started swinging again. The cool air fanned Denton's face and stirred the papers on the desk, so that they fluttered like leaves in a gentle breeze. "And in the meantime," Mr. Brown resumed, "here are some pamphlets regarding the duties you will be expected to perform, which I advise you to study attentively." He passed a bundle of booklets, neatly tied with yellow tape, over the desk. "I shall examine you orally on pamphlets three and four on Wednesday at ten a.m."

"Yes sir."

"The first two pamphlets merely give general information and so forth."

"Yes sir."

"That does not mean they can be disregarded."

"No sir."

"If your answers are satisfactory, you can start accompanying one of the established officers on his rounds."

Denton looked down at the grey cover of the top pamphlet. There was a dark ring-stain on the corner and he imagined some previous probationary officer placing his glass there late at night while he swotted anxiously for the next day's examination.

"You will be expected to make some headway with the Chinese language, too. No doubt you have been told that? You will find a list of approved tutors in the mess. You may choose any one. Your fees will be paid by the service, of course. The details are in the first pamphlet."

18

Denton nodded, glancing down at the ring-stained cover again, as if he expected to see the details there without having to open it.

"Your salary is paid in arrears," Mr. Brown went on, "If you have not yet arranged a bank, I suggest the Hong Kong and Shanghai Bank or the Chartered Bank. Both British and thoroughly reliable."

"Thank you, sir."

"They are on the Bund, of course." Mr. Brown's light blue eyes met Denton's for the first time with disturbing directness. "Your contract is probationary at present, as you know, but with application, Mr. Denton, I see no reason why you should not be substantiated at the end of two years."

"Yes, sir, I'll try."

"Stranger things have happened," Mr. Brown added obscurely, stroking his moustache ruminatively again. Just above his lip the flowing hairs were stained a dark yellow by tobacco. "Mrs. Brown and I would be glad if you could join us for dinner next Tuesday," he said at last, as if the ruminative pause had been to consider whether Denton merited the invitation. "Will that be convenient?"

"Oh, thank you sir. Yes, very convenient. Er, about what time?"

"Mrs. Brown will send you a card. We usually dine at nine p.m." He turned his head to glance at the clock again, then adjusted the papers on the desk. "Well, that will be all for now, Mr. Denton. Your quarters are quite satisfactory, you say?"

"Oh yes, sir," Denton stood up. "Very satisfactory." He thought of his clothes still lying on the bare mattress.

"I don't suppose you've seen much of the city yet?"

"No, sir. Although we did see, I mean..." Denton hesitated then went on. "I mean we passed, er, an execution on the way from the ship." His voice hushed slightly as he said "execution," and the image of the head swinging round on its queue swept over his mind.

"Really?" Mr. Brown's scanty eyebrows rose. He took up his pen and examined the nib again. "I would hardly have thought that was necessary," he murmured. Then he leant forward, opening the file he had been writing in when Denton entered. "Well, then, Thursday at ten o'clock."

"Yes sir. Thank you, sir."

19

He glanced up as Denton opened the door. "Ten o'clock *precisely*, Mr. Denton."

4

"Be with you in a minute." Mason too was writing at his desk in his own, smaller, office. "Got to finish off these damn reports. There's a paper over there, if you want to have a look at the local news."

Denton sat down obediently in a cane chair beside the window and picked up the newspaper. The indemnity for the Boxer rebellion had definitely been agreed, the *North China Daily News* announced on its front page. The Dowager Empress had received the new German ambassador in Peking. In Shanghai, the American consul had given a reception in the international settlement to celebrate Independence Day.

Mason's pen scratched on while he grunted and sighed at his desk, occasionally muttering irritably under his breath.

"What does 'Bund' mean?" Denton asked timidly when he saw Mason leaning back in his chair, sucking the end of his pen.

"What?"

"'Bund'?"

"Sort of embankment place. Indian term, originally. Got all the good-class buildings in it. Consulates and banks and the big hongs and so on. Not to mention the Customs House, of course." He yawned, scratched his scalp with the end of his pen, examined it, and then leant forward to write again with a sigh. "Shanghai Club, all those places. 'Bund' is Hindi, actually."

"Have you been to India?" Denton asked, impressed by Mason's knowledge.

"In my time," Mason grunted, frowning as he wrote, as if to discourage further questioning.

Denton turned the page. Twenty-three pirates apprehended in Bias Bay had been handed over to the Chinese authorities. He read on quickly, to push away the bloodstained images that immediately leapt into his mind. Under *Wanted Known*, Ah Chew, ladies' tailor, announced immediate attention and promised "instant visitings." Church Services were listed in a solemn little ornamental border—

"Oh, that'll do for now," Mason growled, shoving back his chair. "Come along, let's go back to the mess. Time for tiffin."

5

Mason kicked his way through the crowded, clashing shafts of the badgering rickshaws and settled into one further away from the gate, leaning back sweating under the canvas canopy. "Never take the first one," he advised Denton loudly, "They always charge more." He took off his topee and wiped his forehead with the back of his hand.

It was noon, the heat stared balefully at them from the cloudless sky, from the narrow, parched streets, from the flat walls of the houses. The coolie pulled them along bumpy, rutted alleys and beside stagnant little canals, stinking with refuse. Stalls and dark cave-like shops lined every street. Coolies with long bamboo carrying-poles, women with crushing loads of stones in baskets on their backs, children, dogs and whining beggars pressed noisily all round them. Occasionally another European passed in a rickshaw or a sedan chair, eyes narrowed like theirs against the heat and light.

"Where d'you come from?" Mason asked suddenly, taking another cigar out of his tunic pocket. This time he did not offer one to Denton. "Enfield? Near London, isn't it?"

The rickshaw lurched into a pot hole and Mason fell against Denton. "Blithering idiot!" he shouted at the coolie. "Why don't you look where you're going?"

The coolie's head shook briefly in apology. Or was it incomprehension, or mere helplessness?

"Look-see! Look-see!" Mason called out threateningly. "You damn well look-see, or I'll kick your behind!"

The coolie shook his head again, hunching his shoulders abjectly. His subservience seemed to mollify Mason. He gave a satisfied but still warning little grunt and leant back again, lighting his cigar. "What got you into the Customs service?" he demanded, tossing the still burning

21

match aside as he settled himself more comfortably in the seat.

Denton edged along to make more room for him. "It was an accident, really," he began.

"Hey, look at that," Mason interrupted, nudging him with his elbow. "Not bad, eh?"

A sedan chair was being carried past by two bearers. The curtains were open and Denton caught a glimpse of a doll-like oval face with quick, dark eyes and rouged cheekbones framed by shiny black hair. Mason twisted round as the chair swayed past, his eyes gleaming as they had at the execution. "Not bad, at all, eh?" he sighed as he turned back, blowing out a long jet of aromatic blue smoke. "That's what makes being here worthwhile."

Denton looked at him inquiringly, puzzled.

"Sing-song girl," Mason explained obscurely. "They make a fortune. Cost it, too."

"Sing-song girl?"

"That's the translation." He said something in Chinese. "Sing-song girls."

"Oh, they're singers?"

Mason glanced at him sideways. "That's one of their accomplishments," he agreed, preening his moustache with his knuckle and pursing his rosy lips into an ironic little smile. "Here we are. Hop out, you're smaller than I am."

They walked together up the stone steps of the large building that Denton had scarcely noticed when he first saw it, his eyes still numbed by the execution. It was an imposing building, he recognized, in the same style as the Customs House. *Imperial Chinese Maritime Customs Officers' Mess* he read over the entrance, feeling a faint lift of pride that he belonged to it.

"Let's change your money first," Mason nodded across the lobby. "At the desk over there. Then you won't have to rely on me to pay the rickshaw boys."

6

The dining room was cool and dim, two large punkahs stirring the limp, moist air beneath the high ceiling. Delicate large-fronded palms, and rubber plants with glossy, thick leaves stood along the walls and between the rattan

22

tables. White-jacketed waiters moved noiselessly about in black cloth slippers. There seemed to be thirty or forty young officers in the mess, drinking and eating in separate groups. Mason took him a table in the corner, introducing him off-handedly to the two officers already sitting there. One was called Jones, a tall, fair-haired man with a downy moustache. Denton didn't catch the other's name, and was too shy to ask.

Mason ordered from the handwritten menu in a disdainful voice that suggested the food couldn't possibly be much good. Denton tamely said he'd have the same. The steward, an old man with a short grey queue, nodded silently. His slippers shuffled away over the tiled floor.

"Where d'you come from?" Jones asked Denton, as they began to eat.

"London," Mason answered for him, packing his mouth with rice and diced chicken.

"Enfield," Denton qualified mildly.

"Near enough. Ah Koo!" Mason snapped his fingers, calling out across the room. "Soya sauce!"

"How did you get into this outfit?" Jones dabbed his downy moustache with his napkin, looking up at him with slightly bloodshot eyes.

"It was an accident," Mason answered for him again.

"Well, I was going to be a teacher," Denton spoke quickly and quietly, toying with his rice, "I'd just done one year in a training college, actually—"

"Ah Koo! Soya sauce!" Mason called out again.

"—And then my father had an accident at work, so I had to give it up. And I just saw an advert in the paper and..." He shrugged and sipped some of the beer Mason had insisted he should share with them. It was only the second time in his life that he'd drunk beer, and he shivered at the bitter taste. Jones, losing interest, turned to talk to Mason in a low voice that excluded him.

"What sort of accident was it?" asked the small, dark man, whose name he hadn't caught. He had a mild, even, slightly nasal voice.

"At the small arms factory. He was testing a rifle when the barrel burst."

"Ah Koo! One piecee soya sauce!" Mason shouted irritably. "Come along, man! Chop-chop!"

The dark man nodded, scrutinising the moistened point of the tooth-pick he was using. "I started as a sailor.

23

Strange what brought us all out here in our different ways."

"Money," Mason said emphatically.

The dark man inserted his tooth-pick between his teeth without replying, which Mason seemed to take as a tacit denial.

"Cash," he said belligerently. "That's what brought us here." He took the soya bottle from the steward and shook it vigorously over his plate.

The dark man probed the gaps between his teeth reflectively.

"Not that there's much of that by the time you've paid your chits, eh?" Jones said pacifically.

"Anyone can make a pile out here," Mason asserted through bulging cheeks.

"Do you mean the bonus on contraband seizures?" Denton asked hopefully. He planned to send some of his salary home to his parents each month.

Mason glanced at him under his reddish brows and swallowed deliberately before answering. A thick, blackish trickle of soya sauce ran down from the corner of his mouth and he dabbed it with his napkin. "That, and other things," he said, with the same ironic smile that he'd given when he spoke of the sing-song girl's accomplishments. He turned to Jones, who had pushed back his chair. "Are you doing the auction, Jonesy?"

"Smith's stuff? Yes. Three o'clock in here. Why?"

"Nothing." Then Mason jerked his head at Denton without looking at him. "Except *he*'ll want to buy some stuff."

"I haven't got much money to spare," Denton began doubtfully.

"Who cares? Pay by chit." Mason waved his fork grandly. "Cash is for coolies."

"Er...how do you bid?"

"I'll bid for you, if you like," the dark man said reassuringly as he dropped the broken tooth-pick on his plate. "You just tell me what you'd like, and I'll do the bidding." He spoke in a monotonous, lulling tone of bland, sapless benevolence, but Denton was grateful.

"Well, perhaps some chair covers and curtains?" he suggested cautiously. "Would that cost very much?"

"Depends who's bidding against you, doesn't it?" Mason said, with a mocking flick of scorn in the rising

24

inflection of his voice. "Come on, let's go to the tailor's first, get you fitted out."

The tailor's was a dingy narrow room without windows, reaching back from an unpaved street into ever darker and mustier gloom. Six or seven Chinese men bent over sewing machines, working the treadles incessantly with their feet. Scraps of cloth lay scattered on the floor, which looked as though it had never been swept. The walls were grimy. Thick black cobwebs hung down from the ceiling. On a bare round wooden table near the back of the room stood several bowls with greasy chopsticks beside them. The table was littered with grains of rice and what looked like chicken bones, stained with a dark sauce. There was a smell of engrained dirt mingled with the heavy scent of incense which was drifting slowly up from some joss sticks smouldering dimly away at a little smoky red altar against the back wall.

A small man in a long grey gown shuffled towards them, bowing and hissing through his teeth. His face looked old, the skin thin and taut over his cheekbones.

"One piecee uniform for my friend, same same me." Mason ordered. "You makee one day fitting how muchee?"

The tailor glanced at Denton with a momentary gleam in his brown eyes. "Today very busy," he said impassively, gesturing to the hunched backs of his workers.

"Never mind busy. How muchee?" Mason demanded curtly.

The tailor's eyelids flickered. "Forty dollar."

"Forty? You must be mad! You before makee for me twenty-five dollar!"

The tailor smiled faintly. "Long time makee for you. Now more dear."

Denton, standing self-consciously beside Mason, grew aware of the workers' faces half-turned to listen while they sewed on at the same busy speed, pulling the cloth this way and that beneath the stabbing needles. There were smiles on their pale faces. One of them coughed and spat nonchalantly into a spittoon.

Mason damned the tailor, expostulated, threatened to walk out, and finally grudgingly offered thirty after the tailor had crept down to thirty-five. "You makee chop-chop tomorrow night finish. Fitting morning time. Otherwise no pay."

The tailor inclined his head a fraction and took a tape measure out of his sleeve. He hadn't raised his voice once in response to Mason's blustering. He'd bowed often and folded his hands courteously in front of him, yet his face had been unmoved, almost as though he hadn't even been listening. Denton sensed that he'd got the price he wanted and that Mason was put out. It was the first inkling he had that the Chinese were not all servile.

"Well, he knows your uniform allowance is forty dollars," Mason muttered as the tailor's light, bony hands deftly measured Denton. "Artful blighter knows how much you'll have to spend on shoes and a hat. He knows how much he can squeeze you for."

The tailor called out the measurements to one of the workers, who jotted them down on a scrap of paper. Denton wondered how the tailor could measure him without even seeming to touch him, his hands were so light and nimble.

"Tell him which side you hang 'em," Mason grunted as the tailor measured his inside leg.

"Sorry?"

"Oh never mind."

Denton blushed, thinking that after all perhaps he had understood. "Er, didn't you say I ought to get a stomacher as well?"

"Right, one piecee stomacher," Mason patted his paunch. "How muchee?"

"Five dollar."

"Three."

The tailor was measuring the width of Denton's trousers. "Four-fifty. Special for you."

Mason was evidently losing interest. "Four," he said, taking out a cigar.

The tailor stood up shaking his head mildly. "No can do. Too muchee workee."

"Oh all right then you blasted robber. Finish tomorrow, all right?" He bit his cigar and turned to Denton. "That leaves you just enough for the hat and shoes. They've got it worked out to a tee."

"Well it is much cheaper than in England," Denton murmured. "And I suppose he's got to pay all these workers here..."

Mason surveyed them indifferently, breathing out a blue curl of cigar smoke. "You can bet he doesn't pay *them*

26

much, if he pays 'em at all. Food and lodging probably, that's all. It's dog eat dog out here you know."

"Lodging? Where?"

Mason snorted. "On the floor. Where d'you think?"

7

"Now what am I bid for these curtains?" Asked Jones, leaning forward over the table, resting his weight on his spreading finger-tips. "Beautiful floral pattern, almost unused. Hold 'em up, Ah Koo. Up! Up! That's right. Shall we start at five dollars? Who'll start us off at five dollars?"

Ah Koo, barefooted, stood on the table, holding the curtains up one after another, his arms trembling with the strain. His wrinkled face smiled self-consciously, as if he were both embarrassed and proud of his prominence.

"These curtains graced our departed friend's sitting room and bedroom," Jones was saying. He paused to glance round the room with an anticipatory leer. "Eight lovely drapes from Whiteaway and Laidlaw's. And when they were drawn, who knows what sights they saw?"

A loud suggestive laugh from Mason led a snigger round the room. One of the stewards snaked his way between the tables, balancing a tea-tray on his hand. He set it down by the dark man, whose name Denton still didn't know. Denton glanced over his shoulder as he signed the chit. *R. Johnson.*

"Six dollars I hear," Jones called out. Ah Koo's arms quivered more and more unsteadily as he struggled to hold the curtains up, fold after fold. The smile on his face was growing fixed with the effort.

"Seven," Johnson said.

"Eight," called Mason. "Why not?"

"Why not indeed? Eight I am bid."

"You've just got some new ones," Johnson murmured, pausing with his hand on the tea pot.

"And why shouldn't I get some more?" Mason asked provocatively. He glanced at Denton. "Can't let 'em go too cheap, can we?"

"Any advance on eight?"

Denton hesitated as Johnson looked at him with raised, inquiring brows. Surely he could do without curtains?

After all there were shutters. But impulsively, vertiginously, he nodded to Johnson.

"Nine dollars." Johnson said, scarcely raising his voice.

"Nine fifty."

"Only one dollar bids, Mr. Mason," Jones licked his lips. "We're going up by single dollars only."

"Ten, then," Mason shrugged carelessly.

Johnson glanced inquiringly at Denton again. Denton rubbed his chin, blushing. Everyone was looking at him. He knew Mason was bidding against him on purpose, and he felt challenged. But he couldn't afford to spend much.

"Any advance on ten over there?" Jones asked hopefully.

Denton recalled the gleam in Mason's eyes at the execution that morning, and some small corner of his mind hardened. He nodded to Johnson.

"Eleven."

"Eleven dollars? Mr. Mason? Any advance? No? Sold for eleven dollars."

Mason laughed loudly, looking round with eyes that sneered and yet at the same time seemed to seek approval. "Well, that'll help pay old Smithy's bar debts, anyway." he said.

Johnson leant closer to Denton. "I knew he wouldn't go higher, once he'd bid nine fifty," he murmured placidly. "He was getting careful."

"Next item, chair covers. Same design as the curtains, excellent condition, look. With antimacassars thrown in."

Mason didn't bid again, and Johnson got the chair covers for Denton at six dollars. "He's a funny fellow, old Mason," Johnson whispered. "He was just trying it on, to see what you'd do. He does that with everyone, he doesn't really mean any harm."

"And last but not least," Jones called out, "a solid teak desk, which you see in front of me. Three drawers, top one lockable. Our departed colleague penned his billy-doos on this desk. And if you're lucky you may find one inside still."

"Get on with it Jonesy," a voice called out in weary encouragement.

"You can sign a chit and give it to Jones, he's the mess treasurer anyway," Johnson was saying to Denton.

"I'm trying to work out what it comes to in English money."

"About two pounds altogether." Johnson stirred his

28

tea rhythmically, round and round, the spoon clinking against the same place on the cup each time.

"No offers for this beautiful solid teak desk?" Jones asked plaintively, with a show of incredulity, over the rising sound of inattentive voices. People had begun to leave the room. "No offers at all?"

Denton gulped. "Ten dollars," he called out in a high, unsteady voice.

"Ten dollars?" Jones cupped his ear. "Did I hear ten dollars?"

Denton nodded.

The desk was his.

"Well you soon got the hang of it, didn't you?" Johnson said encouragingly. He drank his tea down and wiped his lips with the back of his hand. "Tibby Mason must've put you on your mettle. Did you really want that?"

"I suppose I'll want to write letters and things in my room sometimes," Denton replied unsteadily. He felt his heart thumping slightly with surprise at his own audacity.

8

He sat in his nightshirt at his new desk, stroking the thick yellow varnish with his finger-tips. The curtains and covers lay neatly folded on the armchair. He glanced round at them once more, then dipped his pen in the ink bottle and began to write.

Dear Mother and Father. Arrived safely today, after hot but interesting voyage. Keeping well, hope you are too. Also hope you got the letters I have been sending. Weather here is very hot and sticky. Was met off the boat and shown—paused, thinking of the severed head swinging round on its queue, then went on—*a few sights on the way to the above address where I am now settling in. Picture on other side shows Customs Headquarters. Have been measured for my uniform already, which they can make in one day. Long letter follows soon. Love, John.*

He left the postcard on the desk and went to the bathroom. Dipping his toothbrush into the round, silvery tin of Dr. Mill's Dental Powder, he started brushing his teeth. He had opened all the windows and shutters. Though it was after eleven o'clock, the street below was just as noisy as it had been in the morning. He listened to the hoarse, outlandish cries and shouts as he contemplated the white foam round his lips in the mirror. Would he ever get used to them, understand them? Darkness had fallen suddenly at seven o'clock, as he had come to expect on the ship, and the steward, whom everyone addressed as "boy," and whose silent presence still made him uncomfortable, had come and lit the gas lamps with a gentle plop that reminded him of home.

He wandered to the window, still brushing vigorously. Oil lamps flared over fruit stalls in the street below and glimmered in the poky little shops that crammed cheek in jowl against each other. Rickshaw coolies shouted their way raucously through the crowd, and a sedan chair floated past, preceded by a man with a lamp. The stall lights flickered over the chair, and through the uncurtained window he glimpsed a woman's face peering out with gleaming eyes. Further along, two British soldiers were strolling in their new khaki uniforms. Denton turned away, suddenly remembering his brother dead at Mafeking. If he'd had a khaki uniform there, instead of that proud scarlet one, the Boer sharpshooters might never have got him.

He had taken a mouthful of water from the tumbler and spat it out into the enamel pail below the marble wash-stand, before he realised that the water might not have been boiled. He brushed his teeth again fiercely, with a big cake of dental powder on the brush, and spat once more into the pail, this time without rinsing. A faint unease stirred in his stomach. Could Smith's cholera germs still be in the room?

The steward had replaced the bucket in the toilet box when he made the bed, and Denton sat on the seat, enjoying the freshness. His stomach was what his mother would have called loose. He got up and washed his hands, brushing his nails thoroughly.

Reaching up to the lamp, he pulled the lever down, avoiding the sticky brown flypaper hanging from it, on which several small black flies were hopelessly mired, feebly wriggling their legs and flapping their wings. The light faded; a blue flame licked round the mantle, then went out with a terminal plop. He walked barefoot to the bedroom, draped the mosquito curtain round the bed and turned the light out there too. Ducking under the curtain, he lay down.

The air was still and heavy, pressing warmly down on him. He was sweating under his nightshirt. He pushed the sheet down to his feet and lay on his back, hands clasped behind his head, watching the dim shadows from the passing lights in the street below flickering across the ceiling.

Closing his eyes, he clasped his hands over his chest and whispered a prayer, as he had done, secretly, every night in his berth on the *Orcades*. He remembered to add a prayer for the executed pirates. His eyes opened again on the flickering shadows. His arms beneath the nightshirt were sweaty. So were his chest and neck. He undid all the buttons down to his waist and pulled the nightshirt open. Forlorn images of home came straying through his mind: his mother in her apron, cooking at the large black grate in the kitchen; his father with his scarred hands crossed in his lap, seated immovably in the corner, silent and brooding. He saw Emily with her parents at the Easter service, her wavy brown hair falling loose beneath her wide-brimmed hat, the soft curls round her neck as she knelt to pray. He stirred despite himself and his fingers brushed the bare skin of his chest as if he were stroking her arm, her shoulder, her throat. To punish himself for his impurity, he forced himself to recall the horror of the execution that morning. But somehow praying for the dead men's souls had dulled the frightfulness, moved their deaths to a different plane, more distant, less disturbing. And it was Emily's lips that came into his mind now, fresher and more vivid than the ritual cruelty that had stunned and sickened him only a few hours before.

He turned onto his side and thought determinedly of the things that had happened to him since he left the *Orcades*, of the new curtains and chair covers and desk, of the pamphlets he would begin studying tomorrow. Soon he was thinking only of his temerity in bidding at the auction, of the *Orcades* sailing on to Japan, of the weird sing-song sound of the Chinese language...A mosquito was whining somewhere near his ear. His watch was hanging by its chain from the brass bedrail, which gleamed softly in the dimness and he wondered whether he'd wound it properly, willing himself to reach up and check. But his lids were heavy now and it seemed such a big, tiring effort...That mosquito was whining by his ear

31

again and he must check his watch, in a minute he would reach up for it...

He woke up with a jolt, his eyes wide and fearful. He was lying on his back, the filmy gauze of the mosquito net veiling the menacing shadows that lurked and shifted round about him. For a moment he wondered why the ship wasn't rocking, where the other berths in the cabin had got to, but then he heard the raucous voices outside laughing and shouting, and something that sounded like a violin only it made weird, screeching, endlessly undulating sounds, not like music at all really, just a continuously repeated wailing. He remembered with a sudden, hopeless, forlorn drop in his stomach that he was not safe on the boat, he was alone in China, in Shanghai. He must think of something nice and peaceful. Like the ship when he left England for instance: the band playing at Tilbury Dock, the people shouting and waving, the paper streamers whirring through the drizzly air. He'd kissed Emily on the cheek, stiffly and shyly in front of his parents, and she'd turned her face away blushing, her fair skin glowing right down to her throat. Perhaps further—no, he mustn't think of that. He thought instead of his father gripping his hat with one clawed, mottled hand and waving with the other, unsmiling; while his mother fluttered her handkerchief briefly then turned jerkily away. The coal black smoke had bellied up from the funnels and, as the gap between the quayside and the sliding vessel widened, their faces, then their whole bodies, had slowly blurred. The deck had begun to creak in the estuary as the level banks of the Thames slowly receded, dimmed, became a faint grey smudge merging with the clouds. And then England was gone.

9

There was a clink-clink of china by his head, and, more distantly, a hubbub of voices, wheels, and donkeys' braying. His eyes opened onto the brilliant, harsh light.

"Tea, master," the steward said, placing a thick white cup and saucer on the locker beside the bed.

Denton's stomach churned at the thought of the new

day and the new things he would have to do in it. He glanced covertly at the steward. He was wizened and crooked-shouldered and very thin. His wrists were like chicken bones covered with loose veiny skin beneath the frayed cuffs of his white sleeves. Why did they call them boys? he wondered, blinking at the spilt brown trickle of tea dribbling erratically down the side of the cup. The steward—the boy—had gone into the bathroom, and Denton heard water splashing into the wash-basin. He realised his nightshirt had become crumpled up above his knees. Shyly he jerked it down to a decent length.

"Ho' water," the boy said, clearing his throat noisily. He carried the toilet bucket out and shut the door.

Denton looked at his watch, still swinging gently on its chain. Quarter past six. He watched the long sweeping second hand ticking round. So he had wound it last night after all. His skin was still moist with sweat, his nightshirt felt damp with it. The sheets smelt faintly moist. He scratched a mosquito bite on his cheek, remembering the whining by his ear before he fell asleep. Lifting the gauze of the net aside—and that too felt damp, it must have got soggy and mouldy from the watery air—he sipped the strong, sweet tea. Had that noisy din outside gone on all night? He listened to the voices, trying to separate them from the confused hubbub of the other noises. A man was calling out the same chanting three notes, repeated again and again. A gong was clashing somewhere. Women's voices chattered stridently against each other. And all the time there was that undifferentiated swell of sound that rose and fell like the sea.

He swung his legs out of the bed and walked across to the veranda. Over the flat roofs of the low houses opposite, he saw the dull sheen of the river, gleaming sullenly in the early sunlight and bristling with masts, sails and funnels, some pouring out long plumes of smoke that rose straight up to the windless sky, others still and sleeping. Sirens and hooters blew, groaning and whooping like living monsters. Sampans moved slowly between the crowded ships, so slowly that they looked motionless, as though they'd been painted on the viscous surface of the river.

Hearing a donkey bray again, he glanced down into the street. There was a train of them plodding along, long ears twitching, loaded with baskets on each side. The baskets were open, and Denton saw they were full of human night-soil. He sniffed and caught the stench, wrinkling his nose. So that was where his toilet bucket went. Yet the hawkers and rickshaw coolies, the sedan chairs and the women carrying live chickens, ducks, bundles of fruits and vegetables bound with twists of rattan, seemed not to notice or care as they bustled along beside or amongst the donkeys, often brushing against the brimming panniers. His nose wrinkled again. He looked back at the broad waters of the river.

There was the *Orcades* gliding steadily downstream, smoke belching from her sloping yellow stacks, strings of coloured flags fluttering from her masts. He watched forlornly as the liner slid remorselessly away behind those bat-wing sails of the junks and the scaffolds of the cranes. For a moment he could see the lower deck where he'd said goodbye to Emily; then with the red ensign breaking at its stern, it was gone. He followed the masts above a warehouse wall, a patched junk sail, and then there was nothing but the drifting, spreading cloud of smoke staining the sky. He felt like a small abandoned child, just as he'd felt on his first schoolday, when his mother had left him in the screeching, shouting, alien Church School playground and he'd watched, paralysed with despair, as she sailed away, bonnet ribbons flying on the raw autumn wind.

"Come on, this won't do," he muttered sternly to himself, and turned to go in. But then there was a loud report somewhere in the street, followed by several others, like the rapid rifle fire he'd often heard from the small-arms factory in Enfield. He looked back startled, images of massacre and revolution tumbling panicky through his mind. But the street life went on undisturbed although the loud reports still banged away spasmodically. No heads turned, there were no police or soldiers, no rampant bloodthirsty mobs. Then he saw that the bangs came from a giant red paper firecracker hanging down from the first floor of a building further down the street. The firecracker was slowly smouldering upwards in a cloud of bluish smoke, intermittently flashing and banging as the little parcels of gunpowder concealed in it exploded. One or two passers-by glanced at the dangling red snake and some children had gathered round it, gaping and clapping their hands over their ears, but nobody else seemed to notice. Even the donkeys, now disappearing, only flattened their ears and shook their heads.

A white fluttering movement on the next veranda caught the corner of Denton's eye. Knowing it must be Mason's, he glanced round, forcing a false, uncertain smile of greeting. But through the iron lattice work that separated the two verandas he saw, not Mason, but a young Chinese girl. She was leaning over the parapet to watch the firecracker, wearing nothing but Mason's tunic. Her long black hair hung down over the white of the tunic, which reached as far as her bare knees. As she leant further over, the tunic moved up, and he saw the shadowy dimples at the back of each knee, the pale curve of her thighs.

His first thought was that he mustn't allow a lady to see him in his nightshirt, but instead of turning away, he stared stupefied at the girl's pale legs and tiny bare feet. Then she turned, and saw him. Mason's tunic was hanging open and Denton glimpsed a small, swelling breast, the round rosy circle of a nipple, a long streak of pale skin and a shadowy darkness between her legs before she casually shrugged the tunic closer round her. She eyed him coolly, her eyes seeming puffy with sleep, and walked back into Mason's bedroom, while Denton gazed stiffly past her.

"Nothing, Tibbee," he heard her chirp in a high toneless voice. "Onlee fi' cracka."

Denton went in and sat on the bed to finish his tea, his mind lurching from upright condemnation of what he'd just seen to turbulent images that went beyond it, images which he resolutely dismissed but which insidiously crept back again and again. He put the cup down and went into the bathroom, the vision of the girl's breast persisting wickedly in his mind.

There was a new bucket in the toilet box. He planted his legs before it sternly and imagined himself contemptuously upbraiding Mason. His own licentious thoughts slowly wilted too as he visualised Mason, shamefaced and crestfallen, turning and slinking away from him in the mess.

When he was dressed and ready to go down for breakfast, his old diffident shyness seized him. He would have to brave a roomful of strangers, who would all look up at him with hard, judging eyes, he would have to choose a table under their watchfulness, perhaps introduce himself, order his breakfast from the steward without swallowing his words. He waited for several minutes with his hand on the door, rehearsing how he would greet strangers, call a steward (*Boy! Boy!*), order from the menu...On the *Orcades* it had all been so much easier, a set meal without any choice at a set table. At last he forced himself to go. Even so, a creak on the boards outside held him back and he hung there listening till he was sure he wouldn't run into Mason or the Chinese girl outside, his brave imaginings of facing Mason down abjectly abandoned. Then he turned the handle gingerly and glanced cautiously through the crack before he slipped out and went down the stairs.

But breakfast went off all right. Johnson waved to him to join him at a table by the wall, and left after a few smiling bland remarks, so that Denton was able to order from the boy without being observed. He hastily chose a boiled egg—the first word he read on the menu—and signed his name to the chit afterwards without any mistake. Best of all, Mason didn't appear.

He decided he could walk to the tailor (he'd memorised the way when Mason took him the day before) which would save him the embarrassment and perhaps humiliation of trying to hire a rickshaw by himself.

When he set off, pretending to ignore the beggars and rickshaw coolies who besieged him as he walked down the broad stone steps, he saw a rickshaw being pulled away, a girl leaning back under the canopy. She glanced round at him with heavy-lidded eyes, very like those of the girl he'd seen on Mason's veranda. But he looked away at once before he could be certain, although he felt sure she continued to stare at him with a frank, inquisitive gaze.

10

On Thursday at ten he knocked on Mr. Brown's solid door and was summoned in. Mr. Brown was sitting, as before, writing at his desk, and the punkah creaked regularly, as before, over his lowered head.

"Let us see how much you have learnt." He closed his eyes and rested his bulging forehead between his hands, meditating for several long seconds, as if he were drawing the questions up from some solemn pool deep in his brain.

Denton licked his lips and waited.

At last Mr. Brown opened his eyes, raising his massive head just enough to rest his chin on the steepled tips of his fingers. He exhaled slowly through pursed lips, stirring the limp grey fringes of his moustache, and cleared his throat portentously. "Mr. Denton, what tax is chargeable on goods exported via Chinese ports?"

"Five per cent ad valorem, sir."

"And 'ad valorem' means?"

"According to value."

Mr. Brown's faint grey eyebrows rose, giving him an implausibly perplexed expression. "But who decides the value?"

"The assessor, sir."

"Correct, Mr. Denton, the assessor decides." His brows slowly lowered, and his eyes closed for a second. "Now tell me, what do you understand by the term 'likin'?"

"Er, it's a tax on anything that crosses the boundaries of a province."

"Anything, Mr. Denton? A donkey wandering in search of grass, for instance?"

"Oh." Denton stirred on his chair. "On specified goods only, sir."

"Exactly," Mr. Brown nodded deliberately, then rested his chin on his fingertips again. "On specified goods only, Mr. Denton. We must be precise."

"Yes sir."

"That is why we are here—to be precise. The Imperial Chinese government has had a Customs Service for hundred of years, Mr. Denton, but it was not precise. It is our duty to inject precision into a loose and apathetic organization that has not known it before and generally does not welcome it now."

"Yes sir."

"Precision, Mr. Denton." Again his brows rose in mock perplexity. "But who decides the amount of likin in cases where the value of those specified goods is contested between the Customs officer and the owner?"

"The assessor, sir?"

"Precisely, Mr. Denton." His eyes gleamed with pride, as if he had led a dull pupil to appreciate at last a sparkling intellectual truth. "There you have it, the assessor again!" He surveyed Denton satisfiedly for a moment and then narrowed his eyes gravely. "Now we come to the question of opium, a question which, together with the question of salt, may be regarded as providing the *raison d'être* of the Imperial Chinese Maritime Customs Service." He paused significantly and moistened his lips. "Under what circumstances is it now legal to import opium into China?"

"When it is handled by a Chinese importer, sir."

"And?"

Denton looked at him, nonplussed.

"Is it legal to import opium into China through a Chinese importer without payment of tax and, if need be, likin?"

"Oh I see, sir. No sir."

"No it is not." Mr. Brown smiled. He unsteepled his hands to toy with his watch chain, glancing up at the clock on the wall. "And in what ways are tax and likin payable?"

"Well, sir, it can be paid on entry into the country, in which case it is specially packed and stamped with the Customs seal..."

"With the Imperial Chinese Maritime Customs seal," Mr. Brown chided him.

"The Imperial Chinese Maritime Customs seal, sir," Denton nodded.

Mr. Brown was easing a gold watch out of his pocket. "Precision, Mr. Denton," he murmured. "Precision, even about titles."

"Yes sir."

He opened the case and frowned down at the dial, tilting his head to one side. "And the other method?"

"To put it in bond, sir."

Mr. Brown glanced from his watch to the clock on the wall, then closed the case and slid the watch back into his pocket, nodding gravely. "What is the regulation governing the importation of opium and when was it made effective?"

"Er, I think nineteen hundred and two, sir. I can't remember the number."

"Notification number two hundred and sixty one." Mr. Brown smiled again, self-gratulatingly. "And it became effective in nineteen hundred and three—this very year of grace."

"I see, sir."

38

"Is there any other method of paying tax and likin on opium imported into the Chinese empire?"

"Er, no sir. Opium from abroad is illegal to be imported," he stumbled and went on, "unless tax and likin have been paid like that."

"It is illegal to import opium otherwise, Mr. Denton. Not 'Opium from abroad is illegal to be imported.'"

"Yes sir."

"Precision in grammar as well as in other things. Always express yourself precisely."

"Yes sir."

"And finally," Mr. Brown stirred in his seat, "to whom must all reports of searches, inspections and confiscations be made in the first instance?"

"To the assessor, sir?"

"There you have it again Mr. Denton! The assessor once more! Always the assessor. Remember that, remember it well." His lids drooped slowly down in satisfaction. "Very well, Mr. Denton, that will do for now. I shall arrange for you to accompany Mr. Mason on his rounds in Upper Section and Mr. Johnson later, down at the Woosung forts."

"Thank you, sir."

"And have you found a suitable Chinese teacher yet?"

"I'm going to start next week, sir."

"I recommend you to apply yourself to it." He glanced sharply up at the punkah, which seemed to be slowing, and struck the bell on his desk three smart blows, still gazing upwards.

The blade began to swing more quickly again. Mr. Brown breathed out through his moustache. "Precision, you see, Mr. Denton. Precision in everything. Our watchword must be precision."

"Yes sir. Oh, and thank you for the invitation. It arrived this morning."

"No doubt you will be sending Mrs. Brown a note of acceptance in due course," Mr. Brown hinted discreetly as Denton rose to leave.

11

They moved from quay through the Upper Section of the wharves, Mason swaggering ahead, Denton following a pace behind, self-conscious in his new uniform. The docks, open to the sloping evening sun, stank of rotting refuse, coal dust, oil, and all the casual effluents of the city that the sluggish muddy waters of the river washed lazily along. Burly Sikh watchmen lounged by the gangways, swinging long wooden clubs, while coolies watched from the shade of the godowns, silent and lethargic, squatting on their heels and smoking cigarettes through wide brown bamboo pipes.

At each vessel the Chinese agent greeted them respectfully and handed Mason the cargo manifest, waiting alertly—often, it seemed, nervously—while Mason lounged in the saloon, assessing duty and demanding in his abrupt, domineering tones to inspect some case or other in the hold. Each agent offered them drinks, cigarettes and cigars with ingratiating politeness. Mason invariably accepted, sticking the unsmoked cigar in his tunic pocket.

"What's the matter?" he asked sarcastically after Denton had declined everything on the first two ships. "Don't you have any vices? Not even one?"

"I don't smoke or drink really," Denton apologised uncomfortably, afraid of exposing himself to Mason's mockery, and simultaneously ashamed of his fear. It was true, he didn't smoke or drink (he'd signed the pledge at the Band of Hope when he was seventeen), but he was also thinking of the regulation he'd studied in the third, tan pamphlet Mr. Brown had given him, in which the acceptance of gifts of any description from persons dealing directly or indirectly with the Customs Service was expressly forbidden. On the third ship, a British India Steam Navigation tramp steamer, its hull dented and rusty, Mason seemed to divine this thought of Denton's. "Well if you don't smoke yourself, you could at least take a cigar or two for your pals," he muttered peevishly as the agent, a slight, young Chinese in a dark blue gown, with swift, shining eyes, offered them three cigars each. "Or is it the rules that are stopping you? You needn't worry about them, nobody gives a tinker's cuss about a few cigars, you know!" He sniffed one of the cigars he'd taken himself, but said nothing, merely raising his brows in derisive amazement, when Denton again refused the cigars offered to him.

It was on that ship that Denton first saw opium.

Mason carelessly ordered the opium consignment opened and took some of the dense-packed brown stuff in his fingers to smell it. "Here, have a sniff." He held it out to Denton. "Best quality Indian. Worth a packet, even after tax."

Denton's nose wrinkled at the rich, greasy smell, which he realised then he'd already encountered in faint whiffs on the waterfront and in some of the streets he'd passed along. Mason suddenly reached forward to tuck a few shreds under the flap of Denton's pocket. "There you are," he laughed, one eye on the agent. "Smuggle some ashore."

The agent chuckled obsequiously, his dark eyes glistening, while Mason went back into the saloon to compute the tax.

When they'd finished with all the ships berthed at the quays, they boarded a waiting Customs launch flying the Imperial Chinese pennant. "*Alexander the First*," Mason ordered the coxswain, a tubby Chinese with a rolling double chin that gave him a comfortable, jolly look. "Number four buoy." Mason held four fingers up in front of the coxswain's nose to ram the number home. "Number four, all right?"

They went forward as the clanking engine started, dark smoke spurting up from the single grimy funnel. The sun was just setting over the skyline, a collection of long roofs and chimneys, black and sharp-edged against the great disc that sank further with every second, like a slowly-winking angry eye.

"That's the French Concession over there," Mason nodded.

Denton gazed at the buildings, lower, older and shabbier than the merchant palaces along the International Settlement's Bund. "Is it interesting?" he asked.

"Depends what you're looking for," Mason glanced enigmatically at him from under slyly lowered lids.

Denton didn't speak again until the closing eye of the sun had vanished behind the buildings in the west. The sky still smouldered, reflecting its glow upon the smooth brownish waters of the river. He glanced back at the International Settlement, growing a dusky mauve and blurred already behind them. "I wonder where the nearest church is?" he said unguardedly, half-aloud.

41

"What?" Mason turned to look at him as though he thought he must have misheard. "What church?"

"Well, the Church of England."

"God knows." He guffawed suddenly at his unintended witticism, and then repeated it to ensure Denton appreciated it too. "God knows. And if He doesn't, who would, eh? There are dozens of 'em. Why? Thinking of getting married?"

"I'll... I'll need to know for Sunday," Denton muttered as if grudgingly confessing to some embarrassing frailty.

"Will you now?" Mason glanced at him, then looked down at the water. "Personally I'd rather do something enjoyable on Sundays," he said at last, drily, brushing the ends of his moustache lightly upwards with the back of his knuckle. Then he took out one of the cigars he'd been given and turned away from the wind to light it, smoking in silence as they drew nearer to the Russian liner.

Denton watched a blue sack-like thing floating in the water just ahead, wallowing almost below the surface. It slowly turned, rose, and sank as though it were being gently rolled and tugged from below. Mason had seen it too, and was leaning forward on the rail.

"It looks like a body," Denton said.

"It *is* a body," Mason answered coolly. He called out to the coxswain and the launch slackened speed.

Mason was right. It *was* a body, floating face down, its trousers and shirt darkened by the water and glistening slightly as it broke the surface. The queue, still neatly plaited, snaked away from the head like a piece of sodden black rope.

Denton's pulse quickened and he found himself holding his breath while he gazed at the submerged face, as if he himself were under the water. The coxswain fetched a boat hook and tried to hook the corpse's shirt with it. But the hook caught in the putrid flesh beneath and a piece flaked off like sodden pastry. A dark thick liquid oozed out.

"Phew!" Mason threw his cigar away. It landed with a little hiss in the water a few feet from the body. "Can bring on board? Bring topside?"

"No can do." The tubby coxswain laughed almost gaily, except that at the same time his eyes were mournful. "He go open, open." He closed his hands then flapped

42

them open several times to express how the body would disintegrate if they touched it.

"Let him go then," Mason said, waving dismissively. "Or her. Can't tell, can you?"

The coxswain gave an obedient little shove to the corpse, pushing it under. It sank slowly, rolling on its side, then slowly rose again, rolling back, so that its greenish, eyeless face gaped at them for a moment, the flesh half gone. It was like a last silent scream for help.

The coxswain walked back to the wheelhouse, trailing the boat hook in the water to clean it. The engine clanked clamorously and they steamed on.

"That's one the slops didn't find," Mason said, his nose still wrinkled above his ginger moustache. "They pick up the corpses by the docks every morning. That one must've floated out. Been in a few days too, by the look of it, although they do rot pretty fast in this weather. Enough to put you off your grub, isn't it?"

Denton swallowed a little sour tide of nausea that was rising up his throat. "What d'you think happened?" he asked.

Mason shrugged. "There are usually a hundred or so bumping along the quays every morning. The slops have a special boat with nets to catch 'em with. Like trawling for fish."

"A hundred?"

"About that, yes. Hunger, disease, gang-fights, ordinary murders and robberies—they all end up in the river. Nice and convenient. Some of our informers end up there too."

"Informers?"

"How d'you think we nab the smugglers then?" He laughed shortly. "We'd never get 'em, the likes of you and me. The Chinks are too crafty for us. It takes a Chink to see through a Chink. We have to buy tips. They'd sell their best friend for fifty dollars, too. That's how we do it."

Soon they came alongside the gleaming white hull of the *Alexander the First*. The gangway trembled and swayed under Mason's weight as he clambered heavily up the steps. The agent was waiting for them at the top, an older man this time, dressed in a long silk gown with full sleeves and wearing a little round hat on his head. "Good evening, Mista' May-song," he smiled, affably rather than deferentially, giving a ceremonious bow that seemed almost mocking as he held out the cargo manifest courteously in both hands. The little finger nail of his left hand was long and curving, like some bird's talon.

"Evening, Mr. Ching." Mason replied with a grudging surly politeness himself. "My assistant, Mr. Denton."

The agent bowed with the same mocking ceremony. "Good evening, Mr. Den-tong, how are you do?" His voice was high and loud, with none of the deference of the other agents.

Denton nodded and smiled awkwardly. He noticed how pale the man's skin was, as though it had never been in the sun, and wondered why Mason so uncharacteristically treated him with a certain respect.

Mason was leafing through the sheets of the manifest, each covered with a strange, looped writing that looked illegible to Denton. Then he glanced up, shaking the sheets together. "We'll sort this out while we're eating, all right?"

"Of course, Mista' May-song." The agent bowed again, folding his hands together in his sleeves, then led the way with short gliding steps, his gown flowing behind him, to the first class saloon.

They had hardly sat down at a table by the window, when the chief steward himself appeared, ushered in by the agent.

"What will you like to drink?" Mr. Ching was asking, smiling that same courteous yet faintly mocking smile as he looked down at them through his rimless glasses. The chief steward snapped his fingers for the wine list.

"Sherry to start with. What about you, Denton? I can't stand vodka, myself."

"Oh, nothing for me thank you," Denton said hurriedly. "Or just a glass of ginger beer?"

"Sherry and ginger beer?" Mr. Ching turned to the chief steward and spoke to him briefly in Russian, leading him gently away.

He speaks Russian as well," Denton remarked tentatively. "The agent."

"Yes. Used to live up near the Russian border." Mason opened the menu and studied it, frowning. "Keep on the right side of him. He knows a thing or two."

Confused by the names on the menu, Denton let Mason order for both of them. The putrefying corpse clearly hadn't put Mason off his grub after all, Denton noticed, nor indeed himself. It was as though it hadn't really been human at all, but some strange decaying fish. Only when he recalled the sightless eyes and exposed teeth did Denton feel a nauseous qualm.

After the meal, Mason sipped a brandy and picked over the box of cigars the steward brought them, while Mr. Ching smoothed the cargo manifest out on the table in front of him. "Wouldn't get this in second class," he nudged Denton as the attentive steward lit the long cigar he finally selected. At last he looked reluctantly down at the manifest's sheets trembling under the fan, and began turning them languidly.

"Here, time you got started," he said abruptly after a while. "Sort out the tax on this lot. I'll check it afterwards." He got up, dabbing his moustache with his napkin and went with Mr. Ching to the far corner of the saloon, where the agent refilled his brandy while they talked quietly, facing each other across the table like card players.

At first Denton thought he wouldn't be able to decipher the script, but as he worked at the pages he found he could make it out after all. He finished with a lift of pride that was only slightly dashed when Mason negligently checked his calculations without comment.

"All right," he burped. "Let's sign."

"Shouldn't we examine one of the cases?" Denton asked doubtfully.

"Hell, I s'pose we'd better," Mason frowned in annoyance. "Have 'em open up a case will you, Mr. Ching?" He turned back to Denton as the agent rustled away. "Teaching me my job now, are you?" he muttered, in a tone that seemed to hover uncertainly between indignation and bantering.

A case was opened in number three hold and Mason checked the contents perfunctorily against the manifest. "All right," he turned away. "Let's sign and be off."

As they were approaching the gangway, Mason suddenly stopped, slapping his pocket. "Forgot my report book" he said. "You go ahead, tell them to get ready. They're probably fast asleep, the lazy devils."

It was night now, violet and soft, the lights glistening along the shore, with little misty hazes of moisture round them. Denton looked over the side at the Customs launch. The coxswain was talking to one of the sailors, looking up expectantly at Denton. The boiler fire glowed on their faces, and the water all round the boat seemed black and still, as if it had been varnished.

"We're just coming." Denton called down. The coxswain moved into the shadow of the wheelhouse and then the engine began its vociferous clanking.

He returned along the empty, dimly-lit companion ways to the dining saloon. Mason was holding a white envelope in his hand, talking to Mr. Ching in a low, tense voice. They moved apart when they saw him. Mr. Ching quickly smiled, but Denton felt he had intruded. "They're ready," he said apologetically to Mason. "Did you find it?"

"What?" Mason stared at him blankly.

"Your report book."

"Oh." His face loosened. "Yes, got it. It was on the, er, on the table there all the time."

They all looked at the table, while Mason slipped the envelope into the inside pocket of his tunic.

"Goodbye, Mista' Den-tong," Mr. Ching said in his high cheerful voice. "Goodbye, Mista' May-song."

Mason buttoned his tunic as he went along. He walked most of the way without talking, but then began speaking with a sudden heartiness. "Extraordinary thing," he chuckled. "The old chief steward on this tub sent me a letter." He patted his pocket as if he was willing to produce the evidence if Denton doubted him. "We used to go round a bit when he came ashore. Nice of him to remember me, eh?"

Once on board the launch, Mason leant silently against the rail, one foot on the neatly coiled rope, unusually self-involved. Denton wondered why he didn't read his letter. There was light enough from the lamp on the mast.

"He's got a very fair skin for a Chinese, Mr. Ching?" he asked across the uneasy silence.

"Mm."

The night air sliding over his face was mild and cool. "I always thought Chinese were yellow, but he's paler than many Englishmen," Denton risked again as the silence between them tautened once more.

"They come in all shapes, sizes and colours," Mason answered brusquely.

Rebuffed, Denton didn't speak again. He recalled the moral distance he'd meant to keep from Mason and turned his head stiffly to watch the dark shapes of the ships they passed, each lit by pale twinkling lights.

The launch put in at the Bund, near the Shanghai Club. Denton gazed up at the long, brightly-lit building with its wide verandas and balconies, from which he could hear the distant, muffled sound of music and laughter, cheerful and assured. He watched two Sikhs in red tunics and white turbans stamping their polished boots arrogantly outside the main entrance, magnificent under the heavy gas lamps as they summoned sedan chairs or rickshaws for the members emerging in evening dress from the open doors. As Denton watched, Mr. Brown arrived in a sedan chair borne by four coolies, with an oil lantern burning yellowly on one of the poles. He inclined his shiny bald head, with its woolly circlet of grey hair, as the Sikhs saluted him and ascended the stone steps with a steady, stately step, as if he knew Denton was watching and wished to impress the dignity of his office upon him once more.

12

He took the letter from the rack with a slight churning feeling in the top of his stomach, and walked slowly into the lounge. He'd recognised Emily's long-anticipated handwriting from a distance, but now that her letter had come, he felt an apprehensive reluctance to open it, as if it might contain bad news. Through the open doors he could hear the soft clack of balls in the billiards room as, his pulse quickening faintly, he pushed his little finger under the envelope flap and tore it open. He drew the letter out.

Dear John,

It is only a fortnight since you left, but it seems an age already. I am back at the college and you will be somewhere in the Mediterranean by now. This last week has been quite hard and I always get a headache in the tram coming home. But I expect I will get used to it. The weather has not been too bad, although I expect you are getting a lot more sunshine than we are . . . When you have got this letter, I expect you will be quite used to your new life. Write and tell me all about it, and how your trip was and everything. I expect you stopped at a lot of interesting places. I wish it was not quite so far away though. Is it very hot? Do the natives understand

English? I always thought Chinese was a hard language to learn, but I suppose you can if you have to. There is going to be another lantern show about the missionaries' work in China next month. I expect I will go.

Mother and Father send their best wishes and ask to be remembered to you.

Love from Emily.

PS I am sending this to the address you gave me. Hope it is right.

As he finished reading, Denton became aware again of the quiet clacking of billiard balls, then of Mason's high piercing laughter. He read the letter through once more, this time painting images to accompany the words. He saw her wavy brown hair, her hazel eyes, the way she held her head a little on one side and forward when she listened.

Folding the letter slowly, he put it back into the torn envelope, smoothing the rough edges of the flap down as if he were trying to seal it again.

They hadn't done much spooning, only holding hands and walking to the Band of Hope together, sitting side by side at lectures in the college and on the tram there and back. But he felt how pure their love was, unsullied by the sordid lusts of such as Mason, whom he heard again laughing loudly and penetratingly in the billiards room. Their love was spiritual, he thought solemnly, spiritual and undefiled.

He stood up, sliding the letter into his tunic pocket, and walked towards the stairs. She would wait for him, he would be faithful to her. Eventually he would send for her...

Lighting the gaslight in his room, he took off his tunic and drew the letter out again. A strange, slightly greasy smell seemed to cling to it. He frowned, holding it close to his nose. Surely she hadn't used scent or perfume—not Emily? Then he remembered the threads of opium Mason had stuffed into his pocket. He felt deep inside until he could pick up the twisted little strands between his fingers. Rolling them between his finger and thumb, he sniffed cautiously. Yes, it was the same smell. Perhaps it wasn't so unpleasant after all—just very, very rich. He dropped the opium into the waste paper basket and wiped his hands carefully with his handkerchief. Opium, he was sure, was wrong, just as intoxicating liquor was wrong—a danger to

religion and morals. Yet, in its rich, heavy way, that clinging smell wasn't at all unpleasant really...

13

The cathedral's pews were nearly all filled when Denton
arrived, and a grave, tall sidesman with watery brown eyes
motioned him to a chair in the aisle. He leant forward,
covering his eyes, and whispered a prayer. When he sat
upright again he had already forgotten the words he'd
muttered, as though he'd prayed mechanically, as unconsciously as he breathed or blinked. He glanced round at
the grey stone arches of the nave and up at the tall stained
glass windows, which the burning sunlight outside struggled to pierce. Everything was new; the dark wooden
pews, the unworn flagstones, the vivid colours in the
windows, the fresh grey pillars. Musing treble notes
wandered up and down the bass drone of the organ like
ivy caressing a great broad tree. Denton thought of St.
George's at Enfield—so much smaller and dimmer than
this magnificent airy building. He thought of Emily in her
pew with her parents, lowering her eyes with a secet smile
when he glanced at her from the choir stalls.

He clung to the poignant image, part-memory, part-
fiction, until his eye was caught by the figure of Mr.
Brown walking up the nave toward a pew near the pulpit.
A tall, stout lady rested her hand on his arm. They
progressed at a stately gait, their heads erect and motionless until they reached their pew, when Mr. Brown handed
his wife in first with a grave inclination of his massive-
browed bald head.

Denton glanced over the rest of the congregation,
sweat oozing from his pores despite the gently-squeaking
punkahs that fanned the air above their heads. All the
people in the nave were evidently rich—taipans, he supposed. You could tell by their clothes, the women in
gorgeous dresses and sweeping, wide-brimmed hats, the
men in faultlessly-cut silk suits. Watching them, Denton
felt vague confused, feelings both of envy and of aliena-
tion. He knew that he wanted to wear fine clothes like Mr.
Brown, to have a sedan chair waiting outside the cathedral, to belong to the Shanghai Club, to be looked upon

49

with awe by people like himself. Yet he felt he was not like Mr. Brown and the other taipans, and never would be. There was some essential difference that would always keep him removed from them, their lives unassimilable. His mind slipped off to the church at Enfield, where the congregation were all workmen and shopkeepers in stiff dark suits with frayed button holes and shiny collars, the grime still under their finger-nails.

Shanghai was beginning to unsettle him. He was becoming dimly aware of possibilities in the distance that had lain far beyond the level horizon of his life even when he'd been accepted for the teachers' training college and his father had said he was out of it now, he'd never have to work in a factory.

To stifle his unease, he joined in the opening hymn with a loud voice, following the choir's tenor descant.

> *Praise Him, praise Him, praise Him, praise Him,*
> *Praise the everlasting King.*

Denton waited, listening to the hushed coughing and the closing hymn books and the shuffling feet, determined to concentrate now on the worship of God. He gazed up at the gaunt face of the Dean, who had turned by the altar to face the congregation. But even while he was watching the Dean's grey head and penetrating, deep-set eyes, his fickle mind had slipped off again, and he was wondering about Emily, his hand surreptitiously straying up to the pocket where her letter nestled. What would she be doing now? Sleeping? What would she be wearing? A nightdress? *And under the nightdress?* a voice whispered, while the memory of the girl on Mason's veranda, her breast uncovered beneath his tunic, floated across his mind. He jerked his mind guiltily back to the Dean, who had begun intoning in a high, strained voice, his eyes fixed in vacant reverence above their heads.

"If we say we have no sin, we deceive ourselves..."

He could feel a warm slow trickle of sweat rolling slowly down his cheek. Behind the Dean, over whose head a punkah moved slowly to and fro as though it were a blessing hand, he saw the choristers turning the pages of their hymn books, the leaves fluttering like little white butterflies.

50

14

Dear Sir,

I am honoured to accept to teach you the Chinese language, mandarin or Shangahi dialect according to you choosing. My fees are $5 per hour, for which you receive compensation from imperial customs service on receipt. I will call at you in your rooms on Tuesday 9th August at the 4 o'clock and esteem your honoured favour.

Wei Lam-tung.

Denton drew his watch out and held it away from him, letting it hang and slowly spin upon its chain. Five to four. He read the letter through again and replaced it on his desk. One of the little green lizards that had so disquieted him on his first day rippled along the wall above his head. He watched it pause in stone-like immobility then dart forward to take a little fly with a flick of its whiplash tongue, gulping it down before returning at once to that watchful immobility.

One minute before four there was a shuffling outside the door and a knock. The boy entered and wordlessly gestured a spare little Chinese with glinting, metal-rimmed spectacles towards Denton.

Denton stood up as the Chinese, dressed in a grey silk tunic and trousers, offered him a small, limp hand. "Mr. Denton?"

"Yes. Mr. Wei?" Denton noticed the long, curling nail on the little finger of the man's other hand—a polished claw two inches long, just like the agent's on the *Alexander the First*. The hands were pale and hairless, paler than his own sunburned, reddish ones, which seemed, with their dark hairs, to be suddenly crude and coarse beside them. The long finger nail and anaemic pallor of Mr. Wei's hands made him wonder a moment whether he could be related to the agent—Ching, wasn't that his name? But Ching was tall and uncomfortably mocking, whereas Wei was short and seemed to be open and eager.

"How do you doing?" Mr. Wei smiled with a bird-like jerk of his neck. A gold tooth winked moistly in his lower jaw. "Please' to meet you." He was holding a leather

51

satchel. He opened it deliberately and took out two books, placed them carefully on the arm of the chair Denton offered him, then perched himself on the edge of the seat as if ready to take flight. "Mr. Denton," he asked, his gold tooth gleaming as he smiled again, "how are you like Shanghai?"

"Very nice," Denton murmured. "It's very hot, of course."

"Very ho'," Mr. Wei nodded emphatically. "Perhaps a typhoon will come. Many rains."

"Oh they bring many—a lot of rain, do they?"

"Quite a lo'. In winter it is col'."

"Ah."

"Very col'. But blue sky."

"Not like England?"

Mr. Wei shook his head, his glasses glinting flatly in the light from the veranda. "Very col'," he repeated emphatically.

They paused. Denton, glancing stealthily at Mr. Wei's unlined, taut-skinned face, was unable to put an age to it, Thirty? Fifty? It could be either.

Mr. Wei's glance met his inquiringly and he looked away, clearing his throat. Yet he had nothing to say, so he waited awkwardly. Outside, a man's voice chanted a hawker's call and he imagined the heat and glare of the street, which the heavy wooden shutters dimmed.

"Mr. Denton, for Chinese lesson, what are you want?"

"I beg your pardon?"

"Chinese language many form, Mr. Denton." He held up his hands, pale fingers outspread, to indicate its variety. "Mandarin, Shanghai, Canton, Fukien..."

"Oh, I see."

"All same writing." His gold tooth gleamed. "Speaking all differen'."

"Yes, well, I think Shanghainese, as that's where I'll be working."

"Shanghai, good." He nodded his head several times as though in approval, then took the lower book from the arm of the chair, holding it out to Denton with both hands and giving a little bow.

Denton half-rose to take the book, and some obscure intuition led him to take it with both hands too. Mr. Wei's gold tooth gleamed as he smiled approvingly again. "Mr. Denton, you will be goo' pupil. Already you take thing

Chinese way. One hand give or take is very ru'. Only for coolie," his hand waved scornfully. "For equal and superior, must give and take with both hand. In China, teacher is superior," Mr. Wei went on, smiling widely. "So you must take from me with both han'. Number one lesson, very goo'."

Denton looked down at the book uncertainly. Was Mr. Wei getting above himself? That suggestion of superiority—how would Mason have taken it? But Wei was speaking again in his precise yet stilted manner, unlike the toneless chanting of all the other Chinese he'd heard speaking English.

"You are official of Chinese Imperial Governmen'," Wei was saying with his gold-winking smile, his bright brown eyes watching Denton alertly behind the magnifying discs of his glasses. "Not like business man, speak pidgin. You must learn proper Chinese, learn character! Three thousan' character enough for newspaper," Wei continued, holding up his hand for attention, three fingers flung out rigidly. "Only for newspaper, nor ver' goo'. How many alphabe' in English?"

"Alphabets?"

"Twenty-six alphabe'," Wei gave him no chance to answer. "Twenty-six alphabe' in English, then all finish. No more to learn. But Chinese three thousan' character, only beginning. Five thousan', ten thousan', still not finish. I think three thousan' much more number than twenty-six? So, you see, to learn Chinese, you mus' work ver' har'." He reached into his satchel. "Here brush, and ink, and paper." He drew them out one by one. "To write Chinese character. Chinese character very difficul', Mr. Denton. You must work ver' har'."

"Yes I will," Denton promised, infected by Wei's enthusiasm despite himself. "I do want to learn to write well."

"To write an' read well, goo'." Mr. Wei nodded encouragingly. "Now we star' lesson." He perched further forward, his hands on his spread knees, and gazed unblinkingly at Denton. "Chinese language not like English language."

"No..."

Wei held up his hand for stricter attention. "If same sound have differen' tone, make differen' word. Listen." He moistened his lips and spoke a few words slowly and distinctly, his voice rising and falling in that strange sing-song that Denton heard all round him in the streets. "Now I say again." He repeated the sounds, slowly and distinctly again. "You hear the same or differen'?"

"The same," Denton said promptly.

He shook his head, smiling his gold-winking smile again. "The tone is differen', so they make differen' word'. One mean 'I know Chinese people', the other mean 'I eat Chinese people'. Therefore tone in Chinese language ver' importan'. Now we begin to learn tone'."

15

Unable to find any small cash, Denton paid off the rickshaw with an extravagant tip and walked apprehensively towards the wide stone steps that led up to the porch of the Browns' house. There was a balustrade each side of the steps, from which coloured paper lanterns hung on slender, swaying bamboo slips that had been fixed in the stonework. More lanterns swung gently on the veranda. Voices murmured behind the open windows. Denton fingered his bow tie anxiously as he climbed the steps. He peered up irresolutely at the lighted, empty porch.

"Ah. Mr. Denton, it must be." The tall stout lady he'd seen with Mr. Brown at the cathedral appeared in the hall, dressed in a long black evening dress with billowy lace sleeves. "How kind of you to come." Her voice was stout too, booming in fact. Denton felt her pale blue eyes measuring him frankly, so that his hand crept up to his tie again, in case it had loosened. "Do come in," she said at last, as if pleased, or at least satisfied, by her inspection.

An elderly houseboy, his skin puckered into an apparently sardonic grin, took his hat.

"Ah Man!" Mrs. Brown commanded, grasping Denton's hand firmly. "Paraffin!"

The houseboy was already bending with a sigh under the black Chinese table with claw feet on which he'd placed Denton's new, and as yet unpaid for, silk hat. He brought out a spraying can and stooped to point it at Denton's ankles, pumping with a slow, wheezing sound. A fine, cold, oily haze enveloped his evening dress trousers, his socks and shoes, all bought with chits, glistening on them in a dew of little silvery droplets. Denton watched, mystified and vaguely alarmed.

"So much better than muslin bags, don't you think, Mr. Denton?" Mrs. Brown asked. "Come along, then."

Denton nodded and mumbled while Mrs. Brown sailed ahead of him towards a large sitting-room, her dress just brushing the floor behind her. "The mosquitoes are quite terrible this year, we simply have to do something. It's all these canals, of course, I keep begging the municipal council to fill them in, but nothing ever gets done."

Denton followed obediently in her train, awed and bemused, a distinct smell of paraffin rising from his feet. He saw Brown's round shining dome, with its fringe of grey curly wool, and twenty or so men and women, all splendidly dressed, who turned their heads and paused to survey him as Mrs. Brown led him in. He stood meekly beside her.

"Now this is Mr. Denton, Arthur's latest griffin," she announced in her booming tones, and proceeded round the room, naming every person in the same loud voice, as if she thought he was deaf. Denton smiled stiffly, shook hands stiffly, bowed stiffly and mumbled how d'you do to one guest after another, forgetting every name as soon as he heard it. But near the end of the round, his cheeks rigid with his taut artificial smile, he found himself facing Everett, his fellow-passenger on the *Orcades*.

"Hullo, how are you getting on?" Everett asked, his round, ruddy cheeks, like little apples, crinkling as he smiled.

"Oh, you two have met already, have you?" Mrs. Brown interrupted. "Well, you can have a little chat later. I want you to meet some other people first, Mr. Denton."

Soon Denton was sitting beside an elderly lady whose sagging cheeks were pallid with powder. She had merely nodded when Mrs. Brown introduced him, and now, fanning herself with fierce jerky energy, she turned her back on him to continue an edgy discussion with the couple on her left. The rapid movement of the fan in her mottled hand seemed to match a growing exasperation in her low, cracked voice. Another houseboy, with a dour unsmiling face, offered him a glass of sherry on a silver tray. "No thank you," Denton said, but the houseboy seemed not to hear, obdurately holding the tray out in front of him. So Denton took the glass, shrinking back into his seat to avoid the elderly lady's bony elbow. He sat uneasily sipping the sherry which, like the beer Mason had ordered for him on his first day, and despite his pledge at the Band of Hope three years before, he was too timid to refuse.

55

Suddenly the old lady turned to him, fanning herself with vigorous impatience. "So you're in the Chinese Customs?" she began accusingly.

"Er, yes. That is, I've just joined," he answered deprecatingly. "It's only probationary for two years..."

"I've never understood why we should give them any help at all," she cut him off sharply. "Such a corrupt, barbaric government." Her fan became even more excited as her voice hardened. "And as for that woman...the Dowager Empress...!" She sniffed up the spite she seemed unable to express in words. "It would never have been allowed if Queen Victoria were still alive," she snapped finally. "That I am quite sure of."

Denton had no reply to give her, but in any case she had turned away already with a scornful shrug, as though looking for something more worthy of her steel.

At dinner he sat between two middle-aged ladies whose names he never caught. They talked to him so infrequently and perfunctorily that he was able to attend to all the knives and forks and the two wine glasses watchfully and without blundering. When the ladies suddenly got up to leave, Denton was about to follow them. He'd felt so thirsty that he'd kept on drinking the wines the boy poured for him, and he thought muzzily that those who were staying must be holding some meeting which he wasn't invited to. But Everett caught his arm and pushed him into the seat beside him. "Come and sit with me," he said loudly, then muttered, "Port and cigars, the ladies are withdrawing."

Denton flushed and nodded, humiliated. But now he was sitting next to Mr. Brown, who appeared at first astonished to see him there, regarding him puzzledly for some seconds while he stroked his luxuriant grey moustache. Then, as port, brandy and cigars were set on the long, richly glossy table, the perplexity cleared from his eyes. "Tell me, Mr. Denton," he asked, selecting a cigar, "As a young fellow just out from home, what do they think of the China Question now?"

"The China Question, sir?" Denton felt himself sliding down through blank featureless waters while Mr. Brown's pale blue eyes rested expectantly on his, as if following him down from the rim of a well. "The China Question?" He clutched desperately at broken straws. "Well, sir, I think that, er...the new King has a different attitude to Queen Victoria's. I think," he added doubtfully.

"*From* Queen Victoria's," Mr. Brown said precisely, pressing his lips together under the brushy grey fringe of his moustache. "I must say I'm surprised by what you say. Personally, I disagree entirely with the imperialists."

Denton nodded respectfully, as though he too might have said the same thing if he'd presumed to offer an opinion of his own. He watched Mr. Brown turn aside as the boy lit his cigar, then lean forward again, blowing out a jet of greyish blue smoke while he rubbed his bulging brow reflectively. The boy had filled Denton's glass with port and he drank it down, still trying to quench the thirst he'd felt all evening in his stiff hot clothes. His eyes were beginning to smart from the smoke, the humid heat, and the alcohol he'd unwisely drunk. As he waited uneasily for Mr. Brown to speak again, it seemed to him that the room was beginning to waver in a blurry mist. Part of him felt an apprehensive tremor at this strange experience, but part seemed unconcerned and careless. He watched the boy fill his glass again and watched his hand reach out and raise it to his lips.

"Have you commenced your Chinese lessons yet, Mr. Denton?"

Denton blinked, moving his head slowly to still the misty swaying of the room. "Started on Tuesday, sir," he said, trying carefully not to slur his words. "One lesson a week."

He was conscious of Mr. Brown's eyes resting on him again, and felt he ought to say something more. "The Chinese Question is very difficult," he added uncertainly.

Mr. Brown's eyes seemed to widen and cool slightly. "It is said to be so," he said distantly. "But it was the Chinese language we were discussing."

"What do you think of the opium trade, sir?" Everett asked suddenly as the silence grew longer and heavier after Mr. Brown's last remark.

"The opium trade?" Mr. Brown turned slowly to Everett, "My government—that, the Chinese government—allows it, we know it is harmless when indulged in moderation, and it fosters international commerce..."

Now Denton began to feel tired as well as muzzy. His lids kept sliding slowly down over his eyes and he had to open them with a start, only to feel them slowly slide down again a few seconds later. He nodded vaguely as Mr. Brown's voice flowed past him in a murmuring river of sound.

"We cannot take his choice from the individual," Mr. Brown was pronouncing judicially, "even from the humblest peasant or coolie, without diminishing him in his essential nature. Free trade, Mr. Everett, is closely associated with deeper freedoms—Mr. Denton, I fear I am boring you?" Denton awoke with a start.

When they returned to the drawing room at last, Denton managed to seat himself between Everett on one side and a group of four or five people on the other, who only occasionally interrupted their discussion of servants and horses to glance curiously at him, when he would smile confusedly with bleary eyes and they would turn away with lifted brows and continue.

Everett stood up to leave at last, and Denton rose too, treading on one of the ladies' shoes, and mumbling apologies as she winced and stared at him under raised, curved brows.

"You must come again," Mrs. Brown boomed to Everett, then, more coolly, "I hope you are getting along in your work," she added to Denton.

Denton walked a little unsteadily down the steps beside Everett, while the boy hailed a rickshaw for them both. The paper lanterns were still softly glowing, but their luminousness seemed tired now, hazy-rimmed.

"You know, I'm afraid I may have made myself a bit ill with all that wine," Denton confessed blurrily. "D'you think anyone noticed? I'm not used to it, you see."

"Oh I shouldn't think so," Everett answered casually.

He turned to look at Everett anxiously, the words tumbling out of his mouth almost before he was aware of them. "I'm not used to it, you see, and they kept filling up my glass. D'you think Mr. Brown noticed anything?" Before Everett could answer, another nagging thought that had been vaguely troubling Denton all evening rose up like a bubble to the surface of his mind. "And what's all that about muslin bags Mrs. Brown told me? Do they catch mosquitoes in them or what? And spraying me with paraffin—what was the idea?"

"You tie the bags over your ankles." Everett smiled patronisingly. "It's just to stop the mozzies biting you. Like mosquito nets." He leant back, wrinkling his nose as they passed by a festering little canal in which the pale, bloated body of a dog floated on its side. "Some people prefer paraffin, other prefer muslin, that's all. We've got both in our mess."

"We don't have anything in our mess." Denton felt obscurely deprived and aggrieved. "I hope I don't catch malaria."

"Malaria? What's that got to do with mosquitoes?" Everett peered into his face. "You really have had a bit too much."

"No, I read about it in the paper in England," Denton persisted doggedly, straining to remember through the mists that were rolling across his mind. "Before I left home."

"No, it's from the swampy air," Everett said decidedly. "You've only got to smell it."

In the thick moist heat, with the coolie panting in front of them between his wooden shafts, amidst the shadowy figures, the weird cries of the Chinese, the ripe, rotting, alien smells, Denton's mention of home had tugged loose a little avalanche of self-pitying images. What with malaria and cholera and all those other diseases, he wondered desolately whether he'd ever see Emily or his parents or home again.

16

Johnson was teaching Denton snooker. Lining up his ball carefully on the black, Denton swung the cue gently. The ball kissed the black on the wrong side and rolled smoothly away into the pocket.

"You lifted your head," Johnson explained consolingly. "You lifted your head as you hit it. Otherwise you might've got it." He sipped from the beer he'd placed on the edge of the table, smacked his lips, and leant over to make his shot. The cue slid easily forward over the crook of his finger and thumb, the ball seemed to run inevitably towards the black, there was a click and the black sank into the pocket.

"Well, if we could have a table down at the Woosung

forts next week," Johnson said encouragingly as he finished his beer, "you'd soon get the hang of it."

"What's it like down there?" Denton asked. "I saw them when I arrived, but I couldn't really make much out."

"Just a guardpost really. We go down there to make sure they don't discharge contraband before they get into the harbour." He paused as one of the boys approached and muttered to him. "Where?" Johnson asked, glancing round towards the door. "All right, bring him up to my room."

He turned back to Denton with a faintly excited smile. "One of my informers wants to see me," he said quietly, as if he didn't want the others to hear. "Come along, you might find this interesting."

Denton followed him up to the second floor. At first glance, as Johnson turned the gaslight up, Denton thought the room was completely bare. But looking round again, he saw three straight-backed wooden chairs, which reminded him of a schoolroom, and a watercolour of a sailing ship pinned to the wall. Still, the room was cheerless. There weren't even any curtains. He felt obscurely that its featurelessness was in keeping with the level, monotonous landscape of Johnson's character.

Johnson gestured to the chairs, neatly placed against the wall. "Make yourself at home," he said. But as he remained standing himself, Denton merely smiled, then went across to the painting. It was of a three-masted ship with many sails, all billowing before the wind. The sky was blue except for some fluffy, yellowish clouds, there were sea-gulls curling round the mastheads and flecks of white foam on the choppy blue water.

"How d'you like it?" Johnson asked behind him.

"Very nice."

"Did it myself."

"Really?" Denton felt he ought to show added interest now, and he stepped nearer, peering at it closer. The figurehead on the bowsprit was a mermaid with golden, wavy hair that fell loosely down round full round breasts with little red nipples. He was slightly shocked. All the mermaids he'd seen before had had ringlets that decently obscured their nakedness. He couldn't reconcile this immodesty with what he knew of Johnson. But perhaps it was all right in art? he wondered doubtfully.

"See the mermaid?" Johnson asked with innocent pride. "Life-life, eh?"

"Yes. Yes it is," Denton agreed hastily, looking instead at the row of portholes running along the vessel's side.

There was an almost inaudible rapping on the door. Immediately, a short, lean Chinese slipped inside and closed it. He glanced briefly askance at Denton, then stepped swiftly to the corner, where Johnson followed him. They began speaking in quick, furtive whispers. Denton watched the man's queue twitching as he shook or nodded his head in reply to Johnson's slow, careful questions. It was as though he was trying to convince Johnson while Johnson was sceptical and dubious. He was dressed like a coolie in a cheap, patched black tunic and wide floppy black trousers that ended above his ankles. On his bare feet he wore rope sandals, and Denton noticed how his toes kept curling and uncurling all the time, as though they were squirming with uneasiness. After some time, Johnson counted some notes out into his hand, snapping each one cautiously between his finger and thumb. The man's lips worked silently as he counted the money in time with Johnson. He stuffed it into a pocket inside the waist of his trousers and left, glancing briefly at Denton without expression. There was a white scar on his temple.

"Three o'clock tomorrow morning," Johnson said, putting his wallet away. "A cargo of salt. Not very big, but worth catching. Want to come? It's right down river, past the forts." His faintly nasal voice was still mild and even, as though he was merely inviting Denton to another game of snooker.

17

The journey downstream took over an hour. They travelled in the same launch that had taken Mason and Denton to the *Alexander the First,* with the same chubby coxswain, whom Johnson called "Lolly" in a tone that was at once familiar and colourless. Standing with Johnson in the prow, where the thick warm air fanned their faces, Denton kept patting and feeling the weight of the revolver he'd drawn from the Customs House armoury. "Not that we ever use them of course, but..." Johnson had said in his drab, monotonous voice.

Two Chinese Customs men with ancient rifles and wild-looking swords squatted in the stern of the boat, chatting loudly with the coxswain. The light from the boiler, glowing on their high-boned cheeks and slanting eyes, gave them, Denton thought, a lurid, sinister appearance. Sparks like little fireflies occasionally darted over their heads in the black smoke streaming from the funnel, and the sparks seemed to increase the fierceness of their looks. Yet all the while Johnson talked on in his amiably inexpressive voice about the hikes he'd taken round Shanghai last winter. As if they were only out for a picnic.

Soon after they'd passed the dark, broken heaps of the forts at Woosung, where the solitary yellow light gleamed on the smooth silk of the water, the launch slid slowly into a little creek and lay still with its engine scarcely turning. There were two hours to wait. The humid heat weighed on Denton's lids. He kept dozing off, despite the dull throb of tension in his stomach, to wake with a startled jerk as his head, loosening on his neck, lolled to one side or the other. The Chinese Customs men and the coxswain were all quiet now and seemed to be asleep. Only Johnson was still alert, humming softly to himself as he watched from the bow.

Denton slithered from one half-awake dream to another until Johnson's hand on his arm awoke him. Johnson's head was cocked on one side, his eyes turned up as though he was listening. Denton listened too. At first he could hear nothing except the run and slap of the water against the boat's hull, but then the soft plash of oars and a steady creaking sound carried faintly across the river. His stomach lifted. There was something menacing about that repeated creaking and plashing.

Without a word the two Chinese had risen together in the stern and gripped their useless-looking rifles. Johnson hissed to the coxswain and a second later the engine rattled and clanked. The deck shook and quivered as the launch thrust out of the creak at full speed. Almost immediately ahead were two sampans, low down in the water. The oarsmen were frantically trying to reach the bank before the launch could intercept them, rowing with a single oar from the stern. But the launch closed on them easily, and when they saw it was hopeless, they gave up, leaning on their oars as the launch came alongside them. The coxswain called out, translating for Johnson, and in a few minutes the sampans had been taken in tow, while the two smugglers sat dejectedly in the well of the launch, bound back to back.

Denton felt let down. It had all been so quick and ordinary.

"They can row quite fast with that single oar, can't they?" Johnson said pleasantly. "If we'd left it much later, they'd 've got clean away."

Denton glanced at the nearest prisoner. His face in the flickering light of the boiler was leathery and grim. It seemed all shadows below the eyes, as if the cheeks had been hollowed out by hunger or disease. His lids looked inflamed, the whites of his eyes bloodshot. The man stared out vacantly over the river, while beside him the two Customs men were playing a game with little narrow playing cards no wider than two fingers, laughing boisterously. The coxswain listened, grinning widely, turning his head now and then to join in the banter.

Johnson was lighting his pipe. "What will happen to those two?" Denton asked him.

"Oh well, you can't tell with a Chinese court." He drew and puffed, the tobacco glowing bright and dull in the charred bowl of his pipe. "Depends if they've got any pull, really."

"But isn't there a set penalty?"

"Anything from death to being in the cangue for a bit. That's like the stocks, the cangue." Johnson looked at his pipe, pushed the smouldering tobacco down and placed the moist stem back between his teeth. "It's a shame really, isn't it? They're probably opium addicts, have to smuggle to get the money for their opium." He shrugged with detached resignation, still as uninvolved as if they'd been talking about a picnic spoilt by rain. "Bit of a shame, but there you are."

Soon he was wondering aloud about the possibility of taking a trip to Hankow at Christmas, with the bounty from the capture. "You can have some lovely hikes round there, you know, when the weather's cooler," he said equably. "Have to watch out for bandits, of course."

Denton only half listened, gazing again at the prisoners' faces. They didn't look as though they'd have much pull. His eyelids drooped treacherously. How sore and

63

heavy they felt. How sticky his skin was, despite the gentle fanning of the air. As he rubbed his eyes, he was reminded of the bloodshot eyes of the prisoner nearest him. He glanced at him again. The man's eyes stared out blank and motionless over the dark water and the dark, empty fields. As though the darkness had got right inside his eyes, inside his head, Denton thought. Johnson's voice flowed on uninterruptedly while Denton only half-listened. Then suddenly, as if a light had gone out, the misty shapes before his tired eyes were blotted out by sleep.

18

Dear Mother and Father,

Thanks for your letter. Sorry to hear Father has not been well lately. I hope it will soon clear up. I have more or less settled in here now, although some things still take a bit of getting used to. The food and climate affected my stomach for a time, but I am keeping well, apart from a few minor upsets.

You should see my quarters. They are rather grand, as I think I told you on my last letter. I have my own bedroom, living room and bathroom. The living room and bedroom have verandas and you can look over the houses opposite to the river and docks. I obtained some curtains and chair covers complete with antimacassars in an auction in the mess. They used to belong to someone who has now gone home.

The new work has kept me rather busy. It is often interesting. The port here is actually the third largest in the world. We have to inspect all the ships before they are allowed to unload cargo or sail. Sometimes we get meals on board, and then it is always in the first class saloon, which is often pretty grand!

I actually took part in the arrest of some smugglers last week! We caught some people in sampans (small boats) who were smuggling salt, after waiting in an ambush for them until three in the morning. Very exciting, my first capture! You get a bonus of 10% of the value of any contraband you catch, but I don't suppose I'll get much of it this time as I was really only taken along for the experience of it. But next time perhaps I'll make a real haul!

You would be amazed at the number of well-to-do people there are here. I had dinner with the deputy assistant commis-

sioner a week or two ago. He lives in a grand house with lots of servants, and I had to get evening dress for it. There were a lot of good class people there. The table seated twenty-four!

I have offered to join the choir in the Anglican cathedral. It is supposed to be the largest and best in Asia. So I shall be able to keep my voice in practice. I met the Dean after service last Sunday. He is friendly and I am going to have tea with him the first Saturday next month. He does not know any of the clergy at Enfield, though. He has been out here fifteen years.

There is a native city and an International Settlement (mainly run by the British of course!), and a French Concession in Shanghai. The native population is about three quarters of a million and the whites altogether about twelve thousand. The French Concession is supposed to be rather scruffy, by the way. I have not seen it yet, except from the river.

The enclosed photograph shows me in my full working uniform. How do I look? I am having lessons in Chinese, which most people say is impossible to learn. But we get a special increment if we do learn, so I am going to try!

Must close this now to catch the next ship.

Love from

John.

P.S. Just received your letter posted in July. Glad to hear Father is better. Had a nice letter from Emily in the same post.

Denton placed his pen in the ink well and leant back as he read the letter through. He had taken his shirt off, but his skin was still moist with sweat. His forearms felt slippery against the grainy wood of the desk.

He read the sentence. *They used to belong to someone who has now gone home* with a little satisfied pursing of his lips. He imagined himself casually mentioning it to them a few years from now, when he returned bronzed and senior in rank to marry Emily. *"You remember that letter when I said I'd got some things that used to belong to someone who'd gone home? Well, I didn't want to worry you, but actually..."*

He slipped the photograph into the envelope, folded it and slid the letter in after it. Sealing the thick creamy flap and writing the address in a hand that was larger and bolder than usual, he reflected how little he'd really told his parents. But then he couldn't very well tell them of the dark and deadly side of things—they'd only be upset and

65

worry. He couldn't tell them that he'd seen a man's head chopped off, that he slept in a dead man's bed and wrote on a dead man's desk, that corpses floated in the river and were netted like fish every morning, that beggars held up dead babies to pluck your heart strings. He couldn't tell them of the girl in Mason's room, of the "honey boats" that carried the nightsoil up to the farming villages at dawn, the nightsoil that was packed round the vegetables he subsequently ate, boiled of course, in the mess.

He pushed back his chair and put on his shirt. There were some things one just didn't tell, he thought, with a touch of pride at his own manliness, one simply had to pretend.

Tell who, pretend to who? His parents, or himself? Or the whole world? It wasn't until he was halfway down the stairs, tapping the hard, sharp edge of the envelope against his palm, that the disturbing question occurred to him. And then, after a moment's dim and uneasy pondering, as he reached the tiled lobby, it was the impropriety of the grammar that lingered in his mind, not the question itself. "Tell *whom*," he muttered under his breath. "Pretend to *whom*."

19

The week at the Woosung forts passed slowly and vacantly for Denton. There was so little to do, it was like seven Sundays, he thought. Only without church. When they were not inspecting the junks and barges that infrequently put in for Customs clearance, Johnson would go wandering round the old stone buildings, many of them creeper-covered ruins that hadn't been touched since the British captured the forts in the opium wars sixty years before. Although it was late September and the sun was lower in the sky, the steamy heat seemed just as relentless. Yet Johnson would scramble tirelessly over fallen parapets, peer through crumbling gun embrasures and explore overgrown paths, even at midday when the sun was fiercest and his clothes were drenched with sweat. At first Denton went along too, unwilling to seem unsociable; and, despite the heat, he too enjoyed exploring the place, especially when they followed tracks that led to intensely green paddy fields with peasants working in them, or to placid fish tanks, or sudden little temples, half-derelict and no bigger than a room, in which sweet-smelling joss sticks from some unknown worshipper were still burning amongst the cobwebs and litter. But Johnson's insistently monotonous voice and interminable commentaries on everything they saw began to grate on him more and more. There was nothing, no matter how obvious or insignificant, that escaped Johnson's laboriously detailed explanations. "That butterfly only lives for six days," he would announce as Denton watched the fluttering spread of its gorgeous wings among the leaves. "It lays two hundred eggs." Or "That's a joss stick. They burn for over an hour." Denton had only wanted to stand and look, to absorb the scene through his senses, his imagination, to feel it working on him through the silence and the heat, but Johnson would be counting the bricks aloud or calculating how long ago the joss stick must have been lit.

So he began to make excuses. He had letters to write, he would mutter a little awkwardly, or his Chinese to study. And Johnson, unperturbed, would walk off alone along one of the almost overgrown paths, taking his sketch book with him.

"What's happened to those two smugglers?" Denton asked him as they sat at tiffin one day in the bare but cool stone hut that served as their mess. Johnson had just come back from one of his "hikes," his face red and glistening with sweat.

"Oh, I haven't heard. It usually takes a few months at least before they come to trial. I'll have to give evidence then, unless they're satisfied with my written report." He shrugged, picking up a shred of chicken with his chopsticks, which he was patiently teaching Denton to use. "You never can tell, they might be off scot-free by now. I might never hear of them again. And it'll take at least a couple of months before I get my bounty for the salt, too. Won't be much, of course, but I should be able to hire a boat to get me up to Hankow." His jaws munched slowly and regularly—rather in the way he talked, Denton thought. "Hope it comes through before Christmas. Look, try picking up a bean with your chopsticks. Like this. That's a good test of your skill."

Denton felt a little prick of disappointment and hurt that Johnson unquestioningly assumed the bounty would all go to him, but he tried to reason the smart away. After all, he told himself glumly, as the bean kept slipping off the tips of his chopsticks, his fingers aching with the effort

67

to control them, after all, he'd only gone along to watch, he'd been no help at all, so why should he expect any of the bounty to come his way? He laid his chopsticks down on the plate almost sullenly while Johnson methodically, obliviously, demonstrated with his own how you must hold the bottom one tight with the crook of your finger and thumb against the middle knuckle of your second finger.

"Have you got any plans for Christmas?" Johnson asked casually. Denton sensed an invitation was in the offing to join Johnson on his trip to Hankow and inwardly he resisted it. He looked away uncomfortably as the boy took the plates, guilty over the chagrin he felt about the bounty, guilty that Johnson's blandly persistent friendliness was so tedious. Could it be that overbearing, immoral Mason and wordly-wise Jones secretly interested him more? "There was some talk about going on a houseboat and doing a bit of shooting," he said vaguely, continuing to avoid Johnson's mild, solicitous gaze. "Mason and Jones were talking about it. I don't really know of course. I might be on duty, I suppose." He glanced apologetically at Johnson's still perspiring face.

Johnson's brown eyes glimmered in their depths, but then he nodded and smiled wryly, almost as if he'd expected all along that Denton wouldn't want to join him. After a few moments' silence he set off for the river bank with his sketchbook, the wry but not unfriendly smile still on his lips. Watching him walk away with his firm, energetic stride, Denton thought remorsefully how solitary he looked, recalling too that he never seemed to be with anyone for long. In the mess he would join a table and converse in his affable yet lifeless manner, and then, when the meal was over, he would be left sitting there by himself. And in the billiards room or the lounge, it always seemed the same—eventually he would be left alone while the others had formed groups with their backs towards him. Was that why he'd been so friendly to him, because he was shunned by all the others?

20

Sitting at his desk one evening, learning his vocabulary for his next Chinese lesson, Denton kept letting his eyes stray to the photograph of Emily propped against the wall in front of him, next to the picture of his parents. After he murmured each word aloud three times in what he hoped was the right tone, he would try to write the character, then allow himself to gaze at the misty, sepia-coloured portrait in its oval frame. He would purse his lips in an imagined kiss on Emily's, which he couldn't see properly as the photograph was taken in profile, and imagine the moist fresh pressure of her mouth as she responded. Sometimes his eyes would close and he would imagine her body pressing against his, soft and round and giving. Then, before his imagination had stirred him too far, he would open his eyes and check the strokes of the character he'd just drawn.

He was drawing the character for "like" when there was a cheerful double-knock on the door.

"Come in?" He half-turned, brush in hand.

It was Johnson. Denton's brows rose slightly in surprise. Since that week at the forts, there had been a faint coolness between them, though more on his part than on Johnson's. Denton had started to avoid him except when others were there as well, feeling a slight, but distinct and solid wall inside his chest which he had to surmount whenever Johnson approached him with his affable benevolence.

"Hello." Johnson closed the door and smiled blandly. "Busy?"

"I'm learning my Chinese." Denton dipped his brush in the ink and waited, his hand poised.

"Ah."

"For tomorrow's lesson."

"I didn't know you were working at it." He came across to the desk and looked over Denton's shoulder.

"Just one lesson a week." Denton held himself rigid, as though afraid Johnson was going to touch him. He gazed steadfastly at the moist, pointed tip of the brush.

"Jolly good," Johnson said approvingly, yet absently. He leant further over to examine the character; yet, again, he seemed to do so absently. "It rather looks as though we've got an unpleasant job to do," he said, straightening up.

"Oh?" When Denton glanced round he saw that Johnson

69

was smiling his usual equable smile, whatever the unpleasant job might be.

"Yes. That fellow that gave us the information about the salt-smugglers—remember him?"

"Yes?" *It wasn't "us" when you were talking about the bounty*, Denton thought with a fleeting sense of recollected smart. *It was all "me" then.*

"It looks as though he may have been murdered."

"Murdered?"

"Mm. They want us to go and identify the body." Johnson went on dispassionately. "Won't take long."

"Us?" Denton exclaimed in alarm. "But I hardly even saw him!"

"Well, it does help if there are two of us," Johnson insisted amiably. "It's a bit difficult to identify them if they've been mutilated, as I gather this one has. I mean, you might've noticed something about him that would help."

Denton felt a tide of sick fearfulness washing up his stomach. "I didn't even look at him," he protested weakly.

"The police are downstairs waiting," Johnson went on as if he hadn't heard. "Won't take half an hour. The mortuary's just round the corner. You'll be back at your Chinese in no time."

Despite his unwillingness and his squeamish apprehension, Denton tamely pushed back his chair, slipped on his tunic and began silently buttoning it. Johnson leant over the desk again, gazing at the photographs.

"Your parents?" he asked equably.

"Yes."

"And your sister?"

"I haven't got a sister." He compressed his lips, then surrendered under Johnson's smiling, innocently inquiring eyes. "It's my, er, fiancée, actually." He looked away uncomfortably.

"Oh, fiancée?" Johnson strolled towards the door. "Very nice," he added perfunctorily.

An English inspector and a Sikh constable were waiting downstairs, the inspector sitting in a cane chair, impatiently slapping the arm with the flat of his hand, the Sikh standing monumentally by the main door. "Ah, there you are," the inspector said gruffly as he got up. "Shall we go?"

70

The Sikh led the way through the narrow streets, the others followed three abreast. Hawkers were selling from their stalls beneath hissing paraffin lamps—tea, food, fruits and vegetables—and a fortune-teller sat against the wall beside two old men squatting over a Chinese chess board, while a silent crowd stood round them, watching each move. Denton glanced at them all abstractedly and scarcely heard the strident, bargaining voices all round him, his mind tremulously foreseeing every kind of mutilation that a body could suffer; but Johnson was as undisturbed and detached as ever; talking on in that monotonous, faintly twangy voice of his. The inspector merely grunted noncommittally while Denton walked slightly apart, as though an invisible film separated him from both the street and his companions. "Old Derek's all right," he remembered Jones saying as they left Johnson picking his teeth in solitude at the dinner table one evening. "Only he does drone on and on, doesn't he?" That droning jarred on him now more than ever.

Denton felt a new soft, squelchy quiver of fear as the Sikh led the way past a blue-glazed gas light into the mortuary. A few Chinese in white overalls were gossiping loudly at the back of a large hall, in which were several rows of almost empty benches. At the other end of the hall, guarding a gloomy corridor, a clerk sat at a high wooden desk, making entries in a register. The inspector spoke to him curtly and the clerk ran his finger up and down the columns of one page after another.

A wailing noise started abruptly at the far end of the corridor and everyone glanced round, except the clerk, whose finger was still running up and down the columns in his register. A frail old Chinese woman in black tunic and trousers was led out by two younger men who held her by the arms. She was throwing her head about and shouting wordlessly, yet her eyes seemed quite dry. Some of the attendants gossiping at the back looked incuriously round at her as they talked without any change in their voices. The police inspector glanced sharply at her, frowning.

"Number thirty-four," the clerk said at last.

The inspector and Johnson followed an attendant while Denton went along behind them, clutching at every delay.

The air in the corridor seemed cool although there were no windows. The attendant opened a door and they walked into a cell-like room, in the walls of which were little tunnels with cloth flags hanging down in front of them, each cloth with a number stencilled on it in black paint. Here the air was really cold and for the first time since he'd come to Shanghai, Denton shivered. The attendant looked slowly and lazily for the appropriate flag, and Denton felt his heart thudding softly, his fingers clenching, as, with a bored sigh, the man lifted the cloth and pulled out a stretcher on silent, rubber wheels. A naked body lay on the stretcher, packed in ice, with many congealed stab and slash wounds on its waxen face and chest. Denton shuddered as he looked at the arms. Both hands had been severed at the wrists.

"Twenty-two wounds," the inspector was reading from the card pinned to the stretcher at the mutilated head. "Hands missing, face seriously disfigured. Found in Soochow Creek near Garden Bridge, seven fifteen this morning. No identification marks, about thirty to thirty-five years old." He turned to Johnson, laying the card down and wiping his fingers fastidiously. "This your chap? How long's he been missing?"

"I haven't heard from him for two or three weeks," Johnson reflected in his detached, twangy voice. "But this chap's in such a mess it's really hard to tell."

"I suppose we've got his finger-prints," the inspector grunted. "Otherwise they wouldn't've bothered to chop his paws off. Looks as though they didn't like the look of his face much, either."

Denton gazed at the corpse while the other two talked. Strangely enough, now that he'd seen it, it wasn't so terrible after all, he felt with a surprised, buoyant sense of relief. The rigidity of the limbs, of the feet stiffly sticking up, the waxy pallor of the skin beneath its almond surface, the blocks of ice on which it lay, and which were packed round it, even between the legs, all seemed to dehumanize the corpse. It was hard to conceive of that lifeless marble thing as the living, breathing, furtively swift informer he'd seen a few weeks before in Johnson's room. Denton's gaze moved a little guiltily up the legs to the genitals, drooping from a little triangular patch of black fur between the spread thighs like a piece of limp gristle with a thick, crooked blue vein in it. So the Chinese weren't entirely devoid of body hair, the thought came to him, as though that were the issue he'd really come to settle. The belly was flat, the ribs starkly visible beneath the skin. Finally he gazed at the stumps where the hands should have been, blue round the skin and red inside, with jagged-edged faces of white, crushed bone. Instead of the horror he'd felt at first, now he felt only a distant repulsion, as if he were in a butcher's storeroom. The stab wounds in the chest were blue round the edges too, and he thought with what force the knife must have been driven into the flesh. The wounds' mouths were crusted with dried blood.

It's like a piece of meat, he thought. *It's just a piece of meat.* And although his heart was thudding steadily against the hollow wall of his body, he no longer feared he would faint or throw up. The face had been slashed all over. The contusions and ridges from the cuts made it almost impossible for him to compare the lifeless, disfigured visage with the dimly-remembered face of the informer. Besides, the lifelessness seemed so absolute that he couldn't really believe it had ever been alive. That was what took the horror away. At the actual moment of death, with terror gripping the muscles and screaming through the eyes, it might have been different.

"What do you think, John?" Johnson used his Christian name for the first time, with a familiar little smile.

Denton shook his head slowly. "I don't know..." He felt them both glancing at him for some sign of weakness, but he pretended not to notice, looking thoughtfully down at the head again, the sightless eyes, dead and pebbly, the skin all round them lacerated and swollen. Then he noticed a little whitish line from an old scar across the temple, and instantly recalled seeing the same mark of Johnson's informer when the man had hurried past him to the door.

"Yes, it is the same man," he said suddenly and decisively. "That scar on his forehead—I noticed it in your room that night, just as he was leaving."

They both bent over the head, while the attendant hawked loudly and impatiently behind them.

"This one, you mean?" the inspector pointed.

Johnson pushed out his underlip consideringly. "Well, it could be," he pronounced almost grudgingly at last. "I can't say I really remember exactly, but...yes, it could be."

"I'm sure it's the same scar," Denton said coldly, as if his words had been doubted.

The inspector stood back and gestured to the attendant, who was now belching quietly. With a bored, disdainful shake of his head, the man rolled the corpse back into its grave-like slot.

"Well, we can try and locate some next of kin, then," the inspector said briskly. "You haven't got any ideas, I suppose? No? Just let me have his name and any address you've got for him, would you? Chilly in here, isn't it?"

As the inspector opened the door, Denton saw a little grey shape scurrying along the wall. It ran over the inspector's shoe and disappeared into the corridor.

"God damn it! A rat!" the inspector shouted with sudden intensity, as though for all his apparent unconcern, his nerves had really been stretched taut in there. The attendant slammed the door after them, chuckling in his phlegmy throat. "Him too cold," he muttered. "Him not likee cold."

"Pity about that, if it really was my chap," Johnson ruminated evenly on the way back to the mess. "He was quite a useful informer. Don't know if I'll find anyone as good to take his place. Still I suppose something 'll turn up ... If it really was him, of course."

"I'm quite sure it was the same man," Denton said shortly, nettled by Johnson's persistent doubt.

Johnson didn't reply. He had stopped to bargain with a grey-haired woman hawker who was squatting beside a basket of oranges.

"Here you are, have one," he said as they walked on. "Yes, I didn't know you were engaged. Of course a lot of people are when they first come out here, but then it often all falls apart."

Denton cupped his palm round the globe of the orange without answering. Johnson's voice had seemed to express satisfaction, relish even, about the disintegration of engagements.

"What are you doing next Saturday, by the way?" Johnson asked obliviously as they turned towards the steps of the mess. "I was wondering whether you'd like to come for a little stroll, see a bit more of the place. Bit too hot still for a real hike, of course."

Johnson had avoided looking at him while he spoke, perhaps to make the invitation seem more casual. But there was almost a pleading note in that flat, monotonous voice as he ended.

"I'm afraid I've got another invitation," Denton excused himself thankfully. "I'm going to tea with the Dean of the cathedral," he added with a touch of pride.

"The Dean?" Johnson repeated with an indifference Denton felt sure was feigned. "Well, some other time then, eh?"

It was not until he was going to bed that Denton thought of the rat again and imagined it nibbling at the frozen corpses in the mortuary. Apprehensively, with a suddenly shivering back, he looked round the skirting board of the room before he turned out the light.

21

The Reverend George Eaton had an emaciated, ascetic-looking face, but the cakes his amah set before Denton in the Deanery were rich and plentiful. And it wasn't till the plate was empty, Denton having politely declined the last cake—which the Dean promptly popped whole into his mouth—that with preliminary throat-clearing he broached spiritual matters.

"Well, John," he said as he dabbed his thin, crumb-laden lips with his napkin, "Shanghai is very interesting of course, but it does offer many..." his lids lowered tactfully "...many temptations. Which it is often hard for young men to resist out here. Immorality, particularly in relations between the sexes, is, I'm afraid, a byword." He paused to confront Denton uncompromisingly with his deep-set hazel eyes. "A byword," he repeated sternly. "As I expect you may have noticed."

Thinking of the Chinese girl in Mason's room, Denton blushed, as though he himself were guilty. Perhaps he *was* guilty, the thought occurred to him as Mr. Eaton finished, for his recollection of the girl was somehow fascinating and thrilling. "Well, yes," he said uneasily, "I have noticed something of the kind."

"A byword." The Dean nodded emphatically, his eyes still probing Denton's. "Our Christian Youth Fellowship is a bulwark against that kind of temptation."

Denton recalled the high, rouged cheekbones of the Chinese girl, her pale, slim legs beneath Mason's hanging tunic. Were Emily's legs as pale and slim? He caught himself blushing again under the Dean's disconcertingly unblinking gaze. "Er, as a matter of fact I'm engaged," he muttered defensively.

"Already?" The Dean's white brows arched in disapproving incredulity.

"Oh no, not out here," he spluttered hastily. "I mean before I left home. We got engaged before I left."

"Ah, I see." The Dean's eyes relaxed their grip, and slowly let him go at last. He leant back with a sigh of relief, folding his hands behind his back. There were damp sweat marks under the arms of his white cassock. "And when is your fiancée coming out to join you?"

"Well, she has to finish her course first—she's training to be a teacher—and then it's, er, well, a question of money really."

The Dean nodded understandingly, then, glancing up at the failing punkah over their heads, called out in an unexpectedly sharp voice. Slowly the punkah's wing-like flapping quickened and the cooler air fanned their faces in continual draughts once more.

"These people are really incorrigible, you know, John," he smiled resignedly, shaking his head. "Always going to sleep. One mustn't blame them too much of course, but it's most irritating. The heat has affected their pulses over the centuries, you see. Their pulses are slow and languid now, they are completely enervated. But we are making gradual progress." He held up his hand when Denton nodded, as though warding off any interruption, however sympathetic. "We are making gradual progress. My friends in the out-stations tell me, for instance, that more and more of the natives are joining their churches. We may yet see a truly Christian China in the not too distant future. Not I, perhaps," he smiled a theatrically wry smile, shaking his grey head again in rueful recognition of his years, "but you may. And it is people like you who must set the example, John. The white man, the Christian in China. We are all of us missionaries in our way, not just the clergy."

The Dean turned to look at the amah, sleek and plump in her white tunic and wide black trousers. She was calling in a quiet, sibilant whisper from the door, smiling widely.

"Master, the man come."

The Dean rose with sudden energy and went to meet a tall, thin Chinese in a long grey silk gown who was already gliding into the room. The amah's whisper, and the Dean's haste, as if he didn't want Denton to see his visitor, suggested something confidential, or even secret, and Denton stood up awkwardly, ready to leave.

"Good afternoon, Reverend," the Chinese said loudly, his eyes smiling behind his rimless glasses. Then, after only a moment's hesitation. "Good afternoon, Mr. Dentong. How is my friend Mr. May-song?"

Denton frowned in puzzlement, then, noticing the man's long, curved nail, suddenly remembered. It was Mr. Ching of course, the agent from the Russian ship.

"You know each other?" the Dean asked, on a note of almost displeased surprise.

"I have met Mr. Den-tong in the lines of duty," Ching answered, smiling gaily. "If I may have a few words with you, Reverend, I will not intrude on your pleasant chatting any longer."

The Dean ushered him out of the room without a backward glance, closing the door behind them. Denton sat down again, gazing up at the white-washed ceiling, where the punkah, as if on a signal, was wearily slowing and resting. He felt his nerves slackening and resting too, and realised how tense he was with the Dean, as tense as he was with nearly everyone, he thought sadly.

When the Dean returned a few minutes later, the punkah at once began its regular sweep again. "A little business matter," he apologised. "A little property I am negotiating to buy in Hongkew. If you ever have the opportunity to invest in land in Hongkew, John," his voice strengthened, losing that faintly disconcerted and embarrassed tone it had had when Ching was in the room, "I strongly advise you to do so. I understand that property prices are bound to appreciate there as Shanghai continues to expand."

"Oh I see."

"Yes indeed. And now that you're contemplating matrimony," he wagged his finger genially. "You have an obligation to think of the future, eh?"

"Yes, I suppose so," Denton smiled sheepishly.

77

"Now where were we? Oh yes, the Christian Youth Fellowship. We're having our next meeting on Thursday. A little talk about the doctrines of Dr. Pusey and the position of the Church of England with regard to the sacraments." His voice, alert and energetic when he talked about property, was taking on its stately, pious tone again now. It put Denton fleetingly in mind of a man changing into his stiff best suit after work. "Mr. Fenton will start the discussion. A missionary near Hankow. A deep thinker, I believe, as well as a tireless missionary. And his topic is of fundamental importance, of course."

Leaving the Deanery half an hour later, so unlike, in its white, lofty spaciousness, the cosy picture that the word drew in his English mind, Denton wandered aimlessly down the narrow, unpaved alleys towards the Bund. He held his hat in his hand and walked in the shade that the walls threw from the sloping afternoon sun. Rickshaw coolies hailed him importunately, hawkers eyed him appraisingly from their stalls, women labourers heaving heavy stones on their backs staggered past him towards a new building, sweat oozing down their cheeks and straining necks. It was too late for the concert in the park and too early for dinner in the mess. He felt a slow, heavy swell of dejection rolling over him as, reaching the Bund, he watched fashionably-dressed men and women sauntering away from the park gates and climbing into cabs or sedan chairs, to be carried laughing and smiling away into the evening. It was a nameless dejection that had been growing quietly inside him while talking to the Dean, a depression that seemed to crush him silently with its suffocating weight. An old beggar-woman accosted him, mumbling words he couldn't understand and insistently shaking a scratched and dented red tin box in which a few copper cents rattled together. Her wretched little box, symbol of the hopeless, dreary life it represented, seemed suddenly to epitomise his own life too, although he couldn't have said why. He took out a dollar and recklessly dropped it in the box, as if he could buy off his own depression with such extravagant generosity. At once more beggars appeared, women, children, men without arms, blind, deaf, dumb, diseased and deformed, young and old. He stood helplessly, gazing at the seething, beseeching, clinging little crowd, shaking his head against their insistent whining murmur, while the homeward stream of Europeans flowed steadily past him from the park, their eyes stiffly unseeing or ironically amused. He knew that he ought to go back and practise his Chinese or write another letter home. But the image of his silent empty rooms, of the mess where the rest of them would be drinking, playing billiards or vacantly lying back in the cane chairs of the lounge, yawning with boredom, only added another dark weight to his depression. He ploughed impulsively through the softly plucking hands of the beggars and stepped into a waiting rickshaw.

"Where to, master?" the coolie asked, lifting the shafts. He was a young man, not much older than himself, with a wispy moustache that gave him a sardonic, mocking expression.

Denton didn't know. He pointed vaguely along the Bund.

The coolie nodded, heaved against the bar and trotted off. Watching his sandalled feet slap on the hard uneven road, Denton looked away over the river a trifle guiltily. A long white liner was swinging slowly round in the middle channel, turning to sail downstream away from Shanghai. The setting sun glowed on its side, gleaming brokenly on the portholes and washing the white paint with a faint rosy hue. The sight of the liner leaving, perhaps for England, sent a pang through him and he suddenly understood his dejection. He was lonely, that was all. The letter he'd been waiting for from Emily hadn't come and there wouldn't be another mail ship for a week. It was Saturday afternoon. If he were in England, he'd be walking with her beside the Lea perhaps, or going to her parents' for tea. For a moment he wanted just to talk to someone, just to tell someone about Emily and him—he even considered going back to the mess and calling on Johnson. But no, that wouldn't be any use. He stared at the river, where the liner had completed its turn. A deep, mournful bellow from its siren tore the hanging stillness of the air. He wished longingly that he could be on board, sailing home. The coolie slowed his steps and glanced back over his shoulder, as though divining Denton's thoughts. But Denton waved him on, and the man grunted as he quickened his pace again. The back of his shirt was dark with sweat.

They came imperceptibly to a part of the city he hadn't seen before. The change was subtle but definite.

79

The streets seemed even narrower, the canals more filthy, the smells stronger and more rotten.. Then the rickshaw swung under an arch into a main street, and he saw the name—*rue* Molière. He was in the French Settlement. He looked about him wonderingly, and even a little anxiously— the French Settlement was full of crime, so people said. But there was something appealing about it. French names appeared on the shops, a French sailor with a red pom- pom in the middle of his hat was strolling along the street, and he heard the rapid, voluble murmur of the French language being spoken behind him. Looking round, he saw that it was a lady and a little fair-haired girl in a rickshaw. The lady was holding a parasol slantwise against the last rays of the sun and the little girl was peering round its scalloped edge as she talked. There was some- thing calm and peaceful about them that caught his heart and he kept secretly looking back.

Soon the lady's rickshaw stopped outside a large house, set back behind a white-washed wall, through which streaks of an older, darker, colour showed. Denton watched the lady step gracefully down, holding her bunched, grey skirt in one hand, resting the parasol on her shoulder with the other. The little girl followed her, skipping through the arched entrance in the peeling wall. He felt a sudden impulse to tell his coolie to stop, to take him back, so that he could watch the two of them walking along the drive to the house that lay concealed behind the peeling wall. But he said nothing. He let them float away like some vision— what sort of vision he couldn't say. A vision of serenity, perhaps? He felt some perceptible lightening of his self- pity, as though the lady and the little girl had left a promise of comfort for him as they slipped so peacefully away.

After a short time the coolie's pace slackened again and he stopped outside a tall narrow house with green- washed walls, lowering the shafts expectantly. Denton looked from the coolie to the house. The door was open and a very large Chinese sat toad-like beside it in a cane chair on the shaded porch. At first Denton thought he was asleep, but then one lid slowly opened, followed by the other. The man regarded him unwinkingly from under the wide brim of his straw hat.

The coolie gestured Denton to get down, panting lightly. "What is this?" Denton asked in his lame Shanghainese. The coolie replied unintelligibly, gesturing again. The huge man on the porch heaved himself ponderously out of his chair, and Denton heard the wood creak and groan. He was grossly fat and rolled from side to side as he walked, his whole body quivering at every step. He glanced from the coolie to Denton, his face immobile except for the flickering of his little brown eyes. *"M'sieur?"* he asked in a calm, even voice. *"Vous désirez?"*

Denton shrugged. He had never heard a Chinese speaking French before, and it seemed outlandish. At the same time there was something insolent in the fat man's examining, undeferential gaze. "Do you speak English?" he asked.

The fat man turned his head slowly to the coolie, ignoring Denton, and spoke to him quietly. Then he turned slowly back, gazing unblinkingly into Denton's eyes again. *"Vous désirez une jeune fille?"*

"I don't understand," Denton said blankly, in English, then in Shanghainese.

The man sighed impatiently and brought his round, heavy face closer, speaking slowly and distinctly as if to an idiot. "You...want...this?" he slapped his groin suggestively.

"What? No!" Denton pulled back indignantly, as if he'd been hit.

The gross man turned away, shrugging his massive shoulders indifferently. He muttered something to the coolie, at which the coolie, glancing back at Denton, gave a short, derisive laugh, then waddled quivering back to his chair, where he slowly subsided. Again the chair creaked and groaned.

"Go back," Denton said weakly, but the coolie laughed, gesturing again to the open door. At the same time footsteps sounded down the dark, wooden stairway inside the hall and a man came out into the light. He was a European, dark-haired and sallow, about thirty years old, with a slim, black moustache. He walked swiftly down the path and away, glancing momentarily at Denton. *"Bonsoir, m'sieur,"* he nodded casually, raising his elegant straw hat with a brown silk band round it. There was a white carnation in his lapel.

The coolie was gesturing encouragingly again, but Denton adamantly shook his head. "Bund!" he said tensely, making a turning movement with his hand. "Bund!"

81

The coolie shrugged at last, and picked up the shafts, wagging his head slowly in amused disbelief.

The rickshaw lurched into a pot-hole, as if the coolie was no longer bothering how he pulled such an unworthy passenger, and Denton glanced stealthily back at the house. Beneath his almost panicky abhorrence, he was secretly enticed by the allure of that open door with its vague, carnal promise. His heart was beating more rapidly as he felt a guilty sense of regret and self-reproach that he hadn't dared enter. He tried resolutely to think of Emily, of the Reverend Eaton's exhortation, of the Christian Youth Fellowship and Dr. Pusey's doctrines, but all the pure and earnest images that he summoned up seemed pale and drab against the forbidden excitement of that open door beside the gross and sensual Chinese. In a quarter of an hour, he thought bewilderedly, he'd passed from the serenity of the lady with the little girl to the sordid turmoil of lust—how was such a thing possible?

The evening stretched out before him, stale, lonely and empty, and the dark crushing swell of his depression rolled over him once more.

22

In November the heat at last began to weaken, like an iron hand slowly loosening its grip on the city. Denton could wear his uniform without immediately sweating. Even at midday, the evenings were cool, and at night he slept now beneath a light cotton blanket. The mosquitoes were less troublesome too, as if the drier, cooler air was too thin to carry them.

Mr. Brown seemed moderately satisfied with his progress, though not to the point of inviting him to dinner again, and not long after the Moon Festival, when the Chinese wandered through the street with coloured lanterns hung on springy twigs, Denton had been able to write proudly to his parents that he was no longer merely a *training* probationary inspector, but a probationary inspector in his own right, inspecting vessels in his own section of the wharves, often without any supervision at all. His Chinese, too, had been improving, and Mr. Wei, who always perched on the edge of the same chair in his room, his head alertly cocked like an eager little bird, was able to hold simple conversations with him in the language.

It was in November, too, that the Shanghai Race Club held its annual meeting. A party of officers went on the last day, when the best horses and riders were competing.

"They're gentlemen riders, of course," Johnson explained to Denton, as they stood by the paddock watching the horses being led round. "They don't have professional jockeys or anything like that here."

Denton nodded, moving a little away. His coolness towards Johnson had begun to turn into a mild revulsion, as though Johnson were always standing too close to him, brushing his sleeve, or accidentally nudging him. Besides, he was irritated by Johnson's quiet, smug assumption that he was in all things Denton's guide and tutor. He turned to Jones, who was discussing with Mason which horses to bet on. "Whose colours are they?" he asked, pointing to a pony that had just come in.

"Jardine's. And that's the Bank's. Moller's over there. That's Moller riding himself." Jones raised a quizzical eyebrow. "You a betting man?"

Denton shook his head deprecatingly. "I've never been to a race before."

"I'd put twenty dollars on Jeremiah, Jonesy," Mason said confidently, looking up from his card.

"Do you know a lot about horses?" Denton asked with grudging respect. Horses had always signified gentlemen and aristocrats to him.

"Used to be in the cavalry," Mason threw out as he moved away.

"Really? Where?"

But Mason didn't answer, walking towards the stands as though he hadn't heard.

Jones leant towards Denton confidentially. "One thing it doesn't do to ask too much out here is where people were before they came," he breathed in Denton's ear. His breath smelt of beer. "You going to bet?"

Denton shook his head. "No money to spare," he said with a show of regret, although in fact it was his moral scruples that prevented him. Noticing that Johnson had clamped onto someone else now, he edged away, strolling with Jones towards the stands. Crowds of jostling Chinese thronged the stalls. Hawkers were selling tea and bottled drinks that lay in metal boxes of slushy, melting ice.

Bookmakers bawled out the odds while their assistants took money from the men and women who clamoured round them. A melon-seller was deftly slicing the great round fruit with a long thin-bladed knife into perfect half-moon segments. "Thats what they stab people with," Jones said nonchalantly. "Goes right through and out the other side. Sharp as a razor." Denton thought of Johnson's informer with his twenty-two wounds.

They sauntered on, past the mounted Sikh policemen to the Europeans' enclosure. Denton gazed up at the taipans in their boxes, their finely-dressed wives and daughters twirling their parasols in gloved hands or playing with the ribbons of their hats. One of the girls looked a bit like Emily, he thought, except, he conceded reluctantly and only half-consciously, she was prettier and far more elegantly dressed.

"No good looking that way, old man," Jones said, tilting his hat forward over his eyes. "They're not for the likes of us."

Denton flushed again. "I'm engaged to a girl in England," he said stiffly.

"So we've heard, so we've heard," Jones smiled, stroking down the silky ends of his moustache. "But what the eye doesn't see the heart doesn't grieve over, eh?"

Denton had had only five letters from Emily, each a little shorter than the one before, each somehow a little more constrained, as though the miles and the months that separated them had laid an autumn coolness on their feelings. But the changes were so gradual and Denton himself so unwilling to acknowledge them, except in unguarded moments of loneliness, that he hadn't yet realised what they might mean. He was re-reading the letters, his imagination supplying the glowing colours which they lacked in reality, when Mr. Wei arrived one day, out of breath and uncharacteristically late for his lesson.

"The rickshaw coolie, very stupid," his gold tooth glistened in his apologetic smile. "He bump a foreigner. Very angry. Indian policeman hit him for his clumsy." He laughed, a nervous, breathless little giggle, but behind his glinting, steel-rimmed glasses, Denton detected a gleam of resentment and humiliation.

Where are you going? the first exercise began. *I am going to the tea-house.* Denton paused before saying the two sentences, mentally rehearsing the different rising and falling tones that he so easily confused.

"No, no, Mr. Denton," Mr. Wei chirped spryly, his habitual alertness recovered, "You must do by feeling, not think before say."

"I've never been to a tea-house," Denton said irrelevantly, abruptly taken by the realisation. "Can you take me to one?"

"A tea-house?" Mr. Wei giggled. "You will not quite like it, I think."

"Why not?"

Mr. Wei's hands fluttered deprecatingly, "Foreigners do not go to such place. Only for Chinese."

"But I'd really like to go."

"You like to go?" Mr. Wei's voice, his whole face, expressed polite disbelief. "I do not think."

"Really I would," Denton insisted.

Mr. Wei shook his head, chuckling to himself at the very idea as if it were the naive illusion of an eager but uninformed child. Yet at the end of the hour he referred to it again, as though he'd been silently reflecting on it during the interchanges of *I am going to a tea-house. Is your brother in the tea-house?* "You want to see Chinese tea-house?" he asked circumspectly, as if Denton couldn't really have been serious.

"Yes, I'd like to very much."

He scratched his cheek lightly with his long, curved fingernail. "When you are free?"

"Yes, when I'm free."

Mr. Wei looked puzzled. "When you are free?" he repeated less confidently.

"Oh, when *am* I free?" Denton raised his hands. "Any time. Now?"

Mr. Wei cocked his head. "I am going to a goo' one after my lesson. If you wish, we can walk. It is not far."

But outside the building he hailed a rickshaw, deciding, over Denton's protests, that it would be too far for him to walk in the sun. His manner to the rickshaw coolie was curt and decisive. To Denton, accustomed to his fluid courtesy, it seemed almost arrogant. He hadn't suspected that frail little man was capable of such authority.

The coolie ran them along the bank of the Soochow Creek, the waters thick with sampans and barges, then over a little wooden hump-backed bridge, past the outstretched hands of the beggars who rose in a swarm at the summit where the coolie could hardly pull the rickshaw. Mr. Wei's face, normally so expressive, assumed a stony impassivity as the beggars' hands clutched at their feet, their clothes, their hands, with limp, pleading gestures. It was as if he didn't want to recognise even their existence. But then his mouth and eyes relaxed as they left the murmuring beggars behind and passed along an unfamiliar street. "Mr. Denton, are your parents still live?" he asked. "How many brother you have?" His eyes shadowed sympathetically when Denton told him his only brother had been killed in the Boer War. "Where is he bury?" he asked solicitously. "You have made arrangement for bury in family grave with your ancestor?"

"No, he's buried in South Africa. It would have cost too much to bring his body home."

Mr. Wei's eyes opened wide in pained astonishment at Denton's answer, and he was silent for some time, as if out of deep but puzzled delicacy for his family's humiliation.

They came to the tea-house. It was an old stone building with gold characters painted on a faded red background over the carved wooden entrance. Here too beggars and rickshaw coolies crouched, watchful for prey, while unkempt dogs prowled in the gutter for scraps of food. Denton's adventurous enthusiasm sagged. On his own he wouldn't have given the building a second glance, it was indistinguishable from the seedy slums on either side. Now he'd have to go in, and probably get food-poisoning as well!

There was a wooden screen just inside, facing the doorway. "To keep bad spirits out," Wei explained. "Chinese people think ba' spirit' only fly straigh' line. So bounce off screen and go out door." He smiled, as if he didn't believe it. Behind the screen a large hall opened out, full of round wooden tables in partitioned areas, while at the back were stairs leading to private rooms. The place echoed with the clatter of crockery and the exuberant noise of shouted coversations, orders called to the scurrying waiters, greetings shouted, and above everything else, like a castanet continuo, the clacking and scraping of mah-jong tiles. Mr. Wei led Denton to a table in the corner. He was the only European there, and his back tingled under the frankly curious gaze of a hundred eyes while the hubbub continued round them without pause.

He sat down uncomfortably. Before they came to the place, he'd expected something cool, refined and with a quiet, gracious air, but this was as noisy as the street outside, as pulsing with raucous energy and life. And the floor looked none too clean, either. What about the cups they were carelessly slapping down on the table? He rubbed his finger surreptitiously along the edge of the table and was relieved to see it was reasonably clean. He looked round warily, regretting his rashness. The Chinese here had none of that submissive deference his experience of them so far had led him to expect, and the lack of it disturbed him. It was almost as if they were deliberately flouting his western superiority. Even Mr. Wei himself seemed to have changed. He called for tea in a loud, sharp voice that meant to be obeyed and exchanged shouted greetings with customers at nearby tables. They kept calling out questions about Denton that he couldn't understand, but which he could tell were bantering and familiar. Their eyes, meeting his, smiled or stared without flinching.

An old man in a long blue gown, with glasses resting on the tip of his nose sat down beside Mr. Wei, asking him curiously about the foreigner and throwing smiling, unabashed glances at him. Soon he was joined by another, younger man, then by a third. Smiling at Denton with candid interest, but never addressing him, they plied Mr. Wei with questions about him that his beginner's Chinese could only help him guess at. It was like being discussed as a boy by his uncles and aunts round the kitchen table. When he tried to answer a question one of them asked him directly—an easy one about his age—they nodded and smiled at him encouragingly, commenting loudly to each other about his ability while Mr. Wei's eyes shone with proprietary pride in his pupil.

The tea arrived. Remembering Mr. Wei's instructions in Chinese etiquette, Denton tapped the table with his middle finger when the waiter poured the steaming green liquid into his rice-patterned cup. The watchers murmured in surprised approval, turning to the nearby tables, from where steady eyes had been observing him too, and recounted his proficiency in Chinese customs as well. Before long there were several more men sitting at the table, ordering food, testing Denton's Chinese, and discussing it uninhibitedly amongst themselves. Their warm, congratulatory smiles seemed to be touched with a jesting, patronising surprise that a foreign devil could make anything at all of a civilised language like Chinese.

Although he felt uncomfortably on show, Denton was dimly aware of a new dimension forming in his mind as he sat amongst these inquisitive, lively people. Already, after only a few months, he'd come to expect the Chinese to be subdued and deferential towards him, to call him "master" and to wait on him, to empty his toilet box and pour his hot water. When they didn't conform, as the fat man outside the brothel hadn't conformed, he'd been shocked, as if by a subordinate's insolence. But there, amongst Wei's genial friends, who plainly thought of him as no more than an outlandish, if good-natured, barbarian, he felt the brittle mould in which Shanghai had cast his ideas beginning to crack. Perhaps these people weren't so different from himself? Perhaps they weren't naturally inferior? Beneath their unabashed and curious gaze, he began to wonder, to doubt. It was hard to assume superiority when you were yourself being regarded with patronising benevolence by those who were supposed to be your inferiors.

Gradually the interest in him diminished and the customers drifted off to their own tables, to their tea and mah-jong, as casually as they had first drifted to Wei's. Denton sat thoughtfully sipping the pale, faintly bitter, tea, in which a white jasmine floated round and round, until Mr. Wei called for the bill.

"Please let me pay," he asked, but Mr. Wei would not allow it. "Next time, then?" Denton suggested.

"You would like to come again?" Wei smiled happily.

As they were leaving, a waiter was escorting a singsong girl through the hall towards one of the private rooms. She had rouged cheeks and black glossy hair that reminded Denton instantly of the girl Mason had pointed out to him on his first day in Shanghai. She glanced with momentary surprise at Denton as they passed and then she was gone. A musician followed her, carrying a twostringed Chinese violin with a gourd-like soundbox and ornately decorated pegs.

Wei noticed Denton looking after them, and offered to arrange for the girl to sing.

"Oh no," Denton declined, flustered. "I wouldn't understand."

"If you not like, can sen' away," Wei suggested. "Never

88

mind understanding. Chinese music only soundings, never mind words."

"No, really. Another time, perhaps."

Wei summoned a rickshaw. They travelled back through a maze of alleys Denton had never seen before, alleys in which large houses with tiled pagoda roofs would suddenly appear beside little wooden huts that clung to their walls like sores. With each turn the lanes seemed to get narrower, the crowds more dense. Wei stopped the rickshaw outside a long low brick building with a blue-tiled roof. Trees grew round the entrance, their branches, old and twisted, resting on the curving eaves. A faint sweetish smell came from the heavy wooden doors.

"This is my clan burial house," Wei said, smiling his winking gold smile. He pointed to the doors. "In there is the coffin I give my parents."

"Your parents are dead?" Denton inquired with a sympathetic softening of his voice.

"Not yet. When they die, the coffin ready for them." He smiled proudly. "They are very happy for coffin, cost a very lot, very goo' coffin." While he was speaking four coolies entered the building straining under the weight of a heavy wooden coffin like a moulded, polished tree bole. The same sweetish smell came from that too. The coolies staggered and sighed as they pushed the double doors open and bore the coffin inside.

"When they die," Wei was explaining cheerfully, "we bury them here first, then take bones back to home village. Grave is all ready, very ol', goo' outlook." He nodded satisfiedly several times before sharply ordering the coolie to move on.

"Mr. Denton, are you buy coffi' already for your parents? And funeral clothings? No?" He shook his head in amazement at English indifference to their elders' welfare. "In Chinese we say dying is plucking the flower of life. Do you have such poetical sayin' in England? I think it is very expensive to have bury in your country. How much are you pay, Mr. Denton?"

That night in the mess, in a thoughtless moment that he instantly regretted, Denton told Mason and Jones about his visit to the tea-house. "It was quite interesting, really," he ended lamely and defensively as he saw a leer forming under Mason's ginger moustache.

"Oho, slumming it with the natives, eh?" Mason mocked.

"You'll be wearing a pig-tail next, I wouldn't wonder. Watch out your eyes don't start slanting."

23

On Saturday afternoons, if he wasn't on duty, Denton would write his letters home, a long one to Emily, a shorter one to his parents—he had no one else to write to. He wrote every week, even when he found he had nothing to say. Perhaps it was only to relieve the heavy loneliness of those dull, blank hours after tiffin, perhaps it was merely to cling on to the links with them that he sensed were slowly weakening. Often, ransacking his brains for new bits of information, he would gaze out from the veranda towards the Bund, trying to conjure up their faces—especially Emily's—amongst the forest of masts and funnels, as if the sight of the ships that sailed to England would work some magic on his imagination. But he couldn't picture Emily clearly any more, her face was fading in his memory like an old photograph. He could no longer imagine them taking up where they'd left off with her shy farewell kiss on the deck of the *Orcades*. He could no longer visualise her joining him in Shanghai—not next year, not the year after, not at all, except in some vague fantasy in which her face was dim and misty, the surroundings unreal. Despite himself his letters to her began to sound hollow even as he wrote them. And yet she could be brought back vividly and painfully by some sharp splinter of memory or a chance thought or word. If only she would write more often!

Sometimes he would be disturbed in his writing by the sound of a woman's voice laughing on Mason's veranda. Perhaps Mason's baritone would answer the woman teasingly, and then there might be a silence, a hush almost, followed by a little smothered scream of laughter from the woman. Denton would get up again and pace the floor, muttering indignantly. Yet at the same time he felt a prurient, thrilling desire to peep from his own veranda at the woman on Mason's.

Was it the same woman? What was she wearing? Not Mason's revealing tunic again? But it was when the voices quietened later and there was no sound or stirring for an hour or two in the somnolence of the afternoon that the distraction was, curiously, at its worst. Purge his mind how he would, the same lascivious images would come back again and again in that suggestive silence, images no less sinful for being vague and ill-informed. He imagined the girl he'd first seen there, soft, filmy clothes slithering off her shoulders. He saw her on the bed, a bed just like his, her breasts rippling as she raised her arms to embrace Mason and pull him down on top of her, her lips parting for his, her black hair spread like a fan on the pillow beneath her. Or was it not Mason he imagined sinking down on her softness, but himself? He jerked his mind guiltily away from all these images and forced himself back to the dull dead words on the page in front of him. He could go on determinedly with his letters, and yet his mind would still stray, he would still catch himself gazing dreamily at the wall, his head slightly cocked, listening for the first drowsy sounds of their awakening.

Then at last it would come, the lazy, unhurried yawning of Mason on the veranda again, his languid murmurs followed by the girl's brighter replies. The street below would be throbbing with the usual noises—hawkers, coolies, rickshaw boys and bearers of sedan chairs, servants, cooks, beggars, masters, mistresses and children, all talking, laughing, shouting and complaining in their quick, shrill voices. But in all that clamour, his keen ear unerringly picked out the low, playful or indolent voices of satisfied lust next door.

Sometimes he took Emily's last letter out and read it through, to return his mind to purer thoughts. But while his eyes were scanning the words he now knew almost by heart, his imagination would sidle off to titillating visions of the Chinese girl's swelling breasts, her round pink nipples, the smooth flat paleness of her belly and the exquisite darkness between her thighs.

It was on one of those Saturdays early in December, when the sun was so weak that it was welcome now and Denton would actually seek it in the room, pulling his chair closer to the window, that Ah Koo came in with his laundry. Denton was sitting, unfinished letter in hand, gazing out over the veranda at the paling blue of the sky as the sun went down. He was half-consciously listening for the awakening sounds from Mason's room. After the usual giggles and laughter there had been a silent stillness there for over two hours. Denton had even begun to wonder whether they'd slipped out and stealthily crept away—as if they knew he was listening, or cared if they knew! But then they came, the mutterings and sighs and yawnings, the easy, indulgent murmurs. He looked down at what he'd written with an effort of concentration, but his eyes were soon unfocussed as he strained to hear.

Ah Koo cleared his throat loudly and swallowed. "Master wantee young gir'?"

"What?"

"Wantee young gir'?" He stood with Denton's pressed shirts neatly folded over his arm. "You wantee, I bring. Very young. First time gir'."

"No." Denton frowned indignantly, his cheeks tingling.

"All same Mr. Mason. I bring young gir' Mr. Mason, he not likee, send away. I bring you other one gir', very goo'. Mr. Mason same same you?"

"Certainly not!"

"Not wantee?"

"No. Not wantee." His confusion had robbed Denton momentarily of even the simplest Shanghainese and he stumbled into the pidgin he was trying to grow out of.

"Wantee young boy?" Ah Koo's face seemed utterly impassive. Nothing moved in it except his mouth. There was neither disgust nor gloating in his eyes, nothing but the faint shrewd glimmer of inquiry. He might just as well have been asking where the shirts over his arm should go. "Not wantee gir', not wantee boy?" he asked, shaking his head faintly.

"No." Denton turned away. A low, throaty giggle sounded voluptuously from Mason's veranda, almost as though the girl had heard Ah Koo and was doing her best to help him corrupt Denton. Mason's voice muttered something, then he laughed.

"You wantee, you say," Ah Koo said, unabashed, as he opened the wardrobe and put the shirts carefully away. "All same same Mr. Mason. He very likee. Say Ah Koo bring young gir', I bring chop-chop. I bring you same same. Never mind boy or gir'."

Denton had ostentatiously bent his head over his letter again, but now he turned round and spoke in carefully rehearsed Shanghainese. "I do not want girl, I do not want boy."

Ah Koo listened to him from the door, his corrugated

face still impassive. "You wantee, you tell Ah Koo," he said. "Japan gir', Chinese gir', Portugal gir'. Ah Koo bring chop-chop."

A few days later, Mason paused by Denton's table in the mess, where he was sitting with several other young inspectors. "Ah Koo's a bit worried about your health, you know," he said, leaning on the back of Denton's chair.

"Ah Koo?"

"Yes. Wonders if there's something wrong with you." He surveyed the expectant, grinning faces all round the table. "Says you don't care for girls."

Denton looked back at his half-empty plate silently, feeling his cheeks beginning to flush.

"Perhaps you prefer boys?" Mason suggested. "Only Ah Koo said you weren't interested in them either." He laid his hand companionably on Denton's shoulder.

"You know perfectly well I'm engaged," Denton said, his voice wavering between a show of amusement and a show of indignation. He wanted to shrug Mason's hand off and yet at the same not to antagonise him—rather to treat his teasing casually, as though he was indifferent to it, or even faintly amused himself. After all, it is only a joke, he told himself uneasily.

"We know perfectly well you *say* you're engaged," Mason answered, winking at the others. "But some of us are beginning to wonder if that isn't an excuse. In any case, even if you are engaged," he straightened up, brushing his moustache with his knuckles and glancing significantly round the table again, "you need to get a bit of practice in, don't you? I mean it might be years before she comes out here, mightn't it? You wouldn't want to disappoint her, would you?" And while he basked complacently in the sniggers that rippled round the table, his heavy hand patted Denton's shoulder amicably as if to assure him that honestly, he was only joking.

24

When Emily's letter came at last, he felt a little quiver of fear as though he knew already what it would say. She hadn't written for nearly two months and Christmas was only three weeks away, so when he saw the slim small envelope peeping out of his pigeon-hole that morning as he left for duty, he tried to tell himself it must be her Christmas greetings. But there was an unbelieving anxious tremor about his fingers as he tore the flap open.

He read it in the rickshaw that was taking him to the Lower Section wharves. It was only one page long, and when he saw that, he felt his illusions fluttering away like plucked feathers. She was very sorry, she wrote in that clear large hand without a sign of emotion, but she did not think she could ever be his wife. She had come to realise that she could not bring herself to leave everything in England to live in Shanghai. And he ought to know from her first, because people would be bound to tell him anyway, that she had met someone recently, nobody he knew, to whom she thought she was better suited. But she would always have the fondest thoughts of him and hoped that he would not blame her too much, and might even one day be able to think of her kindly.

He read the letter through twice, the first time with his heart thumping unsteadily, the second time with it still as a stone. Then he folded it carefully in the same creases, slid it back into the envelope and buttoned it away in his tunic pocket—the very pocket in which he'd put her first letter, close to his heart. The air was cold, although the rising sun was warm on his face. He gazed dully at the alleys and streets, the cold dark waters of the canals, at the rickshaw coolie's back with its bony wing-like shoulder-blades sticking up under the torn cotton jacket, at the pyramid of mandarin oranges on a hawker's stall, and at the cabbages and spinach lying higgledy-piggledy on another stall while a woman with torn grey hair and a hunched back sprinkled water over them to make them look dewy and fresh. For some minutes, it seemed, he thought of nothing but what passed before his eyes, as though her letter had slid straight through his mind without leaving a trace. Then, slowly, her words began to recur, as if they hadn't disappeared at all, but had only been taking their time to sink into his brain, to take root. They began to echo in his ears, as though she were quietly speaking to him, to form themselves in her handwriting across his eyes, and he felt a blank, numb chill stealing over him that set the muscles of his face into a rigid, grim mould. *I knew it*, he thought bitterly, staring at the great stolid walls of the godowns coming into view along the quayside. *I knew it all along.*

But then, after those few minutes of bitterness, he boarded his first ship and had to force himself to work. And he started checking the manifest with a determination that closed his mind down as if with metal shutters and left it bare of any thought or feeling except the details of tax, likin, seals and signatures.

He went through the morning without once opening his pocket and re-reading her letter—without even touching it through the cloth of his uniform. At tiffin in the mess, he deliberately sat next to Johnson, knowing that Johnson's stream of banalities would flow on unprompted and distract his own mind with its soothing trivia. He even shared a rickshaw with Johnson back to the wharves, the first time in weeks, and listened to his detailed, unhurried account of the hikes he planned to make round Hankow over Christmas.

His last inspection of the day was of a small opium cargo from Bombay. At the head of the gangway a European stood beside the ship's Chinese agent, a man whose sallow face and dapper appearance seemed vaguely familiar to Denton.

"Good afternoon," the European greeted him with a slight accent. "I am the owner of the cargo if you have any questions. This is the ship's agent, but they never know anything." His voice was smooth yet tense, as if it might grow warmer or cooler suddenly, without warning—the nervy voice of a volatile temper. Looking through the manifest, Denton briefly, hazily, tried to recall where he'd seen the man before, till the spidery figures and letters, inscribed, in ink that was almost brown, by some clerk in Bombay, took over the forefront of his mind.

He examined the opium without comment and computed the tax and likin, accepting the cup of coffee which the owner impatiently told the agent to bring before they had even reached the saloon.

"How long have you been here, Mr....?" the owner asked, sipping coffee himself.

"About six months." He thought of Emily's letter and looked away from the man's face, which was peering at his across the table. Six months—in just six months she could forget him and take up with someone else! He felt his eyes darkening with self-pity.

"I have been here six years," the owner declared proudly.

"Have you?" How would he spend the evening? The long empty hours? There was the weekly Christian Youth Fellowship meeting, but—"In six years I have made myself rich," the man was saying, peering closer into Denton's abstracted face and smiling with almost boyish pride. "I came from Russia with nothing, and now I have a business, a house on Jessfield Road, servants, money in the bank...Jessfield Road, you know? Only rich people." He opened his hands, palms up, as if he were a magician performing a trick. "You wait and see, I will be a millionaire. My name is Ephraim, Jacob Ephraim. How do you do? One day you must come to dinner with me." He thrust out his hand, his brown eyes glowing with friendly warmth.

Denton shook it stiffly, distrustfully.

"And what is your name, may I ask?"

"Mine? Denton."

"Denton? Are you from England? Yes, I thought so. One day I am going to buy a ship from England. John Brown makers. Secondhand. I will start a fleet."

Denton nodded inattentively, returning to the report he was writing in his book. And just as he was writing down the time of his inspection, he remembered suddenly where he'd seen this talkative little man before. It was on that Saturday, a couple of months before, after tea with Mr. Eaton, when the rickshaw had taken him into the French Concession. This was the man who'd come out of that house with the green shutters and the gross Chinese at the door. This was the dapper man who'd greeted him and walked casually away as if he'd done nothing to be ashamed of. Denton frowned in disapproval at the memory and a moment later thought *Then I was still engaged to Emily, she hadn't written that letter yet.*

"What is the matter?" the man's voice broke in sharply. "You don't like to talk to me? Because I am a Jew?"

"What?"

"Because I am a Jew? You despise me, is that it?" Ephraim's eyes had suddenly grown fierce with resentment and his sallow skin was heavily flushed.

"Not at all!" Denton answered hastily. "I was busy, that's all."

"You think, he's a Jew, he's only interested in money, don't you?" Ephraim went on as if Denton hadn't spoken, his eyes burning brighter.

"No—"

"Well, I was a teacher in Russia. In Odessa. Not for money, for love of learning!" He rapped the table imperiously with his knuckles, to compel Denton's attention. "The Cossacks killed my father, so I came to Shanghai, and yes, I said, yes, I will make money now, because money is security. That is why." He nodded emphatically several times. "Money is security for us, Mr. . . . ?"

"Denton."

"Denton. Money is security and power, and we have been without it. That is why Jews make money. Not greed, but safety. We have to survive!" He nodded emphatically again. "There is only one safety for a Jew: get rich. I have learned my lesson, Mr. Kenton—"

"Denton."

"Denton. I have learned my lesson and I am not ashamed. I am making money and nobody can harm me. I feel safe. That is why I make money. *You* have no need to. So you have no right to look down on me. I tell you I would rather be a schoolteacher—"

"I was going to be a schoolteacher too," Denton said drily, closing his report book.

"What? A schoolteacher?" Ephraim's indignant flood ebbed as suddenly as it had risen. The angry light drained from his eyes and was replaced by one of sympathetic curiosity. "A schoolteacher? Why are you here, then? Why did you stop?"

"For money too. I didn't have enough to carry on with my training. I had to give it up." He thought bitterly of what else he'd lost.

"A teacher?" Ephraim shook his head wonderingly. "In that case you cannot have any prejudices against the Jews. Your country had Disraeli for prime minister." He announced that as if Denton himself might not know it. "But in Russia they think we are all bad, evil, cheats, robbers, murderers. Do you know they believe we kidnap Christian children and sacrifice them? Russia!" He wrinkled his nose distastefully. "Barbarians! They think we are all Shylocks, you see? They are still in Shakespeare's times, so backward!"

Denton nodded uncertainly.

"They think our religion is superstition," Ephraim was saying excitedly, his moist lips smiling derisively as he spoke. "But what about Christianity? Three gods in one— absurd! Whereas Jewish customs are good ones. Circumcision, for instance. You think it silly? Well, a famous German doctor has proved it prevents cancer of the sexual organ!" He paused to gaze directly into Denton's eyes, as if expecting to see astonishment and admiration there instead of confusion and embarrassment. "I have a copy of his paper in the *Zeitschrift für Chirurgie* at home, I will lend it to you. You will be interested to read."

"I don't know any German," Denton said quickly.

"Never mind," he waved the difficulty aside. "You can make it out. I will lend it to you. Where are you going now—after this ship?"

"I've finished for the day now." Again he thought of his empty room and the letter in his pocket. A disconsolate, self-pitying tone had slipped into his voice.

"You have finished work? Good! We will have some tea at the Central Hotel. Or the Astor House. You know the Central? It is near my office. The Astor House is the most expensive. I go there too. Which do you prefer?"

"I'm afraid I can't."

"Another time, then, I will bring you that article, you will be very interested."

Denton retreated under the barrage of Ephraim's words. The little man kept bringing his face closer to Denton's, gazing at him searchingly so that Denton had to keep drawing back. As Ephraim was ushering him towards the gangway, still talking and gesticulating volubly, he suddenly checked himself and stared harder at Denton's face. "We have met before, haven't we?" he asked almost suspiciously. "I have seen your face."

Denton hesitated. "Was it in the French Concession once?" he asked pointedly. "I think I may have seen you coming out of a house there."

"Ah!" Ephraim's eyes widened with recognition. "I remember, you were just going in as I was leaving. Yes, I remember very well. What a good house it is, isn't it? How did you find it?"

"Oh, I wasn't going in!" Denton protested hotly. "I'd never go to such a place."

"But you *were* going in!" Ephraim declared. "You were just getting out of your rickshaw!"

"No, it was a mistake. The rickshaw took me there by mistake. I'm—I *was* engaged then. To someone in England." He looked quickly away, his cheeks and lips setting hard.

"You *were* engaged?" Ephraim's voice warmed with sympathy. "What happened? Your betrothed has died?"

"No, no," Denton waved his hand. "Nothing like that. We, er, well, we broke it off." He couldn't bring himself to admit that he'd been jilted, but Ephraim seemed to understand anyway.

"She let you down? Then you must go!" He followed Denton nimbly down the narrow, springy gangplank. "Otherwise you will have bad blood—spots, pimples, acne." Denton, averting his face, imagined him scrutinising his impure complexion. "The girls are all clean, I know for a fact. All the girls there, every one."

Denton nodded coldly at the bottom of the gangway. "I must be going."

"I'll walk along with you. My chair's over there. Oh my friend, you must not be miserable and dull over a love affair." He gripped Denton's arm suddenly with surprising strength and held him still a moment, gazing earnestly into his eyes. "Why, I lost my betrothed in the pogrom of ninety-five. And what did I do? I went to a house, I chose a girl that looked as much like her as I could find—not that she was like one of those girls, you know," he qualified hastily, "but the general features—and I cried all night with her. And in the morning—pouf! I was better." He blew out his lips, kissed his fingers as if bidding his fiancée farewell, and then stroked his thin black moustache complacently. "So you must not be miserable about a love affair Mr....?"

"Denton," Denton said reluctantly, unwilling to allow this strange, immoral man even the intimacy of knowing his surname. He looked down at Ephraim's hand still gripping his arm.

Ephraim relaxed his eager grip at last and walked beside him till they reached his sedan chair. "We will have tea together, Mr. Denton, we have so many interesting things to talk about." And he shook Denton's cold but unresisting hand before turning to the bearers squatting idly in the last warm patch of fading sunlight. "Chop-chop!" he shouted peremptorily. "Central Hotel! If no chop-chop, me makee muchee bobbery!"

At the Christian Youth Fellowship that evening, after a discussion on the furthering of missionary work in China, the Reverend Eaton made a brief announcement about the new movement for young boys that had been started by Colonel Baden-Powell. The fifteen young men and women—Denton had counted them to prevent himself from thinking about Emily—listened respectfully while Mr. Eaton, his eyes glancing more and more often at Denton, explained what the new movement was. The little congregation nodded their heads piously. They were all schoolteachers at the new municipal schools, or the sons and daughters of missionaries; and Denton couldn't help feeling guiltily that their piety was tedious and insipid. The truth was, he had been growing more and more uneasy at the Christian Youth Fellowship and somehow Emily's letter had intensified his unease.

"A truly Christian idea, worthy of the heroic defender of Mafeking," Mr. Eaton concluded sonorously, "with great possibilities for attracting young native boys to the right ideals, while at the same time giving them valuable training in, er, in practical affairs and so on. Boy Scouts, Colonel Baden-Powell suggests these associations should be called. And I hope that some of you"—he glanced at Denton again—"will consider giving up some of your time to promoting a Boy Scout troop here in Shanghai. Who knows, perhaps Colonel Baden-Powell's service to the empire will be matched by a corresponding service to the Christian religion?"

Mr. Eaton had turned directly to Denton. "John, you've been very quiet tonight. What do you think about it?"

"I don't know," Denton answered disconcertedly. "I think, er, perhaps one of the schoolteachers here might be the best person to organise something like that." He stood up abruptly. "Excuse me, I have to go. A very interesting evening. Sorry I can't stay longer." He hurried out of the church hall and hailed a rickshaw, anxious to be gone before anyone could follow him.

Later, when he sat in his room gazing at the bare walls, after he'd read Emily's letter again, he began to feel a kind of peace, as if he'd known all along that it was going to happen, but was only now ready to acknowledge it. As though a long anxious time of waiting for bad news had ended with the relief of certainty. And after all, he had to admit, perhaps he'd been growing cooler himself. Was it really only his pride that was hurt? He got up, put the letter together with her photograph and her other letters, tied them all tightly with a piece of brown, coarse-fibred string, and put them away in the top drawer of his desk, the only drawer that locked.

As soon, within a week, he began to feel free and detached, as if the tie that had bound him to Emily had really been a restraint, a bond that he'd unconsciously wanted to be released from all the time. Without her photograph in its oval frame to remind him, he forgot about her for days on end. At first that disturbed him. Did it mean he was heartless? Then even that ceased to worry him. She belonged to England and a part of his life that was finished. He never replied to her letter.

When Wei asked, self-deprecatingly and with elaborate apologetic suggestions that it wouldn't really be worth his while, whether he might like to visit another tea-house, Denton asked instead to be allowed to pay for a meal in a restaurant. After many courteous demurrals, Wei gave in and took him to a restaurant by the river in Hongkew. The place was richly decorated, though in colours that Denton found garish, and every table was partitioned off by bamboo screens over which the laughter and voices of the other guests came in boisterous gusts of noise. They ate spicy dishes garnished with hot peppers and drank sticky, burning rice wine—Denton soothed his uneasy Band of Hope conscience by telling himself that he drank it as a social duty, not for pleasure; and indeed he didn't like the slightly nutty flavour or the burning in his mouth. Wei's eyes grew a little bloodshot and his pale cheeks were flushed. He insisted Denton should hear a sing-song girl, and this time Denton didn't refuse.

After a few minutes a slight young girl was escorted in, with a blind fiddler who found his way uncannily behind her. The fiddler sat cross-legged on the floor and began to play the two-stringed violin while the girl sang. At first the music seemed shrill and unmelodious to Denton's ear, the girl's voice flat and toneless. But the longer he listened, while Wei drank glass after glass of the clear rice wine, the more he was captivated by the plangent sounds of the girl's voice and the charm of her lowered, oval face. Wei gave her some money and she left while Denton was stumblingly asking in Shanghainese for the bill.

"Mr. Denton," Wei asked as they left, "Do sing-song girls sing in English dinner parties?" He promised to teach

Denton to play mah-jong and to take him to the best Chinese opera in Shanghai.

They went to the same restaurant the next week and the week after, and each time Wei engaged the same sing-song girl to sing her plaintive songs, while the hubbub of voices and laughter, the clack and slither of mah-jong tiles sounded exuberantly round them. Denton watched her while he listened and began to know the expressions of her child-like face, the way she tilted her head when she sang, even the curls and vortices of her delicate ears. He drank the rice wine too, almost with enjoyment, and was scarcely troubled by his Band of Hope conscience.

25

After Christmas the weather hardened. The winds that blew off the Siberian ice swept southwards over China all the way down to Shanghai, and the nights were frosty, though the days, as Wei had promised, glittered under bright blue skies. Beggars, coolies waiting to be hired, and drifting opium addicts clustered on the sunny sides of the streets now, wrapping themselves up in rags and newspapers to keep out the cold. These with money wore thick quilted jackets that made them look like clumsy animals as they moved. The girl-babies exposed on the rubbish heaps during the black-ice nights and the homeless street sleepers who gave up in the cold were often half-frozen in the morning when the municipal cart came round to collect them. The mosquitoes and flies vanished, though, and the decaying summer smells in the rank little canals were bitten back by the cleansing cold.

Mason, Jones and Clark, another officer, had hired a houseboat to take them up the river past Soochow for some shooting at the end of January. But Clark caught the 'flu and the others asked Denton if he would like to go in his place. It was an invitation that had been hanging vaguely about like an unwanted relative since Denton's first few weeks in Shanghai, when Jones had been quite friendly with him. But then Jones, perhaps following Mason's lead, had taken to mocking him slyly for what Denton supposed they thought was his priggishness. Since Emily had jilted him, though, he had relaxed his rigid moral austerity, and though he was never more than coolly amiable, Jones' teasing had grown milder, almost good-natured. Denton sensed he had been asked now only because nobody else was free and they needed someone to share the expenses, but nevertheless he accepted.

Even so, Denton suspected the invitation wouldn't have been revived but for the illusion both Jones and Mason had that he'd lost his virginity after the New Year's Eve party in the mess. Although the ladies of senior Customs and municipal officials had been there, the party had been much more boisterous than a tame Christmas celebration held the week before. And Denton, slightly drunk despite the pledge, had announced that he'd "broken it off" with his fiancée. It was at the end of the evening, when the ladies had all gone and Denton's head was wobbly, and Jones had suggested visiting a "house" to mark Denton's "liberation," as he called it. Denton had gone along with the crowd of them as far as the entrance of the place, in Bubbling Well Road. But as the others climbed the stairs, he'd slipped stealthily away, trembling with both fear and desire. Then he'd wandered the bitter streets and alleys by himself, all the way down to the docks where the sailors' brothels were, veering between fearful desire and disgusted remorse.

He passed several brothels, his head turned sternly aside at the last moment, while girls chirped at him from the open, dimly-lit doorways. In the end, tired and cold, his eyes sore, his mouth dry, he'd found his way back to the empty mess with its jaded decorations, and gone to bed feeling as guilty as if he really had followed the girls up the seedy mysterious stairways he'd glimpsed as he passed.

The next day was Sunday. He sang in the choir at the cathedral and prayed with a sick empty feeling in his stomach for forgiveness of his craving lust and drunkenness. Yet, while he prayed, the image, not of the sordid places he'd seen the night before, but of that more allur-ing green-shuttered house on *rue* Molière, where he'd first met Ephraim, had kept stealing seductively across his mind. And that image had brought another with it, the image of the article on circumcision in the German jour-nal. Ephraim had accosted him on the waterfront one day in the dead of the year between Boxing Day and New Year's Eve, and insisted on lending him the journal with its strange Gothic script. "I have been looking for you every day," he exclaimed almost accusingly. "Now you must have tea with me." Unable to think of an excuse, Denton had let himself be led into the Central Hotel by the voluble Jew and prevailed on to drink lemon tea in a glass. "Just like the Russians. Lemon tea and vodka—the only things they have produced in a thousand years," Ephraim had declared loudly, with a glint in his brown eyes, daring anyone to deny it. Stiffly and hesitantly he'd sipped the tea under Ephraim's quick, warm encouragement, and listened, reluctantly at first, to his spontaneous, child-like self-revelation, to his eager offers of friendship, talk, hospitality and happiness, all of which Ephraim was certain were his to give. And gradually he'd thawed, despite his brittle shyness, as he listened to Ephraim's continuous flow of ideas and anecdotes—about his business, Odessa, the Russian pogroms, the rituals of the Jewish religion...Sometimes, in his enthusiasm, Ephraim had gripped his arm again with that unexpectedly powerful grip. At first Denton had stiffened and recoiled, but by the time he got up to go, he'd grown so used to it that he scarcely even noticed it. He'd taken the German journal back to the mess, and, although no one could read German there, he'd kept it discreetly out of sight in the top drawer of his desk, beneath Emily's letters and photograph.

The houseboat was a long barge-like vessel towed by a steam launch with a patched, faded, junk sail about its cabin. The three of them sat in the sunlight, protected from the wind, and watched the fields slide slowly past, brown and rich, waiting for the next sowing. The scattered villages they saw, cowering under the bare branches of leafless trees, looked poor and shabby, as if all the wealth of the country went into the land while the people lived like cattle. The huts were dingy, windowless and unpainted, the walls cracked and flaking as though they had mange. Peasants leant on their hoes and gaped at them as they passed.

Jones knew a German businessman in Soochow and he arranged for the houseboat to be moored at a jetty near the house his friend had leased. The jetty was empty except for a few covered sampans in which whole families huddled, gazing at them over their rice bowls with the listless envy of the wretched for the unreachably rich. The street behind the jetty was empty too, although it was early afternoon.

"Funny," Jones said, feeling his wispy moustache that never seemed to grow any thicker. "You'd think there'd be quite a lot of people about at this time of day." They walked down the street to a two-storied Chinese house, the freshly-painted shutters all closed. Jones knocked on the door and a dog began barking inside, loudly and fiercely. After some time, while they glanced up and down the deserted streets, there was the sound of a shutter being unbolted and opened on the first floor. An amah appeared, grumbling and sour-faced, as the shutter swung open and clashed back against the wall.

"Mr. Henschel?" Jones shouted up, first in English, then in a Shanghainese that Denton was advanced enough by then to know was very bad. "Where's your master?"

The woman shook her head peevishly, pointing down the street and shouting down to them in an angry, complaining voice.

"What's the old girl jabbering about?" Mason asked.

Jones shrugged.

"Something about some bandits, I think," Denton said uncertainly. "I can't understand her accent very well. It must be a dialect."

The shutters slammed shut and they heard the bolts squealing as she tortured them into their sockets. They stood looking at each other.

"Well, she pointed that way," Mason said, nodding down the street. "Why don't we go and take a look?"

They began walking on slowly, uneasy in the eerie silence.

A suspicion began to tug at the corner of Denton's mind. Hadn't the amah used the word for "kill"? Was it another execution they were going to? Or had the bandits killed someone? The emptiness of the street unsettled him as they strolled along. The silence was sinister, unnerving. He glanced back. The launch and the houseboat looked small and remote at the little jetty.

They came to a canal with a hump-backed bridge over it. The street went on, was crossed by other streets, passed over more canals. And everywhere the place was deserted, except for a toothless old beggar the other side of the bridge, whose head was shaking uncontrollably as he gazed up at them, silently holding out his box. They didn't even bother to question him, it seemed so hopeless.

"Looks a bit rum," Mason muttered, his normal hectoring tone subdued. He was unsettled, too. "Where is everybody? The place looks in pretty good shape, they can't have had any trouble."

It was true, Denton thought, the place *was* well cared for. The houses were neatly and freshly white-washed, and the little stone steps that led down to the canals were firm and sharp, unlike the crumbling quays they'd passed on their way upstream.

"Venice of China," Jones murmured. "That's what they say this place is. Only where the hell are the Venetians?"

Then Denton heard, far away, that sudden yell of a thousand exultations that had haunted his first nights in Shanghai. "Why don't we go back and wait at the boat?" he suggested quickly, knowing instantly what the sound had meant.

But Mason had heard it too. "There's a meeting going on somewhere," he said slowly. Then his eyes brightened. "By god, I know what it is: they're holding an execution or something. Everyone's gone to the execution, that's what the old girl meant—they've caught some bandits! Of course! Come on, I bet your friend's there, Jonesy, having a grandstand view."

And Denton followed them. Unwillingly, his stomach already turning apprehensively, he followed them all the same. For against his rising sense of horror, another sense contended, a sense of fascinated awe. Men were about to die today as he would have to die some day or other. And indistinctly, inarticulately, he wanted to learn about death from them.

After some minutes, the streets began to be alive and full again. Everyone was hurrying in the same direction, laughing and excited, in holiday mood. And now they could hear the full throaty roar of the unseen crowd ahead, shouting *Kill, Kill, Kill,* with delirious joy.

At last they came to the execution ground. It was a square outside the city wall, with fields and little canals stretching out beyond it, and a small, squat temple with some stone huts nearby, about half a mile away on a muddy road. The sides of the square were crammed with people, standing, craning their necks, shouting, talking and laughing light-heartedly, as at any spectacle. Hawkers

106

were calling out their goods in drawn-out chanting voices, more and more people were pushing and jostling their way to the front, and children were climbing the plane trees and clambering up the stone walls, fighting and shoving each other to get a better view.

Near the front of the crowd was a tall European wearing a green hat with a feather in it. "There's Henschel!" Jones exclaimed. He shouted and waved to his friend while the people near them gaped and giggled at the foreign devils with their weird foreign voices. The tall figure turned, stared, and then waved back, taking off his hat, shouting unintelligibly over the tumult of the crowd. He seemed to be beckoning them forward, but it would be impossible to push their way through.

"Perhaps it's all over?" Denton asked hopefully.

But then the crowd in front of them began to part and they saw some Manchu bannermen roughly shouldering people aside to make an alley for them, beating them with their rifle butts if they were slow to move. The bannermen gestured the three Europeans to follow them and they walked as honoured guests through the wondering, murmuring crowd to where Jones' friend was standing.

"The captain here is a friend of mine," Henschel said after shaking their hands with a formal little bow. He was very fair and sunburned, speaking in a voice that was nearly accentless, except that he clipped off every word before he started the next. "They have caught some bandits who rob our mule trains and kill the escorts and so on. So he has asked me along to see justice done. Come and sit beside me."

A batch of prisoners was being assembled for execution. They stood in a wretched cluster, each with a placard fixed to a pole that was tied to his back, on which his crimes were written in large characters. The soldiers were unfastening the placards and throwing them nonchalantly down in a heap on the ground, then ripping off the men's shirts. Some distance away, where the executioner was waiting, a man was setting up a wooden tripod. It took Denton some seconds to realise that he was a photographer. The man ducked under the black velvet cloth mantling the tripod, then marshalled the docile prisoners fussily in front of it, just like the annual Sunday School outing at Enfield.

"I must show you some of my pictures," Mason was

107

saying. "Taken in Shanghai." As if to compete with Henschel he brushed the ends of his ginger moustache up with his knuckle.

The captain wanted the bandits' crimes to be shown on the photograph, so the poles had to be collected and dealt out to the prisoners again. The placards wavered unsteadily above their heads. But now they had to be moved back several feet, the photographer pushing them again like a nervous schoolteacher. They shuffled obediently, their dull, lacklustre eyes fixed on the shiny lens. Denton could just make out some of the characters on the placards. *Murder, Piracy, Abduction,* and many others he couldn't read. But their shivering bodies looked so thin and weak— how could they possibly have robbed and murdered?"

"Really these people are impossible," Henschel laughed again. "They are supposed to have started over an hour ago."

At last the photographer was satisfied. He ducked under his cloth, peered out again, motioned the two men at each end closer in, then ducked under the cloth once more, holding his hand up beside the camera. Sheep-like, the prisoners stood still, blinking at the photographer's raised hand.

"Watch the birdie!" Jones called out lightly.

The photographer pressed the bulb. The prisoners stood patiently, slack and shivering. *How can they possibly be going to kill them,* Denton wondered, *after taking their pictures like on a Sunday School treat?* But his swiftly thudding heart told him they would do it quite simply, without a moment's reflection on the monstrous irony of it all. *After all, this is China,* he told himself, as if that somehow lessened the horror of it.

At last the photographer emerged from his cloth, smiling contentedly and waving at the prisoners with a gesture that might have meant goodbye or thank you.

A low, excited mutter rose from the crowd as the guards began leading the first prisoner towards the executioner. The prisoner was limping and dragging his foot. One of the guards pushed him, not roughly, but as if to help him along, doing him a service. But the push, no more than a nudge really, was enough to make him stumble. He fell in front of the executioner, his face on the bare earth and with his hands tied behind his back he couldn't raise himself. A little titter ran through the crowd.

Then the same guard helped him to his knees, in the same almost courteous manner. He knelt there dumbly, his head lowered as if he dared not raise his eyes to look at the executioner. Like a man kneeling in prayer before his god, it seemed to Denton, except that his hands weren't clasped in front, but bound behind him.

Henschel turned to Denton and spoke quietly into his ear. "If they have not paid enough squeeze, he uses a blunter sword." The sunburned skin round his eyes crinkled as he smiled, as if he thought it terribly amusing.

Denton turned away.

A man pulled the prisoner's head forward by his queue while the two soldiers heaved his bound arms backward. How pale his neck was at the exposed nape, where the sun never reached! The crowd hushed with that tense stillness he remembered from his first hour in Shanghai. Denton saw, or thought he saw the quick shadowy pulse of the man's blood at the side of his neck. The executioner hadn't lifted his sword yet, there were still seconds to go, seconds to live through. Beyond the kneeling victim he could see the waiting prisoners. Like him, they were looking on. Even they couldn't wrench their eyes away.

Now the executioner was ready. He raised his sword slowly higher and higher till it seemed to hang down his back from his clasped hands. Denton's heart pounded violently. His teeth were clenched. He felt his nails digging into his sweating palms and yet he could do nothing to loosen them. One, two, three seconds he counted, his body taut, unbearably taut, his teeth gritted, willing the man to strike and simultaneously wildly praying that some miracle would prevent him. Then the executioner's body seemed to relax faintly, a scarcely noticeable loosening of his muscles, and Denton thought for a brief, dizzy moment that the miracle really had happened. But no, it was only that he was looking at the photographer, who had now turned his camera towards the kneeling victim. The man pulling on his queue and the two soldiers holding his arms back had all turned like the executioner to face the camera, and even the victim himself was twisting his head slightly to stare up at the photographer's hand as it slowly raised from behind the black cloth. The four faces, expressionless, staring, like amateur actors posing in a Band of Hope tableau such as he'd often seen with Emily on St.

George's Day, hung there in the silence; then, as the photographer's hand steadied, Denton saw the executioner's body grow tense again, the curved blade of the sword, which had wavered a little in his grip, grow firm and still. *I'm going to be sick,* he thought frantically, the blood pounding in his ears, the choking horror surging up his throat. He saw for an eternal moment the victim screwing up his eyes and wincing, the shadowy pulse throbbing in his half-turned neck; then the sword slashed down with a little whirr through the air and with a clean chopping sound sliced the head right off. It happened so quickly that for a fraction of a second the head still seemed to be there after the blade had passed through the neck; then it parted as the man holding the queue staggered back.

Denton wanted to scream, to run away, to escape this obscene ritual, but he couldn't move. The very thing he dreaded seeing held him to his seat. He waited for the next victim. He waited like the rest, breathless to see how he would die, whether he would plead or scream. His eyes were fastened to the man by invisible chains as the soldiers heaved and hauled him stolidly towards the headsman. Other soldiers were forcing back the people who had been dipping their cash in the blood of the first victim. The man's trunk lay still, the head a few feet away from it, blood still leaking from the wound onto the hard earth. Already it looked so still and small, he could hardly believe it had ever been alive. The young man stumbled past the corpse as if he hadn't noticed it. His eyes were wide and empty and the mouth was hanging open slackly, as though he were walking in a trance. Denton stared compelled; compelled by the elemental emotions of terror and awe.

Suddenly the man began to hang back, moaning and muttering, his eyeballs rolled up wide and white as if he were in a fit. The crowd seemed to hold its breath as the headsman's assistant stepped forward, grabbed his queue, and yanked him headlong forward, his feet trailing and flapping helplessly. The headsman raised his sword hurriedly while the soldiers hauled back on the man's bound hands. They seemed nervous now, tense and anxious because of the victim's panic. The photographer was under his cloth again, but the headsman wouldn't wait. The victim seemed to give up, kneeling tamely at last, and the headsman swung the sword down with a massive grunt. Yet just as the blade hurtled downwards the man jerked

110

spasmodically back, twitching his queue out of the assistant's hands. The blade swerved as the executioner tried to follow the movement, but it smashed into the back of the man's head. He fell to the ground screaming like a wounded animal—Denton thought of the abbattoir at Enfield, where once, when he passed, he'd heard a pig screaming and squealing. The man's whole body quivered and shook uncontrollably and again the whole crowd seemed to catch its breath. The executioner shouted at his assistant and they both tried to drag the man up onto his knees while the two soldiers stood nervelessly by. But it was impossible, there was no strength left in the man's body, he collapsed as soon as they hauled him up. Then they began kicking him wildly, yelling and swearing at him. His faced was turned towards them and Denton thought that his neck must be broken, his head jerked and twisted so strangely at every kick, like a broken-stemmed flower. His eyes were popping, still turned up so that the pupils had almost vanished, and bubbles of blood frothed round his lips. His mouth seemed to be contorted into a wild impersonal sneer.

At last the headsman stopped kicking, his rage exhausted. He planted one foot on the man's shoulder, the other beside his head and swung the sword again. But the earth was in the way, he couldn't get a clean stroke and the blade clanged against a stone without severing the neck. He bent his knees then to get a flatter stroke, but it wasn't until the fourth or fifth blow that he got the head completely off.

When it was over, nobody spoke. The crowd remained still and uneasy. Nobody came forward to dip his cash in the blood. Nobody believed his blood could be lucky. At last the executioner called impatiently for the next victim.

There were eleven executions altogether, eleven loppings of eleven heads. Afterwards, while the crowd slowly dispersed, limp and exhausted, Henschel insisted on introducing them to the captain of the soldiers. The captain bowed and smiled, but said only "Thank you for your coming," in a thick, embarrassed voice before with another bow he left them.

They strolled back in a deep, drained silence towards Henschel's house. The crowd had thinned by now, and the streets were gradually reassuming the usual appearance of

111

a Chinese city—hawkers squatting by their stalls, rickshaws and sedan chairs moving past, coolies bearing great loads at each end of their carrying poles, walking with that swinging, bouncing gait that seemed to lift them along.

Suddenly they came up behind a thin, stooping man who was walking more slowly with his bamboo carrying pole, as if he were carrying a delicate load. When they looked more closely, they saw that a swaying human head had been tied by the ears to each end of the pole, blood still dripping and splashing in thick congealing blobs onto the street. The spattered trail of dark red splotches followed the man as he walked with short careful steps, but none of the Chinese he passed seemed to notice him, except for a gaggle of children in rags and bare feet, who ran just behind him, gaping and giggling at the bobbing heads. The man himself seemed indifferent to them, his eyes set on the distance, his queue jerking rhythmically with each shuffling step.

"Christ, now I've seen everything," Jones said with an uneasy laugh. "Don't tell me he's going to boil them for soup."

"No, he is taking them for burial," Henshel answered, stepping fastidiously over a drying splash of blood. "He must be a relative. I expect he has paid my friend some squeeze money; their heads are supposed to be stuck on poles at the city gates."

Mason wrinkled his nose. "You'd think he'd want to wrap them up or something," he said. "Hardly the kind of thing you'd want the neighbours to see, I would have thought."

"Oh, they do not think like that," Henschel replied carelessly. "They are not like us. Death does not mean much to them, their lives are worth so little."

They travelled further upstream the next day, past Soochow, and Henschel joined them, riding along the banks of the Imperial Canal, a shotgun strapped to the shoulder of his Mongolian pony. At midday they moored the boat and ate tiffin in the little saloon, the sun warming them through the windows. Denton watched the junks and barges moving slowly past, pulled by coolies whose backs were bent almost parallel with the earth.

"Isn't this the canal that goes all the way to Peking?" he asked.

"No idea," Mason said, finishing his beer. "Let's see if we can get some birds for dinner."

They followed Henschel across the dry, hard, rutted fields, past a squalid village to a wooded rise where he said there were plenty of partridges and pigeons. Jones had left his gun behind; there was something wrong with the trigger. Mason walked beside Henschel, carrying his. The peasants were digging and hoeing, working with long-handled hoes and mattocks. They turned and raised their heads to watch the foreign devils striding across their land, yet without altering the rhythm of their slow, patient digging. Denton listened to the clink of stones and the grate of hard earth as the mattocks came down on each downward swing. It reminded him for a moment, as the sun glinted on the shiny metal blade of a poised mattock, of the sound of the headsman's sword biting into the earth the day before.

A partridge lumbered up suddenly from a furrow behind a narrow grass verge, its wings beating loudly like a desperate heart. Henschel and Mason fired at the same time. The bird's wings folded and it plumped down to the earth. Simultaneously a woman yelled, and the peasants working the fields all round them began shouting and gesticulating, running towards them brandishing their tools.

"You must have winged one of them," Jones said, licking his lips uneasily. He had picked up the dead bird and was holding it uncertainly by its feet.

They were soon surrounded by the peasants who muttered and scowled with a kind of jocular truculence that Denton couldn't make out. Were they really angry, or only pretending?

A woman was pushed forward, large-boned and tall, by a heavy, broad man with a set face and glaring, angry eyes. The man began shouting at Henschel and Mason, while the others growled behind him. The woman was massaging her back and wincing with pain, looking at them dumbly as if she had no other part to play.

Henschel smiled. "I think he is her husband. He says we hit her." He was undisturbed by all the threatening looks and accusations. "It happens quite often," he shrugged. "Ten cents for each pellet is the rule. Sometimes they get in the way deliberately."

"How can we tell how many pellets hit her?" Mason

asked, relaxing his trigger finger slightly. "They'll be asking for fifty dollars!"

"She has got to show us the marks." Henschel took a hooked pipe out of his pocket and began filling it deliberately with tobacco. The crowd paused to watch him, even the woman's husband, whose face was stiff and flushed. Henschel put his tobacco pouch away slowly, then smiled round at the circle of faces, some of which were already starting to crease into grins. "One hole, ten cents," he said in broken Chinese, clenching his teeth down on the stem of his pipe and yet still managing to keep his smile. He held up the fingers of both hands. "One hole, ten cents."

Some of the peasants began to titter, nudging each other and glancing at the injured woman and her husband.

"First see, then pay," Henschel gestured to the woman. "First see, then pay." Then he added quietly in English, "And I hope she has had a wash recently."

The titter became a ribald laugh. Only the woman and her husband didn't join in. She was still wincing and massaging her back. Her husband stood and glared, as if he hadn't heard them laughing all round him. His eyes blinked—it might have been with tears of rage—and he shook his head sharply.

Henschel lit his pipe, sheltering the bowl with his cupped palm. "I would believe there are at most twenty pellets in her," he said between puffs, glancing with a sly, measuring look at the woman's body. "That is worth two dollars. Give them two dollars." He turned to the woman's husband. "Twenty holes," he said in Chinese, throwing up both hands twice with fingers outstretched. "Two dollars."

"Why me?" Mason asked sulkily. "It might have been you that hit her." But he fished in his pocket and held out two dollars in front of the man's face, as if he expected him to sit up and beg for it like a dog.

The man shook his head fiercely while the woman watched in silence, rubbing her back more gently as the pain apparently lessened. The peasants looked from the silver coins gleaming between Mason's thick, reddish fingers to the man refusing them.

"If she has more holes, let her show the marks," Henschel said, breathing a wreath of blue smoke up into the air. "Show more hole, give more money," he offered negligently in Chinese.

The crowd grinned and muttered, repeating his words

to each other. But the man shook his head sullenly. He knew he was defeated, but he wouldn't give in and take the money.

"She'll never show her bum," Jones said with a relieved laugh.

"All a show for money," Henschel said confidently.

"Give him a couple of dollars more and let's leave them to it," Mason suggested. He swung his hand round to Henschel, who, after a noticeable pause, added two more dollars.

Mason held the four dollars out to the man, but again he shook his head obdurately, his eyes glowing. The coins were in the palm of Mason's hand. He tilted his hand slowly till the coins slid off one by one onto the cold earth. They lay there gleaming.

"He will pick them up when we have gone," Henschel said, examining the smouldering tobacco in his pipe. "Shall we go? Don't look round—ignore them."

They turned and walked back towards the boat, followed at an increasing distance by the peasants. After a while, when he could no longer hear them, Denton covertly looked round in spite of Henschel's advice. The man and his wife were still standing there staring after them. As he turned back he saw some boys stooping to the ground at the man's feet, picking up something and then darting away. The man didn't seem to move an inch, as if his resentment had turned him to stone. Denton felt obscurely ashamed, sullied, as though it was he who had hit the woman and dealt with the man in that supercilious manner.

Taking a more direct way back, they followed a path that led them closer to the village. The huts were of mud and unpainted wood, patched here and there with sacking and tin. Some of the roofs seemed to have caved in and those huts were derelict. There was a smell of dirt and decay, a pungent odour of pigs and stale urine.

"Pfui!" Henschel turned aside onto another path, that skirted the village. "It would not be surprising if they had every kind of disease here. Let us keep clear." They passed rows of freshly planted cabbages, the roots of each one neatly plastered with human manure, and left the dogs and the children behind.

"I wouldn't keep a pig in that filth," Mason growled with contemptuous distaste, "Never mind human beings. Why don't they clean themselves up a bit?"

"Do you think they *are* human beings?" Henschel asked lightly, rhetorically.

"That man didn't pick up the money," Denton interjected with a faint, hard edge to his voice. For some reason, he felt he had to defend them. "Some kids ran off with it."

Mason grunted. "More fool him."

"I suppose it was a matter of principle for him," Denton suggested weakly, yet not ready to give up completely. "I mean losing face or something?"

"He'd never have let her show her bum to us," Jones laughed gaily, swinging the partridge jauntily now. "I knew he wouldn't."

"You didn't look so sure of yourself at the time," Mason muttered surlily. "You were ready to run for it."

Jones flushed, but didn't answer and Henschel smiled a sly complacent little smile.

That night Denton went to bed early while the others drank in the saloon. He lay in his narrow bunk reading by the light of the smelly paraffin lamp. The shadows flickered from the unsteady wick and he kept glancing up at the cabin walls and window as if somebody had moved across the light. When at last he turned down the lamp, he looked almost apprehensively out over the moonlit rice-fields towards the darkened village, where not a single lamp was shining. He imagined he could still see the man standing there with his silent wife beside him, glaring fiercely across towards the houseboat. Denton was frowning as he closed his eyes to sleep. He wasn't enjoying this trip, he had to admit. It was a mistake, he wished he'd never come.

26

After duty Denton often drank tea now at the Central Hotel, where Ephraim frequently joined him. Denton would drink the Russian tea with a slice of lemon in it that Ephraim had introduced him to, while Ephraim, if it was after five o'clock, would order nothing but vodka. For a time Ephraim was his only friend, for he had grown more solitary since his expedition with Mason and Jones on the houseboat. They had ended the journey coolly, Denton declining to shoot and reading instead in his cabin, while the other two drank and gossiped with Henschel after the day's slaughter of birds and sometimes rabbits. Back in Shanghai, he avoided both of them, as well as Johnson with his assiduous attempts to become his mentor. And he began to skip the Christian Youth Fellowship meetings, pleading special Customs duties as his excuse. He continued to sing in the choir, though, and attended every service punctually. The blending of the voices under the dark beams of the cathedral still filled him with a melancholy satisfaction in which he released the emotion of his loneliness and yearning for...for something else, something more, he didn't know what. Since Emily's jilting of him he seemed to have been living in suspension, waiting, restless, discarding the ways of life he'd been brought up in and worn unthinkingly like his clothes, but putting nothing in their place.

He took to roaming the city at night, the long crowded streets of the international settlement, the seedier boulevards of the French settlement, the narrow canals and alleys of the Chinese city. Often he passed the entrance to the house on *rue* Molière where he'd seen the lady in grey with the little girl, and it seemed to him that somehow that was an emblem of what he was searching for. But equally often he would go on, towards the house on the other side with its green shutters and mysteriously enticing everopen door. He would glance in and then saunter past, as though uninterested in what the doorway promised; yet his heart always beat faster. The fat man with the level voice was gone, but another, older, man sat in the same chair now, forever reading a Chinese newspaper, from which he would slowly raise his eyes at every passer-by. The lady with the little girl, elegant, serene, remote—he never saw again.

His feet seemed to carry him to places of temptation solely in order to allow him to turn away at the last moment. He was torn between half-acknowledged lust and half-abandoned chastity. Once, in the sailors' district by the docks, two young, effeminate-looking Chinese youths accosted him, smiling in a strange, uncontrolled manner, as if they were drunk—except that Denton had never seen a drunken Chinese.

"You wantee fuckee-fuckee?" one of them asked.

"What?"

"Fuckee-fuckee?" One took his arm familiarly while the other groped for his groin.

He shook them off violently, shocked. They shrugged and sauntered away indifferently, giggling to each other, their gait unsteady. It was not until later, when he'd overcome his quivering repulsion, that he realised that they were intoxicated not by alcohol, but by opium.

Yet still he sought out the same places, and always alone, to see and yet avoid them, to titillate his desires and frustrate them. Faces peered provocatively at him from doorways, rickshaw boys called out invitations from their shafts—"Very clea', Portuguesee, Filipino, what you want?" —girls brushed against him longingly in the street, laying their hands on his arm with a caressing, feather-light touch. He was frightened of them, yet he couldn't keep away. In his room, he would listen more keenly, tantalised, for the chuckles and murmurs through the wall at week-ends or whenever Mason was off-duty. On his visits to restaurants with Wei, he watched the sing-song girls with long furtive glances, especially the one Wei had sing for them the first time. Noticing his half-concealed interest, Wei often suggested that restaurant and often engaged the same girl to sing. Denton knew her name now: Su-mei.

The weather grew colder. He wore his overcoat in his room at night when he sat down to study his Chinese.

One evening in February Ephraim joined him at his usual corner table at the Central Hotel, behind the glossy green leaves of a palm tree. He was rubbing his hands together and smiling gleefully. "Today I have made twenty thousand dollars, my friend." He sat down and gripped Denton's arm with his familiar pressure. "Twenty thousand in one day!"

"Oh? How?"

"How does anyone make a profit? By buying cheap and selling dear!" He gazed at Denton goggle-eyed, shaking his head amusedly at his naiveté. "By buying cheap and selling dear! The only law of business, my friend."

The waiter brought him his vodka unbidden, and Denton listened with a twinge of envy while Ephraim recounted with self-congratulatory chuckles and extravagant gestures how he'd held onto a consignment of opium because he was sure the price was going to rise—and of course he'd been vindicated. As he drank, he became more voluble, more expansive, his mobile, slightly sallow, face glowing with warmth and pride. "You see, we Jews must have a national home—that is why we work to make money. To found our national home where we can be safe from the Cossacks. Have you seen our magazine in Shanghai? *Israel's Messenger*? You will like it, an educated man like you. I will bring you a copy to read. It has many interesting pieces, not just for Jews, but everyone. Politics, art, literature . . . It is the organ of the Zionist movement in Shanghai," he added, as if that were its ultimate distinction.

"In English?" Denton asked cautiously.

"Of course. There is a translation of that article on circumcision in the next issue."

As he drank his way into the fourth or fifth vodka, always vainly pressing Denton to join him, he switched without a pause from the Zionist movement to the future of Shanghai. "Mark my words," he gripped Denton's arm again, "Shanghai will be another city-state like Venice or Florence in the Renaissance . . . You know?"

Denton nodded vaguely, unwilling to betray his large uncertainties about Italian Renaissance city-states.

"We are growing like them, and for the same reasons," Ephraim rushed exuberantly on. "From nothing we are already the third largest port in the world, the largest city in China—"

"Isn't Peking—?"

"Peking? Pah! Finished! Shanghai, I tell you, will be a merchant state as powerful in world trade as Venice was in Italy. It is the door to China. And we shall hold the key to the door." He filled his glass again from the bottle (the waiters knew that he never wanted a glass of vodka, but a whole bottle). "Look at our government. Who rules Shanghai? China? Of course not. Britain? You British founded it, but it is not a British colony."

"The foreign consuls?" Denton suggested mildly.

"Pah! What can they do? The power has passed to the Municipal Council—a merchant oligarchy. There you are— Venice without its Doge! We even have the canals!"

"Without its what?" Denton asked unsurely.

"Without its Doge. *Duce,* a leader, a chief. Ah, one day I shall sit on that municipal council, you mark my words. And we will control China from there, the whole China." He drank with a flourish and smacked his lips, leaning back with closed eyes to savour his dream.

Denton was still uncertain. Who did Ephraim mean

by "we"? "Do you mean the Jews will have a national home in China?" he asked hesitantly.

But Ephraim hadn't heard him. His mood had suddenly changed, his brown eyes frowning now. He shook his head sadly, recalling perhaps the vicissitudes of life in Odessa. "Ach, what are you doing, Jacob, always talking and talking?" he upbraided himself in a melancholy voice. "It will all pass, it will all pass. Venice fell, Florence fell, even Jerusalem fell... So why won't Shanghai fall too?" He sighed heavily, resignedly, pushing out his glistening underlip. "So what are you doing, always talking and talking about your national homes and your Shanghai like Venice? Ach, ach, ach..."

Denton watched in embarrassed silence while Ephraim lamented, rocking slowly back and forth on his seat. But then, as suddenly as it had come, the mood passed. He leant forward, finished his glass and screwed the cap on the bottle, calling for the bill with a peremptory snap of his fingers. He paid as always in cash. "Never pay with chits," he advised Denton early on. "Never pay with chits. They always cheat you." He stood up, took the half-finished bottle under his arm and walked with Denton towards the door. "Tonight, I shall celebrate with a girl," he said decidedly. He stopped to peer into Denton's face. "What about you?"

Denton shook his head uncomfortably, looking away from the lighted porch, on which palms and rubber plants stood like doormen, to the darkness of the river beyond the Bund. "I must be getting back to the mess," he said.

Ephraim gazed at him reproachfully. "Ach, you're not still thinking of that girl in England, are you?"

"No."

"She's gone." He ignored Denton's denial. "Why don't you forget her? Come," taking Denton's arm encouragingly, persuasively, in his grip, "I know just the girl for you."

But Denton, as always, pulled himself away. He watched Ephraim climb into his sedan chair and wrap himself round with a rug. Ephraim waved nursing the vodka bottle on his knees. The chair swayed as the bearers moved off. To the house with the green shutters? Denton wondered. An oil lantern glowed on one corner of the chair. Denton watched it bobbing away, imagined it arriving at the house, saw Ephraim getting out, being greeted by sensuous girls with long hair and high, rouged cheeks...

He heard his name called in Chinese. The sound came from the rickshaws clustering across the road from the hotel. He looked across at them, frowning. His name was called again, quietly and urgently. He walked down the steps and into the shadows where the rickshaw coolies were squatting between their shafts, smoking or dozing, wrapped in rags and old sacks. Again he heard his name called, and this time he made out the podgy figure of Kwai, the coxswain of the Customs launch he'd first been on with Mason.

"Mister Denton," he hissed from the edge of the rickshaws. "Come quickly." He was smiling excitedly, the bringer of good news. But then he always smiled, as though he thought the whole of existence was a genial comedy. Every officer except Mason called him Lolly Kwai. Mason, refusing to be so familiar with any Chinese subordinate, called him curtly by his name alone, if he troubled to use even that.

Lolly Kwai nodded into the shadows thrown by some plane trees. "This fellow says there will be some smuggling tonight."

Denton peered into the trees, but couldn't see a thing. "Where?"

"On the *Alexander the First*."

"But I checked their cargo this evening. They're sailing tonight."

Lolly shook his head, smiling broadly. "Come and talk to the man. He wants money." He led him past the trees to another rickshaw standing by itself. A young Chinese with a wisp of beard straggling from a large mole on his chin was leaning back in the shade of the raised awning. He scarcely glanced at Denton, the whites of his eyes flickering once in the dark and then remaining still. He looked only at Lolly Kwai, his face half-turned away from Denton as though he didn't want to be seen. The three of them whispered in Chinese, Lolly Kwai smilingly translating into pidgin when Denton couldn't follow. There were a hundred bales of cotton outside a godown on the wharf where the *Alexander the First* was berthed. Just before she sailed, having already got Customs clearance, they would swiftly load the bales and so avoid paying tax on them.

"What about the wharf police?"

The young Chinese shrugged meaningfully.

"I have the launch ready," Lolly Kwai turned to Denton.

121

"We can catch them from the river. They will have look-outs on the shore."

Denton felt his stomach crumple. He was unsure and diffident. He tried to remember how Johnson had handled the salt smuggling all those months ago.

"We must hurry," Lolly Kwai urged. "They sail in one hour."

"How much should I pay him?" Denton whispered uncertainly in English.

The informer's eyes flickered again, as if he'd understood. But he said nothing.

Lolly Kwai held up five stiff, plump fingers. "Fifty dollar."

"I haven't got that much on me," Denton said worriedly. "I'll have to draw some more out."

The Chinese spoke rapidly to Lolly Kwai, so quickly and quietly that Denton couldn't understand a word, Lolly Kwai turned back to Denton. "Twenty-five now, twenty-five afterwards?" he suggested.

Denton handed the money over. The man's eyes watched tensely as Denton counted it out, then he slipped it into his quilted jacket without checking it. As he did so, Denton recalled the handless stumps of Johnson's informer in the mortuary. The man slid out of the rickshaw and merged with the night, his black cloth slippers making no sound on the paved street—the first street to be paved in Shanghai.

Lolly laid a restraining hand on Denton's arm until the informer had had time to get well away, then led him to the launch. As they steamed the half-mile down to the lower section wharves, Lolly, his face glistening in the light in the well of the launch, explained how they could catch the smugglers red-handed. Denton nodded gladly, grateful that he was taking over. He felt he was hollow, acting like a puppet; but he couldn't have acted by himself. Lolly gave orders to the two men in the bow, who were flapping their arms across their chests against the cutting chill of the breeze off the water.

When they neared the vessel, Lolly stopped the engines and had all the lights put out. It was a moonless night, and they drifted almost invisibly down toward the *Alexander the First*. Lolly grinned and pointed. A file of coolies were trotting up a gangplank at the stern, carrying the bales on their shoulders and dropping them on the

122

main deck. They were working silently, their usual grunting chant hushed. As the launch drifted towards the white, rusty hull of the ship, Denton could hear the bales thumping dully onto the metal deck above him.

It wasn't until they had gently bumped against the ship's side that they were seen. There was a soft yell, and the coolies dropped their bales and fled. Denton followed Lolly Kwai up some iron rungs onto the quay. How cold and smooth the rungs were he thought detachedly, surprised that he should notice such a thing at such a time. The gangplank lay on the ground where it had been hastily thrown when the last coolie had run off. Lolly led the way up the main gangway amidships.

Denton, following, saw the ship's agent awaiting them, the same smooth, pale Mr. Ching, in whose presence he'd signed the customs clearance a few hours before. "Good evening Mista' Den-tong." His rimless glasses, always set a little down his nose to give him a quizzical, scholarly expression, glinted as he smiled. He spoke a little breathlessly, rubbing his hands together inside the full sleeves of his long, quilted gown. "Is something wrong? It is very cold, I think."

"You've been loading without authority?" Denton said unsteadily. Against his will a polite note of questioning had slipped into his voice.

"Without authority?" Ching's eyebrows rose in hurt amazement. "Surely no, Mista' Den-tong."

"What were those bales you were just loading, then?" Denton still felt unable to be brisk and authoritative against Ching's elastic, courteous friendliness. He glanced after Lolly and the two men who had gone aft to find the bales. Without Lolly's presence, he felt smaller, unprotected.

"Are not those the bales we have already pay tax?" Ching's eyebrows rose again in pained incredulity.

"May I see the manifest, please?" Still he was asking, not demanding.

Ching led him politely to the first class dining-saloon and ordered some coffee for him while the manifest was sent for.

As Ching laid the papers before him, Denton noticed he was drawing a long white envelope out of his full sleeves. Ching held the envelope half-covered, half-revealed as he spoke. "I am sure if there is any mistakings they

123

can be quickly arrange'," he said, smiling, his eyes on Denton's.

Lolly Kwai appeared in the doorway, and the envelope disappeared into the wide folds of Ching's gown. He waited courteouly while Lolly Kwai murmured into Denton's ear. "Twenty-nine bales cotton. Under tarpaulin. More below."

Denton nodded, scrutinising the manifest. "There doesn't seem to be any cotton down here at all."

"No cotton?" Ching shook his head in disbelief. "No cotton, Mista' Den-tong?"

"See for yourself." He pushed the manifest across. At last his voice was strengthening. Was it Lolly Kwai's presence that stiffened it?

Ching bent and studied the sheets for some time, turning them backwards and forwards and shaking his head in a show of perplexity. At last he straightened up, smiling still. "A misunderstanding, Mista' Den-tong. They must have thought the cotton is already cleared. I tell them to unload at once. Some more coffee? Brandy?"

"I'm afraid I'll have to report this, Mr. Ching," Denton said. "The ship can't sail until the matter's been investigated. It appears those bales are contraband."

"If they are unload', Mista' Den-tong?" Ching's voice was wheedling now. "You will let the ship sail? It is high cost of pay dues in port." Again Denton glimpsed the white envelope as Ching turned away from Lolly Kwai. It was just like the envelope Mason had taken from him that time when they'd inspected the ship together.

"I'm sorry. I have to withhold clearance from the ship now." Denton heard himself uttering the official phrases as though he were reciting from the pamphlets Mr. Brown had given him in his first week. "And we shall have to leave a guard on board too." His voice still sounded too polite and apologetic, but there was a stubborn core to it now. He stood up with a faint, throbbing feeling of elation. He felt he'd carried it off after all. He could tell from the momentary, hesitant glimmer in Ching's eyes like an actor's who'd forgotten his lines. And from his smile too—it had lost its pliability and become fixed. Even his supple voice had run dry.

As he went down the gangway, Lolly Kwai turned to him with his cheerful smile. "Mr. Ching big friend Mr. Mason." he said, in a pidgin that seemed to mock itself.

"Mr. Mason not likee this bobberee." His breath steamed on the air as he laughed.

27

"On the firs' day of Chinese New Year, all the family must have dinner together." Wei paused while some firecrackers banged and flashed nearby. "After thir' day visit relative'." He was nursing a small potted tangerine tree on his lap, the little orange fruits quivering on their stems as the rickshaw jolted over the ruts and holes in the road. His spare, bony shoulders pressed against Denton's when the coolie suddenly swung the shafts round to avoid a sedan chair borne out of the little alley by four trotting bearers. "Everyone must have new clothe' to wear and relative' give money to children. Good fortune token, it is called."

Some grinning boys threw a firecracker at the rickshaw wheels and the coolie swore angrily at them as the explosion sent flame and smoke round his legs. Wei nearly dropped the tangerine tree which was wrapped in red paper.

"And after the third day," Denton smiled, eager to display his knowledge, "students must visit their teachers and pay their respects."

"You are very goo' pupil," Wei nodded approvingly. "You have learn' a very lot."

"And the money packets are red for good luck, and the money inside them must be new money," Denton went on. "And that tangerine tree is for your family, for prosperity in the coming year."

Wei began speaking in Chinese now, smiling encouragement. "If you go on like this, you will become my best pupil."

It was Denton's turn to act as host, so he paid the coolie when they reached the restaurant. Firecrackers were exploding again nearby and he covered his ears, recalling his first morning in Shanghai, when he woke up to the banging of firecrackers and thought it was gunfire.

Wei smiled, cuddling his tangerine tree with both hands in front of him, so that his face was half-obscured by the lattice of its branches. "This is nothing. They are only practising." He spoke in Chinese still. "When the holiday really starts, it will sound like a battle."

As they went up the stairs to the restaurant, where

Denton's appearance was no longer a novelty, Denton thought of Su-mei, the sing-song girl. He visualised the curve of her cheek, the black fringe of hair across her forehead, the slightly roguish glances she'd given him the week before. Something quickened in him, a faint rippling thrill. He quite enjoyed her singing now, although she didn't seem to have a large repertoire and he knew all her songs. And it was only her clear, sharp voice really, he told himself, that he was eager for, not the way she held her head and smiled, or half-smiled, at him.

The waiter led them to the partitioned room where they always ate. Denton turned to Wei. "I've never met your family," he began indirectly, in his best Chinese, feeling for a way of finding out whether, as Wei's student, he should visit him after the third day of the holiday or not.

"Oh, they will not interest you," Wei answered hastily, giving the tangerine tree to the waiter to put on the floor, "They are only women and children."

Was that merely a polite disclaimer or definite discouragement? Denton toyed with his chopsticks, probing for a more certain answer. "Do all your students visit you on the third day?" he asked more directly.

"Not foreigners, it is only for Chinese students," Wei said decidedly. "I don't think foreign devils should do it." He had used "foreign devils," the ordinary, derogatory Chinese epithet for foreigners, unconsciously, then, realising his error, laughed in embarrassment. "As we are speaking Chinese, I forgot that you are a foreigner."

Sometimes he was open and easy with Denton, sometimes reserved and polite. At restaurants, as he ate and drank, he usually became more open. This time, he drank more than his normal amount of wine, and began to talk freely, changing to English as his thoughts surpassed Denton's still limited ability in Chinese. His cheeks became slightly flushed and his voice louder as he talked above the clack of mah-jong tiles and the boisterous laughter rising over the partitions all round them. He even applauded Su-mei when she came to sing for them and gave her a New Year's money packet—usually he scarcely acknowledged the sing-song girls he engaged except with a curt nod. While she sang, he told Denton about his two wives, who were always quarrelling, and about his family in their village in the northern part of Kiangsu. Once they had been big land-

126

owners, but his grandfather had mortgaged all their land except the ancestral house in his losing passion for gambling.

"What happened to him in the end?" Denton asked, his eyes on the curled strand of hair that fell cunningly down in front of Su-mei's ear.

"The creditor' take all the lan', and my gran'father kill himself. Throw himself down the well." His eyes were misty behind his glasses, whether from emotion or wine, Denton couldn't tell. Wei's father had come to Shanghai when the British came and became a clerk in Jardine Matheson's. Now he was old, he'd stopped working and lived with his sons, smoking opium and waiting to die. He'd wanted to buy back all the land his father had lost, but he'd never made enough money. Besides, he'd always been too fond of opium. Some people should never take it, they found out too late that they couldn't do without it. Wei enjoyed it himself, but never too much. He held up the heavy pewter wine jug. "You see, I drink, but I am not get drunk," he said, beaming hazily at Denton. "The same with opium—I take but no' too much. But if get drunk on wine like foreigners, you must not take opium." He let the jug down with a thump and splash.

Su-mei sang again. Wei left to talk to some friends in another room, walking with a cautious steadiness that seemed to belie his confidence in his imperviousness to wine—yet he would never show any other sign of intoxication. Denton lolled in his chair, the wine fumes wafting through his own head too. He watched the rise and fall of the girl's breasts under her silk gown, the spot of rouge that emphasised her high, prominent cheekbone, the full scarlet of her slightly pouting lips. Demons slipped the idea into his mind of placing his hands over those breasts. He blinked the demons away. In his pocket he too had a red money packet for her, but he hadn't the nerve to give it. Now was the time, while Wei was out of the room, but though his fingers were round the little packet, he couldn't draw it out. The demons slipped the fantasy of his hands over her breasts into his mind again, and this time he didn't dismiss them so quickly. But still he couldn't get up and give her the packet with the customary words.

She stopped singing and sat with her head slightly bowed, her hands demurely folded in her lap. He sipped some more wine and cleared his throat. He kept glancing at her and then away again, his fingers closing and unclosing on the little red envelope. Then her glance met his as she looked up at him from the corner of her eye. "You like me?" she asked quietly.

"Yes," he answered lamely. "You sing very well."

Her eyelids drooped again. "Not very well," she murmured conventionally.

Suddenly he hauled the packet out of his pocket, got up clumsily and gave it to her with both hands, mumbling the New Year greeting. Her fingers touched his as she took it. She inclined her head and smiled the response. She put the packet away without opening it, folding her hands demurely in her lap as Wei came back into the room.

Later that night, while Denton was leaning over the veranda in his overcoat, watching the anticipatory firecrackers flash and burst in the street below, there was a loud rap on the door. Ah Koo opened it as Denton turned round and, set-faced, with a flinty nod of the head, gestured Su-mei into the room.

Denton stared at her, startled, thrilled, alarmed. She stood looking at him with slightly bowed, submissive, head until the door had closed. He heard Ah Koo's long, phlegmy cough growling away along the corridor.

"What are you doing here?" he asked bewilderedly in Chinese.

She looked up with widening, surprised eyes. "You said you like me. You didn't want me to come?"

"No—I wasn't thinking"—he couldn't recall the word for "expecting"—"you would come."

Her shoulders lifted slightly. "You want me to go?" she asked simply, as if she was about to turn and leave.

"No...I don't know...Sit down, please." Had he secretly expected her to come? What else did it mean to say "I like you" to a sing-song girl? Yet the idea hadn't even brushed the surface of his conscious mind. He felt himself trembling slightly, helpless, like a man dreaming he is teetering on the brink of some precipice.

She was sitting on the edge of the chair at his desk, perching as if ready to fly, glancing at the picture of his parents. "Your mother and father?" she asked calmly.

"Yes."

"How old are they? Are they very rich? How many sons and daughters?" She took the picture off the desk as

128

he answered each question, frowning at it with a little smile at the edge of her lips. She held in gingerly, as if she thought it might play some trick on her. "Is it safe to have these pictures made? In my village, people said the machine that does it makes you sick."

He laughed, closing the veranda doors and taking off his coat. "No, it is safe. Even the Empress Dowager has had a picture made of herself." It was all right, he thought, he would merely talk with her a little, there was no danger of . . . "Where is your village?" he asked more easily.

"Beyond Ningpo," she shrugged. It was the same with all of them—the boys, the rickshaw coolies, the cooks. Whenever you asked them where they came from, it was always "Ningpo more far." It was a kind of evasion, a drawing of the curtains over their own space, like the faint, shuttered rigidity that their eyes assumed when your probed too far. And yet they thought nothing of asking how much you earned or what your suit cost!

"How long have you been a sing-song girl?"

"Three years."

"How did you become . . ." He faltered. "How did you become this thing?"

"Sing-song girl?" She laughed, a fluting, mocking little laugh, "My parents sold me." She placed the picture carefully back on the desk.

He nodded vaguely. He'd seen the little girls standing in docile rows in the Chinese city, waiting to be sold as slaves. At first he'd been shocked and indignant; but then, as Wei had blandly explained things to him, he'd felt his moral certainties begin to crumble. It was part of their way of doing things, he began to think, a way that foreigners couldn't understand, but which *they* would accept as inevitable for ever—or at least until some cataclysm overturned the whole of society. And how could you expect that to happen? Everything was so fixed, so immemorially old. Each succeeding generation seemed to have stamped the lines of tradition further in, so that now they could never be dug out. Impoverished parents sold their daughters, Wei had said, to buy food for those that were left. Sometimes they had a better life that way—they might become a concubine for one of their new family's sons, and so escape the life of drudgery they would otherwise have lived. Sometimes of course, he acknowledged with a fatalistic shrug, they might have a worse life.

129

It depended on the family that bought them. At least it was better than starving or being killed at birth. Denton hadn't asked him whether he had girl slaves himself. It was one of the many things about Wei that he didn't know.

"My teacher was good," she went on casually. "I was with some actors first. I can act as well." Her face turned to him like a schoolgirl's proud of her achievements.

"You sing very well. Your voice is beautiful."

She smiled, holding her hand to her mouth to suppress a giggle.

"What is the matter?" he asked in his stilted Chinese "Why are you laughing?"

She shook her head, glancing up at him under half-closed lids. "You said my voice is beautiful-to-look-at," she said at last, "not beautiful-to-hear."

He laughed and slapped his forehead. "I always make that mistake. It is because in English there is only one word for both things."

"Both things?" She gazed at him incredulously. "How can one word mean two things?"

"Well..." He tried to think of an explanation, but his Chinese wasn't up to it. "We just do have one word for both kinds of things," he repeated lamely at last.

She shook her head, either in continued disbelief or in simple amazement at the existence of so primitive a language. Then she got up. "May I look at your rooms?"

He followed her round the living room as she gazed at the chair-covers and antimacassars, fingering them wonderingly, the curtains, the veranda, the print of some European river scene that he'd bought in a junk-shop some weeks after his arrival and hung on the wall—to remind him of home perhaps during those first melancholy, nostalgic weeks. He stood close behind her while she silently regarded it. It was as though he could feel her body through the long gown she wore, as though it summoned him to touch it. And yet she seemed unaware of her body's attraction, standing oblivious, with her head tilted, without even a sideways glance at him. He could hear her breathing; he dared not step closer. His heart beat faster as she strolled unconcernedly into the bedroom.

She pressed her hand down on the bed. "So soft!" she exclaimed, shaking her head slowly as if she disapproved.

Denton swallowed and licked his lips, his heart thudding wildly.

"I sleep on wood," she said, turning to him. "With a quilt. Do all foreign devils have such soft beds?"

"It's not very soft, really," he got out breathlessly. "They have softer ones in England."

She sat on the bed and smiled up at him, and then, as if to tantalise him, got up and wandered back into the living room. He felt his heart slowing. A confused weight of both relief and disappointment seemed to drag on his chest.

She was fingering the chair-covers again, consideringly. "This is expensive?" she asked. "How much did you pay? Does all this belong to you?"

But before he could answer, she looked up at the gaslight hissing faintly beneath its shade and let out a little gasp of wonder. "Is that the new Western light?"

He nodded, reaching up to touch the dangling chain with its ring on the end. "If you pull this, the light is smaller."

She hooked her forefinger delicately inside the ring and pulled cautiously. The flame diminished and the room grew dim. He was standing beside her, his eyes fixed on her ear, small and flat, with a golden ring gleaming softly in the tiny lobe.

"How do you make it bigger?" she asked, turning to him. The faint blue flame seemed to glow in the shiny pupils of her slanted eyes.

"Pull the other end."

She smiled as the flame hissed, growing white and bright again. She began pulling first one and then the other, her eyes glistening as the light dimmed and strengthened. She looked round at him, her lips parted in a smile. Her teeth seemed to glisten too. He imagined his tongue thrusting between them. Still smiling, but mischievously now, she pulled on the chain till with a little *plut* the gas went out.

"Is it broken?" she asked, suddenly anxious.

He couldn't answer at first, feeling her breath beside him, the faint stir and rustle of her clothes. The firecrackers in the street outside, the cries and shouts, the booming of a ship's siren on the river, all seemed to take on a new distinctness in the silence between them.

"Is it broken?" she asked quietly again.

"No, we must burn it with a match," he said at last.

"*Burn* it?"

"*Light* it," he corrected himself. She was looking up at him, still smiling, although the child-like, contrite anxiety

131

lingered in her pupils. His eyes were on her lips. Suddenly he had lowered his mouth onto hers. He felt that the dreamer on the precipice had fallen, was rushing downwards through the giddy air. He pulled her body close against his. Her arms twined round his back.

She leant gently away from him after a while, although her arms still held him. "You want to be with me?"

He nodded, pulling her back towards him.

But she held her face away as he tried to kiss her mouth again. "How much will you pay me?"

"I do not know. Twenty dollars?"

She nodded faintly, placing her hand over his mouth as he tried for her lips again. "You give me the money now?"

She took the note from him and put it somewhere in her gown, then walked into the bedroom and started to undress. The lamp was unlit above the bed. She glanced up at it and paused. "You like the light on or...?"

He shook his head. Now that she was undressing, he was tense and uneasy. He'd never imagined further than holding her naked in his arms, and he knew there was more to it than that. But how did you do it, exactly? What did you have to do? Her clothes slithered off her, revealing first her breasts, then her slender waist, then her slim shadowy hips. She looked at him questioningly as she stepped out of her underskirt and laid it carefully over the chair. In the dim, erratic light from the window, her skin looked so pale—not with an anaemic whiteness of Ching which was dry and sickly, but with freshness and life beneath it.

"Aren't you going to undress?" she asked.

He began pulling at his buttons, trying to appear nonchalant and experienced.

She had put her hands up behind her head to loosen her hair, and now, with a little toss of her head, she let it fall down below her shoulders. "Do you like me?" she asked, with that faintly anxious look in her eyes again.

"Yes."

"Am I like foreign women?"

"I don't know." He thought of Emily. Su-mei wasn't like her. "No, not like foreign women," he said unevenly. "Smaller. More beautiful."

She shook her head and smiled, glancing down at her body wonderingly. He had never seen a woman naked before, not since the time when, coming home early from school, he'd opened the scullery door to find his mother standing in the old zinc tub washing herself. He'd no more than glimpsed the pasty flabby cheeks of her buttocks, the quivering flesh of her blue-veined thighs, before she'd noticed him and shouted him angrily out, muttering fiercely to herself behind the swiftly slammed and bolted door. Su-mei's body was so different: smooth, firm, small.

She lay down on the bed, one leg stretched out, the other drawn up. "You would rather have a girl with lily feet?" She asked.

"No." He was pushing at his shirt buttons, forcing them through the holes. Lily feet. He hadn't seen bound feet uncovered, but the sight of rich Chinese ladies shuffling along on them, supported by an amah at each side, had made him imagine they would look like deformed hooves.

She lifted her leg and turned the ankle, pointing her toes. "I was not born to be a lady. None of my sisters' feet were bound either." She looked down at her turning foot with a smile, as if she liked what she saw nevertheless, then lay back again, spreading her hair out on the pillow like a black shiny fan. One arm lay carelessly out-stretched on the bed, where he would have to lie, the other across her body, her hand just over her groin as though she were modestly covering herself. He'd got his shirt off now and her eyes surveyed his chest between half-closed lids. Shy and uncertain of himself, he turned his back to pull off the rest of his clothes, tugging fiercely at his shoelaces, which he'd stupidly pulled into a knot. He heard her giggle behind him and blushed, imagining he must seem as repulsive to her as his mother's body had to him. When at last he turned round, she had rolled onto her belly, her face turned towards him, her hair half over her face. Was that the right way? He didn't know. He lay down beside her. She didn't move. But she wasn't laughing at him now, her eyes, between the long dark strands of hair, looked serious—grave, even. The firecrackers and street noises seemed louder again, each one sharp and distinct. What should he do? He noticed detachedly the soft gleam of the brass bedrail. Perhaps if he kissed her again, it would all happen, somehow. But instead of kissing her, he found that his hand was on her buttock, shaping itself round the cold smooth mound and slowly stroking it. *Now I've started*, he thought with that same detachment with which he'd just now noticed the gleam of the bedrail, as if his

133

body were going of its own accord and he were merely a
passenger in it. *Now I've started. I can't go back.* Her eyes
were watching him still, there seemed to be the shadow of
a smile about her lips. Should his hand move up or down
now? He felt her leg move slightly under his palm, like a
cat arching its back against your hand when you stroked it.
He felt himself stirring too. He leant over to kiss her back
and his hand slid down her thigh as he did so. Her skin
was smooth and cold on his lips. But what next? It was
between the legs, he knew, but where exactly, and how? In
his demon dreams he'd sometimes imagined himself lying
on top of a woman kissing her mouth, her breasts. But she
was upside down for that. All the time he was wondering
what to do, he was kissing and licking her back, his hand
was caressing her legs with rising pleasure and desire, as if
his body knew perfectly well what his mind did not. He
pressed her side gently and she rolled over onto her back,
flicking the hair out of her face and closing her eyes. He
leant over to kiss her and as he did so his hand covered
her breast. Another mound, smooth and swelling. He
heard her draw in her breath as he pressed against the
hardness of her nipple and her excitement roused him
still further. Her lips opened for his. They seemed to
grow warmer and moister the more he pressed against
her, the more he brushed his palm across her nipple.
Suddenly her tongue slipped between his teeth, withdrew,
then slipped in again. He lay on top of her now, his stalk
digging into her belly. She laid her arms lightly round his
back. Her fingertips brushed delicately along his skin, up
and down his flanks. That was as far as his imaginings had
ever brought him. For a brief moment he paused, uncertain how to go on. Again that detached sense of being a
spectator of his own body came over him. He seemed for a
second to be seeing himself from above—he had a definite
image of his own back as he sprawled on top of her—and
he wondered remotely how such grappling would be important or exciting, and then, as she pressed up against
him with her hips, he succumbed again. His lips found
her breasts now, the hard little nipples were urging themselves between his teeth and he felt his stalk lunging at her
thighs, blindly and wildly. But her legs were tight together
and he couldn't get in. Was it the wrong place? he wondered uneasily.

But now she was moving beneath him, gently easing

him over onto his back. She knelt over him while his straying hands stroked her head, her cheeks, her shoulders. Her hand was on his stalk, her hair brushing his chest as she kissed his throat, his nipples, his belly. Her hand was playing with the tip of his stalk, pressing and squeezing it, sliding her fingers softly up and down. Slowly he let go, surrendered, abandoned himself to this delicious sensation that seemed to be melting his body with pleasure. His eyes were closed, his fingers were tangled in her hair, she had her lips over his stalk, she was kissing it, licking it, moving down to the root and up again to the very, exquisitely thrilling, tip. Her lips were closing over the tip, were sliding slowly down it once more, further and further down till he could feel the back of her throat like a warm velvet cushion against the tip of his stalk. And all he'd known, the thought drifted like a wisp of cloud across his mind, was that you kissed in bed!

He felt his stalk thickening and trembling, the sap throbbing up, but then, as if she too had felt it with her agile lips, she slipped away and rolled over onto her back, pulling him close on top of her. Her legs were spread wide apart now, and his stalk was between them, probing and thrusting assuredly now, as if he'd known all along where the place was. He felt her take him between her finger and thumb and guide him into the warm, ready, moistness of her body while the other hand, behind his neck, pulled his mouth down onto hers.

Desire suddenly flowered in every fibre of his body. She led him on, rocked him, teased him, charmed him with her licking of his throat, his ears, with caressing movements of her legs, with the lift and surge of her whole body as he plunged wildly into her. At last, with a long moan, he spent himself in violent shuddering spasms that were echoed in her, quivering through them both again and again until, finally exhausted, his head on her shoulder, he felt his mind sliding away into a vast, empty calm.

The loud bursting of firecrackers and the strident angry yell of a woman in the street outside penetrated the heavy layers of his sleep. His eyes opened slowly. His mouth was half-open on her round smooth shoulder still, as though he'd fallen asleep in the act of biting it. The room seemed darker now, the street, after the outburst that had woken him, quieter. He wondered how late it was. He stirred luxuriously against her body and raised his head.

She was gazing up at the ceiling, her face still and reflective. He kissed her throat, sniffing the faint, unnameable scent of her skin, and looked into her eyes again. The dim light in her dark pupils changed as she pulled back from her faraway thoughts, whatever they were, to look up at him. She smiled slowly, her lips just moving at the corners, a lazy, dreamy satisfied smile. He let his fingers trail gently over her lips, her chin, her cheekbones.

"How old are you?" he asked.

"Sixteen Chinese style. Fifteen western style. Chinese children are one year old when they are born."

He nodded.

"I would like to have a house with gas lamps like this one day," she murmured thoughtfully. Was that where her thoughts had been? Her eyes slipped back to him questioningly. "Do you want more?"

"More?"

"Me? If you pay, I will."

A cold wave of disenchantment broke over him and he shook his head.

She seemed to sense his changed mood. She got out of bed with a little shrug and gathered her clothes together. He would not look at her. He lay with his head turned away, gazing at the bare wall. He heard her washing herself in the bathroom.

"Can you give me fifty cents?" her voice asked, small and clear by his head.

"Fifty cents?"

She was dressed, looking down at him, her hands deftly pinning her hair behind her head. "For Ah Koo," she said. "Otherwise he will not let me in next time. I must give him something."

He couldn't reach his jacket. She held it out for him. He pulled out a dollar and gave it to her.

She was ready to leave. He watched her dispiritedly.

She walked to the door, then turned and raised her hand to wave, with a childlike flutter of her fingers. "Shall I come again?" she asked, almost shyly. "Did you like me?"

He hesitated. "I will see you at the restaurant," he answered evasively. "I will tell you then."

When the door had closed, he listened for the sound

of her footsteps, but just then the iron-bound wheels of a heavy cart were trundling past outside. He got out of bed and went to the bathroom. The tiled floor was wet where she'd stood. He could see the dark print of her foot near the door. He stood in the same puddle and washed himself with the same cold water. *Suppose she wasn't clean?* He soaped and soaped, shivering in the cold night air.

He hurried back to the bed and covered himself with all the blankets, keeping away from the side were she had lain. Suppose he'd caught something from her? The wave of guilt and disgust that had been looming over him toppled and broke. He prayed for forgiveness, imagining God as an all-seeing Reverend Eaton. Yet even as he prayed, obscurely hoping that if he truly repented, God would protect him from disease, her voice came back to him—*Shall I come again?*—and with her voice, the image of her face, her body, reviving the memory of her lips on his, her thighs closing round his thrusting stalk.

Far away he heard firecrackers banging and crackling like distant gunfire and as his sore, exhausted lids closed, he imagined her being borne away in a rickshaw, flashes and smoke all round her while she turned and waved and asked, "Shall I come again? Did you like me?"

28

When the clink of his teacup woke him in the morning and he opened bleary eyes onto the mean, cold light, a wave of stale distaste and uneasy guilt washed over him again, together with a lurching sense of fear. He sipped the strong, sweet tea that Ah Koo had brought him and listened to him pouring the hot water into his basin in the bathroom. *I have committed fornication, I am unclean,* he thought with grim Biblical rhetoric. *And I've probably caught some disease from her, too.* He lay down again and closed his eyes when Ah Koo came out with the toilet bucket, unwilling to face his blandly inquisitorial gaze. *Unclean, diseased,* the words thumped accusingly through his mind. He remembered with a sudden stabbing keenness the boys at school who at fourteen or so, just before they left, would start sniggering about the smell of girls, which ones would let you put your hand up their skirts, which ones had

137

"started" and which hadn't. He'd kept himself pure and intact then, but now he was no better than they were, he had come down to the same thing in the end. Disease—he knew nothing about it except from the bragging he'd overheard in the boys' toilets. It could drop off, he remembered one boy with carrotty hair saying, showing off his new-found knowledge.

But how did you tell if you were infected? How long did it take to show? He put his hand down cautiously and felt himself, as if there might be some difference already. And while he did so, Mr. Eaton's face seemed to loom over him, minatory and indignant, hurling down denunciations and imprecations.

The door closed quietly behind Ah Koo. Denton propped himself up on his elbow again and finished his tea, his stomach turning softly with remorse and anxiety. A long black hair lay on the pillow. The sheets were stained. There was a sour smell about them. They were the emblem of his sordid lapse. He pulled the bed apart and heaped the unclean sheets on the floor. Perhaps if he washed himself in his shaving water, he might kill the germs? Or was it too late? He washed himself anyway, examing the limp and flabby little thing for any signs of disease. The tip looked a bit red, he thought. But that might only be because he'd been rubbing it so hard with the soap. Undecided, he poured the water away and shaved in the cold water, searching his face in the mirror for telltale signs of debauchery. And though all he saw was a pair of worried brown eyes with solemn, wide pupils, he couldn't convince himself that the wages of sin weren't already gathered there. He cut himself badly in his usual place, on his Adam's apple, and, as he staunched the blood with the new styptic pencil he'd got from Watson's, he vowed to God, whom he still visualised with the hard, unforgiving brow of the Reverend Eaton, that he would never see Su-mei again if only he could be free of disease. The nagging question, *how did people like Mason and Jacob Ephraim manage?* he pushed aside into an obscure corner of his mind.

For five days firecrackers banged out their salute to the Chinese New Year. All the shops were shuttered and half the boys disappeared from the mess. The weather was cold and dreary and each drab day the same images of guilt and retribution harried Denton, assailing him while he was at work, while he was eating in the mess, in the lonely hours of the night when he lay awake sleepless, and in the thin, chill light of the morning, when he woke tired from the fitful sleep that had come at last in the small hours before dawn. A faint, relentless churning of his stomach, the accompaniment, if not the essence, of his guilt and fear, stole over him time and again, whenever his mind was empty. It came to seem as natural and familiar to him as breathing. He felt he would never feel calm and unworried again.

At last, unable to endure the anxiety any longer, he decided to see a doctor. *If I'm all right,* he promised that stern Providence with the rigid, righteous face of Mr. Eaton once more, *I'll never do it again. And if I'm not, please let me get better and I'll make up for it, I'll make amends.* Yet several more days passed before he could work up enough courage to make an appointment. He chose a Dr. McEwan, whose surgery was on the edge of Hongkew, where many of the sailors' brothels were. He shouldn't be too expensive, Denton thought. Or too censorious. In the meantime Sunday came; Denton sang fearfully in the choir and prayed with aching penitence at morning and evensong. He avoided the Reverend Eaton's eyes, but sitting in the choir stalls, his feet cold on the chilly flags, he glanced often over the irreproachable heads of the congregation, especially Mr. Brown's sedate bald dome with its woolly grey circlet of hair, and his wife's stately wide-brimmed hat. They seemed more remote than ever from him, superior not only by being "good class," but also now by their virtue. He felt he had no right to sing in the choir even, that he was a hypocrite whom the Reverend Eaton might at any moment turn to and denounce with burning eyes.

Dr. McEwan was disconcertingly young—he looked hardly more than five years older than Denton. But he seemed fifteen years older in his manner. Thick black hair grew low down on his forehead and a bristly moustache sprouted belligerently on his upper lip. "Yes, Misterr Denton?" he asked in a faint Scottish brogue, looking up suspiciously beneath knitted, heavy brows, as though he expected something unsavoury already from one glance at Denton's hangdog face.

"Er...I think I may..."

"Yes?" The heavy brows drew even closer together.

139

"Inadvertently, I mean...I may have been in contact with...with a disease."

"That's probably true of all of us, Misterr Denton," he grunted. "Did you have any particular disease in mind, or do ye want to be checked for every blessed one? It'll be mighty expensive if ye do."

"Well..." Denton smiled feebly at his sarcasm, his cheeks smarting.

"Been to a brothel, I take it?"

"Oh no! Nothing like that!"

Dr. McEwan's flush deepened with impatience. "Well, what, then? Pish, man, I can't treat a patient like this! What's the trouble?"

"Well, it *was* a bit like that," Denton conceded shamefacedly. "Only it wasn't a..." His voice failed him at the word Dr. McEwan had uttered with such no-nonsense briskness.

"Right then, ye've been with a woman." His eyes glittered irritably. "Why didn't ye say so? When was it and what are your symptoms?"

"Well, I don't seem to have any symptoms yet—"

"When was it?"

"Last Monday."

"A week ago? Good grief man, ye won't have any symptoms in seven days. God may have made the worrld in six days, but venereal disease takes a wee bit longer. The woman was a prostitute, I take it?"

"Oh no, not at all!"

Dr. McEwan glanced at him sharply. "Ye don't mean a respectable woman, surely?"

Denton looked away. "A sing-song girl."

"Sing-song girls are prostitutes, Misterr Denton."

"No, she was different," Denton stammered weakly. "I mean she...she..."

"She only does it when she wants to, eh?" He laughed sardonically. "A high-class lady, no doubt. Well, you're probably all right. It's the lads in the cheap places by the docks that are more likely to catch a dose—and I doubt ye've been there by the look of ye," he added witheringly. "I'd better have a glance at ye all the same. On the couch please and drop your trouserrs."

Denton lay obediently on his back, ridiculous and vulnerable, gripping his lifted shirt-tails in both hands. He gazed up anxiously past Dr. McEwan's shoulder as he leant over to examine him. A large black fly was flitting erratically round the motionless blade of the punkah that hung from the ceiling. Dr. McEwan's hand felt cold. Denton's body stiffened slightly in recoil at the impersonal insult of his touch.

"Pish, man, there's nothing wrong there," the doctor straightened with a sigh. "It's your conscience that's bothering you, not your health. And I'm not the man to cure that." He glanced wrily down at Denton as he spoke, and Denton caught the definite warm scent of whisky on his breath. He dressed quickly, his chest light with relief, shivering slightly in the cold of the unheated consulting room.

"Keep away from the cheaper places, if ye can't keep away from it altogether," Dr. McEwan advised drily at the door. "You'll be running very little risk if ye just use your noddle. And come back to see me in six weeks' time, just to be sure."

Again, as he passed the doctor, Denton caught that warm smell of whiskey on his breath.

His health assured, Denton determined to keep his vow. He attended the Christian Youth Fellowship on Thursdays and covered his inward yawns with a outward expression of piety. He went to choir practice on Friday evenings and both services on Sundays. On Saturdays, to escape the sounds of Mason's love-making in the afternoon, sounds which had become agonisingly disturbing now that he understood their meaning, he left his room and walked along the Bund. There was the municipal band to listen to in the public gardens, and, in the evening, the brass concert from the balcony of the German Club, the players smoking cigars and drinking great stone tankards of beer between pieces, looking down on the shifting crowd that gathered in the street below with genial, well-fed smiles. And on weekday evenings he worked at his Chinese.

Wei had gone away for three weeks, to visit his ancestral village for the New Year celebration. When he returned, he suggested their usual restaurant for their weekly dinner. But Denton asked if they could go somewhere else for a change. He didn't want to meet Su-mei again. Images of her face and body tempted him still at every unguarded moment, especially when he lay in bed at night, and he felt he wouldn't be able to resist her if he saw her in the flesh—still less so, now that he knew the

141

fears which had been the greater part of his guilt were groundless.

Wei took him to another restaurant in the old Chinese city, where the streets were so narrow that two rickshaws could barely pass. He began telling him, while they ate their Peking duck, about some Chinese revolutionary called Sun Yat-sen who had been imprisoned in the Chinese Embassy in London and escaped with his life only by throwing messages into the street, which some passer-by had found and taken to the police. Wei was just describing how the handwriting on the notes was recognised by an Englishman who'd been Sun's teacher, and Denton, listening, was just taking a slice of the brown, crackly-skinned duck from the dish between them, when he saw Su-mei being ushered, past their table by the head waiter. Their eyes met. He felt his outstretched arm pause while something throbbed for an instant in his chest, as it might have if he'd just missed a step.

"... he is in Japan now," Wei was saying, "waiting for a chance to return..." His eyes followed Denton's gaze, but he went on smoothly with scarcely a break, switching however for some reason into English. "He has many wester' idea', such as democracy and other new thing'. The Manchu try to kill him, but I think she—*he*—win in the en'."

Denton nodded absently, noting detachedly how Wei, like so many Chinese, often mixed up the genders of English pronouns, Chinese having no genders itself. But he could not have repeated Wei's last sentence—that little grammatical error was the only thing he'd heard. His arm trembled slightly as he dipped the slice of duck into the black soya sauce and watched his chopsticks carry it to his mouth. Su-mei had gone on, into one of the private rooms; but, as she passed, the faintest smile had touched her lips, and her eyes had lingered on his for one appealing second before she looked away.

"Sun was educate' in the British colony of Hong Kong," Wei went on. "Therefore he was learn' many wester' liberal idea'."

Denton didn't respond and for a few moments they were awkwardly silent. Then Wei swallowed his rice wine with screwed-up eyes as it burned his throat, and coughed, smiling at Denton indulgently as he reverted to Chinese.

142

"Your mind is on other things. Shall we ask if she is free to join us later on?"

"No, no," Denton blushed, shaking his head too emphatically to be believed. "I'm sorry, I was only thinking..."

"She has a good voice and she is good to look at," Wei urged gently.

"Yes, but not for me, not just now. If you want to hear her...?"

Wei shook his head, his shrewd little eyes smiling in their pale folds of skin. "I have two wives already, that is enough for me."

After the almond soup and the oranges, when they had wiped their hands with the steaming towels the waiter brought them, Denton stayed sitting as long as he dared without being discourteous, hoping he might see Su-mei leave, or at least hear her voice. Wei waited patiently, talking still about Sun Yat-sen although he must have known Denton was only half-listening. But Su-mei didn't appear again and his strained ears heard nothing except the usual lively clatter of a Chinese restaurant. *Just as well,* he told himself at last when he got up to go. But why then did he feel so disappointed, so forlorn?

He was writing a letter home late that night when he heard a sudden shouting and screaming in the street below. There were men's voices, angry and harsh, and a woman's, shrieking wildly in protest. He raised his head, listened a moment with a frown, then lowered it again. Then he jumped up. The woman was calling his name, screaming between what seemed to be blows. And it sounded like Su-mei's voice. He pushed the veranda doors open and leant over the rail. It was Su-mei. She was cowering against the wall while two men struck at her with their fists and feet. People passed by on the other side of the street, gaping but indifferent.

Denton shouted out, but nobody heard—the men went on striking her at will. He dashed out the room, down the stairs, through the lobby. Mason and some others were coming out of the lounge, attracted by the noise.

"What's going on?" Mason asked.

"Quick, they're beating a girl!"

He rushed past them down the steps. Su-mei's hair

143

was loose and she had fallen to her knees. One of her assailants, a vast heavy man, was slapping her face with his open hand, while the other, grabbing her hair, was swinging her into the blows. There was blood on her mouth. Denton felt an immense surge of anger carry him over the threshold of violence. He slipped his arm round the smaller man's neck and swung him round against his braced leg, flinging him to the ground. The fat man stopped, his hand raised to strike Su-mei, and stared at him with flat, expressionless eyes. It was like being stared at by a toad. Denton heard Mason and the others running up behind him, cheering loudly, hallooing like huntsmen. Su-mei raised her head slowly, whimpering. She put her hand up tentatively to touch the blood at her lip and looked down at her fingertip wonderingly, as though she couldn't believe it.

Denton glared at the fat man, panting heavily while the other scrambled to his feet. It was the man he'd seen at the house with green shutters in *rue* Molière. He recognized him at once. The same small unwinking eyes stared like opaque beads into his.

"What's going on?" Mason shouted. "Kick their teeth in!"

But the two groups merely stared at each other like two packs of dogs, the Chinese silent, the British, except for Denton laughing and threatening at the same time, secure in their colour and their numbers. Denton's heart was pumping wildly, his pulse thumping unsteadily in his ears. He'd never struck a man before, and he felt elated and fierce, as if he'd broken some barrier that had been hemming him in.

"Get out!" he said with jerky breathlessness to the toad-like fat one. "Go on, get out!" He didn't even realise he was speaking in English.

The great bulk didn't move. He stared calmly at Denton a second longer, then spoke slowly, in the level, throaty voice that Denton immediately recalled from before. *"Cette fille,"* he said slowly, *"Cette jeune fille à moi."*

"No!" Denton shouted fiercely. He stabbed his chest with his forefinger. "Mine! Understand? Mine, you fat brute!"

The man stared back at him with a cold insolence that seemed almost dignified. His massive head shook slightly, the long queue quivering down his back.

144

"Hear what he said?" Mason swaggered forward. "Go on, push off! Come round here again, you'll land in prison. Get it?"

The fat man's eyes flickered in his moonlike, immobile face as he glanced swiftly from Mason to Su-mei to Denton.

Denton dragged out his Chinese at last—he seemed to have lost it all at first, as though it didn't belong to this savage, elemental layer of his self. "Go away or I will have you arrested," he said distinctly, trying to control his heaving breath.

The man moved his eyes again, without turning his head, to watch his companion draw closer to him, then let them swivel back to Denton. "This woman works for me," he answered in Chinese, staring coolly into Denton's eyes. "It is nothing to do with you." He nodded faintly to the other man, who seized Su-mei's arm. She gave a shocked little yell, then stiffened, pursed her lips and spat deliberately into his face.

"Let her go or I kill you," Denton said. His voice was under control now, low and level. He knew with the same elation as before that he would hit the smaller man if he didn't let go. He felt the violence throbbing up behind that broken barrier.

The man let go after a moment and slowly wiped the spit off his face.

"Good for you, Denton," someone muttered behind him.

Su-mei was trembling and white-faced, though no longer whimpering. She touched the blood with her finger again and looked down at it with the same detached wonder.

"Proper little spitfire, isn't she?" Mason said admiringly. The others laughed.

"She owes me money," the gross Chinese went on stolidly, as if nothing had happened since he last spoke. "One hundred dollars."

"You working for the Red Triangle?" Mason interrupted belligerently, first in English, then in broken Chinese.

The fat man's eyes shifted slowly to Mason then back again. He didn't answer, except for a faint, scornful lowering of his lids.

"Because you'd better watch out if you're not. This is

Red Triangle territory." Mason said, again first in English then in Chinese. "This town belong Red Triangle."

Again the fat man's eyes shifted to Mason while his face remained motionless, still turned towards Denton. He looked back again, as though a fly had momentarily disturbed his concentration. "One hundred dollars," he repeated in his husky, even voice. "She owes me one hundred dollars."

Su-mei was winding up her hair, breathing heavily and unsteadily. "I don't owe him anything," she said sullenly. "He's lying."

Denton took a handful of change from his pocket and counted out ten silver dollars.

"Hey, don't give him anything!" Mason protested. "He's just a pimp trying to make a bit out of the girl. Give him a kick and send him packing."

But Denton held out the coins. The fat man's eyes moved a fraction, then he shook his head. "One hundred dollars," he said.

"Liar!" Su-mei muttered. The man's muscles hardened under his cheeks, but there was no other sign that he'd heard her. His eyes remained, flat and demanding, on Denton's. Denton recalled Mason's dropping the money in front of the peasant outside Soochow. He tilted his palm and let the coins slide off one by one. He was standing so close that several of them landed on the fat man's cloth slippers. But the man didn't flinch. His rigid baleful expression didn't change. The other man stooped, though, and rapidly gathered them up.

"Now leave her alone," Denton warned the fat man. "I know you, I'll send the police to get you if you touch her again. Or the French police. I know where you come from."

For the first time the man's eyes changed. A different, darker light glimmered in them for a second, then they were flat and still again.

"And if the police do not have you, the Red Triangle will," Mason sneered.

"Not enough," the fat man said, ignoring Mason. "She owes me one hundred dollars," but then he turned suddenly with surprising speed for so ponderous a body, and walked swiftly away, gross in his swaying, waddling gait. The small man trotted after him.

"Christ, what a fatty!" Mason shouted. "Be far quicker if he lay down and rolled!"

Denton led Su-mei back to the mess. A crowd of Chinese onlookers had collected and now, as they slowly dispersed, they followed them with their eyes, gawping silently.

"Nice-looking piece, though, isn't she?" Mason nudged Denton and leered. "Where'd you find her? Didn't think you'd got it in you, frankly."

Suddenly Denton's limbs were trembling. He felt he must be wobbling as he walked. "What...what was that about the Red Triangle?" he asked in an unsteady voice, passing over Mason's dig.

"Red Triangle? One of the big triad gangs." Mason brushed up the ends of his moustache, eyeing Su-mei frankly across Denton's front. "Anyone operates in the International Concession without their say so, he's likely to end up in the river in no time. I expect that's what scared old fatty off," he added complacently. "Not the police bit. They always reckon they can buy off the mashers. But the Red Triangle's different. Shouldn't think she'll have any more trouble from him." He leant forward, eyeing Su-mei again. "What's your name, dearie?"

Su-mei didn't answer, dabbing her mouth with her hand. Her eyes stiffened faintly as though she disliked the assuming familiarity of his tone.

"She doesn't speak English," Denton said curtly.

Mason shrugged and nudged him again. "You know old Ching's supposed to be something big in the Red Triangle. He didn't like the way you handled that business with the *Alexander the First,* so I've heard. I'd watch my step there if I were you."

Denton recalled Lolly Kwai's enigmatic remark as they left the *Alexander the First* after discovering the contraband. *Mr. Ching big friend Mr. Mason.* "I suppose you didn't like it either?" he asked pointedly.

"Me?" Mason glanced quickly away, his voice growing slightly hollow. "Why should I care? It's no skin off my nose."

They were climbing the steps now. The waiters and desk clerks who had been watching from the lobby whispered to each other and grinned.

"I'd better take her up to have a wash," Denton murmured self-consciously.

Mason had recovered. He smirked round at the others. "Oh yes, give her a wash," he winked. "And then it'll be bed-time, eh? Time to put her to bed."

Denton led her up the stairs while the rest sauntered back to the bar, laughing and joking, ostentatiously calling out, "Goodnight! Sleep well."

He leant against the bathroom door, watching Su-mei wash her face and dab her swollen eyes. She explained what had happened in short emotionless sentences, examining her face in the mirror while she spoke. The fat man was Pock-mark Chen, one of the leaders of the Green Triangle triad in the French Settlement. The Green Triangle were challenging the Red Triangle on the borders of what had always been their territory—the International Settlement. She used to pay protection money to the Green Triangle when she lived in the French Settlement, but since she'd moved into the International Settlement, she'd been paying the Red Triangle. Now Pock-mark Chen was trying to make her pay the Green Triangle as well. How could she pay both? At first he'd just demanded money and she'd kept putting him off. Recently he'd threatened to disfigure her if she didn't pay. She touched the cut on her lip gingerly and felt the bruise on her cheekbone.

He took her into the living room and sat her down opposite him.

"Why don't you go to the police?" he asked.

She pouted and smiled simultaneously. "What good would that do? They'd only laugh."

"Well, what are you going to do, then?" He felt elated and pleased with himself. He had saved her from being disfigured, he would protect and advise her. His sleeping with her—that was done with. He was atoning for it now. And yet his nerves tingled when he looked at her. The bruise and the cut, which was still bleeding slightly, somehow made her even more appealing than before. He imagined his hand stretching out to brush her cheek. "You will have to do something," he said slowly, struggling to find the right Chinese words. "Otherwise more bad will happen to you."

She shook her head. "It will be all right now. He will not touch me if I have foreign-devil friends. That is why I was coming to you tonight, after I saw you in the restaurant. But they caught up with me." She paused and

148

glanced up at him under puffy lids, her head slightly bowed. "You did not want me any more? You never asked for me again."

"No, not that," he said quickly, evasively. He felt suddenly guilty, for all his pure resolution, before the submissive reproach of her voice. As though he had betrayed her by staying away.

"It does not matter," she went on. "So long as they think you are my friend. It does not matter if you do not want me."

He felt his resolution melting and sat silent, chewing his lip uncertainly.

"Do you want me to go now?" she asked in a small voice.

He shook his head, still not trust himself to speak.

She was gazing at him inquiringly. "You do not like me like this? My face is ugly now?"

"No, it's good," he said. "Good to look at."

She smiled, and winced as she smiled. He imagined his lips on her bruise. He would be tender and gentle with her... He forced the seductive dream away. "What are these triads—the Green Triangle and the Red Triangle?" he asked quickly, in a stiff, brittle voice. He had heard of them, but only vaguely.

"People pay money to them for protection," she said simply. "If they do not—" She shrugged.

"Who pays?"

"Who? Everyone. Shops, restaurants, businesses, opium divans, sing-song girls, even hawkers. Everyone."

"And you pay the Red Triangle?"

"Of course. This is their territory."

"They do not protect you very well against the Green Triangle, though."

"The Green Triangle is getting stronger," she admitted. "But if I do not pay the Red Triangle—" She shrugged. "And how can I pay both? I wish they would fight it out and then everyone would know who to pay. As it is—that is why I came to you." She glanced up at him with an appealing yet frankly practical look in her eyes. "They will not hurt me if I am with a foreign devil."

Denton was silent. *Send her away now, keep clear,* a prudent voice whispered insidiously in his mind. *Remember your vow,* a weaker one added faintly. Yet he thought of her erect, rosy nipples, of her body arching beneath his.

"I will go if you like." She stood up suddenly, as if she'd read his thoughts in his downcast, irresolute eyes. He looked up. She was fumbling with her delicate fingers in a tiny silk purse. "I will give you back the ten dollars," she was saying in a small, defeated voice. A smooth jade bracelet, milky-green, trembled on her wrist. He remembered she'd worn it in bed with him that night. It was the only thing she hadn't taken off.

"No, I don't want the money," he heard his voice say. His resolution and his vow dissolved. He stood up and held her hand, closing the purse. How small her hand was, how slim and vulnerable the fingers. She followed him unresistingly towards the bedroom.

29

His vow once broken, Denton abandoned it for good. He became Su-mei's acknowledged protector and she spent several evenings a week with him—Ah Koo even agreed to accept a smaller tip from her because it was so regular. Denton stopped going to church from one day to the next, not even troubling to send any excuse for his absence. In the fires that Su-mei lit in him, his conscience and religion, all the weight of that unexamined childhood teaching which he'd carried so solemnly and unreflectingly throughout his life, burned to grey and powdery ash. Not that he deliberately rejected the old beliefs and myths—he merely ceased to have any use for them and let them fall away.

The formal break didn't come, though, until a month later, when the weather became suddenly warm and humid again, hurrying into spring. He was on his way to the mess one afternoon, when he saw Mr. Eaton on the Bund. It was too late to avoid him, the Dean's eyes were glinting with recognition already. He had to lift his hat and smile.

"Ah, John, we haven't seen much of you lately." His piercing, unsettling gaze fixed sternly on Denton's eyes.

"Er, no, I'm afraid I've been very busy," Denton murmured, his voice trailing away, uncomfortable in its deceit.

Mr. Eaton's face seemed to hang there waiting, his eyes slowly hardening with disbelief. Denton looked awkwardly away to the knotty tracery of a banyan tree's roots that gripped the stone wall beside them like grey twisting tentacles, "I expect I'll be more free soon." he said dully, his face flushing. "I hope so."

Still Mr. Eaton's face loomed there, his eyes dark with censure.

Denton abandoned pretence, refusing to let himself be made to feel guilty. "Well, I must be getting along." he said breezily.

Mr. Eaton inclined his head a fraction in cold, mute, condemning dignity.

I am corrupt, evil, degenerate, Denton said to himself, testing his conscience. But the words were like snowflakes, fluttering away without weight. He was thinking already of Su-mei's pale skin, the mole on her wrist, the milky green bracelet she never took off, the artful rocking and swaying of her hips. Soon he heard the tap, tap of her shoes coming along the corridor.

He grew more assured, as though Su-mei's influence extended beyond the erotic to the whole of his personality. He no longer hesitated or shrank back so much in his dealings with agents and ship's officers. He gave instructions with authority. He bore Mason's and Jones' chaffing patiently and indifferently—or even with pride when Jones admitted his envy, seeing Su-mei arrive in a sedan chair one sultry evening (she wouldn't travel in a rickshaw now—it would have made her lose face as his mistress). And he grew steadily more fluent in Chinese, the vivid Shanghainese of Su-mei which often shocked Wei with its crude vitality. "Nothing like a sleeping dictionary for learning the language," Mason said, hearing Denton bargaining with a rickshaw coolie by the docks—for whatever Su-mei might think, Denton didn't give up travelling by rickshaw himself. Not merely because it was cheaper. He found sedan chairs too luxurious, effeminate even, preferring the steady hard ride of the rickshaw to the soft undulation of the sedan chair.

Recognising the change in himself, Denton recognised the cause too. Sometimes he lay awake at night thinking of his life before he met Su-mei—so narrow, so tight, so drab and dry. And he would marvel that a woman could have worked such a change in him. And not even a woman really, but a mere girl of sixteen! He would turn to put his arm round her and fall asleep smiling on her shoulder.

Not only did he bear Mason's and Jones' chaffing patiently, he even began to listen to their stories of debauchery with a knowing look, as if to say *I'm not shocked by all this, I'm a man of the world too.* And it was in recognition of this change—"By god, you really have grown up at last," Mason said, wiping the beer froth off his moustache with the back of his hand, "I thought you never would" —that Mason and Jones offered to take him to an opium divan. There was a challenging tone in Mason's voice when he casually asked, "Like to come along with us to a place in Hongkew, smoke a pipe or two?" The challenge, Denton indistinctly recognised, was to his new, apparent manliness, to see if it wasn't only skin-deep after all.

They set off in two rickshaws, Mason and Jones leading while Denton followed alone in the second. His coolie was an older, stringy man, reminding him of the man who'd pulled Mason and himself on his first morning in Shanghai. That coolie had had grey threads in his queue too, and the knobs of his backbone had stood out under his worn shirt in the same way. But so many of the rickshaw coolies were thin and bony, especially the older ones. He recalled how squeamish he'd felt then at being pulled along by a human horse. Now he thought nothing of it. Had he grown callous, he wondered with a twinge of the earlier squeamishness, or simply more realistic? How would this man live, for instance, if he didn't pull a rickshaw? He imagined the thousands of rickshaw coolies in Shanghai lying starving by their empty shafts, and then their wives and children clustering round them, starving too. He watched Mason and Jones' rickshaw turning into the sailors' area, sagging on Mason's side, the coolie straining with bowed head as he pulled them up a slight incline. It wasn't right, he thought, but like so much else in China, it couldn't be changed.

The open drains were smelling again in the warmer weather. The canals flowed sluggish with scum and stinking refuse. The rickshaws stopped outside a shabby stone house in an alley that Denton had often walked through struggling with unassuaged lust before Su-mei had become his mistress. *Blue Heaven Tea-House* the faded gold characters proclaimed over the porch. Beside the door, a small metal plaque announced that the premises were licensed by the

Municipal Council for the sale and consumption of opium, licence number 178. Across the unpaved road, workmen were squatting on their heels, hammering sheets of glittering tin into long cylinders like drain-pipes. American, British and French sailors strolled in groups, boisterous and yet uncertain, up and down the alley, peering up the dark stairways of open doors or clustering dubiously round the painted old women who sat on little stools beside them. Mason surveyed them scornfully. "Look at 'em, they're scared to go in," he said loudly, brushing the tips of his bristly moustache up with that familiar gesture of his knuckles. "Safety in numbers, I suppose. I sometimes wonder how sailors get their reputation." He walked into the tea-house with an exaggerated swagger while the nearest sailors, a group of Americans, watched with the wary eyes of tourists suspicious of the natives.

Here there were no sailors, no foreign devils at all, except for the three of them. Despite its shabby façade, the tea-house was furnished richly with antique black-wood tables and tall inlaid screens. Spittoons of florid china stood by every table and waiters wandered in their soft shoes through a heavy atmosphere of silence. Scrolls hung down from the walls, faint, misty mountain scenes, bamboo branches, and over-life-size birds. The customers too were rich, to judge by their silk gowns, their lean, refined faces, their slim, pale hands with heavy rings, and the long, curved fingernails that confirmed their gentility. There was something strange and church-like about the silence. Denton had never been in a tea-house before that wasn't noisy and exuberant. But here there was a reflective, tranquil, almost religious silence. And the customers were all solitary, too. He'd never seen that before. Each one sat alone at his own table, not even glancing up at the three foreign devils, silently self-involved, as if at prayer. The steam from the teapots rose like incense before their immobile faces and hooded lids. At the back of the sombre room, by the stairs, some joss sticks burned before a red and gold altar. The banging of the hammers on the sheets of tin outside sounded through the doors like the regular muffled clanging of gongs.

Mason led the way up the staircase to the first floor. An attendant wafted them into a dark little room with a fluttering wave of his hand. Blackwood couches with hard porcelain pillows on them were arranged round the three

153

walls. Mason and Jones lay down on their sides, their heads resting on the pillows. Denton took the empty couch.

"Why these people never invented soft pillows I cannot imagine," Jones complained.

"They keep their money in them," Denton said, glad of the chance to show off his knowledge. "That's why they're hollow. Then they sleep with their hand in the hole and no one can get at their money without waking them up."

"Thanks for the lecture, professor," Mason sneered.

"Take my hat off to anyone who can sleep with his head on this thing," Jones went on grumbling. "If you ask me it's a kind of torture."

"You'll be comfortable enough in a few minutes," Mason muttered peevishly. "Don't make such a song and dance about it, for god's sake."

Denton's heart was beginning to thud lightly in uncertain excitement. A little oil lamp was burning with a low flame in the middle of the room and a single joss stick was smouldering away beside it, dropping a long curling leaf of grey-white ash onto the floor. Its heavy smell mingled with a richer, greasier one, a smell that seemed to permeate the whole room, as if it was in the floors and walls, not just hanging in the air. Denton recognised it at once as the sweetish odour he'd smelt that day when Mason stuffed a shred of raw opium in his tunic pocket. Only here it was much stronger. The dulled clanging of the metal-workers' hammering sounded through the closed window.

"Five dollars each," Mason said gruffly. "Better give it to me now."

A young girl wearing a long gown came in. She was carrying a tray of pipes and some dark opium pellets which looked like molasses. She took the money silently from Mason and knelt to prepare the pipes, turning the wick higher in the lamp. Her child-like eyes were solemn and absorbed as she moulded the little pellets onto the long needle. Mason lazily reached under her gown and squeezed her calf. She went on moulding the pellets, with only a faint quiver of her lids. His hand slid further up her leg as she held the opium over the flame. Still she seemed to take no notice, until, when the opium was ready, she put it in the bowl of the pipe and, brushing his hand away as she turned, offered him the pipe first. Each of them inhaled three times, dragging the smoke deep into their lungs. Denton was last. As he inhaled, he looked up at the girl's

154

face. She couldn't have been more than fourteen years old. Her grave, child's eyes seemed indifferent to him, concentrated on the bowl of the pipe. As he breathed in, he noticed how her own flat nostrils flared, as if willing him to breathe deeper—or was she imagining it was herself inhaling?

He felt nothing. He was just going to say, *This stuff must be poor quality, it's not doing anything to me*—he had the words in his head, waiting ready-formed—when suddenly he realised he was going after all. There was a slight giddiness and then he was gone.

All the time he knew where he was, he could even hear the dulled hammering of the metal-workers, but it was as though he was detached from his body, from his sensations, a waking spectator of his own dreams. As the room moved gently about him, taking on new, marvellous shapes and colours like a shaken kaleidoscope, he could still feel the sweet greasy smell in his nostrils and knew, or thought he knew, with startling clarity exactly what was happening. Strange, vivid colours swept over his eyes and his ears were full of harmonies he'd never heard before, and yet it was the same dark room with the burning oil lamp and the glowing joss stick—he could see them clearly. And the same clanging of the gong-like hammers drifted up from the street, which he knew perfectly well was outside the window. His mind remained as still and clear as a mountain pool while all the varied colours and sounds danced across its surface. And his eye was in the pool, looking up at the dancing colours through the cool, heavy, lucid waters. The young girl with the grave, attentive eyes and the flaring nostrils became Su-mei, although she was still herself, and he was looking at Su-mei in her. Yet though her face gave him much pleasure, he had no desire for her, no desire at all except for his serenity to continue while her face smiled down over the pool and the colours and sounds danced across it. And even that desire was muted, passionless. The girl was offering him the pipe again. He wondered whether it was a few minutes or several hours that had passed. The pool grew slowly darker...

The lamps were being lit in the tea-house below when they walked down the dark stairs out into the early evening. The metal workers were eating their rice, squatting in a

155

circle in the shade of their workshop. Red lanterns glowed over the bloody carcases in a butcher's stall further down the alley. Groups of sailors—the same sailors, it might have been—were peering up the same stairways and haggling indecisively with the same old women. The western sky was stained with all the fading lights of sunset, orange and green and silver-blue. The cries of the food hawkers, raucous and coaxing, rose all round them. Yet the whole world seemed unbearably drab and dull to Denton, as if all the sounds and colours of life had been coated with grey mud.

They hailed rickshaws, and this time it was Mason who travelled alone while Jones and Denton followed together. Jones' eyes were slightly glassy still. "Ah, I sometimes think that's better than a woman," he murmured drowsily, his voice scarcely audible above the hubbub of the streets. "Only you mustn't do it too often, you know. Once a week maximum, or you'll end up like those addicts over there." He nodded at several men squatting on their haunches against a wall. Their faces were sunken and deeply scored, with shadowy caverns for eye-sockets, from which their red-rimmed eyes looked apathetically out, shiny and blood-shot. Their hunched bodies looked emaciated, their arms and legs like fragile, brown sticks. They seemed unaware of what passed in front of their eyes. A filthy mongrel dog with a wagging curly brush of a tail sniffed at one of the men's folded, bony hands, but there was no change in his liquid expressionless eyes, no movement in his skeletal fingers.

"They might as well be dead," Jones said, pityingly and contemptuously at the same time. "They don't know where they are any more."

But perhaps their real gaze was inward, Denton thought, on colours and sounds like those he'd just been seeing, on that absolute serenity. No wonder they didn't want to return.

Mason looked back over his shoulder. "You know I dreamt I was having that girl," he called out. "It came from feeling her up before we sniffed, I suppose."

"She was young enough to be your daughter," Jones laughed.

"They mature early out here. Look at John's girl. Only a year or two older, isn't she?"

156

"She's sixteen," Denton acknowledged curtly, foreseeing a gibe.

But Mason's rickshaw lurched suddenly to avoid a palanquin escorted by four bannermen, and Mason turned back hastily to grab the side. Denton glimpsed the long straggly beard of a mandarin and two almond eyes glancing incuriously out at him beneath an elaborate hat, then the official had gone, the bannermen calling imperiously out for people to make way.

"Isn't the Chinese government going to ban opium soon?" he asked Jones.

"They keep talking about it, but they'll never do anything." Jones yawned suddenly. "Too much money in it. Besides, half of 'em are addicts anyway. All those eunuchs in Peking and so on."

"I can see how you could easily become one," Denton meditated aloud, still tinged with the drowsy flush of his intense yet tranquil visions.

"Become a eunuch? So can I. Get a hammer and slosh 'em."

"An addict."

"Once a week," Jones held up his forefinger and wagged it admonishingly. "Once a week and no more. That's the absolute limit."

"Have you ever smoked opium, Su-mei?" he asked her the following evening. He raised himself on his elbow to look down at her.

She gazed up at him warily, her eyes opaque. "Why?"

He shrugged. "I had some last night."

"Did you like it?"

He nodded. "It was..." his Chinese failed him. "It was strange," he said at last.

"Opera singers take it," she murmured, brushing the hair away from her eyes. "One day I will be an opera singer."

"Do you know how to make it?"

Her lids drooped slowly, giving her a sly, mocking look. "You want me to?"

He bent his head down until his lips brushed her nipple. "Maybe. One day."

"If you teach me English, I will."

Her limbs loosened under his touch. She let her fingertips trail lightly along his flanks, down to his thighs.

157

Her nails brushed across his skin like the claws of a kitten, sharp yet playful.

30

His renewed friendship with Mason was precarious from the start, and Denton was always uneasy with him, like an actor playing a role that didn't suit him. So he felt almost a sense of relief when it began to cool a few weeks later and resumed what seemed a more natural state of distant neutrality.

Going to Mason's office to give him some documents that the clerk had mistakenly placed on his own desk, Denton found Ching in the room, about to leave. Ching smiled as genially as ever at him, scratching his pale, taut cheek with the long, curved talon of his little finger nail. "Good afternoon, Mista' Den-tong. How are you do?"

Denton nodded, while Mason smirked connivingly, "I'll see what I can do then, Mr. Ching."

"Thank you, Mista' May-song. Thank you," Ching answered affably as he closed the door.

Denton gave Mason the papers.

"Ah, thanks, old chap." He glanced down at them inattentively. "Er . . . Funny man, old Ching, you know . . ."

"Yes?"

"He's just been talking to me about that spot of trouble on the *Alexander the First*—you know, when they were loading that night you came along."

"Oh?"

"Yes. It cost the company quite a packet, apparently."

Denton shrugged as Mason looked up, drumming his fingers on the papers Denton had just given him.

"Seems to think you might have it in for him."

"No. Why should I?"

"That's what I told him." He paused, cleared his throat and glanced away out of the window at the river. "You know, with your girl and a sniff of opium now and then, I expect you could do with a bit of extra income now and then, couldn't you?" He looked back at Denton, winking and slapping his pocket. "I mean, you wouldn't turn the odd favour down if someone offered it to you and nobody was any the wiser, would you? Know what I mean?"

Denton hesitated, embarrassed rather than tempted. He'd heard rumours, he'd seen Ching passing an envelope to Mason on their first visit to the *Alexander the First*, and there had been the hints Ching had dropped to him over that contraband cotton. But this was the first time a Customs officer had approached him. Although there seemed to be a veiled threat behind Mason's words, his tone was so genial and natural that it seemed hard to be curt or indignant. "Well, I don't know," he muttered uncomfortably, as if it was he who was the guilty one. "I mean, I don't really need anything extra, you know."

"Oh come on," Mason cajoled him blandly. "It's not as though we're overpaid, is it? Everyone take a bit, you know."

"Well, all the same I don't really want to get mixed up with that kind of thing," he said apologetically.

"What sort of thing?" Mason chivvied him. "It's the way of life out here. You're practically expected to, I mean, in England it'd be a different matter, but out here..." He waved his hand largely. "Way of life. When in Rome, you know, sort of thing."

But Denton refused to yield. "I've got some papers to see to," he said woodenly, turning to the door.

Mason sighed loudly in helpless resignation. "Well, there's none so blind as those that won't see, so they say."

In his own office, Denton tipped his chair back and gazed up at the ceiling with the sense of having avoided an unpleasant social duty rather than a moral catastrophe. *It's the way of life out here,* he thought, watching two large black flies flitting round and round on the listless air. *When in Rome.* And yet he wasn't tempted. He wondered why. Just because it was dishonest? But suppose nobody suffered from it, as might often be the case? Would it still be wrong? He felt his mind groping for a certainty that wasn't there. It was queer, unnerving, when you kept on asking why. He couldn't see through the mists these repeated questions rolled over his mind. Yet if he imagined himself being offered an envelope like Mason was, something stiffened in his arm as if to push it away. Was that all it was—just an instinctive recoil? Or merely a reaction he'd been taught as a child, like his religion? But he'd given up his religion easily and painlessly. Could he give up his honesty in the same way? One day he'd have to find the time to study philosophy and ethics, the meaning of life and that sort of thing, to try and find the answers to all these questions. It would be good to get out of all this dim uncertainty into something definite and secure. One day he'd really do that, when he had time.

He let the chair drop forward with a bang and turned to his forms, sighing in the heat.

Mason never mentioned the subject again, but they gradually cooled to each other once more, though at first without any open break. It was merely that Mason never invited him to smoke opium again and they avoided each other in the mess. It was not until some months later that they actually quarrelled, when they were both on duty one breathless June afternoon on adjoining sections of the wharves. Denton was going to his office when Mason called him from the corridor, his heavy face damp with sweat. There were motes of dust sliding through the sunlight that slanted relentlessly in between the slats of the bamboo blinds.

"I say, John." His voice was unusually friendly, wheedling almost. "They've put the *Marseilles* in berth nine?"

"Yes, there's been an accident on the cranes at ten. They can't work them, apparently."

"Oh, accident, eh?" Mason brushed the tips of his moustache up thoughtfully, frowning down at the sheaf of manifests in his other hand. "The thing is, I know some of the chaps on that boat, I was expecting to have a chat with them. Tell you what, I'll do the *Marseilles* and you do the *Wonosobo*." His faced cleared. "Got the manifest, have you? Here's the *Wonosobo*'s."

Denton looked down at the papers Mason was holding out. "I think, as it's berthed in my section," he said slowly, with an almost reluctant dryness, "perhaps I'd better do it myself."

"Why?" Mason's face began to darken beneath its shiny glow of sweat. "Not much to ask, is it? No need to be such a stickler—after all, it would've been in my section, but for this blasted accident anyway, wouldn't it?"

"Yes, but all the same," Denton persisted, hardening as much against Mason's hectoring as against the corruption he suspected lay behind it. "All the same, I think I'd better do it, as things stand."

Mason stepped nearer, bringing his face close to Denton's. "Now listen here, old man, I've got a special reason to do the *Marseilles*." His voice was quiet but unpleasantly tense, his eyes gazing hard at Denton's. "As I've already told you. I want to have a chat with some of the chaps on board. Got it? They're friends of mine."

"Friends of Ching too?"

"Ching?" Mason stiffened. "What are you getting at?"

"Nothing," Denton stared obstinately down at his papers. "Couldn't you talk to your friends while I inspect the ship?"

Mason's neck began to swell, and the veins stood out on his forehead. His cheeks became florid. "You trying to insinuate something, old man?" he asked threateningly.

"No," Denton's voice was blank and dead. He took a sudden breath, as though he was about to jump from a height.

"Well, then..."

"But as I've been given the *Marseilles,* I'll just have to inspect it, unless I'm ordered not to. That's all."

"Oh you will, will you? Well, listen here, Mr. Holy Bloody Denton," Mason was speaking now with loud, angry irony. A passing clerk glanced at him in timid awe and hurried on down the corridor. "Just you listen here. I don't think you've quite got the hang of things out here yet. I'm your senior in rank, right? You're just a probationary inspector, right? You're not established yet, are you? You could be kicked out quite easily, and don't you forget it. Well, as your senior in rank, I say *I'm* doing the *Marseilles.* So I *am* doing it. And you're doing the *Wonosobo.* If you don't mind."

Denton frowned down at his papers, his cheeks flushing. "My orders—"

"Or if you *do* mind, for that matter. Now take this bloody manifest."

"My orders are to inspect all the vessels in my section." Denton said doggedly.

"Well, I'm giving you another order!"

"You realise I'll have to report this to Mr. Brown?"

"Well, go along and report it, then," Mason said in high, sneering tones. "Run along and report it then, there's a good boy." Then, as Denton turned away, "Only don't forget he's on leave. And don't forget to let me have the *Marseilles'* manifest first, either. All right?"

Denton went instead to the Superintendent of the Wharves. He was kept waiting outside his office while the clerks covertly eyed him and whispered smilingly to each other as if they knew already what was going on. Denton waited uneasily, licking his lips. How was it that he felt almost guilty for being there? He had to keep reminding himself that it was Mason who had something to answer for, not himself. And yet he still felt uneasy.

Superintendent Smith was burly, irascible and said to be a heavy drinker, which the hectic flush on his face suggested was true. He'd never got far in the service and was bitter about it. He'd been a "tide-waiter," and "outside" man, for most of his career, and the "inside" men, who could pass examinations, had taken the top jobs and sat in cool offices while he was sent to remote posts from one end of China to the other.

A voice boomed angrily behind the heavy wooden door and a clerk scurried out with anxious, humiliated eyes.

"Now what's all this nonsense about, Denton?" Smith's protuberant, bloodshot eyes stared at him impatiently. "Mason wants to do the *Marseilles*. What are you making a fuss about it for? Can't you arrange a swap between yourselves without running to me?"

"It was my section, sir," Denton began falteringly, on the wrong foot already. "And I..."

"You what?"

"I didn't see any good reason for changing ships."

"Good god, is that all?" Smith shook his grey head in mock amazement. His fist rose and thumped the desk in front of him, making the pens and pencils quiver. "Mason tells me he wants to speak to a friend on the ship. Isn't that a good enough reason? What's wrong with that? A bit of a swap, that's all."

Denton hesitated, pressing his lips together. He sensed he was about to cross some boundary, although he couldn't have said what exactly it was.

"Well? Don't mind walking a couple of hundred yards to the *Wonosobo*, do you?" Smith laughed bluffly, his ill-temper apparently draining away at the sight of Denton's abashed hesitation. "Young feller like you? Bit of exercise'd do you good!"

"Did Mr. Mason tell you what he wanted to talk to these 'friends' about?" Denton said at last, plunging suddenly across the unknown boundary.

"What d'you mean?" Smith's thick brows contracted like two stiff grey brushes. "Talk *about*? What d'you mean? Are you trying to accuse anyone of improper conduct, Denton?" He jutted his chin forward over the desk grimly, the brief, false heartiness swept from his face. "You'd better be careful what you're saying, you know. That's a serious matter. Have you got any evidence?"

Denton swallowed. "I only meant that Mr. Mason's reasons didn't seem good enough to me, sir."

"Oh, they didn't, didn't they? They didn't seem good enough?" He leant back slowly, nodding, his head on one side. "So they didn't seem good enough to you, Mr. Denton, eh? Well, let me tell you something, lad," he leant forward again, speaking in a growling whisper, "Let me tell you something. They're good enough for me. And if they're good enough for me," his voice began to rise slowly, ominously, "they should bloody well be good enough for you!"

Denton stared rigidly in front of him, at the brass buttons on Smith's uniform. "You are satisfied with Mr. Mason's reasons, then, sir?" he asked stiffly.

"That's just what I've been saying, isn't it, lad? How many times do I have to repeat myself?" He glared at Denton with those bulging, bloodshot blue eyes that seemed to have a film of anger over them. "And what's more, I don't like young officers getting above themselves and coming in here suggesting all sorts of things about their brother officers, without a shred of evidence! I don't like it at all! Is that clear?"

Denton felt the muscles growing rigid in his cheeks. "Yes, sir." After a pause, he heard his voice speaking sarcastically, almost of its own accord. "Very clear."

"And don't you cheek me, young feller!" Smith's voice rose to a shout and his eyes bulged dangerously, as if they might pop out. "Just yes sir, no sir, understand? I don't want any of this suggestive 'Very clear' stuff from you. I don't know what you're thinking, lad, but you'll keep you tongue under lock and key if you know what's good for you! Understand?"

"Will that be all, sir?" Denton heard his voice as if speaking of its own accord again, small but unbending.

"Yes it bloody well will."

He felt Smith's eyes glowering at his shoulders still as he opened the door and went out.

31

Two weeks later, Denton was transferred to a different section of the port, along the French Bund. He was on night duty, and he shared the patrol of the whole section with Johnson. Johnson seemed oblivious of the change Su-mei's alchemy had worked on Denton, and even of the passing of time; he still treated him like an inexperienced griffin and saw himself as a benevolent paternal advisor, impervious to Denton's distant off-handedness. "If there's any help you want with those forms, just sing out," he would offer in his friendly, monotonously deadening voice. Or, "Have you done the manifest for the *Camboge*? I'll check the duty for you if you like."

Denton put up with it, only occasionally frowning with irritation and answering curtly when Johnson's mild persistence spoiled his concentration.

One night in July, when the moist heat hung like a still, vaporous curtain and a typhoon warning signal had gone up in the harbour, Johnson's launch broke down. He joined Denton on Lolly Kwai's boat for the journey back to the Customs House. "Looking forward to your first typhoon?" he asked avuncularly "We had a really bad one a couple of years ago. There were ships blown right onto the Bund. Not *against* the Bund," he went on with his maddening talent for needless exposition. "Actually *on* it, on the road itself." He waited, smiling, to see the effect of his revelation on Denton's face.

"Yes, I heard about it," Denton said carelessly. "By the way, what happened to those two smugglers we caught last summer?" Maliciously, he emphasised the word "we" —Johnson had taken all the prize money.

"Didn't I tell you?" Johnson's equanimity was undisturbed. "They were strangled. I had to go to the Chinese court in Chapei to give evidence. Rather an unpleasant way to die. They do it slowly." His flat, even sympathy made strangling sound like a mild digestive discomfort. "I had a wonderful hike round Hankow on the prize money. I suppose you got a bit too, for that cotton on the *Alexander the First*?"

"Yes. So did Lolly Kwai, of course." Denton glanced back at the wheelhouse.

"Ah yes. You'll find he's jolly useful," Johnson said encouragingly, as though Denton had only arrived a day or two before. "I expect your fiancée will be coming out soon?"

Denton hesitated. Johnson must have been the only officer in the mess who didn't know it was all over—who didn't even know about Su-mei. He felt a pitying thought, like the flutter of a bird's wing, stir his mind. Johnson was so isolated that he didn't even know that. He was so boring because nobody talked to him, and nobody talked to him because he was so boring. Behind his dull, perpetually good-natured smile, he lived a solitary life of crowded ostracism. "No," Denton said, his voice relenting slightly. "As a matter of fact it's all over. We've broken it off."

"Oh, all over, is it?" Johnson nodded, as though the news was unsurprising and unremarkable, like a change of plans for the summer holidays. "Well, there are plenty of things to do out here of course." He began to hum a tune in his nasal, toneless voice.

Denton felt his brief, vague ripple of pity had been wasted. He looked away at the lights of the French Settlement, his mind passing from Johnson's indifferent "plenty of things to do" to the thought of the green-shuttered house of pleasure in *rue* Molière, which Jacob Ephraim still praised so highly, and then to Pock-mark Chen and Su-mei. She'd been right, she'd had no more trouble with him. Apparently the Green Triangle weren't strong enough to challenge the Red Triangle after all. And his own status had protected her from Pock-mark Chen. She continued to pay the Red Triangle, but she wouldn't tell him how much. When he'd remonstrated with her occasionally in the early days for paying at all, she'd stared at him with a child-like amazement, as though he'd suggested she should walk out into the street without her clothes on. "They're just extortioners," he'd said. "No," she protested. "They look after people." To her it was like paying tax to an unofficial government, one that could protect her in fact from the real one—or so she believed. Yes, that amazement was child-like. Although she could be shrewd and wise about some things, he thought of her, and it flattered him to do so, as a child. She was still only seventeen, Chinese style—he'd bought her a gold hairpin on her birthday—but her parents had sold her in a famine as soon as she'd begun to menstruate and she must have been used by many men since then. Yet she still seemed unspoilt to him, unspoilt and even innocent. Those early times when she'd seemed merely mercenary had soon passed. Now she never asked him for money. He gave her some every week and she took it, in that curious face-saving way that forbade her to thank him; but she never asked for it. Sometimes she bought him little presents with the money he gave her, or that she earned as a sing-song girl, like the seal on which she'd had his name engraved in Chinese characters, and the little ornaments she'd placed about his room. Of course she only sang in restaurants now, she had no other "protector" as she called him. And she was clever, too—the way she picked up English! Quicker than he'd learnt Chinese in the beginning—though he hadn't had a "sleeping dictionary" then, of course.

As he idly watched the dim lights of the quays slip past, haloed with misty rings, he noticed something moving near the shore. His glance slid over the vague shape, moved on to a ship, then slid back again. The shape was a string of sampans moving quietly along beside the wharves, with only one weak yellow lamp flickering in the leading boat.

He called softly to Johnson, who was on the starboard side of the bow, cooling his bland, smug face against the breeze the launch itself was making. The air smelt of fish and oil and the heavy sulphurous smell of the Chinese factories in Pootung on the other shore.

"Yes, what is it, old chap?" Johnson asked brightly.

Denton pointed. "Those sampans look a bit suspicious. Let's go in and look at them."

Johnson gave the order to Lolly Kwai at once, while Denton was still turning to the wheelhouse. Denton suppressed the twinge of irritation he felt. He watched the sampans moving unconcernedly along in the dark. Either they hadn't noticed the launch, which was unlikely, or else they had nothing to hide. But Johnson was smiling with the faint, complacent air of alertness that was the nearest he came to excitement—*he* seemed to think there was something in it. "A little prize money would come in handy," he murmured, narrowing his eyes. "I haven't had any since Easter."

They drew closer. Denton could see now that there were four sampans altogether, with two men in the leading one. One sat in the bow gazing incuriously at the approaching Customs launch; the other was barely rowing at the stern, just stirring the water to guide the little convoy closer to the wharves as it floated down on the current. The sampans were heavily loaded, but the two

166

men's obvious unconcern convinced Denton they must after all be perfectly innocent.

Lolly Kwai hailed them. "What are you carrying in those sampans?"

"Silk bales." The one rowing spat into the water.

"Where to?"

The man nodded at a large Fukienese junk moored at a pontoon a couple of hundred yards downstream.

Johnson interrupted Lolly's next question in his own flat, awkward Chinese. "Where is the silk going?"

"Foochow."

"Have you paid likin?"

The two men stared at him blankly.

"Likin!" Lolly shouted bullyingly. "Have you paid likin?"

The bigger one looked at the other questioningly. They both shrugged.

"I'll have a look," Denton said. But with a "No, you might fall in and you can't swim," Johnson had already dropped neatly down onto the sampan, which was almost awash with the weight of its cargo. "You keep an eye on these chaps, see they don't make a bolt for it." His smile had become the slightly superior smirk of the schoolmaster who was alive to the pranks of the children and was showing a colleague how to deal with them. But there was an acquisitive sharpness in his eye as well, and Denton guessed he was after the main share of any prize money there might be going. Lolly Kwai must have thought so too; he was muttering something disparagingly under his breath. They leant over the rail, watching Johnson struggling with the corner of an old, frayed sail that had been lashed across the cargo. He turned and gestured to the two men, who were watching him wih sullen indifference, to untie the knots. The bigger one moved unwillingly forward and reached for something on the deck. Johnson bent over the rope again. Suddenly the Chinese straightened up and hit him with some sort of club. Denton heard the heavy, smacking thud on the back of Johnson's skull and the soft, almost drowsy, gasp that he immediately gave. His body sagged at once as if it had turned to jelly, and slithered down over the side of the boat into the river. At the same time both men dived over the other side and swam away into the shadow of the nearby wharf.

There were perhaps two seconds of startled silence

while they stared at the gently widening ripples where Johnson had slid beneath the water, then Lolly suddenly shouted and two sailors jumped in. They dived, surfaced, shouted, dived and surfaced, again and again. Denton gripped the rail, his arms quivering, staring numbly at the black water where the sailors' heads kept bobbing up, then vanishing. He felt a tingling on his scalp at the back of his head, just where the blow had struck Johnson.

All around him there were shouts, questions, answers. Someone brought a lamp and held it over the water. The light glistened peacefully on the silky surface while the shouts grew less excited and the two sailors in the river spent a little longer breathing gulps of air before each dive. Gradually they all became silent, and the two sailors stopped diving altogether, clinging to the side of the sampans. Lolly Kwai looked at Denton inquiringly, his usually genial face lugubrious.

"Perhaps he swam to the shore?" Denton suggested, unbelieving himself.

Lolly shrugged, then shook his head. There had been something conclusive about the way Johnson had slid down below the surface, as though his body had been weighted with lead. "It is a long time already," he muttered.

Denton drew his watch out and examined its large dial under the lamp. Twenty past three. They'd been searching for nearly an hour already. He imagined Johnson floating near the bottom with the same bland smile on his face, only his eyebrows faintly raised in surprise. He closed the watch with a snap and put it away. "I'll have to report it to the French police," he said dully. "Take the sampans in tow." His limbs had stopped trembling. As the boat got under way again, he stared down at the dark, oily water with the last unreal hope that Johnson might yet suddenly pop up his head and wave to them with his cheerful, self-satisfied grin. But at the same time he felt a tremulous, rising sense of relief. Suppose *he* had boarded the sampan instead of Johnson?

While he was making a long, detailed statement to a French police officer who chewed his pen in ferocious concentration as he tried to translate Denton's sentences into official French, Lolly got the covers unlashed from the impounded sampans. The cargo was nothing but sacks of sawdust. He shook his head gloomily when he showed them to Denton by the grey cheerlessness of the first light.

"It was a trick. No silk at all. They wanted to get Mr. Johnson." He paused, thrusting out his underlip and scratching his slightly stubbled chin. "Mr. Johnson or you."

The typhoon came and the harbour emptied as all the ships steamed downriver to ride the storm out in the open sea. But it wasn't a bad one, the winds were no stronger than a gale at home, and there was only the continuous rain that fell steadily for two days and nights from a sky vast with clumsy, tumbling grey clouds. The canals flooded onto the streets and sedan-chair bearers walked waist deep in muddy water; the rickshaw and wheelbarrow coolies couldn't work for a day until the floods subsided. Watching the rain from his window, Denton saw a wheelbarrow go floating down the street at the height of the flood, with an anguished coolie plunging after it.

Then the clouds began to thin, to fall apart and let in gaps of blue. The rain eased, and by the evening of the third day the sky was clear and serene, a pale greenish blue with a faint orange tinge where the sun had set, as though that too had been washed by the rain.

Four days later, Johnson's body floated to the surface, bloated and decomposing. It was picked up by the river police three miles downstream, against the walls of the Bund. Denton was called to the mortuary to identify the body. The dingy waiting room didn't seem to have changed since the first time he'd gone there with Johnson himself to help identify his informer's body. The same clerk was yawning over the same maroon-coloured ledger, the same attendants were chatting and playing cards at the back of the hall. It almost seemed as though the same mute, hollow-eyed men and women were still waiting on the same bare benches for their missing relatives to be brought in.

A senior police inspector turned towards him with a smile of recognition. "Hello, Denton, haven't seen you since that dinner at your chief's house. How are you getting on?"

It was Everett, the man who'd shared his cabin on the *Orcades* coming to Shanghai.

"Just been promoted," Everett said proudly, glancing down at the shiny new pip on his shoulder. He gave

Denton a cloth to hold over his nose. "I'm afraid the body isn't really cold yet, it still smells."

Denton gazed at the distorted and rotting corpse. The swollen features retained hardly any trace of that insistently affable smugness that Denton had come to detest. It was not a *face* he was looking at, Denton thought, but the putrid carcase of a face. Only the short, dark hair seemed the same, as though it hadn't died at all. Looking at the hair alone, still dripping on the ice, you could imagine Johnson had just been in for a swim. Denton pressed the cloth closer to his nose. It had been soaked in some strong disinfectant stuff, but he could still smell the powerful sickly-sweet scent of decaying flesh that he'd first caught in the burial house Wei had shown him last summer. When the attendant turned the head, Denton saw a livid, ulcerous bruise at the base of the skull.

He looked away with a sudden queasy turning of his stomach. "Yes, that's him," he muttered. "That's about where he was hit, too."

Outside, while the two atendants shuffled indifferently past on sandalled feet, carrying in another corpse, Everett paused for a few "inquiries," as he called them with a slightly self-important inflection in his voice. "I suppose you didn't get a good look at the man who struck him?"

"No, it all happened so quickly. He was quite big, that's all."

"Would you know either of the two men again?"

Everett was jotting down his replies in a little black notebook, and the official act, the official tone of voice, irritated Denton. He shrugged. "No, it was pitch dark." He watched a stone-eyed young Chinese being led into the mortuary by a police corporal.

"Would anyone have known he was to be on the launch at that time?"

Denton's chest caught suddenly with the awakening of the thought that Lolly Kwai had left to sleep in his mind. "He wasn't supposed to be there at all," he said slowly. "He only came along because his boat had broken down."

Everett glanced up at him, then continued writing. "Looks as though they were after you, then," he said as he closed the book. "Shall I take that?" He took the cloth which Denton had been absently holding in his hand and dropped it in a rattan basket.

"They?" Denton repeated. "Who?"

"In your line of business," Everett shrugged, "there are bound to be people it's dangerous to offend. As in mine."

Denton thought of Ching scratching his pallid cheek with that talon of a nail in Mason's office. Obviously Mason was taking bribes and Ching had wanted him to buy Denton off too. They were both put out by his refusal perhaps, but this... He shook his head incredulously, and yet he kept seeing Ching's face, his faintly ironic smile, mocking his unbelief.

"I think it was only meant as a warning," Everett was saying soothingly. "It probably just went too far. They hit him too hard, that's all."

"Unless they knew I can't swim."

"Oh no, if they wanted to finish someone off, they could do it quite easily. But they don't like drawing too much attention to themselves by killing a foreign devil." He paused as the stone-eyed Chinese came back down the corridor followed by the corporal, who was noisily clearing his throat and looking for somewhere to spit. The man's eyes were perhaps a little stonier, his mouth a little more stiff. "It'd be different for a Chinese, of course," Everett went on. "They don't mind killing them—nobody takes much notice. Know anyone who might have a grudge against you?"

"I may have got on the wrong side of a ship's agent called Ching—"

Everett's eyebrows rose. "There are all sorts of stories about him," he said with a note both of respect and of warning. "I should watch your step if I were you."

Denton felt suddenly as though his back was exposed— he even glanced round over his shoulder at the patient yet hopeless relatives waiting on the benches. "How? What do you mean?" he asked uneasily.

"Well, just don't run any risks, that's all," Everett said coolly. "I'll have this statement copied out," he went on at once, before Denton could answer. "And then if you'd come to the Central Police Station to sign it..."

"It was Ching," Su-mei said simply when he told her that night. She pulled the long, gold pin he'd given her for her birthday out of her hair and held it between her teeth while she reached up for the smaller ones.

"How do you know it was?" Again he felt that feeling that his back was exposed, vulnerable.

She shook her head. He took the pin from her mouth. "How do you know?"

She shrugged. "He is high up in the Red Triangle. You made trouble for him and he got Mason to try to bribe you." She shook her hair loose. It fell down in a loose glossy mass round her shoulders. "You must be careful."

He felt sure she was right, but still he didn't want to believe it. "How can he be so dangerous? He is only a ship's agent! And Mason—"

"He does many things," she interrupted matter-of-factly, gazing at her face in the mirror. Her eyes switched to his reflection beside hers. "Every Chinese in Shanghai knows about Ching. You foreign devils never look behind things."

He made a dismissive gesture with his hand. "Stories, that is all," he tried to scoff. "Only stories."

She shook her head, watching his reflection with cool eyes. "He is not like Pock-mark Chen. He is an important man. You foreign devils never understand."

32

Johnson was the first European to be murdered in Shanghai for two years, and the *North China Daily News* carried a report of the inquest on its front page. The verdict was murder by persons unknown. The next day the paper's editorial, recalling the atrocities of the Boxers, urged the foreign powers to consider stationing a permanent garrison in the city. There was an announcement on the same page that the Shanghai Volunteers would welcome recruits from every foreign nationality and every walk of life.

Customs officers were authorised by Mr. Brown to carry revolvers at all times when on duty, instead of merely when going on a raid. Denton learnt to shoot accurately with his on the police firing range and began to feel heroic. But often he felt that exposed feeling, as though someone were creeping up behind his back.

Johnson's possessions were auctioned in the mess. There were fewer people there than usual, and Jones, in his last week as mess treasurer, began the auction in a voice that was strangely subdued. There wasn't much to buy, but as the last item, Jones announced, with a little smirk, that some unusual paintings had been found in the bottom of a sea chest that Johnson had kept under his bed. "Always tightly locked," he added, stroking his slim moustache.

"Let's see them!" Mason called out, but Jones, still smirking coyly, said the committee had decided they should not be publicly exhibited. Any officer who was interested could examine them on the table, where they were at present placed face down.

There was a snickering, yet still constrained, pause for viewing. Only Mason seemed unaffected by Johnson's death, and he was soon giving a loud, lewd commentary, while the others merely chuckled. The paintings were all crude erotic pictures of women, each done in great detail, but in violent colours, as if Johnson had hated what he so carefully depicted. Johnson had never been known to have a woman in his room and Denton, gazing with fascinated disgust, wondered what he might have done to one if he had. He tried to imagine what it must have been like to live through the furtive turbulence and twisted rage that the pictures represented. But he couldn't. All he could visualise was that bare room of Johnson's, with the carefully made but empty bed. And the picture of the sailing ship he'd seen on the wall, with those realistic woman's breasts on the figurehead, breasts which now seemed so significant. He could hear the note of pride in Johnson's voice when he'd said he painted the picture, and that too seemed significant now. But what was it like to have lived his remote, distorted life—to have been him night after night alone in his room? That, he couldn't imagine.

Mason bought all Johnson's pictures for two dollars each. A week or two later, he claimed to have sold them to a Chinese brothel-owner at a two hundred per cent profit. "If you ever go there, it'll remind you of the poor old blighter," he declared at the bar, his eyes for some reason straying blankly over Denton's as he spoke, without a glimmer of acknowledgement.

The murderers were never found, but there were no more attacks on Customs officers and gradually they all forgot Johnson's death, or put it safely away in the past, in history. Ching disappeared from the docks, no longer

173

acting as the Russian line's agent. In any case, Russia and Japan were at war, and no more Russian ships called at Shanghai. Su-mei said he was living in Chapei, in a house surrounded by bodyguards.

The heat of summer slowly eased. On the afternoon of the autumn lantern festival Denton went into the street of the silversmiths to buy some earrings for Su-mei. He wandered in and out of the long, cave-like shops until eventually he found an old silver pair of rings, shaped like heavy tear-drops, which the bald, bowed shopkeeper with crafty little eyes said had come from Peking. Usually, in spite of Ephraim's repeated strictures, he paid by chit, but this time he had a fair amount of cash on him. The shopkeeper squinted at each coin and rang it sharply on the counter before he wrapped the earrings in red paper and gave them to Denton.

As he left the shop, the usual swarm of beggars clustered round him, stretching out their hands and whining with quiet, insolent insistence. Most of them, he knew, were professionals, especially the ones with babies in their arms—at least they were all living infants this time—carefully calculating how to work on the guilt of the sentimental rich. But one man was so mutilated, professional or not, that the callous of indifference that had gradually hardened over Denton's natural sympathy was abruptly softened. The man's legs had been cut off high above the knees, and the stumps were covered with worn leather patches. He was dragging himself along by his hands, trailing his stump behind him, and his arms and shoulders had become large and powerful. He glared at Denton with an accusing, bitter stare, as though he were personally responsible for his amputated legs. *Yet, he is a professional,* Denton thought detachedly. *But what else could he be?* He gave him a dollar. The beggar rang the coin suspiciously against the cobble stone and then dragged himself off without a word, as if he thought he'd got no more than his due. *And perhaps it is his due,* Denton thought, half-guiltily feeling the expensive earrings in his pocket. *Perhaps it's even less than his due.* The other beggars crowded round him more thickly now, waving their hands determinedly under his face and fixing their eyes demandingly on his. He pushed his way through them. "No, no more," he said curtly, striding on. He couldn't give them all money. Was he responsible for all the suffering in the world?" "No!" They took notice, shuffling along beside him, whining and plucking his clothes. "No more!" He was shouting now. And then abruptly, involuntarily almost, he had stopped and was dropping the rest of his change into their outstretched hands, young, old, clean and dirty, ashamed at the same time of his weakness, his sentimentality. As if those few cents would solve any problems! As if charity was the answer! But then what was? All the money was gone, but still the soft, plucking hands reached out and the whining voices cajoled and coaxed him. He shook his head again and brushed through them, climbing into a waiting rickshaw. The coolie regarded him with a sly, calculating look. Good for a big tip, his eyes seemed to say.

"Where to, master?" he asked in pidgin.

"Chinsan Road."

"Long way, master. You pay one dollar?"

Denton shrugged. He'd given so much away, why bother about fifty cents more or less now? "This time I will pay one dollar," he said in Chinese. "But don't think I don't know it should be fifty cents."

"You speak Chinese? Very good." The coolie grinned, put out his half-smoked cigarette, placed it carefully in his pocket then lifted the shafts.

As the coolie pushed his way through the still hopeful beggars, shooing them gruffly and scornfully away, Denton noticed two people gazing at him from across the road. They were a man and a woman, both taller than the average, dressed in faded black cotton trousers and jackets. The woman wore a peasant's wide-brimmed dun straw hat. The man had slung his by its cord over his back. They were gazing at him with a solid, diconcerting stare, but it wasn't until the rickshaw had passed and he'd turned back to look at them again that Denton recognised them. It was the woman who'd been hit by buckshot that day they'd gone shooting with Henschel outside Soochow—she and her husband. They were still gazing after him with that disconcerting stare, neither hostile nor friendly. The memory of the shooting revived his obscure sense of shame about it and he turned away uncomfortably. What had brought them to Shanghai? he wondered. Had they lost their land, or sold it, as so many of the peasants flooding the city had done, and come in search of work? Their unnervingly dispassionate stare stayed in his mind while he fingered Su-mei's present in his pocket. Were they too blaming him for their fate whatever it was? But their gaze hadn't been accusing. It had been a curious one, rather, as if he were some brilliant exotic fish displayed in a tank, interesting but useless. And that too made him uneasy. Sometimes he felt he never knew where he was with these people. So many of them seemed to have the Great Wall in their eyes, even the humblest of them, from which they could look down at you with cool indifference as mere barbarians, foreign devils. Even Wei. And Su-mei? He pushed the question aside. He didn't want to think like that about her, especially not tonight.

Su-mei had brought an orange lantern with her for the festival. She lit the candle inside it and hung it from the veranda railing. Denton had ordered dinner in his room and they sat across the little table she had bought him, their knees touching, teaching each other new words in Chinese and English. When they had finished eating and were sipping the last of her favourite strong green tea, he laid her present on the table beside her.

"T'ank you," she said in the high, level tone in which she spoke English, tilting her head and smiling faintly. If he hadn't known her better, he might have thought she was hardly pleased at all. But he understood now that she would have found it demeaning to be more effusive. She leant forward across the table to let him put them on her. "If I wear them tonight, you will not dare bite my ears in case you swallow them," she said simply, in Chinese now.

He smiled, but her face was still, as though she'd meant it seriously. She put her hands up to feel the earrings hanging from her small pink lobes. They looked like two little silver tears tugging gently at them. He took her hands as she leant back. "Su-mei?" be began.

"I want to look at them in the glass."

"Wait a minute." He held her wrists tighter. His tanned hands, with the dark hair sprouting at the knuckles, seemed enormous on her smooth slender wrists. How odd, too, that her skin was actually paler than his. "If I moved out of the mess, we could find a place to live together in."

She glanced up him with a sly smile in her half-lidded eyes. "You want to marry me?" she asked mockingly.

"You know what I mean." Of course he hadn't thought of marriage. He too smiled at the idea.

She eased her wrists out of his slowly slackening grip and went to the mirror in the bathroom, turning her head from side to side. The silver gleamed, dangling in the shadowy hollows beneath his ears.

"Well?" he asked.

"Very beautiful." She raised her hands to adjust the earrings.

"What do you say about finding a place to live together in? Several people here have done it."

She held up the hand with the little dark mole on it. "Do you know Chinese people think this is very good, this mole here? When my father sold me, he got a better price because of that."

"Su-mei!"

She went back to the veranda and leant over the rail. Below, orange, red, blue and yellow lanterns jogged and swayed along the street as children carried them towards the little hill that was the highest point nearby. The children were shouting and laughing as though there were no such thing as poverty and starvation and the selling of children.

"Well?" he asked again.

"And still be a sing-song girl?"

"I would have enough money for both of us. You could give up your room in Hongkew."

"I have given it up already. I have let it to someone."

"Let it?" he glanced round at her frowning. "Where do you sleep when you don't stay here?"

"With a friend." She was looking steadily over the rail, avoiding his eyes. "I pay her—"

"Him or her?"

"Her," she repeated sharply. "I pay her half what it costs her. So I make money out of the other place."

He paused, trying to visualise this girl who was only sixteen by western reckoning, and who was such a child in some ways, hard-headedly devising profitable schemes that he would never have dreamt of. "So we can move together," he said uncertainly, feeling that she had gone suddenly out of focus, acquiring a new dimension. "You have given up your room already."

"But if I stop being a sing-song girl, I will lose all my customers," she went on in a practical voice. "Then one

177

day you will go away. And what will I do without my customers?"

He felt a sudden doubt that seemed to make something crumble in his chest. "Su-mei, your customers—you don't...? I mean you only sing for them, don't you?" he asked suspiciously.

"Since I have been with you, yes." She spoke lightly, as if that was irrelevant. "But what will I do when you go away? Besides—"

"I will not go away," he said bravely, and felt he meant it.

"Of course you will," she answered flatly. "Foreign devils always go away. One day you will marry a foreign woman. You will have to."

She was gazing directly at him now, challenging him to deny it. He looked away from her assured brown eyes, down into the street with its nodding lanterns. He wanted to deny it, to take up her challenge, but something cold and heavy blocked his voice. Living with a Chinese girl, a sing-song girl at that—of course it could only be temporary, no matter how much he liked her. He felt the chill hand of reason pulling him back, the same chill hand that was guiding her. It was like a cloud suddenly covering the sky, draining the colour out of everything. She was right. In the end he would go away. Of course she was right. She couldn't rely on him.

Her eyes were still on his face. He glanced up at the earrings glistening against the glossy jet of her hair. "You could keep on with your customers and still live with me," he said hesitantly.

She gave a definite little shake of her head that made the earrings quiver. "You would want a place at least as big as this, and an amah to look after it—it would cost much more than you pay here." She glanced back over his rooms with a remorseless practical eye. "Too expensive," she concluded. "You would pay more to someone else and you would have to give me less. Then I could not pay for my singing lessons. Or else I would have to send less to my parents."

"Your parents!" He stared at her. "But they sold you!" He knew about her singing lessons, her ambition to become an opera singer, and he enjoyed the thought that he was helping her with his money in that, although the only Chinese opera he'd ever attended had seemed a gaudy, clashing cacophony to him. But sending some of his money to her parents—that was different. She'd never told him about that.

Yet she seemed amazed at his astonishment, gazing at him, with wide, uncomprehending eyes. "Of course I send them money, they are my parents!"

"And they sold you!"

"Otherwise I would have starved. And so would they. Now I can send them money." She spoke slowly and patiently, as if explaining a simple problem to a little child.

He heard several voices laughing and talking suddenly in Mason's room. They sounded boisterous and exuberant, with the shrill, uncontrolled hilarity of drunkenness. "Shall we go in?" he asked abruptly. He didn't want to see their leers or hear the gibes they'd be bound to make if they saw Su-mei.

She took the lantern in from the veranda and hung it on the wardrobe door in the bedroom. How little he knew about her, he thought, as they undressed. How little he understood. Her parents sold her, and yet she sent them money as a matter of course. She even made it sound as though they'd done her a favour in selling her. Perhaps they had. He shook his head perplexedly.

She lay with her head on his shoulder, and he, on his back, gazed up at the pale shadows on the ceiling looming and shrinking weirdly as the candle flame inside the lantern flickered. He cupped his hand round her shoulder. "Tell me about your family," he said slowly.

Her shoulder shrugged lightly under his hand, as if to say, "Why should you want to know about them? What business is it of yours?"

"How many brothers and sisters have you got?" he persisted.

Again her shoulder shrugged. "Two half-brothers and a half-sister," she said expressionlessly. "Three younger brothers and two sisters."

He added them together in his head. "Half-brothers?" he asked puzzledly. "Half-sister?"

"My father had two wives at one time. My mother is the number two wife."

"He must have been rich then, to have had two wives?"

"He was a rice dealer. When the Boxers came, they took all his rice. He was ruined. Then there was no trade

179

for several years because of the Boxers. Everyone was starving. They say the peasants ate their dogs first, then the rats, then the girl babies. My father sold me when I was thirteen, I was the oldest girl. The Boxers killed the number one wife," she added as an after-thought. "When they took the town. They raped her and killed her. Many men. But my mother was my father's favourite wife." She said that as though it somehow lessened the horror of killing the first wife.

All the same she had been speaking in a dull, inexpressive voice—almost grudgingly, as though she resented having to tell him. A loud sally of laughter carried into the room from Mason's veranda, discordant and loutish after Su-mei's bare and unself-pitying words. Unself-pitying and grimly realistic, he thought. She'd mentioned the first wife's death last because it was less important for the family than the loss of the rice. Without rice they starved, but her father had a second wife—and could get another if he was ever able to afford it again. And anyway the second wife was his favourite.

His hand left her shoulder to fondle the earring which lay in the hollow of her neck. He pressed it gently against her skin, rolling its little tear-drop mass to and fro.

"You're hurting," she said in the same level voice.

"What's happened to your family now?" He was still rolling the earring to and fro. "The Boxers were all killed in nineteen hundred, weren't they?" He glanced down at her face. She was looking up at him warily, her slanted lids almost closed, as though she thought he might suddenly jerk the earring or tear it off her ear. "What are they doing now?" he asked again, holding his hand still.

"My father owes a lot of money. He has to work for the people he owes it to, until he has paid it all off. My brothers are working too. They give him money to help pay."

"And your sisters?"

"Married." She stirred. "I send more money than my brothers do," she said simply, without pride. "I make more."

"What does he look like, your father?"

She shrugged, and he felt her cheek move as she smiled.

"Old."

He imagined her father selling her, taking her to the

dealer, showing off her good points, the little mole on her hand for instance, while the dealer smirked into his beard, knowing that hunger would force her father to take his price in the end. He couldn't visualize her father, but he saw the dealer as a bony old man with a straggly white beard and moustache. Did her father kiss her goodbye? No, he wouldn't do that. Did she cry? How did they treat her?

The candle in the lantern went out. The room was dark except for the reflected moonlight filtering through the shutters. Again a guffaw of laughter from Mason's room. In the dark it sounded louder. "What happened to you when you were sold?"

"The dealer sold me to an opera company. But they broke up, they lost all their money. They wanted to sell me to a brothel, but I ran away. I stole some money from them. It was in Tientsin. I got on a train to Shanghai. It was the first time in my life that I'd been on a train. The only time. I think I was more scared of the train than of being caught. And when I got to Shanghai, I became a sing-song girl." She sighed, as if telling her story had tired her.

"How long ago was that?"

"Two years. I came because it was a long way off. People said they would not be able to catch me in the foreign settlements. Because of the foreign police."

He had the sense that she had come to him across some immense plain in which everything was dim and strange. Would his life seem equally strange to her—his banal, narrow and sheltered life in Enfield?

"And did they catch you?" he asked.

"I would not be here if they had." She raised herself suddenly on her elbows and looked down at him, resting her chin on her hands. "You send money to your father?" she asked.

He nodded. *But they didn't sell me,* he was just about to say, but then checked himself. After all they weren't starving either. He gazed up past her head at the ceiling. How did her parents live? What sort of work did her father do? He'd been in Shanghai over a year and he'd learnt the language and yet China seemed just as inaccessible to him now as the day he arrived. "Do your parents know about me?" he asked.

"No." She was leaning her head on one side, unfastening

181

the earrings; first one ear, then the other. "They would be shocked to know I went with a foreign devil. I was frightened myself, only Wei told me it would be all right."

"Wei told you to come to me?" His voice rose with pique. Hadn't she come of her own accord? What business was it of Wei's?

"Wei told me you would not hurt me." She rolled onto her back suddenly and opened her arms. "See? I have taken them off after all. You can bite my ears if you like."

33

The first motor car to arrive in China was unloaded at Quay Five in the Lower Section wharves in December nineteen hundred and four, while the winter sun shone brightly on a cold morning that it could not warm. Denton, on duty there, watched with interest, but little excitement, as the coolies broke the crate open and revealed the strange horseless carriage, black and shiny, to an invited group of businessmen and reporters. Two photographers were there too, delaying the ceremony while everyone stood rigidly facing them, paralysed smiles on their faces. The photographers fussed beneath their black velvet hoods and the smiles grew more strained, until at last the photographers pressed the bulbs and the staring faces came back to mobile life again. Then a young griffin from Jardine's climbed into the thing and sat at the wheel, wrapped up in a leather coat and cap with a scarf round his throat. They couldn't start the engine yet, but some photographs were taken of the coolies pulling the machine along with ropes while the young driver steered, one gauntleted hand on the wheel, the other raised in precarious salute.

Denton returned to the Customs House by rickshaw. The coolie laughed and muttered to him about the strange, useless western contraption they'd just seen. Denton leant back against the padded seat, looking out indolently at the façades of the consulates as the coolie trotted past at an easy, steady pace. First the Russian consulate, tall with turrets and spires, then the German with its colonnaded

182

verandas, then the smaller ones, Dutch, Portuguese and Belgian. Each one seemed to assert, by its size and position, its country's stake in Shanghai. The most stately of them all was the British, he felt with a throb of pride. Its architecture was not grand like the Russian or German, but it stood in the most dominant position near Garden Bridge, set in wide rolling lawns like a country house at home. It didn't have to clamour for attention by making grandiose gestures. It merely stood there, serene and slightly remote, secure in the knowledge of its own preeminence. The other consulates you could almost mistake for business houses or clubs. But the unpretentious British consulate couldn't have been a vulgar hong. It was the manor house round which the city had developed. Denton thought he would mention this to Jacob Ephraim when they next met. Jacob was always praising the Germans for their science and their culture, but he'd have to admit they'd had precious little to do with the building of Shanghai. When it came to government, administration and the running of an empire, the Germans simply weren't in it. Even the French, although they were always a bit shabby in Shanghai, had done more than the Germans.

He gave the coolie a tip and went towards his office with a vague glow of well-being warming his body. After all, it did feel good to belong to a nation that counted.

The glow cooled a little when he noticed several of the clerks in the large outer office eyeing him rather impertinently and smiling behind their hands as he passed. He stared at a couple of them until they lowered their eyes, but, as he opened his door, he noticed they were glancing at him again, still furtively smirking at each other.

He pulled the door shut behind him, frowning in irritation. His irritation grew stronger when he saw the letters and forms he'd signed earlier in the morning still piled on his desk. He was just going to ring for the messenger when he noticed a white envelope addressed to himself leaning against the ink well. It was an official envelope, with the seal of the assistant commissioner across each of the flaps. He felt a faint stirring of unease in his stomach as he turned the letter over in his hands, the same stirring that he'd felt when he took Emily's last letter from his pigeon-hole in the mess. The muttering and tittering of the clerks suddenly seemed significant and ominous to him. He had to push himself to slit the envelope.

He drew the letter out and took it to the window to read.

Dear Mr. Denton,
    The commissioner has come to the conclusion, after careful consideration, that it would not be in the best interests of the Service to offer you a permanent contract in the Imperial Maritime Customs Service. Your employment will therefore terminate upon the expiry of your probationary contract on June 30th 1905.

                              Yours faithfully,
                              W. Brown
                              Assistant Commissioner.

Stunned, Denton stared down at the letter, while the words went on echoing in his head. He felt as though he were sagging and crumpling where he stood—as though something was running out of his body, something more vital than blood. He read the letter through again, then looked up out of the window. The sunlight lay as before on the cold dirty waters of the river, ruffled here and there by cats' paws of wind; there were the same masts and smoking funnels, the same rigid arms of the derricks, the same junks and barges clustering round each ship. But though they hadn't changed, they all seemed suddenly distant now, as though with those few lines on that crisp piece of paper, they had moved into another dimension, outside his life. He watched a sea gull swooping low over the wake of a tramp steamer that was sailing slowly down the channel towards Woosung; but his eyes were nerveless, and it was the cool, wounding phrases of the letter that he really saw.

Why? Why? He shook his head uncomprehendingly while his eyes mechanically followed the dipping and wheeling of the seagull. Why? What have I done wrong? "Not in the best interests"? Was it Mason? Or Smith? Surely they wouldn't do a thing like that? "Not in the best interests." The sea gull passed from sight behind one of the new Whampoa Docks godowns. He read the letter through once more with that frantic, irrational hope that he might after all have misunderstood it. But no, it was plain and curt—they didn't want him. He folded it slowly and slid it back into the envelope, his eyes smarting, his cheeks stinging with humiliation. So that was why the clerks had been looking at him like that outside! Of course—they knew already! They always knew first. He'd lost face, he was down, so they could smirk at him with impunity and make their mean little souls feel large by sneering at him. Well—he turned to the desk and banged the bell sharply, one, two, three times.

He stood waiting, his pulse throbbing in his wrists and ears. He still had the letter in his hand. He slipped it into his pocket and banged the bell again. He banged it so hard that it hurt his hand. He imagined the clerks outside watching his door and grinning at each other. He'd half a mind to go out and—*And what?* His mind and will stumbled into a soggy blankness. He saw himself sinking into a swamp. Whatever he said or did, they'd always get the better of him with their elusive, silent mockery that he'd never be able to get hold of and pin down. And he'd slowly sink deeper and deeper into the swamp.

At last the messenger came, shuffling in with a cigarette burning half-concealed in the cup of his hand. He lounged by the door, not even troubling to shut it, his brows lifted a fraction in dumbly insolent inquiry.

"Why haven't these letters been taken away?" Denton asked in a tight, rising voice, his eyes stiff with resentment.

The man, who only yesterday had bowed and smiled ingratiatingly when he came in, now merely gazed at him silently for a second before lifting one indifferent shoulder. "Too busy," he muttered.

"Well, take them at once!" Denton's voice snapped tensely—more tensely than he'd meant, betraying his emotion. He saw the man's lips twitch in amused superiority as he shuffled idly forward and took the papers lazily one by one. "And if you're too busy tomorrow, I'll see you're dismissed. Understand?"

The messenger shuffled out as though he were deaf.

Denton listened to the door closing, squeaking on its hinges as it had done for weeks. He'd kept asking for the

185

hinges to be oiled but nothing had happened. Now, he thought with a self-pitying catch in his chest, now he needn't bother. He gazed down at the torn edge of the blotting paper on his pad, the pad that was now no longer really his at all. *"It would not be in the best interests of the Service."* The phrase kept sliding through him like a knife. He glanced over the furniture of the desk, the pens, the pencils, the volumes of Customs regulations, the calendar, the Chinese dictionary, the unfinished report forms, the neat pile of official writing paper—all that a few minutes ago was his by right; and now was only lent him. By some trick of memory he suddenly recalled the crowd of beggars that had swarmed round him that day only two months ago when he bought Su-mei those earrings for the moon festival. He remembered how he gave away his change, first to that legless beggar with the sullen face, then to all the others, and how he'd seen that peasant couple from Soochow. Their faces seemed to form and dissolve in the dark wooden grain of the desk. Had they come back to him now because of some unconscious association his mind had made already—because today he'd slipped a step nearer them? *"Not in the best interests."* They didn't want him. *Why, why, why?*

Abruptly, he sat down, chose a sheet of paper from the middle of the pile, where neither dust nor sunlight had reached to discolour it, and wrote a note asking for an appointment to see Mr. Brown.

When he told Su-mei that night, he was still stunned, incredulous, unable to think the decision was final. Su-mei listened in silence, then, raising her head, looked directly at him. "Will you go away?"

It was the first time he'd thought of the practical consequences of the letter, and immediately he shied away from them. "I'll have to see Brown first," he shrugged. "Perhaps they'll change their minds—perhaps there's some mistake."

Her lids half-closed as she looked down again. "Why should they change their minds?" she asked dispassionately, refusing to encourage his delusions.

He shrugged again irritably. "How do I know?"

"Then you will go away," she said with dry conclusiveness. It was as though a door had shut between them.

186

He turned the polished brass knob and went in. Mr. Brown sat at his desk, stroking his moustache pensively. He was reading in a file, his domed head, with its woolly circlet of grey hair, slightly inclined, his brows faintly drawn together. "Mr. Denton?" he inquired, without raising his eyes. "Please sit down."

Denton sat. A page rustled beneath Mr. Brown's turning finger. He read on unhurriedly for half a minute, then looked up, closing the file. Denton made out his own name on the stiff green cover.

"You wished to see me?"

"Yes sir, about ... About termination of my contract."

"Yes?"

"Well, sir, I don't understand this letter." Denton pulled the letter out of his pocket.

Mr. Brown gazed at it in his hands, making no move to take it. "You do not understand the letter, Mr. Denton? Is it unclear? Is it ... imprecise?"

"No, sir, it's not that. It's ... I mean, I don't understand why my contract is being terminated. The letter doesn't really give any reason."

"No reason?" Mr. Brown clasped his hands slowly on top of the file. "The reason given, was it not, was that the commisioner does not feel a permanent contract would be in the best—"

"Yes, sir, but it doesn't say why not."

"—in the best interests of the Service," Mr. Brown finished, lowering his eyelids faintly in displeasure at the interruption. "I may add in amplification that your immediate superior officers have reported that in their opinion your temperament is not entirely appropriate for the Imperial Maritime Customs Service." His shoulders rose in a brief, resigned shrug. "In the light of those reports, I am afraid there was nothing more to be said."

"But can't I be told why?" Denton asked helplessly. "What have I done wrong? Is my work unsatisfactory?"

Mr. Brown gazed down at his clasped hands, drawing Denton's eyes too down to their pale plumpness. "Mr. Denton, it is not your work exactly, but your temperament." He frowned lightly for some seconds and then looked up. "I don't know if you play cricket at all, but

187

I'm sure you know enough about the game to agree that a man may be an excellent batsman and yet never be included in the team, simply becase he does not quite..." he glanced up at the ceiling, searching for the exact word, "...he does not quite *blend* with the other members of the team. The captain's job in such a case is to see that his team still functions. He cannot afford to play the best batsman, or still less a merely quite promising one, if the rest of the team will not play with him. I'm sure you can see the analogy I am drawing. *Do* you play cricket, Mr. Denton?"

"No, sir."

"However, the analogy is quite clear, I expect?"

"Suppose that the player doesn't blend because the other players are cheating and he isn't?"

"It is not cricket to cheat, Mr. Denton. Nor is it cricket to slander other members of the team because you are not chosen to play yourself." He leant slowly, ponderously, back, regarding Denton with a closing look that signified the interview was over. "That is all I have to say."

"Who says I don't blend?" Denton asked rebelliously. "Superintendent Smith?"

Mr. Brown glanced at the clock on the wall and felt for the gold watch-chain that hung across his soft, round paunch. "I cannot discuss the details of a confidential report of this nature with you any further, Mr. Denton." He drew out his watch, opened the gleaming gold case and checked the clock against it. "Personally, I may say that I regret this decision had to be made." His lips turned down at the corners as he peered over his paunch to slip the watch back into his waistcoat pocket. "However, given the nature of the report"—his eyes slid to the file for a moment, then up to Denton's face—"given that, I am bound to say that no other outcome was conceivable."

"How can you judge someone when he's not even allowed to speak in his own defence?"

"This is not a trial, Mr. Denton." Mr. Brown had drawn a handkerchief out of his breast pocket. He began wiping his fingers fastidiously on it, and Denton recalled for years afterwards that the handkerchief was a pale blue silk with white spots on it. "It is a decision by your superior officers, arrived at according to the appropriate procedures, about your suitability for a permanent contract. And I must confess I was not entirely surprised by the report that was made on your temperament, having regard to your somewhat...erratic behaviour at my own residence soon after your arrival in Shanghai."

Denton flushed, remembering how fuddled with wine he'd become at the Browns' dinner party. "I simply wasn't used to wine then, I'd never drunk it before!" he protested. "You can't hold that against me, it isn't fair!"

"I merely observed, Mr. Denton, that in the light of that incident the report did not surprise me. But in any case, as to the question of fairness," Mr. Brown said, replacing his handkerchief and arranging it carefully, "I must remark that sometimes...that sometimes one has a larger duty to consider than simple fairness to individuals. Good day, Mr. Denton."

"What larger duty, may I ask?" Denton was surprised himself by the flick of sarcasm in his voice.

Mr. Brown's massive forehead shook almost imperceptibly from side to side, and his lids lowered with the mildest, but definite, display of annoyance at Denton's insubordination. "Good *day*, Mr. Denton."

At the mess, as he walked through to the lounge, several officers seemed to be watching him covertly, and the voices suddenly died in the group by the bar where Mason sat, his portly buttocks bulging over the tall bamboo stool. Mason's head half-turned towards him, and Denton heard him mutter something at which the others smiled. He walked on through the doorway, his face rigid, his cheeks burning. Sitting down in an empty corner, he picked up the *North China Daily News* and ostentatiously pretended to be reading it. But his eyes scanned the words uncompre-hendingly, as if they were written in a foreign language.

Someone began playing *Home, Sweet Home* on the piano in the bar, with many flourishes and trills. Denton knew the words were syrupy with sentimentality, but still they sprung ambushes in his chest and throat. How would he help his parents now? In their last letter his mother had added a secret postscript under his father's laconic good wishes, *"Your father is*

189

not at all well." Well, how would he help them now? *"Wherever I wander,"* the words sang forlornly through his head, *"There's no-o-o place like ho-o-me."* Indignation, shame and self-pity mingled in a sudden flood behind his eyes. He held the paper higher to shield his face and blinked back the shame and bitterness.

After a few minutes he got up and walked out; through the bar, across the lobby, up the stairs, his head erect and stiff, forcing himself not to hurry. Su-mei wasn't coming that night. He lay down on his bed without undressing and gazed up at the pale, anonymous shadows wandering across the ceiling. The indifferent, raucous sounds of the street that he'd long ceased to notice sounded strangely loud and distinct to him now, as though he were hearing them for the first time—or the last. It was cold. He kicked off his shoes, and the hollow clump they made on the floor seemed desolate to him. He pulled the blankets up to his chin and stared up at the ceiling once more.

34

Although Su-mei had taught him the vivid colloquial speech of Shanghai, she had never learnt to read or write beyond the level of a child. So he'd continued taking lessons with Wei, and was slowly mastering the Chinese script. At the end of the next lesson, just after Christmas, he was subdued and inattentive. He explained to Wei apologetically afterwards, that he would be leaving the Customs Service soon. "I'll be going back to England, I suppose—I'll have to stop having lessons."

"Leaving Shanghai?" They always spoke Chinese now, unless Denton was lost for a word. Wei's lids flickered momentarily. "I shall be sorry to see such a good pupil leave."

"I shall be sorry to go. But I have to." Denton's fingers fidgeted with the watch-chain that looped into his fob. He glanced up. Wei's half-hooded eyes were watching him alertly, yet without curiosity. "The fact is," he took a sudden breath and rushed on awkwardly, "I am not being given a permanent contract in the Customs Service."

Wei's lids flickered again. His expression did not change.

"They don't want me," Denton added bitterly.

Still Wei sat quietly watching him with those alert yet incurious eyes. It had cost Denton some humiliation to admit he was being sacked, but apparently it had aroused neither sympathy nor interest. "Well, there it is." He gestured clumsily with his hand.

Wei stood up spry and erect. "Shall we go and have some tea? There is a new place just over the Garden Bridge."

Even when they had settled down in the rickshaw, Wei uttered no word of sympathy. Denton stared sombrely at the coolie's shoulders as he heaved on the shafts and hauled them over the hump of the bridge, past the beggars soaking in the midday sun. Wei perched beside him, his thin lips pressed austerely together. Occasionally his sharp little eyes darted sideways glances at Denton behind his steel-rimmed glasses, but Denton obstinately ignored them, staring unresponsively at the patched tear in the coolie's threadbare jacket. *I suppose I've lost face with Wei too*, he thought sullenly. *Soon even the coolies will be sneering at me.*

Wei had said the tea-house was just over the bridge, but the coolie loped along from one alley to another into parts of the city Denton had never set eyes on before. As the streets grew narrower the sun was often shut out, and the shadows were numb with cold. At last they came to a larger building; red banners were streaming down the front blazoned with golden Good Luck characters. The smoke of fire-crackers still hung about the entrance and beribboned baskets of flowers had been placed along the steps. Wei led the way in, being met by a smiling, bobbing waiter who led them to a table by the window and waited with exaggerated deference for their order. "It only opened today," Wei said, as if he sensed Denton's surprise at the respect they were being shown. He ordered spring rolls, one of Denton's favourites, and a strong tea "to keep the blood warm in the cold weather." A young boy brought them hot, moist towels. They wiped their hands on them in silence.

At last when the tea had been poured and they had

sipped from the cups, Wei leaned forward, sucking his lips in before he spoke. "Why does the Customs Service not want you?"

Denton sipped the dark green, bitter tea again before he answered. "They said I did not..." He couldn't think of the Chinese for "blend," "did not *fit* with the other people," he said at last.

Wei nodded, belching softly as he put his cup down.

"You think they were right, then?" Denton asked ironically.

Wei waited while the waiter placed the steaming basket of spring rolls on the table. He took up his chopsticks and delicately broke off a piece from one of the rolls while he spoke. "Yes, perhaps you did not fit with them. Perhaps you were...awkward to deal with?"

"Awkward?"

"Perhaps you were offered presents and did not take them? That might make you awkward for some people."

Denton smiled wryly. "Of course that is what I suspect, but I cannot prove it. I only ran my head into a brick wall."

Wei looked up, puzzled and concerned, at Denton's head. "You ran into a brick wall?"

"No, no, not like that. It is an English saying. It means I keep trying to make progress, but I cannot."

"I am running my head into a brick wall," Wei said reflectively in English, testing the metaphor as though it was a wine. He nodded approvingly, then returned to Chinese. "It was unlucky for you that you crossed Ching."

"Ching? How do you know about that?"

Wei smiled modestly, placing a piece of roll in Denton's bowl with his chopsticks. "People talk," he said evasively. "It is Ching who does not want you in the Customs Service." His chopsticks toyed with a morsel abstractedly, dipped it in the soya bowl, then raised it to his mouth. "He found you awkward to deal with." He swallowed and licked his lips.

"I can't believe that Ching runs the whole Customs Service," Denton protested with a smile. At the same time he was strangely consoled by the thought. Suppose Ching really had engineered it all? It turned him into a martyr instead of a failure.

"What was the name of that foreign devil officer who was drowned?" Wei reminded him gently.

"Johnson?"

"Yes, Johnson. Perhaps it was an accident that he died, but it was not an accident that he was hit—except perhaps that he was mistaken for you."

Denton laid his chopsticks down and gazed out of the window thoughtfully. "That was only a single incident, done by someone outside the Service. It would be very different if the Red Triangle, or Ching, or whoever it is, actually controlled the whole Service as you seem to be suggesting." But even as he heard his own sceptical tones, he thought of Mason's way with Ching whenever he'd seen them together—hand in glove and yet respectful, deferential almost.

"It would be too expensive to control the whole Service," Wei agreed, as if that were the only objection to doing so. "It is only necessary to..." His lips pursed a moment and he gazed at the tips of his chopsticks, in which he held a shred of chicken. "To make certain people in certain positions indebted to you. Those people can be asked to prevent someone's promotion. And of course it is in their interest to prevent it in any case, if the person is awkward to deal with."

"I can't believe that Brown is indebted to Ching," Denton said flatly, thinking of the Browns' stately passage up the aisle of the cathedral when he used to sing in the choir. But the image of their immaculate decency led him on to the Dean and he recalled with a little quiver of doubt how he'd seen even the Reverend Mr. Eaton conversing in that discreet, almost stealthy, way with Ching. Were they just discussing an innocent piece of business, or...

"You must realise that in China we do not see these things in quite the same way as foreign devils do," Wei was saying. He spoke in that same detached, practical way that seemed tacitly to exclude Denton's moral concern as irrelevant and unrealistic sentiment, like a girl's horror of the slaughterhouse but enjoyment of pork. "It does not seem strange to us to give gifts or to accept them. If a policeman stops a rickshaw coolie because he has not got a licence, the coolie will offer him some money to let him go. And the policeman will expect it. It is the way we do things. They say in England that does not happen, but I ask myself how any other way is possible. It is very...flexible, you see. The policeman gains, the rickshaw coolie gains as

193

he does not have the bother of going to court and paying more, and he will also remember to get a licence before it happens again. In your country perhaps the government takes the money as a fine that the rickshaw coolie here gives to the policeman. And then the government gives it to the policeman as pay. Chinese do not see very much difference. But do rickshaw coolies really not give money to policemen in your country?"

"There are no rickshaw coolies in my country," Denton answered drily. He was silent for a few seconds, hearing again Mr. Brown's rotund, indirect phrases, *"Personally I may say I regret"* . . . *"the rest of the team won't play."* He looked up at Wei uncertainly. "How big a part does this giving of gifts play in Shanghai?" he asked. "How much does it control?"

"In Shanghai?" Wei's Adam's apple moved up and down as he swallowed his last piece of spring roll. "Many foreign devils believe it is the Municipal Council, or the foreign consuls that rule Shanghai. But in China, things are never so simple. It is not the foreign devils, it is not the imperial viceroy. Or not them alone. It is like those old Chinese wine vessels with three legs." He spoke didactically now, with that condescending tone that Su-mei's voice also sometimes took on—the tone of a Chinese explaining the subtleties of his life to a crude and naive barbarian. "The foreign devils are one leg, the viceroy is another leg, and the third is the people like Ching. Only that leg is invisible. And because it is invisible, many foreign devils like you do not believe it exists. But without that leg the pot will not stand."

He poured some more tea, first into Denton's cup, then into his own. The tea was only tepid now, and tasted too bitter, but Denton swallowed it anyway.

"You see, my brother owns a business—a very small business—in which I also have a share." Wei's eyes glanced full into Denton's for a second, as if he wanted to impress his brother's business upon him. "Every month we have to give gifts—to government officials, to policemen, to the Red Triangle. The third leg of the tripod."

"What would happen if you didn't pay?"

Wei shook his head and smiled indulgently at the very idea of such a thing. "It is how we do things," he said with a shrug.

They were quiet again for some time. *So I have tripped*

194

over the third leg, Denton thought with a rueful little smile. Wei, noticing his smile, looked at him expectantly.

"What sort of business is it that your brother has?" Denton asked politely. He looked round as a sing-song girl was ushered up some stairs to a private room. What would become of Su-mei? he wondered with a needle prick of pain. She would become someone else's mistress eventually. Someone would take her up and she would pass to him because she had no other way to live. He imagined someone else holding her in his arms, but though he could see her clearly, the other figure was only a vague, misty shape. He couldn't visualise his successor—did that mean it wouldn't be anyone he knew? The thought somehow comforted him.

"A very small business, of course," Wei was saying. "We are not like the big hongs. We buy and sell—jade, rice, tea, silk. So far we have been trading inside China, but we are thinking of trading with other countries now." Again he glanced full at Denton as if to impress that upon him too. Then he appeared to study the tips of his chopsticks for some seconds, holding them abstractedly over his empty bowl. "As a matter of fact," he went on casually, "we are looking for a foreign devil to be our agent with foreign customers." This time his glance lingered even longer on Denton's face, and there was no mistaking it. "If you are leaving the Customs Service," Wei went on slowly, picking his words carefully like someone crossing a stream on slippery stepping stones, "it may be, perhaps, that you would like to remain in Shanghai and ... engage in some business?"

Denton sipped the bitter, lukewarm tea again while Wei watched him beneath his lowered lids. "What sort of business, exactly?" he asked slowly.

Wei's thin lips twitched into a relieved smile, as if he'd been afraid Denton might reject the idea curtly as beneath him. He shifted forward a little on his seat and leant across the table. "Would you like some more tea? Spring rolls? No? How did you like them?"

"They were really very good. The best I've tasted for a long time."

"I am glad. The restaurant belongs to us." His eyes glimmered with pride and pleasure at Denton's evident surprise. He began to explain his proposal.

Denton's glance strayed round the room as he listened,

taking in the decoration, the tables, the hurrying waiters, with a new interest. So that was why they'd had such prompt service, such deference.

Wei spoke fluently and smoothly now for several minutes. They believed they could sell Chinese goods to the west at a lower price than the big hongs like Swire and Jardine's, because the hongs were being fleeced by their Chinese compradores. The Weis wanted to sell directly from Shanghai to foreign stores and so undercut the foreign hongs. But they needed a foreigner to help them obtain orders. They would appoint Denton as their sole agent for one year if he agreed. In that time he would make contacts with foreign firms and obtain orders after sending samples of their goods. If the orders justified it, he would be appointed for a further two years. He would get ten per cent of all sales negotiated. If the business grew, he would have to travel abroad, of course. "You could become a very rich man," Wei concluded as he leant back.

"Or a very poor one," Denton smiled dubiously. "I do not know anything about business." *Work for a Chinese firm?* he was thinking. *The idea's unheard of. As well marry a Chinese. But then why not?* Something leapt in his chest at the thought of actually doing it. It would pay them back if he made a success of it!

"In business, doing is learning," Wei said. "And besides, we need someone we can trust." He laughed, a relieved little chuckle, and Denton realised again how apprehensive he must have been about approaching a foreign devil like that, even one he knew. Many would have felt insulted and sent him packing. "And if you do not fit with the Customs Service, you must at least be trustworthy. In any case," he added with a realistic shrug, "many foreigners would not want to work for a Chinese business."

"I will think about it," Denton promised at last. "Thank you for asking me."

"But first you must meet my brother," Wei said, taking out his watch. "Otherwise how can you tell? He will be there now. You are not too busy?"

They took a rickshaw deep into the mazy streets and alleys of Chapei, where the buildings were crumbling and decayed. The low walls, once whitewashed, were scabby and blackened, the low archways set into them giving onto darkness and dirt. The canals were sluggish and clogged, and the open drains were thick with refuse. Denton saw several rats moving slowly and without fear amongst the scraps of food, scarcely pausing to glance with their shiny button eyes at the passers-by. The rickshaw stopped at a large godown backing onto a smelly canal, on which a couple of sampans were moored. The entrance to the godown was barred by sliding brown horizontal poles as thick as a man's arm, as if a giant had placed his ladder at the doorway. Wei's brother appeared, bowing and smiling. About a dozen people, women, children and young men, sat at a large round wooden table, eating their midday rice. Two of the women held babies on their laps, who stared at him with wide, amazed eyes. The table round each bowl was littered in the Chinese way with the nibbled bones and discards of each person. Beyond the table, in the windowless gloom, bales of silk were stacked untidily, and sacks of rice and tea, open cases of jumbled jade ornaments. Denton gazed at it all, wearing an artificial smile to conceal his scepticism. Could a living really be made out of such a junkheap?

"I will think about it," he said again, less promisingly this time. It looked worse than the secondhand market in Enfield. How could they imagine they'd be able to do business with foreign firms in the west from a rotting godown where the whole family lived, in a rat-infested corner of the Chinese city? He thought of Jardine's building on the Bund, and Swire's. They were like palaces. The whole idea was preposterous. And yet there was that restaurant which Wei said they owned. While he stood there confused, his cheeks aching with his artificial smile, a young man—one of the brother's sons, he supposed—hawked loudly at the table, then got up and sauntered past him to spit out into the street. The rest went on shovelling in their rice, holding their bowls up to their mouths and scraping it in with their chopsticks.

"Rents here are very cheap," Wei remarked as they climbed into another rickshaw, sensing Denton's misgivings perhaps.

They wound slowly through the crowded alleys, so narrow, cold and damp that it seemed the sun could never reach into them. *But still,* Denton kept thinking, *there is that restaurant.*

They came onto a broader street and the rickshaw coolie pulled up abruptly to let some Manchu bannermen past. They were swaggering with an almost theatrical gait, escorting some criminals in cangues. The prisoners shuffled past clumsily, their heads and hands locked in the holes of the wooden boards on their shoulders. They had those dull, empty eyes that Denton had seen before in the faces of the condemned prisoners at the executions he'd watched. He felt a weight dragging suddenly on him as the bannermen prodded them along with their rifle butts. In the usual way, the prisoners' crimes were painted on placards fixed over their heads.

Wei began describing the business again as the rickshaw coolie leaned against the shafts when the grim little convoy had passed, but Denton couldn't get those faces, with their lustreless, unseeing eyes, out of his head. They seemed to crowd his mind so that there was no room for Wei's words, and Wei, feeling his preoccupation, if not understanding it, soon gave up.

They had not gone much further when they came to an open space and the coolie paused again, gesturing with a wordless, but satisfied, grunt to the little crowd in the center.

"What is it?" Denton asked.

"Nothing much," Wei answered quickly. "Go on."

But the coolie pointed again and, as the people in the crowd moved, Denton saw two more bannermen beside a young woman tied to a tall pole. There was a pulley at the top of the pole, from which a taut, thin wire ran down on one side to the woman's waist, where it seemed to be fastened, disappearing in the overlapping folds of her tunic. On the other side, the wire was tied to a large basket that swung gently to and fro where it hung a few feet above the ground. The basket seemed to be heavy. Its weight was pulling the wire tighter around the woman's waist. At first Denton couldn't understand it at all, although his pulse had quickened ominously. Then he saw a pile of massive stones beside the base of the pole, and one of the bannermen approaching it. He lifted one of the stones with both hands and, staggering under its weight, heaved it with a crash into the basket. Denton saw the wire quiver as the basket jerked and sank a little lower with its new burden, tightening the noose round the woman's waist. He heard her give a little squeaking cry, like a rat in a cage. Some of the onlookers tittered. The bannerman stood by the basket slapping the stone dust off his hands.

"It is a penalty for adultery," Wei said quietly. "Can you see the notice on the pole? The wire slowly tightens under the weight of the stones until she dies."

"It will cut her in half?" Denton asked, sickened, yet unable to turn away.

"No, no," Wei answered soothingly. "She will suffocate first."

The coolie grunted again, watching the other banner-man heave a stone into the basket. The woman's body twitched as the wire jerked and quivered. A trickle of blood came out of the corner of her mouth and ran slowly down her chin. She was sagging now, her hair hanging across her eyes, as if she were unconscious. But again he heard that faint, squeaking cry.

Someone called out mockingly in the scattered crowd and there was another, uneasy, titter from the rest of them.

"Go on!" Wei ordered the reluctant coolie. "Haven't you seen enough?" And yet it seemed to be more distaste than indignation, let alone pity, that was in his voice.

"It seems a cruel way to punish such a human failing," Denton said unsteadily after a time. As he said it, he was ashamed of the mildness of his tone.

But the coolie turned his head back reprovingly. "Not cruel, sir, not at all! She deserved it, betraying her husband!"

"Watch where you're going," Wei said curtly. "We do not need ignorant fools like you to teach us."

The coolie shrugged and heaved on the shafts, muttering sullenly under his breath.

Denton kept seeing the image of that thin, taut wire slowly cutting through the woman's flesh. "How long does it take?" he asked heavily.

"It depends how quickly they put the stones in." Wei smiled a tight, dry little smile. "You see, she must give presents too. Even to die."

When Su-mei undressed that night, he noticed a little red weal round her waist where she must have tied her underslip too tight. He told her about Wei; then, when he lay down beside her, about the woman. He kept tracing the faint and fading groove in Su-mei's slender waist as he told her, imagining a wire slowly tightening round her body, cutting deeper and deeper beneath the weal that his stroking fingertip could still just feel. She lay on her side,

199

her head propped on her hand, listening and watching expressionlessly.

"I suppose she may not be dead even now," he said, holding his finger still at last on her skin. "Even now." He saw the bannerman casually slapping his hands free of the stone dust after dropping the stone in the basket, and heard that inhuman squeal of pain from the woman's parted lips. "I don't know if I want to stay in Shanghai after all. All this torture, all this corruption. I don't know if I could stand it. How do *you* stand it, Su-mei?"

At first she didn't answer, her eyes gazing past him at some distant thought. Then, as he watched her, the light came back into her eyes and she looked at him with full attention again. "You should ask Wei for fifteen percent," she said decidedly. "And accept twelve and a half."

He flopped over onto his back away from her. "Is that all you can say?" he asked coldly.

He felt her shoulders lift in a disclaiming shrug. "I cannot alter the other things."

"You sound as though you don't even care about them."

"In my village," she said detachedly, "they would have put that woman in a pig basket and tied stones to it and thrown her in the river." Her dispassionate tone implied some rebuke to him, as if he were meddling with things that didn't concern him.

"And you?" He scrambled through his mind for the word for *condone*, but had to give up. "You *accept* that?"

"Am I the empress to change the laws?" She stared at him a moment, her dark eyes suddenly flaring with resentment. "Of course I accept it. I cannot just go away like foreign devils can! I have to accept it."

They fell asleep without touching, silent and separate. But after his first, deep sleep, Denton awoke and reached across the bed for her. "You know, I've just realised Wei knew all along I was getting the sack," he murmured. "He was going to ask me about his business today before I even told him. He was going to take me to his restaurant and introduce me to his brother. It was all planned. How did he know?" He had the uneasy feeling that Wei was some kind of benevolent spider, catching him and entangling him in the delicate threads of his web. "How did he know?"

200

"People talk," she muttered sleepily. "Ask him for fifteen per cent."

35

At the end of his last day in the Customs Service, Denton took a rickshaw to the Central Hotel. He stretched out his legs under his usual table and sipped the lemon tea the waiter brought him. The brass-tipped wooden blades of one of the new electric ceiling fans, which the management now proudly advertised in its brochures, whirred over his head. He closed his eyes under its cooling breeze and wondered fatalistically where he'd be in a year's time. In the end, as nothing else offered, he'd swallowed his misgivings about the Weis' business, and agreed to work for them. He'd taken Su-mei's advice, though, and asked for fifteen per cent commission. Wei's resistance had surprised him. Behind the façade of elaborate courtesy with which he'd always treated Denton, he was wily and tough, and Denton was reminded of the sharp way he often had with a coolie or a waiter. Denton had had to settle for ten per cent on the first ten thousand dollars' worth of orders and twelve and a half on the rest. "You're too soft," Su-mei had said, but Denton was glad to have got anything. His contract, with Wei Brothers Ltd, in Chinese and English, had been signed and witnessed. It ran for one year. At first Wei had demurred at the expense of a contract— "What need to pay lawyers if we have already agreed?" But then, smiling bleakly at Denton's western caution, he'd reluctantly acquiesced.

Denton had sent samples of their goods off with a carefully re-written prospectus to a hundred stores in London, New York, Paris, Berlin and Vienna—Jacob Ephraim had willingly translated it into French and German, improving it, he said, as he did so. He'd rented some rooms from a Chinese landlord in the cheapest end of Bubbling Well Road. Now he could only wait. In six months, if he couldn't pay the rent any longer, he would fall on the charity of the Municipal Council, which maintained a fund to ship destitute Europeans back to their homelands, where their impoverishment wouldn't lower the white man's prestige in the eyes of the yellow. He reckoned the money he'd saved, and the passage money from the Customs Service which he'd added to it, would last six months at least, especially now that Su-mei was refusing to take any more money from him. He reached forward to sip his tea, then leant back again. It was to be the last tea he'd take there, he vowed, until he began to make money. He felt in his pocket for the stiff new business cards he'd had printed for himself. Their hard, clean edges were strangely reassuring.

Suddenly a hand gripped his shoulder and Ephraim's voluble tones, purring with delight, poured over him.

"How is your business going? Haven't you started yet? You will be rich, I can tell. Come and meet my fiancée."

"Your fiancée, Jacob?"

"Yes." His warm dark eyes glistened proudly in his sallow-skinned face.

"I didn't even know you were engaged!"

"How could you? It only happened yesterday." He nodded towards a corner table, where a large, stern foreign woman in black was sitting with a demure dark-haired girl, watching them doubtfully. "Her father's starting a cotton mill in Hongkew," Jacob explained, turning back. "Oh, we shall be rich, we shall be rich, what did I tell you? You must come to the reception when we are married." He pulled Denton up by the arm. "Come along and meet her. I can't ask you to the wedding as you're not a Jew, but you'll come to the reception, won't you?"

The large, stern woman, his fiancée's mother, continued to eye Denton doubtfully as Jacob introduced him, as if she were being asked to buy something she didn't really want. Her droopy, crêpe-skinned throat was sheathed in a thick pearl choker, and several gold bracelets slid down her wrist and clashed together when she distantly shook Denton's hand. Her daughter, Sarah, was small, though plump, with an olive skin that seemed to have been untouched by the sun, like a fruit that hasn't ripened. Her fingertips scarcely brushed Denton's palm as she shyly shook his hand.

Denton stood smiling awkwardly while Jacob harangued the two women in Yiddish. "No good trying to talk to them," he said at last as if it had been Denton speaking all the time. "They only speak German and Yiddish." He waved his hand proprietarily over the two women's heads while their eyes, bright-beady and dark-apprehensive,

202

strained to catch the meaning from his expansive gestures. "The marriage is in October. They have only been here six months."

The mother sipped her coffee, her eyes still pursuing Jacob's eloquent hands, and cast a brittle smile at Denton from time to time. The daughter had a crumb of cake on her lower lip, which her tongue, peeping hesitantly out, at last succeeded in dabbing up. After that her liquid eyes looked less apprehensive.

Jacob gripped his arm and led him away as swiftly as he'd brought him, so that Denton scarcely had time to smile goodbye. He leant confidentially over the table as he pushed him into his seat again. "What about your commission? Did you get them up to fifteen per cent?"

"Twelve and a half after the first ten thousand dollars' worth."

"Twelve and a half?" He wrinkled his nose as if the figure actually smelt. "They are cheating you. But never mind, you will succeed, I'm sure you will." He leant closer, inclining his head towards the other corner. "What do you think of her?"

"Very—"

"Beautiful, eh? Rolling in money too, I shall be a millionaire—didn't I tell you that once? Docile, as well. No nonsense, knows her place." He nodded meaningfully. "I'm the boss and she knows it. What about you? Still got that Chinese girl? Good, when you're in business you need it more. Because of the strain. Don't go without it." He gazed into Denton's eyes earnestly. "Go without sleep, go without drink, even go without food. But not without a woman. Believe me, I know." He glanced suddenly up at the fan, frowning. "And don't sit under these electric fans, they go too fast. They'll give you pneumonia with their cold air. They should have kept the punkahs, much more natural." He looked round irritably, as if searching for someone to complain to. But instead he must have seen his future mother-in-law. She was gazing at him under faintly lowered brows, tapping the table with her beringed fingers. "I must go now," he gripped Denton's arm briefly and moved away. "Come to the reception, we'll send you an invitation. At the Jewish Club." He was calling out half-way across the room now, in a high, exuberant voice, unaware of the turned heads and disapproving stares he

203

was attracting. "Not the wedding, mind. You're not a Jew. Only the reception."

Denton stayed in the hotel until seven o'clock, when the brief twilight gave way to the violet of night. His old tin trunk and a few other belongings he'd acquired were waiting for him in the lobby of the mess, and he wanted to collect them inconspicuously, when most of the officers would be in the dining-room. The gas lamps had been lit and the first couples had begun to appear in evening dress when he walked down the steps of the hotel and called a rickshaw. As he climbed in, Big Ching started chiming from the illuminated tower of the Customs Building. He listened pensively to the brazen notes shimmering over the velvet dark of the river and the ships' glistening lights, each with a misty halo on the humid air. Were the chimes warning him or merely bidding farewell?

When the coolie halted at the mess, his neck and back slippery with sweat, Denton felt he couldn't get down and take that last step that would mark the end of his career. He sat there for some seconds, paralysed. But when the coolie glanced round at him expectantly, resting his shafts on the ground, Denton forced himself out. "Ten cents if you find me a barrow," he said dully. "I've got some baggage to take on."

The coolie nodded, wiping his neck and face with a dirty grey strip of cloth. Denton heard him hawk and spit behind him as he walked tensely up the stone steps to the lobby.

Ah Koo was waiting by the desk, his puckered face as motionless as ever.

"Put my things in the barrow, will you?" Denton said tightly.

Ah Koo glanced past him down the steps. "No barrow," he said.

"It's coming," Denton replied in a taut voice. "Hurry up." It was a still night, thick and sultry, the day's heat trapped in the moistness of the air. He felt a trickle of sweat rolling smoothly down the side of his cheek.

Ah Koo put his trunk into the barrow and placed the other packets round it. The barrow coolie rearranged them all, with a superior, expert air. "Where to, master?" he asked when he was satisfied. "Which pier?"

"No pier. Bubbling Well Road. Follow me in the rickshaw."

The man's brows rose faintly and he shrugged, turning to adjust the barrow strap over his shoulders.

In his hurry to be off without being seen, Denton forgot to bargain over the price with him. He turned to Ah Koo and dropped a last dollar into his waiting palm. Ah Koo muttered perfunctory thanks, then stepped closer. "You want an amah for your new place?"

He hesitated. He hadn't wanted to spend the money, but Su-mei had said he must have one. She'd find him an old woman, she'd said, who couldn't ask much.

"Third cousin," Ah Koo murmured, watching his eyes. "Very cheap."

"Cheap? Doesn't she know anything, then?"

"Knows a lot. Good worker."

"Why so cheap then?"

Ah Koo shrugged. "Maybe she likes a good master more than a lot of money."

Denton heard voices in the lobby behind him. His back prickled. "All right, bring her round tonight," he said quickly. "I'll talk to her. You know the address?"

Ah Koo nodded. Denton walked swiftly down to the waiting rickshaw. As he was getting in he heard Mason's voice calling out.

"Hey! Going already? What's the hurry? Aren't you going to stand us all one last round of drinks?" A subdued, perhaps even ashamed, snigger followed from the people with him. Denton half-turned. Mason was gazing at him innocently; the others, smiling sheepishly, avoided his eyes. He turned back and walked on.

Mason called out again, with the same pretence of innocence. "I say, old chap, what address shall we tell that piece of yours if she comes asking?"

Denton walked a few more paces, then abruptly turned round to stare at Mason's button eyes, his bulging, ruddy cheeks, his bristling ginger moustache which he was just brushing upwards with that characteristic gesture of his knuckle. The gas lamp in the entrance to the mess was streaming straight down on his red-brown hair. By some trick of the light it seemed that the other faces had receded into indistinctness behind Mason's. For some seconds they stared at each other, and the mock-innocent air seemed to slip off Mason's face to reveal a triumphant

205

vindictive glare. Denton wanted to shout some taunt back, to hurl some stinging insult at his cold, vengeful face. But he could find no words—Mason's figure seemed to fill his mind and smother any other thought. An inarticulate thick anger choked his throat. As he turned back helplessly, Mason lifted his hand in an ironic farewell.

Denton got into the rickshaw, watched curiously by the coolie and the barrow coolie who muttered and chuckled together. "Bubbling Well Road," he said again in a strangled voice.

He had two rooms and a kitchen, with a privy in an uneven, cobbled courtyard, across the middle of which ran an open drain, crawling with cockroaches. Water had to be collected from a pump. It was true, he thought as he looked despondently round the shabby rooms, he did need an amah. They cost next to nothing and it would give him more time to work. He lit a paraffin lamp and began unpacking his trunk in the airless bedroom. The little window was open, but no breeze came in, only the sounds and smells of his Filipino neighbours, quarrelling while they cooked their evening meal. His shirt was soon clinging to his body with sweat.

There was a knock on the door. Ah Koo stood at the threshold, with a woman just behind him. When Denton motioned them in, he saw with astonishment that she was the peasant woman who'd been hit by the shotgun pellets. The woman seemed leaner now than he remembered her, leaner even than when he saw her at the moon festival. But he recognised her at once, and the brief glimmer in her eye, though it was quickly replaced by that concealing Chinese blankness, showed that she recognised him too.

Ah Koo spoke self-importantly in pidgin, clearly to impress his status on her and give himself face. "This one already long-time amah," he said. "Very goo'. Goo' workah."

"Where did she work before?"

"Shanghai. English family."

Denton glanced at the woman again. She was plain, but strong and honest-looking. He remembered her standing in the street of the silversmiths with her husband, watching him with that strange incurious gaze. Now she glanced from one to the other as they spoke, and again it was a strangely incurious gaze, as though she had no

206

desire to try to understand what they were saying, but merely wanted to look at their faces.

"How long work Shanghai?" he asked.

"Two year. Makee-learnee two year. Now very goo'."

Denton's lips twitched into a little triumphant smile. "She live Soochow more far, before now. Not work amah. Her husband very tall. Come Shanghai last year."

Ah Koo's eyes blinked briefly in amazement. Then, recovering, he muttered another lie as though the first had never been spoken. "I teach already. She know wester' cooking, very goo' workah. You try. Not likee, send away, I get other one."

The woman turned her flat incurious gaze from Ah Koo to Denton, as if waiting to see the expressions he made when he replied. *Ah Koo will take a cut from her wages,* he thought. *If I take her on.*

"Where her husband now?" he asked, giving himself time to consider.

"Go away, be sailor. Big ship."

"Before he farmer?"

Ah Koo shook his head. "No land. Work for other one. Now no more work, come Shanghai, be sailor."

We've both come down in the world, Denton thought wrily. Ah Koo's matter-of-fact summary brought momentarily back the image of his own father unemployed in Enfield, and not keeping at all well as his mother kept writing. His parents' image had faded steadily in his memory, like a photograph going brown with age. He hadn't told them his contract had been terminated. He'd merely said he'd been offered a post in an export firm. He turned to the woman and spoke to her in Shanghainese. "What is your name?"

She frowned, trying to understand him. Clearly she couldn't speak Shanghainese very well.

"Ah King," Ah Koo interjected. "Very strong."

"Ah King," she said, as though he hadn't spoken.

There was a clatter of dishes from the Filipinos, something smashed, and after a second's blank silence, the quarrelling voices burst out louder and angrier, Denton and the two Chinese listened a moment, turning towards the window.

When he looked back to her, Denton saw she was smiling faintly at the commotion, her eyes crinkling at the corners. It was the kind of smile you'd give to children's

207

quarrels and misfortunes, he thought. And then he felt he was going to take her. "Ah King," he said. "Can you cook?"

Again she frowned. He could see her eyes moving as she filtered his words through the sieve of her own dialect. At last she nodded. "Chinese food," she said in heavily accented Shanghainese.

"Western food can do. I teach," Ah Koo added at his elbow. "You tell, I teach."

"All right, I'll try you," Denton said as if he'd only just decided, and against his better judgment at that. "You cook, clean, wash. You can sleep in the kitchen. I'll pay you..." he avoided Ah Koo's eyes "...five dollars a week."

The woman frowned intently, then turned inquiringly to Ah Koo. He spoke rapidly to her in that dialect Denton could hardly follow. She nodded, and Ah Koo looked back at Denton. "Five dollar no can do," he said regretfully, as though he'd been trying to persuade her. "You pay six dollar, master?"

"Five-fifty," Denton said definitely.

Ah Koo spoke to the woman again. She looked from him to Denton and nodded. "I try," she said in stilted Shanghainese. There was a composed tone in her voice as though it was she that was going to test him, not he her. He realised that she had not lowered her head at all, but looked at him quite frankly all the time, as she had with her husband in the street of the silversmiths. What had they been doing since then, he wondered. How had they lived? She seemed to be wearing the same clothes, and, yes, definitely she was thinner and paler.

"How about food money?" Ah Koo asked him, in Chinese now.

"I'll give her money for the market. She can buy her own food out of that, as well as mine."

Ah Koo began translating into her own dialect. She nodded her understanding before he'd finished, but he bore authoritatively on. Then he spoke to her in Shanghainese, portentously and slowly for Denton to hear too.

"This master is very good. You work well and he will give you a lot of good fortune money in the New Year." He glanced back at Denton for confirmation.

Ah King lifted her possessions, a small bundle tied up in a coloured cloth, with the handle of an earthenware rice pot sticking out of the top. She went straight to the kitchen and stood looking round, arms akimbo. "Master wants evening rice?" she asked.

Su-mei didn't come until late the next night. Denton heard her shoes tapping on the stones outside, but Ah King got to the door before him. The two women stared at each other in surprise, the slight, painted girl with her delicate skin and the tall sunburned peasant with her queue hanging loosely down her back.

"Come in," Denton said in English.

Su-mei stepped past Ah King without a word and walked into the room Denton was to use as both office and living room. She sat on a black-wood stool. For some seconds they looked at each other, constrained by Ah King's presence in the kitchen. The Filipinos were talking again, quarrelling perhaps. Ah King was washing dishes, banging them noisily. She had left the door to the kitchen open.

"Who is that?" Su-mei asked at last, in Chinese. She jerked her head contemptuously towards the kitchen.

"My amah. I got her yesterday."

"How much?"

"Five-fifty a week."

Her face had stiffened slightly, yet enough, under her rouge, to make it appear mask-like. "I would have got you one for four," she said in a rigid, clipped voice. "You're too soft."

He shrugged. "You weren't here."

"I said I'd find you one. I could have got an older one for four dollars a week."

He shrugged again. "Is that what troubles you? She isn't old enough?"

She let her eyelids droop in silent scorn and glanced round the room. "Where does she sleep?"

He smiled. "You're jealous."

"Where does she sleep?"

"In the kitchen. You are jealous, aren't you?"

"Not of that," she said sullenly. "Not what you think."

"Well, there's no need to be."

She shook her head irritably as if a fly had been bothering her. "You should have let me employ one for you."

"You weren't here."

"Now she'll think...*She*'ll be jealous of *me*. If I'd

employed her, she'd have given me face. Now she'll only... she'll think I have no rights here, she won't treat me properly."

"Nonsense." He noticed the noise in the kitchen had lessened. Was Ah King listening? He got up and shut the door. "Besides, you were not here to employ her, as I keep telling you."

"How could I be here? If I do not take your money now I have to work more. That does not give you the right to humiliate me like this!" Suddenly there were two large tears in the corners of her eyes. She sat sniffing like a little girl, her hands, curled up into fists, pressing against the tears.

He watched her in baffled irritation. At one moment he wanted to shout at her, at the next to embrace her and stroke her cheeks. He sat helplessly, waiting for her to stop.

And, quite quickly, she did. She began dabbing her eyes with her knuckles. Silently he offered her his handkerchief. She looked up at him after a time contritely, holding the handkerchief to her eye. "What is that you are playing with?"

He looked down at his hand. "A button. Off my Customs uniform. I cut it off yesterday." He hadn't even realised he was playing with it. He must have taken it out of his pocket while she was crying and been fiddling with it unthinkingly between his finger and thumb.

"Cut it off? Why?"

He shrugged. "A keepsake. I don't know really. For luck perhaps."

"A button for luck?"

"Well, it stopped you crying, didn't it?"

She laughed suddenly, against her will it seemed, then stood up, still smiling. "Let us go to the night market and have our fortunes told. Then we shall really know if we will be lucky or not."

In the night market, Su-mei listened with an awed and anxious face while the lean, shrewd-eyed old man went through his ritual of palmistry and fortune sticks. She was going to be rich, the old man told her, squatting beside the sooty oil lamp as he pored over her hand. She would have many children.

"Sons or daughters?" she asked nervously.

He pored over her palm again; teasing her, Denton thought.

"Mainly sons."

When Denton drew the sticks and offered his hand too, the old man sighed and shook his head at first, as if the foreign devil's fate was too obscure for him to see. But then, turning his head this way and that, he appeared at last to discern something through the mists. It was wealth and many children for him as well.

"What a surprise!" Denton scoffed. But Su-mei's eyes glistened with satisfaction.

"Don't you realise he tells everyone the same thing?" he asked as they travelled back in a rickshaw.

"Of course he doesn't. Why should he lie? A fortune-teller told my grandmother her daughter was going to die, and she did. Different people have different fates. It is just that we are both going to be lucky." She pressed her leg against his suddenly. "You remember you asked me about smoking opium together, months ago? Shall we do it tonight?"

"Tonight?" He stared in perplexed amusement at her eager, happy face, happy because the fortune-teller had told her she was going to be rich and have many children. How could she believe it? Did Wei believe it? Did they all? But then he'd believed the absurdities of the Christian religion until a year ago. After all it was easy to believe in nonsense. And now she wanted to smoke opium with him.

"I have the things in my friend's house," she was saying. "We could stop there and pick them up. It will be to celebrate your new life."

"How long have you had the things, then?"

"Months and months. Ever since you talked about it. But you never asked again, so I sometimes smoked it by myself."

"Why didn't you tell me? Why didn't you remind me?"

She pouted. "Foreign devils are strange about opium. Sometimes they want to smoke it and sometimes they get angry and will not touch it."

That night he fell asleep beside her with the greasy smell of opium in his nostrils and its slow, contented dreams colouring his mind.

211

PART TWO

36

"What is all this noise, Mr. Lo?" Denton called in Chinese from the door of his office. "What is going on?"

The three clerks had deserted their desks and were shouldering each other at the open window, peering down into the street and chattering excitedly—so excitedly and so loudly that they didn't hear him. From the street below, the sound of the new Shanghai Tramway Company's clanging bells rose intermittently above their chatter.

"Mr. Lo! Haven't you got any work to do?"

Lo, the senior clerk, glanced round with a start, then tapped the others' shoulders. They all went back to their desks, smiling embarrassedly. The paper in the American typewriting machine on Lo's desk fluttered in the breeze from the electric ceiling fan. Again the tram bell clanged outside and Denton heard the metal wheels grinding along the tracks. Beside that now familiar sound, he heard other ones, a few peremptory shouts and a swell of subdued murmuring, as of the crowds waiting at the races.

Watched discreetly by the clerks, he went to the window himself. Two lines of imperial soldiers with rifles and fixed bayonets were escorting a column of prisoners along the street, holding up the trams, barrows and rickshaws. An officer rode at the head of the column on a black horse. The murmuring had come from the hawkers and shoppers, the waiting coolies and the passengers cramming the obstructed trams' windows. They were all watching the column shuffle past.

"Condemned prisoners from the rebellion," Lo said at his side. "They're taking them to the new execution ground."

"Sun Yat-sen's rebellion, you mean? That was in Canton, two years ago!"

Lo leant deferentially on the sill beside him, and he heard the other two behind, peering over Lo's shoulders. "Yes, but they send prisoners to be executed in different cities, as a warning. It takes time."

Denton watched the bowed, defeated heads pass beneath him in the ruthless July sunlight. They were all in cangues, some singly, others yoked two or three together in one. The cangues seemed to pull their heads even lower. Condemned men always walked with that same mechanical, trudging step, he thought, as if withdrawn already from the world. The sun's brilliance, striking back off the road, dazzled his eyes. One of the clerks burped behind him.

He shifted his gaze to the people lining the street. They parted as the soldiers passed, then flowed together behind them like water behind a ship. He saw two photographers taking pictures. There was something different about the mood of the onlookers. They were quieter than the crowds that usually followed condemned pirates and bandits. They weren't jubilant or jeering. There was nothing festive, no excitement. Their subdued murmur could be one of awe or even sympathy, he realised. His eyes focused on the soldiers. Even they seemed subdued, as though they felt half-guilty for what they were doing, for being there at all.

The clerks themselves were watching from the window with a kind of solemn respect now, so different from the excited chatter Denton had heard at first. There was a moment's silence, after the column passed from sight, as at the end of a play, then they went back to their desks once more. The trams started moving again, jolting and clanging. He would ask Wei about that Sun Yat-sen, Denton thought as he turned away from the window. He suspected from the way he talked that Wei secretly sympathised with him.

Lo lifted the lid of his glass and sipped his tepid green tea reflectively, as if still under the spell of the procession. Then, licking his lips, he held his slim sallow hands poised over the keys. Still he didn't start typing, his hands hanging there, fragile and still like a butterfly's wings at rest.

"I want all those invoices ready for the mail today," Denton said, more sharply than he'd intended. "Don't forget." He went into his office, took his panama hat off the hat-stand and glanced at his face in the mirror. It had grown fuller in the past three years. It made him look more mature. There were little vertical lines on his forehead, just above his nose, and faint horizontal ones that deepened as he raised his brows. His eyes were the same, though, deep-set and brooding, gazing back at him from

215

an impenetrable depth like a wary animal peering from its lair.

He took the *North China Daily News* from his desk and went out. "I'll be back after I've taken Mr. Larsen to his hotel," he told Lo. "About four o'clock."

Lo nodded, his fingers fluttering lightly now over the clacking keys. Denton walked out into the sunlight, raising his hand for a passing rickshaw. *Why should I look like that in the mirror?* he asked himself as he stepped in. *I'm doing all right. I'm doing very well.*

"Where to, master?"

"The Customs Building." He leant back in the shade of the canopy and took off his hat to let the passing air cool his head. In front of him the coolie's knotted shoulders glistened with sweat. Denton watched the man's queue swinging as he trotted along.

Yes, in those past three years he'd done very well. The Weis' order books had filled up steadily and, after that first uncertain year when he'd lived in that slum in Bubbling Well Road, he'd been making more money than he'd ever dreamed of. Wei had been right, their prices were undercutting the big foreign hongs. They had more buyers than they could sell to. Now he had a hundred thousand dollars on deposit in the bank, a small house in the green fields of Jessfield Road, an office with three clerks on the border of the Chinese district of Chapei—and he was on his way to meet the first foreign buyer to visit Shanghai, a buyer who represented a new chain of stores across America from San Francisco to New York. Why that uneasy look in the mirror, then?

The coolie pulled up abruptly as a tram clanked over the points round the corner in front of them, the driver ringing his bell and staring superciliously down at the lowly rickshaw-puller. The coolie cursed him hoarsely. The driver looked through him impassively.

"They'll kill us all and take our business as well," the coolie grumbled, half to himself, half to Denton.

"Ah well, it's progress," Denton murmured unthinkingly.

"Progress? Progress won't fill my rice-bowl!" the man grunted angrily, wiping his forehead with the back of his hand as he leant against the bar again. "And they don't have to pay protection money either."

Denton looked down at his paper uncomfortably, feeling vaguely responsible for the progress that was threaten-

216

ing the rickshaw coolie's rice-bowl. He checked which berth Larsen's ship would arrive at. Number ten. It wouldn't take long from there to the Customs Building. "Protection money?" he said absently, looking up again. "Which triad is number one now, the Greens or the Reds?"

The coolie glanced round at him suspiciously. He had a tired, wrinkled face, with red-rimmed eyes. "How do I know?" he answered grudgingly as he turned back. "They say they're joining together now. Like lips and teeth."

"Who? Ching and Pock-mark Chen?"

The coolie trotted on for some time in silence, as though he hadn't heard. Then he half-turned his head. "Are you police? What d'you want to know for?"

"No, I'm not police."

"I don't know anything about it."

"I'm not police."

"Well, whether you are or whether you're not," the coolie muttered stubbornly as he pulled the rickshaw over a stagnant, weed-covered canal, "I still don't know anything about it. It's just what I've heard, that's all."

Denton watched his bobbing head and flicking queue as he pushed his way down the narrow alleys towards the Bund. There had been several battles between the Reds and the Greens, he knew from the papers and from Su-mei, but he hadn't heard anything about a truce, let alone a coalition. He wondered idly whether the Weis paid as much in protection money as they paid him in commission, and who they paid it to. And whether the Tramways Company paid as well, despite what the coolie said.

The rickshaw swung round and suddenly the Soochow Creek appeared, junks and sampans floating like painted brooches on the smooth, glittering cloth of its surface. Su-mei had done well too, he reflected. She was becoming quite a well-known opera singer now, one of the few women in an otherwise male company. She was talking of joining an all women company soon—it was going to be the new thing, Shaohing opera. He smiled at the thought of her playing a man's part. But then why not, since men traditionally played women's parts in China? Yes, she'd done well. Perhaps that fortune-teller had been right. Now she had her own apartment with an amah and her own palanquin with two bearers. She too still paid protection money to the Red Triangle. At first he'd tried to get her to go to the police, but she'd always shrugged, as if to say,

"What good would that do?" When he'd mentioned it to Everett, newly promoted to superintendent, he'd shrugged too. "Frankly, she'll get better protection from them than from us," he'd admitted. "It's worth her while to pay a bit for it. The triads are just too big for us."

Sometimes he almost wished she hadn't done so well. She no longer depended on him, she was always at rehearsals or performing, she smoked opium with the other actors in the company, she played mah-jong for high stakes, she was often tense or moody; there was a shrillness sometimes about her life, as though she were living it too loud and too fast. He missed the girl she used to be, childlike, wayward and impulsive. Sometimes he saw the girl in her, but too often she seemed to be concealed beneath the smart varnish of a successful actress. And yet she was only twenty—nineteen by western reckoning.

He remembered the first time he'd seen her perform, on a little temporary bamboo stage, her face painted into a vivid mask. There were only four other actors, all men, accompanied by a few gaunt musicians playing two-stringed fiddles, lutes and cymbals. There had been as much speaking, or declaiming rather, as singing, and, as far as he understood it, the dialogue was earthy. Had she stood out then, or had he only imagined it? Her teacher, an old blind actor called Chin, told him afterwards that her voice was good, but it was the expressiveness of her gestures that appealed to Denton most. When Wei heard about it, he gave a tight little smile. "That kind of opera is very vulgar," he said. "Only for peasants and coolies." Yet Denton preferred it to the splendid Peking operas Wei sometimes took him to. For one thing, the music was simpler and there was less of it—and Chinese music still clashed on his western ears.

The coolie was pulling him past the back of the Shanghai Club now, and, as he glanced up at the walls, which beat the heat back down onto the narrow street in majestic indifference, he recalled with an inward wince one reason for that mistrustful expression he'd caught in his mirrored eyes. Only six months ago, he'd written to apply for membership. Wei had been gently insinuating he should do so for some time, convinced he would make connections there that would help the business. For Wei was ambitious—he was determined that his Chinese hong would rival the foreign hongs like Jardine's and Swire. Back had come a stiffly formal reply from the secretary.

"I refer to your inquiry of November 7th and wish to inform you that there are no application forms for membership of the Club. Names of prospective members must be put forward by not less than two full members of the Club of at least five years standing. Prospective members are interviewed by the committee, after which the application is approved or otherwise."

"But I don't know any members," he had to tell Wei. "Not in that way, anyway" (he remembered that Mr. Brown was a member of long standing). So Wei, who as a Chinese was not allowed to cross the threshold, couldn't get in by proxy either. And Denton had had to concede that the little prosperity he'd attained, about which he'd made his parents in Enfield so proud, was insignificant in the estimation of the Shanghai taipans. It galled him to lose face with Wei, and it galled him to lose face with himself. "Never mind," Wei had said mildly. "Perhaps it costs more money." Like most Chinese, he believed that everything in Shanghai had its price. "Perhaps next time you should offer presents to the members of the committee?" he had suggested hopefully.

Denton looked across at the side of the Club as the coolie pulled the rickshaw down onto the Bund. Cabs, palanquins and rickshaws waited in a neat line under the shade of the trees, and two large black motor cars stood on the road, liveried chauffeurs snoozing in their seats. The rickshaw coolie nodded at the cars, muttered something derogatory about them and spat as he passed. The Sikh doorman eyed him from the shade of the porch with magnificent disdain.

"Did you see the prisoners being marched to the execution ground?" Denton asked, wondering what the coolie had thought about that, whether he too sympathised with them.

"Prisoners? What prisoners?"

Waiting for the passengers from the American ship to disembark, he saw Jones going through the gate to the Customs offices. He glanced away at once, but Jones waved.

"Hello, what are you doing here?" he greeted Denton cheerily. "Long time no see."

"I'm waiting for someone," Denton answered coolly.

"Oh, waiting for someone, are you? I've just come back from leave, bought myself a little house in Kent. You knew old Tibby Mason'd left the Service, didn't you? Got his own estate agency now."

"Yes?"

"Doing pretty well too, I believe. Of course he's got his fingers into quite a number of pies, old Tibby. What are you doing?"

"Nothing much." Denton recalled that last evening at the Customs Officers' mess and Mason's triumphantly vindictive glare. He gazed over Jones' shoulder stiffly.

Jones frowned slightly, his hand rising to finger his weedy moustache with a gesture that Denton instantly recalled. "Nothing much?" he asked uncertainly. "You must be doing something. I see that little piece you used to have is getting a bit of a name for herself, isn't she?"

"She's doing all right."

Jones' frown deepened and he fingered his moustache again. "Not very chatty, are you?"

"I have no reason to be."

"It wasn't me that got you eased out of the Service, you know! You needn't look at me like that."

"Well, who was it, then?"

"How the hell should I know?" Jones' light skin, not yet tanned again by the Shanghai sun, darkened sullenly. "Well, I see it's a waste of time talking to you," he muttered and moved abruptly away.

Denton watched him go, his long-dormant resentment mingling with an irritatingly guilty sense that he'd taken it out on the wrong person. He turned to look at the first passengers arriving.

There they were, wide-eyed, expectant, pleased, bemused, searching, anxious. Friends went forward raising hats. Touts clustered round the ones that looked lost. Denton took out the photograph Mr. Larsen had prudently sent him and studied it once more. Grey hair, full face with straight, thin lips, and a pince-nez, he recited to himself for the tenth time, and looked up to scrutinise the faces one by one.

A man with a face that marched the description, yet somehow didn't resemble the two-dimensional photograph, came through the hall. He was peering round anxiously and questioning the porter, who carried his cases in stolid silence. A pince-nez dangled on the black cord from his neck. Behind him, a young woman with short, fluffy fair hair followed another porter, gazing coolly about her. Larsen had said he was bringing his wife, but that couldn't be his wife—she was no older than Denton. He looked down at the photograph again doubtfully, and, when he looked up, the young woman was pointing at him while the man fumbled for his pince-nez.

Denton stepped forward. "Mr. Larsen?"

"Yes." He dropped his pince-nez, his face sunny with relief. "Mr. Denton? How do you do, sir. Pleased to meet you. This is my daughter, Mary-Ellen."

Mary-Ellen put out her hand and smiled frankly. "How do you do, Mr. Denton?" she said in a low, relaxed voice that seemed unconsciously to mock her father's nervousness. Her eyes, Denton noticed, were very wide and blue.

"My wife's mother passed away, so my wife wasn't able to come with me," Mr. Larsen was saying eagerly, little flecks of saliva on his lower lip.

"Oh, I'm sorry."

"Thank you, sir. She was a fine old lady, ninety-five years old."

"Ninety-five?"

"I brought Mary-Ellen in her mother's place. She's just graduated from Wellesley." His pale watery eyes gleamed proudly. "She's very interested in China, she took some courses."

"Is it always as hot as this?" Mary-Ellen asked as they both turned to look at her.

"No, it's just the summer. I've booked rooms for you at the Palace Hotel. Is this all your luggage?"

Mr. Larsen pressed his pince-nez onto his nose again and counted the pieces twice while his daughter smiled at his fussiness.

Denton arranged for the cases to be taken to the hotel and turned back to them. "Would you like to go by car, cab, or rickshaw? It isn't far."

"I think I'll take a rickshaw," Mary-Ellen said firmly.

"Well, what do you think, Mr. Denton?" Larsen asked dubiously. "Are those things safe?"

They settled, or Mary-Ellen settled, on two rickshaws.

221

Mary-Ellen declared she'd go in one while the two men talked business in the other. Larsen gave in after some hesitant, fond murmurs, on condition that she travelled in the front one, where they could keep an eye on her and see she didn't get lost.

Denton pointed out the main buildings on the Bund and Larsen retailed their names in a loud voice to his daughter. "That's the British Consulate, Mary-Ellen! That's the Hong Kong and Shanghai Bank—the one with the lions outside it. And that's Jardine's, a very big company!"

Denton left them to unpack, arranging to call for Larsen at seven. "Mr. Wei has invited you to dinner. I hope you like Chinese food?"

"Never tried it," Larsen said with a game smile.

"I have," Mary-Ellen said. "I like it."

Denton hesitated.

"Oh." Her eyebrows rose in two fair arches. "D'you mean I'm not invited?"

"I'm sure it can be arranged," Denton said awkwardly. "Only I'm afraid you'll be the only lady there."

"Oh, Mary-Ellen wouldn't want that," Larsen began.

"I wouldn't mind at all," Mary-Ellen smiled composedly. "If it's not too much trouble, Mr. Denton?"

Larsen accompanied him to the door, lowering his voice. "Say, Mr. Denton, could you give me a lead on how to deal with these Chinese?"

"Oh, Wei speaks pretty good English," Denton answered vaguely.

"I mean about etiquette and so forth?" Larsen pressed his pince-nez onto the bridge of his nose and blinked through the lenses nervously.

"Well, they're, er..." He paused, nonplussed. What *were* they like? "They're rather formal and reserved at first."

Larsen nodded slowly, taking this in, it seemed. The lenses of his pince-nez were thick, magnifying his eyes behind them. They were the same colour as his daughter's, only milder. "Are Chinese allowed here in the hotel?"

"Well, no, not normally," Denton said uncomfortably. "The two races tend to live separately except when they're actually doing business," he went on quickly, as though it was as much the Chinese who didn't want to enter the hotels as the Europeans who kept them out.

Larsen was still blinking and nodding as he digested

222

what Denton had said. He brought his face closer to Denton's, so that Denton felt compelled to step back a pace. "We have a similar situation in the United States," he said understandingly at last.

"It's quite common for Europeans to eat in the better-class Chinese restaurants." Denton assured him.

"Europeans?"

"I mean white men. To the Chinese we're all Europeans."

"Well, I certainly am looking forward to meeting this Mr. Wei," Larsen said. "And doing business, hey?"

"Goodbye for now, Mr. Denton," Mary-Ellen called out in her low, assured tones.

Passing through the lobby, Denton met Jacob Ephraim coming in. He was sweating and vexed, mopping his face with a mauve silk handkerchief. "That cursed motor car has broken down again," he spluttered vehemently. "I told him not to buy it! I said the Chinese know nothing about such machines, they'll break it in no time, I said! But no, my stupid, obstinate father-in-law must always know best! And this is the second time this week! Does the driver know what to do? Pah! He's never seen an engine before in his whole life! A farm boy, a peasant! He's probably lighting a joss stick beside it now. I tell you," he gripped Denton's arm forcefully, "motor cars will not last in China. We have rickshaws and barrows and cabs and sedan chairs— what do we want motor cars for? The Chinese can't handle complicated machinery, you mark my words. I know, I've seen the Russians. Come and have a drink."

Denton shook his head. "I can't, Jacob, I've got to get back to the office."

"Ah, that reminds me." Jacob glanced round, then leant close to Denton's ear. "I have a tip for you. Buy shares in Isaacson Mills. You'll double your money in a week. I've bought a thousand. They're going to be taken over by Jardine's; their shares will go up like a rocket when the news gets out. Buy today, as soon as you can. Tomorrow may be too late." Glistening little beads of sweat were still forming on his forehead and he looked up at the fans reproachfully, as though they were deliberately shirking. "I hate those things, always too slow or too fast. The old punkahs were much better. Did I tell you Sarah is expecting again? This time it'll be a boy. Come and have a drink."

His grip tightened on Denton's arm and his glowing brown eyes urged him towards their usual table.

"No, I must arrange things with Wei." Denton detached himself firmly. "We've got an important buyer here. Congratulations, though."

"Don't forget that tip." Jacob let his arm go unwillingly. "I wouldn't tell everyone. Keep it to yourself."

Denton warned Wei about the complication of Larsen's daughter and, as an afterthought, asked him about Isaacson Mills. Wei too had heard the rumour. On a giddy impulse, before he'd had time to consider it carefully—indeed, to avoid considering it at all—Denton picked up the telephone that he'd had installed only a few weeks ago at the opening of the Shanghai Telephone Company's first exchange, and instructed his bank to buy fifty thousand dollars' worth of Isaacson shares. When he hung the mouthpiece up, his hand felt limp and unsteady. *I mustn't think about it,* he thought. *That's half my savings. I mustn't think about it.*

Ah King had laid his clothes out on the bed. When he'd bathed and dressed, he went down onto the veranda and called for a whisky. She brought it on a tray, as he'd taught her, with a jug of iced water. "Any messages?" he asked.

"No messages."

"None from Miss Su-mei?"

She shook her head dourly. "No messages."

Su-mei had been right—or perhaps she'd made herself right. The two women hadn't taken to each other. "Miss Su-mei has broken a cup," Ah King would say with an immobile face, her eyes gazing blankly into his. Or, "Has Miss Su-mei taken the silver letter-opener? I can't find it." And Su-mei for her part would ignore Ah King or else speak to her cuttingly, curtly requesting more tea or another pillow for the bed. "Why don't you get rid of her?" she would demand after a silent, inconclusive struggle between them. "She's so sullen. Look at my amah." But he wouldn't let Ah King go. She was loyal, honest, hard-working—and not sullen at all, except about Su-mei, whom she plainly considered to be merely a sing-song girl. One day, her frowning brow seemed to promise, Denton would tire of Su-mei; and then Ah King would have the pleasure of shutting the door in her face. She was proud of Denton's prosperity, too, from which she got, every Chinese New Year, her own percentage as good luck money and a rise in salary. But she grudged the money he spent on Su-mei. "One day you'll be sorry," she muttered once when she saw a silver bracelet he'd bought for her. It was the nearest they came to a quarrel. Apart from the matter of Su-mei, where each had learned to tread softly, they never disagreed. She had become indispensable to him, providing meals, dealing with workmen, tradesmen and beggars, bargaining with his money at the market and running his house as if it were her own. She never mentioned the shotgun incident near Soochow, when they first set eyes on each other. But he was sure she remembered it.

"No messages," she said again stolidly, in a tone that suggested he had no right to expect any.

'If Miss Su-mei's amah comes, tell her I may call after dinner, if it doesn't get too late."

Ah King barely nodded as she turned away. Su-mei's amah was never allowed even into the kitchen.

He drank his whisky slowly, watching the darkness filling the sky as the sunset faded. In a few minutes it was all over and the cicadas were beginning their incessant nightly chirping. A bat flitted the length of the veranda. A mosquito whined by his ear and he felt them biting his ankles. He got up to go. "Ah King," he called out. "Light a mosquito coil in the bedroom."

She didn't answer, but a man's voice sounded in the kitchen. Denton pushed the door open curiously. The man turned. Denton recognized him at once; tall, stern, a little heavier than before, but otherwise unchanged. It was Ah King's husband. He had not appeared once at the house in the last three years, and Ah King had never mentioned him, evading Denton's occasional questions with vague, laconic answers. Denton had assumed he'd left her.

They looked at each other for some seconds. It was disconcerting, the way he didn't lower his eyes but simply stared straight back unsmilingly at you. And he remembers too, Denton thought.

"So you're back," he said at last.

"Yes."

"Been to sea?"

"Many places." He hadn't learned to speak the Shang-

225

hai dialect as well as Ah King. He still had his Soochow accent.

"Are you going again soon?"

"Next week."

Denton nodded. There was nothing more to say. The man wasn't exactly hostile, but indifferent to him. It made him feel obscurely an intruder in his own house. He turned to Ah King, who was watching him uneasily, as if her husband's brusqueness unsettled her too. "Your husband can stay here with you until he goes again," he said.

She nodded and murmured her thanks, still uneasy and constrained, and he left without looking at the man again. He would have stayed whether I'd said that or not, he thought as he went to the door. What a boor. I should really have thrown him out.

But he knew that was a fantasy. He couldn't have told him to go.

The dinner was a success. Wei had ordered bland Peking food in the best private room of his own restaurant, and Larsen, who'd confided to Denton on the way there that he had a sensitive stomach, ate it with relish. Only the wine he refused—not for his stomach's sake, he explained, but for his soul's. Denton had to expound his puzzling notion to Wei in Chinese, who smiled sympathetically and clucked his tongue while a faint vagueness passed over his eyes. Wei was courtly and bland himself, and when he mentioned he was thinking of sending his oldest son to an American university, Larsen was completely won over. Wei's brother smiled amicably and occasionally interpolated giggling remarks about Larsen's spotted tie and dangling pince-nez, which Wei freely translated into complimentary phrases. They both treated Mary-Ellen with distant politeness, a distance less of reserve than of caution, as though the low-voiced foreign woman who lolled so unconcernedly in her chair were some mysterious and unpredictable animal. So it was Denton who, as he'd hoped, had to entertain her. She listened with a lazy, amused smile to his account of life in Shanghai and China, and asked him to show her how to use chopsticks, which she'd only tried once before, while her father, after one clumsy attempt, fed himself with a spoon. All the time, Wei was subtly complimenting Larsen, deferring to his views and diligently playing on his foibles. Denton was intrigued to

226

see how easily Wei seemed to be manipulating the American. Was that how he'd manipulated Denton himself when he got him to act as his agent? The wine fumes were misting his mind, and he refused to think about it. Anyway, it didn't matter now. At the end of the meal, Mary-Ellen took out a cigarette and lit it, despite her father's whispered remonstrances. "Why, all the girls did it at college," she drawled, pushing back her chair and crossing her legs. "It's not as though it's opium." She smiled a slow collusive smile at Denton as the four men and the waiters gazed wonderingly at her. It was the first time he'd ever seen a woman smoking a cigarette, and it seemed somehow shocking, although many Chinese women smoked pipes.

Arranging to take Larsen to visit the Wei's new and more imposing premises on Nanking Road the next morning, Denton wished them both goodnight at the hotel. He let his glance linger a moment on Mary-Ellen's face. She looked back at him with ironic amusement, as if to say, You and I understand this is all a joke, don't we? The corners of her eyes crinkled slightly with her smile and she ran her fingers through her short fluffy hair. As he turned away a shade of regret passed over his mind at the thought that she would be leaving Shanghai in a few weeks' time.

Two chair coolies were outside the hotel, and he treated himself to a ride home with them instead of going by rickshaw. The springy, swaying motion of the chair lulled him, and he closed his eyes, listening to the slap-slap of their feet on the ground and the creaking of the wood, almost as though he were in a boat. When they put him down in Jessfield Road, he gave the panting bearers a large tip and sauntered into the house with a warm feeling of contentment lying over his tiredness like a comforting eiderdown.

"Miss Su-mei came," Ah King said, grimacing as she bolted the door behind him. "She wanted the opium pipe."

"Oh?"

"I said I didn't know where it was."

"It's in the cupboard in the bedroom," he frowned. "You know very well."

"Well, if she'd taken it," Ah King muttered, tacitly

227

admitting she'd known perfectly well where it was, "she might not have brought it back."

"Oh rubbish." He climbed up the stairs, ignoring her murmured protests, determined not to let her ruffle his contentment. The hot air was still and heavy in the house—he was sweating again by the time he'd reached the top landing. All the same, he thought as he pulled off his limp clothes, he didn't like Su-mei to use opium by herself. That was how you became addicted. So perhaps it wasn't so bad that Ah King hadn't let her have the pipe, after all.

He lay down naked under the mosquito netting. The sheet had absorbed the sultry moistness of the air, he could smell it as he turned and lay on his side. As sleep dragged him heavily downwards, he heard Ah King moaning rhythmically in the servants' quarters, the muffled sounds floating in through the open windows. He half-woke, then let sleep pull him downwards again. It was probably her husband driving into her to produce an heir. Like every good Chinese. His last drowsy thought was whether he'd ever have an heir himself.

37

He spent most of the next few weeks with the Larsens, arranging business, at which Larsen proved to be after all as shrewd as Wei, or taking them round the city and the surrounding countryside. Mary-Ellen bought a hand-painted parasol, which he bargained for on her behalf, a jade necklace and antique pieces—vases, bowls and carvings which Denton had to confess he knew nothing about. "She took a course in Oriental Art at Wellesley," Mr. Larsen explained with mingled pride and perplexity. "But how you tell the good from the bad in all that stuff I really don't know." They went to the Episcopalian church, though Mary-Ellen protested idly, "I don't believe a word of it, I never go at home," and they called at the American Consulate. The rest of the time they spent with Denton, sometimes with Wei there, sometimes alone. Larsen's sightseeing was stolid and dutiful, but Mary-Ellen viewed everything, especially the antique shops, which Denton had rarely visited before, with a detached, quizzical fascination. Even the squalid and festering canals in the slums of the Chinese city, even the scabby hordes of beggars that swooped down on them, attracted her in a way. "I know it's terrible, but they do look kind of picturesque," she said in her languid drawl, while her father anxiously warned her to hold onto her bag. Coming back from a dinner at Wei's restaurant one night, the rickshaw coolies took them nonchalantly down a street of brothels and opium divans near the harbour. Larsen stared round him in speechless, embarrassed shock, but Mary-Ellen looked back at Denton and laughed. "They say New Orleans is like this," she said. "I'd love to see it." Her father's ears seemed to grow red—even the back of his neck.

On the evening of the second day, Wei had drawn Denton aside and asked whether Mr. Larsen would like a sing-song girl. He could have one sent to the restaurant or to his hotel room. Or perhaps Mr. Larsen would prefer to try some opium and visit the street of the flower girls—or the girls on the boats? "I'm not sure he's interested in that kind of thing," Denton had advised tactfully. "In any case, not with his daughter here." Wei's raised brows had registered his surprise. Wouldn't a daughter want her father to be given pleasure? he seemed to be mutely asking. And why should her father care what she thought anyway? Wasn't it enough that he fed and clothed her? Wei had two wives, and he found the married lives of Europeans mysterious. "Why is it that in the west a man cannot take a concubine?" he asked puzzledly. "What is the harm?"

"Well, if that Sun Yat-sen succeeds in getting western ideas into China, it may happen here too."

Wei smiled incredulously and shook his head. "Only useful western ideas," he murmured with assurance, scratching his cheek with his long curved finger nail.

Denton gave a farewell dinner for the Larsens at Jessfield Road, on the evening before they left for Peking. Ah King had cleaned and polished all day. In the evening she put on her best white tunic and black trousers. In deference to the foreign visitors, she also put on black cloth slippers instead of going barefoot as she usually did during the heat of summer. She lit mosquito coils in every room and also insisted on spraying the visitors' ankles with paraffin when they entered the porch, on which she'd hung orange and yellow lanterns. But Denton wouldn't let her fasten muslin bags on the guests' feet as well, although she'd bought some from Whiteaway Laidlaw's on Nanking Road, near the Weis' new office.

Mary-Ellen tried to thank her in Chinese, lifting her skirt when Ah King sprayed her ankles. Ah King looked up with an uncomprehending but not displeased glimmer in her eyes. The smoke from the mosquito coils curled upwards in heavy flat blue layers, lightly scented. "Are they joss sticks?" Mary-Ellen asked, and laughed at herself, showing her regular white teeth, when she discovered her mistake.

Wei came on the stroke of eight, and the Ephraims, in their newly-repaired motor car, at a quarter past. Sarah Ephraim looked fat and placid, her arms heavy with diamonds and silver. Jacob nudged Denton. "Have you seen how Isaacson shares are going up?" he whispered. "Sell next week, they've gone too high."

"Pity you couldn't bring your wife with you, Mr. Wei," Larsen said heartily.

"Which one?" Jacob muttered, while Wei smiled and shook his head sheepishly. "In China, wifes stay at home," he said. "Beside, she is not quite suitable for foreign meal, since she does not spea' English."

A cook from Wei's restaurant prepared the food, but Ah King served it, while Denton poured the French wine he'd ordered from Watson's—Ah King, so reliable in other ways, often confused the glasses and filled tumblers with wine, wine glasses with water. Larsen still refused wine, but Mary-Ellen took half a glass, ignoring her father's hushed reproaches. Jacob drank nothing but vodka, and as the sweat began to bead on his forehead, became more and more eloquent about the future of China, a future in which European Shanghai was to play the dominant role. "An economic zone along the Yangtze river, under western control," he declared. "That's the first step."

"How do you know so much abou' China, Mr. Ephrai'?" Wei asked curiously, when Jacob paused to drink. "You must read a lo' of Chinese book' and spea' to many Chinese people?"

Jacob could neither read nor write Chinese and his spoken Shanghainese was almost unintelligible—as Wei well knew. But Jacob was not at all abashed. "No need to read what Chinese books say, they know nothing about it," he answered off-handedly. "You people don't understand economics. It's not in your history, any more than it is in

230

the Russians'. That's why the Japanese beat you both so easily."

Wei's smile stayed unchanged while his pale skin darkened beneath it.

"Economics," Jacob said. "Organisation! That's what you need!"

"Would anyone like some more wine?" Denton asked hastily.

They were drinking their coffee in the cooler air of the veranda when Ah King called Denton in an urgent sibilant whisper.

"Miss Su-mei," Ah King said stonily, jerking her head sideways towards the dining-room. "I said you were busy, but she won't go away."

Su-mei stood by the open window, looking out. Behind her the table was still littered with the forlorn and stale debris of the meal. Perhaps she'd deliberately turned her back on it, he thought as he went in.

She glanced round when she heard his steps. Her eyes glittered and her face was set, as if she were crying.

"What is it?" he asked anxiously in Chinese.

"What is it? What is it?" she echoed him fiercely. "I wait for you for weeks, I send my amah and she is told you are too busy with a foreign woman to see me, you will not even let me have the opium pipe, and now you keep me waiting like a servant! And you ask me what is it!"

He saw it was not tears glittering in her eyes, but rage. "But I couldn't see you, Su-mei," he said in a low, tense voice. "I had these people to look after—not just a woman. Who kept you waiting anyway? Not me!"

"Pah!" she blew out her lips in disbelief. "And why do you hide the opium pipe? Who is this foreign woman?"

"She's the man's daughter—a businessman, I've told you already!" He was angry himself now, angry because he felt guilty after all for enjoying Mary-Ellen's company even though he couldn't have avoided it. "And the opium pipe is in the cupboard in the bedroom. I told Ah King she should have let you have it."

"Ha! Ah King does what you tell her!"

"Not always."

"Get rid of her then!" she said triumphantly, catching him in her trap.

He glanced back at the half-open door, through which he could hear the broken murmur of their conversation

231

on the veranda. If he could hear them, they must be able to hear Su-mei and him. "Look, I must go back to them," he said, lowering his voice. "I'll come and see you tonight when they're all gone. I'll bring the pipe. I can't talk to you now."

"No, of course not! I'm not the kind of woman you can have in your house when your friends are here!"

"Quiet, Su-mei! Please!"

Her eyes flashed at him, angry and bitter. "I don't want you to come tonight. You stay with your friends!"

"Get out!" He was surprised himself at the hissing venom that had rushed into his voice. "Don't you dare come here making scenes like this again! I certainly won't come tonight!"

She glared at him a moment, then tilted her chin and stalked past him on her golden sandals, her heels clicking loudly on the floor. He saw Ah King watching from the hall, a grim vindictive glint in her usually tolerant eyes. "Ah King, why aren't you looking after the guests?" he asked sharply. She turned, half-smiling, her shiny, plaited queue quivering with pleasure, it seemed, as she went out to the veranda.

He watched Su-mei from the window as she walked swiftly down the path to her waiting chair with its yellow lantern. And already, as the bearers hoisted the poles, he felt another twinge of guilt for his neglect of her over the past weeks. Not that he could have been with her anyway, but she'd simply gone out of his mind—he'd scarcely thought of her at all. Still, she couldn't go on making scenes like that, he excused himself as he walked back to the veranda. Perhaps Wei was right—women with bound feet couldn't come storming up at you, they had to sit and wait.

When all the guests had gone and Ah King was silently clearing away the last scattered cups and saucers, he hesitated, drawn to Su-mei in spite of everything. But no, he mustn't give in, he must let her know who was master. After all, where would she have been now without him, if he hadn't protected her from Pock-mark Chen?

Yet still he wavered. The thought of lying beside her and smoking opium, then stroking her languidly till the desire rose—

"Where is your husband?" he asked Ah King abruptly.

"Gone away again."

"Already?"

"Already." She picked up a cup from the floor by the chair where Mary-Ellen had sat. "Are you going out, or shall I lock up?" she asked with exaggerated casualness.

"Lock up." Then angry at her unconcealed smile of satisfaction, he snapped at her over his shoulder as he left the room, "And who told you to say I'd gone out with a foreign woman?"

"If you were out with the foreign woman," he heard her muttering as he stamped up the stairs, "why shouldn't I say so? Nothing to be ashamed of in that, it's only natural."

38

The next morning he woke up tired and sluggish, a deep throbbing ache above his left eye, a queasy feeling of distaste and nausea in his stomach. He should have gone to Su-mei, he thought repentantly as he shaved himself bleary-eyed before the mirror. But then why should he? She would just have to understand that she couldn't behave like that and get away with it. And yet, as he splashed the remaining lather off his face, round his ears and cheek-bones, he thought how appealing that fierceness in her eyes had been. Then he thought of Mary-Ellen's wide blue eyes and ironic detached smile. Well, he would let Su-mei wait a little, anyway.

His coffee tasted bitter to him and he left half the cup undrunk. The sun seemed fiercer than ever as he accompanied the Larsens to the North Station, and the throbbing in his head was getting worse, pounding right through his skull so that he could hardly bring himself to answer their last questions and thanks. He turned in relief, even from Mary-Ellen's casually amiable wave as the train began to clank out of the station and the steam, seething up from the boiler, let out a sudden head-splitting shriek. He called a chair, then changed his mind and clambered heavily into a rickshaw. The faster ride on wheels seemed suddenly imperative for his sore, pounding head.

"Kwangtsao Road," he told the coolie; but then the office, now that he visualised it, seemed far too hard and hot for him, he didn't see how he could get any work done that day. "No, Jessfield Road," he called out, and let his tired lids close as soon as he saw the coolie's head nod. How could the man run bare-headed in the sun all day? he wondered. How could he stand it? A case of have to, he supposed as he slumped wearily back against the struts of the canopy.

His head was definitely getting worse, the hammer blows thudding more and more powerfully. Perhaps he was in the sun? But when he opened his eyes he saw that the canopy was safely over his head. Yet still the light seemed unbearably bright all round him, bright and burning as if he were in a furnace, while all the other people teeming in the alley seemed cool and dim, watching from dark shadowy distances while he alone was pulled through the incandescent merciless heat.

Then he felt the uneasiness in his stomach becoming turbulent, a sudden wave of nausea wallowing up his throat. He swallowed and forced it down again, closing his lids. But it came back, stronger than before, irresistible. He lurched forward as the nausea swept a dizzy greyness over his eyes. He knew he had to get his head between his knees, but the greyness made him feel faint and he felt himself reeling. He opened his eyes frantically, looking for something to hold on to, but everything was giddy now, tumbling hazily round him. He had one definite, detached vision of the coolie's bony feet trotting impersonally between the shafts, then of the spokes whirling round on the wheels, and then the greyness became a blinding white mist and though he knew he was falling he had no fear, no feeling at all except the desire for that terrible shuddering quake of nausea that was convulsing his stomach to be over and finished with so that he could breathe again.

He tumbled out of the rickshaw and pitched onto the road, hearing his head thump painlessly on the stones.

The coolie jerked to a stop, lowered his shafts and stared. A crowd quickly gathered to gaze down at the sprawling, unconscious foreign devil. Women hawkers in black trousers and tunics, still holding their notched bamboo scales, left their stalls to examine him, coolies with their carrying poles still swaying from their springy stride stopped and stared down with dispassionate curiosity, beggars with grimy hands and keen eyes shuffled forward, children scraped their bare toes in the dust.

"Is he dead?" the rickshaw coolie asked. "He hasn't paid me."

"Where was he going?" an old woman with a missing tooth asked.

"Jessfield Road. I started by the station."

The woman shook her grey head slowly, gazing calculatingly down at the foreign devil, whose face was bleeding from where he fell. "You've taken him more than half-way. How much did you ask?"

The coolie didn't answer. Suppose the foreign devil was dead? Then there'd be the police, and he'd be in trouble as he hadn't paid this year's licence fee yet. But if the foreign devil wasn't dead, he might get a reward for taking him on. On the other hand, he must have money on him—perhaps fifty dollars. He could go through his pockets somewhere on the way. He visualised the bamboo grove by the Bubbling Well cemetery. But if the man was dead, he'd best get going while he could.

"Perhaps it's cholera," another woman suggested.

"Do foreign devils get cholera?"

If it's cholera, I'm not touching him, the rickshaw coolie decided. He backed slowly away and lifted his smooth, worn shafts.

Suddenly the foreign devil moved. He hauled himself up onto his hands and knees, gasping heavily, and started retching. The nearest people shifted their feet back a little, watching expectantly.

Denton became intermittently aware of their feet, brown, bare, calloused and dirty, as he shuddered with spasm after spasm, spitting and panting between each paroxysm. He was cold and shivering although he knew remotely that the sun was burning on his back. Chilly drops of sweat were weeping on his forehead. His jacket and shirt were soiled and he could smell the vomit on his hands. He tried to get up after a while, but his legs were too wobbly and he sank down again. "Call a doctor," he wanted to say, but he couldn't get a word out—his voice was nothing but harsh fetid breath gasping against the roof of his mouth. He let himself droop onto the ground again and lay there with eyes closed, panting, while the distant, curious voices muttered round him.

Then some time later, it might have been a few minutes or half an hour, he heard a woman's voice speaking Chinese with an English accent. "What is wrong?" the voice was asking crisply, reminding him of starched aprons and the smell of newly-ironed laundry. "Where does he live?" With one last effort of his fading strength, he raised his head once more and saw a plump, sunburned English face, bare-headed, with flat fair hair that seemed to be white-hot in the sun. The woman's blue eyes looked terribly pale, he thought, in that sunburned face. He'd never seen eyes of such a pale blue before. His eyes closed and he felt his head drop. "Where d'you live?" the woman asked matter-of-factly, laying her hand on his forehead. "Can you hear me? Where do you live?"

"Forty-six Jessfield Road," he got out in a hoarse whisper, before the world went grey and he fainted again.

He was conscious intermittently, between long periods of nothingness. He knew he was being heaved into a rickshaw, and that his feet were dragging along the ground as they lifted him in. He heard the woman's crisp cheerful voice again, but not what she was saying. And then there was the kaleidoscope of brilliant, fierce heat and sudden shade, thrown by the sunlight on the thin membranes of his lids as his head lolled back and the rickshaw limped and jolted along past buildings and trees.

Then he was being lifted out and he saw Ah King's face peering down at him with startled, anxious eyes, and he thought he'd never seen her show any emotion towards him before. But then everything went achingly black again until he was lying on the bed and the Englishwoman's voice was calling out "Water! Quickly! Towels!" and hands were fumbling with his clothes, pushing and pulling him like a sack. "It's only a touch of the sun," he muttered thickly, or thought he did, but nobody answered.

He dozed. His head was burning, his eyelids were sore. When he woke up, though, he was shivering and the retching started again. His stomach twisted and quivered, but he had no more to throw up. Yet still his stomach cramped and convulsed itself until a few reluctant threads of yellowish watery liquid were flung out of his mouth. His head fell back on the pillow and, breathing quick, shallow pants of relief, he closed his eyes again.

"It's cholera," he heard a man's voice declaring later, an irritable voice that sounded vaguely familiar.

His eyes drifted open. It was Dr. McEwan bending over him, holding his limp wrist and frowning down at him with that same impatient expression on his whisky-flushed face. Light seemed to blaze behind his head as though Denton were still lying in the open on the ground. He winced and closed his eyes.

"Aye, it's cholera, I don't doubt. Where've you been eating, man?" McEwan demanded accusingly. "What's that over there? A cholera belt? Useless! Throw it away!"

Denton heard Ah King's voice then, and the blithe, precise tones of the Englishwoman. McEwan began speaking again, but now his voice seemed quieter. Denton slipped away into a feverish sleep. But though he slept, he seemed to be aware of his body all the time, burning, dry and burning. He felt he was a shrivelling leaf curled up in a baking oven. He could feel the heat scorching all round him.

And through the heat he knew there was something he had to do, something important, but he couldn't remember what it was...

For several days he lay in a delirious trance, vomiting and soiling his bed. His lips blistered, his tongue grew dry and harsh, his skin burned and his body ached and shuddered, growing feebler and feebler as it wasted away. Night and day the bamboo blinds were drawn and he was intermittently aware of the dazzling slatted sunlight on his eyes in the morning and the quieter light of the afternoon. Sometimes he half-woke when the room was nearly dark, and he heard the low hiss of the gas lamp in the ceiling. Occasionally voices came to him over immeasurable distances, McEwan's, curt and irascible, the strange, cheerful Englishwoman's, Ah King's low mutter and the quiet murmur of Su-mei's tones. Sometimes, when they had sponged him down or raised his head to spoon in some liquid, against which his racked stomach knotted in shocked but weak revolt, his lids fluttered open and he saw Su-mei's face hovering over him, her hair hanging forward round her cheeks. But his eyes felt like glass and it was as though he saw her through a thick window which swiftly darkened. He understood he had cholera and he thought of "Old Smithy" whose rooms he'd had in his first days in Shanghai. Was he going to die too? He was too feeble to be afraid. The questions seemed not to concern him, he was already so distant from life. Would they auction his things? He dreamt he was telling Su-mei she could have the opium pipe for herself. And the button off his uniform that he always kept in his right pocket, she could have that too for good luck. But then it seemed to be Mary-Ellen Larsen he was telling, not Su-mei...

And all the time something kept nagging at the edge of his mind. There was something he had to do, but he couldn't remember what it was. Something terribly important...

On the fifth day he stopped vomiting and his heavy lids opened to see clearly at last. He was alone in the room, his body no longer burning, but sweating gently onto the sheets. It must be evening, he thought, the light was dim and he could smell the scent of a mosquito coil, heavy and fragrant. He gazed weakly at the dimming sky through the irregular slats of the blinds. On the white ceiling above him, a tjik-tjak clung motionless, its green tail slightly curled. He could see its bulging little eyes and its flanks faintly, rapidly, moving as it breathed.

Denton slowly moved his hands and rested them on his own tired, sore flanks, as if to reassure himself that he too was breathing. Yes, his ribs did move in and out regularly, he must be getting better. He closed his eyes, smiling faintly.

He slept a long, dreamless sleep, waking to the sound of a spoon clinking against china. It was dark outside, the cicadas were chirping their incessant jarring notes, and the gas lamp was hissing above the bed, giving a soft dim light. He felt as if he'd just returned from a long journey.

"Drink this." It was Su-mei's voice. He turned his head slowly. She was sitting by the bed, stirring something in a bowl. It was one of the rice-pattern bowls. He gazed wonderingly at the translucent grain shapes in the porcelain, as though he'd never seen them before.

Su-mei smiled, holding the spoon to his lips.

"What is it?"

"Rice water."

He sucked it off the spoon while she supported his head in her cupped palm.

"More."

He shook his head faintly, but she eased another spoonful into his mouth. He sucked up the warm watery rice again and then a third time, until she let him slump back on the pillow.

"No more," he protested weakly, closing his eyes. He heard her clothes rustle as she moved, and then the gentle

238

chink of the bowl being put down. All these sounds, he thought. I haven't heard them for so long. It's as though I'd just been reborn. "How long have you been here?" he asked after a time. And the sound of his voice was strange and new too.

"Today? I've just come. No performance this evening."

He felt her hand take his on the sheet while she slowly stroked it with her fingertips. He smiled faintly. It was what she used to do when he lay exhausted after love.

"Remember?" she asked.

He nodded. "Don't stop."

Then it came to him, what he had to do, what had been troubling his mind all the time he'd been ill. The Isaacson shares! He opened his eyes and looked up at her. She was gazing at the window, smiling lightly as her fingers traced wandering paths across his skin. "How long have I been ill?" he asked.

"Nearly a week."

"What day is it?"

"Saturday." Her fingers were stroking his head. "Saturday evening."

His eyes closed exhaustedly again. "I should have sold some shares," he muttered despondently. "They've probably dropped." *Half my savings,* he thought.

"Isaacson shares? Ephraim sold them for you."

"Sold them for me?" He opened his eyes and frowned up at her. "What d'you mean?"

"Ephraim and I."

"How could you sell them? They were in my name."

"I copied your signature. Ephraim said you had to sell them, so he had Lo type a letter and I signed your name on it. I copied your signature thirty times first, then I signed the letter. Ephraim said they were nearly double what you paid for them."

"My god." He held her small hand a moment in his large but feeble grasp. Then his eyes closed and he fell asleep.

By the next morning he could sit up in the bed, propped against the pillows. Su-mei had gone, but Wei and Lo had visited him briefly and Ah King told him, in brief snatches while she cleaned the room, how he'd lived through the past week. A missionary Englishwoman had brought him

239

back with a rickshaw and sent for Dr. McEwan. Twice she had come to ask how he was, but not in the last three days.

"What was her name?"

Ah King shrugged, sweeping noisily in the far corner of the room. "She said she'd come back."

He listened to the broom-head knocking against the wall as she swept. How comforting it sounded. He let his lids close to listen to it better. He'd never realised how firm and comforting the simplest, most ordinary sounds could be. He felt the sweat gently dewing his face, and the mild dampness of his nightshirt against his body. How comforting that was too, to feel his body moist after all that scorching dryness of his fever.

Ah King was muttering in the corner. He opened his eyes. "What?"

She shook her head, making her queue twitch fiercely, then stopped sweeping to look at him sternly. "It's time you got married," she declared. "No wonder you get ill if you haven't got a wife."

"Marry Miss Su-mei?" he asked mischievously.

She snorted, turning her back to go on sweeping. "Not her. Chinese marry Chinese, foreign devils marry foreign devils."

"But she helped make me better."

She banged the broom hard against the wall without answering at first, then she turned to face him again, almost scowling. "She held your hand while I did the work," she said grimly.

"She did more than you think," he answered in a curt voice, then closed his eyes, pretending to be tired again. But as he lay there, the pretence became real. His lids really were heavy and his mind thickened. He dozed until she woke him with some more sloppy rice for lunch.

In the afternoon Dr. McEwan came. "Ye'll need to build yourself up," he said tersely after examining him. "It was a close-run thing."

"It shows what a good doctor you are," Denton smiled, lying weakly back on the pillows.

"That's as may be." He frowned as though Denton had insulted rather than flattered him. "And if ye believe that, perhaps it'll make it easier for you to pay the higher fees I'll be charging you from now on." His tone seemed to hold Denton responsible for the increase. "But no doubt with your killings on the stock market," he went on testily, "ye'll find it easy enough to pay them anyway." A warm breath of whisky wafted over Denton's face.

Su-mei came and sat with him every night when she wasn't performing, and every afternoon when she was. In the mornings Lo brought him the office mail and took his instructions. One day Jacob came briefly, standing by the door and speaking in uncharacteristically hushed and anxious tones, as though Denton's life were still in danger.

"I can't come any closer because of my family, much though I'd like to," he apologised. "it is possible to be infected just by breathing the air of the sickroom. Your shares are all right, eh?"

"Yes. Thank you for that, Jacob. It was very—"

"Well, if you'd died you wouldn't have needed the money, but I thought you might survive." Jacob spoke dubiously, suggesting a relapse was imminent.

"Yes, I'm much better now, so it was the right decision. I'm getting up tomorrow."

Jacob advanced a step into the room, pulling out a handkerchief which he held over his nose and mouth. "Don't get up until the doctor says so." The handkerchief made his voice sound muffled and adenoidal. "On no account get up—"

"He *has* said so."

"He has?" Jacob peered at him suspiciously. "Are you sure? You don't look strong enough to me. That can overstrain you, you know. The latest medical view is for a long convalescence after serious illness. It helps to avoid complications. I was reading an article only the other day. When did this MacQueen qualify?"

"McEwan."

"When did he qualify? They don't keep up when they come out here, they lose touch. You should tell him to read this article, it's in a German journal. Oh, and no women for six weeks. That's most important. No women for six weeks at least." He wagged his finger in warning as he retreated. "The orgasm is most debilitating, that has been absolutely proved. Absolutely. Not for six weeks now, remember. Not till you are strong enough to stand it."

It wasn't until he'd been up for two days that the missionary Englishwoman called again. He was sitting in the

241

living room, still too weak to walk about, while Ah King, trousers rolled up to her knees, swabbed the tiled veranda floor. She put her head round the door. "Missionary woman coming," she said grumblingly. "I can't let her in, my feet are all wet."

"Tell her to walk in. Call out from the veranda."

She called out peevishly, muttering to herself about people calling at all hours of the day, and went on splashing the water about noisily.

"Don't be bad-tempered," the Englishwoman's voice sang out cheerfully behind Denton. "I won't cause any trouble." Her Chinese had a strange inflection to it, apart from its English accent. As though she were singing a psalm, Denton thought.

"Well," she changed to English. "How are we today? Don't get up, you look as though you'd drop dead if you did. I think your amah's rather jealous of lady visitors, by the way."

Denton wouldn't have recognised this buxom, smiling woman, her face perspiring freely, as the one whose dimly-perceived head had bent over him against the blinding white of the sky after he'd fallen out of the rickshaw. Her face had the same sun-burned plumpness, the same light blue eyes, but he hadn't noticed the boyish smile then, the snub, freckled nose and the double chin that quivered like jelly when she laughed. But then he'd only had a glimpse, he reflected, before he passed out.

"It was very kind of you to help me the other day," he began awkwardly—awkward because the recollection of his incapacity was somehow humiliating to him.

"Two weeks ago," she laughed.

"Two weeks, then. I can't imagine what would've happened to me if you hadn't come along."

She sat down opposite him. "I expect you'd have been robbed and left to die," she said with a jolly laugh that set her chins shaking again. "But I'm glad to see you're better now. I knew it was cholera, of course, the minute I saw you lying there and puking."

"Did you? How?"

"Oh." She pulled a large handkerchief out of the pocket of her long plain dress and began unaffectedly drying her face with it as though it were a towel. "Lot of it about this year, you know. Five thousand dead in the Chinese city."

242

"Five thousand?"

"So I believe. But they still keep coming in. Place will burst at the seams soon. Is your amah a Christian by the way?"

"My amah? No. Why? Is Christianity a protection against cholera?"

"It has been for me," she said calmly. "You should talk to her about Our Lord."

Denton hesitated under the firm, still cheerful, gaze of her pale blue eyes. There was something disturbing about the assured directness, the light of conviction in them. "I'm afraid I'm not religious," he said almost apologetically. "Not any more."

"So I supposed." She stuffed her handkerchief back into her pocket. "But in that case you can't have been really religious in the first place." She looked at him quizzically. "I'll pray for you," she said with a smile that might have seemed ironic, but for the ingenuousness of her voice. "Pity to save your body if we can't save your soul. Bit of a waste. I'll pray for both of you."

Denton stirred uneasily under her steady gaze. The idea of her praying for him seemed vaguely threatening. He imagined her on her knees somewhere at night, her eyes screwed shut, concentrating all her energy on him while he slept, willing him to repent. "I'm sorry," he said suddenly. "I don't even know your name."

"Pulham, Janet Pulham. No, don't get up. You might die and it would be an awful waste if you hadn't been reborn." She got up herself and shook his hand with mock solemnity. "How do you do, Mr. Denton?" Her hand was firm, still moist with perspiration.

"How long have you been in Shanghai, Miss Pulham?"

"Oh, three and a half years. The Lord called me to do His work here." She made it sound as natural as an invitation from the British consul. "Which reminds me, I must be on my way." She pulled a watch out of her other pocket, the chain fastened to her dress by a safety pin.

"What kind of work is it exactly?"

"A mission for orphaned and abandoned children," she said, winding the watch. "Girl slaves too, when we can find them. You should come and see it. Number Thirteen, Canton Street. We need some money, by the way. It may be the Lord wants you to give us some." She got up, dropping the watch into her pocket again.

"Thirteen, Canton Street?" Denton repeated mechanically.

"It's called Jerusalem House. Ask any rickshaw for it. Only they call Jerusalem Chi Loo Sun. Funny, isn't it?"

She paused by the veranda, where the mop was still sploshing and swishing to and fro. "Ask your master to tell you about Jesus," she smiled at Ah King. "You'd be surprised what he knows."

Ah King looked up at her less dourly, resting on the mop a moment. She gazed consideringly into the frank, jolly eyes of the Englishwoman, then went back to work.

Miss Pulham turned to Denton. "Well, goodbye for now. No doubt we'll meet again soon. I'll pray for you, remember. I don't want to have saved your life for nothing. Oh, and that concubine of yours. I'll pray for her too. You'll have to marry her, you know. Or stop using her. It's against God's law, you know that, don't you? Goodbye. Thirteen, Canton Street. Don't forget, if you want to give money. Jerusalem House."

Ah King appeared with wet feet at the veranda door, wringing the mop out over the bucket.

"How does that woman know so much about me?" Denton asked.

Ah King shrugged. "Every time she came she asked so many questions." She gazed after Miss Pulham with the same considering, curious gaze, as if she were watching a weird new creature from some distant jungle.

39

It was as though the cholera had purged him of some ingrained cautiousness of spirit, some petty fear of large ambitions. As though the dark rush of death's wings when they passed him by had inspired him with a new energy, a new boldness—perhaps a new realisation that his time might be short. He was hardly recovered before he began to speculate on the stock exchange, encouraged by the success that Jacob Ephraim's tip had brought him. He had doubled his savings while he hung between life and death, and he took his recovery and his gains as an auspicious omen. This time he left only a quarter of his money on deposit at the bank, and bought more shares with the rest.

He recalled how, long ago, the Reverend Eaton's austere features had gleamed with a more human light when he spoke of the property he was buying in Hongkew. And Mason had started an estate agency when he left the Customs Service. Now Janet Pulham had mentioned the inflowing tide of immigrants into Shanghai from the surrounding province, a tide that anyone could see just by travelling through the lanes and alleys of the Chinese city.

Businesses were sprouting everywhere; factories and mills were opening every month, absorbing the flood of starving workers. Eaton and Mason had seen it coming, he realised. Land was the thing, it was bound to rise in value as it became scarcer. He consulted the Shanghai Desk Hong List, a plain red-covered annual that he'd always thought dull before, and sorted out the companies that owned property near the harbour. He obtained copies of their prospectuses and accounts and selected four companies with land along the river or on Soochow Creek. Without even asking Jacob's or Wei's advice, he bought heavily in the companies' shares. He confided only in Su-mei, and then only after he'd already bought them. "You were right," she said. "The fortune-teller said you'd be lucky."

It was the day the old Empress Dowager died in Peking, but that didn't shake her conviction. "She was a Manchu," she shrugged, "not a real Chinese. Their luck is different."

In two years the price of his shares quadrupled. He became rich without working and with his riches he became richer still. He turned now to the cotton mills, the silk factories, the wharves, the transport and telephone, gas and electricity companies. He invested in all of them, and in the hotels, and the construction companies that were building them. He invested three-quarters of his now substantial savings again, and, while the Weis' orders continued to increase his regular income, saw himself with the equivalent of ten thousand pounds a year from the interest on his shares alone. He had become rich, simply and immediately, just by having enough money to invest at the start—and by having the will to risk it, a will that his cholera seemed to have forged in him, like a flame that toughens soft metal. I worked harder in the Customs Service and at the beginning for Wei, he reflected as Su-mei prepared the opium for them one night in her apartment. And yet I would never have become rich by working hard. It was a fact anyone could see if they stopped to think about it; but it was one thing to see it abstractly and quite another to watch it working out in your own life. The experience disturbed him sometimes, especially when he passed those grim, bleak factories where workers could not earn in a lifetime of ten or twelve hours a day what he got from his shares in a year. There was something flawed in the world, his puritanical conscience whispered, if money could grow simply from money, and not from work. But the uneasiness passed, leaving only a smudge on the calm skies of freedom and security that his wealth had given him. When Su-mei lay down beside him and handed him the pipe, he was thinking already that he would stick out for a flat fifteen per cent commission from Wei when he made his next contract.

He inhaled and passed it back to her. Soon they were drifting off into that emptiness in which the world and all its flaws was for a time annihilated.

He bought a house on the Bund, not far from the British Consulate, and let his other one to a Baghdad Jew who traded in opium. The new house was larger, and Ah King, with a year old son now, recruited a gardener and a makee-learnee amah to help her. The gardener, Cheong, was one of her cousins from Soochow; he never came inside the house except to eat and sleep, preferring the space and solitude of the garden. For months Denton never heard him talk; it was as though he was as dumb as the plants and trees amongst which he spent his life. When, one autumn morning, he asked Denton if he could buy some more glazed flower pots, it was as though he'd broken a vow of silence.

The new amah was a hollow-cheeked girl with timid eyes. Ah King brought her in to Denton, speaking pidgin English to impress her in just the way Ah Koo had spoken pidgin when he brought Ah King to the squalid tenement in Bubbling Well Road.

"My cousin number three girl," she introduced her, pushing her forward.

"Where from?"

"Ningpo more far." Ah King glanced at her disparagingly. "Makee-learnee. Very cheap, I teach. Other one know too much, I no likee, not workee same-same me, cost too many money. This one cheap, I teach, everything right."

The girl waited with anxious, downcast eyes, stealing occasional shy glances at Denton or Ah King.

"What did she do before?" Denton asked.

"Father sell to bad man. She run away."

"Bad man?" He thought of brothels, of Su-mei's beginnings.

"Show your hands," Ah King commanded the girl in Chinese.

Obediently the girl held them out. All her fingers were swollen and cramped, the joints red and sore.

"Small piecee factory," Ah King said impassively in pidgin again. "Makee silk."

Denton nodded. He knew her story from her hands. She'd been forced to spin silk from cocoons over pans of boiling water. The steam from the water prevented the threads from breaking. Girls were sold and sometimes kidnapped for that; after a few years their hands were crippled from the steam and there was nothing left for them except to become beggars when their owners threw them out. They couldn't work in tea houses or brothels because their looks had been ruined by years of work in steamy, airless cellars, where they were sometimes chained together to prevent them running away, and forced to eat and sleep in the same room. The *North China Daily News* had recently reported a case in which a girl, whose arms had grown so thin that she'd been able to slip her chains, had escaped and been found by the police. The unsuspected back-street factory where she'd been kept prisoner was only a mile from the magnificence of the Bund.

"Put your hands down now," he told the girl in Chinese, momentarily sickened again by the existence of a world with such gross flaws in it. *But I'm not responsible,* he soothed himself hastily. *I didn't ruin her hands.* He knew already that he was going to take the girl on, but his next question sounded heartlessly doubtful, as if in disclaiming responsibility he had to become callous as well.

How can she work with those hands?"

"Can work," Ah King maintained phlegmatically. "I teach."

"All right, we try." Then, as an after-thought, "What's her name?"

"Ah Sam."

"Ah Sam. Number three." He glanced at the girl again. She looked weak and phthisic. I hope she doesn't have tuberculosis, he thought.

He began to entertain in his new house. The garden overlooked the public gardens and the river, and often the guests would drink their sherry or port gazing out at the lights of the harbour and Pootung on the other banks, lights which ended in a sudden deep blackness that spread unendingly onwards, as though the rest of China had been blotted out. Ah Sam helped Ah King serve the drinks, holding the glasses with extravagant care in her thick-jointed, stiff-fingered hands.

When there were no wives present, Su-mei appeared; when there were, she did not.

Most of Denton's guests were exiles, exiles not merely from their lands but from their earlier lives. Ephraim, an émigré from school-teaching, Wei from humble clerkdom in Jardine's, others from the sea, from humdrum existences in England, America or the colonies, Denton himself from the mean respectability of Enfield and the dulling routines of the Customs Service.

Jacob had been studying natural history, and one evening, drinking his vodka in the cool of the garden, where the bauhinia petals glowed palely in the dusk like ghostly stars, he suddenly broke into Denton's conversation with an American banker from Peking.

"You know what elvers are?" he asked, looking round at the others, his brown eyes gleaming in the light of his match as he lit a cigar. The flickering flame threw weird, leaping shadows on his face, giving it a changing, restless cast, at once cunning and melancholy. "You know what elvers are? They are young eels. At a certain time in their life, they feel a need to swim away from their home waters, where they were born. They swim blindly, three thousand miles across the Pacific, to a place they've never seen, where they have to breed. They mate, they live, they lay their eggs and then they die." He drew on the cigar a moment before he went on, and looked round at their faces, relishing the effect of his pause like an actor in the theatre. "They are like us here in Shanghai. The only difference is that we think we are free. Free to come and go. But look at us. We're no more free really than the elvers are. We're just human elvers, moving about as blindly as they do. Human Elvers, nothing more."

Among his new acquaintances, Denton found two who would put him up for the Shanghai Club. Now that he felt sure his riches would qualify him, he wanted to retrieve the face he'd lost with Wei. Something else prompted him as well, something stronger but as yet more obscure. For now that he had money, he was already beginning to feel it wasn't enough. It was the key that opened doors, but it was not the rooms the doors gave on to. He wanted to find out about those rooms, to see what they held. Sometimes he felt stifled by money alone and the pursuit of money that took up most of his life, and even Su-mei couldn't assuage his restlessness then, his impatience and dissatisfaction. In the Club you could meet the foreign consuls, the taipans and bankers who ruled Shanghai. Was that what he wanted—power, influence? He didn't know, his thoughts were too dim and unacknowledged, hidden beneath the obvious motives which he shared with others. "Join the Shanghai Club? Of course!" Su-mei said. "It gives you face. People will see you're rich."

He was asked in a polite note to meet some members of the committee.

"This way, sir," said the boy, bald, stooping, and with dark pouches under his eyes. He led him along the carpeted hall, up the wide stairway and along the landing, his head deferentially on one side, occasionally glancing back over his shoulder to make sure Denton hadn't lost him.

"Oh, Mr. Denton." The chairman half-rose from his deep arm-chair to shake his hand, while the other two gazed guardedly up at him. "How kind of you to come and see us. This is Mr. Keston and Mr. Green."

Mr. Keston and Mr. Green both smiled perfunctorily, half-rising in their turn to shake Denton's hand. Keston, with a fleshy, purplish face, had a moist, limp handshake; Green, lean and dark-haired, crunched Denton's knuckles briefly.

"Would you care for a drink?"

Denton glanced at the tall glasses in front of the three men. "Thank you. Whisky and water, please."

The boy, waiting behind Denton, slippered out. Denton glanced surreptitiously round the room. The walls were panelled in dark heavy wood. Photographs of solid, heavy men in stiff white collars hung at eye-level all round them.

He felt their blank, collective scrutiny focussed on his shoulders as he looked back at the chairman, who, after a few uncertain sideways glances at the other two, gave a prefatory cough.

"You have been in Shanghai a long time, Mr. Denton?" His grey eyes met Denton's, then drifted off towards the faces assembled on the walls.

"Seven years." They knew that. They knew everything about him. "It's a formality," Jacob had assured him. "They only want to see if you've got any Asiatic blood in you." Jacob himself refused to join any club except the Jewish Club. "You pay good money and get bad food. What is the point of such extravagance?"

"And you came here first in the Imperial Customs Service?"

"Imperial *Maritime* Customs Service," Denton said, remembering Mr. Brown and his preciseness. "That's right."

"You must know Sebastian Brown, then?" Keston asked, as if Denton's correction had reminded him too. His voice was dark and rich. Denton thought vaguely of a slab of fruit cake when he heard it.

"Yes, he was Deputy Assistant Commissioner when I came."

Keston's sagging lids folded half-closed over his blue eyes as he nodded. "Gone to Peking now, of course, hasn't he?"

"Yes." Denton glanced away out of the mullioned window at the hard blue sky. It was winter, the afternoon sunlight was just beginning to fade. A bird slid down through the air—a sea gull. He recalled suddenly the sea gull he'd watched from his office in the Customs Building just after he'd read Brown's letter telling him his contract wouldn't be renewed. He looked back at Keston. "I'm afraid we've lost touch with each other now," he said.

"Oh he still comes down to Shanghai occasionally," Keston said.

"And then you left the Customs Service?" the chairman resumed gently.

"Yes, I've been in business for the past six years."

"How long do you anticipate staying in Shanghai, Mr. Denton?" Green's voice was sharper—as if, whatever the others might think, *he* wasn't going to be taken in easily.

"Indefinitely."

"Let me see." The chairman cleared his throat as he

glanced down at the sheet of paper on the arm of his chair, "Your business is...?"

"I have an export agency."

"Oh yes." He had taken out his glasses and placed them on the end of his nose, raising his eyebrows as he peered down through them. "With Wei Brothers."

"Isn't that a little unusual?" Green asked, leaning back to regard Denton sceptically.

He'd expected to be asked that. "Yes." He returned Green's stare with a smile that he tried to make disarmingly modest. "But then Shanghai would never have been founded if people only did things the usual way, would it?"

"Hm." Green looked down. He opened his mouth as if to speak but then reached for his glass instead and raised it without drinking.

The door opened quietly and the boy brought Denton his whisky.

"Of course I have rather more interest in my investments now," Denton went on with rehearsed casualness. "Though I expect Wei Brothers will expand pretty rapidly in the next few years."

"I see." Green's lips puckered at one corner. He drank silently at last as Denton lifted his glass.

"Thank you," Denton smiled over the rim at the chairman.

"Are you, ah..." Keston hesitated, glancing at him with heavy-lidded eyes that looked as though he was about to wink. "Are you...*married*, Mr. Denton?"

"No, I'm not...*married*." Denton lingered too before the last words. He thought of Su-mei kneading the opium pellets. A faint, complicit smile appeared on Keston's full, red lips and his lids drooped a fraction lower, as if to acknowledge that he too was a man of the world.

The chairman affected not to notice. "Do you belong to any other clubs? The Polo Club or...?"

"No, I don't ride much." He swallowed and cleared his throat uneasily. Could they tell that he'd never been on a horse in his life?

Green leant forward, hunching his bony shoulders. "Er, Mr. Denton, your association with the Wei Brothers is as you say a little er, unusual."

"Yes?"

"I wonder what you think about the...well, whether

251

you would like to see that kind of business association extended to the social sphere?"

There was a silence as the other two watched him closely. Denton smiled understandingly and drank again, gazing at his glass with a contrived, considering look, before answering. He knew that was the real question he'd been invited there to answer, and he'd rehearsed his reply to it several times in his day-dreams. They knew about his association with Wei, and that could be justified by the wealth it had brought him. They must know about Su-mei too, and that was no problem—most of them had a Chinese mistress. So long as they kept their Chinese women tucked away out of sight, there was no problem. What they were worried about was how far he would go. Would he let the side down? Would he *marry* a Chinese for instance—not Su-mei of course, that was out of the question, but one of Wei's daughters, say? Would the day come when he brought a Chinese into the Club and made a fuss when requested not to do so? Mixing the races like that— it was blasphemy to speak of it. The Chinese would lose their respect.

"Oh, I don't think that would be a good thing at all," he said reflectively at last, as though he'd never dreamt of the idea before. "The occasional dinner at a Chinese restaurant, perhaps, to entertain business people—as I do myself. But a general social mingling of Europeans and Chinese is really out of the question, isn't it?" He glanced up at the chairman, smiling disparagingly at the very notion. "To put it bluntly, the Chinese are different from us, even the better educated ones, and it simply wouldn't do to pretend otherwise. As a matter of fact, I think the Chinese themselves would agree." He was squirming inwardly, but he smiled.

Green listened with his head slightly on one side, glancing at him askance as if doubting his sincerity, but the other two nodded and murmured their approval.

"You see, we like to be sure." The chairman smiled, taking off his glasses and folding them slowly. "We like to be sure that anyone we elect to the Club would have—how shall I put it?—*congenial* views. That he would be compatible with the other members. So I was very pleased to hear your opinion on that question. As I'm sure we all were," he glanced at the other two. "I'm sure you're right, of course. I mean the Chinese simply don't have the same standards as we do, and, as you say, one can't very well ignore that. After all, a club is a bit like a family, and we can't have too many heterogeneous individuals in it, or the family will be disrupted, so to speak."

Denton nodded sympathetically. Heterogeneous, he thought. I must look that up.

"That's why we felt we ought to meet and have this little chat with you, you see, to find out whether we'd get along together. Very good of you to come."

"Not at all."

"And of course it also gives us a chance to see whether you'd really like to join this, er, this family, so to speak. After all, there are a number of other clubs and so on that some people might perhaps prefer to..." His voice faded, as though, with the best will in the world, he just couldn't believe such an improbable suggestion.

Denton too smiled his incredulity. "It's been a great pleasure to meet you," he said, conscious of the faint sceptical look still glinting in Green's eye.

A week later he was invited to pay his entrance fee and first subscription to the Shanghai Club. It was then that he remembered *heterogeneous* and looked it up in Chambers' Dictionary.

He dined there in the Jacobean-styled dining room once a week, at first by himself, then, as time passed, with other members. There, or in the long, panelled bar, they began to ask him about the stock exchange and the growing fortunes of the Wei Brothers, who had just opened a large department store on Nanking Road, in competition with the staid English firm of Whiteaway Laidlaw.

"Are they thinking of getting listed on the Exchange?" asked Gilbert, a junior director of Jardine's. "They're getting very big."

"They'll stay out as long as they can, I should think, but eventually they'll have to raise capital, and then—"

"Capital for what?"

"They're planning banking, insurance, and a shipping company."

Gilbert raised his sandy eyebrows, and Denton felt a little surge of pride and satisfaction. He was a person of some account, then, he thought. The following week Gilbert invited him to dinner. It was there he first met the British and French consuls.

*   *   *

Now he had the means and status of a gentleman, he felt he ought to acquire some of the accomplishments as well. The consuls, the taipans, the bank directors all rode their own ponies. Many of them raced them themselves at the annual race meetings, and galloped across the unsown winter fields in the paper chases that took the place of fox-hunting. If he was to be their equal, to fulfil that unformulated ambition to have power, to exert influence, he would have to be more like them. He decided to take riding lessons.

He had himself fitted out with breeches, jacket and hat and arranged tuition in a small and inconspicuous riding school at the end of Jessfield Road, where the city streets trickled away into the fields. Ah King shook her head disapprovingly as he left self-consciously for the stable one Thursday afternoon in December.

On his third lesson, the instructor, a retired sergeant-major from India, was letting him walk the horse back to the stables when Mason cantered up on a large black horse and reined in suddenly as he recognised Denton. "Well, well, if it isn't old Denton," he said in a mocking voice, brushing up the bristly end of his moustache in the way he always used to. "Taking riding lessons now, are we? Quite the gentleman, eh?"

Denton had seen him at a distance several times in the past five years, but this was the first time they'd come face to face since that evening when he collected his luggage from the mess. Mason seemed fatter, the skin stretched taut over his cheeks, which were flecked with little broken red veins as if they were beginning to pop.

For a weak moment Denton was tempted to smile, as if there'd never been any trouble between them that a little chaffing couldn't put right. But then the memory of his humiliation returned, hot and stinging. "Let me get past," he said coldly, nudging his pony forward with his spurs.

"Oh, want to get along, do you? No time to talk, eh?" Mason's mocking turned into a sneer. "Well, off you go then, mind you don't fall off." And he suddenly slashed Denton's horse with his whip.

The horse reared, then bolted. Denton lost his seat and clung on helplessly, reins lost, feet dragged from the stirrups. He heard the instructor yelling behind him while his face was buried in the horse's furry neck and he slid further and further round, clutching frantically at the coarse greasy hair of the mane.

At last the horse pulled up. It shook him off by a ditch then ambled away to graze, the reins trailing along the ground.

Mason galloped up ahead of the instructor as Denton got shaking to his feet, bruised but unhurt. His round button eyes were alarmed at first, but when he saw Denton was all right, he laughed.

"Pride cometh before a fall, eh?"

The sergeant-major dismounted and gathered the horse's reins. "You shouldn't've done that, sir," he said, stiffly yet respectfully.

"Done what?" Mason stared at him, all insolent innocence.

"Could've been a nasty accident, setting his horse off like that. Inexperienced rider an' all. And you'd've been responsible, sir."

"Oh rubbish!" Mason said nonchalantly, yet with a faintly guilty laugh. "I hardly touched the old nag. He shouldn't've been off the leading rein, anyway, if he's so bloody helpless."

The sergeant-major's lips pressed together.

"Let me get on again," Denton said unsteadily. When he'd clambered up he turned to Mason, who was backing his horse away. "You keep clear of me, Mason." His voice came out in uneven jerky spurts and he could feel his pulse thudding in his ears from shock and anger. "I'll get you for this one day." Afterwards he thought oddly ashamed that he could only find such banal and trite words to express his rage, and he rehearsed cold biting insults in his mind on the way home, as if he might get another chance to deliver them. But for the moment he'd become speechless.

Mason laughed, an overloud, bluffing laugh, and cantered off.

Denton persevered doggedly for six months, until he could ride well enough to go out on his own in the fields round the city. He even joined the Paper Hunt Club and rode his own Mongolian pony at the rear of a pack of horsemen hallooing across rice paddies, streams and open country till they arrived steaming and shouting back where they'd started. Then he bought a motor car and left his pony in the stables, to be exercised by the sergeant-major and eventually sold. He realised he would never sit well on a horse, he would never equal the taipans that way. His car was the nine hundred and forty-fifth car to be licensed in Shanghai, a Daimler from England. Jacob Ephraim, who had just persuaded his father-in-law to sell their car, recommended their chauffeur to Denton. "He's not much good, but as good as you'll ever get in China," he said. "And you needn't pay him as much as we did. Your car's smaller."

Su-mei loved riding in the car. On weekends they often drove out into the countryside, Su-mei always urging the driver to go faster while Denton, watching her shining, excited eyes and parted lips, her hair fluttering against her forehead in the wind, recalled the eager, wondering look she'd had when she first lit the gas lamp in the Customs mess seven years before. She was twenty-three now, a well-known actress, and sometimes moody and spoilt. But she could still be as child-like as she had been then, and when she was he loved her as much as he'd ever done. Besides, she'd helped to nurse him through the cholera and helped sell those shares, without which he might never have become as rich as he was now. Since then he'd never considered leaving her, although occasionally he thought of Mary-Ellen Larsen and sent his best wishes to her whenever he wrote to her father. And her father made a point of telling Denton what his daughter was doing—she was "going quite far into oriental ceramics," he wrote in a postscript to one letter, "whatever they are exactly."

On their drives, Su-mei would take him to tea-houses in little towns where they'd hardly ever seen a foreign devil before, and she'd sit at the table with him drinking tea and ordering cakes, revelling in the gaping curiosity of the waiters and the crowding peasants peering mutely in through the doorway.

One October weekend, soon after the moon festival, they drove further than usual out towards the north, staying overnight in a ramshackle inn on the great canal. As they left the next morning, Su-mei said thoughtfully, "This is near my village, only another ten li or so."

"Shall we go there?"

256

"No," she shook her head decidedly. It was as though she'd closed the door to a private room.

They drove on another twenty miles before turning back. As they drove, they came across a ragged dirty column of people straggling along the long empty road towards Shanghai. They were men, women and children, their shoulders hunched, their faces gaunt, their bare feet covered in a fine grey dust like ashes. They trudged on, mile after mile of them, in crushed silence, their eyes empty and motionless, exactly like condemned prisoners.

"Hunger marchers," Su-mei said. "They used to come through our village every year. The harvest must be bad this year, there are so many of them."

"Where are they going?"

"Shanghai," Chan, the driver answered for her. "Those that don't starve."

The column plodded on beside their polished windows, like some great sick insect crawling on a hundred unsteady legs. Faces turned, eyes watched them, with remote exhausted curiosity. They seemed too involved in their long painful weariness to feel any envy, or even surprise, at the strange, shiny machine or the strange rich passengers inside it.

The flawed face of the world again. Denton pulled a handful of change guiltily from his pocket.

"Don't stop," Su-mei warned Chan. "They'll all try to climb in."

"They haven't got the strength," Denton said curtly. But he let Chan drive on, scattering the money out of the window. Dropping it out like that made him feel more guilty, as if he were flinging his charity away contemptuously. He could have taken some notes out and dropped them too, but something restrained him—meanness? Or a fear of seeming sentimental to Su-mei and the driver? "Whatever you give them," he said almost apologetically, as if to excuse himself to the marchers, "it won't be enough, will it?"

He looked back. The marchers were clustering in little groups now, the rhythm of their miserable procession broken. They were scrabbling in the dust for the coins, squabbling feebly amongst each other. He turned back, sickened. "What did you use to do in your village when they came?"

"Lock everything away and put up the shutters," she

said dispassionately. "My mother said they'd steal everything if they got into the house."

But they were starving! he thought protestingly. But he didn't say it. He knew she would only shrug her shoulders and say "They weren't our people, we had enough troubles of our own." He didn't want to hear her say that in her detached, fatalistic voice—she who still sent her parents half her money, and would send it all if they asked for it.

"They give their children mud to eat," Chan half-turned to Denton. "It fills them up and stops the hunger pains. Of course they die sooner."

"Mercy mud," Su-mei murmured in the same dispassionate voice. "Mercy mud, they call it."

The road was clear for a while, and then they came upon some more marchers, it seemed a family, halted on the verge. One of them, a woman, was lying on her side, as if she'd fallen. The others, a man and several children, stood beside her, looking down apathetically. Denton reached into his pocket for some more change, but the car was already far past them. He drew his hand out slowly and let it lie empty on the seat.

40

Wei had taken a third wife and built a new house in Chapei large enough for all three wives and their eleven children. His third wife was only seventeen—sixteen by western reckoning—sleek and demure, and she walked on her bound feet, only three and a half inches long, with that swaying, tripping shuffle that Wei found so seductive. Her amah always accompanied her, an old woman with grey hair, whose pallid face was a web of anxious wrinkles. The amah bent forward from the hips as if on a hinge, and she had to crane her neck far back in order to see ahead. The constant stretching seemed to have lengthened her neck; Denton was always reminded of a tortoise when he saw her.

Wei had decided to take this girl as his third wife against the wishes of the other two, but he'd consulted a couple of astrologers and they'd both recommended it. It wasn't a third wife his other women disapproved of, but his choice of a well-bred girl with bound feet. He could have had any girl slave for a concubine and they would have been able to order her about and exact face from her. But Wei had picked the youngest daughter of a family that had suddenly been impoverished, and the girl considered herself their equal. Her family had even been able to persuade Wei to let the girl bring her amah with her; the two of them fought a silent bitter war against the first and second wives. The struggle was so fierce that for a time Wei took his third wife away and lived with her in a separate apartment in the old city. That made the other two lose so much face that they had to swallow their resentment and beg him to return. Then he'd had the new house built, in which they were all to live in harmony. The site was chosen carefully for its fung shui, and Taoist priests in yellow robes performed elaborate and expensive rites before they moved in. The building was modelled on the ancestral home which his grandfather had gambled away, with green tiled pagoda roofs, a hall for the ancestral tablets, and separate apartments for each of his wives. Denton saw it for the first time when he was invited to dinner there in the week before Chinese New Year.

His car had broken down, so he had to travel by rickshaw. The coolie had folded the canopy away, and Denton could see the star-pale sky clearly between the hemming-in walls and overhanging roofs of the houses. The cold bit hard, and a keen, icy wind cut through his clothes. The coolie's panting breath misted on the air before the wind snatched it away. The stars glittered frostily. Occasional fire-crackers flashed and banged in the alleys as the rickshaw's solid tyres whispered over the smooth parts of the road and jolted over the rough. Denton felt warm despite the cold. For the first time he'd been drinking at the head of the long bar of the Club, where by tradition only taipans and consuls could gather. Gilbert had invited him, and the British consul had asked if he'd heard anything from Chinese business people about rumours that Sun Yat-sen was planning another revolt against the Manchu dynasty. "Those chaps usually have their ears pretty close to the ground, you know. Bound to find out what's going on before we do." And then all his shares had registered gains that week, except those in Holt's Wharves, which he'd sold off as they seemed to have peaked. But best of all was that Gilbert had sounded him out about standing for the Municipal Council at the next election. There was the difficulty that he'd planned to visit his parents in England, which would mean he'd be away for several months, but Gilbert had said if not next year the year after. And he'd asked him to join the board of one of Jardine's companies. So he was really becoming someone who mattered. He imagined his parents' faces when they saw his boxes labelled First Class. Who would have thought it when he left in 1903? He wasn't vain, but still money and success were certainly something.

Two servants met him at the gilded wrought-iron gates and a string of lanterns led the way to the main hall. Wei, dressed in fine silk robes, greeted him with eyes heavy with that contented fullness Denton knew came from love. A great round table had been set for Wei's three wives, his brother and his two, and all the cousins and nephews who'd been brought into the business over the years. They ate Peking food with unleavened white bread, and the men drank rice wine and brandy, growing flushed and boisterous as the dishes followed one after the other. The younger cousins played count-finger games with that loud simple enjoyment that Denton always found embarrassingly childish and immature. Wei's first and second wives looked on dourly, barely acknowledging third wife's formally propitiating behaviour with curt nods or a flickering of lids, as she picked out the greatest delicacies and placed them in their bowls with their own chopsticks, eating little herself. But it was formal propitiation only, Denton could see. Every now and then the young bride would glance slyly at Wei, as if to say, "See how submissive I'm being to them, but still they hate me."

As the concluding tureen of soup was placed on the table, Wei turned to Denton, scratching his cheek lightly with his long, curved nail. "What are the foreign devils saying in the Shanghai Club?" he asked smilingly, his face, too, flushed from the wine.

"Tonight they were asking what's happened to that revolutionary Sun Yat-sen."

Wei sucked some soup up with noisy relish before he answered. "Sun Yat-sen has married one of the Soong daughters in Japan."

"The bible printers?"

Wei nodded. "He sent his first wife away as part of

260

the settlement. She's gone back to her village." He sighed, glancing coolly at first and second wife. "She must be very unhappy, she has lost so much face."

The two women's lips tightened momentarily. Second wife stared stonily across the table, but first wife's eyes swivelled briefly to the young bride, cold and accusing.

Denton too glanced at third wife. She sat with her head slightly bowed, smiling coyly.

He smiled too, speaking in English, which none of the women understood. "You see, Sun has only one wife at a time. These western ideas are catching on."

"Catchin' on?" Wei looked puzzled at the expression, then laughed as his eyes cleared. "That will no' las'." He spoke in English as well. "For him perhaps it will, he is a Christian, but for China no. Here, too many women. What happen' to them if man canno' have two wife?" He looked at Denton challengingly, smiling and confident in his logic. "More girl chil' will be kill'. There will be more girl-slave."

"Did Soong's daughter have bound feet?"

Wei's eyes grew opaque behind his glasses. "In China people do no' think women beautiful if they have big fee'," he said evasively. "So if girl' do no' have boun' fee', canno' marry rich man." He shrugged and sucked some more soup up, then adroitly changed the subject, speaking in Chinese again now. "As for Sun Yat-sen"—he belched softly—"In China there are always rumours."

He seemed undecided whether to go on or not, and looked at Denton under his lids consideringly, as he did when he was negotiating a new contract. "The Soongs have a lot of money," he said at last, enigmatically. "If the Soongs give Sun their money—" He clamped his lips together, leaving the rest of the sentence unspoken. "The Manchus are worn out, degenerate," he continued after a moment, leaning closer to Denton as though afraid of being overheard. "They can't last much longer. You know what we say—they have lost the mandate of heaven."

One of the nephews had a new camera from America, that could take pictures by artificial light. Everyone had to sit still, staring at the lens, bulging and shiny as a fish's eye, while he kept fiddling with little switches and levers. At last he was ready. The taut, lifeless smiles were fixed again, there was a sudden flash and they were photographed for the first time in Wei's new home.

"Now for some opium," Wei said. "Let's leave the others."

He led Denton through several halls into a small room where three blackwood opium divans stood with their hard porcelain pillows. The young third wife followed behind them, tripping on her bound feet. Her amah accompanied her as far as the door.

"Do you remember when you wouldn't take me to an opium divan because I wasn't Chinese?" Denton asked.

Wei grunted, lying down on his side. "I wasn't sure about you then. Some people should never take it. My brother, for instance, he hasn't taken it for ten years."

Denton waited for him to explain why, but this time Wei didn't go on.

Third wife prepared the opium, warming it over the little kerosene flame.

"This is the second best thing in life," Wei sighed, watching the little treacly wads of opium softening in the heat. "The first is money. Make money, get rich. That is best of all."

"What about having a young third wife?" Denton asked, sniffing the enticing, greasy smell. "Isn't that good too?" He looked at the girl's face as he spoke. There was no movement, not the flicker of a muscle in her intent face, and yet her very stillness showed she was listening.

"That is third best," Wei answered carelessly, not even glancing at the girl. "It can't be as good as opium, because women always make trouble, however much they please you. Opium is simple. And money"—he took the pipe and inhaled, closing his eyes—"money is what makes the others possible."

Next week, just before the start of the New Year holiday, Denton bought Su-mei a silver bracelet and a heavy red silk gown. She was going back to her village for the feast, and he brought the presents round to her the evening before. Ah Leng, Su-mei's amah, met him at the door with a strangely sullen face and he frowned as she grudgingly let him in. "Where's your mistress?" he asked coldly.

"In the bedroom. Asleep."

He watched her impatiently while she bolted the door with exaggerated care and walked past the spirit screen towards the bedroom. "I'll see if she wants to see you," she muttered insolently, leaving him standing there with the parcel in his arms. He looked down at the red crêpe paper in which he'd wrapped the presents himself, a confused uneasiness and annoyance stirring behind his eyes.

Su-mei came at last in the kimono he'd bought her at Christmas from one of the new Japanese stores in Hongkew.

"What's the matter with your amah?" he began irritably, then stopped. Her lids looked heavy and swollen as though she'd been crying. "What's wrong?" he asked, suddenly concerned. "What's happened?"

She slumped down on a chair without answering.

"Su-mei, what's wrong?" He sat beside her, holding the parcel on his knees. It seemed too large there, unwieldy and out of place. The paper rustled as he put it on the floor. "Come on," he coaxed her. "What's happened?"

She lifted her shoulders, staring away from him down at the floor. He heard Ah Leng's slippers hesitating in the hall, then slithering on towards the kitchen.

He touched her arm, but she shook his hand off with a quiver of revulsion. The gesture was so sharp that he started back himself. He stood up, exasperated and impatient. "Well, if you don't want to tell me, I'll go." He nudged the parcel towards her with his shoe. "Prosperous New Year," he said tartly.

He has passed the spirit screen when she spoke at last in a dull level voice. "I'm pregnant."

"What?" He turned to look at her. Something seemed to leap then drop in his stomach. He'd heard what she said, but he asked again blankly. "What?"

"Pregnant." She was gazing down still at the floor, not even glancing at his present.

He walked back to her, suddenly conscious of his feet on the polished floor, of the steps his legs were making, as though he'd never noticed such things before. His stomach curled. "How do you know?"

She shrugged. "How every woman knows."

He sat down beside her again, gazing unseeingly at the red paper parcel.

"I can get rid of it," she said.

Her hands lay on her knees and he looked at the jade ring on her little finger. When did I give it to her? he thought absently. It was strange, he could recall very well slipping it on her finger, but when was it? And where? And while he gazed at the ring, another thought was running through his head, heavy and insistent. You can't

263

marry her, the words formed by themselves, as if it were someone else speaking. That's absolutely impossible. And he saw Green's face, lean and suspicious as he'd leant forward in the Shanghai Club, "Would you like to see that kind of association extended into the social sphere?" And Keston's rosy lips with their complicit smile, too. "Are you...married, Mr. Denton?"

Suddenly she bent down and took up the parcel, picking at the knot in the golden ribbon that tied it. "I can get rid of it," she said again.

It seemed a long time before he answered. He felt he was dragging the words up reluctantly from some great clinging depth. "Isn't that dangerous?"

She shrugged. "They say if a foreign devil makes a baby with a Chinese woman, it may have a tail and be covered all over with hair."

"That's rubbish!" He laid his broad pink hand over her fingers and held them still. The crêpe paper rustled.

"I've seen it in the paper."

So had he, in the ill-printed, flimsy sheets that tried to stir up anti-foreign feeling. Cartoons of horrified mothers being shown their monstrous babies by outraged midwives while the long-nosed, bearded foreign father smirked diabolically in the corner, rubbing his hands. "The papers are full of lies," he said. "You've seen Eurasian children yourself, here in Shanghai."

She snorted. "Half-breeds! Look at them! Miserable little things!" It might have been pity or contempt in her voice; or both.

"Well, they haven't got tails. They're not covered with hair."

"They probably keep the worst ones locked up at home. Or throw them away."

"Throw them away!" he repeated scornfully.

"Well, what else would you do with them? Chinese always throw away the freaks." It was as though she was taunting him, daring him to deny what she was saying.

"Su-mei, you know perfectly well it wouldn't be a freak, so stop saying that, will you?" He raised her hand and squeezed it till she winced. "And you mustn't do anything to...to get rid of it. Not yet, anyway."

"Why not?"

"I want to ask a doctor first."

"A foreign doctor?" She pulled her hand away. "I've

heard of them. Making women undress and then pawing their bodies!"

He thought of the little naked statuettes, one hand modestly covering their groins, with which Chinese ladies consulted their doctors, pointing to the affected part of the statuette, which was a surrogate for their decently-clothed bodies. "I'll only *ask* a doctor," he promised. "I won't bring him to see you."

"What's the use of asking him, then?" she said perversely.

When he left later that night, she still hadn't unwrapped his parcel. They had gone round and round, over and over it, and decided nothing. At one moment she said she was going to a Chinese doctor immediately, at the next she was resigned to accept whatever happened. Then the thought of the hairy freak she was sure she'd bear made her hysterical, so that Ah Leng came running, scolding and crying herself. Then she would blame herself for her carelessness, and a moment later sullenly accuse him of trying to murder her with the enormous foreign devil he'd deliberately planted inside her. He went away exasperated and dispirited, feeling as though a stone had been placed on his chest. Why not let her get rid of it? he asked himself as he watched the rickshaw coolie's legs running before him and listened to the clicking of the spokes. Why not? It's their way of doing things. All around him the fire crackers exploded joyfully.

"Do ye realise what you're asking me to do, man?" Dr. McEwan asked indignantly, his brown eyes widening in his hectically florid face. "Risk being struck off, just to help you out of a scrape with your lady-friend? Pish, ye've got a nerve!"

"I was only asking your advice," Denton answered stiffly. "I'm not asking you to do anything. She has her own doctor."

"Well, why waste your money coming to me, then?"

Denton paused, hesitating. His eyes took in the soothing quiet comfort of the chairs in McEwan's new consulting rooms, a comfort that seemed so much at odds with McEwan's prickly manner. "I want to know how safe it would be to..." His voice wilted beneath McEwan's hard bristling glare.

"Well, my advice to you is that no decent doctor would perform an abortion, if that's the word you're

265

looking for. And any doctor that would perform one is pretty likely to be incompetent. That's my advice and ye'll find it's pretty expensive too." He folded his arms. "Was there anything else ye came to see me about?"

That morning Wei had given Denton a print of the photograph they'd taken at his house. Stern faces with rigid smiles stared blankly out of it with a faintly hostile expression. They all looked brittle and lifeless, sitting frozen at the great round table; nobody would have guessed how boisterous and exuberant they'd been a few minutes before. He examined his own face. That was taut and stern too, the contrived smile artificial and joyless. But it differed from the others in the eyes. There was that wary, withdrawn look in them that he so often caught in the mirror, the expression of someone absent or lost—or rather of someone who suspected life might set some trap for him at any time. Well, that was right, he thought. A trap had been laid, and sprung.

Su-mei had gone to her village, taking New Year gifts for the family that now depended on her. When she came back he would have to decide—not whether to marry her, but whether to let her keep his child, which would then grow up as an outcast belonging to neither race, or else to risk an abortion. He lay awake in his empty house—the servants had all returned to their parents' homes for the festival—and listened to the barrage of fire-crackers that crashed and battered through the night, picturing himself as the father of a half-breed child, or Su-mei pale and dying from a botched abortion. You could put it in an orphanage or some sort of home, he thought. Wouldn't that be best? That was how many Europeans arranged things. He remembered Jacob Ephraim saying so, and he should know—perhaps he'd done it himself. He imagined asking Jacob about it, but he felt ashamed at once, so that his fingers and toes curled involuntarily under the bed-clothes. Not because Jacob would think anything of it, but because Denton would have to hear himself *say* what now he was only thinking, that he wanted to abandon his own child to poverty and misery. And saying it would make it real, would bring him face to face with it. *His own child.* How strange that sounded.

On the first day after the holiday, before Su-mei had come back, while the servants, weary from all-night feasting

266

and paying their respects to their relatives, were working sluggishly and peevishly at even the simplest tasks, a messenger from the P & O office brought a letter to the door. The envelope had a black border, the address was written in his mother's hand. He took the letter from Ah King into the study, a room on the second floor with few books but a large desk and a filing cabinet. He wanted to be alone when he opened it; death was a private thing. His stomach lifted and fell as he stood there for some seconds holding the letter unopened. *Father,* he thought, trying to visualise the pale, embittered face as it had been nearly eight years ago. *So he's gone.*

His arm trembled slightly as he slit the flap open. He drew the letter out slowly, with the half-conscious, childish, thought that nothing would really have happened until he read it in black and white. It was just one page. He had been taken poorly, been sent to hospital and died on the fourth night. *I wish you were here,* her last sentence read. *I feel I cannot cope.* He folded the letter slowly and slid it back into the envelope. He sat down by the desk and gazed out of the window at the ships in the harbour. "We are like elvers out here," he heard Jacob's voice in his head. Elvers. He hadn't known that word till then, hadn't even heard it. A tall Foochow junk was drifting downstream past the moored cargo ships, its ribbed grey sails almost motionless, stirring and flapping only occasionally like great lazy wings as some light wind touched them. Soon it would be summer again, he thought. He gazed at the junk and the black-clad people moving idly about on its deck, recalling haphazardly what he could of his father's life. But all he could see, really, was the blackened grate with coals glowing behind the bars, and his father sitting in the chair with the torn leather back—and he couldn't make his face come clear.

In the evening, when he went to Su-mei, she too was irritable and tired from the feasting and visiting and the long journey back, as well as from her concealed anxiety. She looked at him with peevish inquiry as soon as they were alone.

"Keep it," he said. "We can't risk...doing something about it."

"Suppose it's a freak?"

"Don't talk nonsense."

267

She stared down at the floor between them, her eyes doubtful and yet also relieved. "What shall we do when it's born?"

"Let's wait till then." He spoke impatiently, not wanting to discuss or explain, afraid she might weaken his resolve. The decision had grown in him almost unconsciously while he sat in the study after reading his mother's letter. Secretly he hoped she would lose the child before it was born, but he felt he couldn't bring himself to interfere with it now. Different reasons bound him: fear, the sense of his father's death, which obscurely deepened his horror of taking life, and an indecisiveness that held him back from making any choice that was definite and irreversible while he could still delay. After all, he told himself, I could still change my mind next week. It wouldn't be too late. Or we could have it adopted eventually. He couldn't say which thread of reasoning was stronger—he was scarcely aware of some of them, they were in the half-light of his mind. Above all, he wished it had never happened.

He booked passages to New York and London on a P & O liner sailing in November, and wrote to his mother that he'd be there in the new year. If nothing happened, the child would be two months old by then, and the whole business would be settled one way or another. He had to go to America first to set up an office for Wei; besides, he wanted to invest in the New York stock market, and he would need to find a good broker. And afterwards he would do something about his mother, arrange things for her. The thought that he would meet Mary-Ellen Larsen again in New York was curiously pleasing. Perhaps in the end everything would turn out all right.

41

Su-mei did nothing to protect the baby before it was born. She wore no charms, she put no knife under the bed, she pinned no dragon pictures on the wall. She consulted no fortune-tellers at the night market and did nothing to try to ensure that the child would be a boy. "What does it matter?" she would answer listlessly when Ah Leng reproached her for her indifference. "It'll be a hairy monster anyway, and we'll only have to get rid of it or chain it up."

She kept on singing at opera performances until she couldn't hide her swelling belly any longer, and then she declared she'd never sing again. She bought no clothes for the baby and made no preparations for the birth. It was Ah Leng who arranged for the midwife and bought clothes and a rattan cradle.

When Denton visited her, Su-mei would often be languidly playing mah-jong with women he'd never seen before, whom she would sulkily introduce collectively with a wave of her hand as her "friends" or "people from the company." Sometimes he smelt the cloying scent of opium when he arrived and noticed the moist brightness in their eyes. At other times she would be sitting discontentedly alone, staring out of the window over the shimmering, sultry roofs of Chapei towards the thin, bright glitter of the sunlight on the curving river far away.

"Have you told your parents?" he asked.

She shook her head and snorted derisively.

"Will you ever tell them?"

"They've got enough trouble," she shrugged. "Besides, I might die, and then they can find out when you send my body back to them."

"Why should you die?" he asked irritably. "You're not ill."

She let her heavy lids slide down over her eyes till only a slit of white and brown was showing. "They say foreign devil babies are so big they split us open and we bleed to death."

"Who says?"

Another shrug. "I read it somewhere."

Yet her persistent leaden moroseness sometimes relented, and she would say with sudden hopeful buoyancy in her voice, "Ah Leng saw a half-breed girl yesterday, in the French settlement. Quite pretty, she said."

He realised then that her sullenness, her listless depressions, were rooted in fear. She really was afraid she would bear a monster, a freak, and that it might split her slim-hipped body open. Her morose pessimism was a way of preparing herself for the shock, the disgrace, and even her death. She was trying to inure herself against it in advance. But whenever he tried to reassure her, she would turn away sulkily, refusing to listen. Perhaps she *should*

269

have got rid of it, he began to think, now that it was too late.

For the last two months she wouldn't let him into her bed, whereas before that she'd often clutched him to her fiercely and goaded him on as though she wanted him to dig the child out of her body. Now, "Go and find another woman," she would say bitterly. "Make another monster." And yet her eyes seemed to plead with him not to go, to stay with her and bear her moody perversity. "When Sarah is past her sixth month, I go to the house in *rue* Molière," Jacob had told Denton once, gripping his arm as he always did in moments of self-revelation. "It is unhealthy to check your desires. If my wife is not hungry, is that a reason for me to starve? The great German philosopher, Nietzche, says we must gratify all our desires. I have a review of his work in a German paper Sarah's sister sends us. And that house really is safe, by the way. You don't catch anything there."

Several times Denton was tempted to follow Jacob's example, but each time the memory of that pleading look in Su-mei's eyes, like the look she'd thrown him when Pock-mark Chen attacked her, restrained him. *I don't mean this,* her eyes seemed to urge. *Whatever I say, it's only because I'm afraid.*

But once, near the end of her eighth month, he did walk out angrily and told a rickshaw to take him to *rue* Molière. She hadn't even wanted him to touch her, and jerked her hand away from his as if he were unclean. "All right, then," he'd said resentfully. "I'll go somewhere else."

He hadn't been down the street for more than a year, but it hadn't changed at all. Nothing in the French Settlement ever did change, except to grow a little older and seedier. The door was still open with its dimly sinister allure, and the paint was still green, though more faded now, and peeling off the shutters. A man sat in what might have been the same bamboo chair, glancing up at Denton as he walked down the path towards him.

"Vous désirez, m'sieur?" His eyes surveyed him with a fatigued courtesy, as if he'd asked the same question a hundred times already that night.

Denton remembered the sense of incongruity he'd felt when he first heard Pock-mark Chen speak French to him. "A girl," he said abruptly in Chinese.

The man led him into the hall and gestured him to sit

down. "Chinese, Portuguese, Filipino, Japanese?" he asked. He took out a toothpick and examined the point with narrowed eyes, holding it away at arm's length as if he were long-sighted. "Europeans cost more. What kind do you want? Young? Older?"

Denton hadn't sat down yet. He looked round the bare hall, which was lit by a dim gas lamp. A broad staircase led up to the next floor and he heard girl's voices gossiping, idle and bored. He thought of the women he sometimes found at Su-mei's. There was the smell of opium here, too.

The man waited, inserting the toothpick between his lower front teeth and regarding Denton inquiringly as he probed with it, his lips slightly drawn back. "You like lily feet? Anything you like, I can get it for you."

"How much?" Denton asked dully, his desire all gone.

The man smiled, removing the toothpick. "That depends on what you want. Come upstairs and take a look, see which one you like." He inserted the toothpick again. "All nice girls. All very clean. Come and see." He stepped towards the stairs and turned his head, waiting for Denton to follow. "Would you like a drink? Come upstairs, no hurry, you can take your time."

Denton hesitated, then suddenly turned and walked hurriedly away.

"Come on upstairs, sir," the man called out quietly behind him, quietly and reproachfully. "Just come and have a look."

The rickshaw coolie was squatting between his shafts, gazing vacantly down the road, his jaw moving slowly as though he were chewing. Denton got in and gave him Su-mei's address. The man sighed and spat, lifting the shafts wearily without a word. He was old and narrow-chested, his legs looked no thicker than Denton's arms. Denton glanced back as the rickshaw moved off at a walking pace. The man was sitting in his chair again, crossing his legs. Was that really what Jacob liked, to go and choose a woman like that? There must be something wrong with him, he thought, he must be perverse. He imagined Jacob's bright brown eyes and moist, labile lips, and they seemed suddenly repulsive to him, like those of a reptile. And yet, beneath his disgust, Denton felt a furtive, tingling thrill, a secret longing to go up those stairs and choose a woman with a lordly disdainful nod and...

The rickshaw was passing the house where, years ago, he'd seen the lady with the little girl walking through the arched entrance in the wall. Then too he'd been racked between lust and something else—what was it?—that the lady with the girl had seemed to symbolise. What was it? Not purity exactly. Peace? Then and now. Had nothing really changed, then?

He gave the old man a large tip when he got out at Su-mei's apartment. The man took it wordlessly. The lights were out and nobody answered the door. He waited a few minutes and then left, going slowly down the three flights of stairs. The old man was still squatting there between the shafts with the same vacant stare, as though he'd been tethered there like a horse. Denton let him take him home, although this time he gave a smaller tip.

The baby was born on a September evening. Ah Leng came to tell him just before nine. He heard her chattering excitedly with Ah Sam at the kitchen door, not daring to cross the threshold while Ah King was there. Ah King was sitting with her back towards the door, feeding rice to her son. "It's only a girl," she said disdainfully, before Ah Leng could speak herself.

"We can get rid of it if you don't like it," Su-mei murmured weakly, turning her head as soon as she heard him come in. Her cheeks were flushed and moist, and there were tired, mauve shadows under her eyes. Her jet hair lay braided on the pillow. "We can leave it at the orphanage. It's no good trying to sell it, nobody would buy a half-breed girl." Her lower lip quivered suddenly and her eyes turned back to the little bundle in the cradle beside the bed. "Only make up your mind quickly," she added plaintively.

The midwife had bound the child up in its swaddling clothes so tightly that it couldn't move at all. It looked like a little rigid mummy. The pink, wrinkled face, neither Chinese nor European, puckered as he gazed down at it and gave a little snuffling whimper. Its hair was dark, almost as dark as Su-mei's. He couldn't see its eyes beneath its screwed-up lids.

"Girls are bad luck," Su-mei murmured again, looking up at him with fatigued, questioning eyes. Her voice had sounded contrite, as though it was her fault that on top of everything else she'd produced a girl. "Do you want to get rid of it? It hasn't got a tail, though."

The snuffling whimper grew into a coughing, broken wail, helpless and desperate, as though the child had understood Su-mei's words. "Feed the baby!" Ah Leng urged. "Feed it." Su-mei's eyes looked up at him anxiously still, the question still glimmering in her wide dark pupils. The wailing grew more frantic, long howls punctuated by shuddering gasps for breath.

"Well you'd better feed it, hadn't you?" he said unsteadily. "We can talk about it afterwards."

Ah Leng put the baby to her breast. It was stiff and quivering now, its face and head red with breathless screaming. It's having a fit, Denton thought, and then the howls suddenly ceased in mid-breath as, with a little choking sob, its lips closed round her nipple. Su-mei's face softened as she looked down at it snuggling at her breast and sucking greedily, its breathing calmed now to deep contented little grunts.

He stayed with Su-mei until she fell asleep soon after one in the morning. Every half hour or so she had shuddered with the after-pains, her face stiffening and wincing. So much pain for such a little thing, he kept thinking, glancing from her to the cradle, which Ah Leng was rocking and crooning over ceaselessly. So much trouble. He couldn't think of the swaddled baby as "she," still less as his. It seemed an alien greedy little animal that would suck Su-mei dry, feeding on her like a parasite. He felt a dull resentment against it, rising as Su-mei's own sullen hostility seemed to dissolve. As her face grew softer, her eyes warming when she looked at the child, so his grew stiffer and more withdrawn. She no longer asked him whether they would get rid of it, as though her own mind at least was settled.

When she'd fallen asleep, he walked through the empty streets and alleys back to his house—empty except for the sprawled figures that lay sleeping on the ground, under trees, by doorways, or along the banks of the canals. He hesitated outside the door, then went round the house and sat on a bench in the public gardens. He'd forgotten his key, and he didn't want to wake the servants and face their inquisitive looks. He gazed out at the lighted ships meeting their lighted reflections on the still dark surface of the river. The air was cool and dry. In a few weeks they

273

would have the first chills of autumn. He had to think about the child, what to do with it. He loosened his collar and gazed at the river, thinking of Su-mei's anxious eyes, of the child's greedy sucking lips, of its old-looking wrinkled face. But what to do with it—his mind was blank and empty. Big Ching chimed the hours, a Chinese policeman passed, then a Sikh, both giving him a lingering, uncertain look. *Slops* he thought irrelevantly, *that's what Mason used to call the police, slops.* But as for the child—still his mind was empty. At last the sky began to pale down the river, and then a faint rosy streak appeared beneath the paleness. He saw mist lying on the water by the other bank, with the stark jibs of cranes and factory chimneys rising behind them as if they grew out of the air. He got up and walked towards Hongkew, taking the first rickshaw he found, its coolie shovelling in the last of his morning rice before lifting the shafts.

"Holy Family Orphanage," Denton told him.

The coolie was fresh, the morning was still young and cool, and the streets were clear. They whirled past shuttered stalls, and empty barrows stacked in rows or clustered round the early morning food stalls. Several times the coolie loped past bodies lying inert, as Denton had seen them in the middle of the night. How many of them would get up as the sun warmed them? How many would be carted away to be buried in shallow unmarked graves? The coolie grunted suddenly and shied away from something, making the rickshaw lurch. It was an old woman, lying beside the gutter, one frail, skinny forearm covering her eyes while the other lay stretched out beside her. Denton noticed how scant her hair was. He could see the skin of her scalp through the sparse grey threads.

"Was she dead?" he asked, twisting round to look back.

"Probably," the coolie panted. The woman hadn't moved.

He got down at the square opposite the blank stone face of the orphanage, and watched from the coarse sackcloth awning of a food stall that was still boarded up. Nearby, some coolies were squatting, playing with narrow playing cards that were no wider than a man's finger. They had slept on the street too, but they had got up. Now they were waiting for the stall to open and sell them their rice and tea. They glanced at Denton curiously, then went on with their game.

The sun strengthened and the sky brightened minute by minute. He watched the brightness sliding gradually down the orphanage wall, from its tiled roof to the top storey of open shutters, then down to the next storey, illuminating a large stone statue of the Virgin Mary holding the infant Jesus. Beside the closed brown doors below, a little alcove had been let into the wall, in which there was a wooden shelf with a basket on it. He hadn't been waiting long before a woman approached the shelf, carrying a little bundle in her arms. Quite matter-of-factly, as if she were weighing vegetables, she placed the bundle in the basket and then reached up to pull a chain. A bell jangled inside the building. Some of the coolies looked round, hands poised with their cards, then turned back to their game, calling out for good luck as they threw their cards down. Denton watched the woman walk away. She didn't look poor, she was well enough off to have new sandals and a tunic that wasn't faded by frequent washings and the sun. She didn't look back until she was about to turn into an alley that led off from the square. Then she paused, and after a minute or so, while she was still watching, the shelf moved in the wall, swinging round like a piece of stage scenery into the inside of the orphanage, while another empty basket was brought round on another shelf. She'd got rid of her baby. The orphanage would never know where it came from, nor would the child.

In the stall behind him, a man started hawking and coughing, then a bolt was drawn back with a harsh grinding squeal. One of the coolies called out that they were hungry, and a sour, sleepy voice, clogged with phlegm, muttered that they'd just have to wait. Denton walked away, the coolies eyeing him and nudging each other, murmuring in low chuckling tones.

He wandered along the side of the Soochow Creek, watching the sampans loaded with vegetables paddling down towards the markets. Then he struck off through the slums, past green, slimy canals smelling of decay, and huts cobbled together out of rotting planks with tin roofs. The sun was higher now and he began to sweat. Children with rickety legs and sunken, wide eyes stared at him as he passed and whispered into each other's ears. Inside the huts were more children, and women cooking on wood

275

fires, glancing out of the grime and smoke with a lustreless, indifferent gaze.

Suddenly he came upon a municipal cart. Two policemen were laying a dead street-sleeper onto it. It was a man, not very old, but with very hollow cheeks, his limbs bony and emaciated. They handled the body neither reverently nor callously, but rather as if it were a rolled-up carpet which they didn't value highly yet didn't want to damage. There were other bodies in the dray already.

The constables glanced at him hesitantly. His clothes were expensive and he was a foreign devil, but he was rumpled, unshaven and walking aimlessly. He might be one of the remittance men it was safe to ignore. On the other hand—They decided to greet him. "Good morning, sir," they called out with guarded respect.

Denton nodded and then paused, answering in Chinese. "Tell me, where is Jerusalem House? It's near here, isn't it?" It wasn't until he'd paused to speak to them that he'd thought of Janet Pulham and her mission. Was that what he'd been looking for since he left the orphanage? It suddenly seemed as though it was.

"Jerusalem House?" They looked at each other, then shook their heads.

"In Canton Street?" he prompted them. "Where the English missionary woman..."

"Oh, Che Loo Sun," they smiled and pointed. "Down there. The Englishwoman, yes. The baby bag."

"Baby bag?"

"That's what they call her." They grinned and turned away as the driver flicked the horses' flanks and the cart trundled forward.

He found Canton Street and walked slowly down it, keeping to the shadowed side where the night's coolness still lay like a fading mist. It was a mean street, even for that part of the city, the houses broken down and crowded, smelling sourly of grime and decay. Dogs slunk amongst the rubbish in the open drains, lifting their heads warily as he passed. They were lean and unkempt, their dirty, matted fur worn away with patches of mange. Their eyes were rheumy, leaking yellowish-green matter at the corners. From inside the houses came the complaining whimpering of babies, and slurred growls from their mothers. A man emptied a slop bucket under Denton's feet. An old woman, dirty, uncombed, and with mindless eyes, sat by a heap of garbage while a young girl picked it over, dropping her findings in a dented tin.

Near the end he found Janet Pulham's mission, an abrupt, clean stone building with a crude picture of Jesus painted on a board outside it. Jesus, with a western nose but slightly slanting eyes, was surrounded by Chinese children and gazing down at them with an expression which, failing to be compassionate, gave him a girlish simper. *Suffer the little children to come unto me* had been daubed in red, uneven, characters above his head. Behind the shutters he heard children's voices reciting in singsong tones. Saying their prayers, he supposed. If we got rid of it, it might come here, he thought, gazing at the shutters, glad that he hadn't been seen. Then what would become of it? The voices stopped and he heard the rattle of tin plates and mugs, then a woman's voice—not Janet Pulham's—speaking firmly and loudly, with a slightly strident tone.

He turned away, the fatigue of his sleeplessness suddenly overcoming him with its soft, dragging weight. His lids felt sore and his mouth was dry. He walked back up the street, hoping to find a rickshaw—but who could afford a rickshaw there?

Then he saw Janet Pulham coming towards him. She was walking with an ungainly, mannish stride, a large canvas bag slung over one shoulder.

"Goodness, look who's here," she said cheerfully, shading her pale blue eyes against the sun. A lank strand of hair hung down by her ear from beneath a wide-brimmed, yellowing straw hat. Her hair seemed darker than he remembered, and there were little lines running from the corners of her eyes and mouth, lines that seemed to express good humour as much as age. "What brings you here, Mr. Denton? At this time of day too!"

He shrugged, hesitating. "I happened to be walking this way, and I thought I'd just see if...if I could find your place."

"Ah." She moved her bag round from her hip to her front. "Well, now that you've found us, see what *I've* found this morning." She held the flap open for him to look inside. It was a new-born baby, a strip of dirty cloth loosely wrapped round its middle. It lay still and quiet, a tiny fist clenched by its mouth. "Found it on the rubbish down the street." Her head came close to his as she too peered in.

She was breathing slightly heavily, as though she had a cold. "They know I come looking, so they leave them there. Another girl of course."

Denton gazed at the little pink nails. The hand was very still. "Is it all right?" he asked doubtfully.

"All right?" she laughed. "I wouldn't be standing here talking to you if it was all right! No, I was too late this time. She's stone cold." She let the flap down and looked up briskly. "At least I got there before the rats and the dogs. I expect the parents wanted me to find her. They know when I make my rounds, and they put them out just before I come. Can't afford to keep them, you see. I should think this one was dead already. But I often find live ones. Mostly girls, of course." She glanced at him with that quizzical expression he recalled from before, as if she were about to tease him. "I've been hoping you might come round one day. I'd like you to give us some money."

His eyes couldn't leave the little bulge at the bottom of her bag. *Baby bag*, he thought. *Baby bag*. "Do people ever *ask* you to take their babies?" he asked slowly. "Or do you always have to go out and find them?"

"They bring them sometimes. Leave 'em on the steps usually." Her eyes gleamed mischievously. "Why, have you got one to offer?"

He felt himself blushing as he shook his head and smiled at such a ludicrous idea, uncomfortably conscious of her steady, ironic gaze.

She looked at him for some seconds more, as though she expected him to speak, then glanced down at the bag and patted it with a little sigh. "Well, better get along, arrange a Christian burial for this little mite. D'you want to come in and see the place?"

"I'd like to, only I'm rather tired. I've been up all night and..."

"All right," she shrugged equably. "Come another time. Why not give us some money now, though?" She smiled at her own audacity. "Shameless, aren't I? Have you got any with you?"

He drew out his wallet. "How much would you like? I suppose I still owe you something for saving my life."

"As much as you can spare. The widow's mite, you know. Or in your case, the bachelor's. Yes I suppose you do owe me for that, although you did send a cheque, didn't you?"

"Yes." He took out forty dollars. There were ten left. "I'll send you another. Will this do for now?"

"Thanks," she smiled matter-of-factly, crumpling the notes as she pushed them into her pocket.

He hesitated, looking down at the crisp edge of the last ten dollar note peeping out of the wallet. A sudden warm flood of emotion seemed to gush up in him, repentant and yearning, breaking the dams of his reserve. It was as though his childhood had returned and he was with his mother in church, taking communion when he was innocent and naive. I want to be on your side, he thought forlornly, however absurd your beliefs are. I want to do the right thing. But I'm afraid I won't.

She was smiling at him, as if she knew what he was thinking. But he couldn't say it aloud, what was in his mind. It would sound sentimental, he'd be embarrassed. He shrunk away from her encouraging blue eyes—that lightest of blues—drawing the ten dollars shamefacedly out of the wallet. "Here, have this as well. I don't need it."

"How're you going to get home?" she asked, taking it nevertheless.

"I'll walk."

"All that way up Jessfield Road?"

"No, I've moved. I'm on the Bund now."

"Ah," the irony returned to her smile. "Going up in the world, eh? Still got the same amah?"

"Yes."

"And the same concubine? You should marry her or stop it. You know the commandments."

Denton flushed, looking away. "I must be going," he said stiffly. It was relief that he could be annoyed with her. He felt thankful he hadn't made a fool of himself with that wave of feeling a minute before.

"All right, then, Mr. Denton," she answered tranquilly. "I'll pray for you again."

He walked back through the alleys, raucous now with the clamour of day. His mind was numb, numb with tiredness, numb with a quiet horror at the helpless cruelty of life. He walked past the train of donkeys carrying night soil over Garden Bridge without even turning his face away. He thought of the dead baby girl in Janet Pulham's bag and the live baby girl in Su-mei's bedroom.

He shaved and bathed and washed all the weariness and grime away, leaving only the memory of it like a dull

279

pain in his head. He ate a large breakfast, ignoring Ah King's inquisitive glances, and had Chan drive him round to Su-mei's apartment. She had just fed the baby. A drop of pale, watery milk trickled down from her nipple, and the baby's pink, wet lips dribbled with the same pale whiteness. He couldn't look at the baby with affection. He felt nothing for it. But he knew that made no difference.

"You'd better start looking for a baby-amah," he said, before she could voice the question lurking in her apprehensive eyes. "Or will Ah Leng do?"

42

The ship moved slowly downstream in the crisp November twilight. Denton felt the deck quivering faintly beneath his feet and listened to the remote throbbing of the engines. The buildings of the Bund slid slowly past, lights glowing in their spacious windows. The Shanghai Club, McBain's Building, the Hong Kong and Shanghai Bank, the Chartered Bank, Jardines, Butterfield and Swire—each one massive and powerful, they seemed like vast idols looking complacently down on the pygmies slavishly toiling for them on the junks and sampans, the lighters and cranes of the docks below. Somewhere behind those grimly smiling idols, whose stony faces the creeping dusk was quietly softening and blurring, Su-mei would be sitting with their child: Li-li, or Lily, a stranger who was estranging them. He could pick out now the narrow strip of his own house, by the Netherlands Bank, where Ah King and Ah Sam would be cleaning up the mess of his packing and leaving. He pictured Ah King scolding her wilful son for jumping on the easy chairs, while Ah Sam's swollen-jointed hands eased the dust-covers over them. He looked at the sloping lawn, its greenness fading in the dusk, and thought he saw someone moving under the trees—the silent Cheong probably, sweeping the leaves with his slow, absorbed care.

The public gardens, the girders of Garden Bridge, the waters of Soochow Creek flowing into the river—why did he feel no regret at leaving this place that had given him all his wealth? Why this relief to be free of Su-mei and her daughter? Her daughter—he could hardly being himself to acknowledge she was his as well. The house was disappearing behind the bend in the river. As he watched, a small yellowish light appeared in one of the windows, as if someone had lit it to say goodbye. He pictured Su-mei watching the gas lamp being lit for the first time seven years ago. And it seemed as though his life had grown stale since then, stale for all his success. He no longer took in the bleak grim shapes of the wharves and cranes in Hongkew, the muffled thumping and clashing along the docks. He was looking inward, on the scenes of his life with Su-mei. Her glancing up at him as she sang in the restaurant, the click of her shoes outside his room, her playfulness, her eyes shining with pleasure at the fortune-teller in the night market... It all seemed to have changed, to have lost its flavour. Was he jealous of the child he himself had persuaded her to keep? She loved it now as fiercely as she'd feared it before its birth, while he saw it only as a responsibility that would always be dragging behind him. Or was it just that they were tiring of each other? Or was his disenchantment part of a larger disillusionment with life itself? His mind wandered from one uncertain thought to another, and only the sense of dissatisfaction stayed the same. The trouble is, I don't really care about making money, he thought with a dawning feeling of enlightenment as the dinner gong sounded behind him. That's what it is. It's not enough, I want to do something with it. He should have taken Gilbert up more enthusiastically when he suggested he might stand for the Municipal Council. Why not? He remembered Jacob saying years ago, gripping his arm for emphasis, "Shanghai controls China and the Municipal Council controls Shanghai." Something like that, anyway. He felt as though a door was swinging slowly open in his mind, a door he'd been dimly looking at for years. He'd built up a business career, why not a political one too? Already he could see himself in the council chamber, making a speech that would influence the whole city, the whole of China... He turned to go to the dining saloon. And then, as he walked along the scrubbed boards of the deck, he saw the steward carrying the gong along in front of him, and for a moment it was as though time had slipped back and he was on the *Orcades* approaching Shanghai eight years before. He could see with utter distinctness the spotty, arrogant face of the young steward beating the gong for breakfast as they sailed up the river that July morning. He could see his face and he could feel his wonder and naiveté, his apprehensiveness, again. But all that is past, he told himself. You must move on.

"Now sir," Larsen's eyes gleamed hospitably behind his pince-nez. "I insist on your staying with us over the Christmas holidays."

"But really, I've booked a hotel, it would be troubling you to—"

"Not at all, how could we leave you in a hotel at Christmas time?" His breath steamed on the frosty air outside the cavernous and gloomy customs shed, and he stamped his feet in the snow. "Mrs. Larsen wouldn't hear of it, would she, Mary-Ellen?"

"Of course not," Mary-Ellen said, pushing her hands deeper into her muff. She smiled lazily, as though she was stretching and yawning. "You'll just have to cancel your hotel I guess, Mr. Denton." The cold had brought the pink out on her cheeks, and her halo of fair fluffy hair was crowned by a round fur hat. "Do you know how to skate? We can go on the lake near home."

"Now Mr. Denton may have a lot of work to do," Larsen warned her in a heavy paternal tone, as though she were still a child.

"Oh no, not all that much," Denton said.

Mary-Ellen disregarded her father with a little unperturbed shrug of her eyebrows, as though, if he must treat her like a child, she would treat him like a dotard. "Not so much work that he can't go skating once or twice anyway," she drawled, looking not at her father, but at Denton.

He sat between them in the cab, listening to the long-forgotten sounds of wheels hissing through the slush, while Larsen pointed out the sights to him.

"That's the new Opera House over there, Mr. Denton," Larsen pointed; and Denton recalled how three years ago he'd been pointing out the buildings of Shanghai to Larsen while Larsen relayed their names to Mary-Ellen in the rickshaw ahead of them. It was as though they were playing a game, he thought, and had just changed ends.

"Do you go there often?" he asked.

"Not very often," Larsen said regretfully.

"Not at all," Mary-Ellen murmured, in a voice just loud enough for him to hear. She was gazing through the other window, paying no attention to the sights her father was pointing out. Denton could see a languid smile on the corners of her lips, as though she was secretly amused. At the same time he seemed to feel a casual, unconscious pressure of her arm against his; not artful, but warm and friendly.

"We were sorry to hear you were ill after we left Shanghai," Larsen said, rubbing his gloved hands together.

"Oh yes, cholera."

"Cholera?" His eyes widened. "Are you better now?"

Mary-Ellen laughed aloud. "That was three years ago! He'd be dead by now if he wasn't better."

Denton realised that he hadn't yet spoken directly to Mary-Ellen. He turned to her again, "What have you been doing in New York since you came back?"

"Oh Mary-Ellen's been going into things Chinese in a big way," Larsen answered proudly for her. "She really caught a bug out there in China."

Denton looked back at Mary-Ellen interrogatively.

"Oh just some work I do in the museum here," she said off-handedly. "Restoring pots and things...They didn't want women in there, but I talked them round." Her eyes narrowed slightly and her casual nonchalant tone was replaced by something keener. "I guess they realised I knew more about it than they did, after all that stuff I saw in Peking—have you seen it?"

"I never really had much time to look at things there," Denton said, apologising for his ignorance. "I was always very busy whenever I was there." His voice faded with the sense that his apology didn't really excuse him. Besides, he was being disingenuous. He'd visited Peking only once, and that was just a few weeks ago, when the boat had put in at the north-east port of Tientsin for a few days. He'd taken a train to the capital city and followed the recommendations of Thomas Cook and Sons' *Guide to Travellers*. And the truth was, he'd been disappointed. The temples with their decaying stones and idle monks, the unreal palaces and lakes, the drab walls of the Forbidden City frowning over the maze of huddled houses in their narrow, dusty lanes, even the Altar of Heaven and the Great Wall itself—he saw them all with a rising sense of dissatisfaction. Every one of them seemed to symbolise stagnation and apathy—or to embody it, rather. Give me Shanghai, he thought, where everything bursts with ener-

283

gy, not this dead museum. And he recalled Ephraim's prophecy about Shanghai once more. Only in the Temple of Confucius, with its elegant tree-lined courtyard and its quiet rows of steles listing the names of candidates successful in the imperial examinations, did he sense a different atmosphere, something enduring and undecayed like a cathedral at home. And on his last evening, something different again: the street of theatres and flower girls, jostling and vital with noises and cooked food smells and coloured lanterns. That was more like Shanghai, but of course it wasn't what you were expected to go to Peking for.

"Too busy, eh? Like me," Larsen was saying with a jocularity that sounded half-solemn. "Young girls can go around looking at things like that, but us men have to make the money, eh, Mr. Denton?"

Denton smiled perfunctorily. Mary-Ellen was saying something about Ming vases in her lackadaisical drawl, and Denton tried to recall when exactly the Ming Dynasty ended. When she turned to regard him with a questioning look in her wide, ironic blue eyes, he had to look away a little ashamed. "I'm afraid I don't know much about all that—I've been so busy, Miss Larsen."

"Right, sir!" Mr. Larsen said emphatically.

Mary-Ellen's eyes glittered faintly at her father. Then she looked back at Denton. "Do call me Mary-Ellen. After all, we've known each other for years."

"Mary-Ellen," Larsen admonished her roguishly, like a playful bear, "Mr. Denton will think you're being rather forward."

"Oh no, not at all," Denton answered hastily, noticing Mary-Ellen's lids lowering disdainfully at her father's clumsy humour. "Miss—Mary-Ellen's quite right. I mean it's three years ago that we first met, isn't it? I hope you'll both call me John?"

"John," said Larsen slowly, as if trying it out.

"I knew your J stood for John," Mary-Ellen said languidly, turning to look out of the window again. And again her arm seemed to press gently against his, as if she felt it quite natural to touch him.

Denton felt a little ripple of gratification that she'd been wondering what his initial stood for. "Well, I don't know much about Chinese art," he resumed. "But of course I'd like to find out about it."

284

"You must come and see what we've got in the museum," Mary-Ellen said, rubbing at the misted window with the back of her gloved hand. "What about tomorrow?"

"Now let Mr. Denton get his breath first," Larsen began to expostulate.

"John," Mary-Ellen said, letting her lids droop disdainfully once more as she glanced with a little collusive smile at Denton. It was as though she were saying *We'll just have to endure my father, you and I.*

It was Denton's first holiday, the first Christmas he'd spent away from Shanghai in the nine years he'd been there. Last Christmas, there'd been the usual party at the office—a sprig of fir from a hill tree, orange and soda drinks from Watson's Soft Drink Company, biscuits and slices of cake from the Chinese confectioners down the road. It was a wan affair.

"Happy Christmas," the Portuguese manager had smiled and bowed his glossy curls when Denton had forced himself to look in.

Mr. Lo had bowed too, offering him a glass with both hands. "Happy Christmas, Prosper' New Year."

"Yes, well . . . Thank you very much." He'd drunk with a stiff, uneasy smile while the clerks all watched and giggled nervously themselves.

"Now we shall take photograph," Lo had proposed. "For future reference." It was a joke he repeated every year. They had all tittered politely.

And afterwards he'd dined at the club with the other bachelors, in an air heavy with stillborn cheer. For Su-mei had been performing in Soochow, and he never accepted invitations to families at Christmas—it always made him feel like a poor relation. (Last Christmas, he thought, last Christmas his father had still been alive and Su-mei wasn't pregnant yet. How his life had changed. And, as always, it had changed in ways he'd never suspected.) But it hadn't seemed to matter, that cheerlessness, until there in New York he found himself taken up by the Larsens, and in particular by Mary-Ellen with her ironic drawl and careless, casual pressure of arm or leg—a pressure so careless that she never even seemed to notice it.

She took him, first with her plump, grey-haired mother, then—despite her raised brows—alone, to the museum, to the park, to the theatre, where the D'Oyley Carte

Company were performing *The Mikado*, and to the ice-covered river, where he found he could still skate, though not as well as she. A crowd of relatives arrived from distant parts of the country, and they sat down fifteen to dinner after the Christmas morning Episcopalian service, at which Mary-Ellen showed her indifference to religion by gazing constantly up at the roof with a superior smile on her lips while her leg seemed to touch Denton's lightly as though to say *You and I, we're above all this.*

Perhaps this is what I've been missing, he thought as she leant across the littered table to whisper some calmly derogatory remark about one of her aunts. Her hair brushed his cheek, yet she seemed unaware of it. He imagined her momentarily in his house at Shanghai, at his table, with guests ranged all round it between them. For the first time he imagined her in his bed, embracing him without guile or coyness, but with an amused little laugh, simply because she felt like it.

She was saying something again, her lips parted, showing her regular, moist white teeth, and he wondered what it would be like to kiss those lips. As if she'd read his thought, he saw her eyes glimmer with teasing irony. "You weren't listening, were you?" she accused him, laying her hand remonstratingly on his for a moment.

"I was distracted by..." His voice faded. He didn't quite dare to say what he was distracted by, with all the aunts and uncles apparently straining to catch his words.

"I was just saying how much I'd like to go back to China," she said. "It's so dull here in America. So conventional."

The Larsens invited him to their house in New Hampshire after Christmas. He'd finished his business, and his mother was expecting him in England, but the Larsens were pressing and Mary-Ellen's cool, tantalising manner intrigued him so much that he postponed his sailing for two months. *I've been delayed by business* he wrote to his mother, with a twinge of guilt as he thought of the cold, lonely house with the gloomy kitchen. But after all, he allayed the twinges of guilt, this might be important to him, it might change his life again. He felt a subterranean excitement, as though beneath the placid, tedious surface of the Larsens' life, Mary-Ellen and he were each boring a tunnel towards the other.

They travelled up to New Hampshire in the train, the snow deep outside the carriages, silencing the woods and hills with its dense smooth blanket. Her mother and father went to the restaurant car.

"Would you really like to go back to China?" he asked her suddenly, after they'd sat silently gazing out at the white undulations of the hills for several minutes. Their silence had made him tense, although she seemed at ease in it.

She didn't turn to look at him but he saw her glance at his reflection in the window. Her fair fluffy hair was curling around the nape of her neck, above the fur collar of her coat. "Yes," she said with a faint shrug. "Yes, very much."

"Well," he heard himself blurting out, "Why don't you, then?"

She turned to him now with a languid, teasing smile. "Yes, why don't I?" she echoed him.

He felt as though he'd asked her to marry him—and yet that he hadn't really asked her at all. The question and her answer hung in the taut air between them, yet neither had actually formed the question or the answer. Her parents came back, and they began talking about the village they were passing, from whose chimneys blue wood-smoke rose up in perpendicular curls on the windless air. And while they talked, Denton kept watching Mary-Ellen, wondering, between dutiful nods to her parents, whether the subterranean tunnels they were boring had really met or missed each other and gone on. He kept glancing at her, but he couldn't tell, she gave nothing away except an occasional ambiguous, sly smile. With all her lazy candour, there always seemed to be something remote about her, something she withheld from him. All her gestures were like that too, ambiguous between sensuous promise and careless indifference. Was that what fascinated him—that he never quite knew where he was with her?

He spent more time alone with her, walking in the woods where the bare branches sagged under their burden of snow, or skating on the frozen streams. Their voices echoed as sharply as axe-blows across the dry, biting air, and, apart from the dull cracking of the ice or the sudden snapping of an overburdened branch, they heard no other sound. When they rested, she would smoke a cigarette, complain about the stifling provincialness of American life, dilate on her passion for Chinese art.

In the old farmhouse, built by Larsen's grandfather when he came across from Sweden, Mary-Ellen would sit by his side, a book of Chinese porcelain on her lap, explaining the different styles and periods while he listened inattentively, looking for some recognition of that moment on the train. And sometimes she would smile as if she too recalled it, while at other times she could pause in midsentence, her eyes hardening faintly at his abstractedness.

They spent hours together, yet when they returned to New York, he was still unsure how they stood. It was exciting but unnerving to be so intimate with her and yet not to be intimate at all. It wasn't until the night before he sailed that he brought himself to allude to that brief exchange in the train again.

"Would you still like to go back to China, Mary-Ellen?"

She nodded, glancing frankly into his eyes this time. "You know I would."

"Well, we'll have to arrange it then," he said unsteadily. "I mean, I'd like it too."

He took her hand, and she let it lie in his, yet she didn't return his pressure and only smiled at him mockingly. "Would you now?" she asked coolly. "All right, then."

He pulled her to him. She turned her face at the last moment, with that same mocking glance, so that he kissed her cheek rather than her lips. Yet she didn't try to move away. When he let her go she smiled goodnight and walked out of the room, and still he didn't know whether she'd wanted to be kissed or not.

He knocked on the door of Larsen's study. Larsen was there with his wife, drinking hot milk. Did they exchange glances as he came in?

"I would like to marry Mary-Ellen," he said. "I've just asked her."

"Why John, this is a surprise!" her mother exclaimed, in a tone that showed it wasn't.

Larsen's lips were rimmed with milk. "But did she accept you?" he asked archly.

"Yes—at least, I think so."

"Just like her," Larsen chuckled, his pince-nez trembling then slipping off his nose. "You'll never know where you are with her, John, I'm sure we don't. Like when she said she wished she could have been George Sand the other night. Now who in the world was George Sand?"

Mrs. Larsen went to find Mary-Ellen while her husband poured Denton some warm milk despite his protests. Denton hated warm milk.

"Of course I accepted him," Mary-Ellen said, calmly lighting a cigarette. "The only condition is that I want to be married in Shanghai, out of the clutches of all my deadly aunts and uncles."

When Denton sailed the next day, an announcement of their engagement had already been sent to the *New York Times,* and it had been settled that he'd return to America on his way back to Shanghai. "To finalise the deal and exchange contracts," as Larsen said with his cumbrous sense of humour. Perhaps there was a faint sense of relief in his voice too—relief that they were getting their wayward, unpredictable daughter off their hands.

It wasn't until he was alone on the boat and the grim, smoky docks were beginning to blur, that Denton reflected on Mary-Ellen's character again. He'd never imagined a woman could be so natural and unaffected, so indifferent to conventional opinion. She'd taken it all so casually—as though she were merely accepting an invitation to dinner, not to marry someone and live at the other side of the world. Again he thought of her in his bed. Those blue eyes and that fair Swedish skin seemed to promise a new kind of sensuousness for all her offhandedness when he'd touched her. He imagined her giving herself to him without fuss or coquetry, as if it were the simplest, most natural thing in the world.

And he would be able to entertain important people in Shanghai now, he thought, people Su-mei couldn't be introduced to. He'd be able to break out of the narrow world of money-making into the wider world of people like Gilbert and the foreign consuls, a world where he could play a larger part.

In all his thoughts about Mary-Ellen, he was conscious of the shadowy reproachful figure of Su-mei. But then he couldn't marry Su-mei, they'd known that from the beginning. There'd always been only one status she could ever have with him. But he wouldn't abandon her, as so many Europeans did their mistresses when they brought a wife out from home. He'd settle an allowance on her and the child, he'd make sure Lily was educated and didn't want.

289

Would he tell Mary-Ellen about her? He suspected from casual matter-of-fact remarks she'd made that she might have guessed already, and certainly wouldn't condemn him. "Of course Chinese society always had concubines," she'd said, shocking her mother who drew her brows down and tutted her lips with a flustered shaking of her head. "And when Europeans went out there they naturally followed the Chinese customs, if they weren't married already. The Chinese were always more realistic about these things of course, while here in America we're so censorious and hypocritical." What else could that be but an acknowledgement and acceptance of the facts? He'd explain it to her one day, he thought vaguely, not seeing any need to do so at once.

And Su-mei? That chapter of his life was ending anyway when he left Shanghai. She must have known that herself. She'd accept the new situation provided she didn't lose face. And yet, when, thinking coldly of her like that, he visualised her face, her walk, her black hair on the pillow, he couldn't fend off a sense of sadness and remorse.

43

"Oh it's you," she said, opening the door wider. "Come at last, have you?"

He glanced guiltily at his mother's grey, lank hair, her pale cheeks and lustreless eyes. Guiltily as if he were to blame for her ageing, her loneliness. When she bent with a sigh to straighten the doormat he saw that her shoulders had grown round, almost into a hump.

"I'm sorry I had to delay," he said awkwardly. "It was business and..." He shied away from telling her about Mary-Ellen yet.

"Well come along in, it's cold." She shut the door first, then distantly let him kiss her cheek. Her skin felt papery and smelt of soap. There were grey hairs growing on her upper lip. "I s'pose you're too grand now to come in the back way?"

"No, I just didn't think..." he said apologetically. "And with my luggage..."

How dingy the hall seemed, smelling vaguely of damp plaster. The flowery wallpaper he'd long forgotten was still there, with strips peeling from the corners like worn-out memories. She'd refused to take more money from him since his father had died, saying her widow's insurance was enough, but the house smelt of drabness and poverty, and he felt guilty for that too, as well as for her loneliness and her age. He followed her past the front room, the door closed as always, into the kitchen, where the life of the house, such as it was, had always gone on. Nothing had been moved there, nothing had changed except that everything seemed smaller and darker than he remembered it. His father's chair stood in its place by the oven, yes, with the same L-shaped tear unmended in the black leather skin of the upholstery. He felt a little shock when she sat down on it with another sigh. No one had ever sat in that chair except his father, as long as he could remember.

Her eyes caught his expression before he could conceal it. "Oh your father won't mind. He's out of it now," she said in a listless voice. "Well, what kept you in America? You look thin, aren't you eating enough? The kettle's nearly boiling," she bent forward to riddle the grate. "I s'pose you'd like a cup of tea?"

He stumbled out the news of his engagement. She heard it without comment. Almost without interest, it seemed. "So you'll be staying out there a good long while yet, I suppose? I'll be dead and forgotten like your father by the time you come back again."

"You know you could always come out there," he began, watching her warm the teapot—it was a different pot, not the old brown one with a chip in the spout. That at least had changed since he'd gone away. Something was different.

She didn't answer at first, emptying the scalding water down the cracked scullery sink, then spooning the cheap small-leafed tea out of the same dented caddy. "A fine lot that'd cost me," she said at last. "Going out there to all those dirty yellow people. As if I'd got the money for that."

"It wouldn't cost you a penny. I'd pay your trip of course. And you'd be staying with me—us."

"In the same house with a couple of newlyweds? I should think so! No I'll stay here. Too old to go gallivanting round at my age."

The kettle started boiling at last, steam hissing from

its long, swan's-neck spout. Drops of water fell onto the grate and spat as they sizzled on the hot iron. "Your father's well out of it," she said shaking her head again as she poured the steaming water into the pot. Her knuckles, whitening as she gripped the kettle handle, looked large, and yet smooth, as if the years had both swollen them and worn them down. "He always was the lucky one. Apart from his accident. It's me that's got left behind, I'm the one that's got all the worry of carrying on alone. One son killed in South Africa and the other thousands of miles away in China as well..."

He opened one of his cases and took out the present he'd brought her.

"What's that then?" She peered at it across the table.

"It's a Chinese painting." He unfurled it and held it up. "It's painted on silk."

She gazed at it for a few seconds. "Well, thank you," she said, almost cursorily. "Don't know where I'll put it though, I'm sure. What is it, birds?"

"Yes, birds. I'll hang it up for you." He rolled the scroll up again and laid it on the table. "All it needs is a nail. Just tell me where you want it. I've got some material for you too, packed away. Shantung silk. You can make yourself a dress."

"Oh I can't see to sew any more. It hurts my eyes." She stirred the tea and put the spoon down on her saucer. It was covered with wet, dark, clinging tea leaves. She gazed at them for a while, her brow wrinkled into a frown, then "Your father's ashes are in the scullery by the way," she went on matter-of-factly, as though the tea leaves had reminded her. "On top of that cupboard by the window. He wanted the ashes scattered in the fields over Bulsmore Lane way. I thought I'd leave it till you came. I can't go out all that way by myself. Why he couldn't be buried like everyone else I'll never understand. He always was one for having his own way, he just had to be different. Look how he never even went to church, not from one Sunday to the next."

Her voice had grown querulous. He felt uneasy hearing her speak like that of his father. She was hinting at disagreements and dissatisfactions he'd never known about. And he didn't want to know about them. He wanted obscurely to preserve the myth of childhood intact, to think they'd never quarrelled, they'd always been united,

292

even if only in unhappiness. "Well, I suppose he didn't believe in religion," he began cautiously, trying to defend his father without offending her.

But she'd gone on already. "I want to be buried in St. George's," she was saying, "When my time comes."

"Oh you've got years and years to go," he said overloudly, uncomfortable now at her talking of her own death. And yet while he spoke, he recalled Wei taking him to see the coffins he'd had prepared for his parents. *Plucking the flower of life* Wei had called death. Why was he so coy and deceitful about it when his mother spoke as naturally of it as Wei had?

"Years and years?" she repeated scornfully, "Months and months more likely. I can feel myself sinking week by week. Don't worry, you won't have to put up with me much longer. What sort of birds are they on that picture, then? D'you get a lot of birds out there?"

He stayed with her just over a month, sleeping in his old room, doing her shopping, buying the milk each morning in the same white jug from the same shop on the corner (though the people were different and didn't remember him), helping her clean the house and scrub the scullery. And gradually her shell of indifference and dogged wretchedness softened. She asked about Mary-Ellen, about Shanghai, about his business. When she was convinced that he really was well-off, she even consented to his paying the rent of the house in future—her widow's insurance and savings would be enough for food and coal, she said.

He asked if she ever saw Emily. "No," she answered with a touch of fire. "And I don't want to, either, after the way she treated you. Living somewhere round here, I think. Got a couple of kids, so they say. Her husband teaches at the grammar. If I met her in the street I wouldn't even pass the time of day with her, after what she did to you. Not that I go out much anyway..." She sniffed and worked her lips scornfully.

"If ever things get too much for you, you must come out to Shanghai," he urged her once, not from feeling, but from duty. For despite her slow thawing, she was a stranger to him now. All the ties that had bound them when he was a boy, even when he left home, had frayed and parted. She had simply become a slightly fractious old woman that he had a duty towards.

293

"When things get too much for me, I'll go to the workhouse," she said stubbornly. And though he tried to move her with a show of coaxing and cajoling, she wouldn't budge. It was a pretence of course. She would never go to the workhouse—he wasn't even sure whether there was such a thing as the workhouse any more. If—when—things got too much for her, he'd arrange for her to go into a home since she wouldn't come out to Shanghai. But he felt guilty again, as no doubt she'd intended him to. Guilty that she wouldn't become a burden, guilty at the secret relief he felt.

On the afternoon of his last day, he took his father's urn down from the cupboard in the scullery. It was a brown tin, with *Enfield Crematorium* stencilled on it in black paint. A cardboard label was tied to the lid with a piece of grey-white string. *A. J. Denton.* He was surprised how heavy it was when he lifted it down. Did a man's ashes really weigh that much?

"You go alone," his mother said. "It's too far for me to go traipsing in this weather at my age."

"We can take a brougham," he offered. "If you'd like to go."

"No," she shook her head decidedly.

He was relieved again. He hadn't wanted her to come, his offer had been half-hearted. He wanted to do it alone and not have her complaining beside him.

He'd put off taking it till the last moment, he scarcely knew why. Afraid perhaps of the theatricality of scattering his father over the fields, afraid of some sudden throbbing jerk of emotion? He walked along the familiar streets, crossed the tramlines and turned down into Bulsmore Lane. There were new houses there now, where the blackberry hedges used to be, but only at the beginning of the road. Further on, the buildings ended abruptly. Denton walked on, carrying the urn in a brown paper bag, recognizing with stinging sharpness all the places where they used to play after school. In that hollow over there, by that stream on the other side, where the broken cart had lain on its side for years, in that thicket that still had the single beech tree in it, looking so small and forlorn now. The wind, cold and raw, sent flurries of icy rain into his face. He climbed over the worn stile into the field. The grass was coarse and dank. He heard a dog barking somewhere behind him, and children's voices calling.

Where should he scatter the ashes? He couldn't imagine his father ever coming that way. But then he knew nothing about his parents really, he realised. Nothing except what his erratic memory gave him back from the age of five or six onwards. Most of their lives had been lived without him, after all. His father had lived a life as long as his before he'd been born, and as long again afterwards. And he knew nothing of it.

He was standing on a little knoll. That would do as well as anywhere. He glanced self-consciously before he drew the urn out of the bag. There was nobody to see him do it. He crunched the bag up in his hand and stuffed it into his pocket. The lid of the urn was stiff, he had to twist with all his strength to loosen it. They don't want to be thrown away he thought half-superstitiously. His ashes want to stay together a bit longer. Then, pressing his lips tight, he took the lid right off and shook the urn upside down, swinging it to and fro as if he were broadcasting seed in front of him.

Immediately the wind snatched the fine, grey powder and threw it back over him in a floury dust. He swung round with a little shudder and let the rest of the ashes out at arm's length. They smoked away, leaving a little heap at his feet which gradually dwindled as the wind winnowed it. How long it seemed before the urn was empty! He gazed down at the little pile by his shoes, relieved to see there were no bones there, only that strangely heavy yet powdery ash. His father's body was really annihilated then, unrecognisable.

The ash on his clothes wouldn't come off. The rain had streaked it over his shoes and his sodden trousers. He put the urn down and took off his coat, shaking it in the wind. But however much he shook the flapping cloth and beat it with his hands, however much he scraped his shoes on the grass and brushed at his trousers, some streaks of grey remained.

He was shivering. He put on his coat and buttoned it up, picked up the urn, tapped it on the bottom and fastened the lid again. Carefully he unravelled the paper bag and slipped the urn back into it. The grass at his feet was grey and powdery, the rain swiftly turning the powder to paste. The little heap, grown sodden and thick, was scarcely blowing away any more. It was like a tiny burial mound. How light the urn felt now.

He could still hear those children shouting. He walked back towards the stile without looking round. Anyone watching me might have thought I was only emptying ash from a bonfire, not performing the last rites of my father, he thought.

He climbed over the stile, resting his hand on the smooth, worn wood, dark and slippery now from the rain. It was those new houses that the children's voices were coming from. There were two of them, both girls, playing with a wooden hoop. As he approached, a woman opened the front door of the house and came out onto the porch to call them in. She was plumpish, about his own age, with wavy brown hair. "Mabel and Doris," she called out. "Come in at once, it's raining!"

Something leapt inside him like a startled animal. He might not have known her face, but he knew the voice at once—Emily's.

The girls went reluctantly in, dragging their hoop along the gravel path. One was about seven, the other five. Both had her brown hair. He couldn't see their faces, he was still some distance away. Emily glanced casually up the road as she followed them in. Her eyes slipped over him without a glimmer of recognition, then she shut the door.

He walked on weakly, glancing covertly up at the house as he passed. It was a semi-detached red-brick villa with gothic windows. The rain had darkened the bricks and was running down the blank faces of the windows like tears. There were some newly-planted rose bushes in the garden. He hurried on as he heard a noise at the door again. He didn't want to be seen, he wanted to bury all that past or to scatter it like his father's ashes so that it became unrecoverable.

"How did you meet father?" he asked his mother at tea that evening. She had cooked liver and bacon for his last night, and the smell even more than the taste reminded him of the past that he wanted to forget.

"How did I meet him?" She was wiping her plate with a thick half-slice of bread and that gesture too resurrected the past. "He was Elsie Waters' brother's friend. Why?"

"Elsie Waters'?"

"Yes." She pushed the dark, dripping bread into her mouth and chewed. "Elsie Waters, my best friend. She died of tuberculosis when she was twenty-one. Why?"

He shrugged, wiping his own plate now. "I just wondered. I wondered why he wanted—why he chose Bulsmore Lane?" He glanced at his scrubbed finger nails, as if expecting to see traces of ash lurking still beneath them.

"Oh, Bulsmore Lane. We used to go walking out together down there." She stopped munching and gazed across the table, her faded eyes on some scene he would never see. "I expect that's why."

Elsie Waters, he thought, your best friend, died of tuberculosis. How little I know you.

"I shall miss you being here," she muttered grudgingly, as if ashamed to admit it, when she climbed up the uncarpeted stairs to her bedroom later. "When you're not here, I keep falling asleep all the time, and when I wake up I feel so alone..." For a moment her eyes were stained, as though she was about to cry, but then her voice strengthened as she turned and went on. "Wind the clock, will you. I don't like it if it stops."

He wound the heavy black marble clock, its engraved brass plate a little dull and tarnished now. *Presented to A J Denton in recognition of his faithful service, August 1902.* There were a few embers still in the grate, but the room was getting cold now. He turned the gas lamp slowly down, watching the shadows dim on the dark walls. The clock chimed on the mantel-piece behind him. Eleven o'clock. For the first time he let himself sit in his father's chair and watched the dying fire as his father must have watched it night after night. So you walked along Bulsmore Lane with her he thought. And you met her through her best friend's brother. All that living that I never knew about, and now you are ashes where you used to walk.

When the cabbie rapped on the door the next morning, his mother's face suddenly broke. She turned her head away and cried, great sobs that wracked her shoulders.

"Go on, don't wait, you'll miss the train," she jerked out between her sobs. "I won't come to the door—go on."

"Where you off to then?" the cabbie asked, cocking his head to examine the labels on Denton's cases.

"Shanghai, China."

"China, eh?" He whistled. "In the navy are you?"

"No."

"China? That's where they do it..." He glanced at

297

Denton's inward-looking eyes, and thought better of it. "Right then. Let's get this luggage stowed away for you."

At Victoria Station, he heard a newsboy shouting something about China. He bought *The Times* from him. Inside were discreet headlines. *Abdication of Emperor in Peking. Manchu Dynasty Falls. China Declared a Republic.* His glance slid quickly to the end of the special correspondent's dispatch. *Dr. Sun Yat-sen is reported to have returned to the south and at every city gate revolutionaries are said to be posted with shears, cutting off the queues which Chinese men have worn for centuries as a symbol of their submission to the Manchu rulers.*

He laid the paper down on his knees as the train jolted forward. He couldn't imagine a Chinese without his queue.

The Larsens met him in New York. Mary-Ellen offered him her cheek, and the unaffected pressure of her arm and leg in the cab. She chose an engagement ring with him, an old Chinese ring with a heavy piece of jade set in its wide gold band. Larsen, in a "man to man palaver," said he was worried about the "upheavals" in China, but Denton assured him that Shanghai at least would always be safe. Then there were relatives to visit, shopping to be done, arrangements to be made. Mary-Ellen endured it all in long-suffering but expressive silence, or with unconcealed sighs. She was to follow Denton in a few months time, when her parents could accompany her, to be married in Shanghai. Nothing would persuade her to be married in America "with all those ghastly pious relatives sniffing into their handkerchiefs and muttering conventional inanities!"

Denton was scarcely alone with her at all, except when they went to meet her best friend, Helen, in a Greenwich Village restaurant. Helen, a small, dark-haired girl, was, Mary-Ellen said, "an even better judge of porcelain than I am—and that says a lot!" They chatted desultorily and awkwardly, Helen saying little. Her shy violet eyes always slipped away whenever they met Denton's across the table. As they were leaving the restaurant, Denton put his arm round Mary-Ellen. She removed it firmly, throwing a significant glance at Helen. "Not in front of the children," she murmured. And her parents were at the dockside with her to see him off, so once more she only offered him her cheek. "Never mind," her cool amused smile seemed to promise. "Once we're alone in Shanghai..."

44

There were several warships moored in the river when the liner steamed up the Whampoa early in March. The great white clouds of spring hung low over the fields and the air wept moisture, which the sun, a dim white disc behind the clouds, burned to a steamy mist. Denton looked out from the boat deck at the city he'd left with such vague dissatisfaction ten months before. Along the wharves of Hongkew he could see new military encampments—British, German, American flags and uniforms. The sight thrilled him, reminding him that great things were happening. The new wireless telegraphy service on the ship had provided the passengers with a daily digest of events in China and the newspapers picked up in Hong Kong had confirmed the sense which the laconic digests gave that the history of Asia was being made before their eyes. Garrisons were being strengthened in all the foreign concessions, ambassadors were trying to influence the uncertain new government in Peking, and there was talk of partitioning the country between the western powers and Japan if the government broke down into anarchy, as most leader-writers seemed to think it would. Denton felt caught up in the excitement. He'd come back just in the nick of time, he thought, as he made out his house flanked by the commanding merchant buildings of the Bund. He had a heady feeling that he might have some part to play in all this turmoil. He saw himself obscurely making a speech in the Municipal Council chamber, conferring with generals and consuls, influencing the destinies of millions...

As soon as the vessel berthed, he noticed the coolies with their shorn queues. The sampan boatmen, too, the dockworkers, the tally clerks, all had short hair now. It was as though they were naked, this symbol of their new freedom. Naked and vulnerable.

Ah King had sent the car, but it wouldn't start for all Chan's cursing and cranking with the starter handle. "Never mind," Denton said, glancing at the bare nape of his neck. "I'll take a rickshaw." It was the first time he'd spoken

Shanghainese for months and it felt strange and foreign to him. Chan gave a surly, half-apologetic grunt, straightening his back with a sigh.

The house was aired and cool, the garden tended, the servants smiling and expectant. He gave each of them a present from Europe—small things that he'd packed on the top of his case so that he'd be able to get at them easily. Ah King's son peeped at him from the dark of the kitchen, his eyes round with awe and curiosity. *Shanghai really is my home,* he thought as he sat down to eat tiffin, *I really do belong here.*

Ah King had cooked his favourite Shanghai chicken. She and Ah Sam hovered round him while he ate, flitting close to the table to fill his glass or take away his empty plate. They asked perfunctory questions about England and his mother, but he knew those were merely the polite preliminaries. When he started his coffee, Ah King at last asked him directly while Ah Sam giggled behind her, covering her mouth with one red, swollen-knuckled hand.

"Is it true you're bringing a wife from America?"

"Who told you that?" He felt he was blushing faintly.

"Mr. Ephraim."

"Yes, it's true. The lady who was here before, with her father. You remember? In the old house?"

She clattered the dishes together and shooed Ah Sam away. "And what about...Miss Kwan Su-mei?" she asked hesitantly, naming Su-mei with formal politeness.

"What about her?" he asked blankly. His tongue had begun to get round the Shanghainese again, as though it needed other muscles than English.

"Will you send—will she go away?"

"Foreign devils only have one wife," he answered obliquely. He glanced at her waist. Was she pregnant again? "Has your husband come back to see you while I've been away?"

"For a few days." She too glanced down at her waist, with a stern kind of complacence. Then she looked up. "Miss Kwan's baby...?" she began.

"The baby will stay with her."

She nodded, then took his coffee cup away. He heard her announcing the news in the kitchen, before the door had closed. Su-mei will know in half-an-hour he thought with a sudden pang. I must tell her first. "Ah King," he called out irritably, "I want a rickshaw. Haven't you had enough time to gossip while I've been away?"

The streets seemed more crowded than ever, the alleys almost impassable. The odours of the canals, of the smouldering joss sticks, of the opium divans, that he hadn't noticed on the short trip from the quay to his house, seemed to leap out at him now, each one embracing him with its own memory. *Yes I belong here* he thought detachedly, trying to rehearse what he could say to Su-mei. He'd kept putting off rehearsing that speech, postponing it from day to day on the boat as it churned sturdily on from England to America, from America to China; and now there he was on his way to see her with the words still unformed. The rickshaw coolie had to go at walking pace, jostling his way between hawkers and beggars, and Denton was grateful for every hold-up, every pause. And yet the words still wouldn't come to him, a great blank wall seemed to bar their path. He leant back in the shade of the canopy—the sun had burned through the thinning clouds at last—watching the coolie's dun straw hat jogging up and down as he trotted or walked or dodged, grunting and bawling out angrily as he manoeuvred the rickshaw past vegetable-sellers, fruit-pedlars, beggars, and old men shoving tea stalls blindly down the centre of the way. Letter-writers sat by the walls, reading their compositions to attentive customers, barbers were trimming hair, a cobbler with glasses on the end of his nose examined the shoe he was cutting with a puzzled, humorous gaze.

"When did you cut your queue?" Denton asked the coolie suddenly while they waited for a donkey with bulging straw panniers to pass.

The coolie stroked the back of his neck with his hand, as though hoping to find the reassuring coil of hair still hanging there. "Some men were waiting by the old city gate one morning, a few weeks ago," he shrugged. "It's the new government. Before they killed us if we didn't have a queue, now they kill us if we do." He rasped a gob of phlegm up into his mouth and spat, leaning into the shafts again.

"What kind of men? Soldiers?"

"Soldiers? No." He swung round into Yuen Fong Road. "Green Triangle, Red Triangle—who knows? I didn't ask."

The road was wider and less crowded. He began to trot again, panting with short, harsh breaths which gave him no chance to talk. Perhaps that was why he'd begun trotting, Denton thought, to avoid any more questions. He tilted his hat against the changed angle of the sun and tried to think again how to tell Su-mei. The coolie's rope sandals slapped rhythmically along on the uneven muddy road.

A hawker was chanting out the price of spring vegetables as Denton got out of the rickshaw at Su-mei's apartment. He tipped the coolie and stood looking up towards her veranda, the sun on his back, listening to the hawker's voice crying with an almost plaintive, wailing sound up at the unresponsive brick walls. Then Ah Leng's head appeared over the veranda balustrade. "How much the cabbages?" she called down to the hawker, then, as he answered, she noticed Denton. Her face changed, whether with pleasure or alarm he couldn't say, and her head vanished instantly. He walked up the stone stairs heavily. He still didn't know how he was going to tell Su-mei, and suddenly he felt guilty and ashamed, as though he was about to betray her. Yet what else could he do? Wasn't it the accepted thing to put away your Chinese mistress when you married someone from home?

Ah Leng was at the door, smiling, holding the baby in her arms. His guilt increased. He looked down at it uneasily. Its hair had grown, dark as a Chinese's. The skin was fairer, though, and the serious, dark eyes that looked up at him were rounder, with higher lids. But, No this isn't really mine, he thought. It can't be. It's hers, Su-mei's. It's nothing to do with me. Ah Leng made to give him the baby, but he brushed past as if he hadn't noticed, pausing at the ghost screen. A new mirror had been hung on it, exactly opposite the door, for evil spirits to see themselves in and rush straight out. "Where's your mistress?" he asked abruptly.

Ah Leng bolted the door carefully, holding the baby in one, crooked arm, before she answered. "At the theatre," she said, unsmilingly now. "She said would you wait." She moved past him, shushing the baby as it began to whimper.

"How did she know I was coming?" he asked, following her into the room. Everything was as it was when he'd last seen her, as though she'd preserved it untouched for his return. The sense of his treachery deepened, and he spoke more curtly to conceal it, angry with himself for feeling it, angry with Ah Leng for guessing what'd he'd come to say. "How did she know when I'd be back? I didn't tell her." It sounded like an accusation.

Ah Leng shrugged coldly, laying the child in its cradle. Outside, the vegetable hawker's voice still rose, hoarse and pleading, echoing off the narrow walls. "She read your ship was coming in the newspaper. The man in the shipping office said you'd be on it. He saw your name on a list." She turned away with another shrug and went to the veranda again, leaning over to shout down in a high piercing voice.

"Hey, how much the little cabbages? Are they fresh?"

She bargained raucously, letting down a little basket on a string and pulling it up with a cabbage in it. Denton sat down, glancing round the room that seemed to eye him reproachfully for his betrayal. His eyes kept being drawn to the cradle, in which the strange creature which he would not think of as his daughter lay, its round eyes gazing up at the ceiling. He turned away to watch Ah Leng examining the cabbage with a dissatisfied wrinkling of her nose, then leaning over to bargain further. "The leaves are going yellow, it's not fresh."

"Not fresh?" the man's injured voice wafted up. "I picked it in Paoshan this morning!"

When she'd settled the price at last, she lowered the money in the basket, pulled up the change and came in. Without glancing at him, she picked up the child and carried it into the kitchen.

The hawker's voice moved on, calling and echoing, gradually fading. The baby began whimpering again in the kitchen. Denton took out his watch. Quarter past three. He would wait till half past, then leave. He could give Ah Leng a message for Su-mei, or he could leave her a letter. A lid was rattling on a pot in the kitchen. His eyes began to feel tired. He was unused to the heavy, moist air, the lulling warmth that seemed to smother him with its gentle weight. He let his lids close, then forced them open again as his mind was about to drift off into sleep. He took out his watch once more. Only five more minutes. He began to hope she wasn't coming.

But then there she was. There was a tapping on the door which he recognised immediately, although he couldn't have said beforehand how she knocked. Ah Leng slid the bolts back, murmuring to her as she came in, and then Su-mei stood before him. She was wearing a long red silk dress. Her hair was drawn back from her face and fastened on top of her head. Some spots of theatre rouge heightened the colour of her high cheekbones. Her eyes regarded him at first with a bright warmth, but then, as he got up slowly with a wry smile, they slowly dulled as if a light had been put out in her head. She just stood there, her lips slightly parted, her eyes downcast, like a prisoner awaiting sentence, and in that moment he felt something dark and leaden plummeting inside his body, as if he knew then once and for all that he was committing a little murder of the heart, a murder that he now recoiled from in horror, but could no longer keep himself from doing.

"Su-mei," he said, his voice dry and uneven. "I've got something to tell you." And even while he spoke and he saw her eyes stir, he was thinking how absurd, how banal his words sounded, like a speech in some melodrama. He sat down and patted the seat beside him. "Sit down."

She shook her head. "I know what it is," she said in a low, lifeless voice.

"You know what it is?" he repeated stupidly. As she wouldn't sit down, he had to stand up awkwardly again.

She nodded, her lids quivering a moment. "When foreign devils come to China the first time, they take a Chinese woman and treat her well, and the woman thinks they are better than Chinese men because they don't treat her like a slave. Then the foreign devil goes away, he has a lot of money now, and when he comes back again he has a foreign wife. And then he is worse than Chinese men, because now the Chinese woman is nothing. Not a wife, not a concubine with some face, but just someone who must go away and never be seen again—nothing." She breathed in suddenly, a long shuddering breath. Her lips quivered, then she swallowed and blinked. He thought she was going to cry, but no, her mouth merely set a little. She looked up at him for the first time. Her eyes neither accused nor condoned. "What about Lily?" she asked tonelessly.

"Su-mei, I . . ." He wanted to explain it all to her, to make her see that things couldn't have been otherwise, perhaps to make himself see it too. But his thoughts ran into a blurry fog and got lost, so that all he could see was her resigned eyes that went through him more keenly than the fiercest accusation would have done. "I suppose it was bound to turn out like this," he got out lamely at last, wondering again at the banality of his words, despising himself for using them.

The baby wailed suddenly in the kitchen, and he saw her eyes turn swiftly towards it. But she didn't move.

"I mean we couldn't have done anything else in the end, could we?" he stumbled on. By saying "we" he was trying to halve the blame. "You always knew I'd have to get married sometime, and..." *And it couldn't be you,* his thoughts said, but he lacked the nerve, the brutality, to say that. "So we knew it would end this way sooner or later," he ended weakly. "Didn't we?"

She didn't trouble to answer. Her lids fluttered briefly as the baby wailed again. "What about Lily?" she asked once more. "It's a pity we didn't get rid of her, isn't it?"

He pretended not to have heard that last bitter muffled sentence. He wanted to get it over with now, to finish it off as quickly as possible. "I'll pay you an allowance of course, but we won't be able to meet any more. I'll see that—" he didn't want to say Lily, as though that would acknowledge a personal relationship he was trying to deny. "I'll see that the child has enough to be looked after and educated. You can send her to a school later on, I'll pay it all, you needn't worry..." He was speaking quickly, nervously, gabbling almost, and yet he felt as though he were miring himself down in mud, his feet clogging and sticking till he couldn't move. "I'll open an account for you in the Bank of China. It'll be all right," he ended unconvincingly, "You'll never have to worry about her."

Su-mei's lips pursed faintly. "Is she pretty?"

"Lily?" he asked unthinkingly before he realised what she meant.

"Your foreign wife."

"I'm not married yet," he evaded her question. "Not till July."

"Will you tell her about me?"

He looked away, across the veranda at the grey wall opposite, brilliant now with clear sunlight. Far away he could still hear the vegetable hawker chanting his cry like some broken-hearted lament. He shrugged at last. "Why should I?"

She slid a swift, sly glance at him under her lowered

305

lids. "Suppose I came and told her? She'd go away, wouldn't she? She'd leave you?"

"If you did that, I'd stop your allowance," he said curtly. "And I'd have you thrown out of Shanghai." It was a relief to be able to fight her, to feel threatened even, if it meant he could feel less guilty. "And don't forget it'll be a good allowance," he added warningly. "You won't be poor."

The baby was wailing again, as if it sensed the magnitude of what was happening. Su-mei's eyes flickered towards it, then she went into the kitchen and came back holding it against her shoulder, patting it gently on the back. "How much will you pay me?" She asked coldly, matter-of-factly, craning her head back to look at the baby's face.

He went to the Club afterwards, but the rooms were nearly all empty, a sombre gloom about their dark, panelled walls and their dark, heavy furniture. He walked out into the sunlight again and took a rickshaw to the Palace Hotel. As he'd hoped, Jacob Ephraim was there, his vodka bottle open in front of him.

"Sarah had her fifth last month," he called out across the room in his exuberant, unselfconscious voice. "Another girl, seven pounds four ounces. I saw your ship come in, I was coming round this evening."

"I've just pensioned off Su-mei." Denton sat beside him, gazing sombrely at his clasped hands as if they'd just throttled her.

"Pensioned her off? Why?" Jacob's liquid brown eyes widened in incomprehension. "I thought you weren't getting married till July?" He splashed some vodka into his own glass, then into the one that the waiter, with a little obsequious hiss of breath, had brought for Denton.

"I'm not."

"What are you going to do for the next three months then? I thought you liked Su-mei?"

Denton shrugged, resting his chin on his hands and gazing across the room at the thick, shiny green leaves of a rubber plant. "It was a strange thing to do," he said, as much to himself as to Jacob. "I suddenly thought it was all wrong, telling her to go, just like that..."

"Wrong?" he heard the ridicule in Jacob's voice. "But you're getting married! Of course she has to go. It is the thing! What did she expect? You have to get married, you

306

couldn't marry a Chinese girl—let alone one like her—she knows that as well as you do! Or she ought to anyway. But why now? You could have waited another three months!" He leant forward abruptly to peer up at Denton, who was still gazing gloomily across the room at the rubber plant's fleshy leaves. "Did you make her an allowance? How much? What? That's much too much, half that's enough, she'll only keep asking you for more anyway, you can't spare that much."

"How do you know I can't?"

"You don't realise how expensive marriage is," Jacob gripped his arm, "How many things you suddenly have to pay for. Servants, dresses, babies, baby amahs, doctors—Sarah's at the doctor's every other day—It's endless. I'm nearly ruined myself and I'm twice as rich as you are." He shook his head at Denton's soft-heartedness and swallowed a burning mouthful of vodka that made his sallow face redden and brought tears to his eyes. "And you've started paying Su-mei three months before you need to!"

45

The city was edgy. Denton could feel it like the breathless stillness before a typhoon. It was in the faces of the Chinese he saw in the streets, in the nervy gossip in the Club, in the subdued caution of the stock exchange. It was in Wei's eyes when he called on him, in the way he glanced at Denton then looked quickly away. For three days running the *North China Daily News* carried editorials about Sun Yat-sen, who had been to Shanghai and was now in Canton. What did he mean when he said the time had come for a new relationship between the powers and China? the editor asked anxiously. Wasn't the existing arrangement mutually profitable? In the Club, Gilbert told Denton at the long bar that Jardines were discreetly moving as much capital out as they could without causing a panic. Only Jacob was unconcerned. "Sun Yat-sen? I saw him in Shanghai, in the French Concession. He looks like a grocer's assistant. The northerners will destroy him, they want to carry on as before. Buy now while shares are low." But Gilbert shook his head dubiously when Denton hesitantly retailed Jacob's views as if they were his own.

307

He was invited to dinner by the British consul. "It is because you know Wei," Jacob said without envy. "And Wei is thick with Sun Yat-sen. They want you to sound him out."

The French consul was there, and the vice-consul of the United States, as well as Gilbert and the chairman of the Hong Kong and Shanghai Bank. The ladies left after the dessert and the men clustered together at the head of the table.

"Make no mistake about it," the French consul said lugubriously to Denton, speaking with that placeless accent that only foreign speakers of English ever achieved. "The western powers are beneath siege in China. It has always been such and will always be it." He was tall and bony, with sharp blue eyes, and at first, before he opened his mouth, Denton had thought he was the American vice-consul. "Here in Shanghai there are fifteen thousand of us, if one is to count the soldiers. Out there,"—and he nodded across the room, where the open windows gave onto the river, then the wharves of Pootung, then the dark, lightless plains that swept down to Canton and Sun Yat-sen—"out there are two hundred million—three hundred, who can tell it?—waiting to rush at the gates, to plunder the rich foreign merchant and ravage his wives and daughters. His wife, I mean." He sipped from his brandy glass, looking broodingly out still at the dark. "Today they are not strong enough. Tomorrow?" And now he shrugged with an expressiveness Denton expected of a Frenchman. "We are a city beneath a siege and we do not know when the enemy will strike."

A white-jacketed houseboy silently removed the crumpled napkin he'd dropped beside his chair.

Nixon, the chairman of the Hong Kong and Shanghai Bank, sitting across the table, was listening with an ironic smile, contemplating the port glass he was turning round and round in his hand. He glanced up at Denton meditatively, allowing the consul's words to drift away with the flat, curling layers of cigar smoke. "Your friends the Weis..." he began with a little chesty chuckle. "I suppose they might know as well as anyone else what Sun is up to really?"

"There's certainly a connection between them," Denton acknowledged. "I believe Wei gives Sun quite a lot of money."

"Ah." Nixon's glass slowed momentarily in its gyrations, then accelerated again. "I suppose you haven't seen much of them since you got back? Too busy picking up the threads and so on...?"

"As a matter of fact I'm having dinner with Wei on Friday."

"You might perhaps glean a few hints then, I suppose?"

"That may even be why I've been invited," Denton said.

"Possibly, possibly..." Nixon nodded, leaning slightly to one side as the houseboy filled his coffee cup. "No milk, thank you." He took some sugar with a golden spoon and stirred thoughtfully. "You know I was up in Peking when the Boxers were buzzing round China in 1900, when they really *were* besieging us in the legations"—he glanced beneath his drooping lids with a faintly mocking smile at the Frenchman. "And I often used to think if we'd only kept in better touch with them at the start, we might have avoided an awful lot of unpleasantness. They weren't a bit xenophobic at the beginning you know. Not in the beginning."

The French consul was pinching his cheek between his finger and thumb, pulling the skin down to give his face a mournful, bloodhound look. "They are out for possessing our goods and our women," he maintained dejectedly, regarding his brandy with solemn eyes. "That is all they desire."

On Friday, as he was dressing after his evening bath, Denton glanced in the mirror of the solid teak wardrobe and saw Su-mei standing at the door watching him.

No, it must be an illusion. He turned round swiftly.

It was not an illusion.

"Su-mei! How did you get here?"

"I haven't forgotten the way yet."

His first words had been warm, as though a part of him had forgotten he'd finished with her—the part that was spontaneous and uncalculating. But her biting tone reminded him, gave him his cue. "You shouldn't have come," he said coldly, turning back to the glass. "What d'you want?"

"Your new wife won't smell me three months from now," Su-mei said. "Even the way your amahs clean, she won't smell me then."

"What d'you want?" he asked more coldly still.

"And if I call at your house I'll still come in the front door, not the back way."

He glanced at her reflection. "Who sent you the back way?"

She sniffed scornfully, tilting her chin up. "Your amah *tried* to send me."

"Ah King?"

"That's what she's called, isn't it?"

He turned round. "Well I didn't tell her to send you the back way. You know I wouldn't do that."

"She thinks she can treat me like a servant." Su-mei's face was stiff. Her eyes glittered. "And you let her do it!"

"I've told you already, I did *not* tell her to do that."

"Well you don't stop her! She tried to send me round to the kitchen. I had to push past her!"

"All right, I'll speak to her."

"'Speak to her!'"

He sighed, putting on his jacket. That instinctive pleasure with which he'd first seen her had become bitter now with her own bitterness. "I have to go out. What did you want?"

She held out a slip of paper which she'd been keeping folded in her hand.

"What's this?" he asked impatiently, as he unfolded it. She had written in unsteady capital letters HONG KONG AND SHANGHAI BANK, 1 QUEEN'S ROAD. HONG KONG. "What's this for?" he looked up at her.

"I'm going to Hong Kong. Send the money there."

"Hong Kong?"

"There is a theatre there. They've asked me to come. It will be good for Lily too."

"Lily? Why?" He frowned down at her childlike letters, and suddenly his irritation was swept away. The regret and self-reproach that he'd felt when he broke with her returned like a dark curtain falling over him. He'd loved her so much!

"Because they have a school there for half-breeds." She said "half-breeds" with a little hardening of her voice. "A church school run by the Christians. Besides, it's a British colony. Safer there than here. If the rebels come, they'll murder all the half-breeds here."

"Who's been telling you that nonsense?"

"The Boxers killed my father's first wife."

"She wasn't a half-breed, as you call it."

She let her lids close disdainfully. "If they killed Chinese, of course they'd kill half-breeds. Send the money to the English Bank, not the Bank of China. Maybe the Chinese banks will be no good now, and lose all my money."

He folded the paper carefully along the same creases and slipped it into his wallet. "When are you going?"

"Next week. You can telegraph money, they told me in the bank. It's much quicker, all you have to do is—"

"I know how to telegraph money, Su-mei."

Her eyes dropped submissively a moment, as if all the fire had suddenly gone out. He gazed at her small, round head with its sleek, black hair and the straight white line of her parting. He had to hold himself back from reaching out to touch her. Instead, "I have to go, I'm late," he said abruptly.

She turned and walked quickly out of the room. He listened to her steps on the stairs. The front door opened and then slammed shut with a bang that shook the house. He heard Ah King muttering angrily in the hall.

The car had been repaired at last. He sat in the back while Chan honked his way between the rickshaws and barrows that scattered to each side as he drove recklessly on.

"Not so fast!" Denton called out.

Chan's shaven head nodded fractionally and he slowed a little before sending the car lurching forward faster again. Denton shrugged in resignation, gazing sombrely out of the open window, letting the warm moist air fan his face and disarrange his hair he'd so carefully combed a few minutes before. An old woman with bowed legs was setting light to paper models for the dead by the side of the street. He glimpsed a paper house, like a doll's house, as the car swished past, and a paper rickshaw, paper money, all just catching fire, beginning to twist and curl in the flames. The woman was standing still, watching with musing eyes in a lined, tired face. Was it her son, or her husband, or even her master perhaps, that she was sending ghostly possessions after, to provide for him in the world of the dead? He felt for his wallet absently in his pocket, and drew Su-mei's little folded piece of paper out, unfolding it on his knee. That might be the last he would ever see of her, that scrap with its childlike lettering the last thing she ever gave him. He was glad for the childlike

311

lettering—it recalled her as she was when he first saw her. That was a better way to remember her. All the same, it was a relief she was leaving Shanghai—she couldn't make trouble for him down in Hong Kong. Suppose she'd just appeared at the door one day when Mary-Ellen was there and showed her the baby?

They were passing the night market now, the hawkers just setting up their hissing yellow paraffin lamps in the violet dusk. His fingers folded the paper and slid it back into his wallet while he watched the tumblers and jugglers limbering up on the wooden stage in the middle of the square.

The car suddenly skidded with squealing tires. Denton looked round startled, to see a large black saloon sliding in its own screeching skid across their path. There was a long, hanging moment's helpless vision of the car irresistibly sliding towards them, and then the thump and smash of metal as they collided.

The two cars bounced off each other and stopped sideways across the road. Three men jumped out of the other car and ran towards Chan. Denton opened the door and stepped out. The three men paused, glanced at each other, at Chan, who sat still and hunched at the wheel, then hesitantly back at their own car. Denton saw a lean pale face with grey hair at the window. Then the door opened and Ching stepped spryly out. He was dressed in western clothes now, and his hair was cut like a European's, but his face was unchanged, except that the skin seemed stretched a little tighter over his prominent cheekbones, as if it had shrunk.

"Mr. Den-tong!" he called out amiably, "Long time, no see! What a nuisance these clumsy drivers make. Your motor car is not badly wounded, I hope?"

Denton looked back at the car. The offside wing was bent and torn, and the headlamp was smashed, dangling down from its polished standard like a broken limb. There was a little lake of icy blue glass splinters on the road. Already a crowd had gathered, rickshaw coolies, barrow coolies, hawkers and their customers, all standing round in a distant but growing circle, silently craning and peering to see the damage, their eyes shifting watchfully from the two cars to the three men, who had now retreated to Ching's side, and then to Denton.

"Can you drive on, Mr. Den-tong?" Ching called out.

"Yes, it's not very bad." He was ashamed to hear himself speaking so civilly to Ching after all that had happened. And yet Ching's bland politeness was like an oil that made friction impossible. Besides, it was a long time ago now...

"Please let us exchange our cards then, and arrange matters in friendly ways. My motor car is also intact. Please."

Denton took his card, printed in Chinese and English, and gave Ching his own. Ching's little fingernail was still long and curved like a hypertrophied talon, and he crooked the finger so that the nail didn't touch Denton when he took his card.

"So I hear you are a rich, important man now, Mr. Den-tong!" Ching smiled affably, his eyes gleaming with a little hint of mockery behind his glasses.

"Not so very important."

"Oh yes, I hear very important," he nodded knowledgeably. "And soon you are to be wedded. My best wishings, Mr. Den-tong."

"Thank you" Denton bowed faintly. "You are very well-informed."

Ching smiled delightedly, "Yes, I hear what are going on. And your friend Mr. May-song is also doing well."

"Mr. Mason is not my friend."

"Not your friend?" Ching's fine grey brows rose in a show of pained surprise.

"We had a disagreement in the Customs Service. Perhaps you heard about that too?" he asked ironically.

Ching shook his head sorrowfully. "A disagreement with Mr. May-song? How unfortunately. Well, I must be going along with it. Goodnight Mr. Den-tong."

"Goodnight."

"Please give my regard to Mr. Wei. You are still *his* friend, I think?"

When Denton got back into the car, Chan was still sitting motionless at the wheel. His pulse was throbbing visibly in a long mauve zig-zag vein on his forehead.

"Do you know who that was?" Denton asked, feeling his own pulse racing slightly now.

Chan licked his lips and nodded, pushing the gear forward with a nervous jerk.

"Lucky for you I was here," Denton said. "They'd

313

have made a mess of you if I hadn't been, wouldn't they? Perhaps you'll drive more slowly now."

Wei's eldest son had just returned from Yale. He sat next to Denton at the great round table and talked enthusiastically about the future of China in rushing, polysyllabic American English. Glancing at his plump, round face, on which the eyes, nose and mouth seemed all to have bunched in the middle, leaving pale expanses of featureless flesh round the edges, Denton tried to recall the shy, awkward youth this moon-faced, cocksure, yellow American had been four years before. But he couldn't visualise the pig-tailed submissive Chinese boy he used to know at all. The transformation had been so powerful, complete with American clothes and an American haircut, that the new appearance had erased even the memory of the old. Was this what was going to happen to the rest of China?

"Now the Manchu autocracy's been finally overthrown," he was saying, "all we need to do is graft a representative democradic constitootion onto China..."

His father listened, head cocked like a little bird, scepticism fighting with pride in his bright little eyes.

"But Ping-kwan," Denton protested listlessly, knowing this was only a preliminary to the main business of the evening, "What difference will that make if nothing else changes?"

"Call me Philip," Ping-kwan blinked genially, almost patronisingly, at him. "I call myself Philip in English. Ping-kwan only in Chinese."

Denton fidgeted with his chopsticks while Philip continued his assured barrage of prescriptions for China, occasionally spitting off his lips in his excitement. The other children and First Wife were chattering away in Shanghainese, while Wei, in the middle, passed like a magpie from one side to the other, picking up the bits of conversation in either language that caught his fancy. Neither Second nor Third Wife was there, and First Wife, dressed in the red she alone was entitled to wear, relished her eminence and authority, ordering the servants and children about sharply—all except her returned-from-America-son.

The last dish was almond soup and as soon as they had finished, Wei led Denton to a room behind the hall with the ancestral tablets. A baby grand piano with the lid

314

raised stood in the middle of the room. "This is for Ping-kwan," Wei said in Shanghainese. "A come-home-from-America present."

"I didn't know he could play," Denton said, admiring the spotless, polished sheen of the wood.

"It's a Bechstein."

"Yes." Denton touched the keys. "They're very good."

"They are the most expensive." Wei was watching him uncertainly as if he wanted to be reassured.

"They're very good," Denton said again. "Where did Ping-kwan learn to play?"

"He hasn't learnt yet. He's starting lessons with Professor G.B. Fenton next week. He wants to understand all about western music. You know Professor Fenton?" The glimmer of uncertainty was still there, making Wei's normally shrewd eyes mild and appealing. "Is he good?"

"I don't know—I expect so."

"How long will it take to learn to play this?" Wei touched the lid gingerly, doubt still lingering in his voice. "It's much bigger than Chinese instruments."

"The bigger ones aren't necessarily harder to play."

Wei looked relieved. He nodded. "Ping-kwan says an American friend learnt in six months. You think that is possible?"

"I'm sure he'd make great progress in six months," Denton said neutrally. He thought of Ping-kwan's moon-face hanging proudly over the keys while his fingers picked out *Twinkle, twinkle, little star.*

"It is the most popular instrument in America, Ping-kwan says. You wife will be able to play it too?"

"No, she never learned," Denton avoided Wei's eyes. "But it is popular, yes."

"Ping-kwan said every lady and gentleman learns to play it in America." Wei's voice had risen slightly as if he doubted Denton's qualifications to comment on American cultural life.

"Well many do, certainly," Denton conceded smoothly. He tried to draw Wei out of his preoccupation with music. "Ping-kwan seems very keen on western ideas?"

Wei's mouth puckered wrily. "A little too keen." He gestured Denton to a blackwood chair, and sat down himself. Denton sensed the preliminaries were over and the time for business had come. "Of course, Sun Yat-sen is also interested in Western ideas, especially since his visit to

315

America." Wei fitted his hands snugly over the carved arm rests of his chair.

"There is a lot of interest amongst the foreign devils here about what his ideas are, exactly..." Denton crossed his legs and tried to sit upright. The severity of Chinese chairs had always defeated him, with their straight, hard backs and austere, unpadded seats. "They say you are one of his closest friends?"

Wei smiled and shook his head deprecatingly, scratching his cheek with his long finger-nail and giving a little disclaiming chuckle.

"I met Ching this evening, by the way," Denton said, reminded by Wei's nail of Ching's. "In fact my car collided with his."

"Collided?" Wei's eyes widened with concern.

"Oh, not badly. Just a bit of damage. He sent you his regards..." Denton glanced at Wei. "He seemed to know as much about me as I know myself."

Wei's face had flushed slightly. He lowered his lids. "Ching had been helpful to us," he muttered sheepishly. "We don't approve of him, but Sun might have been caught by the Manchu if Ching hadn't helped."

It must have cost you a lot, Denton thought, easing his back down slightly against the chair. Aloud, he said "Ching spoke English. He always did with me."

"For some things it is easier to speak English," Wei said in English himself. His eyes were still half-closed, as if he were contemplating the glossy piano that stood before them, a monument to the utility of commerce between the west and China. "Sun Yat-sen is an admirer of many wester' idea', such as patriotism, liberty and democracy... And he see' the advantage of trade with the other country, which the Manchu did not see. He like to have foreign business in China, but"—he cleared his throat apologetically —"I think the foreign soldier on Chinese land will not be suitable any more. The foreigner will have to obey Chinese law, not govern themselves how they want and treating China like their own lan'..." His eyelids rose and he glanced at Denton appraisingly, to see what effect he was having. "When Frenchman or English does murder, he mus' be dealt with by Chinese law, not by foreign consul."

"And undergo Chinese torture as well?" Denton asked, more sharply than he'd intended.

Wei blinked behind his glasses, his face expressionless. "With the new governmen' of Sun Yat-sen, when it comes, the ol' custom' will be change'."

Denton glanced at the reflection of the gas lamp, an incandescent white circle, on the sheeny, sloping lid of the piano. He felt Wei's eyes fixed appraisingly on his face again. "All this will take time?" he asked at last. "After all, Sun isn't even in power yet."

Wei chuckled, relaxing as though some crisis had been averted. "Rome was not buil' in one day."

46

The Larsens arrived in June. Mary-Ellen nonchalantly turned both cheeks for Denton to kiss when they met at the Customs Building; her fair skin was glowing with perspiration from the launch ride in the sun from the liner to the quay-side.

"My, is it always as hot as this?" Mrs. Larsen asked, perspiring too as they shook hands. Wasn't that what Larsen himself had said when they first met five years ago? Denton felt he must have been through it all before, as he murmured an explanation of Shanghai's seasons.

Mr. Larsen called him John, and, after a second's shy hesitation, clapped him on the back. "Mary-Ellen couldn't wait to get here, John," he said, fanning his face with his straw hat.

"I couldn't wait till she arrived," Denton smiled.

"No, she just couldn't wait to get at all those bazaars and places she went to last time," Larsen went on blithely. "You know how she is about Chinese art."

"And all those silks!" exclaimed Mrs. Larsen.

They were to stay at the Palace Hotel until the wedding. Denton sat next to Mary-Ellen in the car. Her leg touched his with that same unaffected intimacy that he'd remembered so often from New York. "Don't give money to the beggars, mother," she drawled. "Those babies are probably dead already. Isn't that right, John?"

Mrs. Larsen gasped in horrified incredulity, gazing out at the jostling crowd of beggar women pressing and whining round the car.

"Yes I'm afraid that's right," Denton said.

"Oh how terrible!" Mrs. Larsen's eyes rounded. She

317

shrank back slightly in her seat, as if afraid one of the little girl corpses might be dropped through the window onto her lap.

Denton turned to Larsen quickly, with a sense of helpless shame. Whatever you did, the beggars came; whatever you did, babies were exposed to die. And you grew used to it and no longer noticed, until you saw the shock on someone else's face. "Mr. Wei's arranged some meetings for you," he said.

"Good, good..." Larsen took off his pince-nez and wiped them carefully on his handkerchief. The clip had left a little red dent on each side of his nose. "I'm looking forward to meeting him again. You're sure this upheaval in Peking won't affect business, John? I sure was glad to see those warships in the harbour." His weak eyes looked apprehensively at Mary-Ellen's unconcerned face.

"Oh no," Denton spoke in more soothing tones than he'd recently been using at the British consul's. "Just a bit of trouble in Peking and Canton until things sort themselves out..."

"Well, we certainly could buy all he's got to sell." Larsen replaced the pince-nez with a decisive little gesture that somehow restored confidence and definiteness to his face. "Provided he keeps the quality up, that is. But we can get down to that while the ladies are shopping, eh? How're you doing on the New York Exchange, by the way?"

"Not bad." Denton felt Mary-Ellen's arm pressing against his as she turned to peer out of the window at a barrow carrying two great pigs bound tight in rattan baskets. He pressed gently back. Larsen was still looking at him expectantly. "Not bad," he repeated absently, "I've done well on the railways."

"Railroads, yes," Larsen nodded. "You bought at the right time. My," he peered out of the open window, "this place sure has grown since we were here, eh, Mary-Ellen? Now what road is this we've just turned on to?"

"Nanking Road. The Palace Hotel is just down here on the left."

"I wouldn't say it's changed *that* much," Mary-Ellen said languidly, letting her lids droop faintly as though her father's excitement was rather naive. She smiled at Denton lazily.

They were married in the American Church. Denton had ordered stiff white invitation cards with silver lettering to

318

be printed for Mrs. Larsen, and she sent them out to all the people on the list he gave her. The wedding was announced in the *North China Daily News* and a press photographer was there to take pictures when they arrived at the church. As Denton stood beside Mary-Ellen at the altar, watching the insouciant smile on her face while she repeated the words of the vow after the severely Yankee pastor, he thought with a faint tug of emotion of Su-mei with Lily in Hong Kong. Yes, the emotion *was* faint and detached now, like his recollections of his childhood and the distant past. It had been; it was no more.

The pastor was looking at him. He bowed his head. Already his collar felt limp and moist round his neck—and they had the reception still to go through. Out of the corner of his eye he watched a glistening pearl of perspiration running down the side of Mary-Ellen's throat, under the collar of her white lace gown. He imagined himself following that pearl with his tongue, and catching it somewhere on her breast. The thought that he'd never seen her body, never touched it, excited him. There was the mystery and the discovery yet to come.

The pastor pronounced them man and wife. He heard Mrs. Larsen sniffing. At least, he assumed it was her. "I'm sweating like a pig," Mary-Ellen said softly as she leaned on his arm walking down the aisle.

The reception was held at the Shanghai Club. The British and American consuls came, and taipans from several of the big hongs, all with their wives perspiring in hats and gloves, fluttering their fans uselessly.

"You must come and see us as soon as you get back from your honeymoon," the American consul's wife said with a maternal smile.

"Of course we will," Mary-Ellen answered composedly. "Now that I know you've got those wonderful vases."

Sarah Ephraim had grown fat since her fifth child. She drank champagne, and giggled, with large, sparkling eyes, golden bracelets clinking heavily on her podgy arms with their dimpled elbows. Jacob took Denton aside, his sharp, inquisitive eyes searching his face. "Any trouble with Su-mei? What did I tell you? It's what they expect."

Nixon of the Bank gallantly kissed the bride, then murmured suavely to Denton as he shook his hand. "You know, I think we could do business with Sun Yat-sen. You might pass it on to Wei—After your honeymoon of course. Where're you going, did you say? Japan? Lucky fellow."

"No, Tsing Tao. Then Peking."

"Oh Tsing Tao. Delightful spot." His glance strayed to Mary-Ellen, who was shaking his wife's hand, withered and bony beneath its white glove, after thirty years in the east. "I'm sure you'll enjoy it there. Of course things were different when we were married," he added wistfully. "Come along Louise, we simply must let the happy couple go, you know..."

Chan was to take them to the station. He swept them furiously away from the Club while the Larsens were still waving and calling good luck at the open windows, so that their faces slipped back from the car in two anxious blurs. He drove as fast and recklessly as ever, his hand constantly reaching for the horn. White ribbons had been tied from the radiator to the roof and a model bride and groom fastened to the radiator cap. The ribbons and model shuddered as the car swerved, accelerating round the corner of Canton Road.

"Did they *have* to put those two dolls in front?" Mary-Ellen asked. "They're so tasteless."

"Well, it's what they do in Chinese weddings," he apologised, taking her hand in his. "The servants did it."

"It's awfully tasteless," she repeated. "You shouldn't have let them, really."

He squeezed her hand. The hot air, streaming in through the open windows, blew her fluffy fair curls about under her new brown hat, and she leant back to look out, her shoulder against his. He lifted her hand suddenly and kissed it. Her lips smiled absently while she gazed out still with her frank, curious eyes. "Look," she disengaged her hand to point out of the window. "That's the shop where they had that Ming plate I was telling you about." As she turned to look back, as if she hoped to get a glimpse of the plate, her thigh pressed against his.

He took her hand again. She let it lie in his passively. The pressure of her thigh seemed to promise something that the cool unresponsiveness of her hand denied. As though she was teasing him unconsciously, he thought, as though her natural unaffected touching and leaning against him was balanced by a coldness that withdrew, pretended indifference, dared him to go further.

"Sometimes I think you're a bit of a flirt," he said, smiling accusingly into her eyes.

"A flirt? Why?" She gazed at him with real amazement. "How can I be a flirt?"

He shrugged, unable to explain at first. Then, as the car swerved into the station. "It's nothing, really. It's just that, well..." he felt suddenly apprehensive, as though he might be going to offend her.

"Well what?"

"It's just that you seem to...well, encourage and discourage at the same time." His voice faded tentatively. Above all he didn't want to offend her, he wanted to take her that night without there being any blemish in the day.

But she wasn't offended. She merely regarded him with a stare of candid incomprehension in her direct blue eyes. "Encourage, discourage? What on earth d'you mean?"

"Oh it's very charming," he added quickly. "It's just that it's sort of unusual too."

She was still gazing at him with wide, puzzled eyes when Chan stopped with an arrogant slither of tyres on the loose stones by the station entrance.

Tsing Tao was a German concession. They'd built the hotel, with German turrets and steep mansard roofs on the edge of the beach. As soon as Mary-Ellen saw the sea, she wanted to swim.

Denton watched from the smooth bare sand while she splashed and swam among the waves that rolled evenly in from the west like shiny, rippling hills. The waves didn't break, but expired foamlessly as they ran up the beach one after the other and sank whispering away in the sand. The setting sun dyed the sky deep red at the horizon, and tinged the surface of the water too, which glistened with an almost silken sheen.

She didn't come out until the sky began to darken, her long costume clinging to her body provocatively. He hadn't seen her change or go into the water—he'd been arranging dinner with the head waiter—and this was the first time he'd seen the shape of her body. After Su-mei's dainty slimness, she seemed full and ripe. He helped her into her bathrobe, letting his hand lie on her slippery shoulder a moment. She paused glancing sideways down

321

at his hand, then shrugged the robe higher. "Now what's to eat?" she asked matter-of-factly.

Denton drank a long German lager while Mary-Ellen bathed and dressed. They ate a Chinese dinner on the veranda overlooking the beach. The breeze that cooled them also kept blowing out the candle on the table, which the waiter, with an apologetic smile, kept attentively relighting while they ate. They didn't talk much. There was a quiet current of tension and expectancy running through Denton, which he supposed, from her toying with the chopsticks and the wine glass, was running through her too. Well, a marriage night is a good idea he kept thinking. She was wearing a high-necked white silk blouse and long black skirt. Her skin glowed from the swimming, which seemed to have washed all her travel-weariness away.

"Aren't you too hot in that?" he asked, admiring the way her full white throat rose out of the frills of her blouse.

"Not particularly." She fingered the mother of pearl button at her neck as if, despite what she'd said, she might want to loosen it, but then laid her hand down again, glancing out at the dark silence of the sea. "I'll teach you to swim," she said. "We'll go in together tomorrow morning."

He covered her hand with his and she left it there motionless, telling him desultorily about the collection of vases she was going to start making as soon as they returned to Shanghai. "Do you think I'll get on with the servants?" she asked as he released her hand to take his coffee cup. "It's strange how Ah King remembered me, isn't it? I'd completely forgotten her."

She sipped her coffee slowly, still lingering over it when the other diners, German diplomats from Peking, had gone with formal, heel-clicking good nights. Denton thought he caught an understanding and admiring glance in the grey eyes of one of them, and he let himself smile an acknowledgement. When her coffee was finished at last, she wanted to walk on the beach. So you're shy after all Denton thought. They walked slowly back and forth along the soft, giving sand. After the third turn, he took her hand. "Come Mary-Ellen." His body was tingling expectantly as he led her inside and up the stairs.

* * *

He waited in his nightshirt on the veranda. The sea was breathing darkly under the rising moon, which had laid a gleaming silvery blade across the gentle waves, all the way to the pale line of the beach. Far out, a single light glistened—a fishing junk, probably. It reminded him of his days in the customs service, of the nights at the Woosung forts with Johnson, when they used to watch the junk lights moving slowly downstream to the open sea. He heard the bathroom door open, he heard the swish of the mosquito net, he heard the bed creak as Mary-Ellen lay down.

She was lying on her back, wearing a long white nightgown. As he went towards her he saw that its lace bodice was negligently tied with a tape, which had come half undone. He could see the pale mound of her breast where the bodice was loose, and he felt his desire rising. She didn't move when he lifted the net, except that her eyes flickered towards him, shining faintly in the moonlight. He laid his hand on her breast and felt the nipple against his fingers. He bent over and kissed her lips. They accepted him coolly, passively. He tugged at the tape of her nightdress until the bodice fell open and both her breasts were free.

She stiffened faintly as he lifted up the nightdress and pulled it over her head. He looked down at the white skin of her body, the full, heavy breasts with the dark circles of her nipples the swell of her hips and curve of her thighs. "Take mine off," he whispered, stroking her nipples with his fingertips.

"What?"

"My nightshirt."

She shook her head. "I can't."

"Take it."

"No, I can't," her voice rose.

He knelt astride her then and fumbled at the buttons with one hand while he caressed her breast with the other. As he pulled the nightshirt off, he heard her suck in her breath and sigh. He sank down on her, pressing his lips onto her mouth, and let his body stretch out along hers. Her lips were still cool and passive, as if she were waiting to see what he would do next. Her body was stiff and tense beneath him. He kissed her throat and slipped his tongue between her teeth. Her tongue didn't respond. Her body didn't loosen. He raised his head to look at her. She was gazing straight up with rigid eyes, her face withdrawn, expressionless. Her glance shifted to him a moment. "Go on," she said drily. "I know we have to do this, but don't think I enjoy it."

He went on. Each night of their honeymoon he went on, but nothing he did could warm her. She endured his tenderness and his fierceness alike with the same remote, faintly repelled, passivity. Each night he spent himself in disappointed solitude inside her, and each night when he opened his eyes afterwards, he would find her gazing up in the dark, waiting patiently, distastefully, for him to have finished. And in the morning, when he awoke, she would be lying dressed in her nightgown beside him, making him obscurely ashamed of his nakedness, so that he would pull the sheet up over his chest.

"It's not that I don't like you John," she said one night, when he lay exhausted and dispirited on her body that was as pale and cold as marble. "It's just that I've never felt like that kind of thing. I've always known I wouldn't enjoy it."

Yet still her arm or leg would unconsciously press against his when they sat or walked together, and for a moment he would think, Tonight it will be different. But it never was different, and in the end he began to withdraw almost apologetically from that friendly pressure, as though she were a stranger and it could only have happened by accident.

She swam every day, and urged him to go in too. But he always refused. Something in him rebelled against the idea of her teaching him, almost as it did when Johnson offered to teach him once at the Woosung forts.

47

They returned to Shanghai in August after three weeks in Peking, which Denton enjoyed no more than the first time. The train wound through the intense green of the paddy fields beneath a great, white, burning sun that seemed to hold the humid air motionless with its blinding stare. Not even the mildest draught stirred through the open windows as the train jolted and dawdled over the points and crossings approaching the city. "There's going to be a typhoon," Denton said, sitting opposite Mary-

Ellen. "Whenever it's as still and close as this..." His voice faded with the effort of speaking. It seemed too much trouble to go on.

She had been dozing. Her eyes opened slowly and she blinked and stretched. "I wish I'd bought that vase in Kweilin," she murmured, licking her lips. "Are we nearly there?"

"You'd never have got it back in one piece."

"All the same..." And she let her lids close again.

He leant his head back against the musty antimacassar and watched her covertly while the couplings ground and squealed through his head. Her lids were lightly shadowed with tiredness, but her brow, glistening with perspiration, was clear and unfurrowed. She had taken off her hat and loosened the back of her dress. He could see the faint purplish mark at the base of her statuesque throat where he'd bitten her the night before in his frantic, vain attempts to arouse her desire. As he watched her, she stirred and sighed, licking her lips again, and the movement of her shoulders and breasts beneath her dress looked languidly voluptuous. How strange it was that she could move like that, in that loose, sensuous way, unselfconsciously displaying her beauty, and yet be unaware of, uninterested, even, in the feelings she was provoking... His own lids closed drowsily. When they arrived in Shanghai, men who saw the unconstrained gestures with which she touched him, the slow contented expression in her clear blue eyes, would never doubt she was a passionate and satisfied woman. Well, that was something, anyway. He couldn't bear the thought of sniggering behind his back. And she'd come round in the end, he told himself. She must. Despite the cold, dark worm of doubt that squirmed in him now whenever he touched her, he believed—he had to believe—her indifference would eventually thaw and melt away like ice on a river.

When he opened his eyes again, she was lolling with her head against the half-drawn blind, her full lips parted, her finger stroking the bruise on her throat, as if she was living in some dream the delight that his body hadn't brought her.

Ah King opened the door. She was wearing her best white tunic and black trousers, her hair was sleek and shiny, and a smile of wary deference creased her usually stern face.

She'd been getting at him to marry for years, Denton thought. Now she was wondering whether she hadn't raised a boulder to drop on her own feet. Her belly seemed larger than before, protruding low down beneath her loosened trousers.

"Welco' home, missy," she said in her best English, her eyes shifting from Mary-Ellen's face to her waist, as if she expected to see the fruits of the honeymoon ripening there already.

"Why thank you, Ah King," Mary-Ellen smiled casually, with that distant ease she seemed to feel towards everyone.

Ah Sam smiled mutely and shyly at the new mistress, ducking her head in a nervous little bow, then hurried out to help Chan bring in the cases from the car.

Letters and cards lay on the table, and he began opening them while Ah King talked to Mary-Ellen outside. The largest envelope contained the wedding photos. He looked down at the stilled faces in their stiff cardboard mountings. How flat and cold they looked! Only Mary-Ellen's expression was natural and unposed, as though she was smiling at a friend, not the cold glass eye of the lens. He felt a brief, mild spasm of irritation that she should look so relaxed and he so taut.

She came into the room and peered over his shoulder. "Ah King wants to have two weeks off when her baby's due," she said. "At least I think that's what she meant— Oh, are those the photos?"

He could feel her breast just touching the back of his arm, and he moved away involuntarily. "They're good of you, aren't they?" he said.

While she was shuffling through them, Ah King came in with the *North China Daily News.* "Look-see picture, missy." She held it out with both hands, open at the social events page.

They looked down at other pictures of themselves— outside the church, at the reception, shaking hands with the chairman of the bank.

"There are more of us than of anyone else," Mary-Ellen said with a lazy kind of pride. "Are we so important? Nobody else has got three pictures in the paper—only us."

Ah King pointed to the picture showing the chairman of the bank. "Very goo'," she nodded emphatically. "Numba' one."

"What shall I tell her?" Mary-Ellen asked after Ah King had gone. She was still studying the newspaper. "See what it says about us? You're a prominent member of the business community. And I'm the daughter of a businessman with long-standing connections with Shanghai."

Denton's obscure sense of irritation was growing. "They write all sorts of rubbish in that paper," he said curtly, turning away to open the other letters. "I suppose you'd better tell her she can have two weeks off. Unless you want the baby born here. But you're the missy, you have to say." And that too seemed to annoy him, that Ah King of course approached Mary-Ellen now for advice and favours, not himself.

Mary-Ellen's eyes glanced up at him curiously, as if she'd caught the brusqueness of his tone but didn't understand it.

"We've been invited to the Bank's box for the first race meeting," he said more mildly, ashamed of his curtness, although Mary-Ellen hadn't seemed hurt by it—merely curious.

"Have we?" she asked uninterestedly, looking at the photos again.

"Lunch with the chairman," he said, with a touch of his own pride now. "It's the first time I've been invited there."

"Lunch with who?" She picked up a letter and began slitting the flap open. "When?"

"The chairman of the bank."

"Oh," she said absently.

"Not till October, when the weather's cooler."

She didn't answer, reading the letter she'd opened with an amused little frown.

"I'm going to have a bath and change."

"What? All right. This is from Helen. You remember Helen?"

"Yes."

He paused by the door, waiting for her to go on, but she was too immersed in the letter itself to say anything about it. He gazed a second at her tilted head, her calm, good-humoured smile, her wide blue eyes. But she's so magnificent, he thought. She must come round, I must be able to reach her.

"She's going to Japan," Mary-Ellen said, glancing up

in pleased surprise. "Imagine that! She's been asked to buy some stuff for the Smithsonian. Netsuke and so on."

"I told Ah King she could have her two weeks off," Mary-Ellen called out from the bedroom later, while he lay in the bath, gazing broodingly down at the body that had failed to rouse her. "I didn't know she had a son already?"

"He lives in their village. Near Soochow."

"Why? Wouldn't you let her keep him here?"

He sat up, watching the water slide off his chest. "It's nothing to do with me. Or with her. It's her husband's mother that decides what happens. Ah King's job is just to produce the babies, that's all. They belong to the mother-in-law. Then when she's a mother-in-law herself, she'll look after her son's children. And make her daughter-in-law's life as miserable as her mother-in-law's made hers." He heard Mary-Ellen murmur something as he stood up, but the sluicing of the water drowned her voice. "It's called the mother-in-law's revenge," he ended, reaching for his towel.

He opened the door, the towel round his waist. "I've just thought of something. For our first party. We'll have the municipal band. They could play on the lawn."

She was lying on the bed, her head pillowed on one hand, her knee raised in an attitude that he would have found provocative if he hadn't already come to know her. In the other hand she was holding Helen's letter. "On the lawn?" she repeated abstractedly. "That sounds nice. Have you finished in the bathroom?"

She swung herself off the bed with an easy, athletic movement. He caught her arm as she walked past.

"Yes?" She smiled, her candid blue eyes regarding him with puzzled curiosity.

She simply didn't understand what he wanted, why he was touching her.

"Nothing," he said, letting her go.

But then she did understand. Her eyes hardened faintly and her smile stiffened. "We don't have to do *that* again, do we?" she asked lightly, in the tone she might have used to say *We don't have to go to that boring dinner tonight do we?*

"Not if you don't want to," he said woodenly.

* * *

328

Next morning, telling Chan to leave the car in the garage, he set off on foot for the town hall. Ah King shook her head disapprovingly. "Why keep a car if you walk everywhere like a coolie?" she grumbled.

"Madam may want to use the car this morning," Denton answered brusquely. It was the first time he'd called Mary-Ellen Madam—tai-tai in Chinese; it sounded strange in his ear, artificial. Never mind, he'd get used to it. He walked out into the sunlight. The air had been still at night, the moist heat enveloping the city like a great stifling blanket, and he'd woken up covered with a film of sweat, his head throbbing. But now the faintest whisper of wind just lifted the leaves of the poinsettia by the steps and there was the merest shading of the sky in the south-east, as though the brilliant blue had been veiled by a fine grey diaphanous veil. The typhoon's coming, he thought with relief. In a few hours it'll be raining.

He walked down Nanking Road, past the jewellers and the silk shops, past the legless shoe-polish boys banging their brushes on their wooden boxes to attract his attention, past the beggars with their tin mugs and their borrowed or dead babies. It wasn't really for Mary-Ellen's sake that he'd left the car, but because he'd wanted to walk anyway, to be alone, to let the confused discontented feelings that filled his head settle into place, present some order that he could view and understand. But when he reached the town hall, wet with sweat, no order had come. There was only the same dim feeling of discontent, of vague disillusionment, that he'd started out with.

"I would like to hire the municipal band," he said to the Portuguese clerk who sat in the office, idly gazing out across the corridor.

"Yes?" The clerk's large dreamy eyes shifted reluctantly. He surveyed Denton's sweating face sceptically for a long, insolent moment, then reached into a drawer with a leisurely movement, bringing out a maroon ledger, a pen and a bottle of black ink. "It costs one hundred dollars per hour," he warned, raising his fine dark brow. "Payable in advance."

Denton laid his cheque book on the desk. "I want it from six p.m. till midnight on Thursday the twenty-third. This month."

The clerk's eyes stirred in their liquid brown depths. Had he misjudged this nondescript person who'd apparently been saving money by walking in that heat instead of travelling by cab or rickshaw? "What name and address?" he asked in a more neutral tone, one that he could steer towards either deference or contempt when he knew who he was dealing with. "You must pay for transport if the address is more than one mile from the town hall."

"Denton. Sixty-three the Bund."

"Yes sir," the clerk said at once, dipping his pen into the ink-bottle. "No charge for transport."

The band played in their white jackets on the lawn, there were coloured paper lanterns hanging from the trees, and the waiters hired from the Palace Hotel were deft and poised as they carried the food and drinks round on silver trays.

"I just can't get used to these chaps without their pig-tails," the British consul said to Denton, taking another glass of white wine from the tray which a young waiter had adroitly insinuated between them.

"It is exactly as if they were scalped," the French consul agreed. He regarded the departing waiter gloomily. "It will be the turn of us foreigners next."

Denton had invited Parsees, Middle Eastern Jews and Wei, as well as the European business taipans. It was the first time he'd dared bring the different races together—all the more daring as he'd asked their wives as well, and it was the European tai-tais rather than their husbands, who drew the most definite social distinctions. But of course only the European wives had come—he'd known the Asians wouldn't bring theirs. Some of the English tai-tais—Mrs. Nixon, the wife of the Bank's chairman, in particular—had looked tartly at the dark and yellow skins of the Asian businessmen and muttered vinegary words about native opium peddlers, as if their husbands' firms had never traded in it. But the British consul—Denton had consulted him beforehand—went out of his way to be genial and charming, so the tai-tais had to swallow their gall.

"So pleased to meet you," the consul had greeted Wei as he entered, alone and in western dress, his smile at once ingratiating and defiant. Both men were uncertain whether to shake hands, each pair of eyes glancing uneasily at the other's hand, until the consul, with what seemed like an inward swallow, offered his first.

Wei bowed. "And how is your King-empera'?" Wei inquired politely. "Keepin' well, I trust?"

The consul's lead was followed by Nixon and the other taipans, who discreetly detached themselves from their disapproving wives. By the end of the evening, while the sweating band played selections from famous operetta overtures for the third time, arranged and directed by Professor G.B. Fenton, by then a limp and wilting figure, lively conversations—or so they seemed to Denton—were going on between the Parsee silk millionaire and the chairman of Jardine's, between Jacob Ephraim and the German consul, between Wei and Nixon. And Mary-Ellen too was moving from guest to guest, making no distinction of race or colour, though she was the only woman to do so.

"A most interesting evening," the British consul murmured as he left, bowing over her hand as if he was going to kiss it, but only lightly brushing it with his straggly grey moustache. "And most valuable, I'm sure," he added, glancing at Denton. "If it weren't so hot, I'd be inclined to say we may have broken the ice, eh?"

Wei, as he left, turned to watch Professor Fenton's final, weary flourishes with his baton.

"How is Ping-kwan getting on with his piano lessons?" Denton asked in Chinese.

Wei nodded, although his eyes looked dubious. "He practises every day," he said cryptically.

Jacob was one of the last to leave. "Well, how does marriage suit you?" he asked, gripping Denton's arm familiarly.

"Very well, very well..."

"Not missing Su-mei?"

"No," Denton answered cautiously. "Why should I miss her?"

"Oh for me the first six months with Sarah were terrible."

Denton glanced sharply at him. Were all white women like Mary-Ellen then, when they first married? After all he couldn't know himself.

Jacob went on, trampling obliviously on Denton's budding hope. "I missed the freedom, you see. The freedom to come and go, to get some variety... But then I said, why deny yourself, Jacob, if it does no harm? After all one takes a wife for one thing and a mistress for another. But I

331

know you are different," he added pityingly, "I know you think there can only be one at a time. It is the English public school tradition isn't it? Fair play and all that?"

"I didn't go to a public school."

"Well, I know you are different anyway." He let go of Denton's arm, glancing approvingly across at Mary-Ellen, who was composedly shaking the Parsee millionaire's hand. "And you've made a good choice. She's a magnificent hostess."

Mary-Ellen's shoulders were bare, and Denton could see the Parsee's eyes regarding her skin with timid interest.

"A magnificent hostess," Jacob was repeating.

He sat under a bauhinia tree when all the guests had gone, gazing out over the Public Gardens at a tramp steamer silently moving on the tide down to the sea. Behind him Ah Sam and Ah King were blowing out the candles in the paper lanterns. Cheong, the gardener, was raking the debris off the lawn with steady, slow strokes, as if it had been the middle of the day. "Leave that until tomorrow," Denton called out, but Cheong shook his head doggedly and went on raking.

"He doesn't like to sleep if the garden's untidy," Ah King said. "He was always like that."

Denton glanced across at Cheong's bowed, absorbed head. It reminded him of some patient animal, a water-buffalo, plodding tranquilly through the paddy fields at its own unvarying pace.

Ah King reached up to blow out the candle in the white lantern above his head. "Why did you put white up?" she asked in that slightly hectoring tone which she used for even the mildest comment. "Very unlucky, to use the colour for mourning."

"It's not the mourning colour for foreign devils."

"White is for mourning," she repeated emphatically, as if dinning an obvious natural fact into his head.

The players were packing their instruments away in their cases. The snap of metal clasps and the listless murmuring of tired voices sounded across the lawn behind him.

The tramp steamer was turning the bend in the river now. The stern light suddenly vanished. A coastal ship, he thought. Bound for Hong Kong perhaps. Hong Kong, Su-mei. Memories of her rippled through his mind, accompanied by feelings of loss, of guilt, of having taken a wrong path which he could never retrace.

He heard Mary-Ellen's dress rustling over the grass. "There you are." She sat down beside him and sighed, "I've been looking everywhere. D'you know what Nixon said to me?"

"What?"

"He said you ought to put up for the Municipal Council. They need someone like you, he said."

"Oh?"

"Because you're not one of the old firm, he said. Because you've got connections with the Chinese, the ones round Sun Yat-sen. There, doesn't that please you? He said it was very far-sighted of you to invite all those Indians and Chinese and so on. Aren't you pleased. You ought to be."

"Yes, I suppose so. Too tired to be pleased just now." He remembered the Parsee millionaire eyeing her naked shoulders with guilty, fearful fascination. *Well good luck to him* he thought bitterly. He turned to look at her. "Aren't the mosquitoes biting you?"

She shook her head. "I've got that new ointment on, from Watson's. Smell."

He put his face close to her palely gleaming skin. It had a strong, lemony scent. What would it taste like? He touched her round, smooth, remote shoulder with the tip of his tongue. It tasted at once oily and bitter.

"Don't," she shivered. "You're tickling. Wasn't the party a success? Aren't you pleased about what Nixon said?"

"Yes." He stood up. His lids felt sore and heavy. "It's nice to know *some* people think I'm all right, anyway."

"Some people?" she stifled a long slow yawn. "What d'you mean? I'm getting that Ming bowl tomorrow by the way, if that man'll only go down another hundred..."

48

Ah Sam came into the dining-room carrying the chicken and fresh cabbage she'd just bought at the market. "The carpenter's here, master," she said. There was a tone of hesitant self-importance in her voice. Ah King hadn't yet

333

returned from the Ching Ming grave-sweeping festival in her village and Ah Sam had taken over her work with uncertain pride.

Denton looked up from the *North China Daily News*, glancing at the clock on the sideboard. "He's early. Give him some tea. I'll be out in a minute."

She stood there still, hesitating. He looked round again. The chicken hung, tied by its leg, upside down and clucking feebly; its brown, dangling head jerked from side to side behind the heavier pendulum of the cabbage. In her other hand Ah Sam was carrying some peaches, the flat Shanghai kind that Mary-Ellen liked. "Can't you leave that bird in the kitchen?" he asked sharply.

"The cat will get it."

No wonder it was jerking its head anxiously round towards the door. "Well, why don't you kill it off at least, instead of letting it just hang there like that?"

"Oh they don't feel anything," she muttered. "They're only chickens, master."

He turned back with a sigh and lifted the paper again disgruntledly. She was still standing there, wanting to speak, but not quite daring. He'd guessed already what it was, but he didn't want to encourage her.

But she clung there like a timid shadow while the bird's wings fluttered weakly. "Master, in the market I heard..." she began tentatively, lacking Ah King's nerve, though possessing all her zest for gossip.

"Heard what?"

She giggled self-consciously. "They say Pock-mark Chen's had Ching killed... They say he's got the Green and the Red triads together now."

He'd just been reading about it—or about some of it anyway. A decomposed and mutilated body, which was believed to be Ching's, had turned up in the docks. An inquest would be held. There was nothing about Chen.

"There's something about Ching," he pointed to the back page. (The headline on the front page, which he'd hardly troubled to read, announced the assassination of an Austrian archduke in a place called Sarajevo.) Ah Sam craned her neck to see the photograph of Ching, taken some time before he disappeared six weeks ago. She couldn't read or write, neither Chinese or English; he translated the caption for her.

Ching Man-kuo, the prominent Chinese businessman, who disappeared last month. His motor car was found abandoned in the Chinese city near the rue Colbert gate in the French Settlement. Two of his bodyguards disappeared at the same time. A police spokesman said last night that foul play was suspected.

"Nothing about Pock-mark Chen?" Her voice had fallen. If a rumour was printed, she thought it must be true. Now she felt let down.

"No." He finished the last of his coffee and got up. "Where's the carpenter?"

"In the kitchen." She followed him out. "You said to give him some tea."

"He can have it later."

The carpenter was squatting on the kitchen steps, watching Cheong watering the plants in the garden. He was a spare, grey-haired man with the reddened lids and hollowed cheeks of a heavy opium smoker. He stood up slowly, smiling and bowing as Denton entered, his eyes dreamy as though still absorbed by some lingering vision in his head. A teakwood case of tools with a tarnished brass lock and handle stood at his feet. "Good morning, master."

"Good morning. Have you eaten?"

"Eaten already, thank you?"

"I want some shelves put up, for books."

The man glanced round the kitchen with a puzzled smile as if he thought the shelves were to be put up there.

"No, the room is upstairs. Come and see."

The man nodded, picking up his box. He had bushy eyebrows which he drew together in an amused, perplexed frown when he spoke, as if he couldn't quite take his occupation seriously. Or was it the idea of bookshelves? Denton wondered.

"You speak Chinese very well," the man said courteously.

"Not very well," Denton responded with the ritual polite disclaimer. "I make many mistakes—Ah Sam, please tell Chan I'll need the car at quarter to eleven, to take me to the Municipal Council meeting."

Ah Sam nodded. She had just got her knobbly hands round the chicken's neck. It beat its wings frantically now, squawking and screeching in desperation as if it knew this

335

was the final moment. Ah Sam tightened her grip. The ginger cat, crouching under the table, watched with unblinking opaque green eyes, its tail swishing gently from side to side with a sinister little whip-like flick at the end of each sweep. Denton flinched and turned away, as Ah Sam wrenched the chicken's neck with a sudden violent twist. He heard a dying indignant shriek ending in a choking gasp. The wings were still flapping. Ah Sam went past him to the door, yanking at the twisted head until it came off while she shouted out to Chan in the garage. "Hey! master wants the car at quarter to eleven." Then she turned back to the sink, holding the torn, broken neck over an earthenware pot to let the blood run into it. And still the reddish-brown wings with their gorgeous soft sheen were spasmodically flapping, the bound yellow legs twitching. The carpenter gave a dry little chuckle beside him, as if mocking the chicken's idiotic inability to realise it was dead. For a moment a memory from far away brushed lightly over the surface of Denton's mind, the memory of a man's headless body twitching on an execution ground.

He led the way upstairs.

Mary-Ellen was just coming sleepily out of the bedroom in her dressing gown. She wrapped the gown closer round her swaying heavy belly as they passed, and combed back her hair with her fingers. "What time is it?" she yawned, glancing casually at the carpenter.

"Just after eight."

She nodded, still yawning, then went slowly down, holding the banister rail.

The carpenter's sandals slapped on the polished wooden stairs behind Denton.

"Madam will have a baby soon?" he asked.

"Quite soon yes."

"You have many children?"

"This will be my first."

"I hope it will be a son."

"Thank you." Denton opened the door on the next landing. "This is the room."

The carpenter looked round with that same perplexed, humourous frown, as though putting bookshelves in there was just as comic as putting them in the kitchen. Denton walked to the window, where his desk stood, swung the window open and looked out at the garden.

Cheong was still watering the plants, his peasant's brown, wide-brimmed hat circling his silent head.

Across the road, beside the Public Gardens, a couple of young baby amahs, twittering to each other in shrill voices, were taking their fair-skinned children out, pushing them side by side in great black prams shaded by wide, tasselled, sun canopies. He looked at them thoughtfully. Mary-Ellen hadn't done anything about getting a baby-amah yet. He'd better remind her—Or would Ah King or Ah Sam do?

"*All* the walls?" the carpenter interrupted. "How high up?" His brows drew thickly together in that amused, puzzled frown again.

"Top to bottom, one foot apart." Denton sat by the desk and looked round while the carpenter jotted the measurements down in a little notebook. The room was bare except for the desk, an old glass-fronted bookcase and the teak cabinet where he kept his accounts. He felt it was his own room. Mary-Ellen's vases and pots, her screens and carvings, her jade and scrolls had gradually taken over the rest of the house and made it hers. But this was his own room, hidden away from her—she never set foot in it—like a hermit's cell. He imagined it as it would be in a few weeks, the walls covered with the books he now kept drying in the storeroom, the works of philosophy, history and literature that he'd been buying over the past two years while Mary-Ellen had been assembling her collection of chinoiserie. For in the two years of their marriage he'd began to read again, as he used to read when he first went to the teachers training college and had meant to become a learned man. Jacob had helped, with his recommendations of those strange new authors like Nietzsche and Freud, and then there were the classics he'd always wanted to read, only the desire had withered in the harsh commercial sunlight of Shanghai. Now that he was well-off and had leisure, the desire flourished again. For a long time he'd been thinking of building up a library, subject by subject. He recalled how awed he'd been when he first entered the principal's book-lined study at the teachers training college—he'd never realised before that a man could own so many books. Now he would have a study himself and everything in it he would understand and value. Was he perhaps unconsciously trying to emulate Mary-Ellen in his own way, to rival her collection of

Chinese art which she'd assembled with such an unerring eye—or so people said? Or was it rather a substitute for that enjoyment of her body that she'd so persistently denied him, so that her pregnancy, whatever else it was, could hardly be called the fruit of love?

"How thick?" the carpenter asked, squatting on the floor now. "The shelves, how thick?"

"One inch. Teak wood."

He nodded, scratching his scalp thoughtfully through his short, wiry grey hair. His lips moved slowly as he calculated, scribbling figures in the book. The dim, dreamy light had left his eyes now, though the lids were still red-rimmed.

And yet he *had* made her pregnant after all, Denton thought, glancing round the white walls again. In one of their ever briefer and less frequent couplings, in which she'd submitted to him with her familiar reluctance, she had conceived. It didn't seem to have changed her, except to make her heavier and slower. She neither welcomed nor disliked the prospect of a child. Well, nor for that matter did he. She accepted it as a temporary and uncomfortable interlude in her life—she didn't seem to think her life would be permanently affected in any way. She'd go on hunting through the antique shops and bazaars, she'd go on entertaining and being entertained at the routine dinner parties, where her easy, candid ways always seemed to create an effect—some were for, some were against, but no one was indifferent. And the child? Well, it would be there, an addition to the household, that was all. No wonder she'd done nothing about getting a baby amah—it hadn't even occurred to her that they might need one.

Yes, *coupling*, that was the word. A clumsy get-it-over-with lunge which her distaste had made *him* indifferent to as well.

"Fifty dollars," the carpenter said, snapping his book shut with a gesture of finality.

Denton smiled sadly, shaking his head. "Twenty-five," he said, in a tone that implied he was being extravagantly generous.

The carpenter shook his head in turn, drawing his brows together again in his puzzled-amused frown, as if to say: Does he seriously think I can live on nothing?

Denton shrugged, looking ostentatiously away out of the window. The British gunboat was rounding the bend now, opposite the customs house. He could see the ratings drawn up on the deck in two stiff white rows. Why am I bothering to bargain like this? he asked himself. As if I cared how much it cost. It's just that he'd think me a fool if I didn't. So he went on. "If that's your best price. I'd better give up the idea, or ask someone else."

"Nobody can do it cheaper," the carpenter smiled regretfully. "You ask another carpenter, he'll tell you more. Wood is more expensive now..." He paused. When Denton didn't answer, he sighed and shrugged. "All right, I'll make it for forty-five. I don't make a dollar's profit, though."

Denton glanced round the walls in mock disparagement of the work involved. He pursed his lips as if debating with himself whether he could afford to go a little higher. "Thirty-five, then."

The carpenter stood up, and lifted his box. "Forty."

Denton shook his head, lowering his lids disdainfully. He watched the carpenter walk to the door and bow goodbye, his puzzled-amused frown now hinting incredulity at such meanness. He opened the door, glancing back at Denton as he went out with one last, mute query.

Denton looked studiously away.

The carpenter took a step, paused, then turned back. "All right, thirty-seven fifty."

"Each shelf one inch thick? Teak wood? One foot apart?"

The carpenter nodded.

"When can you do it?"

He stroked his drawn cheeks, pulling the lower lids of his eyes down and exposing the bloodshot eyeballs. "Two days. Start tomorrow, finish on Friday."

"All right," Denton nodded. "Thirty-seven fifty."

The carpenter smiled, bowing slightly again. "You bargain like a Chinese."

"Not so well," Denton said mechanically. "I'm not clever enough."

"No you're very smart, master. Have you lived in Shanghai long?"

"More than ten years. There's some tea in the kitchen, if you're thirsty."

He looked out of the window again. The sun was rising higher, glittering on the brownish water of the river. Below him in the Public Gardens, a few European ladies with hats and parasols were walking sedately over the grass, sedan chairs and cabs waiting for them in a cluster at the gate. He heard the clang of tram bells on Nanking Road. He ought to go down and get the agenda for the municipal council meeting, with his notes on the motion he was to propose, but his eye was caught by a movement in the Public Gardens, near the azaleas just opposite. A young girl of seven or eight was bowling a wooden hoop along the path striking it carelessly and skilfully with her stick while she skipped along beside it. Behind her, a lady walked in a long dress, her head covered by a broad-brimmed hat with a trailing ribbon. The shadow of the brim obscured her face, so that all Denton could see was an indistinct pale outline. The girl had long chestnut hair, with streaks of a lighter colour in it, held back by a broad white ribbon at her neck.

The lady called out something, and after a second or two the girl deftly caught her hoop and turned, waiting impatiently for the lady to come up to her. Then they walked on together behind the azaleas, the lady lightly stroking the girl's hair. The sun burned down on the lady's hat and the girl's hair, and Denton noticed the lady was wearing long white gloves.

He watched the azaleas, waiting for them to reappear. But they didn't come. The sun blazed down on the leaves and the still, pink flowers, and another couple, two ladies with parasols, passed behind the trees and emerged in the path the other side. But it was as though the lady and the little girl had simply vanished, as though he'd seen a vision. They never reappeared.

He remembered seeing something like that before—a woman and a little girl with that same mysterious glow of serene unapproachability about them. Where was it? When? Yes, it was in the French Settlement. In *rue* Molière, that day years ago when he'd gone in a rickshaw and seen Jacob Ephraim leaving Pock-mark Chen's brothel, before he even knew who either of them was. He paused in mid-step, recalling the woman and girl he'd just seen and the ones he'd seen all those years before, entering the courtyard of that house. Was he getting confused? It seemed as though they were wearing the same clothes then as now, as though they were the same people, untouched by time—as though it really was a vision. His footsteps echoed on the uncovered boards of the dim, empty room. But of course it was just a trick of the memory, a quirk.

It wasn't until he was half-way down the stairs that he remembered he too had a daughter. And yet all through these past two years he'd carried that slip of paper folded in his wallet, the slip on which Su-mei had written the address of the Hong Kong bank in her large childlike letters.

"Mail's just come," Mary-Ellen said equably, as she dipped a buttered bread finger into her boiled egg—an English habit she'd learnt from Denton. "There's another letter from your mother."

"Is there? Have you seen the agenda papers for today's meeting? I left them on the table somewhere."

She was reading a letter of her own. "I put them on the chair. Why aren't there any napkins here?"

He retrieved the papers. "There were two when I came down. You've dropped some egg on your nightdress."

"Have I? Damn. Where?" She parted her dressing gown, tucking in her chin to look down at her nightdress. Peering down like that gave her a double chin. She started scraping at the stain, sucking her spoon between scrapes. "You look like the woman in that Rembrandt painting," he said, in a tone more amiable than he felt.

"No, you mean Rubens."

He was sure he'd meant Rembrandt—that painting he'd seen in one of her books of the full-bosomed woman wading, holding up her petticoat, which hung open at her breast. But her confidence unsettled him. It irked him too. He pressed back the impulse to contradict her, picking up his mother's letter and turning it slowly over in his hand. It felt unusually heavy. "It must be a long one," he said. "I'd better look at my notes first."

Mary-Ellen was dipping another bread finger into her egg. "Not using the car this morning, are you?" she asked. "I was thinking of going out to Tze Ka Miao. There's a new dealer out there, from Peking. They say he's got some good stuff."

"Well, I've got this meeting at eleven."

"You could send it back for me, couldn't you? You can hardly expect me to travel by tram and rickshaw in my condition."

"Yes, all right."

She shook out the letter she was reading, thick mauve paper with a large feminine script on it. "Guess what," she looked up suddenly. "Helen's going to Peking now—"

"Who?"

"Helen Bolton, you know!" Mary-Ellen's eyes glistened. "The girl you met in Greenwich Village. She went to Japan. You know! My best friend!"

"Your best friend." Denton thought of the dark-haired girl whose violet eyes eluded him the whole evening. "That shy girl?"

"With men perhaps. She's opening a gallery with some people. God, why does she have all the luck?"

"Why indeed?" Denton said, without quite knowing what he meant.

49

Denton leant back in the corner, watching the back of Chan's bullet head, spiky with stubbly black hair, watching the glittering cap vibrating on top of the polished radiator grill, watching the warm air shimmering above the glossy black bonnet, which the sunlight had beaten into a dazzling white glare. The car moved forward again and he turned his face to the faintly cooler air that flowed in through the window. He looked down at the papers on his lap; his mother's letter, still unopened, lay on top of them. He pushed his finger under the flap and tore it open. Her handwriting, which had seemed as firm as ever on the envelope, looked strangely shaky on the letter itself, large and quivering, crawling slantwise upwards at the end of each line. There were several sheets, but only a few uneven, widely-spaced lines on each one.

I cannot see to write properly. The house must be a mess because I cannot see to clean properly either ... When you are old you are no use and nobody wants you anyway ... Your last letter took six weeks ... You always say you will be coming back one day, but year after year you do not come. What is to become of me? Perhaps I should have gone to Shanghai two years ago, but it is too late now and I do not suppose I would be welcome anyway now ... I am too old and I would not know how to get a passport and arrange everything even if I

*could afford a ticket...Is it hot even in the winter there? I
cannot stand the heat...*

He laid the letter down and gazed unseeingly out at
the rickshaws, the barrows, the hawkers, the beggars, all
noisily unreeling past the window. She wants to come out
here then after all, he sighed aloud. How she'd hate it if
she did. How I would, too. He glanced down at the cheap,
flimsy blue paper, folding it slowly. Yes, she wants to come,
but she's afraid she won't be wanted. And it's true she
won't. Imagine her with Mary-Ellen for instance. He tried
to visualise her face as he'd last seen it, her rounded back,
her hands with their swollen, worn knuckles.

The car drew up outside the town hall. As he got out,
Denton noticed steam hissing gently from the radiator
cap. "Did you fill it with water this morning?" he asked
suspiciously.

Chan nodded, unconvincingly.

"Well, fill it up again when you get back. Cars need
water like animals. Madam will want to go out later. Make
sure it doesn't break down, she wants to go out to Ka Tze
Miao."

As Denton went up the steps, Nixon arrived in a
Rolls-Royce, the bank's pennant flying from the mud-
guard. Denton waited for him and they walked to the
Council chamber together.

"Well, what'd you think our chances of winning today
are?" Nixon asked in a jovial tone, as if they were going to
the races. "Getting your motion through?"

Denton shrugged. "Not very good, I'm afraid."

"No, I expect you're right," he chuckled. He smoothed
back his silvery hair that seemed somehow too old for his
still fresh-complexioned face. "Must say I don't like the
news from Europe much..."

"Ah yes, that business in the paper..." Denton said
vaguely.

They had reached the heavy panelled doors of the
chamber. "Better if we don't sit together, eh?" Nixon
murmured. "Spread ourselves round a bit. Gives an impression of support from different quarters sort of thing..."

They went to opposite ends of the long, dark table.
Denton sat next to Howard, one of the two Americans on
the Council, who was studying the agenda paper intently,
pulling his cheek out into a pouch with his finger and

343

thumb. At the far end, next to Nokomura, the president of the Japanese chamber of commerce, sat Henschel, the only German, who had been elected at the same time as Denton. His hair was short and military, now, but he still wore his spiky, Kaiser Wilhelm moustache. When they'd first met in the Council, Denton had mentioned their shooting expedition ten or eleven years before, when he'd gone with Jones and Mason on the houseboat. But Henschel had claimed he couldn't remember it, yet with a clouded stare that suggested he remembered perfectly, only he preferred not to be reminded of his humbler years now that he'd risen to be a director of the leading German firm in Shanghai.

Denton glanced round the panelling of the room while he nervously riffled his papers with his thumbnail. The tall, mullioned windows had been opened and the street noises below—cries, hoots, bells, shouts, the grinding of wheels, the steady regular whine of a saw—carried up to the room in a continuous but muted hubbub. Above the table, hanging on long, trembling shafts from the high, white ceiling, hung two slowly revolving fans, their varnished wooden blades stirring the corners of the papers in front of the councillors.

Gilbert, of Jardine's, was chairman that year. He dangled his watch on its chain, frowned down at it, slipped it back in his fob, then cleared his throat, shuffling his papers together and tapping them edgeways on the table. "May we begin, gentlemen?" He fingered the shiny wings of his stiff, white butterfly collar, "Item one, confirmation of the minutes..."

They moved on with coughing and rustling of papers to the second item. "Increase in allocation of funds for the police force," Gilbert read out in his melodious tenor. "As members will be aware, there has been an increase in the number of crimes committed in the settlement in the last two or three years, corresponding with the er..." His humorous brown eyes searched the walls for inspiration, "...with the relaxation of law and discipline that seems to have followed the abdication of the emperor in Peking. The finance committee's proposal is to increase provision for the police force this year by fifteen per cent, which will make a corresponding rise in the rates necessary next year." His forehead wrinkled as he glanced at Nixon.

344

"Would the chairman of the finance committee wish to speak to the proposal?"

"Not at this point, Mr. Chairman," Nixon leant back comfortably, feeding tobacco into his pipe from a worn leather pouch. "I think everything is spelt out in the committee's proposal. I shall be happy to try to answer any questions of course, which members may er..." He waved his hand vaguely and let it finish his thought, which seemed to be that he couldn't imagine what questions anyone could possibly want to ask.

Denton turned the page to examine the wording of his own motion once again, and to run through his notes for the last time. He heard Henschel's stiltedly correct English breaking the long silence that followed the scratch and flare of Nixon's match. How would the extra money be spent? Henschel wanted to know. On recruiting new police constables or in training better the existing police constables they already had? Or on giving them better equipment? He could not find an answer to that matter in the proposal of the finance committee.

Nixon, puffing audibly, his pipe gurgling, suggested the answer to Mr. Henschel's question was that expenditure of the moneys allocated to the...er...force was determined by the commissioner of the police in...er... what he considered the best way, having regard to the...er...situation as he saw it at the time.

Denton covered his ears, studying his notes, while Henschel and Nixon fenced, the one sharp and tense, the other relaxed and genial, at the other end of the table.

Did Mr. Henschel wish to press the matter to a vote? the chairman asked, with only a hint of incredulity.

Not this time, Henschel said at last, after glancing round the table, but he might bring the issue up again at another occasion.

Gilbert thanked Mr. Henschel smoothly for his *vigilant* interest in the finance committee's proposal and took it with a smile that the motion was now carried *nem. con.* He turned his agenda paper over and cleared his throat, while Denton felt his heart begin to thud more quickly. "Item three. The proposal by Mr. Denton to recommend to the ratepayers' meeting that the membership of the Municipal Council be increased by the addition of three Chinese members, to be elected by the Chinese ratepayers." He leant back and gazed musingly up at the gently turning

345

fan. "I believe this is the first proposal to change the Council's constitution since the very earliest years of the settlement's existence—though that is not of course to say that changes are not desirable. Would Mr. Denton care to speak to his motion?"

How high and unsteady Denton's voice sounded as he started speaking, how breathless he became, how swiftly the words he'd been silently rehearsing a minute before slithered out of his mind! But after the first few stumbling sentences, when the sound of his voice in the listening silence unnerved him completely, he became gradually more concentrated on his argument, more assured and steady, so that, instead of listening anxiously to himself, he began to attend more to the thoughts he was expressing, and even as he went on, to feel, to anticipate, to plan their effect on his audience. The sentences began to go right, with a steady logical progression, as he'd rehearsed them before the mirror in the bathroom. And he paused, he delayed, he emphasised as their sense demanded. The changing political situation in China...emergence of a modernising movement...influence of western ideas...A matter of justice, equality...It would make the Chinese partners in the future of Shanghai, whereas, if they were alienated, there could only be trouble and unrest..."If we wish to secure the goodwill of the new China," he ended, with a splash of rhetoric that he hadn't fully rehearsed, "we must surrender some of the privileges that antagonise it. And without that goodwill, I do not see how Shanghai, fourth largest city in the world though it is, can survive. It is now at the crossroads. One way leads to a future in partnership with China, the other leads inevitably to extinction. Venice, Florence, Athens, were all great city-states in their time as well. But they fell because they could not, or would not, adjust to the changes occurring in their world. I hope, I believe, the Council will show today that it has understood that lesson of history."

There was a long silence after he'd finished, and it was that silence, in which he could hear the occasional squeak of one of the fans as it turned and turned, that first taught him the power of oratory. They were silent, he knew, not because they agreed with him, but because he'd put a spell on them, his words had taken their minds over, and until their force had faded, they simply couldn't think

346

any other thoughts. It was a kind of hypnotism. He was exhilarated, triumphant.

It was Jacob who had given him that idea about the Italian city-states, of course, but that was many years ago.

Slowly the papers started shuffling again, there were coughs and throat-clearings, bodies stirred, and he heard again the street noises that he'd been oblivious of while he spoke. It was Henschel who cast the spell off first. "Mr. Chairman," he began in his brittle tones, heavy now with irony, "in the previous item on our agenda we hear how many bad things and crimes are done by the Chinese in the international settlement, and now Mr. Denton is telling us these same people should be members of our Council. Surely criminals are not yet quite suitable to attend our meetings?"

"Oh come, Mr. Denton isn't suggesting that," Nixon got in quickly before the smiles had time to turn into outright chuckles. "Surely he's suggesting enlightened and responsible Chinese should be elected, and do the electing—ratepayers, not triad gangsters."

"And what will stop the Chinese ratepayers from electing any riff-ruff who wants to buy their votes? Perhaps some of them *are* triad gangsters?"

"Riff-raff," murmured Nixon, examining the bowl of his pipe beneath lowered lids.

"Please?"

"Riff-raff. Not riff-ruff."

"That is what I have said? Riff-ruff!"

"Would you please address your remarks to the chair, gentlemen?" Gilbert interposed gently.

"Mr. Chairman," Denton blurted out, "there may be riff-raff amongst the Chinese ratepayers, but equally there may be some amongst the others too. There's no more likelihood of the one than the other."

"Mr. Chairman, does Mr. Denton say there may be riff-ruff on this council?"

"Not at all Mr. Henschel—Mr. Chairman. I'm only saying that er..." Suddenly there was a grey empty space before Denton's eyes. What was it he was saying? His words hung unfinished on the air, wilting. "I was only saying that...that there's no more likelihood of one than the other," he ended weakly, apologetically almost.

"If Mr. Denton will read the appendix to the police commissioner's report, Mr. Chairman, he will see how

347

many crimes are being committed by Chinese and how many by other nationalities."

"Well of course. There *are* more Chinese than other nationalities," Nixon answered jovially. "What do you expect?"

"Mr. Howard?" Gilbert asked. "You wished to speak?"

"Well, sir," Howard began slowly, in a slow, conciliatory drawl, "I don't quite agree with Mr. Henschel here about the riff-raff and so on, but I don't quite agree with Mr. Denton either. I mean this settlement was founded for foreign traders, not Chinese traders, and it's run by our own laws, not Chinese laws. So if a lot of Chinese choose to come and work here, that's just fine, but that doesn't mean they should have a hand in running the place. And there's another thing. If we start admitting Chinese to the Council, even just two or three, or whatever number Mr. Denton says, in a few years' time they're going to want more members. And if we've given 'em the first inch it'd be kind of logical to give 'em the second inch as well..." He pulled out a ruminative pouch of his cheek with his finger and thumb and frowned uneasily. "Well, before you know it they'll be controlling the whole place. And then where would we be?"

Only the other American and Nixon spoke in support of Denton. Henschel led the opposition. Nixon artfully tried to present the motion as an innocuous one, blandly disguising and blurring the controversial points. Henschel ruthlessly exposed them.

Several times Denton intervened to try to correct a misapprehension or misleading statement. But his remarks lacked the assurance of Nixon and Henschel. He hesitated, he considered objections seriously, he acknowledged uncertainties he himself felt, while Nixon and Henschel on the other side, were quick debaters, unhampered by a fastidious conscience.

There were only three votes for his motion. As he left the chamber, Nixon caught up with him. "Not too bad for a first attempt," he smiled, his voice rich and undismayed. "We'll have to keep chipping away at them. You spoke to the motion very well, I thought."

Denton shook his head deprecatingly. "I began to think there must be something in all those objections by the time the vote was taken."

"Oh of course there is, but nobody was talking about the real thing were they?" He stood at the top of the steps, knocking his pipe out against the heel of his shoe. "I mean after all we're only here for the money, aren't we? I happen to think, as you do, that we'll make more in the long run by giving a sop to the Chinese. And the others think they'll make more by digging their heels in. That's all. Except Henschel," he added thoughtfully, putting his pipe away in his pocket. "He's playing some other game. Bit of a fanatic, that chap. Makes me uncomfortable...Still, you gave an awfully good speech at the beginning—justice, equality, all that sort of stuff. Had them gasping and flapping like fish out of water for a time—Ah, there's my motor car. Can I give you a lift or...?"

"No, my own is coming for me," Denton lied hastily. "Thanks all the same."

He waited until Nixon's car had gone, with its streaming pennant and proud number plate—the single figure 1—then hailed a rickshaw. So I was a fool, he thought bitterly as he climbed in, a dupe. All those high-sounding principles—he was just using them as a cover for simple greed.

The rickshaw had hardly moved when a motor car horn began hooting wildly behind it. As he looked round, Chan drove alongside and swung in front of the bewildered coolie. His taciturn, morose face was grinning unnaturally. "Madam's baby has come!" he shouted. "A boy! The doctor is still there!"

The rickshaw coolie gaped, an old man with sparse white stubble on his chin and few yellow teeth in his shrunken gums. Denton gave him a dollar and got into the car.

Dr. McEwan was in the living-room when Denton arrived. He came to the door, a tumbler of whisky in his hand. "She's asleep now," he greeted Denton. "I've taken the liberty of toasting the new arrival by myself. Come and join me before ye go to see him. The nurse is cleaning things up now."

"Are they all right?" Denton heard himself ask perfunctorily. He knew they must be—McEwan would have told him bluntly if they weren't, as soon as he opened the door.

"All right? Of course they are, man. Just a few days early, that's all." He led Denton back into the room, splashed whisky into his own tumbler, then into another

349

for Denton. "Here, drink his health. Have ye got a name ready? Your wife didn't seem to know."

"No, not yet." Denton raised the glass mechanically. "Cheers," he said. His eyes took in the grey hairs spreading out from McEwan's temples like two bow waves, and the stiff, thrusting bristles of his moustache. He sipped and swallowed silently.

"Well ye don't seem very cheerful about it, do ye?" McEwan complained. "Perhaps paternity doesn't suit ye?"

Denton shrugged abstractedly. He caught the whisky smell on McEwan's breath, the filmy glaze over his brown eyes, the deep, permanent flush on his cheeks. "It's a bit of a shock, that's all, when it happens. Takes a bit of getting used to."

"Does it now?" he swallowed a gulp and put his glass down on the mantelpiece. "Well I wouldn't know about that. Go on, man, ye'd better go and see, then. I can tell ye think I'm too drunk to tell whether I delivered a boy or a girl." He held out his hand. "Well, it's steady as a rock, see? Steady as a rock." He kept his hand there for several seconds more, watching it intently for signs of a tremor, then let it drop, finishing the last of his whisky as Denton left the room. "Don't wake her if ye can help it, I've had enough trouble with her already, complaining about the pains all the time. As if ye could make an omelette without breaking a few eggs."

Ah King and Ah Sam were in the bedroom, gazing down at the baby and cooing softly while the nurse, a Eurasian from the Margaret Williamson Hospital, was laying it in its cradle—the only preparation Mary-Ellen had made before the birth. They stood aside for Denton, eyeing him with congratulatory grins that only embarrassed him. He looked down awkwardly at the wrinkled fair face with its soft, white, downy head. So this is yours, he thought to himself numbly. We'll have to arrange a baby-amah now. Or would Ah King do?

He turned to Ah King. "When did you get back?" he whispered. "I thought you were coming tonight?"

"Early train," she hissed. "The baby's like you."

"Yes, like you, master," Ah Sam chimed in.

He shrugged self-consciously, glancing at the baby again, then at the Eurasian nurse. She was almost like a Chinese, with the same slim, dainty build, but her hair and her skin were a shade lighter, her eyes rounder, her nose longer and more narrow. Was that how Su-mei's daughter would look? Where was she now? Thinking of her made him feel guilty, as though it was some kind of betrayal of the son who lay helpless before him. He turned to the bed.

Mary-Ellen's face was dewed with sweat, her skin freckled. As he looked at her, her shadowed eyelids fluttered open. "Oh it's you," she said, unsurprised. "Can't you tell them to go away? I want some rest." Her voice was furry, as though she was thirsty. A smell of antiseptic clung to her body.

He sent the servants off and returned to the bed.

Her eyes had closed again. "Pleased to have an heir?" she asked casually after a few seconds.

He didn't answer. He felt nothing at all yet. "What about you?" he asked.

"It started coming on the way to Tze Ka Miao," she said, wincing slightly. "We had to turn back. I'm sure it's because Chan's such a jerky driver, he went over every pot-hole there was. It's a pity, I won't be able to get out there for weeks now. The man's bound to have sold all his good stuff by then.—Nurse?" Her eyes opened again, the mauvish lids sliding wearily up over the eyes. "Can't we have the fan on? I'm sweating like a pig here."

"No fan," the nurse said decidedly. "Baby will catch cold."

50

They solved the baby-amah problem by giving Ah King the job and engaging a cookboy to do the cooking, although Ah King retained her position as number one. "Her cooking really is a bit limited anyway," Mary-Ellen said. It was Ah King herself who found them the cookboy. After they'd taken him on, they discovered he was a distant cousin. "It's getting incestuous," Mary-Ellen drawled nonchalantly. "Still, if it keeps the peace..."

The baby was christened Jonathan, in the cathedral where Denton had once sung in the choir. The Reverend Eaton had gone to Peking, though he was said to own several properties still in Shanghai, and to the new Dean, Denton was a respectable public figure, not a fallen sinner. Howard, the director of the American Shipping Lines, and his wife acted as godparents. "I'm really sorry I had to oppose you at that council meeting," he kept apologizing to Denton. "Especially on the day your son was being born. Maybe being a godfather will make up for it."

Denton smiled vaguely. He'd lost all his religious belief and felt a hypocrite at the font, but he was a Councillor, he depended on votes to be re-elected. So he'd persuaded Mary-Ellen, who was blithely agnostic and indifferent, to go through with the ceremony.

"What was that in the paper this morning about war in Europe?" she asked, pulling off her hat and throwing it on the seat as they settled in the car afterwards.

"They seem to be getting ready for war, that's all."

The baby was murmuring on her lap. She leant forward and handed it to Ah King, who was sitting beside Chan. "Who are?" she asked. "England?"

"They all are. England, France, Germany. Austria, Russia..."

"All because of that Austrian count being shot? Who's on which side?"

"England, France and Russia against Germany and Austria. It was a duke, not a count. An archduke."

"Three against two?" she asked lightly, leaning her head back. "It that fair?"

They were passing the letter-writers sitting at their tables in the shade, and Denton wondered idly why their clients always seemed to be women. It'll be bad for business," he said after a time. "Share prices are falling like mad." Of course, he thought, glancing back at the last letter writer, before whom a grey-haired amah sat, gazing intently down at the page as he wrote. Of course they're women, because girls are less often educated than boys are. And because they write to their children more often than men do. Like my mother. His conscience pricked him. He'd done nothing about her last letter yet.

"Oh it wouldn't be for long would it?"

"What?"

"If there was a war?"

He shrugged. "Perhaps we'll find out this evening. If the British consul doesn't know, who does?"

"Oh is he coming to dinner too?" she yawned.

"You know perfectly well he is."

They rode on in silence, Denton frowning lightly, as he often did now, so that the two sharp little vertical lines

352

between his eyes had cut still deeper into his forehead. He glanced covertly round at her as she leant in the corner, her eyes half-closed. He thought he could see the flabbiness of a double chin just forming, the first thickening of the flesh around her jaw. No, that must be because of the baby—she'd been eating and resting more—still more—that was all. And yet he couldn't help asking himself what she'd look like in five years' time.

The car stopped for a funeral procession on Soochow Road—a long ragged trail of mourners shuffling along behind a hearse with a large photograph of the dead man on top of it. A band in ill-fitting white uniforms were playing beside the hearse. The weird clanging and wailing, that Denton used to find so discordant, now seemed strangely fitting and appropriate.

"Who's died?" Mary-Ellen asked lazily. "I hope that noise doesn't wake Jonathan up."

"Don't know. Must be someone important though, there are such a lot of mourners. I can't see the picture from here."

Ah King turned. "It's Ching," she said in Shanghainese. Beside her, Chan nodded knowingly. "Lot of Red Triangle bosses there. Those women are his wives."

"What was that?" Mary-Ellen asked.

"It's Ching. That triad boss who was killed."

"Oh," she said uninterestedly. "That was a couple of months ago, wasn't it? He must be ripe by now."

"They had to do post mortems, and then there was the inquest. They can keep them on ice for months on end." He thought of Johnson in the mortuary. "And these funerals take time to arrange..."

He'd never told her about Ching and himself. All of those things that he might have said when he was easy with her had been blocked up by that lack of love, that frigidity that he'd never thawed and now didn't even want to. He watched the four wives in their white mourning robes walking first behind the hearse. They seemed to span four generations, from an old but upright woman, who must have been the first wife, to a young girl of nineteen or so, who walked slightly behind the others. Together with them, about ten other relatives were shuffling along—Ching's sons and daughters, the youngest a baby carried by its amah, the oldest a man of around thirty. Behind them came stolid-faced men with expressionless eyes, the Red Triangle bosses, he supposed. Denton looked at the coffin resting on the hearse. The professional mutes surrounding it carried paper models of houses, motor cars and money for Ching's ghost. He could see the picture clearly now. Yes it was Ching all right, larger than life, with a hint of that mocking smile behind the scholarly-looking glasses.

The hearse passed, then the women and children, then the triad leaders. Still more mourners straggled along behind them, all men, young and old, with set, grim faces and a curiously ambling gait, as if they weren't really sure where they were going.

"Red Triangle," Chan muttered again respectfully. "All big men."

"What's he say?" Mary-Ellen asked, yawning.

"They're all high up in the triad."

"They look as boring as businessmen to me."

"I'm a businessman."

She smiled casually, letting her lids droop for answer. After a few seconds, she opened her eyes again. "Haven't they finished yet? It's getting like a Turkish bath just sitting here like this."

But the rickshaw and barrow coolies in front of them wouldn't move until the last mourner had passed. Nor, Denton knew, would Chan. "You're watching the funeral of a local monarch," he said to her tartly. "This is history."

"It's too hot for history," she said.

The baby began whimpering faintly in his sleep. Denton looked down at him as Ah King rocked and shushed him. A film of dew had formed on his skin and his face was wrinkled in a comically peevish expression. For the first time Denton felt a twinge of tenderness for his son.

"I suppose he'll get prickly heat next," Mary-Ellen said. "Be wanting his feed too. Can't we go yet?"

Denton loosened the top button of the baby's jacket with awkward fingers.

"All right master, I'll do it," Ah King said. Her voice was unusually soft, as if she'd sensed the underlying antagonism between Mary-Ellen and himself, and wanted to allay it.

The last mourners filed past for another long minute in their rambling yet menacing column. Then Chan could ease the car forward again, nudging it between the teeming rickshaws, the barrows, the sedan chairs and the cabs.

"Where did you get your cookboy from?" Mrs. Abbotson asked, inclining her head confidentially towards Denton. "He's awfully good, isn't he?"

"Do you think so?" Denton glanced over her grey hair at Ah Man deftly serving the trifle down one side of the table while Ah King served the other.

"Mm, the pork was delicious."

"Ah King got him for us—he's one of her distant cousins. Like the gardener. It was slightly tricky, because she's still number one."

"Servants are so touchy these days, aren't they?" She leant back slightly so that Ah Man could serve her. "There was a time when they thought themselves lucky to have a job at all. Mark you, I've never heard of an amah being above a cookboy."

Mrs. Nixon, on Denton's other side, turned away from Jacob Ephraim with relief widening her eyes. She'd just caught the end of Mrs. Abbotson's remark. "I suppose it's all to do with this Sun Yat-sen and his revolutionary ideas?" she suggested, waving her hand disdainfully, as though Sun Yat-sen were some vulgar fashion in clothes that decent people wouldn't be seen dead in.

"Yes," Denton had been surveying his twelve guests round the candle-lit table, with Mary-Ellen at the far end by the veranda. "That is, I don't know. But I suppose the ideas are bound to catch on."

Mrs. Nixon bridled and raised her brows. She took a dainty morsel of trifle in pointed silence.

"So nice to have a small party like this," Mrs. Abbotson said blandly. "So much more cosy..."

Denton glanced round the table at the twelve guests again.

"John?" Jacob Ephraim leant forward between Mrs. Howard and Mrs. Nixon, "I was just going to tell Mrs. Howard here you should have Jonathan circumcised. It is a hygienic precaution, not specifically Jewish at all. The Moslems also do it for instance."

Denton gripped his spoon tighter, helplessly conscious of Mrs. Nixon's mouth frozen in mid-bite and of the faces turned in shocked silence towards him round the table, a silence disturbed only by the nervous jangle of Sarah's bracelets and a low, amused laugh from Mary-Ellen.

"It has been medically proved," Jacob nodded emphatically, glancing round the table with delight at the attention he was getting, "medically proved by a German doctor several years ago, that circumcision helps prevent venereal disease and cancer of the sexual organ. *Medically proved*—isn't that so, John? Haven't I told you that before?"

"What an extraordinary idea," Mary-Ellen drawled. "Where on earth did you get that from, Jacob?"

"A German journal—"

"Do you think there really will be a war with Germany?" Mrs. Abbotson asked in a loud, high voice, slightly strangled. "So many of them are quite nice people, I mean..."

"They serve jolly good beer at the German Club," Nixon rolled out sonorously. "Ever been there, Mr. Howard? Wonderful light lagers, just the thing on a hot evening— Not that this excellent French wine isn't better of course, John...Different thing altogether of course."

Gradually the conversation limped into life again, tottering and self-conscious.

As soon as Mrs. Nixon had finished her trifle, which she ate in silence, her shoulder turned ostentatiously towards Jacob, Denton signalled with a twitch of his brows to Mary-Ellen.

Reluctantly, with an ironic upward turn of her eyes, she rose and led the other ladies out. Sarah leant over Jacob's chair as she passed, and whispered urgently in his ear before hurrying after the others, her bracelets clinking.

Abbotson moved to sit next to Denton as the men gathered at the head of the table and Ah Man brought the liqueurs and cigars. "Quite frankly, this trouble in Europe could present some tricky problems in the international settlement, you know," he began. "Brandy please—if it does come to war with Germany, I mean. You see the French settlement can act more or less like any of their colonies anywhere, but we're international here. Constitutionally this is neutral ground." He paused to take a cigar and rolled it rustling between his fingers. "There's that German on the Municipal Council, for instance—what's his name? Henkel?"

"Henschel."

"Henschel, that's the chap," he turned aside for Ah Man to light the cigar. "Well, he'll be entitled to stay there and throw as many spanners in the works as he pleases until he's voted off—*if* he's voted off. And then there's the question of Sun Yat-sen and the Chinese government's attitude. Who would they back? Or would they stay neutral?"

"I suppose if there is a war," Denton said slowly, "I'll have to go back and fight..." For a brief moment he imagined himself in the smoke and fire of battle, vaguely glorious. There was even a little constriction of pride in his chest, and a feeling that he didn't quite recognise then, of relief, of imagined escape from his vague discontents to something definite and full of meaning.

"Good Lord no," Abbotson leant towards him, lowering his voice confidentially. "You'd be much more useful here. Nice to go and see a bit of action and all that, but it'd be quite the wrong thing, really. First of all you're on the municipal council and that's important. Second," he started counting on his fingers now, "You're in with Wei and that lot—valuable lead to Sun Yat-sen. Third—"

"Why do you keep talking about war with Germany?" Jacob interrupted, leaning across the table to catch what they were saying. "Germany is a civilised nation. You English should be allies with Germany. The French are your natural enemies. The French and the Russians." He drew vehemently on his cigar.

"Aren't they civilised, then?" Howard asked.

"Civilised?" Jacob turned up his eyes as he exhaled a mouthful of smoke. "The Russians are barbarians."

"And the French?" Howard persisted. "What about them?"

"The French, Mr. Howard?" Jacob's eyes, caught by a chance flutter of the candle flames, glittered wickedly. "All I have to say about the French is—Dreyfus."

"Look what Sarah's given me," Mary-Ellen said when the men rejoined the ladies. "A beautiful baby book." She glanced with ironically raised brows at Denton. "Look, there's a pocket for congratulation letters, a pocket for certificates, pages and pages for photographs, and here's the page for christening, see?"

"I found it in Kelly and Walsh," Sarah said nervously, uncertain whether Mary-Ellen was mocking her or not. "I hoped you'd like it."

Denton looked down at the book, which Mary-Ellen had open at the Baby's Teeth page now. "Very nice," he managed an appreciative smile to Sarah while Mary-Ellen gazed up at him with brows still more curved with irony.

"I only wish I'd had one for each of my children," Sarah sighed. "You forget so quickly."

"You make it sound as though we'd finished," Jacob protested. "Don't worry, we'll make plenty more."

Mary-Ellen went up to feed Jonathan while Denton said goodbye to Jacob and Sarah, the last guests to leave. Jacob paused on the porch and gripped Denton's arm while the chauffeur waited by the open door of his new motor car—Jacob had long since given up his scepticism about the future of the motor car in China, and had bought a large American Oldsmobile. "Get out of shares," he advised earnestly. "In times of uncertainty, buy gold. I've been buying gold for the last three weeks."

Denton watched the car drive away, its headlights flaring on moths and flying beetles that dashed themselves crazily against the glass. He turned and walked thoughtfully up the stairs, Jacob's words echoing in his mind. Outside the bedroom, Sarah's baby book lay on the floor. He picked it up and went in. Mary-Ellen was sitting yawning on the bed, half-naked, while Jonathan sucked on her nipple with little grunting gulps, his tiny pink fingers curling and uncurling as they dug into her heavy breast.

"What's that?" she asked with a yawn, her eyes half-closed. "Sarah's present? I dropped it on the floor, they can clear it away tomorrow."

"We'd better keep it for a bit, in case she asks about it."

She shrugged, her lids closing again. "Somewhere out of sight, then."

He took the book with him up the next flight of stairs to his study and switched on the new electric light. The opium-smoking carpenter had made the shelves well, and Denton had filled them now with all the books he'd read, or meant to read one day. He laid Sarah's present down on the desk and gazed at it abstractedly. The wine had worn off, leaving him stale and disenchanted. There was Sarah's book, so neatly expressing the kind of life she led. And there was Mary-Ellen's life, and his own. They seemed so different close-up, but when you stood back a little, the differences blurred and all you saw was the sameness of them all. As if you were looking at so many ants. And somehow the memory of Mary-Ellen's so obvious contempt for Sarah's gift angered him then. One ant looking down on another—what an absurd idea!

He took off his jacket and tie, unlocked the new teak cabinet in which he kept his accounts and took them out.

"What on earth are you doing here?" Mary-Ellen asked him when she came in an hour later. "Not working at this hour?"

He lifted his hands carefully from the pages, so that they wouldn't stick to his sweat. "Jacob said I ought to sell my shares and get into gold..." he looked up at her, his eyes blurred with fatigue. She was wearing a pink night-gown, one silken strap slipping off her shoulder.

"I'd just fallen asleep, and then Jonathan started crying," she interrupted, yawning. "He's only just gone off again. He really ought to sleep with Ah King in future. And I think it's time he went on the bottle. This constant breast feeding's such a drag. I feel like a cow."

"But I think I may have left it too late," he went on as though he hadn't heard. "A lot of these shares have fallen so low already. Perhaps I'd better hang on and risk it. Or even buy more while they're cheap..."

She yawned again, uninterestedly. "Well you've always got your agency with Wei and Sons, haven't you?"

"If there's a war, there won't be any orders. It won't affect him much, he's got so many irons in his fire. But it will affect us."

"Why must you be so pessimistic?" she sighed. "Of course there won't be a war."

51

War was declared and the stock-market fell. "Buy gold!" Jacob kept advising Denton, gripping his arm and digging his fingers fiercely into his flesh in despair at his obstinacy. But Denton refused. "Too late now, Jacob, prices are too low," he kept answering calmly month after month, while the value of his investments plunged lower and lower. "Better to buy while they're cheap. The war's bound to end soon."

"Soon? How long did it take England to beat the

359

Boers?" Jacob scoffed. "You think the Germans will be easier?"

But Denton was too far in. He'd bought more than he could afford, gambling on a short war, and now the prices were so low, and gold so high, there was nothing he could do except hang on. Each morning, when he looked at the war news and the stock markets, his lips would tighten and the vertical lines in his forehead draw closer together. Reading the reports of the battles on the western front, he often wished he'd joined up instead of bowing to the consul's pressure to stay in Shanghai. To be wounded or killed in some desperate attack seemed so much better than his remorseless, nagging worry that he woke up to every day.

He told Mary-Ellen they would have to economise, she'd just have to stop spending so much on her pots and vases.

"But they're so cheap now," she protested. "Why don't you sell the car? It's hardly ever working now anyway. And you can get rid of Chan too."

She went on buying just the same. He expostulated mildly, but his complaints lacked conviction. Wasn't he responsible for their troubles? Why hadn't he taken Jacob's advice? Too lazy? Too arrogant? He'd never failed in the past, so he'd thought he was infallible? Well now he knew better, and it was up to him to get them out of it, not her.

She was right of course, he should at least give up the car. He could even do that without loss of face; there were hardly any more spare parts to be had in China now, because of the war, and many a taipan left his car in the garage these days, or sold it to a Chinese compradore—*they* could still manage somehow to import parts through the spidery network of their relatives in Europe and America. So he sold the car and dismissed Chan. Chan merely shrugged sullenly and half-lowered his lids when Denton apologetically gave him notice.

He couldn't bring himself to cut down the other household expenses. He wouldn't save money on the remaining servants, he paid them all their double month's salary at the New Year and even raised their wages as he'd always done in the past. It was partly a gambler's feeling that soon his luck would turn, but more a fear of losing face. He remembered Wei's saying years ago that he'd become half a Chinese. Well, perhaps he had, with a sense of face that he hadn't even guessed he possessed till then.

It was the same proud sense of face that made him pretend to Jacob and all his taipan friends, to Wei and the Chinese, that he wasn't sliding inexorably towards ruin. Nixon had only to look up his account at the bank to see how it had dwindled of course; but then how was Nixon to know what other income he might have? He attended the Municipal Council meetings dutifully as though nothing had changed, and helped to stifle Henschel in his attempts to use the meetings for German propaganda. He sounded Wei on Sun Yat-sen and the Chinese government, he conferred regularly with Abbotson at the consulate, he passed discreet inquiries and hints—"pre-diplomatic feelers," Abbotson called them—from one side to the other. He drank at the Club and entertained almost as lavishly as before at home. And all the time the worry gnawed at him and he felt week by week more hollow, more precarious, as though he were a noble house rotting behind its fine façade. Yet nobody could tell from the way he lived how close he was to collapse. Nobody except the tradesman who never got paid and counted their growing piles of chits with metallic, calculating eyes.

He could mortgage his house when the worst came to the worst, he decided in the second autumn of the war. That would give him enough to pay his debts and live another six months. But then what? He sat in his study, where he spent most of his spare time now, and remembered the Municipal Council's fund for packing indigent Europeans off home. He imagined his chair suddenly, unexpectedly, empty at the council meeting, himself, Mary-Ellen and Jonathan being put in steerage on a tramp steamer bound for America or Europe, Ah King and all the servants leaving the house for the last time . . . Yes, he could mortgage his house when the worst came to the worst, but he shut his eyes and with a gambler's trust clung to the belief that things would never get that bad, he would never come to that.

Sometimes, he thought, gazing broodingly out of his study window at the indifferent river flowing endlessly past, sometimes he thought it was as though his will had been paralysed by his marriage with Mary-Ellen. As though his unhappiness with her had killed some nerve and made

361

him helpless. Sometimes he thought of Su-mei, and the guilt was mixed with longing.

It was at this time that he began to love his son. The thought that Jonathan might be left penniless and unprotected caught his chest with a painful throb that he'd never felt while he was rich and assured. He would often have Ah King let the child take his afternoon nap in the study where he was reading or writing. And frequently he would leave his books to lift the corner of the mosquito net that just stirred beneath the draught from the fan, gazing down at the relaxed, sleeping face of his son while the faint, anxious churning in his stomach went endlessly on and on. He doesn't feel that, he would think, contemplating the boy's fair-skinned arms lying peacefully beside his head, the full, contented lips and dark-lashed eyes. That must be what they mean by the innocence of childhood—being able to sleep like that. And when Jonathan woke, before Ah King came clucking in, eager to take him out in the pram, Denton would lift him and hold him in his arms, as if that sleepy, warm bundle could somehow transmit its carefree contentedness to him.

"Baby's made you wet," Ah King scolded him once. "Why didn't you call me to change him?"

"I can get another shirt."

"Shirts are harder to wash."

At that time of the day Mary-Ellen would be sleeping off the half-bottle of wine she drank with every lunch, and she would be peevish if he disturbed her. So he took off his shirt and worked half-naked until he heard Mary-Ellen calling for her tea.

Sometimes he would walk the streets at night after dinner, telling Mary-Ellen he was going to the club. As if he was reliving his early years in the city, he would be dragged to the seedy alleys by the docks, where flower girls sold themselves for a dollar and opium divans perfumed the smells of the open drains. But again, as if he was twenty once more, he would walk stiffly away at the last moment, shaking his head as they beckoned and called after him.

It wasn't until he attended his second annual dinner of the Volunteers that he finally succumbed, giving up his four-year struggle to be faithful to Mary-Ellen despite her indifference to him "and all that kind of thing."

He'd joined the Shanghai Volunteer Force in the first

few months of the war. It was the nearest he could get to the army in Europe. He always felt a little thrill of pride when he put on his uniform. It reminded him of his first months in the customs service. He slipped so easily into fantasy, imagining himself quelling a riot or fighting off hordes of Chinese soldiers—anything to escape from his own drably crumbling existence.

The annual dinner was held in the drill hall on Paoshan Road. Denton sat next to Edward Smith, the honorary colonel, a wiry old man of seventy, who had made a fortune from opium in the nineties and had never worked since. Smith drank steadily throughout the meal, leaning frequently towards Denton to tell him stories of the Taiping and Boxer rebellions. His voice became gradually more slurred as he talked, so that Denton could hardly make out what he was saying. He only half-listened to the old man's reminiscences, glancing round the tables abstractedly. Last year Mason had been there, on one of the lower tables, a little thinner and somehow crumpled-looking, his moustache longer and almost bedraggled. It seemed as though he was going downhill too. This year he wasn't there. Now that he thought of it, Denton realised he hadn't seen Mason for several months. The war had brought a slump in the property market. That must have hurt him. There had been rumours at the time of the inquest into Ching's death that Mason had somehow gained from his murder. Some of Ching's opium was supposed to have disappeared, that was it, and people said Mason had got it hidden away somewhere...

"Where are you going afterwards?" Smith nudged Denton suddenly.

"Afterwards?" Denton gazed uncertainly into the old man's bleary blue eyes. The underlids sagged down like a bloodhound's, red and filmy.

"Wife expecting you?"

"No, not really."

"Another lady? No?"

Denton smiled wrily. "No." A wraith-like image of Su-mei drifted across his mind as he spoke. She'd been his "other lady," but that was all finished.

"Well, then." He nudged Denton's elbow, puckering his lids into a wrinkled wink. "Come with me. Place in Ningpo Road. Been going for years. They bring the girls in from all over the place. Clean too. Never caught a thing there. Been going for years."

And with a detached amazement at himself, Denton heard himself accepting. Why not? he thought resignedly. Since everything else is going wrong. He felt as though he was making a public acknowledgment that his marriage had failed. Well, might as well do it in style, he thought with a shrug. It felt like a defiant gesture against fate.

But in the cab, sitting next to Smith his spirit oozed away. The man was so old and brittle and drunk that the thought of him crawling and panting over a young girl disgusted him. Yet he couldn't turn back now, he'd only make a fool of himself. He paid off the cab and followed Smith up the stairs into a large upper room with worn red velvet-covered settees and peeling gold-framed mirrors.

"Been going for years," Smith said, slapping the seat beside him with his fragile hand. "Don't know what I'd have done without it. They know what I like." Yet there was a hesitant, almost anxious note in his slurred voice now, anxious as though he was afraid he might after all be disappointed. Denton sniffed the smell of dust rising from the upholstered seat Smith had hit. He looked away without answering. The mama-san was shepherding some girls towards them, her face coyly coaxing, as if she too was afraid they might be disappointed.

A woman took Smith's hand and led him off like a little child. She was one of the older ones, lines showing beneath her rouge, with bored, tired eyes. So that was what he wanted, Denton thought while the mama-san tried to interest him in one girl after another, mechanically listing their attraction in a throaty voice. Smith wanted someone to take care of him. He got up to go, but the mama-san laid a light, restraining hand on his arm. "You like Jap gir'? I got," she rasped expressionlessly. "Portuguese I got. How 'bout this one? Nice Chinese gir'?"

Denton hesitated. The girl she was pointing to reminded him of Su-mei. She had the same pouting, full, lower lip, the same tilt to her head. With a throbbing of remembered desire he chose her. "Very beauty," the mama-san said in husky approval. "Very young. You pay now."

The girl lay submissive on the bed, faked her pleasure half-heartedly as he rose to his, then asked him in pert, sing-song pidgin, "You my likee?"

He nodded, falsely, sober and disgusted again. She

wasn't a bit like Su-mei after all. And the sheets were grey and musty.

"You wanchee pay cumshaw?"

He reached across the bed for his jacket and gave her a dollar. She lay back again, spreading her legs and wriggling her hips, her eyes uninterestedly gazing up at the ceiling, but he shook his head and started to dress.

"No wanchee?"

"No wanchee."

"To tire' uh?"

"Yes, too tired."

She chattered in Shanghainese to the old woman who came to change the sheets as they left. "This one was easy. No trouble at all." But something about the glance he threw her made her pause, as if she suspected he might have understood her, and she escorted him downstairs in silence.

He took the rickshaw home, limp and jaded. Yet he went back again and again to the house, each time chasing the illusory hope its tawdry red velvet and flaking gold mirrors promised, the hope that the love he couldn't find with Mary-Ellen would somehow flower in that tinsel, stagey atmosphere. He went back although he couldn't afford it, as though he was actually deliberately trying to bring his ruin nearer.

And month by month, week by week, his income diminished, his debts grew larger. Next month, he kept thinking, I'll have to mortgage the house. But then he imagined himself calling on the credit manager of the Bank, who till then had always bowed to him when they met; he imagined the credit manager bending low to whisper in Nixon's ear and then Nixon's eyebrows shooting whimsically up. And every month he put it off.

He was never tempted to cancel his standing order to Su-mei. Lily would be five years old now, and he'd no idea what had happened to them both in Hong Kong, whether Su-mei had done well as an opera singer or not. All he knew was that the money was regularly paid and regularly collected. Whenever he thought of her, it was like pressing a bruise. He'd let everything else go first before he stopped her allowance.

Sometimes he thought of the opium pipe wrapped up in the bottom drawer of his wardrobe, where he'd left it ever since he'd married. Once he took it out and held it in his hands. The greasy rich smell still clung to it faintly, and to the cloth it was wrapped in. Suddenly he longed for a smoke again, for the scent of the sticky, melting pellets and the taste of the smoke in his mouth, the swimming, colourful oblivion it would bring to his head. Just to feel a release from that perpetual, insistent worry! Even if it was only for half an hour!

But he needed someone to smoke it with. Not Mary-Ellen, they were too far estranged by now. And in any case, when he'd shown her the things once, soon after their honeymoon, she'd only shrugged indifferently. They hadn't really interested her at all. No, he couldn't imagine anyone but Su-mei handling the pipe again.

And yet it was in that time of estrangement, when he often sought comfort in the routine embraces of indifferent prostitutes, that he made Mary-Ellen pregnant again. It was in November nineteen sixteen that she told him, and by then she was already three months gone. At first he couldn't believe it. "I haven't been near you for months!" he exclaimed. "How can you be pregnant?"

"It was after that dinner at the Ephraims," she said casually. "When you got drunk."

"I never get drunk."

"I don't suppose you'd remember it. But you did anyway. I remember very well, because Sarah asked us about that damned Baby Book she gave us for Jonathan, and we had to pretend we'd still got it. Perhaps that's what put you in the mood when we got home. Anyway, we'll have to find another doctor, now that McEwan's joined up—I think I must have had a bit too much too," she added reflectively. "Otherwise I'd never have let you get at me."

Some dim memory of that inebriated, joyless copulation came back to him, confused and cloudy. "It couldn't have happened at a worse time," he muttered miserably. "Now that we're so short of money..."

"Oh I suppose Jonathan ought to have a brother or sister," she shrugged carelessly. "They say single children are unhappy. Though I wasn't."

"You never are."

"Is that a complaint? I thought men liked it if their wives were happy?"

"It depends what they're happy about." He glanced down at her waist. It must be thickening already beneath that loose dress. "I don't think we're the kind of people to have children," he said dully.

"Too late now." Her voice was as unconcerned and cheerfully as ever. She turned away with a shrug to examine one of the bowls she'd bought in the French Settlement the day before. "Besides, it's not being a parent I mind. It's what you have to do to become one."

"Being a parent for you," he said bitterly, "seems to consist in going to buy clothes for your child when Ah King tells you he needs them."

She laughed, a lazy abstracted laugh of triumph, as she held the bowl up towards the light, admiring its deep green glaze. "If you knew anything about it," she rejoined, her head tilted to one side, "you'd know Ah King has Jonathan's clothes made at the tailor's. I've never gone out to buy any. She manages all that by herself."

Now I'll really have to mortgage the house, Denton thought gloomily as he left in a pony cab to attend the municipal council meeting. There's no help for it now. And yet he still couldn't imagine himself stammering to the credit manager, who would receive him with an ingratiating bow and dismiss him with a cool nod, that he unexpectedly found himself in temporary difficulties... His stomach churned more anxiously than ever when he thought of the child growing inside Mary-Ellen's womb. He watched the pony's mane bouncing and flying, its head lifting and tossing gaily as it trotted along between the shafts, and he thought he couldn't remember now what it was like to live without that persistent unsettling churning accompaniment to his life. His fingers drummed restlessly on the agenda papers he held in his lap.

The opium question had come before the Council many times, but whereas, before, the British government hadn't pressed the taipans too hard, now, the consul had warned Denton in one of their meetings, some definite steps really would have to be taken.

"In view of Sun Yat-sen's opposition to the trade, and the Chinese government's opposition too—though god knows whether they oppose it for moral reasons or economic ones—we're just going to have to do something if we want to keep China neutral in this war, let alone come in on our side." He'd offered Denton a cup of the green tea he always drank at four in the afternoon. "Apparently the Germans are making a fuss about it in Peking," he'd raised his brows to read a document on his desk. "Saying we're using Indian opium to corrupt the Chinese and ultimately to colonise them. Henschel's been writing similar stuff in the German newspaper here, too. The government feels we must show willing."

"Yet most Chinese officials smoke it regularly," Denton had said. "I know Wei does."

"Yes, yes..." the consul had raised his shallow rice-pattern cup, through which the tea showed as a dark, sliding shadow. "But there's all the difference between chaps like you and me having a bit now and then and some coolie who has nothing else to live for turning himself into an incapable addict." He'd sipped and sighed faintly with satisfaction. "I mean a couple of gentlemen at home can have a glass of port and know when to stop, but give the bottle to an ignorant labourer and he's dead drunk in the ditch all day, what?"

Denton had stirred uncomfortably. He couldn't imagine himself as a gentleman in England, whatever he might be, or might have been, in Shanghai. And he thought the consul knew it. He'd drunk his tea silently to cover his unease.

To consider the request of the Chinese authorities to prohibit the sale of opium in the international settlement, Denton read from the agenda paper, *and the further request to make the consumption of opium a criminal offence.* The cab drew up at the town hall, the pony pawing the ground impatiently. How absurd, to make smoking opium a crime, he thought as he got down. As well make drinking whisky a crime. They'll never buy that.

And in the council chamber, chilled with the first frost of winter, beneath the stilled blades of the ceiling fans, the decision went as he'd predicted. *To prosecute individuals for consuming opium,* the council resolved, *would be incompatible with the principles of individual liberty which the Council considers it its duty to uphold*—"Not to mention the money in it," Nixon murmured jovially in Denton's ear—*But the Council acknowledged that a number of opium divans in the international settlement had become undesirable places, encouraging lawlessness and crime, and it would therefore cancel the licences of any establishments convicted of infringing the regulations governing their operation. The Council saw no reason however* to prohibit the sale of opium in licensed premises for private consumption, although it proposed to grant no new licences.

The papers rustled as the councillors turned to the next item. "I hope that'll keep the Chinese quiet for a time," Nixon murmured again, knocking his pipe out against the glass ashtray. "We don't want Sun Yat-sen and co down on our necks."

"It may do for the moment," Denton replied. "But they won't really be happy till they've got London to cut off the supply of Indian opium."

"So they say," Nixon agreed comfortably. "In which case opium would be the one reasonably cheap commodity in Shanghai now that could shoot up in value overnight. Anyone holding a good-sized lot of opium then would be sitting on a gold-mine, what?" He started filling his pipe from the shabby leather pouch he'd always used, while the chairman read out the next business in a dry reedy voice.

Nixon's remark caught in a crevice some way down Denton's mind instead of falling all the way through into oblivion. But it wasn't till he was riding home after the meeting that he recalled it. He was passing the opium divans in Foochow Road, and was just glancing at the faded, smoke-grimed characters of the one on the corner of Honan Road, when Nixon's words, as if released by the sight, drifted up into his consciousness again. And at the same time, as though they'd been waiting patiently for their time to come, the latest rumours about Mason floated up to join them. Mason had gone to ground out near Ying Hsiang Kong, some people in the Volunteers had said, because of a dispute with Pock-mark Chen. Something to do with opium, the opium that had vanished when Ching was killed. "They say Pock-mark Chen wants it, but Mason's the only one who knows where it is. And if he tries to sell it, Pock-mark Chen'll know he's got it. He's in it up to his neck, right up to his neck," he remembered a sergeant, the men's outfitting manager from Whiteaway Laidlaw, saying, a middle-aged, short-sighted man, with a shop assistant's stooped shoulders and deferential manner. He'd spoken with a blend of awe and gloating in his voice, the awe of the timid for those who dared and the gloating of the puny at stronger men's failures. The words swung round and round Denton's head more and more slowly, as though each one needed time to sink in. He's in it right up to his neck. The one commodity likely to shoot up in value... Sitting on a gold mine...

He gave the driver a ten cent tip and walked thoughtfully up the steps to the house. The shrill tyrannical voice of Ah King's mother-in-law sounded from the kitchen. She was visiting Shanghai to buy new clothes for the New Year Festival, and to give Ah King a brief sight of her children. He heard Jonathan's voice burbling, then Ah King's scolding her son, then the mother-in-law's shrill demands again, to which Ah Sam was adding her own loud comments. Odd words and phrases rose clearly above the indistinct barrage of noise, but he scarcely noticed them, starting slowly up the stairs, slowly and carefully, as though a mis-step might spill his half-formed thoughts right out of his head. Mary-Ellen called out something from the dining room veranda, where she was sitting in the winter sun, but he didn't answer. When he eased himself down at his desk and gazed with unfocussed eyes at the notepaper lying on his blotting pad, the scheme had begun to shape itself in his head.

52

The house was out on Ward Road, near the settlement boundary. It stood by itself a hundred yards or so from an old village. There was something desolate and shabby about it even from the distance—the white-washed walls were streaked and dirty, and, as he got closer, Denton saw that the paint had peeled off the woodwork. He picked his way over the frozen ruts of the cart track and turned down the overgrown path that led to the door. He could hear pigs grunting somewhere inside the village, and the disturbed honking of geese. A flimsy rice-paper kite soared high above the roof of the house. The taut string, glinting in the sunlight, slanted back towards the village wall. All the downstairs windows were shuttered, as if the place was locked up and empty. And yet he felt as though someone inside was watching him. He climbed the two chipped, cement steps to the door. A torn kite, like the one he'd just seen, lay fluttering faintly like an injured bird beside them, its worn, frayed string trailing forlornly across the concrete, between grains of cooked rice and scraps of paper that the wind was gradually scattering. He knocked on the door, then stepped back to look up at the walls and windows again. It was one of those characterless, jerry-built houses that had been thrown up in the boom before the war. The cement was cracking round the window frames already. He wondered whether Mason himself had had it built as one of his ventures. He used to advertise week-end cottages for sale or rent in the papers, he remembered.

There had been ten degrees of frost in the night, but now, in the middle of the morning, the sun shining from a limpid sky warmed Denton's back. Only the wind was cold, like a knife blade slipped between his clothes. The pigs were still grunting greedily behind the village wall. There was no sound in the house, and yet he still had that uncomfortable feeling that he was being watched. He glanced at the upstairs windows, but nothing moved. A child called in the village. He stepped forward and knocked again, turning round to look at the decaying village wall and the empty fields. A dog started barking behind the wall, then several more. The geese honked more angrily. Two boys appeared at the village gateway, driving a water buffalo out along the track. The buffalo's snorted breath steamed on the air. The boys gaped at him as they passed, then one of them said something in a low voice to the other and they both laughed, watching him all the time.

Had he left it too late? Had Mason somehow slipped away? If so, his plan was done for. Denton turned back to the door. No, he felt sure someone was there, secretly watching him. He looked for the little circular glass of a spy-hole in the wooden panel, but couldn't find one. Then, as he raised his hand to knock again, the door opened slowly and noiselessly an inch or two, revealing a slice of a Chinese woman's face. The woman surveyed him stonily through the gap between the door and the jamb. He saw her brown, slanted eye move to see if there was anyone with him, then turn back to him again.

"Mr. Mason?" he asked, in English first, then in Chinese.

Her eye stirred faintly and she lowered her lid. "Not here," she said tonelessly in English.

"Tell him Denton wants to do some business with him," he said slowly and distinctly, ignoring her reply. He

371

moved a step closer. "Tell him I have a proposal. A deal. I'm an old friend. Denton. Tell Tibby it's Denton."

Her eye stirred at the word *Tibby*. She knew his nick-name then. Must be his mistress, he thought.

She half-turned her head away, then silently closed the door. He strained to listen, but there was no sound inside. The pigs were still grunting, but the dogs and geese were quiet now. He sensed, rather than heard, a stealthy movement behind the door, and had that haunted feeling again that someone was watching him. He must behave normally, nonchalantly. He glanced casually up at the walls once more, tracing the jagged lines of the cracks. Then he bent down and picked up the kite. The slender frame was broken. He pulled gently on the string. It was caught on something. When he tugged it, it snapped. He wound the end slowly in, round his spread fingers. Then, before he'd reached the end, the door opened on its chain again. This time it was Mason.

"Hello Tibby," Denton said casually, holding the broken kite in his hand. "Is this yours?"

Mason didn't answer. His face moved slightly in the gap as he craned his neck to look each side of Denton. Then he inspected Denton himself. His ginger moustache was unkempt, and there was a thick ginger stubble on his chin, with a few glinting spikes of silver. For several seconds he stared at Denton suspiciously. Then at last he seemed to relax. One eyelid lowered faintly, as if he were about to wink. "To what do I owe the honour?" he asked, with a show of the old irony. But his voice sounded weaker, as if he'd been ill. He loosened the chain and opened the door a little wider.

Denton could see all his face now. His cheeks seemed to have sagged. There were little zig-zag bloodshot veins in the corners of his eyes and the skin beneath had formed dark violet pouches. Perhaps he'd been ill? Mason looked away, frowning slightly, as if resenting his estimating glance. "Are you selling kites now?" he asked sullenly.

Denton looked down at the kite, smiling and shaking his head. He let it drop. They both watched it scrape against the door until the wind carried it trembling against the step, where it caught again. "You haven't been to the Volunteers for some time?" Denton said pleasantly.

"Have they made you recruiting sergeant, then?" There was a trace of the old sneer in his voice, but again it was weaker—tired perhaps. Or was it more bitterness than mockery now? Denton recalled that last night at the Customs Officers' Mess, when Mason's voice had rung out across the hot, sticky evening air with such robust, taunting derision. He seemed a beaten man now, all that zestful malice drained away.

Denton felt his own confidence growing. "I've got a business proposition for you."

"So I've heard." Mason's eyes shifted back to Denton's face.

"I think it might interest you."

"Always ready to talk business," Mason said mechanically. But he didn't move. He seemed to be thinking of something else, his eyes still on Denton's face, wandering from feature to feature as if searching for something to catch hold of.

"If you'd like some ready money," Denton went on, "this might be a very interesting proposition..."

"What's it about, then?"

Denton glanced past his head at the bare room behind him. "Perhaps we could talk inside?"

Mason hesitated, craning his neck again to peer each side of Denton, as though he suspected an ambush. He licked his lips. "Where's your car, then? Haven't you got a car?"

"I didn't particularly want to be noticed."

Mason considered a moment or two, then shrugged. He slipped the chain off and opened the door wide enough for Denton to step inside, then shut and bolted it, replacing the chain. The bolts, Denton noticed, were dark and shiny with oil. They moved silently. The woman he'd seen before was leaning against the wall, regarding him still with the same watchful, blank expression. She was wearing a faded scarlet silk robe that she held wrapped round her with one hand, as if despite the cold, she was naked beneath it. her hair hung loose each side of her face and down her back. On her feet were two incongruously large felt slippers that must have been Mason's. They were woolly and worn. She must have just got out of bed, Denton thought. Mason had an old brown quilted jacket on, the silk padding straggling out of the seams in wispy grey threads. As he bent to fasten the lower bolt, Denton noticed the black, pimpled butt of a revolver peeping out of the bulging pocket.

Mason straightened up with a sigh and led Denton wordlessly into a little room, bare except for a plain wooden table and four chairs that could all have come from one of those cheap street-side restaurants in Hongkew. The floor was of red tiles. A paper calendar hung from a rusty nail on the wall. There were no pictures, no rugs, no curtains at the barred, shuttered windows. Mason sat down on one of the chairs, pushing another one out for Denton with his foot. "Haven't had time to do the place up yet," he muttered, noticing Denton's eyes surveying the room. "Haven't been here long. Want a drink?" Without waiting for an answer he spoke to the woman, who had shuffled in after them and was leaning against the wall by the doorway. "How about a beer? Two glasses."

The woman's lids lowered slightly, then she pushed herself off the wall and shuffled out.

"Well," Mason turned back, "What is this proposition you've got?"

Denton clasped his hands in front of him, glancing round the room again. "If you'll excuse my saying so, it doesn't look as though you're doing too well just at present?"

Mason's lips twitched. He brushed his moustache up with his knuckle and sniffed. "What's it matter to you how I'm doing?" he grunted in a surly, menacing voice, as if warning Denton off. But then he went on in a more conciliatory, though still gruff, tone. "Ups and downs, same as everyone else. Bit down at the moment, like a lot of people. At least I'm not dead, like Jonesy."

"Jonesy?"

"Went back to join up. Didn't you know? Got killed in France, silly bugger."

"I didn't know." He thought of Jones' wispy moustache, and imagined his face pale and lifeless in a field of poppies, his weak blue eyes staring stiffly up at the sky.

The woman came back with a large beer bottle and two glasses. She placed them on the table, which had several ring marks on it, and leant back against the wall again. Denton glanced inquiring at Mason, tilting his head towards her.

"It's all right," Mason grunted. He poured the beer until a foaming head rose above the rim of each glass. "She's one of the family, you might say. You needn't worry about her." He nudged a chair out for the woman. "Why don't you sit down, instead of propping up the wall?" he asked roughly. "Sit down, hey? Sit down." He patted the seat in a clumsy gesture that was almost affectionate. Denton noticed his finger nails were bitten down and dirty. The woman didn't move. It was as though she hadn't understood what he'd said. Or else chose to ignore it.

Mason shrugged and turned back to Denton. He swallowed some of his beer and set the glass down heavily on the table. "Well? What's the proposition?"

Denton fingered his glass without raising it, watching the bubbles of foam on Mason's moustache. "I believe you may have a fair amount of opium?" he began at last. "I'd be interested in buying it, if it's good quality and the price is right."

"Opium, eh?" For a moment Mason's voice recovered its old disparaging sneer. "A respectable municipal councillor buying opium? Aren't you afraid you'll get your hands dirty?"

Denton raised his glass. There were smears round the rim. He turned it fastidiously before he sipped. "There's nothing illegal about trading in opium is there? But of course, if you're not interested . . ." He put the glass down with a definite little plunk and edged his chair back. The legs grated over the tiles.

"I didn't say I wasn't interested," Mason said hastily. "Just surprised. Thought you were too prissy for that kind of thing." He took another gulp of his beer and smacked his lips. Again the foam flecked his moustache, and he wiped it away reflectively, glancing from Denton to the woman and back again. "Why d'you want to buy opium?" he asked, a little less sullenly.

"I'm buying for someone else. He's only interested in a bulk purchase."

Mason's eyes strayed towards the woman again. She shifted slightly against the wall, gazing all the time at Denton, her eyes lowered to little hooded slits in the mask of her face.

"Why doesn't he buy from one of the big dealers, then?" Mason asked slowly. "Tata, Dastur, one of that lot?"

Denton was turning his glass to and fro on the table. He noticed three or four grains of rice jammed in a little crevice in the wood. "He thinks he might get it a bit cheaper from you," he answered with a casual shrug. He raised the glass and sipped again. "Rumour has it you might take a slightly lower price for yours." He watched Mason's bloodshot eyes over the rim of the glass. They seemed to flicker with some emotion—Fear? Anger? Hope? He couldn't tell.

"Oh it does, does it?" Mason's voice rose, but the surprise and protest in it were unconvincing.

He'll sell, Denton thought, with a little stab of excited hope.

"And why might I take a lower price?"

"Two reasons, really." Denton placed his glass down on the table. "Firstly, they say you need the cash. And secondly . . ." he glanced slyly up at Mason, "they think you may not find it easy to sell on the open market yourself, because you . . . well, not to put too fine a point on it, you might have some difficulty explaining how you came by it. You might not even want certain people to know you've got it at all?" He ended on a questioning note, glancing at the woman again as he spoke. "That's the rumour, anyway," he added noncommittally.

"Is it now?" Mason gazed at him for several seconds, trying to read some hidden meaning in his eyes. "And why might I not want that?" he asked uneasily at last. His eyes, too, strayed to the woman, as though she were some oriental oracle. "Why might I find it difficult? And who is this chap, anyway?"

A dog started barking again in the village, the angry, snapping yelps sounded muffled and distant through the shuttered windows. Both Mason and the woman turned their heads to listen, then the woman went to the window and peered through a slit in the shutters. Denton saw Mason lower his hand to the pocket with the revolver in it. But the woman merely shrugged after a while and went back to her place at the wall, pulling her robe about her with a little shiver. Mason turned to Denton again, putting his hand back on his beer glass.

"He's someone who's willing to pay a good price," Denton answered. "Only a hundred taels a picul below the market price."

"A hundred taels a picul below!" Mason's indignation was real this time. He laughed curtly. "You must be joking!"

"Provided there's a substantial amount."

"Come off it!"

Denton placed both hands on the edge of the table, as

if he was about to get up and leave. "Well, if you think you can get a better price..."

Neither of them moved. The woman pulled the collar of her gown closer round her throat, then settled back into her pose against the wall. The faint rustle of the silk sounded distinctly in the room. Denton let his hands slowly relax on the table. "A pity for you Ching got killed, by the way, wasn't it? You worked together, didn't you?"

"Ching? What's Ching got to do with it?"

Denton shrugged. "I thought the two of you had a few fingers in the same pies, that's all. When you were in the customs for instance...Owned quite a lot of opium when he was killed, didn't he? They say some of it disappeared...?"

Mason leant back, brushing his moustache upwards, his eyes flickering uncertainly. "And supposing I could lay my hands on some opium," he muttered slowly at last, "how would I get paid?"

"Half in advance and half on delivery of the full amount. Would that be all right?" Denton followed Mason's glance at the woman. Her eyes gleamed slightly under the slits of her lids. "How much opium are we talking about, actually?"

Mason's eyes regarded him broodingly for some time, then he seemed to come to some decision. He leant forward on his elbows and spoke quickly and quietly, as if, having made up his mind, he wanted to get the thing over and done with as soon as he could. "Listen, this opium, I have got some, and it's perfectly legal, absolutely above-board. I've got papers from Ching to prove it. I can prove it beyond the shadow of a doubt. Only I'm being got at. There are people threatening me. They say Ching owed them money. Or double-crossed them or something. So they want to get their hands on the stuff. I say what's Ching's affairs got to do with me? He sold me the opium and I can prove it. But they've got their finger on me..." He slapped the bulging pocket that was dragging one side of his jacket down. "That's why I'm being so careful. In case you've noticed."

"If you've got the proof," Denton asked coolly, "why don't you just let them sue you?"

"Sue me? They wouldn't *sue* me!" Mason voice rose excitedly. "You know what happened to Ching! It's Pock-mark Chen that's after me, not some little smuggler from

Pootung! Pock-mark Chen! The only thing that protects me now is that I'm white, and I'm not sure how much good that'll do me any longer..." He pushed his half-finished beer aside, as if he'd lost his taste for it, staring down at the table blankly while his lips moved silently with some unspoken thought.

Denton stirred. "Why don't you get out, then?"

"And leave the opium? That's the only money I've got in this blasted hole."

Denton smiled. "We ought to be able to make a deal then," he suggested gently.

"What I'm getting at is this," Mason said slowly, still staring down at the table. "If I do sell this stuff to you, even at that stinking price, I want to be out of here before anyone knows about it, all right? You've got to give me a week before you register the sale. And I want the money in a London bank." His voice had taken on almost a pleading tone now.

Denton leant back slowly, fingering his chin while he gazed up at the ceiling. There were cobwebs in the corners, hanging down in soft, grey festoons. "I expect that could be arranged," he said at last, when he felt he'd made Mason wait long enough. "How much opium are we talking about, actually?"

"About twenty piculs. Finest Indian."

Denton nodded slowly, calculating in his head. It was a small fortune. "How will I get in touch with you? You haven't got a telephone?"

Mason shook his head. "They haven't come out this far yet. And I don't go around much these days. Too risky."

"Well I'll find a way of being in touch when I have to." Denton sipped his beer again. "You can show me all the necessary documents, I presume?"

"Yes." Mason laughed, a shade of the old vitality creeping back into his voice. "Still the customs officer at heart, aren't you?"

Denton pushed back his chair and stood up, glancing at the woman again. "It shouldn't take more than a week to arrange," he said. "I take it you'd be leaving Shanghai for good then?"

"You take it right, we would." He put a little emphasis on the word *we*, as if to reassure the woman.

Mason followed him to the door. There *was* a spy-hole

378

after all, in the wall beside the jamb. They must have been watching him through it for some time before the woman opened the door. Mason peered through it now before cautiously sliding back the bolts and unhooking the chain.

Denton paused on the threshold. "Tell me, why are you called Tibby? I often used to wonder."

"Thomas Brian."

"Thomas Brian?"

"T.B. Tibby for short."

"Oh I see. Well that clears that mystery up, anyway." He walked down the steps and turned back as Mason was already closing the door. "In about a week, all right?"

"All right."

Denton felt a strange, inconsistent, impulse to end on a warmer note. "You know, there are a lot of cracks in the cement of this wall," he said. "Looks as though the whole place might fall down one day."

"As long as it lasts another fortnight or so," Mason said indifferently, his glance slipping past Denton's face to the track behind him. "They mixed the cement with ashes. You know how it is."

The door closed as soon as he'd finished speaking. As he turned away, Denton listened for the sound of the bolts, but he could hear nothing except his own footsteps on the still, hard ground. As he walked down the rutted track towards the city, the geese started honking again behind the village wall.

He walked over a mile before he came across a rickshaw near Wayside Market. "The Shanghai Club," he ordered the coolie. He leant back and closed his eyes, listening dreamily to the clicking of the spokes and the slap of the coolie's sandals on the road, as if they were the only sounds in the world. He tried not to think about Mason, he didn't want to let himself hope too much, or too soon.

Before long they were in the alleys of Hongkew, where little Japanese shops were becoming as numerous as the Chinese. They passed an opium divan next to a geisha house. Denton glanced inside. Two old men lay on wooden benches in the gloom, motionless as in a trance. Outside a younger man was squatting in the sunlight, leaning against the wall. His eyes were red-rimmed and vacant. His legs, beneath his flappy grey trousers, seemed thinner than Denton's forearm. Denton looked away. Am I really going through with this? he asked himself. Until then it had been unreal for him, merely a scheme in his mind. But if he went ahead—would the addicts that he saw on every corner lie on his conscience? He thought of his accounts again, of how near to ruin he stood. He knew that he *was* going to go through with it.

He drank sherry with Nixon at the head of the long bar and lunched with him afterwards at a quiet table in the panelled dining-room with its solid Jacobean furnishings. Nixon's brows twitched upwards in surprise when Denton mentioned opium, but he listened carefully without interrupting. "Well, after all we're only here to make money," he said, dabbing his lips with his napkin, "And I must say it's a paying proposition, what?" He leant back to feed tobacco reflectively from his shabby pouch into the scarred bowl of his pipe, while the waiter poured his coffee.

"What about a brandy?" Denton asked.

"Yes. The usual, please..." He was still reflecting on Denton's proposal as he sucked and bit with his yellowish teeth on the pipe stem. "How is Mary-Ellen, by the way? Keeping well?"

"Yes, she's...the baby's due in May."

"Oh," Nixon said absently, watching the tobacco rustle and smoulder as he held a match to it. "Yes, I must say it's a paying proposition, however er...*unusual* it might appear to some people, what?" He chuckled and reached for his brandy.

Denton borrowed from the bank to buy Mason's opium, and joined the Shanghai Opium Merchants' Combine. Imports of opium dwindled over the next few months and the price rose. By the time Mary-Ellen had had their second child—a daughter, Jenny—Denton's holdings had doubled in value. The Combine had cornered the market. They sold sparingly; Tata the Persian, Dastur the Indian, Ezra the Baghdad Jew, and now Denton the Englishman, keeping the price high. When China at last entered the war on the Allies' side, Britain agreed to stop the opium trade altogether. "It's the price we have to pay," the consul sighed over his green tea to Denton. "Otherwise they might've joined the Huns. This puritanical streak in Sun

Yat-sen, you know—just like a Methodist preacher. It doesn't suit the Chinese, does it?"

The Municipal Council reluctantly agreed to close all the opium shops in the International Settlement. But what compensation was to be given to the Shanghai Opium Merchants Combine? Tata, Dastur, Ezra and Denton met in Dastur's office, a room that smelled of curry, in which the creaking fan blew a limp, exhausted draught on their heads. Dastur's dark brown eyes, the whites yellowish from jaundice, glistened as he spoke in his high, voluble voice. His thick black hair swept over his head in deep, glossy waves. The Chinese government had offered fourteen million taels for the Combine's remaining stocks, he reported gleefully. They had bought at under six. "It's still below the present market price," Tata said dubiously, but Ezra reminded him, "There is no market now." "Pah, in six months they'll be buying it at double the price!" "That's too risky," Denton objected.

They accepted the offer, and the Chinese government, with Sun Yat-sen's influence temporarily stronger, arranged to burn the opium on the Pootung shore of the river, opposite the banks and trading hongs of the international settlement. The site was chosen as a gesture to the foreign concerns that had grown fat on the opium trade—not merely the Shanghai Opium Combine, but all the older hongs, Jardine's, Swire and Russell, which had gradually withdrawn from the trade to keep their hands clean for other pickings. But the dark, sweet, greasy smoke blew away from the river, hardly affecting the air on the Bund. Denton, watching with Wei from the veranda of his house, turned confessionally to him. "You know, I'd have been in big trouble if I hadn't bought that opium," he said in Shanghainese.

Wei inclined his head. "If you hadn't bought it, someone else would."

"It seems a pity to burn it all like that. After all, it's a valuable commodity, like tobacco or alcohol, if it's not misused."

"They've gone too far, trying to stop opium altogether, instead of regulating it. Its harmfulness has been exaggerated. A good servant but a bad master, that's all."

Denton nodded, yet while he nodded thought of Wei's father who had died a wasted addict.

"In any case," Wei was going on, "it hasn't all been

burnt. Quite a lot has disappeared, I hear. About half. There were so many officials to handle it."

Denton glanced at him. "I suppose it's still quite easy to get hold of, then?" he asked circumspectly. "For those who want it?"

Wei smiled, his gold teeth glistening. "A little in moderation is always possible."

Wei smiled more rarely these days than he used to. One of the richest men in China now, he had grown a mask of composed gravity over the alert, lively face of a decade before. Denton watched the wind blowing some of the smoke down across the Chinese factories and tenements in Pootung. It seemed symbolic of the Chinese gesture—the smoke blew into their own eyes.

"And now your money troubles are over?" Wei inquired solicitously, scratching his cheek lightly with his long, curved nail. "How much did you make?"

"About a million dollars, after I'd cleared the loan."

"In that case you'll have no difficulty in affording a pipe of opium now and then. What happened to Mason, by the way?"

Denton shrugged. "They both left, that's all I know. There were no ships to Europe, so he took one to Yokohama."

"Pock-mark Chen wasn't pleased about it, so I'm told," Wei glanced warningly at Denton.

Denton's mind slipped back to the house with the green shutters, to the time he'd rescued Su-mei when Pock-mark Chen was only a petty gangster in the French Settlement. Why *Pock-mark*, he wondered. He'd never noticed any smallpox scars on that vast moon-like face. Not then, nor later, when he'd seen him briefly at the stock exchange, or flanked by body guards, at a Chinese restaurant.

"The smoke is clearing now," Wei was saying. "It's surprising how quickly it goes, isn't it?" He might have been talking about the Chinese government's policy as much as about opium. Then he cleared his throat, signifying a change of topic. "Sun Yat-sen will be visiting Shanghai next month. Perhaps you'd like to meet him? There's no need to mention your part in the Opium Combine, though. I've told him about you only as a progressive member of the Municipal Council."

53

"Do you know Dr. James Kant Lee?" the little Cantonese asked, his fine moustache floating on his upper lip like a black feather that the faintest breath might puff away.

Denton glanced out of the window, wondering why they'd chosen a house in the French Settlement for Sun Yat-sen. "Lee? No, I don't think I do."

"Kant Lee," Dr. Sun corrected him mildly. "A very good English friend. My teacher in Hong Kong."

"English?" Denton frowned uncertainly. "Kant Lee? Ah, Cantlie, you mean?"

"Kant Lee, yes." The melancholy eyes smiled at him vaguely, with a kind of troubled gratitude that he'd known the name after all. "He helped me quite much in Hong Kong, and also in London when the Manchu imprisoned me."

"No, I've never actually met him, I'm afraid."

Dr. Sun's tired, sallow lids drooped regretfully. In the adjoining room, Denton could hear Mary-Ellen talking to Madam Sun with that casual ease of hers that he could never master. "I first got interested when I took a course in Chinese art at Wellesley..."

"I hope your meeting with the students was satisfactory yesterday?" Denton asked stiltedly, trying to span the uneasy void of silence that was widening second by second between Sun and himself.

"The university students are very interested in the new ideas," Dr. Sun replied, his voice shy and hushed. "As soon as the war is finished, China will build agai'."

Denton nodded, groping through the blankness of his mind for another uncontroversial topic to bring up. Again he could hear Mary-Ellen's voice flowing naturally along, with Madam Sun's desultory polite accompaniment. He felt a prick of envy and bitterness that everything was so easy for her. "Many things will need building up," he muttered vaguely.

Dr. Sun nodded and smiled, but his eyes glimmered perplexedly as though he hadn't quite understood...

At last Wei coughed gently beside Denton. The audience was over.

"It has been a great honour to meet you, Dr. Sun." He shook the limp, cool hand that the little man extended.

"Thank you for your help to China," Dr. Sun bowed formally. "Wei tells me about it many times."

What help? Denton wondered as he smiled deprecatingly and followed Wei out. A few words at council meetings?

"Dr. Sun became a revolutionary after seeing torture and execution under the Manchu," Wei was saying to him in an undertone in Shanghainese. "It makes him something of a firebrand."

How could such a colourless little fellow be a firebrand? Denton wondered. Aloud, he said "But torture and executions go on just the same as before don't they, it's no different from the Manchu?"

Wei didn't answer. He gestured towards a spruce Chinese man with a baby face and glinting eyes who was just entering the room. "You must meet Chiang Kai-shek," he said.

The two men bowed to each other formally as they shook hands. Mr. Chiang's grip too was limp. But the glinting eyes that probed Denton seemed as hard as flints. They murmured conventional greetings and moved on.

"Chiang is one of Sun's military advisers," Wei explained in a voice hushed with respect.

Mary-Ellen was still talking freely to Madam Sun, who was listening to the large American woman with a tireless, dainty smile on her face.

How she's put on weight since Jenny was born, Denton thought distastefully. She's just let herself go.

Madam Sun's dainty smile took in Denton and Wei now. Denton thought he saw an expression of relief in her eyes as they approached. "Your wife was at college in America?" she asked Denton, as if she hadn't quite believed Mary-Ellen. "Which college were you at, Mr. Denton?"

"Oh he never went to college," Mary-Ellen answered blithely for him. "He's a self-made man."

"North London Teachers Training College," Denton said, glancing frigidly at Mary-Ellen. "For one year."

"Dr. Sun attended the Hong Kong Medical College," Madam Sun said smoothly. "It was very interesting, he says. Did you enjoy it at your London college?"

He prised Mary-Ellen away at last, after she had invited Madam Sun to come and look at all her Chinese things one afternoon.

"I would like to, but Dr. Sun is very busy," she replied noncommittally through her tireless smile.

Mary-Ellen flopped back in the cab waiting outside. "I got on very well with her," she said, fanning herself lazily. "Did you notice the furniture, though? Chinese and French colonial all jumbled together. I've never seen such a mess."

"No doubt she could learn something from your impeccable taste," he said with idle sarcasm, glancing out of the open window at the solitary French gendarme standing by the gate. "I doubt whether she'll come and see your pots and things, though."

"Why? She said she'd like to."

"In China people often say things to be polite."

"You don't say," she drawled ironically. "I'd never have guessed."

"And she wouldn't think your pots and vases are important enough," he went on, nettled. "Or visiting us for that matter. Anyway, they're leaving very soon."

"Are they?" she asked languidly, evidently losing interest. She laid her fan down on her lap and closed her eyes. Glistening little drops of perspiration glowed on her upper lip. "Sometimes I think Chinese simply don't feel the heat at all," she murmured. "There wasn't a single fan in that house."

"They're not as heavy as you are."

"No, isn't it awful?" she seemed oblivious, or indifferent, to the edge in his voice. "Ever since I had Jenny. My dresses have all had to be let out. It wasn't like that after Jonathan, was it?"

Denton didn't answer. He leant back, listening to the clop-clop of the pony's hooves, looking out at the peeling walls of *rue* Molière, with their shaded balconies dozing in the sun. An Annamite soldier was strolling indolently along the pavement. Otherwise the street was almost empty. That was the charm of the French Settlement, he thought, everything being slower and sleepier than in the International Settlement. Perhaps that was why they'd put Sun up there; he looked as though he needed a rest.

His eyes stirred. They were passing the house with the green shutters now, the house where he'd first seen Pock-mark Chen. The door was still open, but the shutters had been closed against the sunlight. In the evening they'd be open again, he thought. One day I'll go there, see what it's like... There was no chair on the porch now.

He leant forward to gaze into the dim hall as the cab passed.

"What are you looking at?" Mary-Ellen asked drowsily.

"Nothing. Just a house, one of the older ones." It wasn't till after he'd said *house* that he realised the pun and smiled to himself.

"Oh." She yawned. "I saw Chan in the kitchen today. What did he want?"

"Wei's offered me one of his cars—the American one. I thought we might take Chan on as a driver again, if I buy it. Apparently you can get spare parts for it—or Wei can, anyway."

"I never cared for him."

"Chan? No, nor did I, but drivers are hard to come by these days. And at least we know his faults. He looked as though he'd been having a hard time of it."

"Did he? I didn't notice." She yawned again and stretched. "God, this weather gets me down. At least a car would be quicker."

Denton grunted. He was looking across to the other side of the street, waiting for the gate in the wall where he'd seen the lady and the girl getting down from a rickshaw on that same day that he'd first seen the brothel. He smiled wrily. On one side of the street, the emblem of lust; on the other the emblem of serenity. His life seemed to oscillate between those two poles. Did other people's too?

The arched gateway slipped suddenly into view. A sedan chair was stopping there now. As the bearers set it down, a Chinese lady stepped out, dressed in elegant, almost theatrical clothes. She turned to speak to the bearers, and Denton glimpsed her face as the cab rolled past.

It was Su-mei.

His heart seemed to check itself then suddenly gallop, while his body remained numb and paralysed. He looked away, staring unseeingly in front of him.

"Did you see that chair?" Mary-Ellen was drawling. "Don't see many like that nowadays, do you?"

He looked back again. Su-mei was just disappearing through the arch. He felt he was quivering, although his hands lay perfectly still on his knees when at last he turned away. He gazed ahead unseeingly. Unseeingly, except that her face and the turn of her head and the gliding movement of her clothes seemed to hover over his eyes, to shimmer there in the cab before him, while Mary-Ellen yawned and fanned herself langorously, pressing her fat white arm unconsciously against his.

He sent the office messenger to buy him one of the best tickets. The messenger knew of course why Denton was going, and smiled appreciatively. "Liang Shan-po tonight," he said. "It's the best one they do."

"Get a ticket for yourself as well, then."

Tactfully, the messenger bought a cheaper seat, far from Denton's.

The theatre was crowded and noisy, the audience commenting and applauding loudly throughout the performance. Denton wiped his hands on the warm towel the attendant gave him, took his melon seeds and tea, and waited patiently for Su-mei to appear. The man beside him was smoking a cigar, talking enthusiastically with his neighbour. Denton listened to the music, softer and more melodious than the Peking Opera. It was a larger orchestra now than when he first saw her perform on the Wing On stage, larger and richer. There was quite elaborate scenery too—he hadn't seen that before. He wondered how he'd like her playing a man. His memory switched him back to the pantomimes he used to go to every Christmas as a boy, when the principal boy was always played by a girl. He sipped his tea and tested a melon seed between his teeth. The casual murmuring all round him nearly drowned the music. Yet everyone seemed to be listening all the same. Every now and then they'd all hush and applaud.

Su-mei was playing Liang, the scholar who eloped with the beautiful Chu Ying-tai. He knew her at once when she came on, and so did the audience. There was a sudden murmur of applause and appreciation at her costume, than an expectant hush. She began her declaration to Chu. Despite himself, Denton almost forgot she was a woman. She had the gestures, the stance, even in a strangely haunting way the voice of a man, or rather a boy. His tea grew cold as he watched her slow, graceful movements and expressive, sparkling eyes, declaring longing and passion so delicately. He almost forgot she was a woman, and yet in everything she did there was something intensely feminine.

Oh my god, Denton thought, can I ever get her back?

Jonathan sat at the great long kitchen table, waiting for Ah King to give him his food. Two pots simmered on the stove with clattering, steaming lids. Ah Man was chopping meat, his small, balding head tilted to one side as he brought the chopper blade slicing down through the white bones and the bloody flesh. Ah Sam was ironing the baby clothes, Cheong, the gardener, was sitting at the end of the table with Chan, silently eating his evening rice. It was the time Jonathan liked best in the whole day, when the servants told him stories or played with him—all except Chan.

Ah Sam, holding up a frock to fold it, examined her swollen knuckles at the same time. The skin was split over them, red and sore. She sighed, glancing at Jonathan. "Silk factory," she said mysteriously, "that's how I got these hands." She held them out crippled and stiff, for Jonathan to examine too, as a soldier might show his battle wounds.

Chan laughed curtly from the other end of the table, his mouth full of rice. "That's why she'll never get married. Who wants a woman with paws like that?"

Ah King put Jonathan's meal in front of him.

"Tell me a story."

"Eat first, then story."

She turned to whisper to Ah Sam as Jonathan picked at the food with his chopsticks. "Guess what. Kwan Su-mei's back in town. She's performing at the Ta Wu Tai."

"No!"

"I heard it in the market."

Ah Man grunted, slapping another quivering red slab of meat on the board. "It's in the paper."

Jonathan watched Ah Sam's eyes widening and gleaming.

"The boss'll be after her like a dog after a bitch," Chan said indistinctly through a mouthful of rice.

"Shh!" They all glanced at Jonathan.

"Who's Kwan Su-mei?" he asked, frowning down at his bowl as he picked at some sticky grains of rice. "Ah King? Who's Kwan Su-mei?"

"Time to get your little sister to bed," Ah King said. "You finish that before I come back, mind. And the milk."

"She'd be too old for him now," Ah Sam said knowingly to Chan and Ah Man. "Five or six years ago now, since they were together. Five or six years."

"Who're you talking about?" Jonathan pulled Ah Sam's sleeve. "Who's Kwan Su-mei?"

"Never you mind," she twitched her sleeve away. "Get on with your food, First-born! It's nobody you know."

Chan burped and sniggered. "It's a bitch your pa used to fancy."

"A bitch?"

"A woman dog," he sniggered again.

Jonathan looked down at his bowl again. Chan's voice always scared him. It always sounded harsh and angry, even when he wasn't really. He began playing with his chopsticks, clicking them together.

"He won't fancy her any more," Ah Sam said over Jonathan's head.

"Why not? If he doesn't get enough of it at home?"

"How d'you know he doesn't?" Ah Man asked, without lifting his head.

"Ask Ah Sam." Chan wiped his lips with the back of his hand. "Ask Ah Sam. She changes the sheets."

They all laughed, all except Cheong, who got up silently, put his bowl in the sink, and went out to the garden.

Ah King brought Jenny in, her eyes small and tired, her head nestling on Ah King's white-jacketed shoulder.

Ah Man and Ah Sam started playing with her, giving her their fingers to hold and shaking her tiny, pink-fingered fist to make her smile.

"She's smiling."

"She's like her mother."

"No, like her father."

"She's sleepy, look."

Chan watched them impassively, his lids lowering faintly as if in contempt. He never took any notice of Jenny, and he never played with Jonathan either. Nor was he like Cheong, who, though he rarely played with them, would often watch them silently in the garden and pick them up with an almost alarmed concern in his eyes if they fell down. Chan was silent too, but his silence seemed vaguely menacing and hostile. Jonathan didn't like being left alone with him in the car when Ah King got out to do some shopping on the way home from their afternoon rides. Once, Jonathan had asked Ah King, sitting in the back of the car, why Chan had that funny mark on the side of his face, and he'd turned round and told him harshly to mind

389

his own business before she could answer. After that, Jonathan never spoke to him directly.

He left the Club soon after eleven that night. The Sikh doorman, stamping his feet against the December chill, turned towards him. "Taxi, Mr. Denton?"

Denton glanced at the cabs, taxis and rickshaws waiting in the dark across the street. "No, a cab please."

The Sikh blew on his whistle, pointing imperiously at the leading cab, and the driver brought it jingling over, snapping his whip. Denton climbed in, dropping a coin into the Sikh's cupped palm, and leant back in the corner. The Sikh closed the door, his bearded, turbaned head appearing briefly in the open window. "Where to, sir? Home?"

"Yes. Home."

"Sixty-three, the Bund," the Sikh called out to the cabman, saluting as the rubber wheels carried Denton away.

The pony's hooves clopped steadily along the road. Denton gazed absently out at the dark shapes of the banks and hongs on one side, and the river lights on the other. He was restless, undecided, and yet he felt his indecision was a pretence, that he knew already what he was going to do, and was merely putting on a show of uncertainty and struggle to appease his conscience. Why else had he left the Club just after eleven, when he knew the opera would be ending?

And so, when the cab was passing the bronze lions of the Hong Kong and Shanghai Bank, smoothed by the hands of thousands of Chinese who came to stroke them for luck, he leant forward suddenly and called out to the cabman in Shanghainese. "Turn down Hankow Road and stop at Ta Wu Tai."

"Ta Wu Tai?" the man nodded and flicked the pony's flanks with his whip.

The road was crowded near the theatre, taxis, cabs and rickshaws waiting along the kerb, while tea and roasted chestnut stalls stood side by side along the pavement. The theatre doors had just opened, and the audience came jostling noisily out, laughing and shouting. Some seized on the rickshaws and cabs, others dodged between them to jump onto a passing tram, others clustered round the stalls. The smell of roasting chestnuts, mingled with the charcoal smoke from the glowing braziers, drifted in through the cab's window. The hawkers were calling out their prices raucously, banging the metal sides of their stalls with heavy iron ladles to attract attention. A tram bell clanged irritably, clearing a way for its clanking wheels through the crowd.

The cabman turned round. "How long are we staying here?"

"I don't know. I'm waiting for someone."

"Get myself some chestnuts, then." He jumped down and pushed into the crowd.

Denton gazed out through the window, searching for her sedan chair. Gradually the bustling crowd thinned. The hawkers called out more insistently, vying for the few remaining customers. Some women had started sweeping the entrance to the theatre while an old, shuffling man wearily bolted the doors one after another. Denton's fingers drummed on the edge of the door. Surely he hadn't missed her? But now all the doors were bolted and the old man had shuffled away.

The cabman was sitting in his seat again, eating his chestnuts. Denton leaned forward. "Do you know where the actors come out?"

"Round the corner."

"All right. Go and wait there."

The cabman muttered something and clucked his tongue. The pony ambled round the corner. And there was her chair, the one he'd seen in *rue* Moliére, painted in red and gold, with an unlit lantern on one of the shafts. The two bearers squatted on the pavement beside it, smoking cigarettes. They glanced across at the cab a moment, the street lamp glowing faintly on their faces, then looked incuriously away again. A dog went snuffling through the litter which choked the gutter beside them—paper bags, tangerine peel, chestnut shells and torn tickets. One of the bearers turned his head aside and spat.

Denton got out of the cab and walked over to the two men. They eyed him inexpressively, as if he'd been another dog.

"Are you waiting for Kwan Su-mei?"

They regarded him with that same indifferent stare, then one of them nodded almost imperceptibly, lowering his lids faintly afterwards as if to dismiss him from his mind. They both drew deeply on their cigarettes. The tips smouldered more brightly a moment.

"How long is she likely to be?"

They glanced at each other silently, then the one who had nodded shrugged. "Depends," he said uninterestedly.

The street was emptying now. A harsh, chill wind scratched through the litter at his feet. Denton heard the pony pawing the ground impatiently, then the cabman growling at it. He took out a coin. "How long do you expect?" he asked.

The same man took the coin and rang it on the chair pole before answering. "Any time now," he said at last.

Then, as he was turning away, he heard footsteps tripping down the narrow, grimy stairway that led up into the darkness of the theatre. He knew it was her, nothing about her step had changed. It was as if she were clicking along the corridor to his room in the Customs Mess again. Or into that first flat on Jessfield Road, where the Filipinos quarrelled every night across the courtyard. He turned to see her step out into the street-light, gorgeous in silk, her make-up still on her face. She emerged onto the dirt and litter as though she were making an entrance onto a stage. *The stage of my life,* he thought. *Let it be the stage of my life.*

She paused, recognising him at once, then came on unhurriedly towards him.

"You haven't changed," he said unevenly, glancing at her smooth face.

She put her hand up to her rouged cheek with a calm little deprecating smile, as if to say: It's only paint, it's not really me you're looking at.

"I saw you in the French Settlement a couple of weeks ago," he went on. "Is that where you live now?"

She nodded. Her hand left her face and the smile slowly faded. She watched him uncertainly now. Her lids had long slanting black lines running up from them, so that her eyes seemed larger, like those of some wild, shy animal.

"I saw your show last night."

Her eyes moved between the black lines and she smiled again. "Did you?"

"It was good."

"What did you think of me playing a man's part?"

"I hope you don't do that off-stage as well."

Her smile widened. "It's the Shaohing style, the new thing."

They stood looking at each other, still uncertain, still questioning. The cabman muttered again to his pony, the harness tinkled. A motor car hooted round the corner in Hankow Road. The two bearers were gazing curiously up at them, their eyes switching from one to the other. She glanced round at her chair at last, as if about to leave.

"Are you going home now?" he asked.

"Yes."

"That's a nicer chair than the one you used to have. Do you remember it?"

She looked at him appraisingly, as though seeing it for the first time, while the bearers went to the shafts and lit the lamp. "Yes, it is better," she agreed.

"Look, come in my cab," he blurted out, feeling he had at last overcome some barrier. "We can talk."

She hesitated. The bearers, who had lifted the shafts, set them down again, turning inquiringly back to her.

"All right?" he asked.

Still she hesitated. He glanced at the bearers. "We're going in the cab," he said briskly. "You can follow us."

Su-mei gave a little shrug of acquiescence, as though grateful she didn't have to make the decision herself, and walked across to the cab. She sat down in one corner, he in the other.

"You look just the same," he said again.

She smiled at him mockingly, as though the privacy of the cab had loosened some band that had held her stiff before. "Hadn't you better tell the man where to go?" she asked quietly.

He leant forward to give the address.

"Your Shanghainese hasn't improved much," she said, with the same, mocking smile. "Are you too busy to speak it now? I know you're something in the government, a taipan. And you have two children, and you race ponies."

"Only one pony. I just bought it, to make myself a proper taipan."

"So you're very rich?"

"I'm all right now. I nearly lost it all, not long ago."

She laughed, an open, friendly laugh. "How could you lose it all? Remember the fortune-teller? You're fated to be rich."

He leant back, smiling. All his muscles seemed to let

go, as if he too had been holding himself stiffly until then. He listened to the squeak of springs, the creak and jingle of the harness, the steady clop-clop of the pony's hooves. She'd taken the trouble to find out about him, then, he thought. The thought was warming. "I suppose I have three children really, not two..." he said slowly.

She didn't answer. He turned to look at her face again, without any constraint this time. Perhaps she had changed after all. Yes, she was more womanly now, her features a little more definite. "How did you do in Hong Kong?" he asked.

"Do what?"

"How did you get on?"

"All right," she shrugged, lowering her lids like shutters against further questions. "It's better in Shanghai."

"And Lily?"

"She's with me here—Is your wife beautiful?" she asked swiftly, as if to deflect him.

"Beautiful?" He looked away into the darkness of the other corner, visualising Mary-Ellen's face. "No, she's not beautiful," he said ruefully. "She was at first, I suppose, but she isn't now..." He gazed unblinkingly into the corner, frowning. He felt her eyes watching him, waiting patiently for him to go on. "It's been a failure," he admitted at last, "a complete failure." He felt relief in saying that. It was as if he'd crossed another barrier.

She was watching him calmly still, as if she expected him to say more. But he shrugged it off. That had been enough. "I'd like to see Lily one day," he said lightly.

"She is your daughter," she said matter-of-factly, glancing away out of the window. Her tone was so featureless he couldn't tell whether she was acknowledging his right or reproaching him. He gazed at the curve of her high cheek, the shape of her nose, the dark mass of hair piled up above the white nape of her neck. She was wearing large silver earrings that swayed and shook with the movement of the cab, gleaming erratically. They weren't the ones he'd given her. He felt a pang of jealousy.

"Do you still have our opium things?" she asked idly after some time. They both looked out of the lighted stalls and tea-houses they were passing now, clattering with noisy talk and laughter.

"Yes. Why?"

Her shoulders lifted faintly and fell.

"I've kept them wrapped up ever since you left. I've never touched them since."

Her brows rose. "Doesn't your wife...?"

He shook his head. "Besides, they were ours. I didn't want to smoke with anyone else."

She turned slowly, smiling with disbelief. "I'm sure you've smoked with lots of women..."

He shook his head again, holding her eyes with his.

The cabman let the pony amble at walking pace as they crossed the *rue* du Consulat into the French Settlement. It was as if he sensed their unwillingness to arrive. They didn't talk much now, as though after all there was no need for explanations. They only looked at each other. When the cab stopped outside her house they waited in the enclosed comfort of the darkness until they heard the slap-slap of the chair-bearers' sandals coming up behind them. The bearers stood panting beside the cab, talking to the driver.

"This is your own chair?" Denton asked. "How much of the house do you rent?"

"I've bought it. All of it."

He raised his brows. "So you're rich too?"

"Not like you."

His mind went back to the night market and the palmistry chart the fortune-teller had displayed, beside the table with the wooden spills. It was so clear he could see the man's shrewd eyes, his lean face and grey hair, as he peered at her palm in the uncertain light of his sooty oil-lamp. It was like a photograph he'd kept in a secret album of his mind, to open today. He took her hand. "The fortune-teller was right about you, too?"

"He said I would have many children," she said detachedly. She took her hand away.

He opened the door for her. "I'm coming to see you tomorrow. You and Lily. What time shall I come?"

She stood considering gravely, and for a moment he was afraid she was going to refuse. But then she said. "In the afternoon? At four?"

He nodded, leaning towards her. "Perhaps we'll smoke a pipe of opium again soon?"

"Perhaps." She smiled enigmatically. "It's good for my voice."

54

The ponies came clearly into view again on the home stretch, and everyone in the box except Denton leant forward eagerly—Denton and Mary-Ellen, who was indolently drinking her fifth glass of champagne. There were four ponies in the front of the field, their riders whipping them on to the finish. Chips of turf flew up behind them and in the box they could hear the hollow thudding of the hooves for a moment before the crowd's excitement welled up and drowned it. Denton's pony, Jolly Demon, was lying first, the young griffin from Jardine's who was riding it getting up in the stirrups now and whipping fiercely. The shouting in the public enclosure grew wilder as Jolly Demon gradually increased his lead. A great shout went up from the crowd, a shout of triumph in which the groans of the losers were also blended.

"Well I never, we've won!" Mary-Ellen exclaimed with drawling incredulity.

"Congratulations," Mrs. Nixon turned with a vinegary smile. She had aged swiftly over the past five years, with that sudden collapse into wrinkles and bitterness that had always seemed imminent. Now her smile and even her voice seemed forced, as though really she grudged anyone the slightest happiness or success.

"Another bottle of champagne please," Denton said to Ah Man, who had deserted the large hamper to peer over the railing himself.

Ah Man was grinning to himself as he uncorked the bottle.

"Did you bet on it?" Denton asked in Shanghainese.

"Fifty dollar," Ah Man nodded. The cork popped out and the light frothy wine bubbled over the neck. He wrapped a napkin round the bottle and refilled the glasses, still grinning happily to himself.

"Aren't you going to lead Jolly Demon in?" Mary-Ellen asked, raising her brows ironically. "The proud owner?"

Denton left his champagne untouched and went down to the paddock. The young griffin, polite and golden-haired, leant forward to pat the pony's lathered neck.

"Thanks awfully for the ride, Mr. Denton," he said as he swung easily out of the saddle. "Enjoyed it very much. That soft going seems to suit him."

Denton stroked the pony's steaming white muzzle. "Come up and join us in our box. Have a glass of champagne."

"Thanks awfully."

"Must be thirsty after all that."

"Yes, it is thirsty work," he agreed respectfully.

Denton handed the bridle to the mafoo and turned away. The young griffin—he could hardly recall his name—accompanied him attentively.

The Nixons congratulated the young man, he genially, she with ice in her voice. Mary-Ellen offered him a glass of champagne.

They leant over the rail to watch the next race. Ah Man, unable to squeeze himself in, took off his black cloth slippers with an apologetic glance at Denton and stood in his bare feet on a chair. The race started. The crowd roared, then settled down to an expectant, hushed murmuring.

Denton sipped his champagne again, contemplating the row of backs presented to him. Mary-Ellen's wide hips seemed to press, unconsciously no doubt, against the mud-spotted white breeches of the young griffin. Mrs. Nixon's shoulders looked slightly hunched and shrivelled. Ah Man stood dangerously on tip-toe, craning his neck, while the chair rocked...

Denton's eyes watched them, but his mind floated away to Su-mei and her daughter—his daughter too. Lily was eight now, a withdrawn, grave-eyed girl who called him "Uncle," spoke English stiltedly like her mother, and watched silently from the corner of the room whenever he visited them.

"She's suspicious of everyone," Su-mei said once, drawing her close to plait her hair, "Like you." She'd put Lily in the Thomas Hanbury School for Girls—*founded for the education of Eurasians, but other students are now received,* he read in the prospectus Su-mei showed him—and the monthl[y] sum he'd been paying Su-mei all those years was n[ow] going into a fund for her. So far, he'd visited Su-mei [on]ly decorously, in the afternoons, or gone riding with her [in a] cab. He wanted to court her, not assume he still ha[d] rights to her that he'd forfeited by marrying Mary-[Ellen]. She'd become a well-known actress in a small way, [and]

397

didn't want her to think he might treat her as a flower girl, to be visited only for the pleasures of "clouds and rain." Besides, he was apprehensive about touching her. Since his marriage he'd known women only as passive means to pleasure, sometimes fierce pleasure, and he was afraid he might not be able to recapture the playful tenderness with which he'd loved Su-mei before. And all the time Su-mei said nothing of clouds and rain, but only watched him with her sleek hair and slanting eyes, a smile of quiet mockery or just simple amusement on her lips while he talked to her of the past seven years and fingered her delicate-fingered hand, which he occasionally took in his. And whenever he came, Ah Leng, the amah she used to have before, opened the door with a smile and brought them tea as if nothing had happened, as if he'd never left her ...

The race was ending. The same swelling wave of excitement was rising higher and higher in the stands beneath them. Looking up, Denton realised he was smiling, that same secret smile of satisfaction that Ah Man had had when Jolly Demon won. He got up to look over Mary-Ellen's shoulder, but he was too late. The wave had risen and broken in another howl of triumph. *You'd think they must all have won,* he thought. But Ah Man's face was glum as he stepped quietly down from the chair and slid his feet into his slippers.

"No luck?"

Ah Man shook his head miserably. "Bad horsee," he muttered in morose pidgin. "That horsee bad joss."

Nixon drew his chair up beside Denton's and leant towards him affably, yet with a confidential lowering of his voice. "Well, d'you think we should try for Chinese members on the Council again? Bit of a puzzler, what?" He felt in one pocket for his pipe, then in the other for his tobacco pouch. "Feelings have been running pretty high amongst the Chinese recently, wouldn't you say? See their point, mind you. They eventually come in on our side in the war and then the peace treaty calmly gives a slice of land to Japan. As if they'd been on the losing side,

Denton nodded. "The Weis are certainly furious."

"Good barometer." Nixon drew reflectively on his pipe. "The odd thing is, it's the Japs we should really worry about, you know. They're going to push us
398

out if we're not careful. They'll be doing what we didn't have the nerve to do." He glanced up at Denton. "Colonise China, I mean. And if they do, there'll be no more room for the white man here than there was for the French when we took over India." He crossed his legs and puffed for some time. "So it seems to me we might do a lot worse than try to get the Chinese on our side, as far as we can, and that's why I'd like to see us making another gesture in the Council, what?"

He had to pause as Jacob Ephraim came in with Sarah behind him. "Congratulations!" he clapped both hands on Denton's arms as though he was going to hug him, his bright brown eyes sparkling in the faint folds of his skin. "I knew your horse would win."

"Ah, but did you bet on it?" Nixon asked jovially. "Knowledge without investment, as the philosopher says, like a virgin produces nothing—Forgive me ladies."

Mrs. Nixon's lips puckered, while Sarah waved her hand vaguely, as though she didn't quite understand what there was to forgive.

"I never bet," Jacob said definitely, releasing Denton's arms. "The profits are too uncertain."

The last race had been run. Denton gazed out at the square shadow of the clubhouse lengthening across the racecourse. Ah Man had begun packing the remains of the picnic into the hamper, his face still set and glum. Without saying anything, as if by a common instinct, they all began to leave.

Jacob held Denton back when the others had gone, gripping his arm with a sidelong glance at Ah Man, who was leaning morosely over the hamper. "You're getting yourself talked about," he whispered sibilantly.

Denton stiffened. "Talked about?"

"Shh." He nodded significantly towards Ah Man, gazing intently into Denton's eyes. "Su-mei. You're not being careful enough. She'll get you into trouble."

Denton shrugged his arm abruptly as if to shake Jacob off. He'd never done that before, enduring his grip, like his flowing homilies and advice, with amused patience. But Jacob's mention of Su-mei had invaded a secret place in his mind, and his first instinct was to protect it. He regretted the movement at once, and tried to check it, but it was too late—Jacob let his arm drop as though it had been cut off.

"I'm telling you for your own good," he said harshly, no longer whispering. He stepped back a pace. "In Shanghai you can do anything, *if* you don't do it openly."

Denton tried to conciliate him. "All I've done is call on her a few times."

"And drive in the street with her. Openly! As if you weren't married, as if she weren't a..."

"Weren't a what?" Denton's own voice hardened now.

"You know very well what! And you a municipal councillor! You could be voted off next week if the word has spread!" He hurried out, letting the door slam shut behind him. When Denton followed, he saw him clutching Sarah's arm, almost pulling her away, leaving the Nixons and Mary-Ellen with a curt goodbye.

By the time Denton had caught up with the others at the door of the clubhouse, Jacob was already stepping into his new American car. He stared past them without acknowledgement as the car drove away, his face rigid and taut, while Sarah questioned him with uncomprehending, anxious eyes. Sniffing the acrid smell of the exhaust, Denton remembered again how once Jacob had declared the car had no future in China. Everything about him was definite but mercurial, he thought. In a week he would have forgotten the offence that now seemed so deadly.

"Excitable fellow, Mr. Ephraim," Nixon murmured with a condescending smile. "Got some strange ideas, wouldn't you say?—Well," he raised his hat, "we must talk again about that other little matter some time. We really ought to see what can be done, what? Thanks so much for a fine day's racing. And congratulations of course."

Ah King brought the children in to say goodnight while Mary-Ellen soaked in her bath. "Talk-story, Talk-story," Jonathan wheedled him in Shanghainese while Jenny regarded him sleepily, sucking her thumb.

"All right, I'll tell you a story," he gave in, taking a child in each arm.

But the phone rang before he could start. It was Nixon. "Something rather extraordinary's happened," his voice began slowly in the ear-piece.

Denton, in the second or two before Nixon went on, imagined riots, assassinations, civil war, in swift vivid images. But the reality was less catastrophic, and still less probable.

400

"There's a fleet of Russian warships sailing up the river. White Russians—refugees from the Bolsheviks. They've come from Vladivostock, apparently. Want to land and settle here. Twelve thousand of them. I suppose it means an emergency meeting of the Council. Must say I don't like the idea of shiploads of presumably impoverished Europeans landing here, though... It'll lower our standing with the orientals, just when we need to keep it up. I mean, how are they going to live? Imagine a white doorman or rickshaw boy—god knows, even a beggar. Not to speak of the women."

Denton took the children in his arms again and went out onto the veranda. "Look," he nodded out at the river. "Princes and princesses, all the way from Russia. They've come from the snow and the wolves."

The children gazed out wide-eyed at the convoy of dark, dimly-lit warships creeping slowly, meekly, past the bright, white liners of the west. The blurred shapes of hundreds of men, women and children lined the decks, gazing silently back at them through the cooling dusk.

55

"What do you want Lily to do?" he asked as she held the needle in the flame. "When she grows up?"

Su-mei shrugged and frowned at the same time, turning the needle to and fro. "Not to be sold. Not to become a sing-song girl," she said with brittle detachment. "To marry a rich man, if anyone will have a half-breed."

"She'll never need money, why d'you talk about being sold and all that?"

"Who knows what she'll need?" But she smiled and tossed her head as if she disbelieved her own doubts. The opium was treacly on the needle, ready. She placed it in the bowl of the pipe and handed it to him demurely with both hands, bowing her head in mock submission—"As a concubine should," she said teasingly.

They smoked three pipes each. Unused to it, his mind grew light and tranquil at once, while everything in the room around him seemed to become freshly clear and definite, as if he were seeing it all for the first time, the tired habits of ordinary vision peeled from his eyes.

401

"What did your wife say when you got the things out from the wardrobe?" Su-mei asked serenely as she made the third pipe.

"She didn't see." As he answered, he wasn't sure whether she'd asked the question a long time ago or just before he spoke. It might have been a half-an-hour, he thought. Time seemed to expand and contract, to have lost its rigid scale. And space too. He reached out towards the silk of her dress—its deep scarlet folds seemed to have taken on a new intensity and moved by themselves across the room, as if colour could travel by itself, alone. But he couldn't touch it. It was too far away after all. No matter, she was coming nearer now. She placed the stem between his lips again and he inhaled deeply for the last time, holding the smoke deep down in his chest.

"It's better like this," she said, expelling her breath first, pausing, then inhaling through the pipe with a long deeply-drawn breath, her eyes closed. "This way the smoke goes deeper."

"I'd forgotten." Again he couldn't tell whether it was a second or an hour after she'd spoken that he was answering her. He laid his head down on the pillow and watched her face for another measureless time. Through the spacious clarity that both brought him close and yet detached him from her face, from the lamp, from the smoke-blackened pipe, the pillow and the couch, he slowly realised that she was loosening her hair. And the way she turned her head from side to side as she pulled her braids apart seemed like the movements in some ritual dance. "It's time for clouds and rain," he heard himself say—or thought he did, for she didn't answer. She didn't even glance at him, intent on her hair, her head leaning forward, her eyes glancing upwards, her arms raised behind her neck in their full, bright sleeves like two gorgeous wings. But then, as she shook her hair free at last, she took his hand and led him into the bedroom. So she'd heard after all—or was it she that had spoken, not him?

"Am I the same?" she asked when they lay side by side, their eyes slow and heavy from the clouds and rain. It was some time before he answered, and he knew it now, allowing the minutes to elapse deliberately, as though all his thoughts, the whole world, had slowed under the weight of that pleasure. He noticed the border of the

402

curtain fluttering faintly in the breeze by the window, and was reminded of a butterfly's wings as he replied at last. "When you went away—when I sent you away—I thought you'd become a little spoilt sometimes. But now..." he shrugged, turning to hold her head in both hands, looking into her full, heavy eyes.

"Now what?"

"Now I realise how stupid I was to send you away."

"If I was spoilt, you should have corrected me," she said gravely, with only a glimmer of mockery in her eyes. "—And here," slapping the bed between them, "how am I here? Am I the same?"

"Let me think..." He let his lids close so that he could stroke her face consideringly, then her throat, her shoulders, her breasts. "Yes, the same," he said judicially as she in turn stroked his body delicately with her finger-tips.

He took a rickshaw back, along the French Bund and then into the International Settlement. It was after two in the morning and he'd found the rickshaw at an all-night food stall after walking for half a mile with a springy, light-headed energy despite the cold. The coolie's padding sandals and steady panting, the rumble of the wheels and the clicking of the spokes, were the only sounds beside the sleeping black water of the river. Those, and the occasional blast of a ship's siren echoing across the harbour like the bellow of a restless animal. He looked out over the French quays at the grey, rusting ships of the Russian armada, still forlornly waiting to discharge the last of their cargo of dispossessed aristocrats. The night was frosty, and the street lamps sent out glittering splinters of light at intervals along the road. The coolie's breath steamed on the air. He ran well, balancing the shafts finely. And the rickshaw—Denton glanced down at it—looked clean and new, the brasswork gleaming.

It was over a mile, and the coolie ran all the way. Denton gave him a fifty-cents tip as he got out. The coolie panted his thanks. "A long run," Denton said.

"Long," he nodded. "Better at night, though. Nothing gets in the way."

"And a nice rickshaw."

"Oh," he smiled, glancing back at it appraisingly. "It's new, that's what. Paid a hundred bucks for it."

"A hundred?" In all these years, he'd never thought what a rickshaw might cost.

"Hundred and ten. Took me two years to make that much. Before, I rented one. Sometimes I only made thirty cents a day. Hard. They squeeze you, those bastards."

"So you're making more money now?"

"Yeah." He smiled. "Saving up for another one. Then I'll rent that out, squeeze some other mother's son...Only they're going to increase the licence fees, so they say."

Denton knew. It had been before the Council twice already, and was coming up again. "Who are?" he asked casually.

"The foreign devils." He glanced at Denton apologetically and smiled. It was a young face, not yet worn and disillusioned. And yet it had the peasant's cunning. He was going to squeeze whoever rented his second rickshaw every bit as hard as he'd been squeezed himself. "The taipans, I mean," he went on. "They're raising the fees. To get money for the Russians," he jerked his head scornfully at the river. "They squeeze *us* to pay for their brothers to come and live here for nothing."

"A lot of Chinese refugees come here too, don't they?" Denton asked mildly.

The coolie laughed good-naturedly at the simplicity of that argument, a laugh that suggested Denton was really far too artful to be taken in by it himself. "How can Chinese be refugees in their own land?" he asked rhetorically. He picked up the shafts with the satisfied air of a man who has just produced an irrefutable demonstration.

"Where did you learn about all this?" Denton asked, watching him turn the rickshaw round, handling it with watchful care. "Licence fees and the Russians and...?"

"The communists tell us."

"Communists?"

"They come round. They tell us things. We're going to have a union. They say there'll be no more taipans soon."

Denton turned and walked up the drive to his house. It must be freezing, he thought, listening to the dry, hard sound of his shoes crunching the gravel. About thirty street-sleepers would die of the cold that night, according to the statistics laid before the Council every year by the Benevolent Society. And out there in the harbour were the last and poorest of the Russians—their rations slowly

404

running out. And every day more Chinese crowded into the city, to work, to beg, or just to starve more slowly than they would outside.

He let himself in quietly and stood listening. The light was on in the kitchen, seeping beneath the door. He pushed the door open. A bowl of half-finished rice stood on the table with two wooden chopsticks, rice grains sticking to them, laid together across it. The flickering green tail of a tjik-tjak slithered off the table as he approached. He frowned at the servants' carelessness, putting the bowl in the sink and filling it with water to keep the cockroaches out. As he switched the light off, he heard Ah King's voice raised in her room, immediately answered, and suppressed it seemed, by the stern voice of a man. He recognised her husband's deep tones at once. So he was back again—to get another child, presumably.

The children still slept together in the same room, Jenny in her cot, the toys from her third birthday party lying round her on the blanket or fallen on the floor. She was sucking her thumb again in her sleep. He eased it, pink and wet, out of her mouth, and her lips slowly closed, pouting slightly as though even in her sleep she knew she'd been deprived. He picked up the furry teddy bear that had fallen on the floor and laid it beside her on the pillow. Already her thumb had crept back into her mouth; her lips were sucking comfortingly on it, making a faint kissing noise. He turned to Jonathan, who had sighed suddenly in his sleep, and pulled the blanket up round his shoulders.

He was still fresh and alert from the opium. I have a third child, he thought, gazing down at them both with almost impersonal eyes. A child I scarcely know. For a moment he imagined the third child lying there beside those two. But no, it was impossible. Even in the tranquil after-mood of opium and love, the idea of a half-Chinese child beside the white ones seemed a jarring disharmony. He went stealthily into the master bedroom.

The beside light was still on. Mary-Ellen had fallen asleep over a book. She must have had a bath, the large pink towel was still wrapped round her, rumpled up above her knees. She'd sprawled on her belly across the bed, so that it would be impossible to get in without disturbing her. The room was hot. She always turned the radiator on too high in winter, and refused to open the windows even a crack. He switched the light off and undressed swiftly by the faint light of the stars that shone through the filmy curtains. The same melancholy siren sounded from the river, like a cow lowing for her calf. He went to the window and looked out. Ship after ship lay moored in the harbour, lights glittering on their masts. Almost opposite him, a tramp steamer was still loading, lamps flaring down over the junks and barges clustering like insects round its hull. On the far shore, the wharves and factories were lit up too. Only when he raised his eyes and looked far away could he see the immense darkness that surrounded the city. Whenever he looked out beyond Pootung like that, he had a sense of both awe and exhilaration. Shanghai—Asia's greatest city, built in only sixty years from stagnant canals and yellow mud. The greatest city, and yet still so tiny on the edge of all that vastness.

He turned reluctantly to the bed. Mary-Ellen's face was towards him, her mouth half-open. Despite his distaste for her now, he could see the remnants of a ripe lusciousness about her body, like a fruit that has dropped off the tree and just begun to rot. He could understand how, five years ago, when she was still firm, she had tempted and challenged him for all her coldness. Yes, even now she was like those fleshy women in that book of French Impressionists she had; only older, without the glow of youth.

She stirred and opened her eyes drowsily as he climbed into bed. "What time is it? Where've you been?"

"At the club."

"Huh."

He couldn't tell whether she was expressing disbelief or indifference—or both. "Did you know you look a bit like a Renoir woman?" he asked quickly, to turn her mind away from himself. Not that she cared what he did, but he recoiled from the thought of her casually sneering at him. If only he could fall asleep instantly, like a flame blown out, fall into a dream of Su-mei!

"Do you mean Renoir or Rembrandt or Rubens?" she drawled patronisingly. "They all begin with R you know."

"All of them," he said, closing his eyes.

He felt the bed shake as she unwound the towel and dropped it on the floor. "I suppose it's all right for me to be like this now?" she murmured in the same ironical, drawling tones.

"Like what?"

"No nightdress. You've changed, you know."

"Have I?"

"You leave me alone now," she yawned lying down beside him. "I'm beginning to feel quite safe with you...Two or three years ago I wouldn't've dared. I guess you're getting past it, eh?" She patted his groin complacently, with a self-satisfied air of quiet triumph in her voice. "See? Nice and docile now, aren't we?"

He felt a gust of resentment and bitterness at her taunt, at the triumph in her voice, at her complacent assumption that she'd emasculated him at last.

"Is that what you think?" he said, knocking her hand away. "Yes, that's what you've always wanted, isn't it?" He rolled on top of her suddenly, imprisoning her wrists and biting her arms, her lips her throat her breasts. "Well you're wrong, you bloody bitch!"

At first she fought back; but the more she struggled the more she aroused him, and at last she gave up and went limp, as if she were shrugging to herself and saying "Well what does it matter, it's so insignificant anyway?" He rammed himself into her furiously, battering against her distasteful indifference until with a groan and shudder he spent himself inside her. He withdrew at once and turned away from her, feeling sullied and suddenly weary.

"That felt like rape," she said coldly.

"It was bloody well meant to."

"I hope you won't regret it then..." She yawned, as if, although the whole thing was too trivial to discuss, still one minor detail should be mentioned. "I haven't taken any precautions."

"Well wash yourself out then," he muttered coarsely. "The last thing I want is another child from you."

"Me too," she drawled sarcastically. But she didn't move, and in a minute or two he heard her breathing deeply and peacefully, almost snoring. Damn you, does nothing ever affect you? he thought bitterly. Not even rape?

He lay awake till dawn, disgusted with her, disgusted with himself. If only I could leave her, he kept thinking, staring up at the grey cheerless light stealing across the ceiling from the windows. And take the children with me. Go and live with Su-mei. But always he felt that jarring disharmony of the half-Chinese child and the white children, of the scandal and the ostracism that would follow. He saw Jacob's angry, offended eyes glowing down at him from the ceiling. *You can do anything, if you don't do it openly! You a municipal councillor!*

It was the end of the afternoon, the children were hot and tired. Ah King watched from the shade of the car as they played listlessly with Jenny's new ball, the yellow one she'd got for her third birthday. Jonathan was jealous of his sister, especially when they came to Jessfield Park, because it was always she who sat on Ah King's lap now instead of him. So he kept snatching the ball away from her, holding it above his head teasingly while she stumbled after him with outstretched hands, pleading, close to tears.

"Give her the ball, First-born," Ah King called out warningly. "Don't be selfish!"

He threw it carelessly at last, when Ah King's voice had grown dangerously angry. The ball hit Jenny's knees. She crumpled and fell on her face. For one second she lay there amazed, then she sat up and bawled.

Ah King slapped him hard, dragging him away to the car. "I saw you do that, First-born! I'll tell your mother!"

"I don't care," Jonathan sobbed bitterly, pulling back against her and beating her hand, which only gripped him more tightly. He was sobbing, not just at the smart of her slaps, but also at the unfairness of it, when he hadn't even meant to knock her down.

Jenny sat on Ah King's lap in the car holding the great yellow ball with both hands, gazing out with tear-washed wondering eyes at the fruit-stalls, tea-stalls, meat-stalls of the market, at the mend-shoe men, the letter-writers and the barbers. Jonathan sat remote and scowling in the corner, stifling his sniffs of humiliation and injustice. "I hate you, I hate you, I hate you," he kept muttering whenever they looked at him, but Ah King only chuckled, while Jenny after solemnly considering him a moment, would hug the ball closer to her and look away out of the window again.

Chan nodded down Bubbling Well Road, half-turning his head. "Big rickshaw meeting down there," he said. "Protest Against The Licence Fees Meeting."

Ah King leant forward, peering over Jenny's head at the barricade of empty rickshaws and wheelbarrows that blocked the road further down. "Go down Chengtu Road," she said.

"Too late."

She shook her head anxiously. "Chungking Road, then."

The coolies were meeting at the recreation ground, their rickshaws and barrows protecting them like a hedge while police looked on with long clubs in their hands. A foreign-devil police officer halted the car, peered inside, then shouted at Chan in a high, nervous voice.

"Turn round and go back, you fool!" His face was sweating and flushed. "Didn't you see the sign?"

"What sign?" Chan muttered.

"They'll stone your car, idiot! Turn round, go back to Siccawei Road! Risking children's lives like that!"

Jenny cowered against Ah King's bosom, scared by the excited anger in the man's voice. Jonathan felt his chest pounding with sudden fear, while Chan, cursing under his breath, turned the car round, swinging from kerb to kerb and braking fiercely. A ragged, defiant shout rose from the coolies, growing gradually louder and more menacing. Jonathan knelt up to look out of the oval rear window as the car drew away at last. Three rows of police were slowly approaching the barricade, wearing steel helmets and carrying round wicker shields on their left arms. Suddenly, as if at an order, a barrage of stones was hurled at them. Jonathan watched them sailing through the air in calm peaceful arcs. Two or three of the policemen staggered and fell down. Then the car turned into Siccawei Road, and Jonathan saw all the shops were boarded up. "What were they doing, Ah King?" he asked weakly. "Why were they fighting?"

"Oh now you want to speak to me, do you?" Ah King said jerkily. She was holding Jenny tight to her breast, patting her shoulder with quick little fluttering pats.

Chan spat out of the open window. "Could've sworn I saw your old man in that crowd, Ah King?" He glanced at her in the mirror with a knowing leer.

"My old man's at sea," she said curtly.

Denton was making a phone call when Ah King brought the children in.

"There was a fight," Jonathan said, braver now he was safe.

"Jonafan frow' the ball at me an' I fall down." Jenny prepared to cry again, her voice wobbling already.

"What is it, Ah King?" he asked as he hung the receiver up.

"Rickshaw coolies and the police. A foreign devil policeman scolded Chan and we had to go back..."

"Yes I know, they've just been telling me," Denton took Jenny on his lap. "Better not go out tomorrow." He let Jenny turn the pages of his book.

"Jonafan knock' me down," she stated with wide-eyed gravity, no longer wanting to cry—she was absorbed in laboriously pushing the pages over one by one with her whole clumsy-fingered hand.

Jonathan had gone to the window. "Policemen!" he called out excitedly. "Policemen with big guns!"

"Well, you've done it again," Mary-Ellen said breezily a week later when she came in at lunch-time.

He glanced at her with a sudden qualm of misgiving in his stomach.

"I'm pregnant." She took a chocolate out of the box on the sideboard and crunched the dark, crackly paper in her hand. "You ought to've left me alone, don't say I didn't warn you. Want a chocolate?"

He gazed down numbly at the Afghan carpet she'd bought a few weeks ago. "Are you sure?" he asked dully. The uneasy qualm had become a stone dragging him down.

"McEwan is." She took another chocolate, then closed the box. "I'm four months gone. I hope you're pleased." Her jaw clicked slightly as she munched the chocolates. She dropped the crumpled papers on the table in front of him. He watched them slowly open up again, like the stiff petals of some poisonous flower.

"I'm not pleased," he said sullenly. He felt as though he'd just been told he'd got some incurable disease. Well, that's just about what it is, he thought.

"Want me to get rid of it?" she drawled. Her jaw clicked again and she paused to suck the sticky chocolate off her teeth.

He closed his eyes and rubbed his forehead. "I certainly don't want you to have it."

"Because McEwan says it's too late. Not that he'd have anything to do with that kind of thing anyway, he said."

"When did you see him?"

"This morning."

"Four months! Why didn't you go sooner?"

She shrugged lightly. "Why didn't you leave me alone? I never exactly encouraged you, did I?"

He was thinking of Su-mei while he spoke, thinking of her with a kind of longing, a weakness almost, as though she were suddenly further away from him, gradually receding. "You could at least have gone to McEwan sooner," he said bitterly. "Now I suppose we've got no choice."

"Oh now it's there, it might as well stay there, I guess," she shrugged. "They're not much trouble, are they?"

"Not for you, they're not, no." He got up suddenly and went out onto the veranda. Jonathan was digging intently at something in the garden. Why couldn't it have been Su-mei? he thought miserably. If it had to be one of them, why not Su-mei? I might have thrown everything up and gone to live with her if it'd been her. But now . . .

"Oh, and Helen Bolton's invited me to Peking," she was saying casually. "Remember Helen Bolton?"

"Your best friend," he said woodenly. "When? Now?"

"Next week, I thought. I don't want to leave it too long in my condition."

"I suppose you wouldn't want to take the children with you?" he asked bitingly, turning to glance at her.

"Get them out of your way, you mean?" She shook her head, "No, they wouldn't enjoy it, being dragged round the antique shops in this heat. Besides, Jonathan's going back to school next month, isn't he?"

"Well how long do you plan to be away for, then?"

She shrugged, pursing her lips. "About six or eight weeks."

There was a strangely elated tone in her voice, one that he'd never heard before. "You sound like a girl going to her first dance," he said.

"I suppose Ah King will look after them just as well as I could?" she asked ironically, ignoring his remark.

"Better," he said.

Ah Sam sat on the kitchen step beside Ah King, watching the children playing on the lawn. Inside, Ah Man's chopper sounded regularly with quick, sharp thuds as he diced the pork for dinner. Chan lounged in a broken basket

411

chair under the dappled shade of the bauhinia, his eyes closed, a cigarette dangling from his lower lip. Cheong's wide, round hat moved slowly at the other end of the garden, where he was bending over the bougainvillea.

"Master's opium pipe has gone," Ah Sam announced importantly, glancing at each of them in turn. "I opened the wardrobe drawer this morning, and it's all gone—pipe, lamp, everything."

"Come away from those bushes, First-born." Ah King called out warningly. "There might be snakes there. Play on the lawn, you hear me? Like Jenny." She scratched the mosquito bite on her ankle, narrowing her eyes to gaze out over the river at the blinding metallic sky, which glowed like a white-hot bowl enclosing the earth. "Typhoon coming soon."

Ah Sam sighed, crestfallen. She'd been sure her news would create a stir. She began massaging her swollen-jointed fingers, pouting slightly.

But then Chan grunted, blowing a funnel of smoke up into the air. "I bet I know where the pipe's gone to, then." He settled himself lower in the chair, folding his hands over his belly.

"My grandfather died of opium," Ah Sam said, almost with pride, still massaging her knuckles. "He got so thin and dry he was like a piece of paper that's been left in the sun."

Nobody spoke for some time. Then, "The boss made a lot of money out of opium," Chan muttered with grudging admiration. "Remember when he was nearly done for, let me go and sold the car? He made a deal with that foreign devil, used to work with Ching. Bought him out and sold it at ten times what it cost him."

The regular slicing thud of Ah Man's chopper paused. "The opium was Ching's," he said. "The foreign devil swindled Ching out of it, and that's how the boss got it cheap."

"It was after Ching died," Chan declared belligerently. "How could it've been his? If it was anyone's, it was Pock-mark Chen's. He hasn't forgotten it, either."

"How would you know?" Ah King asked lazily. "I suppose you're high up in the Green Triangle?"

Chan blew another funnel of smoke up into the air in contemptuous silence.

"Yes, you could've puffed him over," Ah Sam said.

"He just stopped eating. Even my mother could carry him in her arms like a baby. Only thing he'd take was opium. Of course I was only a kid, then."

"Jonathan? Jenny?" Mary-Ellen called from the veranda, "I'm going to the French Club. Want to have a swim?"

Ah Sam and Ah King glanced at each other, "Master say no go out, missy," Ah King called out. "Still some people fight. Rickshaw coolie fight policeman. You better go bime bye."

"Oh it's all right now. We'll keep on the big roads. Chan, you catchee car front-side chop-chop. Where are their swimming things, Ah King?"

"Very hot, missy," Ah King said unhappily.

"That's why we're going swimming!"

Ah King glanced at Ah Sam again, eyebrows raised, while the children went indoors, Chan heaved himself out of his chair, cursing under his breath.

"She never takes them swimming," Ah Sam protested.

"She'll be wanting to give them a treat before she goes away," Ah Man said.

Ah Sam lowered her voice still further, glancing from one to the other. "Do you think she's pregnant again?"

"*I* am, I know that," Ah King answered flatly. "That's enough for me."

At the end of the garden, Cheong straightened his back a moment and stretched, then spread his legs wider and bent over the bougainvillea's thorny brancnes once more.

56

The old, brass-tipped fans creaked as they turned in the dark, oak-panelled bar, and Denton shifted slightly so that he stood beneath one of them, feeling it stir his hair. He sipped his whisky, only half-listening to Green and Nixon talking beside him.

"If the Council's going to give in to a bunch of rioting rickshaw coolies and student riff-raff, we might as well all go home tomorrow," Green declared, his eyes intense in his long face. "Licence fees haven't been raised for over five years now, have they? What on earth are they moaning about? Born tired, half of 'em, if you ask me."

"Well..." Nixon glanced at Denton for support, "I agree the Council shouldn't have given in, not given them everything, anyway... But on the other hand, Norman, we certainly don't want a lot of strikes and riots just now, do we? And of course, letting all those Russians in has rather created a... well, a situation, what?"

"Riots and strikes!" Green's knuckles whitened round his glass as he clenched it tighter, and Denton remembered the force of his handshake over ten years ago, when they'd first met at his interview for admission to the club. What had happened to the others? The plump, good-natured one—Keston, that was it—had been killed in the war, and the chairman had retired and gone home. As they all would one day. And what would have happened to Su-mei and him by then?

"Call out the Volunteers!" Green was asserting loudly. "They'd soon slink home with their tails between their legs!" He had gone grey quite suddenly, in the last year or so. "And as for Sun Yat-sen and that lot, who do they think they are? If you ask me, the only sensible thing to do is for all the western powers to carve this country up between them, like we did Africa in the last century. The Chinese'll never be able to run things themselves, they're too lazy and corrupt. And Sun Yat-sen'll turn out to be just another petty little warlord. What d'you think, Denton?"

"Actually, it's the Japs who are likely to do any colonising," Nixon murmured.

Denton dragged his mind away from Su-mei and from Mary-Ellen on the Blue Express to Peking. Both Nixon and Green were watching him expectantly. He answered reluctantly, with a disclaiming shrug. "Well, I've met Sun Yat-sen a couple of times here in Shanghai," he said slowly, frowning down at his glass and wondering how to go on. "He didn't seem very impressive, I must admit. A bit anaemic, somehow..."

Green grunted with pleased surprise. Obviously, he hadn't expected Denton to back him up.

Denton slid his empty glass round and back on the polished counter. "All the same," he said reasonably, "I suppose the Chinese ought to be allowed to govern themselves how they like, don't you think?" He was thinking of Green's proposal a minute ago to colonise the country. "It's not as though they're a lot of primitive savages, after all..."

"I'll believe that when I see them stop spitting in the streets!"

Jenny sat on Ah King's bed, lifting her arms. "Ah King, carry me, carry me."

Ah King was standing on the thin bamboo-shavings mattress, reaching up to fix the picture of the dragon on the wall. She took the nail out of her lips and hammered it into the soft plaster.

"Ah King, carry me," Jenny chanted monotonously. "Carry me, I want to be carried..."

"Just wait a minute, I'm busy." She leant back to regard the picture. It was a fierce, horrifying dragon, snarling and spitting fire. "Nice, ah?" she asked.

Jonathan had crawled under the unplaned wooden planks of her bed, and was trying to move the trestles that supported them.

"Leave that alone and come out of there!" Ah King called out sharply. She stepped off the bed and slipped her sandals on again.

"Carry me, carry me, carry me..."

Ah King looked at the picture again and nodded approvingly. It would scare a thousand devils away. She spread the carrying cloth out on the bed. "Jonathan, you come out of there and help put Jenny on my back. Come on now."

"There's a knife here."

"Leave it alone."

"What's it for?" He crawled out, his hands grey with dust, holding up the knife.

"Leave it *alone*, I said. Put it back or I won't take you out. Exactly where you found it."

"Well, what's it *for*?" Jonathan demanded impatiently. "Tell me what it's for!"

"Put it back first."

He crawled under the bed again, between the rough wood of the trestles. Down there in the dust and the gloom it smelt different from the rest of the house, different from the kitchen and everywhere. A musty, woody smell. He laid the knife down in the same place, where its shape was outlined in the soft fluffy dust. "All right, what's it for?" He turned round, to see Ah King's face upside down, peering suspiciously at him to see whether he'd put it in the right place. "What's it for?"

"For?" Ah King straightened up, sighing. "It's for the same thing as the dragon." She sat Jenny on the carrying cloth and squatted down with her back to her, tying the lower ribbons round her swelling waist. "Frighten devils away from the baby."

"Baby?" They both looked at her. "Where?"

"Here," she patted her belly. "Now lift her up Jonathan."

Jonathan helped heave Jenny onto her waiting back. Jenny put her arms round her neck while Ah King crossed the upper ribbons over her breast and tied them underneath Jenny behind her. When she stood upright, Jenny's weight, sagging in the sling, pulled the crossed ribbons right, making her breasts prominent beneath her loose blouse.

"Missy doesn't have pictures and knives and things," Jonathan said sceptically.

"Foreign women are different." She shrugged Jenny higher up her back and tied the ribbons tighter. "Now . . ."

"Don't devils come for their babies?"

"How do I know? Foreign women are different," she repeated. "Come along."

As Denton was leaving the club that afternoon, he met two elderly men coming in. He stepped back, holding the door open for them, and realised they were Mr. Brown and the Reverend Eaton.

Mr. Brown's circlet of woolly hair and his drooping moustache were pure white now, and there were heavy wrinkled pouches under his eyes. The Reverend Eaton was stooping and thin, his austere cheeks still more gaunt than before.

"It must be fifteen years since we met," Denton said drily.

"Precisely sixteen," Mr. Brown corrected him. "We are unlikely to meet again. Mrs. Brown and I are returning to England tomorrow."

"What a pity." He had recovered enough to give a little ironic smile. "And the Reverend Eaton?"

There was a pause. Then, "We are leaving on the same boat," the Reverend Eaton said coldly, fingering his clerical collar.

"Come on Jonathan, eat up." Ah King nudged the bowl

closer to him. "Chinese chow, don't you like it? What are you waiting for? Jenny's nearly finished hers."

"All right, all right," Jonathan said irritably. He picked up a pea with his chopsticks and laid it carefully on the table. Then another one which he put next to it, and another, making a little train. He looked across at Jenny. She was doing the same with the last three peas in her bowl. He scowled at her. "Copy-cat!"

"Jonafan said copy-cat."

"Jonathan, eat your food and stop playing."

"I don't like it."

"Don't like it? You asked for it! You eat it up now or I'll give it to Jenny."

Jonathan wrinkled his nose, shunting his train of peas slowly along the table.

"Jonathan!"

"All right!"

Ah Sam came into the kitchen carrying the soya sauce she'd forgotten to buy in the morning. "They've put up pictures of cholera flies all round the market. No wonder foreign devils are afraid of flies if they're as big as that where they come from." She put the soya jar down on the table and held up her hand. "As long as my finger, look, they were, in the pictures!"

Jenny poured some of the thick brown soya into her bowl. "What are cholera flies, Ah Sam?"

"What? What? What? What's this? What's that? It's always what with you..." Ah Sam poured herself some green tea, sipped it and covered her glass with a lid. "Foreign devils think flies bring cholera," she said disbelievingly. "The fishman read the writing on the pictures, keep food covered or something, he said it was." She shrugged. "Cholera comes from bad air, that's what I learnt when I was a child."

"First-born, you haven't touched your food yet!" Ah King scolded Jonathan. "You eat it up now or I take it away and give it to Jenny."

"Go on then, I don't care." Jonathan felt his eyes were hot and sore. There was a funny feeling in his stomach. He rested his head in his hands.

"Here, you have some soya on it," Ah Sam said sprinkling the rice under his nose.

Jonathan turned away. The salty smell made him feel sick.

417

"That's why you always get cholera where the drains are dirty," Ah King said. "It comes from the bad air."

Jenny rolled her chopsticks in the soya and sucked them, pulling them across her mouth. Dark brown stains formed round her lips. "Ah Sam, do you cover your glass because of the cholera flies?"

Ah Sam fingered her only ornament, the thick green bracelet on her left wrist. "No such thing as cholera flies," she said confidently. "How could a fly give you cholera?"

"Jonathan! Will you eat your food!"

"It smells horrible." He picked up some soya-stained rice with his chopsticks, toyed with it, and put it down again.

"What is cholera?" Jenny asked. "Is it being sick?"

Jonathan picked up the rice again and put it in his mouth. It tasted foul, nauseating, but he forced himself to swallow it. He could feel it travelling down his gullet, feel his stomach quivering to reject it. He swung his legs off the bench and made for the door. "It's bad, it's horrible!"

"Jonathan! Come back here!"

"I'll have it," Jenny said, pulling his bowl towards her.

"You leave it alone till I tell you, Jenny!" Ah King snatched the bowl back and put it in Jonathan's place again. "Come back here at once, I'll tell master if you don't, Jonathan! First-born!"

But Jonathan had reached the garden already. The sun was fierce, dazzling his eyes, and he felt giddy. His stomach was quivering more now, gathering itself together. *Jonathan! I'll tell master!* he heard Ah King's voice calling distantly, as if through a dense white fog. He was getting more giddy and he felt himself suddenly turning cold. He'd have to lie down, but he must try and get into the shade. You mustn't lie down in the sun, never. How far away the trees had become, how fierce and white the sky, although he felt so cold! I must get to the shade, he told himself, but then his stomach finally cramped together and erupted, spewing a brown bubbly liquid out of his mouth, forcing it up into his nostrils even. He toppled forward onto his hands and knees, gasping and shuddering while his stomach was convulsed by spasm after spasm. And all the time his eyes were open and he could see the blades of grass with the soil between them, and it was as though he was someone else watching the writhing and shuddering of his body.

Cheong stood beside him, holding his widebrim hat out as a sunshade, gazing down with alarmed, helpless concern while Ah King hurried towards them from the kitchen.

Denton came back late from the theatre, where he'd been watching Su-mei in a new role. As the car drew up by the steps, he saw Ah King waiting at the door, an anxious glimmer in her eyes.

He felt something curl up in his stomach. "What is it Ah King?"

"Jonathan, master," she looked at him guiltily, as though it was her fault. "He keeps vomiting. Like cholera."

He hurried upstairs to Jonathan's room, the room of his own which he'd only just been given. One of Jonathan's clumsy, expressive paintings was pinned to the door.

"What's the matter, Jonathan?"

Jonathan looked up at him silently with fevered glassy eyes. His cheeks were burning. He looked up with a pleading, frightened expression. There was a smell of stale vomit in the air. Denton laid his palm on Jonathan's forehead. It was hot and dry. "Open the windows," he said.

"He'll catch cold," Ah King warned uneasily.

"He's too hot. Open them all." He took Jonathan's wrist and felt for his pulse, hearing distantly the clash of the shutters swinging open and the rumbling of the window sashes. The pulse fluttered like a frightened bird under his fingers. Denton timed it with his wrist watch, and while counting the swift thudding beats against the sweep of the second hand, he recalled with irrelevant distinctness the shop where he'd bought the watch less than a year ago, his first wrist watch, and how Jonathan had kept asking when he could have one too. The second hand ticked calmly round, impersonally gauging the agitated pumping of his heart. Jonathan's pulse was more than a hundred and thirty. It was late—twenty past seven. Should he phone McEwan or not? It might be nothing worse than a bit of food poisoning. "Has he drunk anything?"

Ah King shook her head. "He wouldn't eat his supper. Won't eat, won't drink. It's like cholera, master."

"Where's the thermometer?"

She shrugged. "Maybe madam took it with her?"

He hunted through the chests and cabinets until he

419

found it in Mary-Ellen's dressing-table drawer. The little silvery column of mercury rose as soon as he put the thermometer in Jonathan's mouth. It climbed above a hundred and four.

"Tell Chan not to lock the garage yet," Denton said unsteadily. "I'm phoning the doctor. We might have to go and fetch him."

But McEwan said he'd come at once. "There's a fair bit of cholera about this summer..."

57

"He's got a fifty-fifty chance," McEwan said, closing the bedroom door. "Nursing is the greatest help now..." In the grey light of dawn his face looked haggard, despite the permanent flush that seemed to have deepened and spread ever since he came back from the war. "Where can I wash my hands, now?" But he knew the way and Denton merely followed him, his stomach turning anxiously over and over while he watched him soap and rinse and soap again. *Fifty-fifty* the words kept going through his mind. *He's got a fifty-fifty chance.*

"I've sent a telegram to Mary-Ellen," he said, handing McEwan a towel.

"Aye, best be prepared." He rubbed his hands vigorously. "Make sure everyone washes well by the way. Your nurse should be here any time. Then you can get Ah King out of there. He's no conscious much, but her long face won't be making him feel any better. Besides, ye can't trust her not to try some old wives' remedy on him while your back's turned..."

Denton let his sore, dry lids close and for a moment he was asleep, oblivious, where he leant against the wall.

"I'll have a wee drop of whisky before I go," McEwan's voice roused him. "If ye don't mind."

Denton nodded, followed him tamely downstairs, watched him pour himself half a tumbler.

"Ye'll maybe be needing some yourself?"

Denton shook his head, pressing his lips together as if McEwan were trying to force the stuff down his throat.

"No? Ah well..." He held the whisky on his tongue to savour it, then swallowed reflectively. "I'm afraid fifty-fifty may be a wee bit optimistic," he said slowly, glancing up at Denton under his thick, grey eyebrows.

"A bit optimistic?" Denton's heart seemed to stagger. "I see..."

McEwan drank again, then sat down at the table and opened his bag. "He's lost a lot of fluid and his temperature's staying high." He began writing a prescription.

Denton gazed at his grey hair, his hectically flushed cheeks, his thick, unruly moustache moving faintly as he mouthed the words he was writing. "Have we tried everything? Is there any—?"

"Of course we have." McEwan looked up at him sharply as he ripped the prescription off the pad. His eyes had tiny bloodshot veins in them at the corners.

"I mean, money's no object..."

"D'ye think I don't know that, man?" He swallowed some more whisky, his lips tightening beneath his moustache. "Ye could send him to the best hospital in Shanghai and pay a hundred dollars a day if ye wanted to, but ye'll do better keeping him here with a private nurse. Get this prescription made up at Watson's this morning. He's got enough till this afternoon."

As he took the slip, Denton noticed McEwan's hand was trembling slightly. He nodded obediently, folding the paper in two and running his nail along the crease. A bit less than fifty-fifty, he thought numbly. A bit less, a bit less.

"I'll look in at lunch-time. Ye can phone me if there's any change. Ye'd better get some sleep too. You're no good to him falling ill yourself."

Denton nodded slowly. *A bit less.*

"D'ye need something to help ye get off?"

"What?"

"Sleeping pills?"

"No, no, no..." He watched McEwan close his bag, finish his whisky and stand up. 'Would you mind if I got a second opinion?" he blurted out as McEwan went out into the hall.

"Get twenty if ye like." He shrugged carelessly, but his voice had become testy. "They'll all tell ye the same thing."

Denton followed him to the front door. McEwan turned on the step. "Any idea where he might have picked it up? Cholera's a reportable disease ye know. It'd help if we knew where he got it."

Denton shook his head, gazing blankly down at the

poinsettia plants in their firm, calm pots. How can they just go on growing as if nothing had happened? he wondered absurdly.

"No idea at all?"

"Well, I did ask Ah King last night," he said slowly. It seemed so long ago, last night. "Apparently Mary-Ellen took them into the Chinese city, to buy some jade. Before she left. She took them swimming in the French Club and then on the way home..."

"Ah, well there's a lot of it there." His voice softened slightly.

"And Ah King says Jonathan had a slice of melon..."

"What about Jenny?"

"She doesn't like melon."

"Well, that's a bit of luck," McEwan muttered almost to himself. He dumped his bag on the front seat of his small black saloon and climbed in the other side. "Get some sleep," he called out over the clatter of the engine. He nodded and drove off.

As he closed the door, Denton saw Cheong standing in the drive, broom in hand, gazing at him with soft, inquiring eyes. "Not too bad," he said, forcing a smile.

Jonathan moved restlessly on the bed, his eyes eerily half-closed, so that a thin streak of the whites showed between the lids. A faint odour of vomit and diarrhea hung on the air like the sickly scent of some deadly weed. Ah King sat beside him grim-faced, rocking slowly backwards and forwards and beating her fists on her knees as though he'd already died.

"Go and make some coffee." He laid his hand on her shoulder, the first time he'd ever touched her.

She started, then got up and left. He sat down in the chair and watched. Jonathan's head kept turning from side to side and he was muttering hoarsely through cracked, dry lips, but his eyes didn't open. He's fighting, Denton thought, he's not given in yet. He willed him not to give in. After a few minutes, he got up and walked to the window. The sight of Jonathan's rapid breathing and burning skin, of the steady wasting of his strength, seemed to drag the life out of his own body too. The sun was rising outside, stroking the sky and the river with its absurdly hopeful, rosy light. Already the rickshaws and barrows, the trucks and lorries bringing food into the markets, were teeming along the road towards Garden Bridge. Another day. Last night he'd been watching Su-mei at the opera, and knew nothing of all this that was destined to happen. He gritted his teeth and clenched his fists as a sudden treacherous sob shuddered in his throat.

He drank his coffee in the room. He heard Jenny's voice in the garden, and the steady, soothing scrape of Cheong's broom over the lawn. Then Jonathan vomited again, wretched watery stuff, the juices of his stomach—there was nothing else to bring up. Denton wiped his face and sponged him down with cold water, but when he took his temperature, it was still over 104, in spite of all the medicine. He telephoned angrily, demanding where the nurse was.

"Nurse?" said a detached woman's voice. "May I know who's calling please?" The nurse arrived, a cool and impersonal Eurasian, while he was still talking. "It's all right, she's just come," he told the detached voice contritely, and hung the ear-piece back on its hook.

"How is he, nurse?" he asked anxiously. "What d'you think?"

She shook her sleek head and raised her shoulders briefly, whether in ignorance or resignation he dared not ask. "Can I have some tea?" she said, fluttering her pale, half-Chinese lids. "It's very hot today, isn't it?"

At ten o'clock Jonathan was more restless, his temperature had edged up to 104.5. Denton kept caressing his burning forehead, as if he could wipe the heat away.

"D'you think I should get another opinion?" he asked the nurse uncertainly as she changed the soiled sheets. All his resolution had crumbled, he would take any advice.

"Another opinion?" she echoed blankly.

He shook his head and went out to phone. "Please give me the name of someone to get a second opinion from," he implored McEwan humbly "His temperature's still going up."

"I'm bringing Williams along at lunch-time." McEwan's voice sounded strangely gentle, as if all the previous irascibility had run out of it. "Has the nurse come? Then ye should get some sleep."

It's because he thinks there's not much hope, Denton thought as he hung up. He can't be irritable because he thinks Jonathan's going to die. And he stared at the shiny black ear-piece swinging gently on its hook, wishing McEwan had spoken harshly so that there would have been more hope.

"No change," the nurse said calmly when he went back. But he could see himself that the fever had climbed higher. He laid his hand on Jonathan's fragile forehead again. He was moaning thick wordless sounds, his head turning restlessly from side to side

"His temperature's going up, I can feel it."

For answer, she held up the thermometer. "Quite the same," she said patronisingly. She had a book open on her lap, and it seemed obscene to him that she could be reading in that room. But he dared not say anything, not even frown, afraid that if he antagonised her, Jonathan might magically get worse.

A helpless whimper came from the bed. Jonathan was gazing at him with hurt, beseeching eyes, as if dumbly begging him to take the pain away.

He smiled, stroking his forehead tenderly. "It'll be all right soon," he said, his throat catching. "You'll soon be better." But Jonathan's eyes didn't change, there was no glimmer of relief or understanding in them. He hadn't really been looking at Denton at all. His eyes gazed unseeingly past him with that hurt, beseeching light still burning unquenchably in them.

"He can't hear you," the nurse said matter-of-factly. "Time for medicine." She laid a slip of paper carefully in the book to mark her place. He noticed the title—*Jane Eyre*.

"It's the crisis now, Mr. Denton." Dr. Williams, slim, alert and soft-voiced, glanced at McEwan for corroboration. McEwan twitched his brows, still gazing with compressed lips down at Jonathan's sunken eyes and fevered cheeks. "He is very dehydrated, but on the other hand his heart is still quite strong, considering..."

Denton nodded. *His heart is still quite strong.* He clung on to that. *His heart is still quite strong.*

"Er, is the mother here yet?"

"The mother?" For a moment Denton thought he meant some nun with miraculous powers. "Oh. No, we haven't been able to contact her yet." And he was amazed to hear himself utter such a straightforward, factual sentence like that, just like saying the time or ordering a meal. *His heart is still—*

"She's in Peking?"

"What? Yes, Peking. She doesn't seem to be at the hotel she was going to, though. We're trying..."

Dr. Williams waited, but Denton had finished. "Well," he nodded, "I hope you find her soon."

Step by step Jonathan's temperature crawled up, as if his life was retreating inch by inch before the remorseless onslaught of the disease. He was weaker now, his eyes no longer glassy, but opaque, misted. The nurse ordered some food from Ah King and read while she ate. She spooned the medicine between Jonathan's parched lips, registered another rise in his temperature, and returned to her book. Denton began to hate her.

"Is someone else coming to take over for you?" he asked.

"Tomorrow morning," she said composedly, holding her finger at her place. "I will sleep here with the patient."

The patient! he screamed inwardly. *The patient!*

It was dark when he remembered he hadn't seen Jenny all day. He crept out of the room. Ah King was squatting outside the door like a whipped dog. "Where's Jenny?" he asked sharply.

She looked up. Her ungainly trousers splayed open at the waist to accommodate her pregnant belly. "Miss Su-mei is here," she muttered. "Downstairs. She said not to tell you."

Sue-mei was sitting by the window, watching Lily teach Jenny cat's cradle with a red elastic band.

"What are you doing here?" he asked.

"Are you hungry?"

"No," he shook his head bemusedly. "I just didn't think..."

She walked out onto the veranda and stood looking out at the lights glistening in the humid, velvet night. "Ah Sam met Ah Leng in the market and told her about it. I knew your wife wasn't here, so..."

He nodded slowly.

She laid her hand lightly, almost timidly, on his arm. "You look so tired," she said softly.

"Tired? What about Jonathan? You haven't seen him!"

She bit her lip and her hand dropped away. "Do you want me to do anything?" she asked in a small voice.

He looked at her standing there with downcast eyes,

425

and it was as if she were a sing-song girl again, in the restaurant where he first saw her with Wei. "Yes, find me a doctor who can work miracles," he said brittly. He stared away over the harbour. The moon was rising, large and orange, low down over the warehouses at Pootung. Will he ever see the moon again? he wondered, clenching his teeth. He heard the rustle of Su-mei's dress behind him. She said something to Lily in a low voice. When he turned round they were gone.

"Who was that lady?" Jenny asked.

He shook his head. "Just a friend."

"The big girl played with me."

"Did she? Have you have your tea?"

Jenny shook her head, looking up at him gravely. "Is Jonafan going to die?"

He glanced down at her uncomprehending face. She didn't know what death was, but she was scared of the mystery of it. "Ask Ah Sam for your tea, Jenny," he said, taking her hand and leading her out to the kitchen. "I've got to go and see Jonathan. I'll come and say goodnight when you're in bed, all right?"

"Is Jonafan going to die?"

"No, no, of course not" he said, while a voice inside him spoke in time with his thumping heart, *Yes, yes, yes, he is.*

McEwan came again soon after ten. He spoke a word to the nurse, read the thermometer and shook it slowly down, then examined Jonathan briefly. Denton followed his movements from the foot of the bed. His examination seemed so cursory that Denton felt a pale, incredulous glow of hope spreading uncertainly over him. Surely if Jonathan were getting worse, McEwan would be much more careful, he thought, he'd be shaking his head solemnly.

McEwan laid his hand thoughtfully on Jonathan's head as he turned away. He walked to the window and stood gazing out for a few seconds before glancing round at Denton with a raised brow. Denton joined him. A stream of lights flowed below them along the Bund. His nerves tightened and he could feel his heart thudding, like a man awaiting sentence.

McEwan breathed heavily, the scent of whisky warm on his breath. "I'm afraid we've lost this one," he said at last, gently yet firmly, as if to discourage any rebellious hope. "He's going now."

At first Denton didn't understand, or wouldn't. Then, "But he doesn't seem any worse than a few hours ago!" he protested, as though it was in McEwan's power to change the sentence, if only he'd be lenient.

McEwan shook his head. "He's slipping away," he said, looking steadily into Denton's eyes, allowing him no escape. "We can't do any more."

A slow, cold weight ran through Denton's veins, as though his blood had turned to something chill and leaden. And now he believed it—he felt he'd known it all along, from the moment he saw the alarm in Ah King's face.

"It seems so quick," he said brokenly.

"Aye. It is with children."

He looked out over the traffic and the lights glistening on the ships, and the moon, high and silver now, above the river. So he won't see the moon again, he thought, and felt tears swimming in his eyes. He heaved in a deep, unsteady breath and blinked the tears back. A widening, gleaming path spread out from the moon across the dark river towards him, and a junk with faint, glimmering lights was slowly crossing the path, everything about it black—sails, mast and hull.

"How long?" he asked drily, after a long time.

He heard McEwan's hands drop to his side, and imagined how he must have raised them first with a helpless shrug.

"He canna' last too long," McEwan said softly. "His strength's going. He hasn't got anything left to fight it with, ye see. I'm sorry I can't give ye any hope, but there simply isn't any to give. I've seen too many cases like this to be mistaken." He went back to the nurse and whispered to her.

She nodded, glancing collusively across at Denton.

When McEwan had gone, Denton walked slowly to the bed and looked down. He could see the change now that McEwan must have noticed. Jonathan's face had lost its feverish flush. It was pale, now, drawn and waxy. His mouth was slightly open and his breathing was fainter. He'd stopped fighting. There was a stillness coming gradually over him that foreshadowed the utter stillness of death. Denton felt the tears pricking his eyes again. *If only you'd*

427

take me and not him, he prayed to the god he'd long ago renounced. *If only you'd take me instead—*

"Doctor says you should rest now," the nurse said. "He'll be all right for a few hours. Nothing's going to happen yet."

A memory slid into his mind—his mother saying in Enfield, "Of course they wouldn't let me stay in the hospital, the night he died. They sent me away, they don't like the fuss. They told me he'd be all right, but I knew he was going to go."

"You go and sleep," the nurse said again.

"No. Not yet."

"Yes, go and sleep," she repeated, like a schoolteacher with a slow-witted child.

"Shut up." He brushed her out of his mind as if she'd been a fly. He watched the thickening pallor of Jonathan's skin, the occasional fluttering of his lids, the slow setting of his fingers on the sheet. And all the time he kept praying hopelessly to the god he denied, *Take me instead, what has he done? Take me instead.*

He heard the door open. Ah King came in, and he remembered he hadn't said goodnight to Jenny. "Miss Su-mei has brought a Chinese doctor," she whispered. "Very good, very expensive." There was a tone of inquiry in her voice.

"All right," he said blankly, not daring to hope. *Find me a doctor who can work miracles.*

An old, stooping Chinese in traditional dress, with a black skull-cap on his head came quietly in, followed by Su-mei. The nurse stared, rose, was about to protest, but caught Denton's eye and sat down again, shaking her head with an indignant sigh. The old man, slight and pale, glanced at Denton as he approached the bed. He felt Jonathan's pulse, bent down and peered into his eyes, lifting one eyelid after the other, and listened to his breathing. He straightened up slowly and stood gazing down at the growing waxen stillness of his face. Then, glancing at Denton again, he whispered to Su-mei. Denton watched his pale lips moving, and the sparse long grey hairs of his beard. *Find me a doctor who can work miracles.* He began to feel a faint lifting of the weight crushing his chest. The nurse tossed her head and unnecessarily straightened the sheet where the old man had raised it.

Su-mei came to Denton while the old man remained

gazing pensively at Jonathan, his head slightly on one side. "He says it is too late," she said in a still, quiet voice. "He can't do anything."

The weight settled on his chest again. He nodded and turned away.

At about two in the morning, Jonathan's lids opened. He seemed to be gazing at Denton once more. Denton leant over the pallid, peaked face and forced his trembling lips into a smile. But even as he smiled, the last glimmer of light faded on Jonathan's eyes, and suddenly they were as fixed and hard as pebbles. His mouth slowly opened like a door swinging ajar under its own weight.

The chair creaked as the nurse got up. She closed his lids and eased his jaw up with the heel of her hand.

He heard Ah King wailing, he heard Ah Sam talking in a low voice to the nurse, he heard the telephone ringing and ringing, he heard loud voices passing in the darkness along the Bund, he heard ships' sirens blowing and the clanging bell of a tram...

The dawn came, stroking the water and the sky again with its same pointless, rosy caress. The light grew stronger in the room. McEwan was there, the nurse had gone, and men came to take Jonathan's body away. "No!" he said, and looked once more at the face, while they waited, mutely watching him. But it wasn't Jonathan's face any longer, it was a corpse. Only the tousled hair was his, unaware that it no longer had any right to grow, that its time too had passed. He turned away and gestured then to carry on, as they'd known he would. They put him in a box and carried him out of the room with quiet, shuffling footsteps and quiet, unconcerned voices.

The stubble had grown thick and spiky on his chin. He fingered it as he stood by the window, looking out over the Public Gardens, where ladies with their children were beginning to walk in the cool of the morning. Once he'd seen a lady and a little girl with a hoop disappear like a vision behind those azaleas. Once he'd seen a lady with a little girl disappear through the gateway of the house that was Su-mei's now. Once...

"I want ye to take these tablets," McEwan said. "And go straight to bed. There's no more for ye to do at present."

He gazed down at the powdery little discs lying on his sweat-grimed palm.

"Here's some water."

He threw the tablets into the back of his throat and swallowed. "Where's Jenny?" he asked. "I never said good-night to her."

"Ah Sam's taken her to kindergarten. We found Mary-Ellen, she was staying with her friend. She'll be catching the first train. Now go and get some rest."

He thought, not of sleeping, but of waking up. Waking up having forgotten it all, and having to remember it, to learn it all over again. "Where's the car?"

"Ye'll not be needing the car," McEwan began firmly. "Mary-Ellen can't be here before this evening."

"Where *is* it?"

It was in the drive. He told Chan to drive him to Su-mei's. His eyes were open, but he saw nothing on the way there, and remembered nothing afterwards.

"Shall I wait?" Chan asked.

"What? No, no..." He rang the bell.

Ah Leng let him in fearfully, eyeing his unshaven chin and bloodshot eyes.

Su-mei was coming down the stairs, her hair loose, a silver brush in her hand.

"Don't leave me," he said. "I'm going to sleep. Don't leave me while I'm asleep."

He collapsed on her bed, covering his eyes with his forearm, to keep out the light. He heard voices outside, whispering. Then she came in, drew the curtains and lay down beside him. He turned onto his side, put his head on her shoulder and fell asleep.

She didn't seem to have moved when he woke up hours later in the afternoon. He saw her face before he remembered. She was still holding the brush, loosely, in her hand.

Jenny was in the car with Ah Sam when Chan came to fetch him. "Is Jonafan dead?" she asked.

"Yes."

"He's not at home."

"No. He won't be at home any more, Jenny."

"But where *is* he?" she asked worriedly.

He held her on his lap and she leant back against

430

him, sucking her thumb with a wet little cheeping sound all the way home.

Ah King sat on the kitchen steps, beating her head with clenched fists. Ah Sam gave Jenny her tea in the dining-room. Denton watched with empty eyes while she ate. What shall I do with his drawings, his paintings? he wondered. That one of the train on the door, he was proud of that.

The phone rang. It was Mary-Ellen. "I couldn't get a sleeper," her voice sounded distantly through the crackle. "I'm leaving tonight. How's Jonathan?"

"What? Didn't they tell you?"

"Tell me what?" Her voice faded, then floated back "... said he was ill. How is he?"

"He died at two o'clock this morning," he said bitterly.

"What?"

"He had cholera. He got it in the Chinese city when you bought him that melon before you left. When you went to get that bloody jade!" He banged the ear-piece down, turned away, turned back again and lifted it off, letting it hang swinging on its cable, swinging like a hanged man. His limbs were trembling.

"Was that Jonafan?" Jenny asked, her eyes wide and solemn.

"No, Jonathan's dead, Jenny."

"Can't you phone when you're dead?"

"No, not when you're dead. It's like being asleep."

Suddenly she collapsed into tears, pushing her cup away and spilling it over the table. "Well where *is* Jonafan?" she kept sobbing. "Where *is* he?"

58

"One more pipe," he protested as she turned down the flame on the lamp.

Su-mei shook her head, lying back on her green porcelain pillow beside him. "You're smoking too much. You've had four already."

"One more," he protested again, but without conviction. He let his eyes close on the emptiness in his head. At last the weight of Jonathan's death was lifted off him once more. It was like a coolie must feel, he thought dreamily, when he puts down his load and he feels himself suddenly buoyant again, although he knows he'll have to take up the load once more, after his rest. Colours drifted across the thin membranes of his lids, and it was as though the lids themselves were becoming transparent, dissolving into the colours. He heard the distinct clink of the opium pipe being laid on the tray, the slither and rustle of Su-mei's gown, the distant raucous chant of a hawker in the street below, the clop-clop of pony's hooves and the swiftly passing whine and rattle of a lorry. Each sound dropped separately down into the smooth, dense sea of his mind, dropped and vanished, not even ruffling the surface. As though they fell out of existence altogether as soon as they touched him. "I went to Jonathan's grave today," he said after some immeasurable passing of time.

She didn't answer, but he sensed she was listening and imagined the half-lifting of her slanted eyelids. There was something he wanted to tell her about the grave, but the image of her face had overlaid it, whatever it was, and he let it slip away, thinking only of her lids and the slender, arched brows above them.

There was another long emptiness, in which her face melted and vanished, leaving only the warm feeling of light on his eyeballs, streaming through the misty screen of his lids. He saw Jonathan's grave again then, the granite cross promising a resurrection he didn't believe in; it was leaning slightly already, after only three months, like an angel spreading its wings over the little grassy mound, poised to fly. Was that what he'd meant to tell her, the elusive thought? Then there was emptiness again, soothing and healing...

"My wife's friend has come," he said suddenly, without thinking, so that the words almost surprised him himself, as if they brought news to him too.

"Which friend?"

"The woman she went to see in Peking. Helen Bolton. The antique dealer." He thought of the slim, withdrawn woman with the sallow skin and bobbed dark hair, always stepping to one side when they passed on the stairs or in the hall, as if she was afraid he might barge into her. "She seems to avoid me."

"How long is she staying?"

He shrugged. "My wife's planning to open a shop

432

with her here. A sort of branch of the one in Peking, I gather." He never named Mary-Ellen to Su-mei. Calling her his wife seemed to keep her at a distance, to make her a role, not a person. "After the baby's born."

Su-mei's eyes moved away from his and darkened as if a shadow had fallen over her face. "How do you get on with your wife now?" she asked in a still, detached tone.

"I hate her."

She raised herself on her elbow and looked down at him steadily. "A Chinese who was as rich as you are wouldn't live with a wife he hated," she said deliberately, leaving little spaces between her words as though she was considering each one separately before uttering it.

His serenity was gradually deserting him like an ebbing tide. The returning weight of Jonathan's death was slowly settling back on his shoulders. Only three months, he thought. And yet already it's as though he'd never been. "How *can* I leave her?" he asked dully. "She's going to have my child. For the child's sake I can't leave her now—not for hers."

She raised her brows, furrowing her forehead, and gazed past him contemplatively for a few seconds. Then, "So am I going to have your child," she said with that same slow, deliberate distinctness.

Mary-Ellen and Helen Bolton were sitting side by side on the settee when he came back, typed pages spread out on their laps. Helen looked up at him almost guiltily and shifted along the seat a little, as if making a token offer of her place to him.

"It's all right, stay where you are," he raised his hand deprecatingly, sitting in the chair opposite them. "What are you looking at?"

"Particulars of premises." Mary-Ellen's head was still bent over the papers. "For our antique shop."

"Oh." He picked up the paper and opened it, not noticing what he was reading. I'm going to leave her, he thought. Somehow I'm going to leave her and live with Su-mei. It was something he could hold on to, that thought, like a precious stone clenched in his fist.

"It doesn't interest you?" Helen asked nervously, as if trying not to exclude him. "Chinese art?"

"I don't know much about it, I'm afraid."

"Here, look at this," Mary-Ellen touched Helen's knee.

Then, as Helen obediently shifted closer again, "All John thinks about is dollars and cents."

Denton dropped the paper on the floor and got up. "I think about our children sometimes." He corrected himself as he reached the door "our child, that is."

Jenny was in the garden, clumsily riding Jonathan's bicycle. The saddle was too high, and she wobbled dangerously as she tried to pedal. He could watch her using Jonathan's things now without a pang, though that itself sent a pang through him—it showed him again how he was forgetting, how soon Jonathan would be no more than the yellowing photograph on his desk, the fading images in his memory. Ah King was watching too, from the kitchen door, her new son strapped to her back. The baby's brown eyes regarded Denton with a drowsy seriousness, following his movements with slow gravity. Jade Flower she'd called him, so that the malicious spirits wouldn't know he was a boy and try to kill him—girls didn't matter. Su-mei's child would look like that, he thought, only the eyes would be more round, the skin and hair a shade lighter. He thought of it with a warmth he couldn't feel for Mary-Ellen's.

Jenny swerved, skidded and fell off with a loud clatter. She picked herself up, sucking in her breath with pain, but holding back her tears. Her knee was grazed. She held it a moment, wincing, then climbed on the bicycle again. Denton watched the blood trickling down her leg. "You've cut yourself, Jenny," he called out. "Come and have it washed."

"I'm all right." She tossed her head and careered down the path again standing up on the pedals.

"Jenny is lonely," Ah King said.

"Well she won't be much longer."

"A little baby is too young for her."

He glanced at Ah King curiously. Jade Flower's eyes had closed and he seemed to be sleeping now, his head laid on her shoulder. "My first born is starting form one," she said studiedly. "The schools at home aren't much good."

"Aren't they?" He smiled secretly, sensing now where she was leading, but pretending not to follow.

"Schools in Shanghai are much better..." She fiddled unnecessarily with the tapes of the baby-sling. "He could sleep in my room. He could help in the garden. He could

434

play with Jenny if she's lonely..." She looked up at him dourly, as if she were giving a favour, not asking one. "This one,' she jerked her head at the baby sleeping on her back, "he'll be going to my husband's mother as soon as I stop feeding him."

"All right," Denton shrugged. "He can come here. He's too old to play with Jenny, though. What about your daughter?"

She shook her head. "They need her at home."

Jenny came wobbling to the kitchen door, braked and slipped off. "Look it's stopped bleeding now," she said, throwing her fair, sun-bleached hair out of her eyes. "All gone dry."

"Let Ah King wash it anyway. You don't want to get dirt in it."

"Where's Mary-Ellen?" he asked, when he returned to the living-room.

"She's gone up to change." Helen sat tensely on the settee, one hand riffling the papers. She was like a child forced to sit with the grown-ups. "She said you were going out to dinner?"

"Yes." He poured himself some whisky, thinking of McEwan as he did so, McEwan on that first morning of Jonathan's illness. "You'll be all right, will you?" he asked perfunctorily.

"Oh yes, yes, thank you."

"Ah Man will fix you some sort of meal."

"Oh no, it doesn't matter..."

"Drink?"

She shook her head. Her fingers fidgeted with the papers still, while her violet eyes hunted round the room, reflecting her inner search for something to say to him.

He wondered how she could ever have managed to sell things in Peking. "Did you find anything?" he asked, nodding at the papers.

"Oh yes, yes...One or two things that might be..." she smiled fleetingly. "Of course Mary-Ellen's a bit too tired to go around looking at places just now. Especially after the...your bereavement, I mean." She fluttered her hands in a helpless gesture.

"I'd say she's borne up remarkably well," Denton said acidly.

Helen flushed, looking down at the papers again and

435

shuffling them. "It's good though, isn't it? Having another baby so soon afterwards...?" Her voice faltered, as though she wasn't sure it was good after all, now that she'd said it.

"Depends how you look at it." He said enigmatically and sipped his whisky.

He sat beside Mary-Ellen in the Rolls-Royce that had been delivered only two days after Jonathan's funeral. She sprawled with her legs apart, her bulging belly sagging between her thighs.

"I liked the other car much more," she complained. "This one's like a hearse."

Her crassness fell like a hammer on his chest. He stared blankly at the glass partition that separated them from Chan, his lips tightening at the corners.

"I suppose you think that was insensitive of me?"

"Yes."

"It just slipped out," she said in casual apology. "But we can't live in the past, can we?"

He sat silent for some minutes, gazing out at the new Chinese department stores along Nanking Road, their imposing windows crowded by Chinese staring acquisitively at the glittering goods inside. He remembered the old silk shops that used to stand there, one storey high, their rolls of cloth receding deep into the dark and homely back. Things were better before, he thought, encompassing by "things" his whole life before he married Mary-Ellen.

"Let's not stay long," Mary-Ellen drawled. "I'll only fall asleep after a while, in my condition."

He eyed her belly again, without answering.

"It feels like twins," she went on. "I'm sure I wasn't as big as this before. Why do we have to go, anyway?"

"We can't very well not appear."

"You do worry about appearances, don't you?" she said mockingly, as though he were a timid child, afraid to give offence.

He thought of Su-mei. "Not always," he said.

"Not always?" she repeated ironically. "It's all you live for."

"In this case it's a question of politics," he said coldly.

"Politics bore me." She yawned, "Especially small-town politics."

"Would it bore you to know that all those people out there"—he nodded at the thronging window-gazers, the coolies with their springy poles, the rickshaw-pullers, the hawkers and the barrow coolies, but he meant also the vast unseen city sprawling behind them, the workers spinning in the cotton mills, the beggars sleeping in the alleys, the dockers, the labourers, the narrow-chested clerks—"all those people out there will quite possibly tear us to pieces one day if we don't get this 'small-town' politics question right? And anyway, as it happens, Shanghai is the biggest city in the whole of Asia."

She shrugged sceptically, with an indifferent little smile on her lips, but said no more until they passed the Country Club and turned into the Nixon's long drive. "Well, well, I never knew you were so important," she drawled mockingly again "Guiding the destiny of China, as Jacob would say."

Mrs. Nixon welcomed them with her by now habitual sourness—if anything it was more acidic than usual. Denton wondered whether some of the rumours Jacob had been threatening him with had at last blown her way. But she seemed as crabbed to Mary-Ellen as she was to him, so he decided it must be something else—her husband's support of the reformers on the Council, perhaps? She'd always disapproved of that. He joined Nixon and Smith, the new member of the Council, as soon as he could. They were talking with the British and French consuls.

"We 'ave 'ad the Shinese advisers for eight years now," the French consul was saying. He was the antithesis of his predecessor—small, portly and ebullient. "It 'as worked very well. We ask their advice and then we do what we were going to do anyway. Everyone is 'appy."

Hetherington, the British consul, stroked his chin and smiled furtively, as if he was afraid of giving himself away. His glance strayed from one face to the other, searching for clues. He bowed his head in welcome to Denton.

"The question is whether they'll be satisfied as mere advisers," Smith announced with an air of judicial gravity. "After all, they're asking for full membership."

"Ask Denton, what, come in the nick of time," Nixon said genially. "He's the oracle about John Chinaman, eh?"

"Oh, I'm not much of an oracle I'm afraid," Denton disclaimed hastily.

"You see, what worries me," Smith insisted, "is where you stop." He rubbed the top of his bald head with the palm of his hand, as if he were making the kind of signal Denton had seen bookies' touts make at the races. "If you give them advisers, they'll want members. If you give them members they'll want more members. So where's it all going to end?"

"But it won't end." Denton glanced round at them all, amazed by the sudden clarity of his vision. Of course it wouldn't stop; it was obvious now that he came to think of it. How had they been missing it all those years? "They'll take the whole place back in the end, when they're strong enough. We can't expect to hold on here for ever. We'll be foreigners here eventually, just like in any other country."

There was a cold, stiff pause.

"Well, much as I'd like to continue our little discussion," Nixon said after a moment, pouring his blandness into the uneasy silence, "I rather think we ought to move, what? I see my wife's signalling me to get you all to go in to dinner, so..."

They did leave early, Denton as willingly as Mary-Ellen.

Mary-Ellen dozed, legs spread-eagled, while Denton gazed pensively out at the still-crowded streets. The thought that had occurred so vividly to him before dinner hovered in his mind like a bird of omen. All this will pass, he kept thinking, this city won't last, it won't be ours for ever. Some ragged memory stirred in him like a tattered dusty flag, the memory of Jacob Ephraim prophesying years ago in sudden melancholy tones that Shanghai too would pass in the end, like Venice, like Florence, like Rome...

The car swept noiselessly past the Ta Wu Tai, where Su-mei had been playing when he waited for her in the cab, two years ago now. At least let it not pass for her life and mine, he thought, half-praying. It's our place, we belong here.

"What?" Mary-Ellen opened her eyes.

"Nothing," he shook his head, glancing up at the blurred faces in the tram windows; they were all gaping down at the car in admiration and envy. "How long is Helen going to stay?"

"Why, does she bother you?"

He shrugged. "I just wondered. After all, she's got a business in Peking to run, hasn't she?"

Mary-Ellen's eyes closed again. "She's very clever in

438

her quiet way," she murmured with a sleepy smile. "And I get on with her."

Two months later Mary-Ellen had a son, whom they christened Alec. Three months after that Su-mei also had a son. He was never christened, but Denton called him Michael.

Day after day, week after week, Denton waited for the scandal to break. When it did break, he would leave Mary-Ellen and live with Su-mei. But somehow the secret held, for one month and then another, and another. The thought of leaving Alec in Mary-Ellen's casual hands held him back from making a move himself. "I'll give it a year," he told Su-Mei. "And then I'll tell her, if no one else does."

Su-mei shrugged. He spent nearly every evening with her anyway, pretending to Mary-Ellen—not that she cared—that he was at the club. Mary-Ellen had Helen for company.

59

He drove straight to Wei's house from the council meeting, gazing sombrely out at the streets bright in the November sunshine. The hawkers no longer sought the shade, but had folded their awnings away, to soak in the last warmth before the evening chill set in again. As they passed the large new office buildings on Siccawei Road, he started idly counting the White Russian doormen, while the voices and faces of the council chamber still drifted in and out of his mind. *Six*, he thought. *Last week there were only two*. Then he saw an old White Russian woman begging. She was standing with a wooden box outside the revolving doors of the Grand Commercial Store, standing in that peculiar posture of beggars everywhere, cringing and yet obtrusive.

"White woman begging," Chan commented in a voice that seemed carelessly toneless. "Never saw that before."

"Russian," Denton said, as if Russians weren't white. "There are a lot of poor Russians here now." He saw Chan glance at him in the mirror as if about to speak again, then look away uncertainly. The shifting images of the council meeting gave way in his mind to that of the

439

Russian beggar woman. That was the first one he'd seen. There were bound to be more as their savings ran out. And the newer night clubs were advertising Russian hostesses already—so Jacob had told him, with a kind of shocked glee. "The place is changing," he said absently.

Chan half-turned once more, but only nodded.

Wei's great wrought-iron gates were shut. Chan sounded the horn. After half a minute or so, two strange men in western suits appeared, gazing arrogantly past Chan at Denton before they slowly pulled the gates open.

"Who are they?" Denton asked, frowning.

Chan's heavy shoulders shrugged.

The two men, one each side of the car, inspected him again as the car drove slowly through. One of Wei's servants was standing at the wide steps to the main door, bowing apologetically to Denton. A large black Oldsmobile was waiting in the shade of the willow trees. A few leaves had fallen onto its glistening roof, and the driver, also in a western suit, was flicking them off with negligent sweeps of a feather duster.

"That's Pock-mark Chen's car, isn't it?" Denton asked.

Again Chan shrugged, with an unconvincing show of ignorance. "Could be," he muttered at last. The two men who had opened the gate strolled over towards the car as Denton walked up the white, scrubbed steps, glaring in the sunlight, and Denton heard them talking to Chan in level, faintly familiar tones.

The servant kept bowing and smiling. "This way, master," he gestured towards the empty ante-room leading off the hall, a hurried gesture that belied his politeness. Denton had never waited there before, he'd always gone straight in to one of the main rooms. They were trying to get him out of the way, he realised; because Pock-mark Chen was there. "Is Mr. Wei not at home?" he asked pleasantly, pausing where he was on the steps.

"Not yet, not yet," the old man smiled and bowed extravagantly. "Please wait inside, he won't be long."

Denton stiffened. He wouldn't be brushed out of sight like that. He turned round deliberately, glancing over the garden with its still, drooping trees, the gleaming American car and the two men talking to Chan by the Rolls Royce. One of them had his foot on the running board and was calmly leaning through the open window, fingering the fitments.

"Chan!" Denton called out sharply. "Close the windows, please!"

For a moment the three men gazed at him flatly, the one through the windscreen, the other two from the side of the car. Then, as if it had taken that long for him to absorb Denton's meaning, the man leaning inside slowly withdrew his head.

"Close the windows, please," Denton repeated.

Chan moved unwillingly at last, with an uneasy glance at the two men, and slowly wound the windows up. All the while the two men stared insolently up at him, with hard, challenging eyes.

"It's rather warm in the sun," Denton said expressionlessly to them. "Perhaps you'd be more comfortable in the shade by your own car."

Neither of them moved, not even to glance at each other. Then the taller one hawked twice, turned his head faintly aside, and spat over the bonnet of the Rolls into the flower bed behind it, where bright red climbing geraniums were still blooming. The driver of the Oldsmobile had turned to watch, smiling appreciatively, letting the feather duster hang loosely in his hand.

Denton gazed back at them with an impassive face, while behind his eyes he tried to deal with the realisation that he'd gone a step too far. The two men couldn't move without losing face; nor could he. He should have ignored them after telling Chan to close the windows; that would have left them all room. Now it was too late. He gazed stonily down at them and they gazed stonily back.

The servant kept murmuring anxiously at his shoulder, "This way, master, this way." But he couldn't move, he'd have to do something to face them down. Should he tell Chan to drive away and come back later?

Then he heard slow, heavy steps behind him on the tiled floor and a faint, regular swishing sound that he knew must be the brushing together of Pock-mark Chen's trousers where his gross thighs rubbed as he waddled along. He turned round, relieved at least that he could do so now without loss of face.

Another man walked half a step behind Pock-mark, his eyes glancing snakishly from side to side, as if looking for something to strike. Pock-mark stopped a few feet from Denton, wheezing slightly. His obesity made him seem shorter than he really was—his head was level with

441

Denton's chin. His eyes still held that flat, unwinking look. There was not a glimmer of recognition in them, yet—

"Mister Denton, yes?" he asked in English, after a few seconds.

Denton nodded with a faint, ironic courtesy. "Mr. Chen."

Chen's voice was wheezy but monotonous, as though he were repeating lessons. But his English seemed as good as Wei's. Denton recalled their first meeting, when Chen had spoken only French, offering him a girl. He wondered briefly how Chen had learned English and why. An absurd image of his gross form looming over a table and studying English grammar flitted through his mind. And did Chen too remember the first time they'd met? Certainly the second time, outside the Customs Officers' Club.

"I am honour' to make your acquaintance," Chen was saying blankly. "I see your pony often at the race'. He run very fast."

"Sometimes he does." Denton bowed with the same ironic courtesy. "Your ponies are also very fast."

Chen turned his head slightly to listen, as though he was deaf in one ear. "But your pony run more fast than my, last week."

"That was lucky."

"Mr. Denton," Chen went on without any change of tone, while his body guard's glittering eyes still flickered from side to side behind him, "Some year' past you buy opium from Mr. Mason."

"Yes?" Denton's chest tightened slightly.

"There is some mistake concerning this thing Mr. Denton. That opium does not belong Mr. Mason."

"Oh? The papers were all in order, Mr. Chen."

Chen's voice slowed, giving his words greater emphasis. "That opium belong my."

"In that case, as the documents were all in order, and I bought it in good faith, I'm afraid your only legal redress would be to sue Mr. Mason."

Denton had spoken quickly, and Chen, turning his head aside to listen, seemed not to take it all in. "Really," Denton apologised in Shanghainese, "in a Chinese city we should be speaking Chinese—"

"I understand" Chen interrupted sharply, still speaking English. "In my mind, the money you sell the opium for belong my."

442

"I'm afraid that is not the legal position—the law," Denton said slowly and exactly. Although he felt safe, there was a faint trembling in his chest at the menace like a cold gleam of metal in Chen's voice. "If you question—if you do not think the opium belonged to Mason, you would—will—have to go to him."

"Mr. Mason?" Chen repeated with a slow shrug, "Where is Mr. Mason? Perhaps he no longer lives?"

Denton shook his head. "I'm afraid I do not know where he is. It was many years ago, after all..."

Chen gazed at him for some seconds more and Denton saw his own image reflected for a moment on his flat brown eyes. Then he shifted his head a trifle "Anyway, most honour' to meet you, Mr. Denton," he said, his voice recovering its inexpressive monotony. "Is your wife and family well?"

"Yes, very well, thank you."

"And Miss Kwan Su-mei?" He walked on with his massive shuffling waddle before Denton could reply.

The bowing, smiling servant fluttered round him again ingratiatingly. "Master has come back now," he lied, gesturing him in with excessive deference.

Denton followed him thoughtfully. So Pock-mark Chen knew about Su-mei. Well, that wasn't surprising, he must have eyes and ears everywhere. But what was he going to do about it? Why had he mentioned her just then? Blackmail? Denton smiled. He didn't care who knew about it, it was all going to come out sooner or later anyway. He was merely waiting for that to happen, delaying it only for the sake of the children—and that reason seemed to be losing its force day by day in any case.

Wei smiled a thin, tight smile as Denton went in. "You haven't been waiting long I hope?" he asked in Shanghainese.

"No—I met Pock-mark Chen outside," Denton said casually. "We had an interesting little chat."

Wei's eyes slipped away uncomfortably in the wrinkles of his lids and his cheeks darkened with a faint flush as he pointed to a blackwood chair and then sat down himself. "He is very..." he paused, searching for the right word. "...Very *useful* to the Kuo Min Tang. He doesn't like to be known as Pock-mark by the way."

Denton smiled, "No, I imagine not, now that he's such a respectable figure. Wasn't Ching useful also, in his time?"

Wei moistened his thin lips with his tongue. "Many different people are useful these days," he murmured vaguely. "The party needs strong allies..."

Denton nodded, glancing at the scroll behind Wei's desk. It depicted an old man, a scholar, drinking tea in the shade of a tree. There was an atmosphere of contentment and peace about it, as though the scholar's life was leisurely and serene, not the troubled, restless thing that people really lived.

An amah brought in tea and poured it for them.

"Philip will be here any minute," Wei said, sipping with a slight, unself-conscious slurping noise. "He is anxious to hear the news too." He smiled, and Denton, sipping his own pale golden tea, noticed how many more gold fillings gleamed in Wei's mouth now than when they'd first met in his room in the Customs Officers' Club twenty years ago. It was almost the only sign of age in Wei—that and perhaps a slight loosening of his skin over the cheekbones and under the jaw. And yet he must be nearly sixty, Denton thought as he replaced the translucent cup on its translucent saucer.

They'd have to wait for Philip then. The Council's decision, reached after so many delays and adjournments over the months, wasn't going to please them, and he'd have preferred to tell Wei then and there—Philip would make more of a fuss about it with his half-western ways. He glanced again at the picture of the leisurely scholar reclining on the ground with his tea while a servant held the pot.

"It is Ni-san," Wei said, following his gaze.

"Yes. Very nice," Denton said uncertainly.

"And how are your wife's plans for selling Chinese art?" Wei asked, sipping his tea again with the same unself-conscious slurping sound. A faint ironic tinge in his tone suggested that a foreign devil couldn't possibly understand such things, and it was mildly ridiculous of Mary-Ellen to try.

"They've found a place they can convert into a gallery."

"They?"

"She and her friend—Helen Bolton, you've met her, haven't you? She has quite a successful gallery in Peking. My wife's going to run a branch here."

Wei's eyes moved behind the thick lenses of his glasses, but he said nothing. He glanced up as Philip hurried in.

444

"What a crush!" Philip said, watching the amah pour his tea. "The students from Nanyang University are demonstrating, all the way down Avenue Joffre." Unlike his father, he always spoke English with Denton.

"What are they demonstrate' for?" Wei asked.

Philip shrugged, glancing at Denton provocatively over his heavy black-framed glasses as he took the cup from the amah. "Equal rights for Chinese, support the May Fourth movement, boycott foreign goods..." He too drank with that unself-conscious slurping noise, sighing as he put the cup down. "There's plenty to choose from, after all..." He glanced at Denton again, as if he hoped to embarrass him.

Denton sipped his tea. They were waiting silently now and he knew it was time to tell them the Council's decision. "Well, it was a long meeting at the Council," he said slowly, "and eventually they agreed to the idea of a Chinese Advisory Committee, but... I'm afraid they've gone against full membership again." Out of the corner of his eye he saw Philip toss his head. He looked up at Wei. "Unofficially, they hope you'll stand for election as one of the advisers."

"Advisers!" Philip declared scornfully. "We pay rates like the foreigners, and it's our land to start with, but we're not good enough to sit on the Council! Haven't they heard of the Boston Tea Party?"

"Tea Party?" Wei asked perplexedly, glancing at his cup.

"A demonstration against British colonialism in America, a hundred and fifty years ago." Philip's face was flushed. It was also getting podgy, Denton noted detachedly. "It seems they never learn."

Wei seemed to be puzzling still over the idea of a tea party as a demonstration. He scratched his cheek with his long finger nail, shorter, now that the old customs were dying, but still more than an inch long.

"It's intolerable!" Philip brought out indignantly.

"It is not Mr. Denton's fault," Wei reproved him gently. "He was on our side."

Philip's flush deepened, but at first he said nothing, sullenly staring into his cup. Then, grudgingly, he muttered in a thick, sulky voice, "Well he's no longer British, really. He's half-Chinese."

* * *

445

"Ah King, let's take Alec to Jessfield Park." Jenny peered under the sun canopy of the glossy white pram to look at her younger brother. He had just fallen into a fitful sleep, his mouth still puckered as if he was about to cry.

"Shh, he's sleeping, you come away from there." Ah King sat down on the step beside her eldest son, watching him write in his schoolbook.

"Please!"

"What d'you want to go to Jessfield Park for?"

"I want to go out. You can buy me some cake."

Ah King wasn't listening. She was watching the strokes slowly building up characters under Yin-hong's brush, amazing complicated pictures like the ones you saw in the newspaper.

"Ah King! Please!"

"Shh!" she hissed, not even raising her head. How strange it was to see those little spider's legs of ink all joining together like that! What a lot to learn! "What does it say?" she asked when Yin-hong paused to dip his brush in the ink again.

Yin-hong frowned, examining the tip of the brush. "Essay," he said reluctantly, pouring over the text-book beside him.

"Essay," she repeated.

"I'll wake him up if you don't say yes, Ah King."

"Tell her to shut up," Yin-hong muttered. "I can't concentrate."

"Shut up yourself. I'll tell Missy."

"You wake him up, Jenny, and I'll lock you in my room and go out without you."

"I don't care," she shrugged and went back to the pram. "Anyway you wouldn't dare, I'd tell Missy."

"Just you wait and see. Maybe I'll tell Missy first."

"Well I'll tell Master, so there." Alec lay on his back, his curled fists beside his head. She blew softly, stirring the curl of fine, fair hair that hung over his forehead. His lip puckered again, his nose wrinkled.

"Essay," Ah King said wonderingly. "You mean you're making it up?"

Yin-hong snorted. "I'm copying from this book!" He made some more strokes, mouthing the characters as they formed beneath his brush. "What is Jess Fil Pa'?"

"Jessfield Park," she corrected him with excessive articulation. "The other side of town. What does it say?"

446

She touched the book he was copying from. "What does the essay say?"

Yin-hong gave an ostentation sigh and began reading in a slow sing-song voice. "The virtue of the gentleman is like wind; the virtue of the small man is like grass. Let the wind blow over the grass and it is sure to bend."

"Master's a gentleman," Jenny said. "Yin-hong's a small man, because he's Chinese."

Yin-hong went on copying. Ah King looking over his shoulder. Jenny rocked the pram gently up and down on its springs. "Ah King?" she wheedled, "I'll ask Missy if Yin-hong can come too."

"What?"

"To Jessfield Park!"

Yin-hong looked up. "Go in the car?" he asked. Jenny nodded. Under the canopy Alec gave a fretful snuffle.

Ah King considered.

"*Please* Ah King!" Secretly she shook the pram again. "He's waking up anyway."

Ah King squinted up at her against the sunlight, which turned her fair curls into a misty, dazzling halo. "Don't you tell Missy I said yes then, all right? You just ask her yourself. Don't you say you asked me first, mind." She looked down over Yin-hong's shoulder again.

Jenny rocked the pram violently once more to make sure Alec woke up, then ran inside the kitchen before Ah King could change her mind. She ran past Ah Man sitting at the kitchen table painfully deciphering the front page of the newspaper, his new song-bird chirping hopefully in its rattan cage above his head. Past Ah Sam spitting on the iron and sighing as she pressed it down on the collar of one of Denton's shirts. Past Chan picking his teeth by the sink. Past the cat crouched on the chair by the table. She ran up the stairs to the bedroom and gently turned the handle. If only her mother wasn't asleep—she hated being woken up in the afternoon. She certainly wouldn't let them go then.

Jenny eased the door open and squeezed silently through the gap, holding her breath. Her eyes needed a second or two to get used to the dimness. Then she looked at the bed.

Her mother and Aunt Helen were both on the bed without any clothes on. They looked as though they were cuddling each other. Her mother was kissing Aunt Helen's breast, or sucking at it like Ah King's baby sucked at hers, and her hand was between Aunt Helen's legs, which Jenny had always thought was rude. And they weren't just cuddling, but snuggling and wriggling up against each other, and making strange wordless noises, as if they were wrestling like she used to wrestle with Jonathan, only *they* always had their clothes on.

It was Aunt Helen who saw her first. She stared at her a moment, almost as if she was frightened, while her mother still went on sucking or kissing her breast and clutching her with her hand. Then, "Hello Jenny," she said breathlessly, and her mother's head lifted suddenly and jerked round following the direction of Aunt Helen's gaze.

Her mother too looked almost frightened at first, then, "Yes, what is it?" she said in a high, strained voice. "How did you get in here?"

Jenny watched her mother slide away from Aunt Helen, and she thought how big her mother was, how small Aunt Helen. Her mother quickly pulled the sheet up over both of them. Then Aunt Helen closed her eyes like Jenny did herself when she was pretending to be asleep, squeezing the lids tight shut. "Can we go to Jessfield Park?" Jenny was saying while she took all this in.

"Jessfield Park?" Her mother was clutching the sheet up by her breasts. "Yes I suppose so." Her voice was still tight and high. "Who is we?" She glanced round the room anxiously, as though she was afraid she might see someone else there as well.

"Ah King and Alec and me. And Yin-hong."

"Well, I suppose so..." She kept looking round the room still, occasionally glancing at Jenny, then quickly away again.

"What were you and Aunt Helen doing?" Jenny asked. "Having a play-fight?"

"Nothing—yes, a play-fight. Well, not exactly—Aunt Helen wasn't feeling well, and I was trying to make her better..."

"Oh," Jenny said disbelievingly.

Her mother frowned. "How did you get in here? I thought I'd locked that door. Wasn't it locked?" Her eyes glanced at Jenny, then veered off again.

"No, I just opened it."

"Oh. Well all right, off you go then. Don't be late

448

back, I might need the car." She spoke absently, as though she was really thinking of something else.

"All right." Jenny went out and closed the door behind her.

"Have a nice time," her mother called out, in the same absent, distracted tone.

Jenny stood outside listening a minute, trying to guess what they were really doing. She was sure Aunt Helen hadn't been feeling unwell—she was perfectly all right. They must've been playing some secret game they didn't want her to know about. She felt a little thrill low down in her stomach.

Then she heard the key turn softly in the lock, and their voices talking quietly. After a little while it was quiet again. She thought she heard the bed creak—perhaps they were starting that game again. She turned and went downstairs, thinking. Why had her mother been touching Aunt Helen there, if it was rude? Ah King always slapped her if she caught her doing that herself, although she sometimes did because it gave you such a nice feeling.

She skipped through the kitchen, where Ah Sam was still ironing and Ah Man was just folding up the paper with a yawn while the little brown bird sung a tentative trill above his head, watched malevolently by the cat. "Ah King! We can go! I asked Missy!" But she didn't say anything about Aunt Helen being there.

60

"Guess what?" Mary-Ellen greeted him lazily when he came home. The sun had just set on the first warm day of the year, misty and humid, and she was sprawling in a rattan chair on the veranda, a long glass of gin and tonic in her hand. A green mosquito coil smouldered in a saucer at her feet.

"Where are the children?"

"With Ah King I suppose."

"As usual."

She shrugged and drank. "I'm sure they'd rather have a clever mother who does interesting things than a doting zombie like Sarah Ephraim."

He leant over the parapet, gazing at the creeping

449

shadows of the dusk. At the bottom of the garden he could just see Jenny pushing Alec's pram along, beside Cheong with his wheelbarrow. Denton waved, and she waved back. She was lecturing Alec in a prim, schoolma'amy voice, but he couldn't hear the words—only the tone.

"Guess what?" Mary-Ellen drawled again.

"I can't imagine."

"Helen's selling up in Peking."

"Oh?" He watched Jenny pushing the pram across the lawn towards the garage, her face growing gradually more distinct as she came nearer. Something caught in his chest at the sight. It was as though the twilight was much more than twilight, an atmosphere of innocence and carelessness as well, an atmosphere he'd left so long ago himself that he could only occasionally glimpse it now from far away. He turned round slowly as she passed behind the bauhinia trees, and glanced at Mary-Ellen. "And why is Helen selling up?"

"She's coming down to Shanghai." For all her casual drawl, there was a submerged elation in Mary-Ellen's voice. "I've been trying to persuade her for months—"

"I can well believe it."

"—and now she's finally decided."

"What's she going to do in Shanghai—apart from enjoy herself with you?—She's not staying here again, by the way. I've had enough of that."

He meant more by "that" than she understood, or chose to understand. "Why? Didn't you get on with her?" she asked lightly.

"Not as well as you did." He let his eyes stay on hers after he'd spoken, until she looked away. "I'd like a bit of privacy now and then, too."

"She's going to run the gallery with me of course." Mary-Ellen said, lifting her glass. "You needn't worry about her being in your way—there's an apartment over the gallery, she can rent that or buy it."

He walked back into the room, to get himself a whisky. "She'd do better to buy than to rent," he said absently, mechanically. He was thinking that it was only half an hour since he'd left Su-mei and Michael. If it weren't for Jenny and Alec it would have been like passing from summer to winter. But then that was probably how Mary-Ellen felt about him too. At least, if Helen did come, Mary-Ellen would spend most of her time with her, and

450

they'd be still more out of each other's way. So long as Helen didn't live in the house, that would be too much...He poured himself some whisky, then noticed a letter on the sideboard. It was his mother's handwriting, large and shaky. An apprehensive twinge went through him. It was her first letter from the home she'd abruptly decided to enter after her seventy-first birthday. Undertaking to pay the bills hadn't really assuaged the guilt he felt at never renewing his old offer to bring her out to Shanghai—not that she'd have come, he supposed, she was too frail by now. But still—He took the letter with him out onto the veranda. Already the first stars were glittering in the sky as the dusk swiftly faded into night. He heard Ah King calling Jenny to bring Alec and come for tea.

"I thought I'd go up to Peking next week," Mary-Ellen said with forced casualness. "Help her pack up and settle everything..."

He drank without answering, placed his glass on the parapet, and turned the letter over in his hands, reluctant to open it.

"She'll have a lot to do," Mary-Ellen went on, almost as though she was excusing herself.

"And no doubt you can't wait to see each other?"

"What?"

He hesitated, then drew back, letting the words fade from his mind until something less challenging took their place. "I'd have thought Peking was a better place for antiques than here?"

"There's more competition in Peking," she said abstractedly. "And more money here."

He shrugged, expressing his ignorance, and his indifference. "How long are you going for?"

"Well...I suppose the children wouldn't miss me for a couple of weeks."

"I shouldn't think they'd know you were gone, since they never see you when you're here..."

"My! Aren't we waspish tonight?"

Tell her to stay away for good, he thought. Tell her. Tell her. But he drew back again, turning to drink some more whisky. He pushed his finger under the flap of his mother's letter. "I suppose you've got the business side worked out?" he asked, neutrally.

"Half-shares in everything."

"Including the bed?"

The words had slipped out before he'd even thought of them. But now they were out, they hung there between them like a tangible thing which they both stared at, amazed.

She blushed, the first time he'd ever seen her flustered. "What d'you mean?" she asked unevenly.

He shrugged, glancing down at the jagged, half-opened flap. His heart beat faster with the knowledge that he'd only to say one more word and it would be over, there'd be no going back. "Jenny asked me what the two of you were doing in bed," he heard himself say.

"In bed? When?"

He felt a sudden slackening of his nerves, as if some rope that had bound him tight had been loosened at last. His heart had steadied as soon as he'd spoken. "Two or three times she saw you. She thought it was a game you were playing. She wondered what it was."

She was silent for some time, while he slowly tore the rest of the flap open. He glanced inside the envelope, but didn't draw the letter out. The acrid smoke of the mosquito coil wafted across his nostrils. He'd done it at last, he was thinking in the dawning of that release. He'd done it. It had started now, it couldn't be stopped.

"Well, now you know," she said at last, in a calm matter-of-fact voice. "The little spy." Then, her tone rising a little defiantly, "I can't help the way I feel."

He shook his head. "No, I suppose not." He'd never seen her show as much feeling as that before. "And nor can I..."

"Nor can you?"

She was watching him with wide, slightly bulging eyes, and he remembered with a shock how captivated he'd been by them once. Could these really be the same blue eyes, the colour of the sky? "I can't help the way I feel either," he said slowly, glancing back at the envelope. "I have...I have someone else too."

"D'you think I didn't know that?"

He shrugged. So it was ending now, he thought thankfully. At last it was ending. It all seemed so simple.

"Some cheap little actress," she said disdainfully. "A sing-song girl."

"She isn't cheap, as a matter of fact." There was no edge in his voice—it didn't matter whether she believed

452

him or not. It was almost as though he was talking to himself.

She laughed drily. "You never did have any taste."

"More taste than to bring her into your house and into your bed at least."

She was silent for a moment, actually abashed, he thought. Then she shrugged it off. "Well, now that we both know, what are we going to do about it?" She was turning her glass slowly round and round in her hands.

"If you knew about it," he said slowly, "why didn't you say something?"

"If you knew about me, why didn't you?" She was her unconcerned, ironic self again. "It left us both free, didn't it?"

"Well," he breathed out slowly, "there's no need to discuss it now then, is there?"

"I don't want to hear about your sordid affairs," she said with a light, amused scorn. "If that's what you mean by discuss."

"You think yours isn't sordid?"

"Not at all. I'm proud of it." Again her voice strengthened with a depth of feeling he'd never seen before. "Proud of it."

He could still feel his heart thudding softly in his chest. It wasn't going faster now, he noticed, only he could feel it, like the beating of a muffled drum. Well, now it was out and everything was over. His sense of release grew deeper.

She drank, a long, gulping swallow. "Well what are we going to do about it?" she asked again.

He shrugged. "I suppose we ought to get a divorce."

"All right. Only I don't want Helen dragged through any law courts. It's all right for you, your affair's more common."

"Common in what sense?"

"Both senses." She swallowed the rest of her drink in another series of gulps.

"You mean you want to sue me for divorce and me not to defend it?"

"You're such a gentleman," she drawled. "Isn't that what's called doing the decent thing? Besides, imagine how you'd feel if my side of it came out. Lots of men commit adultery, but not many have wives...wives with

453

my kind of interests..." She smiled a little crookedly, and he realised she was a bit drunk. "And think of the children..."

"Well we can work out the details later," he said, nodding his agreement. So he was free at last, that was all he could think.

"I'll leave for Peking as soon as possible—the day after tomorrow, I guess. Thank god this farce of a marriage is over." She scraped back her chair and stood up.

"Yes..." he gave a long, tired, but relieved sigh. "It's been a kind of illness, hasn't it?"

And then he heard her laughing, chuckling softly as she leant on the back of the chair to steady herself, with a fuddled ghost of that smiling candour that used to brighten her eyes when she first came to Shanghai. "Oughtn't we to be making more of this scene?" she smiled, her voice mildly slurred. "You know, throwing things at each other and so on?"

He smiled wrily. "No, we've never had a real scene, have we? You're difficult to fight with." And for a moment his long, deep hatred of her faded away. She could hurt no more, and he felt only a rueful regret for all those mismatched, wasted years. "As a matter of interest, how did you get, how did you become...?"

"Lesbian?"

He nodded.

"You really want to know?" She smiled crookedly again. "My father messed around with me."

"What?" He stared at her incredulously. "Your father?"

"Started when I was fourteen. Surprised?"

He was shaking his head, trying to take it in. "Why d'you think he brought me along the first time he came to Shanghai? Mother wanted to come. He just didn't want her along."

"I just can't believe it! Your father! The old goat!"

"I keep telling you you're naive." She smiled, neither sadly nor happily. "It put me off men."

He drank slowly and thoughtfully, still shaking his head. "But," he turned back to her at last, "In that case, why on earth marry me?"

"How else would I have got to China?" she asked, spreading her hands. "Besides, I thought I ought to give it a try at least. You served both purposes."

He watched her get up with a little heave and walk unsteadily into the hall. He heard her climbing the stairs.

He was still holding his mother's letter, still unread. What would he say to Jenny, he wondered, how would he explain it to her?

61

At first Su-mei refused to move into the house on the Bund. The fung-shui was bad, the house would be unlucky, the servants wouldn't give her face, his first wife's children would curse her...To every reply he made she brought out another objection, or, when objections failed, merely shrugged or shook her head to show she wouldn't budge. "But you've been there often enough before," he protested. She shrugged, as if that was another life. "You're going to be my wife now," he said. "You must live in my house."

"You might go back to your first wife."

"Never."

She shook her head incredulously, yet pleased by the spontaneous vehemence of his assurance. And he began to realise it was because she didn't trust him that she was refusing to move, producing all those flimsy excuses that she propped up again as soon as he'd knocked them down. He'd sent her away once, why shouldn't he do it again? It wasn't poverty she feared—the opera had made her quite well-off—but loss of face. She wasn't going to live in this house and then be thrown out of it. "Before I wasn't much more than a sing-song girl. Now I have more to lose. I must be your number one wife."

"But you will be—you'll be my *only* wife. As soon as I've got my divorce."

She tossed her head with a disbelieving little smile. "And when will that be? Why can't you be divorced today—tomorrow? Give the magistrate a present and he'll do it for you at once, a taipan like you."

He smiled at her still child-like naiveté. "It has to be done by British law, Su-mei. Because I was married under British law. And that takes two years."

"By Chinese law it would be easy."

He shrugged. "This is Shanghai, not China. Foreign devils have their own laws here."

"Well, they have very bad laws, then."

"You'll have to wait till the English court gives me a divorce. I'll marry you the next day."

She began to waver. He formally adopted Lily and Michael, he made a will in her favour. "It's not that," she said, "it's not the money—I don't trust you not to send me away again. If you come to me here, and then stop coming, that's one thing. If I go to your house and then you send me away, that's different—nobody would ever give me face again. Will it be as hard for you to divorce me as it is to divorce your foreign wife?"

"I'm not going to divorce you!"

"Will it?"

"Yes, of course it will—would."

She considered. "In that case, come and live with me here till you're divorced. Then if you change your mind and leave me before we're married, it'll look as though I'd got rid of you."

He sighed exasperatedly. "Su-mei, in the first place I won't leave you, and in the second you know perfectly well this house is too small. There just aren't enough rooms. Not enough for the children, let alone the servants."

She looked at him dubiously, then a light stirred and glimmered in her eyes. "Let's go to a fortune-teller then, like before," she said simply.

So that evening they did go, to the same night-market they'd visited fifteen years before, with its hissing kerosene lamps, its melon-stalls, tea-stalls, sugar-cane-stalls, its crowded kerb-side restaurant, its open-air opera singers and tumblers. The man who'd told their fortunes before wasn't there any longer, but in the same place squatted a younger man who might have been his son, reading a newspaper and smoking a hand-rolled cigarette while he waited for customers.

Denton surreptitiously paid him double the usual amount before he took Su-mei's palm to read it. "We need to know whether we'll have good luck," he said, eyeing him steadily. The man's lids fluttered almost imperceptibly, but Denton felt sure he'd struck a deal.

Both he and Su-mei would have long, prosperous and happy lives, the fortune teller said, poring over their palms and turning them gently this way and that in the flickering light of his lamp. They would be important people—perhaps they were already. Their lives were intertwined—he locked his two forefingers together like

456

links in a chain—their children would respect them, they would be blessed with many sons and they would have grandchildren and great-grandchildren...His voice chanted on in a quiet, reflective sing-song, retailing all the old illusions she'd come to hear, almost as though he were in a trance—except that occasionally his eyes would glance shrewdly up at Denton to check whether he was getting it right.

And Su-mei, her head lowered over her palm, following his long, slim forefinger as it traced the lines, took in his words with grave attention. She, who'd advised Denton as a sixteen year old girl how to bargain with Wei, whose career owed as much to astuteness as to talent, who could see through a plausible fraud long before Denton—she was taken in by this simple trickery!

"Was your father a fortune teller here, too?" Denton asked when the man finished.

He hesitated, then nodded cautiously.

"We came to him many years ago," Su-mei explained. "Everything he said came true."

Did it? Denton wondered. He couldn't remember much about it now, except that he'd said they'd be rich. Well, that had come true anyway.

Su-mei agreed to move to the Bund.

"There's only the problem of Ah King," Denton said, having avoided it till then. "You two never got on before. But she looks after the children—she always has, even before my wife left..."

"Is it true your wife is living with that woman? Like husband and wife?"

"I suppose so, yes."

Her nose wrinkled in disgust. "If you ever went back to her after me, I'd have to kill myself."

"I'll never go back to her. But about Ah King—the children are completely used to her, I couldn't let her go..."

"It's all right," she said calmly. "As I'm to be your wife now, things will be different. She'll give me face. But you'll have to get rid of Chan."

"Chan? Why?"

"He's in the Green Triangle. It doesn't matter for you because you're a foreign devil, but it's different for me."

"How do you know he's in the Green Triangle?" He

457

thought uncomfortably of Pock-mark Chen and his body-guards at Wei's house last winter.

"They've got a way of looking, a way of greeting people, even a way of holding a rice bowl..."

"How do *you* know?"

She shrugged. "I found out. When I was a sing-song girl."

"Well, he always has been rather surly," Denton conceded uncertainly. "And lazy."

"Do you know what they're saying about you?" Jacob leant across the table in the Palace Hotel, where, after many years, Denton had taken to stopping for tea since Mary-Ellen had gone.

"Who?"

Jacob nodded at the tables around them. "Everyone! They're saying you've thrown your wife out onto the street and taken your Chinese mistress to live in your house!" He glared at Denton fiercely while he poured vodka into his glass. "I hear it everywhere!"

"Well, I didn't throw her out on the street. But the rest of it's true. Mary-Ellen's petitioning for divorce."

"Petitioning for divorce!" Jacob slapped his sallow, lined brow and moaned aloud. "Petitioning for divorce! My god, my god, in the year you could have been chairman of the Municipal Council! No, I mean it! If you'd stood, you'd have been elected! And now with this scandal— How can you be so mad? You might even lose your seat altogether!"

"I'm sure I will—I may not even stand for re-election."

Jacob stared at him, shaking his head in horror. "But what was wrong with keeping Su-mei somewhere quiet and leaving things as they were? All it needed was a bit more discretion and everything would have been all right. But you had to flaunt Su-mei at everyone! And now, taking her into your house—!"

Denton shrugged, pressing the lemon down in his tea with his spoon. "We couldn't have gone on like that any longer." In the golden-brown liquid he saw Mary-Ellen's cases standing in the hall. Had it really only been six weeks? He hadn't had a word from her—but then why should he, except that there were things to arrange? When he looked up, Jacob was gulping his vodka, glaring

458

at him indignantly and uncomprehendingly still. Denton smiled—he'd never seen anyone drinking *angrily* before.

"What are you grinning at? You have just ruined your political career, your chance of controlling the greatest city in Asia, the city that controls China—and you find something to laugh about? Is this your English sense of humour? Well it doesn't amuse *me*!"

Denton shrugged. "I was getting tired of all that in any case," he said.

"I kept trying to tell you, you could have had everything," Jacob bore on, "mistress, politics, wife and family—how d'you think other people do it? Look around you! All it needed was a bit of discretion! And now you've thrown the lot away. All you've got now is your mistress, and how long d'you think that will last?"

"And my children. I have them too."

"Bah! You'll always be quarreling with Mary-Ellen about them. They'll never belong to you again." Suddenly he leant forward and gripped Denton's arm with the old force. "Listen, is it really too late?" he pleaded in a low voice, peering urgently into Denton's eyes. "Couldn't you patch things up with Mary-Ellen and send Su-mei away for a bit? Pay her something to keep out of the way?"

Denton leant back, shaking his head slowly in amused amazement. "I don't think you understand what's happened between Mary-Ellen and me," he began.

"Understand?" Jacob's grip tightened. "There are two things I understand better than anyone else. One is the importance of success, and the other is women. And you've made a mess of both!"

"Well that's that!" Chan flung the chamois leather into the pail and watched it slowly open up and sink.

Yin-hong looked up from his homework. He was sitting on the running-board of the Rolls, in the cool shadow of the garage.

"That's that!" Chan spat deliberately through the open doors into the garden, where Cheong was clipping the lawn. Cheong glanced round questioningly, his eyes mild and apprehensive.

"Fuck your mother, I'm not talking to you," Chan said, and the gardener turned away.

Yin-hong gazed up at Chan's sullen face. His pale scar seemed to be throbbing faintly like a living thing.

"I've got the push," Chan said. His eyes narrowed to cold, slanting slits.

"Got the push?"

"Thrown out. Finished." He pressed his lips together, gazing down at the pail. Some air was trapped under the chamois, making the darkening leather bulge above the water. He pushed the pocket slowly down with his bare toe, watching the bubbles squeeze out under the side and burst as they rose. "Sacked for the second time, how d'you like that?" He imagined it was Kwan Su-mei's face under his foot. "It's that bitch of a woman," he said.

"Kwan Su-mei?"

"Got something against me." He pushed downward suddenly with his whole weight. The water poured over the sides as the leather drowned under his foot. "She's got it in for me." The water subsided as he lifted his foot, then rose again as he pushed the soft, pulpy leather down again. He pushed harder and faster, the water splashing out all over his leg, over the car and the floor. He was squashing and squelching Su-mei's face under his foot, slowly drowning her.

"What are you going to do, then?" Yin-hong asked. "Get another job?"

"Do? Job?" Chan paused. He took his foot out and knocked the pail over. The water washed over the hot, dusty floor. "Don't worry, I won't starve. A triad member never starves. They look after each other, they've sworn an oath . . . But we'll get even with that bitch," he went on, for some reason grandly including Yin-hong in the "we." "We'll settle accounts one day, the little jumped-up whore." He kicked the pail away as if it had been a stone in his path and smiled maliciously as it clattered against the car wheel. "Well, never mind that for now. You want to earn a bit of cash, Yin-hong? Want to do a favour for someone in the triad? All right, be at the Woochow Road market, nine o'clock tomorrow night, all right? I'll give you a little errand to run."

Yin-hong nodded, his eyes blankly concealing his pride.

"It's strange," Green declared loudly as Denton passed by the little group at the long, dark bar, "strange how those who claim the Chinese aren't being treated properly seem incapable of treating their own kith and kin in a decent manner."

Denton felt their glances brushing over him, sly and sneering. His cheeks smarted. He'd eaten alone, he'd sat alone in the reading room, people he knew well had gazed past him as he went by. And now this, the cutting insult out of the side of the mouth. He went on a few steps and then turned back, feeling his heart thudding softly against his ribs. They stopped talking as he approached, their eyes stiffly evasive. He noticed a muscle flickering in Green's gaunt cheek. Then Green spoke again, in the same overloud voice, his eyes gazing coldly over Denton's head. "I suppose they'll be asking us to open the *club* to Chinese next. With a special room for *concubines*. Complete with *spittoons*." Their faces smirked, secretly watching Denton's. One or two of them smothered uncertain giggles.

"Were you speaking of anyone in particular, Norman?" Denton asked pleasantly. He beckoned the barman. Inwardly his arm trembled, yet it looked perfectly steady.

"I was speaking only to my friends."

Denton raised his brows. "I thought perhaps you wanted me to hear, you were speaking so loudly. Are any of your friends hard of hearing?"

Green turned his head away in silence.

"Can I get anyone a drink?" Denton asked in a high but level voice, only a little strained. "Norman?"

"I'm just leaving."

Denton shrugged. "Someone else?"

"No thanks."

"Not for me."

"No."

They moved away, some still smirking, some sheepishly, all avoiding his eye. He noticed Walker amongst them, the young griffin who'd ridden his pony once at the races.

He ordered a whisky and soda and stood there alone, sipping it slowly. The group had reformed at the other end of the bar, where by custom only the griffins drank. He heard Green's voice again, loud and hard as iron, rising above the others'.

The barman gave him a melancholy smile.

"I climb over the veranda and watch them," Jenny whispered. "I peek through the curtain. Sometimes she's on top and sometimes he is. But I can't see what they actually do."

"You mustn't!" Lily whispered with shock-wide eyes. "It's wrong!"

"'Course it isn't. I'm only watching." She pulled a strand of her long fair hair down and chewed it between her teeth, gazing up at her half-sister critically. "My father's not really your father, you know. Otherwise you wouldn't have such slanty eyes."

Lily felt her cheeks flush with the old shame, the shame so old it had become a habit, the shame of being neither one thing nor the other. "That's not true, he *is* my father. He told me. And he's Michael's too."

Jenny looked at her sceptically, without answering. Lily's shame turned to resentment under that look. "And don't you dare spy on them again or I'll tell my mother," she said.

"Su-mei?" Jenny bit off a strand of hair and spat it out. "Go on, tell her, then." She smiled up at Lily tauntingly. "Go on."

"And don't you call her Su-mei either! You call her mother like I do."

"Why should I? She's not my mother."

"She is now."

"My mother's in Peking."

"Oh no she's not." Lily's resentment suddenly soared into triumph. "She's in Shanghai."

"She's in Peking!"

"She's in Shanghai. I saw her on Penang Road the other day. With that woman she lives with."

If she's in Shanghai she'd come and see me, Jenny thought with forlorn despair. And yet she believed Lily.

"And anyway, she's not your mother any more." Lily went on severely. "*My* mother is."

Jenny's melting eyes hardened. "Your mother can't be," she sneered.

"Why not?"

"'Cos she's only Chinese of course."

And all Lily's triumph collapsed and crumpled as the old shame burned in her cheeks again.

Dear Sir,

For reasons which I am sure you will appreciate, the committee has reluctantly come to the conclusion that it would be inappropriate for you to remain a member of the Shanghai Club. The committee believes it would be in the best interests of all concerned, and save a great deal of unnecessary unpleasantness all round, if you would agree to resign from

*the Club. However, should you not do so, I regret to have to
inform you that the Club servants will be instructed not to
admit you or serve you after the end of next week. I am sure
you would not wish such an embarrassing situation for all
concerned to arise.*

*I am enclosing herewith your unpaid chits up to the
present time and would be grateful if you would remit a
cheque for the full amount in due course.*

Yours faithfully.

"How can they do that?" Su-mei asked when he showed
it to her with a wry smile.

"Quite easily," he shrugged. "Jacob was right. They
don't speak to me at Council meetings either. I'll be
certain to lose my seat at the next election, if I bother to
stand."

She watched quietly from the bed, her black hair
loose on the pillow. "What are you going to do about it?"
she asked at last. "How are you going to pay them back?"

He sat on the bed beside her, took the letter from her
hand and let it flutter to the floor, "Nothing," he said.
"Absolutely nothing. I'm going to ignore them."

"But you've lost face! You can't let them treat you like
that!"

He shook his head. "I'm finished with them. I'm glad
to be rid of it all. I don't want to spend my life on that
stuff any more. I want to do something else."

"Something else? What else is there for you to do,
here in Shanghai?"

He pursed his lips, considered, shrugged, and then
nodded at the bottom drawer of the wardrobe, where the
opium things had returned at last. "Well, there's one thing
I can do anyway," he said. "Come on, make us a pipe."

It was two and a half years before the divorce was granted.
By that time the scandal had been forgotten. Denton was
no longer on the Municipal Council, his name never
appeared in the papers, he was no longer known in
Shanghai.

"Now you must marry me," Su-mei said when he
explained that the divorce was absolute at last. "So everyone knows I am the number one wife."

"I'll marry you under Chinese law if you like. You can
come to me in a bridal chair, dressed in red."

But she wouldn't hear of that. He must marry her in the same way that he'd married his foreign wife. "Then you won't be able to get rid of me so easily." She spoke with a little self-mocking smile, but he knew she was half in earnest.

"We can't be married in church," he warned her. "Divorced people can't be married in a church."

"Is it still a real marriage if it's not in a church?"

"Just as good. Just as hard to undo."

So they were married at the Register Office. Su-mei's parents had died, her brothers wanted nothing to do with her; Denton asked Wei to come but he found an excuse. In the end only Jacob and Sarah were there as witnesses. And Jacob, still convinced Denton was making a mistake, said he came against his better judgement. However, his eyes always brightened when he saw Su-mei.

Afterwards they flew to Kweilin, the first time either of them had flown. They stared down amazed at the silent land unrolling like a many-coloured carpet beneath them, and at the plane's shadow flitting effortlessly across it. In Kweilin there were calm green waters reflecting steep, mist-wrapped limestone rocks, weird and haunting in their gnarled craggy shapes.

Two weeks later they returned to Shanghai. A telegram, three days old, lay on Denton's desk, announcing the death of his mother.

PART THREE

62

"Yes, I knew your father years ago," Miss Pulham said, wiping a limp, damp strand of grey hair off her forehead. "Used to pray for him in fact..." She gave Lily the pile of hymn books she was carrying close to her shapeless chest, their dark covers faded and spotted with mildew. "Just lay these out on the desks, will you? Two to a desk. Yes, I used to pray for him. That was before you were born. Pray for him to give up his life of sin. And now the Lord sends *you* to help us." She smiled, the freckled, sun-burned skin crinkling round her pale blue eyes. "So perhaps He heard my prayers after all..."

Lily paused, turning her head to listen as she laid the books on the worn, ridge-grained desks. The sound was starting again, that sound of the crowd shouting. It rose from a muffled, distant murmur to a sudden roar that seemed closer and threatening.

"What's that? Are they still demonstrating, Lily?"

"Yes, I think so, Miss Pulham." Lily went on laying out the books with their loose covers and torn bindings. She laid them more carefully and more quietly now, as if afraid of disturbing the hush that had followed the crowd's roar.

"What on earth they're demonstrating about this time I can't imagine," Miss Pulham was saying placidly. She turned to the blackboard and began writing the hymn numbers on it. The chalk kept squeaking and breaking in her hands.

Lily glanced up at Miss Pulham's clumsy, large characters, such as Lily herself used to make when she was a child, and suddenly recalled—perhaps it was because it was a schoolroom here too—recalled Miss Robinson's geography lesson at school last week.

See girls, this is the political map of the world. Page six, see? It shows all the different countries' possessions. See how much of the world is coloured red? That's the British Empire, present here in China and in every corner of the earth.

466

*Africa, see? Asia? The West Indies? Everywhere you look,
you'll see some red. See Hong Kong? That little dot? Who's
been to Hong Kong? You, Lily? Good. Now, see what a great
civilising force the British Empire is, how it's brought law and
order and progress to all those backward parts of the world
All those girls who are British, raise your hands—No, not you
Lily, you can't be British, you're half-Chinese.*

And even now as, with unfocussed eyes, she watched
Miss Pulham's chalk snapping and squeaking under the
pressure of her thick fingers, Lily could feel the blood
burn in her cheeks, remembering her humiliation, remembering the other girls tittering, especially those who'd
raised their hands.

"What on earth are they shouting?" Miss Pulham
asked, hand poised at the blackboard, gazing inquiringly
over her shoulder at Lily. "Can you hear?"

Lily became aware of the throaty, baying roar again.
She listened, then shook her head. "I saw some banners
when I was coming, Miss Pulham," she said. "It was
something about..." she hesitated, obscurely afraid the
whole truth might make Miss Pulham angry. "About unequal treaties," she concluded lamely. What she'd actually
seen was "Beat Down British Imperialism," "Cancel all
Unequal Treaties," "Scrap Extra-territorial Rights." And
she'd seen coolies shouting together with the neatly-dressed
students from the university. She'd seen hawkers and shop
assistants laughing and cheering them on from the pavements, even women and children peering out of the
windows, smiling and waving. It was strange how she'd
suddenly felt a throb of pride in her chest as though she
wanted to shout too, although she wasn't Chinese—she
wasn't even half-Chinese, whatever Miss Robinson said.
She'd got an English name and her father was English,
which was more important than what your mother was.
And anyway she didn't look at all Chinese if she didn't
wear Chinese clothes...

"Oh well, it'll all blow over I suppose," Miss Pulham
said tranquilly. "When they've had a good shout." She
went on torturing the screeching chalk against the blackboard, writing her stiff and awkward characters. "Aren't
any of the other girls in your class interested in helping
the orphanage? Have you asked them?"

Lily shook her head dumbly at Miss Pulham's back.

467

"Have you asked your friends, Lily?" Miss Pulham turned round at last, wiping her chalky fingers down her dress.

Suddenly Lily's lips were trembling and she felt a tearful sob in her throat. "I haven't got any friends," she blurted out unsteadily. "You're my only friend."

"Nonsense, of course you've got friends," Miss Pulham said briskly, wiping her hands down her grey dress still. "Jesus is everyone's friend. Now, it's time to call the children in. Tell Ah To to ring the bell, will you?"

All the time the children were singing in their docile uninterested voices, Lily kept hearing the distant growing swell of the demonstration, the low murmur rising to sudden ragged roars that slowly calmed then rose again, briefly overwhelming the plaintive whine of Miss Pulham's harmonium and the children's singing, making their eyes swivel curiously to the barred windows. Miss Pulham went round the desks, showing the youngest children how to clasp their hands during the prayers before she knelt herself and clasped her own. Lily prayed too, prayed that this time at last she'd have the strength to take that final step. Behind her closed eyes she pictured Jesus as a tall fair man with pale blue eyes like Miss Pulham's, only burning with an intenser light. If she thought of Him as a white man, she caught herself wondering as the prayers ended, did that mean she really was more English than Chinese?

Afterwards, as they went round the empty desks gathering the hymn books, she felt her heart beating faster with the words she'd rehearsed so often in her lonely daydreams, but never managed to make herself say. She felt sure she couldn't say them today either. But then suddenly they tumbled out in a breathless rush. "Miss Pulham, I think I'd like to be baptised."

"Think you'd like?" she sniffed and laughed. "What does that mean?"

"I mean I want to be. I mean I believe in Jesus." Now that she'd said it, it seemed such a strange thing to say, after all the nights she'd thought and thought about it. It seemed strange and small, somehow. But now she'd said it, it was settled, she couldn't go back.

"I've been praying for that," Miss Pulham said in calm, unsurprised satisfaction, as though she'd just got the answer to a letter she'd sent. "You see I'm *not* your only friend am I? Jesus is your friend too." She sniffed at the pile of books, wrinkling her nose. "We'd better put all these in the sun tomorrow or they'll simply rot away. —Now," with scarcely a change of tone, "if you're going to be baptised, we'd better tell your parents about it."

"Oh no!"

"Of course we must," Miss Pulham said decisively. "I don't want your father complaining to me. Or your mother. Besides, it might set an example to them. And in any case I want to ask your father for some money. I've been waiting for the Lord to tell me what to do next about money, and as soon as you said you wanted to be baptised I knew He was showing me what to do."

"My mother won't allow it," Lily protested anxiously. "If we tell her, she won't allow it. Can't we do it secretly—without telling her, I mean?"

"If we tell her you've been reborn in Christ?" Miss Pulham asked incredulously, as though that would be like telling her Lily had won a prize at school. "Of course she'll allow it. Why ever not?"

Lily imagined her mother's face stiffening, her eyes hardening. "We needn't tell her now, though," she protested weakly.

"Of course we must. No time like the present. Will your father be at home now?" She looked down at the watch which she always kept pinned to her dress.

Lily felt the terrible magnitude of what she'd done. Her yearning for God, for salvation, for spiritual union with the Lord—all those rich emotions that had seemed so strong in the private luxury of her imagination, began to flutter away now like rags in the wind. But there was nothing she could do now, she'd said it and she couldn't go back.

She walked tamely along with Miss Pulham, out of the gate and into the street. Perhaps something would happen, she hoped silently, perhaps the demonstration would be in their way and Miss Pulham would give up for today...

The crowd's roar sounded louder now, as if they were only a few streets away. It was a persistent chanting that grew fiercer and fiercer, like a war-cry yelled from ten thousand throats. Lily felt faintly uneasy, but it was the thought of her mother and father meeting Miss Pulham

469

that really worried her. Miss Pulham, cocking her head to listen to the noise, merely shrugged and smiled.

"My mother doesn't know I come here," Lily said hesitantly. "She thinks I stay at school..."

"Now you haven't been telling her lies, have you, Lily?" Miss Pulham chided her lightly. "Not lies about going to help the Lord?"

"No, I just haven't told her," Lily answered wretchedly.

"Well, we'll tell her now, then. We mustn't be afraid to say we're doing the Lord's work, must we?"

It was a few more steps before Lily realised what it was that made the street they'd turned onto seem sinister and uncanny. It was the emptiness. There was nobody else on it, the shopfronts were all shuttered as if a typhoon was coming, all the hawkers' stalls were gone.

"Shall we take a rickshaw?" Miss Pulham asked, oblivious of the desolation.

Lily gestured down the street for answer.

"Oh, not another strike, is it?" She shrugged composedly. "Shank's pony then. They think too much about money, these rickshaw coolies, not enough about their souls."

They walked along in the shade, past the shuttered shops and the stagnant canals, past the dogs lying panting with lolling tongues in the gutter, past the uncleared heaps of refuse over which rats scuttled unafraid. Miss Pulham was humming a hymn-tune as she walked, her breath slightly wheezy, her skin glistening with perspiration. Despite the heat, she had a blithe smile on her face and her sharp pale eyes glanced continually over the rubbish as if she expected to find abandoned babies wherever she looked. She had shouldered her baby bag as they left and every now and then she slapped it with her hand, as the tram conductors slapped their heavy leather purses when they collected the fares.

They were walking towards Maloo. The thunder of the crowd was getting louder and wilder. It seemed to go on and on without pause now. Lily held back a little.

"Perhaps we shouldn't go down there?" she suggested timidly.

"Where? Down towards Maloo?"

"That's where I saw them all marching."

"Oh," Miss Pulham strode on carelessly. "They're only shouting a bit. It's the quickest way, isn't it?"

They turned into Tibet Road. There was a great

crowd milling at the bottom of it where the Louza Police Station was. Lily could see them surging round the dull red-brick walls of the building like a great, foaming tide. Her legs grew weak at the sight, but Miss Pulham strode on, humming her hymn-tunes unconcernedly, her face running little rivulets of sweat. Lily's mouth had gone dry. She saw people break away from the crowd to hurl stones at the police station and then fall back into the mass like the spray of a wave when it struck the rocks.

"What on earth are they up to this time?" Miss Pulham asked indulgently.

Lily shook her head. But in fact she could make out what they were chanting, the chant growing stronger with each beat as they worked themselves gradually into a kind of exultant frenzy. "Kill the foreign devils! Kill the foreign devils! Kill! Kill! Kill!"

They're only shouting, she tried to convince herself, they don't mean it. But then suddenly she stopped dead. "Miss Pulham! We can't go on. We'd better go back."

"Go back? Whatever for? Haven't you seen a demonstration before, Lily?"

Lily's lips trembled. "They're shouting 'Kill the foreign devils'," she said unevenly. "Please, let's go back, it isn't safe!"

For a second Miss Pulham's eyes lost their assured pale light and glimmered irresolutely. She listened to the cries, holding her breath for a few moments. "So they are," she conceded slowly, her breath wheezing again. But then her resolution returned and her eyes gleamed once more with the light of conviction. "Oh, they're just a lot of students, Lily. They're always shouting things." She took Lily's hand and marched on with her down the street. Lily's heart pounded, she wanted to pull her hand away and run back, but it was like in a dream, her legs just went on walking. With mounting panic that made her want to scream she walked on and on, her hand in Miss Pulham's, nearer and nearer the chanting, yelling mob. Now she could see their faces clearly, throats knotted, eyes wide and set, mouths grimacing, as they bayed out, hundreds in one voice, "Kill the foreign devils! Kill the foreign devils!" And through her panic she saw distinctly that many of them were not students, they were not hawkers or coolies, there was something different about them, something disciplined and organised.

Any moment now some head would turn and they'd be seen. She pictured the crowd streaming towards them with that cry in their throats. She pictured them waving knives, cargo-hooks, poles. She pictured herself being butchered beside Miss Pulham. Her heart thumped wildly in her chest, and yet she walked on, not even dragging her feet, walked on as helplessly as in a dream, while Miss Pulham hummed *The Lord's My Shepherd*, a bit more determinedly perhaps, but just as calmly.

Now they were only thirty or forty yards away and Lily's panic leapt madly. She could tell the students' and the coolies' faces easily from the others; *they* seemed older and surer, and, whenever the shouting began to flag, whipped it up again with a sullen, grim efficiency. And while she saw all that, her eye was taken by a black cat that slunk across the pavement in front of them, its belly low, its tail swishing slowly from side to side as if it meant to pounce at any moment.

A line of policemen stood facing the crowd at the gates to the station, a white officer, with Chinese and Sikh constables. They were standing there with rifles, tense and still while the crowd pushed slowly nearer them, throwing stones and lumps of wood, howling that one word "Kill!" in a faster and faster beat till it sounded like one long pulsing yell.

"Oh dear, how are we going to get through that lot?" Miss Pulham wondered, shaking her head in mild exasperation. "They could at least have left *some* room for people to pass by."

Lily's heart pounded, her wrists throbbed, her ears thudded, but still she walked on as if hypnotised, with Miss Pulham's sweating hand round hers. Then she saw one of the policemen stagger and fall as a stone hit him on the side of the head. The crowd jeered and shouted, then surged forward excitedly as if to rush the rest of the police off their feet. Then quite deliberately and slowly it seemed, while the fallen policeman stumbled to his knees, blood running down his face, the other policemen pointed their guns into the crowd and started firing. Lily saw the puffs of blue smoke and heard the deep, loud, jagged reports still as if it were a dream. This isn't real, she thought, it can't be happening. And yet her thumping heart told her it was.

There was a hush, sudden and absolute, in the crowd.

"What on earth's going on now?" she heard Miss Pulham ask bewilderedly. Then the policemen fired again. And again. And again. At once there were yells and screams of fear and the mob that had hung hesitant, unbelieving, at the first volley suddenly turned and ran, no longer a menacing crowd but only terrified people, each with strained, panic-filled eyes and wild, screaming mouths, dashing frantically away from the guns that went on shooting steadily, relentlessly behind them.

They rushed away down the street past Lily and Miss Pulham, throwing them aside and trampling all over them. Lily cowered against the wall, kicked, bruised and shocked, while Miss Pulham, knocked to her knees, was barged this way and that until she too collapsed beside her.

Then, quite suddenly, they were all gone and the street was empty again, the shooting had stopped. Lily looked round fearfully. It was as though a great wind had swept down the road, leaving only the debris of groaning or silent bodies behind it. The policemen were coming towards them now, going from one body to another, turning them over with their boots.

Trembling, Lily helped Miss Pulham up. She was shaking too, her arm quivering against Lily's hand. Strangely, now it was Lily who was calm, calm despite her inner quaking, as she wordlessly held out Miss Pulham's baby bag to her.

Some of the policemen were dragging the bodies out of the road into the shade of the police station wall. Lily saw one of the policemen kick a man, lying near them, his limbs twitching horribly in the sunlight. The man's eyes were open. They seemed to be staring imploringly at Lily. She looked away.

Then she heard the European officer calling out, "Get that girl, she's robbing that lady there!" And almost at once the officer himself had grabbed her arm. He swung her round and she looked up startled into his red sweaty face with a thin dark moustache along the length of his upper lip. "Bag-snatching too are you, you little bitch?" His voice was strident and unsteady. "I'll teach you, robbing a harmless old lady—"

"Don't be ridiculous," Miss Pulham cut in with a high trembling, breathless voice. "She's with me. She's not one of those demonstrators, she's helping me."

"Helping you?" The officer relaxed his grip on Lily's

473

arm. He stared at Miss Pulham incredulously. "But she's a Chink!"

"Her father's English."

The officer scrutinised Lily's face sceptically, then reluctantly let her go. "What's your name then?" he asked brusquely.

"Her name's Lily Denton," Miss Pulham answered for her. "And she lives on the Bund. We were just on our way there—what on earth happened?"

"Happened, madam?" He glanced round at the bodies. "It was a riot, didn't you see? You're lucky they didn't turn on you."

Miss Pulham's voice was still breathless and wheezy. "I've never seen anything like it," she said bemusedly. "They trampled all over us."

The police officer shrugged silently, as if to say: What d'you expect?

"Is it all right to go on now?" Miss Pulham asked.

"To the Bund? Yes. Only keep on the main road. And keep your eye on the girl, otherwise some constable's going to take her in. She looks enough like one of those students, and we're not too fond of them just now, know what I mean? Some of them were only high school kids like her." He gave Lily a long, considering glance. "Her father's English, you say? She looks like a Chink to me."

Miss Pulham ignored him. "Come on Lily." She took her hand and they walked on, each trembling, feeling the policemen's eyes on their backs.

"Don't look," Miss Pulham said, but Lily couldn't help seeing the inert bodies lying against the police station wall like dumped sacks. There was blood on their clothes, on their heads and their faces, and they were all so very still now. Lily felt she was going to be sick, but she had to look, she had to gaze at them.

"Mind!" Miss Pulham warned sharply, and they stepped over a patch of bright red blood, still shiny and sticky under the sun.

They're like me, Lily was thinking, I look Chinese like them. The white policemen couldn't believe my father's English. Something cold and heavy weighed inside her. You'll always be Chinese to them, she thought. It's no use, they'll never let you be English.

*   *   *

"Yes, I remember when your father used to live in Jessfield Road," Miss Pulham was saying a little breathlessly as they walked up the drive to the front door. "I kept telling him to marry your mother, and now he has. Though I must say he took his time about it." She was wheezing and sweating heavily—they'd walked all the way, hurrying through the eerie, abandoned streets in which only speeding police vans seemed to be moving. Miss Pulham had talked desultorily about Lily's father—remarks Lily could hardly follow; the images of those sack-like bodies were too vivid before her eyes. Why hadn't Miss Pulham talked about the riots and the shooting and the corpses? Didn't she care? And yet Lily was grateful—she didn't want to talk about it either.

"Ah," Miss Pulham wheezed suddenly. "And I see he still has the same amah. I wonder if she remembers me?"

Ah King was scowling at Lily anxiously from the open door. "Where've you been?" she demanded roughly. "Your mother's very angry. Been looking for you everywhere. Ah Leng's half-crazy."

"It's all right, she's been with me," Miss Pulham wheezed equably. "Remember me? I brought your master home in a rickshaw, when he had cholera. Years and years ago." She stood on the top step, wiping her glowing face with a handkerchief while Ah King still held the door suspiciously half-closed.

Ah King surveyed Miss Pulham beneath half-lowered lids. Her own hair was still black and glossy, the skin of her large, plain face smooth and unlined. The woman she was gazing at had wrinkled sunburned skin, pouches under her eyes and dull, grey hair. Could she be the bible woman with fair hair that had brought master home with the cholera? She was too old, surely? But then the eyes might be the same—they had the same mad blue stare in them. And foreign devils aged quickly anyway, their skins all shrivelled up.

"Yes, I remember you," she admitted grudgingly, opening the door wider to let them both in.

"Is your master at home?"

"Busy," Ah King muttered sullenly. "Business talk. Very important."

"Oh it can't be more important than what *we've* got to tell him," Miss Pulham said, stuffing her handkerchief into her pocket. "You lead the way, Lily, will you?"

The hand she laid on Lily's shoulder seemed firm and

strong, yet there was an occasional breathy tremble in her voice, as though after all she hadn't completely forgotten the still bodies lying by the Louza Police Station wall.

Lily heard voices in the living room and faltered by the open door, hoping Miss Pulham would go in first and perhaps leave her outside, but the hand on her shoulder guided her firmly in. She glanced apologetically, sheepishly at her father. He was standing by the wireless, listening intently, head bowed, eyebrows raised, while the other two men in the room talked to each other in low voices, themselves gazing at the wireless. They were Ephraim and Wei.

Her father frowned, lifting his hand for quiet. The announcer's English voice sounded faintly from the wireless amidst crackling and whistling and the jabber of other voices edging in. Lily visualised the announcer as a man trying to make himself heard in a room full of people talking incessantly in different languages. The voice strengthened and faded, as if he were approaching, then backing away: "...twenty-five casualties, of which nine were fatal... The mob dispersed at once and the streets are now free of trouble-makers. The commissioner of police however advises all residents to stay indoors unless they have urgent business to attend to..."

"Twenty-fi' dea'," Wei exclaimed sharply.

"No, no," Ephraim said soothingly, "Only nine. Only nine dead."

Wei's face remained rigid, as if he hadn't heard. Then they all turned at the sound of Miss Pulham's voice.

"Excuse me barging in like this with Lily, Mr. Denton," she said in a breezy, determined tone, no longer breathy. "Remember me?"

Denton stared at them both. "Lily! Miss Pulham! What's happened? Are you all right?"

"Oh yes, perfectly all right, thank you." She slapped her baby bag. "Still at it, you see. Though this isn't the old bag. And Lily's been helping us down at Jerusalem House..." She paused, but as the three men only gazed at her in amazement, she went on at once. "I know there's been some trouble on the streets—well, we ran into some ourselves, actually. By the Louza Police Station—"

"Louza Police Station? You were there?"

"Yes. But Lily's got something important to tell you, something that should make you very happy." She turned

476

to Lily. "She's ready to accept Our Lord into her life. She wants to be baptized, she wants to be born again. We came to tell you at once—"

But as their eyes turned from her sunburned, prematurely aged and calmly fanatic face to stare at Lily's, Lily suddenly shook her head, ducked away from Miss Pulham's hand, and ran out of the room. They heard her steps in the hall, racing up the stairs to her room at the top of the house. They heard her door slam.

Denton knocked and Ah Leng, summoned from the kitchen, knocked. Denton spoke quietly, and Ah Leng scolded and threatened, while Jenny and Alec stared and giggled and Michael looked gravely on. But it wasn't until Su-mei returned in the car from her vain search through the streets, long after Miss Pulham had left in resigned disappointment, but with a cheque from Denton, and peremptorily demanded to be let it, that Lily turned the key. "I don't want to be baptised," she kept sobbing incoherently, "I don't want to be baptised. It's no use, I'll always be Chinese."

"I am certain there will be strike', more riot', many trouble'," Wei was saying when Su-mei returned to the living-room. "And the Shinese gover'men' will be oblige' to make trouble too, otherwise they lose suppor' to the communist'."

Su-mei was wearing the new cheong-sam dress that fitted her body like a silken skin, and Wei glanced at it disapprovingly. She sat down, ignoring Wei and Jacob, her eyes set on Denton's face. "What has this Pulham woman been doing to Lily?" she asked sharply in Chinese.

"I don't know. She wouldn't say a word to me."

She pressed her lips together and waited while they went on talking.

"The market dropped fifty points in an hour," Jacob said, screwing up his eyes as he lit a cigar. "Our workers were out on strike before we'd even heard about the riot."

The telephone rang. They watched Denton speaking into the mouthpiece. He covered it and turned to Wei. "The Secretary to the Municipal Council is trying to contact you," he said, with a little ironic smile at his formality. "Do you want to speak to him, or...?"

Wei shook his head decisively

"I'm afraid he's just left," Denton said. "No, he didn't say..." He hung up after a few more words and turned back to Wei. "They're very anxious to find you and the other Chinese advisors. Apparently they can't reach any of you?"

Wei's lids dropped faintly behind the walls of his lenses.

"They're worried about what you're going to do," Denton added.

"I will resig' from being advisor to the Council," Wei said precisely. "Now we mus' have membership. At leas' three member'. Maybe four. There will be other demand'."

"You should never have left the Council, John," Jacob began warmly. "You could have influenced—"

"He did not leave it," Su-mei said drily. "He was throw' out because of me."

"I wasn't thrown out. I merely failed to get re-elected," Denton corrected her mildly.

She shrugged. "It is the same."

Her poised, waiting presence made them all uncomfortable. Jacob and Wei left soon afterwards.

"Well, what has that woman been doing to Lily?" she taxed him as soon as they'd gone. "What is all this rubbish about being baptised?"

"If *you* don't know, I'm sure *I* don't. She wouldn't even speak to me. What did she tell you?"

Su-mei shrugged. "She was in the middle of that riot, did you know that?"

"Yes."

"She saw the shooting. She could have been shot herself."

"I know."

"Well what are you going to do about it?"

"What can I do? It's all over now."

"About this Pulham woman with her ridiculous religion? If it was Jenny or Alec, you'd have never let it happen."

"Don't talk rubbish. You didn't know it was happening yourself."

She looked away without answering, lowering her lids.

Ah Leng appeared at the door. "Master, dinner," she announced. "Ah Man's not back. I cooked it myself."

"Where's Ah Man gone, then?" Denton frowned.

"Gone to look for his son. Not come home yet from the university, Ah Man's wife said. She came here when

478

Lily came back with the bible woman. They've gone to look."

"He's not old enough for the university, is he?"

Ah King shrugged. "He's been there nearly a year."

Denton shook his head in surprise, thinking how little he knew of Ah Man, even after all these years. How little he knew of Ah King's life for that matter, outside his house. What her husband did, for instance, how he lived and where—it was all kept behind a screen like the screen that met you when you entered a Chinese house, to send the evil spirits bouncing back through the open door.

Lily came down to dinner with red-rimmed eyes, only picking at her food despite Ah Leng's coaxing and fussing. "Leave her alone, Ah Leng," Su-mei said at last. "Can't you see she's not hungry?" Jenny kept nudging Alec and grimacing at him, while Michael sat between Lily and his father, looking from one face to another as if hoping to find some clue in them to the silence and abstraction in which his parents ate.

When they'd finished and the children had left the table, Denton poured himself a second cup of coffee and drank it on the veranda, gazing out at the glistening lights of the harbour and the unbroken darkness of the plains beyond Pootung, of the China from which Ah King, Ah Man, and Su-mei too, all came.

"Didn't you like the peaches?" Ah King reproached him as she cleared the table.

He glanced round. They were the flat Shanghai kind that Mary-Ellen used to like so much. He hadn't even noticed them on the table. "I wasn't hungry," he said. He looked a second longer at her impassive face. "How's Yin-hong doing at school?"

She shrugged as she turned away, as if closing a gate. "Very lazy, the teachers say."

"His father will be angry?"

She didn't answer. "I'll leave a peach for you on the sideboard for later," she said, and went on clearing the table in a silence as blank as the plains beyond Pootung.

He looked down on the Bund as he sipped his coffee. The street was still quiet. The rumble and whine of traffic, the grinding, clanging trams, the comforting clopping of ponies' hooves as they drew their rubber-wheeled carriages, the lights on the rickshaws and the occasional sedan chair—everything had stopped. There was going to

479

be more trouble, the persistence of that ominous stillness told him. But he felt curiously detached from it, as if, despite what had happened to Lily, the troubles wouldn't affect him. It was because he wasn't responsible any more. Since his divorce and his marriage with Su-mei, he'd become a no-man, he thought, swallowing the last of his coffee, the grounds sandy on his tongue. He was in between, he belonged neither to the world of the taipans nor to the world of the Chinese. Like the city itself, neither one thing nor the other. He went inside. Ah King took his cup. "Where is tai-tai?" he asked her.

She shrugged. "Upstairs with eldest daughter. You take the peach if you're going to the study. Reading makes you tired. You read too much."

"Is Ah Man back?"

"Not yet."

Su-mei had been right about Ah King, he reflected as he walked up the stairs. They accepted each other, the old hostility was gone, if not forgotten. Even Ah Leng was accepted, although there was an unspoken agreement that she had to do with Su-mei's children only, while Jenny and Alec belonged to Ah King. Everyone preserved face and the kitchen ran peacefully.

The air was so warm and heavy that his feet were dragging already at the first landing. The children were all in bed. He said goodnight to them each in turn, Alec and Michael in one room, Jenny reading in the other. The fans in each room just stirred the thick, moist air as they revolved at their lowest speed, stirred it sluggishly, only enough to dry the sweat off them where they lay in bed.

"Did Lily really see the shooting?" Jenny asked.

"Mm."

Her eyes widened slightly, but she said no more. She was reading a creased and smudged copy of an English girls' comic, over a year old.

He stopped outside Lily's closed door and listened. Su-mei was talking with her, he could hear her firm, intense voice and Lily's unsteady answers. He was about to open the door, but paused and then turned away, going on upstairs to the study. Lily would talk to Su-mei now, but not to him. He'd find out about it all later. And he'd make it up with Su-mei later too, he'd reassure her that he cared for her children as much as for Mary-Ellen's. That was the only thing that ever divided them, her fear that his other children, truly white, truly European, would displace her own "half-breeds," as she called them when the mood was on her, in his feelings. And yet *her* children were the love children, not Mary-Ellen's.

All the shelves in the study were filled with books. He switched on the ceiling fan and looked round them with a sense of comfort and consolation. It had taken him time to get all those books. He spent half his days there now, reading programmatically in history, browsing through popular works on science and psychology, but absorbed most of all in literature; especially novels, which he read indiscriminately, from every part of the world.

He put the peach down on his desk and picked up *Sons and Lovers,* which had arrived from England the day before, flicking the pages over beneath his thumb. On a tall Chinese table in the corner stood the new gramophone, with a cardboard packet of shiny needles open beside it, and a record lying on the turntable. It was Verdi's *Aida.* He wound the handle and set the needle down in the gently spinning groove. The music soared with a slightly metallic sound through the open window, out onto the sultry night.

As the waves of the chorus crashed about him, and he gazed absently out over the Bund and the harbour, the half-formed thoughts that had been brooding in his mind for weeks began slowly forming themselves into definite shapes. They came as images, imbued with feelings that he'd hardly known he felt. There was Mary-Ellen with her candid blue eyes first, sitting in the gallery she ran with Helen Bolton. He'd never seen her there, but he visualised her now, fat and placid, her hair as short as Helen's, running her hands over the curving belly of a vase while she discussed some detail of Chinese pottery with Helen. He saw her with the same sense of detachment, of remoteness, that he felt when he remembered his taipan days. He was indifferent to Mary-Ellen now, as if she were some distant figure from his childhood, as indifferent as he was to Emily with her wavy brown hair in Enfield. He saw Su-mei next, her head pillowed on her hands as she lay in bed, her body as firm as when he first knew her, only a little fuller, a little more ripe. In these past five years, they'd grown together, mellowed. There was less excitement but more peace between them—the only sharpness now in her jealous concern for her children, which sometimes made her cool towards Jenny and Alec. But then, with a little shock as though he'd unexpectedly stepped off a kerb, he felt that perhaps she too was becoming remote from him, that he no longer desired her so much, that their growing together was really only the pressure of habit, of no longer noticing each other, of taking for granted. And then he saw his whole life, his daily study, his business, his family, Jacob, everyone, as if they were slowly drifting away from him, or he from them, as if he could watch them detachedly, without emotion, as if he no longer really cared for them. He felt for a moment that he was numb to this life which they were the texture of, that it had become a life of habit and routine and was going stale.

The music stopped. The needle was scratching and crackling in the last groove. He watched the turntable turning more and more slowly as the spring ran down. It seemed an emblem of his life, still spinning on, but pointlessly, the music over. You're getting middle-aged, he told himself. That's what it is.

He started eating the peach, sucking the juice up as it ran down his chin when he bit into the melting flesh. The gramophone had run right down now, the record had stopped turning. His ankles were being bitten all over by mosquitoes. He got up, lifted the arm off the record, and set it back on its rest, then closed the shutters, lifting one leg after the other to scratch his ankles. Until now I've lived for one thing and the next thing, he thought. But now there aren't many next things left. Everything will be the same. I'm middle-aged. A quiet panic gripped him at the thought of all the years that might be left to live, years that would be playings and replayings of the same record till at last the machine ran down and stopped.

He turned off the fan and went out.

As he went down to the master bedroom he smelt the rich greasy scent of opium coming from the door. Su-mei lay on the hard mattress she'd insisted on having in place of the old soft, springy one. She was smoking, her oblique eyes half-lidded. "Are you angry with me?"

"Why?"

"For saying that about Lily?"

He shook his head, watching her knead a pellet for him. "What did Lily tell you? I heard you talking."

"She's been going to that Pulham woman's for three

482

months. She's like the other half-breeds," Su-mei went on dispassionately, her nostrils flaring at the scent of the new opium. "She wanted to be a European, that's why she wanted the European religion. But then the policeman said she looked like a Chink." She snorted. "So now she thinks she can't be a European, and she wants to be a Chinese after all—a Chink." She handed him the pipe as he lay down beside her.

"I don't think you'll ever believe it makes no difference to me that they're Eurasian, will you?"

She took the pipe after he'd inhaled. "It wouldn't be natural if it made no difference. I expect that's what you were thinking about up there in your study?"

"I was thinking about middle age."

He took the pipe from her hand and drew deeply on it. "I think we need a holiday," he said, the words seeming to speak themselves before he'd even thought them. "Let's take a trip to England. We ought to think about schools for the children anyway..."

"Even the half-breeds?" she asked drowsily, with a sly little smile at the corners of her lips.

Her body was loose and passive when he touched her. She might have been asleep, but for her smiling, parted lips, the slowly quickening panting of her breath and the sudden long moan she let out as she quivered beneath him.

As he floated away into sleep, he recalled the day he lost his seat on the Council. When the votes were all counted, and he'd heard he'd polled fewer votes than any of the other candidates—and the year before, he'd polled more—he'd left the town hall with a wry, defiant smile on his face, his head leaning forward reflectively, his overcoat collar turned up against the sharp winter wind. Well that's that, he'd thought as he strolled along. Perhaps I shouldn't have stood again after all.

Su-mei hadn't troubled to ask him the result. She'd been living with him for three months and the scandal was at its height. She'd followed him silently out onto the veranda, where he'd leant on the parapet surveying the ships lying at anchor in the wind-ruffled waters of the harbour. After some minutes, she'd put her hand hesitantly on his and looked up inquiringly into his eyes, with that faint ironic smile lurking round her lips. "Shall we celebrate with a pipe of opium?" she'd asked.

Now, as he remembered it, he smiled too. Or dreamt he did; for by then he'd fallen asleep.

He woke at the pressure of her hand on his shoulder. Simultaneously he head the noise downstairs.

"What is it?"

"Shh!"

They listened together. It was a lone man's voice singing or wailing monotonously, interrupted by other voices, men and women, as if calling out to the singer to stop, or perhaps to encourage him.

Denton looked at Su-mei's eyes, gleaming apprehensively in the dark. "Are they having a party downstairs or what?"

"Maybe it's robbers?"

He shook his head "Not making that kind of noise." He swung his legs out of bed, pulled on his dressing gown, and stepped carefully over the opium pipe. Turning the key quietly, he eased the door open. Now he could hear clearly—Ah King's voice, Ah Sam's, Ah Leng's, all clamouring and shouting. And the deep voice of Ah Lau, the driver, who had replaced Chan. But there were other voices too, men's voices that he didn't recognise. And above them all, like the screech of some bird trying desperately to escape its pursuers, the wailing shrieking wordless voice that he knew now was Ah Man's.

Oh god, something's happened to his son, he thought, and ran down the stairs. At the kitchen door he came upon Lily staring in, her face pale and rigid.

"What is it?" he asked, but she seemed not to hear him. He pushed past. Ah Man stood in the middle of the kitchen, wailing and shrieking inarticulately, the meat cleaver in his hand. There were tears running down his face and his lips were contorted and slobbery. On the floor was the wreckage of his bird cage, with the little grey bird inert beneath the smashed and twisted struts. Around him, like an audience, stood all the other servants shouting or calling to him while he swung the cleaver to and fro in front of him. Amongst the servants were two khaki-uniformed policemen, one a European inspector, the other a Chinese sergeant. Ah Man seemed to be staring straight at Denton, yet not to see him. Wordless, grunting moans came out of his twisted, dribbling mouth now, like the sounds Denton had heard mongol children make. Then suddenly he swung the cleaver high above his head.

The circle round him moved back, hushing suddenly. Ah Man ran to the kitchen table and brought the cleaver down with all his strength. Ah Sam let out a brief, stifled scream. The blade stuck in the wood, and, as Ah Man, shrieking gutturally, tried to wrench it out, the two policemen grabbed him, one on each arm. They dragged him away, wrestling clumsily with him. The inspector let go as Ah Man seemed to relax. He gripped the cleaver and yanked it out of the table. Ah Man, struggling free, ran at him, but the sergeant had his revolver out now and clubbed him twice on the head with the barrel. Ah Man collapsed soundlessly onto the floor. The sergeant clubbed him again.

"OK, that'll do," the inspector said unsteadily. He glanced at Denton, then back at Ah Man. "Better put some cuffs on him," he panted.

"What the hell is going on?" Denton asked faintly.

He glanced down at the sergeant, who was putting the handcuffs on Ah Man. Blood was trickling down the side of Ah Man's head, just in front of his ear. His eyes were closed and he was breathing heavily with an uneasy snorting sound in the back of his throat. One leg lay across his mangled birdcage. "What the hell's going on here?"

"Chap's gone a bit berserk," the inspector said, slowly recovering his breath. "As you can see. His son was killed in the riot this afternoon—yesterday afternoon, I should say," he added pedantically, glancing at his watch. "We just brought him back from the mortuary and he went off his head."

Denton looked at the ring of Chinese faces gazing from the inspector to him, trying to grasp what they were saying.

"And they say the Chinese are unemotional," the inspector went on, shaking his head resignedly. "He could've killed the bloody lot of 'em."

"You didn't have to keep hitting him like that, did you?" Denton said sourly, glancing at the sergeant.

"He could've killed the bloody lot of 'em," the inspector repeated emphatically. "What did you expect us to do?"

Ah Man stirred. His eyelids slowly opened and he looked up at them with a dull, uncomprehending light in his eyes. His mouth was open too, as if he still wanted to wail. But he made no sound. Blood was leaking faster through his hair now, dripping onto the floor.

Denton heard Su-mei's slippered feet behind him. "What happened to his son?" he asked. "How did he get...?"

"Stopped a bullet, I'm afraid," the inspector said crisply, as if he'd been saying *Stopped a taxi*. "Outside the Louza Police Station. No doubt you've heard about it?"

"It was his only son," Denton said sombrely, "Wasn't it, Ah King?"

Ah King stared at him and he had to repeat the question in Chinese. "Yes," she said. "Only son."

"Should've stayed out of trouble then," the inspector said, not unsympathetically, but as a matter of undeniable fact. He let his glance wander over Lily and Su-mei. "Is the lady of the house here, or...?" He raised his brows slightly at Su-mei with a sort of smirking delicacy.

"This is my wife," Denton said coldly.

"Indeed sir?" the inspector gave Su-mei an ironic fractional bow. "I'm afraid we'll have to cart this chap off to hospital, if you can spare him for a day or two. For observation. What does he do? Cookboy?"

Su-mei nodded.

"Ah, thought as much." A mildly smug tone of detectional pride entered his voice. "Hence the cleaver, eh? Spare him for a day or two, can you?"

There was something subtly different about the way he spoke to Su-mei. He sounded a shade more casual, a shade more familiar.

"What are you going to do with him?" Su-mei asked stiffly.

"Oh, just keep him under observation, see he's all right," the inspector said with a bland smile. "And ask him a few questions of course," he added as if as an after-thought. "My name's French, by the way. Inspector French."

He had turned to Denton as he introduced himself. Denton nodded, without giving his own name.

"Spare him for a day or two, can you?" the inspector went on more coolly.

Denton shrugged. "I suppose it doesn't make much difference whether we can spare him or not?"

"No, I s'pose not," the officer agreed equably. "We'll come back and ask the rest of your servants a few questions too, in the morning." He laid the cleaver down on the table. "If that's all right," he added perfunctorily, absently almost.

They hauled Ah Man up and dragged him out, his feet stumbling beneath him, tripping over the threshold.

"Are they going to put him in prison?" Ah King asked as the police van clattered away.

"No, of course they aren't," he answered impatiently, humiliated by his powerlessness before them and angry because of his humiliation. "They're taking him to hospital, that's all..." He said nothing about the police interrogating Ah Man, or about their returning to question the rest of them—perhaps they wouldn't come after all.

Lily was still standing in the doorway, her eyes wide and shadowed.

"Clean that mess up and throw the bird away before the cat gets it," he heard Su-mei say sharply.

He smiled at Lily and put his hand tentatively on her shoulder. She let it rest there, but her body was tense beneath it and he knew he was no comfort to her. He let his hand drop as Su-mei led her silently up the stairs.

63

"Now that your father's gone away with that woman," their mother said, "I'll be seeing more of you both. I'll be keeping an eye on you." She led the way through the rear of the gallery to the stairs that climbed steeply up to the flat above it. Jenny walking immediately behind her, nodded at her large hips heaving up and down in her baggy green trousers, and mimicked her silently to Alec.

"What're you grinning at?" their mother asked placidly, turning at the landing. But she went on before Jenny had time to make up an answer. "Don't forget to say 'Good afternoon' to Auntie Helen."

"Good afternoon," Jenny and Alec said.

Auntie Helen glanced round at them and smiled faintly. She was wearing trousers and a shirt too, combing her short, dark hair with slow, abstracted gestures. Her eyes looked small and red as though she'd been crying.

"How long are they staying?" Auntie Helen murmured, catching their mother's sleeve as she passed.

But their mother didn't answer, going through into

the kitchen. Auntie Helen gazed after her a moment and then went on combing her hair, staring listlessly at her face in the little hand mirror she'd propped up against a vase on the table in front of her. Occasionally she sighed, as though she didn't like what she saw.

Jenny and Alec sat down on the sofa, gazing uninterestedly round the long, untidy room. It seemed so crowded after their own home—vases, tables, chests, all jammed together higgledy-piggledy, scrolls hanging side by side on the walls or lying half-unfurled on the tables, the drawers of the chests half open... On the arm of the sofa beside Jenny lay a heap of clothes. She wondered if they belonged to the gallery, to their mother or to Auntie Helen. Gingerly she put out her hand and started feeling the cloth.

Their mother came from the kitchen, wiping the sweat off her forehead. "There's no ice again," she complained. Then, when Auntie Helen only looked at her dumbly, "And that blind still hasn't been fixed. The sun's streaming in there."

Auntie Helen's eyes dropped.

"It's impossible to stay in that kitchen in the afternoons," their mother went on irritably. "It's like an oven."

"Why do I get the blame for everything?" Auntie Helen whispered tearfully.

"*Now* what's the matter?" their mother asked in exasperation. "Nobody's blaming you—I was just pointing out..."

"Don't be impatient," Auntie Helen sniffed. "I've got a headache, that's all..."

Their mother sighed. "Not *another* headache?"

"I can't help it."

"Come here then," their mother said with a gruff sort of tenderness. "Let's have a look." She stepped behind Auntie Helen's chair and laid her hands on her neck, massaging it casually, with a firmly rippling movement that Jenny would never have imagined those large pale hands were capable of.

"Can I have a drink?" Alec asked.

"In a minute." Their mother bent over Auntie Helen's head as she stretched and curved her neck, her eyes closed, the lashes moist. 'I'll take them out," she said. "You can have a rest. I won't be long."

"Who'll look after the shop?"

Their mother shrugged. "Close it," she said carelessly. "Come on, children, where would you like to go?"

"The French Club," Alec said at once. "I want to swim in the pissin."

"Piscine," his mother said. "What are you giggling about Jenny? Is that how your father's woman says it? No, you can't go, you haven't got your swimming things with you..." She led the way downstairs. "Say 'goodbye' to Auntie Helen. I'll tell you what—we'll go to a café in Little Moscow."

Her car was parked by the kerb. She unlocked it and opened all the doors to let the trapped, steamy heat out before they got in. Jenny sniffed the smell of the hot leather seats. "Does Auntie Helen have a lot of headaches?" she asked.

"It's her time," her mother said casually. "Know what that is, I suppose?"

Jenny nodded quickly, but her eyes were vague. It was something the older girls whispered about in school, but she hadn't quite understood it yet.

"Come on, get in. It'll be cooler when we start driving."

The smell of exhaust smoke and heat was heavy in the air, rising slowly in humid layers. They looked up at the crowded tram that was passing them, clanking and grinding over the joins in the rails. The passengers, fanning their faces with their newspapers, stared blankly out through the open windows with dulled eyes, as though the heat had dazed their brains.

When the tram had lumbered past, their mother swung out into the traffic, driving down past Bubbling Well Police Station. The barbed wire and sandbags outside the walls had all been taken away now, and only a single constable stood on duty by the gate. "The riots are over," Alec announced importantly, funnelling the air in through the window with his hands.

"Yes, that's right," their mother said absently. "I think we'll go to Maxim's. Have you ever been there?"

Both children shook their heads, the heat forgotten as they gazed out at the French gendarmes, the French street signs, the French names over the shops.

She pulled in towards the kerb, nearly nudging a wheelbarrow over, and drove along slowly. "This is Little Moscow, here."

Jenny and Alec gazed out. The shop signs there were

longer and harder to read even than the French ones. And at the little restaurants and bars they saw something funny. Some of the waiters were white men—strange-looking white men with big moustaches and wide cheek-bones and dark brown eyes. And at the tables, shaded by striped awnings or wide umbrellas, Chinese men were sitting, giving orders to the white men. And the white men bowed and brought them the change and bowed again just like real waiters.

"Here we are, this'll do," their mother said, squeaking the tyres against the kerb. "No need to lock. We'll sit outside in the shade." She led them to a small round iron-legged table with a large umbrella above it tilted against the sun. An elderly Chinese in a dark western suit sat at the next table, with a tall blonde woman in a thin dress. Jenny saw his olive hairless hand brush the white woman's wrist.

Their mother dabbed her forehead with her handkerchief then tucked it away in her pocket. "Well, what d'you want?" she asked as a Russian in a white jacket greeted her, giving her the menu with a stiff little bow. "Lemonade? Cake?" The Russian had thick grey hair, brushed stiffly up from his temples, and a spiky waxed moustache. He smiled at Jenny with a faint lowering of his lids, almost as if he was winking.

"Two lemonades, a tea and some cakes please, Boris," their mother said. She glanced round at the nearby tables and shifted her chair slightly, further into the shade. "Well, how are your music lessons going, Jenny? Violin, isn't it?"

"Piano," Jenny said. "All right."

"It's Michael learns the violin," Alec said. "Jenny doesn't practise."

"I do!"

"What about you, Alec?" Their mother was still glancing round, as if looking for someone. "Aren't you learning anything?"

Alec shrugged. "Don't want to."

"Don't you?" she asked, surprised. "Who's your teacher, Jenny?"

"Mrs. Jackson."

"She smells," Alec said.

"Smells?"

Alec looked at her uncertainly, then risked it. "She farts in the lessons," he said baldly.

But their mother didn't seem to have heard. She was looking round the other tables again. "You ought to have a Russian teacher," she said abstractedly. "Tell your father I said you ought to have a Russian teacher. They're much better. And cheap too. You can get them for nothing."

The Russian waiter brought the cakes and drinks, placing them on the table with a little flourish, bowing to each of them in turn.

"Shall I tell you something about that man?" their mother said as the waiter left. "He used to be a colonel. In the Russian army." They looked round at his stiff, white-jacketed back. "There's a price on his head in Russia," she added, lowering her voice.

Alec tried to imagine the waiter in Russia with a price tag on top of his head. "Why?" he asked.

"Because he's a White Russian."

When she didn't say any more, he turned, still puzzled, to his lemonade, sucking it up through his straw with loud gurgling noises.

"How long's your father going to be gone for?" their mother asked abruptly. "Six months?"

"Five months now," Alec said. "Four months and three weeks."

"Didn't he want to take you with him? Leaving you here in all this heat while they . . . Thought you'd be in the way, I guess," she suggested, with a casually contemptuous little laugh that implied *she'd* never have done such a thing.

"He said we'd got to stay in school," Jenny said loyally. "He's taking us to Japan for Christmas. And Ah Lau takes us out on the boat."

Her mother's lips tightened. She took a slab of cake and pushed it into her mouth inattentively, so that it broke and fell onto her plate. Jenny, gazing under her brows at the lines in her face, decided she must be twenty years older than Su-mei.

"Why do you and Auntie Helen always wear trousers?" Alec asked.

"Just a minute," their mother said, pushing herself out of her chair. "I've got to say hello to someone over there."

"What were you looking at me like that for?" Alec asked Jenny.

"You shouldn't ask questions like that."

"Why not?"

"It's rude."

"Why?"

"It *is*, that's all. You'd have got into trouble if she'd heard you."

Alec tossed his head and wrinkled his nose in disbelief. But he wasn't sure enough of himself to challenge Jenny directly. Perhaps it was rude, like saying "pee." Which reminded him. "I've got to pee," he said.

Jenny didn't hear. She was watching her mother approach a tall woman with short fair hair dressed in a white blouse and black skirt. The woman smiled as her mother greeted her, and her eyes glistened. Her face, which had looked stern and almost hard, softened and warmed. Jenny watched with a fascinated sense of mystery and excitement as the two women talked.

"I've got to pee badly," Alec said.

"Well go and ask where it is."

He peered past her into the dark interior of the restaurant. "You ask," he said uncertainly.

"No. Why should I?"

Alec started squirming on his seat, his face going red.

"You shouldn't've drunk so much," Jenny said severely. "You should've gone before you left home."

"I *did*," he moaned.

"If you don't go now, you'll have to wait for hours and hours."

Alec peered again at the dark interior of the restaurant. In an agony of embarrassment and need he pushed back his chair.

But their mother was coming back to them, light seeping slowly from her eyes, her face setting in the memory of a smile.

"Alec's got to go," Jenny announced. "He's got to go badly."

"Oh god. Come on, then." She took his hand, then let it drop, propelling him in front of her between the tables.

Jenny glanced round her. The elderly Chinese was getting up. He slipped some notes into the woman's hand as he left, and a few seconds later she got up too, pausing at another table where two more young blonde women sat together over half-empty long glasses. How pretty they looked, Jenny thought, watching the way their slim, crossed legs, with high-heeled, ankle-strapped sandals, swung under the table. She tried to swing hers in the same way, proud that she'd crossed them already without thinking—and not because she wanted to pee, either.

Alec and their mother wound their way back between the tables. "Come along then," their mother said. "We'd better be going. I paid at the counter."

A beggar had stationed himself by the car. She dropped some coppers into his tin as she opened the door.

"You know that lady that was on the next table to us?" Jenny began with an obscure sense of daring. "Why did the man give her money when he went away?"

"That old Chinese? Did he?" Their mother pulled the starter. The motor coughed and gurgled. "Expect she was a tart." She pulled again, and this time the engine caught, rattling loudly under the bonnet. "A Russian tart. The place is full of them."

"What's a Russian tart?" Alec asked.

"A Russian tart?" Their mother laughed curtly. "Ask your father when he comes back. He'll know all right. Knows what Chinese tarts are, anyway. Does that woman of his still sing Shaohing opera by the way?"

"Yes." They glanced at each other. "Sometimes."

She grunted, grating the gears as the car jerked away from the kerb. "How d'you get on with her kids?" She glanced at Jenny in the mirror.

"All right," Jenny said blankly.

"All right," Alec echoed. "Michael's good at school."

"What about you? Damn! Missed the turning. We'll have to go along Siccawei Road, now. What about you, Alec?"

"I'm lazy," he said with a disparaging grin.

A hearse was coming the other way, just turning out of the road from the isolation hospital. It was a large black American car, with a polished barrel-shaped wooden coffin inside.

"Is there a dead body inside?" Alec wondered, craning out to watch it as long as he could.

"Probably taking it to the funeral parlour," their mother nodded, yawning suddenly. "What's happened to Ah Man by the way? Is he better?"

"He hardly ever talks any more," Jenny said.

"Never did talk much anyway, as far as I can recall."

"Cheong never says a word," Jenny said.

Their mother yawned widely again. "And your father's not exactly loquacious either. What a house of the dumb."

64

"It's funny," Denton said, gazing out through the taxi's rain-splashed windows at the glistening streets. "I keep expecting to see trams and horse cabs like the last time I was here, instead of taxis and those new trolley buses."

Su-mei was sitting in the other corner, wiping the mist off the window with the sleeve of her raincoat. "I wish I'd seen where you were born," she said.

"It makes me feel old," he went on, as if he hadn't heard her. But then he said, "They knocked it down soon after my mother went into the home. That makes me feel old too. I hardly recognised the road."

They listened to the wheels sizzling over the wet macadam.

The taxi turned into Bulsmore Lane. The houses where he'd seen Emily before the war were still there, but with a sad, dilapidated look about them, the woodwork shabby, roof-tiles missing, the gardens unkempt. He wasn't even sure now which one had been Emily's. He wondered idly whether she still lived there. And the fields where he'd scattered his father's ashes—they were all covered with little houses now, raw semi-detached villas with odd shaped windows and mock Tudor beams cemented into the upper storeys, each one the same as the next.

They watched the street slide past like a ribbon unwinding, the pavements dark and puddled. The driver accelerated with knocking engine past a red double-decker bus and a shuddering coal lorry, a coalman in the back sitting with a grimy black face under the shelter of an empty sack.

"'Ere we are, then," the driver called back through the glass partition. He drew up beside the grey stone walls of the churchyard.

Denton put up his umbrella. They walked through the gateway. He had to lift the gate slightly to prevent it dragging on the ground, and as he did so he realised that he'd done it from memory, before it had even begun to drag. It was the same gate, with the same curved rut worn in the gravel. Something had stayed the same then. And the church was the same too, of course. He gazed up at the spire and the gold figures on the clock. How many thousands of times he must have seen that clock, and how many more thousands must his mother.

Su-mei was wandering amongst the graves. He caught her up. "These are the older ones," he said, nodding at the worn lettering on the stones. "It'll be over there, further away."

The rain came down more heavily, drumming on the taut skin of his umbrella.

They found it in the far corner, a plain granite headstone. *Harriet Denton, Born 13th July 1848, Died 23rd October 1924*. It chilled him to see his own name on a gravestone. He imagined his mother lying still and straight under the shallow grassy mound, staring sightlessly up at the dark lid of the coffin.

"It isn't very big," Su-mei said, glancing round at the neighboring graves. "How much did you pay them?"

"She didn't want anything grand. It was in her will."

She shook her head uncomprehendingly. "There are no ancestors either. Only strangers near."

The rain drummed harder on the umbrella. Su-mei stepped closer to him. They watched the drops bounce off the headstone.

"Are there no special days for sweeping the graves and bringing flowers?" she asked.

"No special days, no. I could have brought some flowers, I suppose, but who would appreciate them? They'd only die and rot."

She shook her head again and gave a little shiver. "I want a Chinese burial when I die," she said.

He stood a little longer, trying to visualise his mother's face, to feel some touch of reverence. But all that came was the thought that he too would one day be like her.

65

Yin-hong had been waiting outside the door for more than half an hour now. His palms were clammy, his stomach kept churning loosely, and his lips were dry. He kept going over the ritual answers in his head, gazing down the narrow, dark stairway at the dazzling oblong of sunlight on the street below. He could just see the sandalled feet of the look-out on the pavement, one crossed over the other. He must be leaning against the wall, smoking probably, one hand on the hilt of his knife that would be concealed down the side of his trouser leg. Across the road, amongst the coolies by the rickshaw stand, the other fighters would be loitering—they too with their long, thin-bladed melon knives. He'd seen them lolling and squatting on the other side of the road as Chan led him to the stairway and gave the secret sign.

Suddenly the peephole slid open. He glanced at it nervously, seeing nothing but a faintly moving darkness, while he knew he was being carefully observed. He licked his lips and wiped his moist palms down his trousers, watching a large cockroach out of the corner of his eye as it crawled slowly across the stone step by his foot, its long slender feelers waving delicately in front of it. He could feel his heart thudding. Surely they'd call him in before—

The chain rattled and the door was abruptly swung open. He saw the roach scuttling back the way it had come as he blinked at the bright lights burning in the curtained, incense-filled room.

It was Chan, waiting to conduct him to the ceremony. Chan, with one sandal on, the other foot bare, and his trouser leg rolled up to the knee. He looked strange and sinister, as though he was limping. His face was still and hard as flint. He merely nodded faintly at Yin-hong to take his place by his side. Yin-hong's pulse thudded softly in his ears. The incense was heavy and thick, almost choking him and making him dizzy. At the same time it gave him a feeling of awe, of reverence, like the feeling he used to get at the Ching Ming Festival, when the family elders kowtowed before the ancestors' graves. But this was more solemn, more awesome. And in his awe he began to feel pride too, pride that he was going to be admitted to the triad, to the greatest society in China, the society which everyone feared and everyone obeyed. If only he got all the answers right! He began rehearsing them again in his head, his eyes beneath his lowered lids taking in the banners of the great leaders on each side, hanging still in

496

the smoke-heavy air, the yellow and green flags of the five tiger generals, the banner of Pock-mark Chen himself. He glimpsed the rice tub on the main altar, painted as red as the blood that would soon flow from his own arm when he took the oath. Every grain of rice in it stood for a member of the society, as many members as there were grains of rice. Chan led him on, his feet shuffling over the stone floor.

Now, as they drew nearer, the incense master chanted the first words of the ritual, the long pale scar where he'd long ago been slashed on his cheek seeming to twist his mouth to one side.

Chan paused, and Yin-hong went forward and knelt before the executioner. He closed his eyes and lowered his head. He heard the sword scrape lightly on the stone floor and the executioner's robes rustle as he moved and raised it over his bare neck. With one blow he could slice off his head. He shivered.

Then the sharp, heavy edge of the blade tapped the nape of his neck, cold and hard. He flinched in spite of himself.

"Which is harder," intoned the executioner, "The sword or your neck?"

"My neck is harder," he answered humbly, his voice sounding still and small in the silence of the room. He felt their eyes all turned towards him, intent and unblinking. His neck was harder, for not even death at the hands of the police could drag the society's secrets from him...

Afterwards Chan took him down the gloomy staircase, out into the blinding brilliance of the sunlight, and led him across the street to the melon stall. "Meet our new brother," he said to the men squatting and lounging there. And Yin-hong formally greeted each one in turn while Chan cut two slices from a melon and handed one to him. The stall-owner looked on unprotestingly, a narrow-shouldered old man with faded eyes, as Chan gave Yin-hong the knife as well. "It's good, it's sharp," Chan laughed at the old man. "Too dangerous for you, you might cut yourself with it."

The old man mumbled something inaudibly and sighed, shaking his head to himself as he propped up the awning over the stall with a bamboo pole.

"And this time we won't be paying for the melon slices," Chan went on loudly, for the subdued rickshaw coolies squatting a respectful distance away to hear. "We're celebrating, all right?"

They leant back together against the stall, sucking the melons and spitting the seeds out onto the dusty, rind-littered ground. Yin-hong ostentatiously tested the melon knife's edge against his finger, while the brothers nudged each other and laughed.

"See that scar on the incense-master's face, did you?" Chan asked Yin-hong, fingering his own smaller scar on his temple. "He got that when he was no older than you are now, fighting the Red Triangle. That was when Ching was their boss, before we did him in."

66

The headmaster's handshake was unenthusiastic, and he didn't trouble to shake hands with Su-mei at all. When Denton started talking, he looked down his nose out of the window, as though he found it tedious to have to listen.

"I suppose the preparatory schools in Shanghai *are* adequate, Mr. Denton?" he interrupted with a sceptical sniff as Denton described Michael's and Alec's education up till then. He drew his eyes reluctantly from the window. "Wouldn't it be better to send them home to an English school to prepare for the common entrance? We've never had Chinese—er, *half*-Chinese," he slid a sidelong glance at Su-mei—"half-Chinese boys in the school before. They may perhaps require a little time to get used to...to English ways?"

Denton wondered whether the hesitation before he said "English ways" had been to check himself from saying "civilised ways." He flushed slightly. "Only one of them is half-Chinese—Michael, that is, the younger one."

"But I understood...?" the headmaster's face was long and thin, with that peculiar English fairness that gave the skin, even in middle age, a clear bloom, as though it had always lived in the rain. He looked from one to the other of them now with an amused, puzzled smiled in his blue eyes, suggesting he'd caught them out in some trivial cheating. "I thought they were brothers?"

"Stepbrothers," Su-mei said coolly. "I am Michael's

mother, Alec belongs Mr. Denton's first wife. I am number two wife. He left the number one wife."

A deep blush rushed over the headmaster's face. Even his ears glowed. he looked down at the file on the desk in front of him. "Oh, I see," he said slowly.

"I'm divorced from my first wife," Denton added quickly, in case the headmaster had any doubts.

The headmaster raised his head and looked away out of the window once more. "They appear to have been born within a few months of each other," he said bleakly. "I hadn't noticed..." He was silent again. Denton imagined him counting the months between them, calculating the depth of this shameless couple's adulterous depravity. Then he took a deep breath and turned reluctantly back to them, putting duty before inclination with an obviously strenuous effort. "Does the...does your son—Michael—speak English well, Mrs. Denton? Forgive my asking, but your own English—well, it's very good for a *foreigner* of course, but..."

"They're both bilingual," Denton said brittly. The headmaster's tacit condemnation affected him despite his resentment of it. He was squirming inwardly, twiddling his hat diffidently on his knees. He could have bought the school up, and yet this patronising, moralistic upper-class Englishman could make him feel like a shabby sinner, could put him in his place, could return him in a couple of seconds to his origins as a mere factory-worker's son. Only because he'd divorced a white wife and married a yellow one, and fathered a child with both at almost the same time. "I think the schools in Shanghai are all right," he went on in a high, strained voice. "I mean, some of my friends' children have taken the common entrance from there quite successfully."

"Ah." The headmaster's cheeks had cooled. They seemed if anything clearer and paler now than before, as though he'd undergone some moral bloodletting. "Of course, I ought to warn you that our fees are likely to be considerably higher by the time..."

"That's of no consequence," Denton said, glancing at Su-mei's face. She was watching the headmaster with the alert, expressionless eyes of a cat crouched watchfully on the branch of a tree.

"Are you married, Mr. Walker?" she asked suddenly as they got up to go.

"Married?" His face flushed again. "No, madam. Nor am I divorced."

They crossed the quadrangle, passed under a low stone arch and came out onto the playing field, walking in silence to a wooden seat that was protected from the wind by the stone wall of the cathedral cloister. They sat down, glancing round at the uneven roofs and walls of the school buildings, at the mass of the cathedral rising behind them, at two boys in white flannels practising at the nets.

The sun was shining through a valley in the fleecy clouds, sending long shadows from the oak trees beside them across the grass. Denton watched a tall, dark-haired boy bowling. His lengthened shadow moved effortlessly before him as he loped up to the crease and delivered the ball with a lazy, graceful action, following it through down the pitch. The batsman hesitated, played forward, dabbed and missed. The ball knocked the off-stump out of the ground.

With all my money I'll never have the poise of that boy bowling like that, Denton thought ruefully. Would Michael and Alec get such assurance here? Smarting still from his interview with the headmaster, Denton wondered if anything else would compensate for it if they didn't. Perhaps Alec had it already. But Michael? His mixed birth was against him to start with, and then he seemed to have inherited his father's angular temperament as well.

"What is that game?" Su-mei asked, "Cricket?"

"Yes. They play it in Shanghai too. On the recreation ground. Haven't you seen them?"

She nodded. "Would Michael have to play it?—Michael and Alec?"

"Yes. Those two aren't playing actually, they're only practising."

"Did you play it?"

"Not like that." He watched the bowler running up again, again his lengthened shadow gliding effortlessly before him. "We didn't have a playing field like this, we never wore whites. We just played in the school yard at break. With a tennis ball. It wasn't a school for the sons of gentlemen."

A sudden gust of wind rustled the oak trees' leaves, billowed the nets and ruffled the bowler's hair. Denton noticed a few leaves sailing off the trees, scurrying over the grass before the wind. They were dying already, blood-red and rusty round the edges. Autumn was nearly there, though the sun still shone mellow and warm. He wanted to get up suddenly, to leave, to go back to the heat of Shanghai at once, to forget that warning of the coming grey, damp chill. But he didn't move. Instead: "Well?" he asked. "What d' you think of it? The school?"

She was quiet for some moments, and then she spoke as if making up her mind. "I would like Michael to go to it," she said in a firm, definite voice. "Otherwise he won't get far."

"What about Alec?"

She shrugged. "He won't have to fight so hard as Michael, will he? He won't have such a hard time?"

"No," he admitted, "I suppose he won't."

"But you'll send him anyway, won't you?"

"I suppose so. I'll have to ask..." As usual he avoided saying her name. "I'll have to ask his mother first. All the same, I don't like the school."

"Why not?"

"That headmaster for one thing—he certainly won't make Michael very comfortable."

"Comfort isn't the point. It will give him a start."

"Perhaps."

They got up to go.

"Are you sure we shouldn't arrange something for Lily?" he asked, as they walked out of the gates into the narrow streets of the town. "She could always go to the same school as Jenny."

"It isn't worth it. In two years she'll be finished with school. Besides, she wants to be Chinese."

"All the same, she should get the same chance as Michael."

"She's a girl," Su-mei said firmly. "What is the point? She'll only get married in the end, even if she is a half-breed. Now that she'll have money."

"How Chinese you are," he said drily, watching the women in a poky butcher's shop all turn to stare at her.

"How English you are," she answered tartly. "You don't see the difference between sons and daughters."

"Well, but suppose Michael hates it over here?"

"He can't afford to. He's a boy."

They walked on silently. The women in the butcher's shop were still staring at Su-mei, nudging each other and

501

muttering amongst themselves. The butcher, in a blue and white striped apron, was looking up too, a long knife poised in his hand. They'd stare at Michael like that, Denton thought, they'd call him a Chink at school and bully him. Would Alec side with him or against him?

They didn't speak again until they were waiting on the platform for the London train. Denton's mind had returned to Shanghai, to the sun and heat there now, to the house on the Bund, to the children and servants, and the smoke rising from the ships in the harbour, rising straight up under the breathless brazen bowl of the sky. "I wish we were going back to Shanghai now, don't you?" he said. "I feel I don't belong here."

67

"Want to know how babies are made?" Paula whispered as Miss Robinson came in. "Come to the gym after school. Ann's coming too."

Jenny glanced at the back of Ann's head in the second row from the front. Her hair was always neatly done into two stiff little braids, she was always putting her hand up when Miss Robinson asked questions, she never forgot her homework, and she always got good marks. Jenny frowned back at Paula dubiously as Miss Robinson gazed short-sightedly round the class, cleaning her large plain glasses on her handkerchief and panting slightly as she always did after climbing the stairs to their classroom.

"Ann?" Jenny whispered incredulously.

Paula nodded, raising her brows, and leant closer. "I found out from my big sister."

"Yes, Paula?" Miss Robinson asked in her brisk, mannish voice as she replaced her glasses, nudging them into place with a little rabbity wrinkle of her nose. "Do you have something to tell us?"

They slipped into the gym by the side door. The long windows had all been closed, and the sun, beating on the glass, made the air stifling. They opened them stealthily, then Jenny and Ann looked expectantly at Paula, who was nearly a year older than they were, and a head taller.

Paula glanced over her shoulder at the door. It was

still ajar. "Shut the door," she whispered. Her voice seemed to be muffled by the hot sultry air.

Ann pushed it shut. "Go on, then."

Paula beckoned them closer, glancing round at the door again. "Well, you know men have things?"

Ann gazed at her sceptically. "*What* things?"

"*Things!*"

"Yes," Jenny said. "What about them?"

"Well it gets all big and they stick it in you. A foot long it gets." She held her hands wide apart to show them.

Jenny and Ann glanced at each other mistrustfully, then at Paula.

"Is that all?" Jenny asked, disappointed.

"Where do they stick it in you then?" Ann's tone was sceptical. "How can they?"

"Here."

"Where?"

"Here. There's a hole."

"Where?"

Paula glanced round furtively, then raised her skirt, pulling out the elastic of her knickers. "In here," she whispered, pointing with her finger. "It goes all the way up into your tummy."

"How d'you know it's like that?" Jenny challenged.

"My big sister," Paula declared. "She goes to boarding school in England. I'm going next year too."

"So am I, the year after." Ann tossed her head, making her braids fly. "What's so special about that?"

"It's the most expensive girls school in the whole of England."

"I'm going soon too," Jenny said.

"When? Which one?"

"I don't know yet. My father's gone to arrange it."

"My sister says they play special games there," Paula said mysteriously. "At her school."

"What special games?" Jenny was thinking of something a foot long going into her.

There was a noise at the door. They looked round, startled. The door swung open and one of the cleaning amahs came in with a bucket of water and a mop. The three girls moved away from each other quickly.

"What are you doing here?" the amah asked, in Shanghainese, setting the bucket down and letting the handle clank against the side. She sloshed the mop in the bucket and lifted it out, watching the water run off with a peevish look on her face. "I've got to clean it up."

"We're just going," Jenny said.

Paula and Ann looked at Jenny inquiringly.

"She's got to clean," Jenny explained. "She wants us to go."

"Fancy knowing Chinese like that," Ann said, between envy and scorn. "It's no good in England, you have to learn French and Latin."

They walked out together, Paula in the middle, clinging to the shady side of Woosung Street, where the fruit hawkers had their stalls. Glancing at the pyramids of peaches, oranges and apples, Jenny recalled a memory that had lain near the surface of her mind for years.

"You know, when they put their things into you?" she turned to Paula reflectively.

"What about it?" Paula asked grandly.

"Do you have to be standing up or lying down?"

Paula considered. "They usually do it in bed," she answered indirectly, unwilling to commit herself too far. "Why?"

"Because I think I saw my father doing it once with .. with my new mother." She'd never said "new mother" before, but she couldn't get herself to say "stepmother." "Only she didn't have a baby afterwards," she conceded uncertainly.

"Your new mother's Chinese," Ann said, gazing at her unblinkingly. "That's why my mother won't let me play in your house."

Jenny flushed. Out of the corner of her eye she saw Yin-hong sitting on a stool at a tea-stall.

"She says Chinese are dirty," Ann went on primly. "We're never allowed to play with Chinese children in case we catch something."

"Not as dirty as you are," Jenny retorted mechanically, but without conviction. She saw Yin-hong starting to grin at her, then check himself and look stonily away. Beside him she thought she saw Chan, their old driver, but she wasn't sure. She too had begun to smile, and her hand had half-risen to wave. But now she looked away herself and let her hand fall.

"My father says the better-class ones are all right," Paula was saying magnanimously.

"Well, but look at the way they live," Ann objected,

tossing her head so that her braids flew stiffly out again. She turned her nose up disgustedly, nodding at the melon rinds, orange peel and pips scattered in the gutter. "That's why they're not allowed in the Public Gardens. And they're always spitting too. My mother says even the women spit. She says she doesn't know how your father could possibly marry one." Again she gazed with blank, unblinking directness straight into Jenny's eyes.

68

"Every time I have a Russian woman," Jacob said, gulping some vodka without apparently even troubling to taste it, "I think of the cossacks." He watched Denton toying idly with his glass, watched him with a flicker of concern in those tireless brown eyes of his that seemed to outlive the gradual aging of his face. "*That's* for the pogrom of eighty-nine, I think. And *that's* for the pogrom of ninety-five...Ah, I pay them back, I pay them back my friend, believe me." He swallowed again, glancing round the crowded tables of the Palace Hotel. "Not that they know anything about pogroms of course, these girls." He laid his hand on Denton's forearm and gripped it reassuringly, "They're far too young. But still, *I* remember, *I* remember all right..." He laughed, leaning back in his chair. "They all tell me they're princesses. Then I speak Russian with them and find out what they really are. Princesses, pouf!" He blew them symbolically away with his fingers. "But nice girls, some of them. They have souls. Not like Chinese women. You know what these Russian girls are thinking. But a Chinese—you look at her face on the pillow and it might just as well be a statue."

Denton's eyebrows rose faintly. "Su-mei's Chinese," he said drily.

"Oh, I don't mean Su-mei," Jacob absolved her with an airy wave and smoothed back his greying hair. "Not women like her. I mean the girls you have for a night. Sing-song—"

"Su-mei was a sing-song girl once."

"Ach, you know very well what I mean," he said unperturbed, tipping the bottle up to drain the last of the vodka into his glass. He drank and sighed, then leant

505

across the table to peer solicitously into Denton's downward-looking, abstracted eyes. "Your holiday doesn't seem to have done you much good?"

"No, I'm all right." Denton stirred and drank. "Bit of a loose end, that's all."

"Loose end?"

Denton brushed it aside with a shrug. "How's Sarah, by the way?"

"Sarah?" Jacob threw up his hands and gazed at the ceiling in a gesture of exasperated helplessness. "Unbearable. Hysterics every day. Fits, tears, moods, depressions—I can't think what's come over her, unless it's the menopause. Nothing to do now the children are all away, perhaps that's what it is. You know what Freud says about the menopause? The only cure is death . . ."

Denton only half-listened, turning his glass round and back, round and back on the swan-white table cloth. It was true, his holiday hadn't done him much good. Ever since he'd come back to Shanghai, despite the Christmas holiday in Japan, he'd felt more and more often that sense of futility that he'd first felt in his study the night of the Louza Police Station riot.

". . . She's always quarrelling with the servants," Jacob was complaining. "We can hardly keep them a couple of weeks. And she used to be so placid. That's why I married her—remember when you first met her? In here wasn't it? This very table for all I know. Remember how placid she was? You wouldn't believe it was the same woman . . ."

Well, you're middle-aged, that's all it is, Denton thought. Things are bound to go a bit stale.

"As long as you can enjoy a woman, though," Jacob gripped his arm fiercely. "As long as you can still enjoy *that*, life is all right, eh?" But then the enthusiastic light failed in his eyes. "Poor Sarah. She no longer interests me." His face crumpled all at once into the creases of its age as he sighed and shook his head sadly. "That's the real trouble with her. Yes, that's the real trouble all right. There's no use denying it."

Age was showing at last in Wei's face too. His hair hadn't turned grey yet—with Chinese that happened much later—but his pale cheeks had taken on a pinched, tired look. His brother had died some years before, and Wei carried on

506

alone as head of the family business, which now had branches in Hong Kong, Singapore and Kuala Lumpur. But Philip, fat and bustling, the father of two daughters and four plump, spoiled sons, was taking over more and more of the daily administration, leaving his father free for his third wife, his secret opium smoking, and his devious Kuo Min Tang politics.

Old Wei went everywhere in his American car now, and never stepped into a rickshaw or sedan chair except when he went into the old city to visit his third wife—in deference to Sun Yat-sen's monogamistic eccentricity, he'd long ago placed his concubines in separate establishments. There the streets were too narrow, and he would leave his car parked in the shade on *rue* Montaubon, walk with his bodyguards through the black stone arch into the Square of the Palanquins and step into a chair to take him down the Street of the Fans. The driver would doze in the car, a newspaper over his head. The bodyguards would flank the chair all the way, only dropping back when they met another chair going in the opposite direction.

It was outside an ivory-carver's shop in the Street of the Fans that Denton met Wei one day in April, when the spring sun was scorching its way through a barrage of heavy white clouds. Denton had come to buy some chessmen for Michael's birthday. He'd seen Wei's car parked on *rue* Montaubon, a troop of beggars waiting patiently beside it—lepers, swollen-headed children, limbless victims of the warlords' battles that had followed the death of Sun Yat-sen. So he wasn't surprised when he heard Wei's voice from a chair that was passing along the narrow flagstones behind him.

"What are you do' here?" Wei asked in English.

Denton held up the chessmen. "For Michael's birthday next week," he explained.

"How much did you pay?" Wei still spoke English, as if he didn't want the bearers or the body guards to understand, though that didn't stop them from looking on with the usual frank Chinese interest. "Too much," he shook his head regretfully. "You can get for less."

Denton smiled and shrugged. "How is your family?" he asked with the necessary politeness.

"Very well thank you. And yours? Have you time for tea? We can go to Woo Sing Ding." His eyes were glistening, the whites faintly bloodshot. Denton guessed he'd been smoking opium with third wife. He walked beside the chair across the zig-zag bridges that frustrated straight-flying evil spirits to the old tea house with its curling roofs. It stood on slender, crumbling stone stilts in the greenish waters of a neglected pond, its open windows seeming to stare at the reflection of its decaying elegance with blank surprise. Beggars followed and squatted outside the door, dulled eyes fixed on the steaming tea-pots, while the bodyguards lounged by the threshold.

"They say Chiang Kai-shek will take Hankow soon?" Denton said with an inquiring lift in his voice.

"He will take Shanghai before long," Wei said assuredly. He held his cup in both hands and drank with his usual slurping relish. "The northern armies will not figh'. They are all demoralise'. Their soldier' are deserting."

Denton nodded. The grey uniforms of the northern soldiers could be found everywhere in the fields these days, thrown away by deserters. The peasants were beginning to use them for scarecrows. He looked down at his jarmine tea, bubbles slowly bursting round the rim of the cup.

"If Chiang takes Shanghai," he asked cautiously, "what about the foreign settlements? There are a lot of foreign soldiers here now."

Wei's face, softened perhaps by the opium, smiled broadly, as it used to twenty years before when he drank mao tai with Denton after his Chinese lessons. His numerous gold teeth glistened amongst the few that were still his own. "He will not touch them," he said. "But they will have to change now at last. More Chinese on the Council, no more foreign control. Otherwise he can make many troubles for the foreigner'. As many Chinese member' as British member'," he added, as if to dispel any illusion.

"And the communists? I thought they were his allies? Won't they want him to get rid of the foreign settlement?"

"Bandits." Wei shook his head decisively. "They will not last. Today, Chiang use' them. Tomorrow—" he slid his hand across his throat, chuckling in an almost gloating way.

Denton looked away, a forced smile precarious on his lips. He'd never seen Wei like that before. He wondered if he'd had too much opium—it was though whatever had usually held Wei back had momentarily slackened, letting something cruel and fox-like appear. Do I really know him? he wondered.

As he was gazing uneasily at the doorway, through which the afternoon sun slanted long, bright, mote-filled beams, two figures suddenly appeared in it, dark against the brilliant light. The figures paused, then strolled in. They were northern soldiers, carrying rifles and bayonets. They swayed slightly as they walked.

Wei, sitting with his back to the door, hadn't noticed them. He leant forward to Denton confidentially, speaking Shanghainese now. "Chen—Pock-mark Chen—is a blood brother of Chiang Kai-shek. He doesn't want Shanghai disturbed. Between them they'll take care of the communists."

One of the soldiers kicked a chair over, and Wei glanced round.

The soldiers wandered towards their table, grinning slackly. Wei became suddenly very quiet, he seemed to shrivel in his skin. Denton's pulse quickened softly. The waiter, coming from the kitchen, stopped where he was, his eyes alert, yet with an obsequious cringing light in them.

Wei sat stiff and still. A muscle twitched spasmodically in his eyelid. Looking back at the soldiers, Denton realised they were drunk. He'd hardly ever seen a Chinese drunk before; it made the sight of these two suddenly more menacing. They stopped unsteadily by the table. One of them gazed at Denton with a crooked smile on his face, the other lifted the teapot lid, peered inside, then dropped it back in place with a little clink that sounded suddenly loud in the tense silence. They handled the cups and saucers in the same way, giggling slightly, their eyes bleary. One of them fingered the sleeve of Denton's jacket. He had his eyes on Denton's all the time, his other hand holding his rifle carefully on his shoulder, finger on the trigger. If I pull my arm away, Denton thought, he might shoot me. Wei's face was set in a rigid polite smile as the other soldier lowered his rifle till the bayonet was pointing at his heart.

"Communists, Kuo Min Tang," the soldier said in a thick northern accent. "We kill them."

Wei's eyes blinked behind his glasses. He stared past the soldier's head and licked his lips. His eyelid was still flickering. Where were the bodyguards? Denton thought wildly, then realised they'd never attack two soldiers. They

509

must have cleared off like the beggars, as soon as they saw them coming.

The man who'd been feeling his sleeve stood up now, an uncertain look passing over his eyes. He doesn't know whether to take the coat or not, Denton thought. He doesn't know whether to risk it. Because I'm a foreign devil. Then suddenly he knew what he had to do. "Waiter, some more tea please," he called out as casually as he could, turning his head slightly. "Two more cups for these gentlemen." He leant forward slowly and pushed a chair out for the uncertain soldier. "Please join us," he said pleasantly. "The tea's good here."

The man was still uncertain, but the waiter had bowed and hurried away, and gradually a relieved light appeared in the soldier's eyes, as though he was glad to have had the decision made for him. He sat down in the chair Denton had offered him, leaning his rifle against the table. After a pause, the other, less willingly, pulled out a chair for himself.

The waiter placed tea on the table, bowing and smiling obsequiously. The soldiers stretched out their legs and drank, sucking the tea up loudly and sighing. They seemed to have forgotten Wei and Denton now, grunting to each other in some northern dialect Denton couldn't follow. They were tall and heavy, with large faces—from the far north they must have been. They wore puttees, but no boots, their bare feet thrust incongruously into sandals. The waiter brought cakes as well, and the soldiers munched and swallowed them while the waiter hovered anxiously behind them. Wei seemed not to move at all, except for that flickering eyelid. His tea stayed undrunk and he gazed into the space between the two soldiers with a politely attentive smile fixed on his lips.

When they'd finished their tea and cakes, the two soldiers shoved back their chairs and got up. One of the chairs fell over. The waiter moved swiftly, apologetically, to pick it up. They sauntered slowly out, belching. Near the door was a small scroll. It couldn't have been worth much, but the soldier who'd threatened Wei yanked it down as he passed and began rolling it up. He stuffed it into his tunic and went on, the waiter ushering them both out with nervous bows, fear and grateful relief alternating in his eyes.

It was some time before the bodyguards showed up

again, with hangdog faces. They glanced remorsefully and apprehensively at Wei, but he acknowledged neither their absence nor their return. When he lifted his cup at last, his hand was trembling and he had to support it with the other hand as well. "They have been executing a lot of people over the past few days," he said, in Shanghainese now. His voice too was trembling. "Mostly political prisoners. They shoot them now. It's quicker. About two hundred yesterday, I heard, Kuo Min Tang or communists, they don't care... At first I thought those two had come to arrest me..."

He drove Denton home in his car. They didn't speak, but Wei kept licking his lips as if they were always too dry. His eyelid still ticked occasionally and there was no trace now of that gloating, vindictive smile Denton had seen just before the soldiers entered the tea house. Wei nodded a subdued, chastened farewell at the gate. "It was lucky you were there," he said slowly, as if it was hard for him to get the words out. "They didn't quite know what to do with a foreign devil. If we'd both been Chinese..." His lips puckered into a dry little smile.

A few weeks later, Denton stood in the crowded gallery of the Shanghai Stock Exchange, watching the shares drop minute by minute. There was hardly time for a price to be quoted before a still lower one was taking its place. People were jostling and shouting frantically on the floor, selling Jardine's, selling Swire, selling Bank, selling, selling, selling. He listened to the feverish hubbub and watched the prices falling, wondering when he should buy in.

A familiar grip on his arm. He turned round.

"There's a rumour Chiang Kai-shek has taken Hankow," Jacob said breathlessly. "It'll be Shanghai next—have you got rid of your shares?"

Denton nodded. "How much lower d'you think they'll go, though? I'm thinking of buying again soon."

"Buying?" Jacob stared at him astonished, the faintly yellowish whites of his eyes growing suddenly wider. "Are you serious? They may be fighting in the streets in six months!"

Denton tilted his head. "No, I think Chiang will leave us alone."

"Because of a couple of warships from Britain and

America and a few hundred soldiers? Pah! He's got German military advisers now. That's why he's winning. These western warships are just a bluff. Or to take off the refugees." He shook Denton's arm fiercely. "Buy gold! Remember what I told you in the war?. Was I right, eh? Buy gold!"

"I have gold."

"Well stay in it, it's going to shoot up."

Denton pressed his lips together and tilted his head again, as if to say I'll think about it. But he was thinking of Wei's opium-loosened tongue at the tea-house in the old city.

Half an hour before the end of the session, he placed several buy orders with his broker. He was to buy some shares now, and more later if the price went lower. The broker, a Eurasian with Parsee blood in him, laid his brown finger thoughtfully beside his long nose, raised his brows, then shrugged.

Denton walked home along the Bund, glancing at the dark and light grey colours of the western warships anchored in the river. Whatever the result, if Chiang attacked, his shares would be worthless; the city's industry would collapse. Not that he'd be ruined, he'd kept enough abroad to live on, he wouldn't make the same mistake twice. He wondered idly what had become of Mason, then thought of Wei's opium-shot eyes at the tea-house. Well in six months I'll be a lot richer or a lot poorer, he thought. I'm risking a lot on that single confidence of Wei's.

It made him feel light-headed. At least it took away that staleness he'd been feeling lately.

He started walking up the drive to the house, then suddenly paused. The front door was wide open, and two police cars were drawn up in front of it. He saw a policeman's khaki uniform inside the hall. He went on with a lurching sense of foreboding. He didn't quicken his steps, he wanted to prepare himself for whatever it was. A traffic accident he kept thinking, one of the children. He visualised a child spreadeagled on the road, a damaged car beside it, though which child it was he couldn't see, and yet still he climbed the steps at his normal steady pace. His eye even detachedly noticed the cracked lens on the headlamp of the nearest police car, and his mind equally detachedly wondered how he could notice a thing like that at such a moment, while all the time he was conscious of his legs mechanically carrying him on up the steps, of the moist smell of the freshly-watered earth in the flower pots, of an English police officer with shiny silver badges in his epaulettes turning towards him, of Su-mei coming down the hall behind the officer with a wild stare in her eyes. It's Lily or Michael then, he thought numbly.

The police officer was Everett. He held out his hand calmly, as if he was merely making a social call. "Long time no see."

"Yes." Denton took in his badges. Chief Superintendent. "What's the trouble?"

"Well, I'm afraid something's happened to your son Michael," he spoke slowly and deliberately, as though allowing time for each word to sink in.

"What is it? An accident?" The images flung through his mind again, only this time the spreadeagled child was Michael and he was definitely dead.

"No, not an accident exactly." Everett paused. "He's missing. In fact, he seems to have been kidnapped."

69

The dawn began to brighten a little gap between the door and the floor. Michael stopped crying. He watched the light strengthen and felt a hesitant glimmer of hope, as though the new day must bring something good just because it wasn't dark any more. As the little room grew lighter, he looked round it again, slowly sitting up on the quilt they'd thrown down for him in the corner. There was a window high up near the ceiling, with a grill of metal bars across it, going rusty at the ends. The window was closed, and an iron shutter had been fastened over it, so that the light seeped in only round the loose-fitting edges. Sometimes he heard steps going past, sandals slapping on concrete, and the low voices of men talking. And now there was the faint murmur of traffic too. It was comforting, that sound, it brought the world of roads and people and safety closer to him. High up in the opposite wall was another grill, but that one was windowless. As the daylight strengthened, he could see the grey-white cement of a blank wall beyond it, with many-armed rusty drain-pipes crawling down it, and a long black electric cable that swung shivering to and fro as though someone was shaking it gently from one of its unseen ends. He looked down at the rough concrete floor. In the corner was the bucket. "For you to piss and shit in," one of them had said, the one with long wispy hairs straggling from the large mole on his cheek. The sharp stale smell from the bucket was beginning to catch in his nostrils; there was no draught to take it away. He went to the bucket again, holding his breath while the bubbles frothed and foamed in it, then sat down on the quilt, his back against the wall. And suddenly he began to cry once more after all, because the bucket stank and he was frightened. Through his sobbing he heard the slap and slither of sandals outside the door again, and then men's voices. One sounded like the man with the wispy hairs. The voices rose as though they were arguing and then fell again. As he sat gazing anxiously at the door, wiping his eyes and sniffing, he remembered how it had all happened yesterday—the black car drawing up beside Ah Leng and him as they left the violin teacher's flat, the two men jumping out and grabbing him...He heard the violin case falling to the ground again as he was shoved in through the open door, he heard Ah Leng shouting and screaming, he heard the case splintering as the wheels lurched over it and the car sped away while they held him down on the back seat, his head covered with that same quilt that he was sitting on now, so that he could hardly breathe.

On the ceiling, a little bright green lizard flickered, stayed, then flickered again. He began watching it.

Everett assured them most kidnap cases were solved "one way or another" within forty-eight hours. They didn't ask what "one way or another" meant.

So "Michael is staying with friends," they lied to Jenny and Alec. Only Lily and the servants knew the truth. Ah Leng wallowed in her guilt in the servants' quarters, but the younger children didn't seem to notice. Su-mei told them the police cars had come because Mr. Everett was an old friend of their father's.

Everett had promised to keep it out of the press, but somebody talked. It was in the Chinese newspapers the next morning, and broadcast on the radio. So they had to tell the children after all. Jacob phoned, Wei phoned, offering helpless sympathy. Three reporters stood at the door all day.

The ransom note arrived on the second day with the morning delivery. It was in a plain, coarse envelope, so cheap that there were tiny slivers of wood pressed into the texture of the paper. It was addressed in Chinese to Mr. and Madam Denton, post-marked in Hongkew the previous evening. All the other letters were bill and accounts. As soon as Su-mei saw it, she knew. She handed it to Denton unopened. "Whatever they want we must give them," she said. He turned it over, weighed it in his hand then broke it open with his little finger. The flap tore jaggedly. A single flimsy sheet of paper was folded inside, with three sentences crudely printed on it in Chinese. *Your son will return unharmed when you have paid one million dollars. Await instructions. If you tell the police spies this, your son will get hurt.*

"Don't tell the police," Su-mei pleaded. She spoke calmly, but with a composure that was almost frightening, like a tightly coiled spring under enormous pressure. The children had just gone to school with a detective shadowing them. "Don't go to the police," Su-mei said again. They could hear Ah Leng still blaming herself in the kitchen.

Denton gazed down at the letter in his hands, wondering that his fingers weren't shaking, that they were holding it as they might have held any bill or letter. He laid it down on the table, imagining the hand that had written those simple characters, that had held the paper and folded it. What was the pen like that the man had used? Had Michael been there watching? Or was it a hoax, was he dead already?

Neither of them had slept until just before dawn for the past two nights. Then they had dozed off in broken fits of exhaustion.

"Don't go to the police," Su-mei said again.

He scraped back his chair. "It may be a hoax. Or they might be able to recognise the writing. We'll have to tell them."

Her lips tightened, but she said nothing as he dialled. He was through almost at once, as though Everett had been waiting for him to ring. "A note's come," he said, not even troubling to announce himself.

"I'm tied up at the moment," Everett's voice apologised

515

smoothly, as if Denton would understand he might have more important matters to deal with. "I'll send someone down to have a look at it. Don't touch it."

"I've touched it already!" Denton's voice rose. "You didn't tell me not to touch it! How could I know till I'd opened it?" He felt he'd ruined one of Michael's chances, and it was all Everett's fault.

"Never mind," Everett's voice sounded soothingly in his ear. "It doesn't really make much difference. Just don't touch it any more, all right? We'll be wanting to interview your servants later on, by the way. Don't let any of them leave, will you?"

Su-mei watched and listened while Denton spoke, her eyes on his.

"They're sending someone round to examine it."

She shook her head. "We shouldn't bring them in."

"They might get fingerprints or something."

"You trust the police too much."

"Would you rather trust the bastards who wrote that letter?"

Her voice rose. "If it's true, they can hurt Michael. What good will the police be then?"

"We don't even know if it *is* true. It's probably a hoax." His voice had risen too. He was afraid she might be right.

"Why should it be a hoax? That's how they do it, isn't it?"

A Chinese detective came at eleven, two hours later, when Denton was about to phone Everett again and ask what was happening. The detective was short and podgy, with stiff short hair, and wore braces over his open-necked shirt. He carried a small leather case in his hand.

"Mr. Denton, Missy Denton," he greeted them in a jolly, confident voice. "I am so sorry to hear your trouble. Do you remember me, Mr. Denton? Lolly Kwai, customs service? Now detective inspector. No more customs already long time."

Then Denton recognised him—the portly coxswain with the genial smile who'd been with him when Johnson was killed. "Yes, yes, of course," he said hastily, then pointed to the letter which was fluttering faintly under the slowly spinning fan above the table. Lolly Kwai had helped him make his first capture in the customs service, he was thinking. Perhaps it was a good omen? He'd begun to cling on to little irrational things like that already.

516

Lolly looked down at the letter, smiling and screwing up his eyes. He seemed to read it through several times, then turned to the envelope and scrutinised that. Looking up at last, he hooked his thumbs in his braces. "The man who write the letter is not the same as the man who write the cover," he asserted confidently. He opened his case and took out a white cloth, wrapping the letter and envelope carefully in it. "Now I take your finger prints please." He laid ink pads and sheets of paper on the table.

"Finger prints?" Su-mei asked suspiciously.

"To elimina'. We want to find the other one' finger-print', not your'. Maybe we have record of the finger-print', then we go and get the man."

It sounded so easy, so routine, that Denton felt a sudden lift of hope. "Do you think you will?" he asked, glancing across at Su-mei.

Lolly took his fingers and rolled them one by one onto the pad, then over the paper. "If they are stupid, we will,' he chuckled.

The hope sank. Denton gazed down dejectedly at the whorled inky lines on the paper.

"Now I take statemen' from the amah," Lolly said when he'd finished. "The amah who was with the boy. How long she work for you?"

"She couldn't have had anything to do with it," Su-mei said quickly in Shanghainese. "She brought him up. Besides, they took one the day it happened."

Lolly held up his hands. "I didn' say she do anything wrong," he protested with a cheery laugh, refusing to switch to Chinese as though he suspected Su-mei of casting a slur on his English. "But we must elimina', Missy Denton, we must elimina'. Maybe this time she say something differen'."

He gave them a damp cloth to wipe their fingers on.

All the time Michael was eating, pushing the rice into his mouth with his fingers, the one with the wispy hairs squatted against the other wall, whistling between his teeth. He didn't whistle a tune; just two notes, up and down, repeated again and again, as if he was calling a dog. Every now and then the whistling would pause, and his wide, dreamy eyes would glance at Michael measuringly, as though guessing his height or weight, or what he was thinking, perhaps. Then Michael would stop eating,

517

expecting the man to ask a question or tell him something. But each time the eyes would turn away ruminatively and he'd go on with his whistling.

It was hard to eat. The rice seemed to lie on a cold shelf in his chest that wouldn't let food go further down, however much he swallowed and tried to force it. When he'd eaten as much as he could, he put the bowl down beside him, careful not to drop any rice grains on his quilt. The man took out a long knife and began paring his nails with it, still whistling those same two notes. Michael looked up at the windowless grating where the lizard usually was. He'd come to rely on it as a sort of mascot. But it wasn't there just then.

"Miss your mum and dad?" the man asked. He was frowning down at his forefinger, watching the nail curl up under the slicing knife.

Michael nodded eagerly, hopefully. Perhaps they were going to let him go then?

The man saw the nod out of the corner of his eye. His brows rose faintly. He held his hand out at arm's length and examined the nails critically, admiring the cleanness of their shape, turning his head form one side to the other to get a better view. "Better write and tell them," he said slowly. "Tell them to leave the police out of it or you'll get hurt." He dragged a crumpled sheet of paper and a pencil stub out of his shirt pocket and passed them to Michael, nudging the bowl out of the way with his bare foot. The bowl juddered over the rough edges of the concrete, making a chinking sound, and a few grains of rice fell off. "Write in Chinese," he said. "Say 'I miss you. Leave the police out of it or I'll get hurt.' Got it?"

Michael felt queer writing to his parents like that. And the bit about getting hurt frightened him. But he tried to write as neatly as he could, as if his mother would be angry if the characters weren't tidy.

When he'd finished, the man took the paper, read it through and got up. As the door opened and a shaft of sunlight blazed in, Michael saw a face behind the man's shoulder, peering in round the edge of the door. He was astonished, it looked just like Yin-hong. But then the face slipped away.

"Yin-hong!" he called out with a leap of hope.

"Yin-hong?" the man asked casually, swinging the door shut. "Who's Yin-hong?" He was whistling through his teeth again as he turned the key in the lock. But soon afterwards Michael heard him talking angrily to someone, as if he was telling him off.

Su-mei beckoned Denton into the living room, away from Jenny and Alec, who were quarrelling peevishly over their breakfast. They could forget. Only Su-mei and he couldn't. Sometimes he wished it was all over, one way or the other, just to be free of this constant draining anxiety.

She held up a flimsy piece of paper with pencilled characters on it. "Look, this is his writing," she whispered. Her face quivered and for the first time since it began, he didn't know how many days ago now, she began to cry. "It was posted in Pootung. Each time it's a different postmark, look."

"I still think we ought to tell the police," he said slowly after he'd read it. He was thinking of Michael's hand holding the paper, gripping the pencil. Only a few hours ago he'd been touching this grubby bit of paper then. He was alive, he thought with a flicker of hope. At least it showed he was alive. he laid the paper down carefully, by the corner of the page only, on the arm of a chair. "It's the only way."

"What have they done so far?" she flared up in a fierce whisper so that the children wouldn't hear her. "What have they done? Taken our finger prints, that's all!"

He heard Alec yell, and then a crash as some plate or cup fell to the floor. Su-mei ran to the door and shouted at them in English "Keep quiet, can't you! You may not care what happen' to Michael, I know he's not English like you are, but I care! So shut up!"

Denton saw their startled faces staring up at her, then she'd slammed the door and was standing by it trembling violently, her hands covering her face. He put his arms round her, but she turned away, shaking her head. Then, after half a minute or so, she took a deep breath and was still again. When she looked at him, her eyes were still bitter. He felt as though something had torn that could never be repaired. There was silence in the dining room, then the sound of Ah King's voice.

"What else can we do, Su-mei?" he asked dully, trying to ignore her outburst. But she seemed suddenly to have become distant from him. We're not together any more, he thought desperately. It's driving us apart. "What else

519

can we do? It's the only way, isn't it? There may be finger-prints, I mean."

"It's not the only way, it's not!" She was whispering fiercely again, holding her clenched fists in front of her face and staring at them intently.

"It is! I'd raise the ransom money, but they never tell us when or where!"

"Because you keep going to the police!"

"How do *they* know?"

"How do they know? They've only got to look!"

He paused, made uncertain by her certainty. "In any case," he changed his ground, "suppose we did pay it and then they didn't...didn't let him go?" They both knew what happened to kidnap victims who weren't released. A Chinese millionaire had had his son posted back to him recently limb by limb, although he'd paid half the ransom. Half wasn't enough. He was too slow about the rest.

"Would we be any worse off?" she asked in a voice as unnaturally calm now as it had been fierce before. "Or do you want to save the money?"

"How *can* you say that?" He stared at her till her eyes shifted away. "If they tell us where to leave the money, the police can set a trap."

"And if they don't tell us? Because you keep going to the police? Or if the trap fails? What happens to Michael?"

He closed his eyes wearily. If only it was over one way or the other, before they were both destroyed. "Either way, it's a risk," he conceded hopelessly. "Calling the police in seems slightly less of a risk, that's all. We've been through this so many times, Su-mei. In the end, we're just in their hands, whatever we do."

"Why don't you ask Wei?"

"Wei?" he stared at her again. "What's he got to do with it?"

"He knows Pock-mark Chen."

"What if he does?"

She was speaking coolly now, as if she'd thought it all out beforehand. "Chen's got thousands of men in Shanghai, many more than the police. Nothing big happens here that the triads don't know about. He could find out where Michael is."

"Chen..." Denton repeated slowly. He thought of that day he ran into him at Wei's house, of Chen's grudge about the opium he'd got from Mason, of that fight they'd

520

had over Su-mei more than twenty years before. He had the sensation of something collapsing inside him, as though his heart had fallen in on itself. Was that why Michael had been kidnapped? Could Chen be behind it? He felt numbly afraid that he was, although he couldn't say why. And if he was, the police would indeed be powerless, as Su-mei kept saying. "Well, even if you're right," he said uneasily, not wanting to come out with his suspicion at once, "it wouldn't be much good. Chen wouldn't be likely to help us. Quite the reverse."

"Not even if Wei asked him?"

He shrugged. "How well does he know Chen?" he said, as if he had no idea himself.

"How well? Like lips and teeth, you know that. They're always doing each other favours..."

Denton nodded and considered. The rattle of crockery being swept into a pan next door brushed across the surface of his mind, the lost, precious world of normality, of everyday life with its trivial accidents so easily put right. And I was complaining about things going stale! he thought remorsefully. "I could ask Wei," he agreed at last. "But we'd still better tell the police about his letter."

Michael *lived* on the quilt now. He slept on it, he ate on it, he hugged it to him when he cried. His hand still clutched it when he stared up at the grey concrete wall beyond the grimy metal grill, at the rusty, crawling drain-pipes, the electric cable that was always quivering as though someone was tugging it, at the lizard that rippled over the ceiling and watched him with it two sharp little eyes. The quilt, with its rich greasy smell and stains, was his companion and comfort. It had begun to smell of him, of his tears and his unwashed body and unwashed clothes. He knew which side was uppermost even in the dark by letting his finger nails explore the seams. He had a special way of folding it when he slept. He knew the places where the filling had slipped down and made it too thin. He knew where it was torn and where one of the seams had opened, letting thin grey strands of the filling filter through. Often he tugged at the strands and drew them slowly out, rolling them into tight little balls between his finger and thumb.

So when they came in after all that talking and arguing or quarrelling outside, his fingers immediately gripped the quilt. He didn't like it when they both came in together, it made him more afraid. It was the same two men as always, the big one with the white scar on his temple and the dreamy-eyed one with the wispy hairs straggling from his cheek who usually brought him food. He'd always hoped to see Yin-hong again, but he never had, and by now he'd begun to wonder if he'd ever really seen him at all.

They closed the door and stood looking at him queerly with that measuring expression that the dreamy-eyed one often had when he watched him eat. The big one had one arm behind his back. The dreamy-eyed one started whistling again, those same two notes, and then they moved slowly towards him.

Michael knew they were going to hurt him. He shrank back into the corner, both hands clutching the quilt now, his heart pounding violently in his chest. "Please don't hurt me," he started to plead, but before he could get the words out they had suddenly grabbed him. He didn't struggle until he saw the meat cleaver in the big one's hand as he took it from behind his back. Not a shiny cleaver like Ah Man used, but a dull grey one, the blade pocked and pitted. Then he shrieked and fought and squirmed against them frantically. The dreamy-eyed one had both arms round him and the big one held his right arm, but Michael kicked and pulled so wildly that the big one had to drop the cleaver to clamp his legs together with both arms. "We'll have to fucking tie him," the big one panted, matter-of-factly, not seeming angry at all. "Otherwise I'll take his fucking hand off."

"In my pocket," the other one gasped. "I'll hold him down."

Michael felt his straggly hairs against his cheek, as the dreamy-eyed one lay on top of him, his garlic breath hot on his face. "Fuck you, stop fighting or we'll chop your head off," he grunted, chuckling good-humouredly as the big one sat on his legs and started tying his flailing ankles. Despite the frenzy of his fear, Michael felt a little tremor of hope in their easy-going casualness. It was almost like being bullied at school, when you knew they were only doing it for fun and they wouldn't really hurt you. The two men wouldn't be so good-tempered if they really meant to hurt him—you had to be angry for that. Perhaps they were only pretending, he hoped wildly. Or perhaps

522

they *were* going to hurt him but not badly—just enough to make him cry. Yes, it was probably only a game after all, because the dreamy-eyed one had laughed when he said that about chopping his head off. He'd start crying at once, so they'd think they'd hurt him already. But his body struggled just the same, whatever his mind dared hope.

Yet once his legs were tied and they could both hold his arms, he stopped struggling altogether, except for occasional little twitches like a dying fish flapping on the stones. He let them bind one arm to his side, watching with helpless detachment. The dreamy-eyed one was whistling again. "That's better," he said, patting Michael approvingly on the shoulder. "We're just going to send your ma and pa a little present. A keepsake, like."

It wasn't till they rolled him on his stomach, his face buried in the quilt so that he could hardly breathe, that he remembered the cleaver. He heard the blade scrape on the rough surface of the floor while they held his free arm out. Then suddenly he knew they were not pretending. They really were going to hurt him as they'd kept saying they would if his father didn't stop telling the police. He screamed again, a sobbing high-pitched scream, trying weakly to pull his arm away. But the dreamy-eyed one sat on his shoulder while the big one knelt on his forearm so that he shrieked with pain now, his bound legs flapping uselessly while the big one curled his fingers up into a fist, all except the little finger, which he stretched out flat along the floor.

"Need three people for this," the dreamy-eyed one muttered. "Two's not enough really..."

"Hold the little fucker still, can't you?" the big one grunted.

"Don't take too little off, they've got to know where it came from."

Michael screwed his eyes shut while they argued. He kept seeing the image of his crushed violin case, hearing the sound of the wood cracking and splintering, the image dissolving into one of his finger crunching and splintering in the same way. "Please don't, please don't," he sobbed and moaned. But his voice was too choked for them to hear, and the more clearly he tried to call out to them, the more he seemed to choke. It was like a nightmare.

"You think you can do it any better, you can fucking try," the big one muttered.

"I told you we needed three."

"Three, fuck your mother!"

"Go on! One good chop'll do it."

"Take *my* fucking finger with it, too!"

Michael made a desperate attempt to curl his finger back so they couldn't get at it, but the big one pressed it down so hard against the floor that he couldn't move it for the pain. All he could do now was sob and flinch in anticipation.

Suddenly, "Got it!" the big one grunted, and at the same time there was a grinding, excruciating blow on his finger, as if someone had jumped on it with metal heels. He shrieked and leapt with agony, but almost at once the blow came again, that crushing grinding pain.

He heard himself shriek and shriek, yet now it was as though it wasn't himself but someone else screaming through his throat. The two men's voices sounded again, from far away it seemed now, and they were getting off him, untying him. "Why did you go to the police, why did you go to the police?" he kept moaning to his absent father between the electric waves of pain that made him scream out wordlessly. Then their voices seemed to go further away, and everything turned grey and dizzy before his eyes. He sighed with unspeakable relief and gratitude that soon he wouldn't feel the pain any more. The fingers of his uninjured hand scrabbled and clutched at the folds of his quilt.

Denton didn't have to go to Wei. Wei came to him that morning. Denton saw his shiny black car draw up, saw him climb a little stiffly out, saw him walk past the policeman, past the cameraman and reporters who were still hanging about for news. He'd phoned them often in the first ten days, but then less frequently, as if it was slipping out of his mind. Unlike Jacob and Sarah, Denton thought with resentment; they still phoned or came every day, even though Sarah's weepy sympathy and Jacob's torrents of advice were equally useless. Yet he'd probably saved Wei's life when those northern soldiers approached them at the tea-house!

So Denton met him with some reserve. Su-mei had gone touring the back streets of Hongkew and Pootung, showing pictures of Michael in shops and rooming houses, despite Lolly's assurance it could do no good. "Whoever keep him, Missy Denton,"—he insisted on speaking English still, "keep him hide away. Nobody see!"

"I was coming to see you," Denton said abruptly. "Su-mei thinks Pock-mark Chen might be able to help?"

Wei frowned through his glasses, his eyelids puckering as though it hurt him to think. "You wouldn't be making a mistake if you asked him to help," he said circumspectly, almost guiltily, his eyes sliding off whenever they met Denton's. "But you must remember he has lost face because of you in the past." He perched on the edge of the chair like a wary sparrow.

"Could he help?" Denton asked bluntly. "If he wanted to?"

Wei's tongue flickered round his lips. "I think it is more a question of whether he...whether he could be *persuaded* to help." He gave a bleak little smile that left the rest of his face unchanged. "After all, he knows many people. Perhaps he would get them to find things out...if you asked him."

He was holding something back, Denton thought. There was something he didn't want to say. The thought hovered on the dim edge of his mind while he went on hesitantly, with a note of pleading in his voice. "Su-mei said—we were wondering whether you'd be able to speak to him for me?"

Wei smiled almost gently, as though it hurt him to say it. "I have spoken to him," he lifted his hands to display his helplessness. "I'm afraid it is best if you go to see him yourself."

"Don't you see?" Su-mei said at once when he told her. "Of course, it's Chen behind the whole thing! He was sending a message through Wei. Twice you made him lose face and he couldn't do anything about it, because you were too important then, or he wasn't strong enough. But now you're not a taipan any more, you're not on the Council, the foreign devils don't like you, they won't make a fuss about what happens to you now. So he can get back at you."

He stared at her, remembering his own suspicions of a few days before, which he'd kept hidden from her. She seemed to confirm it now—she'd even used the same words. "I thought of that a couple of days ago," he said slowly. "But after all these years! And he's so powerful! What could it matter to him now?"

"It would matter to me," she gazed at him with level,

525

hard eyes. "Of course it matters to him. He's sitting there waiting for you to come and beg him—"

"Beg him for what? Do you mean to say he's going to tell me he kidnapped Michael and would I please pay him the ransom?"

"Don't be so stupid. He's allowed it to happen, that's all. And he can make it stop. But you have to beg him first. You have to give him face."

Denton stared down at the floor, his eyes tracing the pattern in the Persian carpet that Mary-Ellen had bought years ago. "That's what Wei was trying to tell me, then?" he asked. "After twenty years Chen still wants to settle a score with me? That's what he was telling me really?"

"With both of us," Su-mei said. "Twenty-four years."

"Twenty-four years" Lily heard her mother saying as she opened the door. She went in, her heart beating uneasily. They looked round at her. Her mother's eyes seemed to have got smaller and brighter, as if she was feverish.

"This parcel just came," she said, holding the little brown paper package uncertainly.

"Came?" Denton repeated nervously. "How?"

"The postman."

"Oh." As Denton took it from her, he felt his stomach curdle. It was coarse paper, tied with rattan. The address had been written in crude characters like the characters on the ransom notes. The black ink had smudged at the end as though it had been done in a hurry. This time it was yet another postmark—Chapei.

They've never sent a parcel before, he thought, trying to calm himself. Perhaps it isn't from them, perhaps it's something else. He watched his fingers carefully loosening the knots.

"Lily, go and see what Jenny and Alec are doing," Su-mei said tensely.

"They're in the garden—"

"Go and see! And shut the door."

Denton waited till the door had closed before he went on undoing the parcel. "It's the same writing," he muttered unevenly. "Isn't it?"

Su-mei didn't reply.

Lily had passed through the kitchen and reached the garden when she heard her mother's short, loud cry, as if someone had stabbed her.

*   *   *

He went there in the car, a quaking sensation running through his limbs, his stomach relentlessly turning and turning. *"Mos' please' to see you,"* Chen's voice had sounded coolly in his ear when at last, after three hours, the secretary had put his call through. *"I do not see your pony race recently. Is he well?"* Denton kept glancing at his reflection in the driver's mirror, his drawn cheeks, his worn, shadowed eyes, the grey in his hair that he'd never noticed before. Could it have come in those two weeks alone? Lau's eyes strayed to the mirror, met Denton's and shifted apologetically away again, as if he'd been caught spying.

Some blind musicians were playing by the tram terminus on Maloo, their blank, sightless eyes raised as though they saw some inward vision while they played their two stringed violins and sang their plangent songs. A boy stood on the pavement beside them, shaking a tin. He was about Michael's age. The car had stopped while a throng of passengers crowded across the road and pushed their way into a waiting tram. Denton's glance wandered to the boy's hands clasping the dented tin. He found himself involuntarily gazing at the fingers. A tremor shook his throat at the memory of the bloody mess of skin and bone, so irretrievably dead, that had lain on the table in the nest of bamboo shavings when he unwrapped the parcel. It must have still been bleeding when they packed it, there was blood on the shavings. He shook his head violently, closing his eyes. And yet, when he first saw it was a finger, he'd felt a moment's relief that it was nothing more—not an ear or a whole hand. Feeling for some change in his pocket, he beckoned the boy closer. The coins rattled in the tin, the boy gave something between a nod and a bow, and, as the car drew smoothly away Denton was left with the image of the perfect set of fingers, however dirty, closing round the tin. The violin's wailing tones and the singers' plaintive voices faded into the clamour of the traffic. He leant back, closing his eyes once more. *"If you wish us to leave the case alone,"* Everett had said, *"of course we will do so. But remember if you do meet their demands, there's no guarantee they'll turn him loose."* He'd spoken a little stiffly, as if his competence was being doubted.

"D'you think we haven't thought of all that?" Denton murmured to himself. He opened his eyes to see Lau glancing inquiringly in the mirror again. "No nothing," he waved his hand. "Keep going."

Two men dressed in western clothes halted the car outside the thick wooden gates of Pock-mark Chen's house. They peered in through the windows of the car before swinging the gates open and motioning Lau to drive in. It was like the portcullis to a castle, except that the house lying behind it was modern and ugly. Denton heard the two men chuckling to each other as the car passed them, glancing at them again, and he knew they were chuckling at him. Were they the same pair that he'd seen at Wei's years ago? He didn't care, he was beyond worrying about humiliation now.

He got out as soon as the car drew up at the ornate and garish porch. "Wait in the shade," he said in a low, heavy voice. Lau's lips pressed together and he looked apprehensively over his shoulder as he nodded.

At the porch another man scrutinised him with pebbly eyes before calling to a servant, who led him wordlessly along tiled corridors, through a courtyard with a pond in it, where goldfish flickered beneath the flat broad leaves of water lilies, into a small inner room. Four deep western-style armchairs, with antimacassars on their backs, were arranged round a glass-topped table, on which heavy, dragon-shaped ashtrays stood. It was like the ante-room to any Chinese businessman's office, solid and dull. The servant gestured casually to the chairs and left him. He sat down. The sun was shining through an open window onto his face, but he lacked the will to change to another chair. He tried to concentrate his mind on what he was going to say, but it was paralysed, as his body was sometimes paralysed in a nightmare. He sat there like a sack, the sun burning his face, his stomach quivering faintly, the image of that mangled finger in his eyes. His face began to sweat after a little while, but still he couldn't get himself to move.

After some minutes he heard short, quick footsteps clacking on the tiled floor. He looked up. A young girl walked past, dressed in a red cheong-sam slit to her thigh. Her cheeks were rouged as Su-mei used to paint hers, and her hair, pulled back and piled high on her head, was held with an enormous golden pin. Her face turned slightly as she glanced indifferently towards him. They were insolent eyes in an oval face of regular, mindless beauty. But her insolence looked like a pretence, as though she was really only a young girl trying hard to act beyond her age. Her face seemed familiar—perhaps she was one of the many film stars of the Shanghai studios. She glanced away when their eyes met, and he listened to the clack-clack of her heels receding down the corridor. Looking down at his lap, he realised with a start that he was stroking the little finger of his left hand—the finger Michael had lost.

At last the servant came back in his soft cloth shoes, and motioned Denton to follow him. Another bodyguard lolling in a chair eyed him cursorily and spat into a spittoon as the servant opened a large wooden door and led him in. It was only as he advanced towards the vast squat figure seated at a desk at the end of the room that Denton realised in the remote back of his mind that none of the rooms he'd passed through had any decoration. No books, no scrolls, no ornaments of any kind except those vulgar ashtrays. Nor had this room. For all the tasteless opulence of the architecture, the whole mansion had a bare unfinished look about it, as though Chen had just moved in, or was just going to move out. And yet he'd lived there for years, guarded by his private army.

Chen didn't get up, but waved Denton to the seat before the desk. He was drinking green tea. The servant looked at him inquiringly before, at his nod, pouring a cup for Denton. It was a western cup, with an ostentatious gold-stemmed rose pattern on it.

Chen made a deliberate show of reading some document through to the end before raising his heavy moon-face. His bulging, unblinking eyes regarded Denton coldly. "Your family are all well Mr. Denton?" he asked in a voice that seemed to rise from his chest, wheezing its way up through clogging barriers of catarrh. Again he spoke English, as if to suggest that Denton's Shanghainese wasn't good enough.

"I've come about...about my son Michael," Denton began at once, scarcely marking the insult of Chen's feigned ignorance. He fixed his eyes on the grey silk tie beneath the rolling bulge of Chen's double chin, a bulge that almost obscured the collar. He couldn't bring himself to look at those toad-like eyes. The knot on the tie helped him to focus his thoughts.

Chen had turned his head slightly to one side as

529

Denton spoke. "Your son?" he repeated, raising his scanty eyebrows.

"The one who's been kidnapped."

"Kidnap'?" The scant brows rose again. "Your son has been kidnap'?"

"It was all in the papers." Denton's voice hardened slightly. He glanced with a brief challenge at Chen's blank, unwinking eyes.

Chen stared back impassively till Denton looked down again. "I am afrai' my poor English...I do not rea' the English paper'."

"It was in the Chinese papers too. And on the wireless," Denton said dully, pressing the resentment out of his voice.

"Yes?" Chen didn't bother to pretend concern or interest any more. "Sometimes I am too busy to rea' paper' or even hear wireless..." He sipped his tea, putting the cup down with a little clink. "Except importan' news. You are not drink? You do not like the tea?"

"No, it's very good tea." Denton forced himself to sip it. It was very bitter.

"I always drink. For the hot weather." Again he wheezed as he spoke. Denton visualised his voice struggling up from the cavern of his chest through clinging webs of mucus. Chen turned slowly back to Denton. "Your boy, he has come back now?"

"No," Denton's voice shook and he had to breathe in deeply, looking down from Chen's massive, unconcerned yet taunting face to the knot in his grey tie again. "They keep sending notes, but they don't say how to pay it. And because I..." His voice wobbled. He clenched his fist with the effort to steady it, then swallowed, went on in a rush, "Because I went to the police they cut off half his little finger..." He gazed at the tie moving up and down on Chen's cream silk shirt as the wheezing bellows in his vast chest breathed. "So I've stopped the police. I've come to ask if you could possibly...if you'd be good enough to help me?"

He'd got it out, his abject plea. But he couldn't force himself to look at Chen's face. He gazed only at the grey tie and the silk shirt stirring together as the mound of flesh beneath heaved and subsided. He saw Chen's hand raise his cup. The hand was heavy and short, the bands of two gold rings and one jade embedded in its fleshy fingers. More than twenty years ago that hand had struck Su-mei. He heard Chen suck the tea up, heard a wheezing sigh of satisfaction and saw the cup lowered again.

"Well, Mr. Denton..." Chen's chair creaked as he ponderously shifted his bulk, and Denton momentarily imagined that bulk lying naked on the slim young girl he'd seen outside, crushing her in a slobbering embrace. "I don't know how I can help—particularly as you are not qui' helpful to me in the past."

"I'm willing—I'd be pleased to settle that other matter now if you like," Denton said quickly, looking up at last. "If you'd be kind enough to help about my son." He cringed at his abasement, but only faintly.

"We Shinese like to settle our debt'," Chen gazed at him with that same hard, unblinking stare, his chesty voice sternly censorious. "Otherwise, how can there be trus'?"

"I paid half a million dollars for that opium," Denton said appeasingly. "If you feel Mason had no right—it belonged to you, I mean—I'd be willing to repay..." The image of Mason's sagging, unshaven face scudded over the surface of his mind while he spoke. "I'm very sorry there has been this misunderstanding," he said meekly.

"It is worth one million, I think," Chen said with heavy emphasis, his eyelids drooping slowly. "Half a million is not enough."

The room was still for some seconds while Chen's eyes held Denton's, challenging him to question the amount. It was so still it felt for a moment as if they were in a glass jar sealed off from the world, a jar that would shatter if they weren't careful. A million dollars, Denton thought, that's just what the ransom note asked for. He looked down, nodding faintly. His pony was worth something, he could sell some property—if only he hadn't bought shares a few weeks ago, he'd have more cash now. But he could raise the money. "If we settled this matter satisfactorily," he asked in a slow, dull voice, the voice of surrender, "Do you think you might be able to help me?"

The bulging eyes glimmered with the merest hint of light. "I have some friend' who sometime' hear about things," Chen said off-handedly. "I do not know if they can find anything..." He shrugged his mountainous shoulders, as though whether they did or not, it would mean little to him. "Perhaps I will ask them..."

531

"I would be terribly grateful," Denton murmured humbly.

"When we have a settle' this other matter," Pock-mark Chen reminded him. He raised his cup again. "When one thing finish', can do the next." His meagre eyebrows drew together as he sucked up some more tea. "You are not drink? The tea is no' good?"

"No, no, it's very good," Denton declared tamely. Submissively he raised his cup.

It took him two days to raise the money. Jacob lent him a quarter of a million and Wei lent more. The bank lent the rest on the security of his house and his overseas stocks—the credit manager politely turned up his nose at his Shanghai shares. He could sell his champion pony, his shares, his gold later, to repay the loan. Jacob and Wei refused to hear of collateral when he offered it—Jacob as though he was insulted by the suggestion, Wei with a quick, embarrassed shake of the head. Wei still avoided Denton's eyes as if he was hiding something from him. But "It is because he is ashame' for you," Su-mei said. "You have lost so much face he does not want to embarrass you by looking at you."

The money was paid to an account off-handedly designated by one of Pock-mark Chen's secretaries. Denton and Su-mei waited by the phone the next day.

Nothing happened.

In the afternoon, Denton phoned Pock-mark Chen and got no further than the same secretary. Yes, the money had been received. No, Mr. Chen was too busy to call.

The next day Mr. Chen was out. The day after he was unavailable. There was no sign of Michael, no note.

"Let's bring the police in again," Denton said tensely. He felt a silent terror crawling through his veins. He dreaded the postman's knock, in case he brought a parcel.

Su-mei wavered, then shook her head. "A little longer," she muttered tight-lipped.

"How long? A day? A week?"

She didn't answer.

He's dead, Denton thought. The words were like lead in his brain. He's dead and we've been cheated.

"Perhaps I should go and see Pock-mark Chen?" Su-mei said wearily an hour later.

"What good would *that* do?" He exploded. "He just wants to keep us dangling on a thread! Probably Michael's already—" He bit the word off just in time.

"Don't ever say that!" she hissed fiercely, glaring at him. "Don't ever *say* it!"

A few minutes later he said quietly, "We'll have to think it, though—Where are you going?"

"Chapei. To ask people again. Someone must have seen him."

"I'll stay by the phone," he said hopelessly.

"What's the matter?" the one with the wispy hairs said, squatting down in the corner.

"Off your chow? Finger doesn't hurt any more does it?"

Michael shook his head briefly, pressing back his tears. The lizard had died. He found it lying on the floor when he woke up. By the time they brought his food, it was beginning to smell. "I want to go home," he murmured unsteadily for the hundredth time. Somehow he'd thought the lizard would bring him luck. He'd imagined they might even go home together when it was all over, although he knew lizards' tails dropped off if you tried to catch them. But now the lizard was dead and the thudding of his heart seemed to be telling him he might never go home after all.

The man had taken out an orange and was peeling it with that wicked long-bladed knife he always carried. "Perhaps they've forgot you at home," he chuckled, tilting his head as he watched the long coil of peel snaking down from his deftly moving blade. "Maybe we should send 'em another reminder, eh?"

He slit the orange and threw half across to Michael. "Try that, it's a sweet one. You can tell by the way it peels."

Su-mei went to Chapei by taxi. She didn't tour the slums where Michael might be hidden though. She went to Wei's house. After talking with Wei for half an hour she made a phone call. She was pale when she came home. Denton saw there was no point in asking her if she'd had any luck. She said she'd go again the next day.

"I knew we'd meet again," Pock-mark wheezed. "I knew you'd be round to see me in the end." His eyes watched her from the door, following every movement, yet without emotion, merely registering. "You've worn well, considering— Don't drop your clothes on the floor like that. I like things tidy."

She watched the fan spinning slowly round and round above her head while the great sweating mass heaved and strained on top of her, crushing her breathless. Michael's finger would've been all right if we'd kept the police out of it, she kept thinking. I'll never forget that.

He knocked her legs further apart suddenly. "Come on, do something for me, can't you?" he panted, the breath clogged in his chest. "Or have you forgotten how?"

He subsided at last. The bed sagged inert. She was slippery with his sweat. She watched the fan blades slowly turning.

"Remember Sai Chin Hua?" he murmured chestily from the bed, his eyes half-closed. "The girl from Soochow, lived with a German general in the Boxer time, when the foreign devils burnt Peking?" It had been too much to say, he had to pause to get his breath back.

She slipped on her shoes.

"Remember?" His head turned on the pillows. The toad-like eyes regarded her unblinkingly.

"No," she said tonelessly. "I was too young then."

"Slept in the empress's bed, they say," he wheezed. "The two of them together... Then he went home to Germany. Know what became of her?"

She was at the door. She shook her head.

He breathed heavily through his mouth.

"She lives in a hovel here in Shanghai... Near the North Station... Starving. Better to trust your own people, eh?"

She heard his breath snorting and whistling as she closed the door.

The soft-slippered servant led her out by the back way. They passed a large porcelain spittoon with a scalloped rim. She paused and spat into it twice.

At half-past three the next afternoon a policeman found Michael on Bubbling Well Road, wandering dazedly towards his home, his hand in a dirty bandage.

"Well, at least it was his left hand," McEwan grunted dourly as he peeled away the cloth. "The finger's infected,

534

we'll have to take the rest of it off." He drank half a tumbler of whisky while they waited for the ambulance. "Pish, laddie, it won't hurt at all," he rallied Michael as he clung to Su-mei. "I'll have it off in a jiffy. Ye'll have an anaesthetic this time, remember."

Everett telephoned while they were at the hospital. Lily took the call. "He wants you to ring him back," she told her father. But Denton didn't. The next day Everett came in person, with Lolly Kwai. Ah Sam showed them up to the study, cracking her red, inflamed fingers and sighing at every step—she'd begun to get pains in her knees now, for which she got poultices from Chinese herbalists.

Everett placed his hat carefully on the floor by his chair. "So you paid the ransom?" he asked Denton. Lolly Kwai stood smiling by the door, as though the whole thing had been a joke.

Denton gazed down at the mirror-smooth surface of Everett's polished toe caps. "No, they must have just let him go."

Everett's brows rose faintly in disbelief. "Could we talk to the lad, see if he can give us any clues?"

"I'd rather not."

Everett's brows rose again.

"He's been through enough. I'd rather he was just allowed to forget it, instead of raking it all up again. Besides, he's already told us all he knows." He glanced from Everett to Lolly Kwai, who was still beaming genially, then back to Everett again. "There were two men, he never heard their names, never saw them before, he's no idea where he was kept."

"Could he describe them?"

Denton shrugged. "One was big, one not so big, that's all. The smaller one had hair sprouting out of a mole on his cheek."

"How about we show him photo' and he tell' if he see'?" Lolly suggested.

"Denton shook his head obstinately. "I'd rather leave things where they are. I don't want anything else to happen. After all, you weren't exactly successful in this case, were you?"

Everett flushed, seemed about to reply, then bent down to pick up his cap. "We can't put kidnappers behind bars if the victims themselves won't co-operate," he said stiffly as he got up to leave.

"I'm sorry, but I want to forget about the whole thing now. And I want Michael to forget."

Listening to the deliberate solid tread of their shoes going downstairs, Denton recalled Michael's puzzled hesitant whispering from the pillow the night before. *'The big one had a scar on the side of his head ... And once I thought I saw Yin-hong, just for a moment at the door. But it couldn't have been him, could it?'* His eyes had been shy and uncertain, almost guilty. As though the thought that Yin-hong might have had something to do with it was somehow disloyal and might make his parents angry.

Afterwards, Denton had asked Ah King if she'd ever heard from Yin-hong since he ran away more than a year ago.

"Never seen or heard from him," she said grimly.

Three weeks later, Ah King was eating her rice and listening to the crackling old wireless that had passed from the living room to the kitchen. Chiang Kai-shek's armies were moving north from Hankow, the announcer said, and a Russian communist adviser called Borodin was prominent on his staff. The northern general Sun was however determined to defend Shanghai against the Kuo Min Tang, and his armoured train, the Great Wall, manned by White Russian soldiers, was streaming up and down the countryside, striking fear into the hearts of all southern bandits and reds.

Her eyes dulled at the news of the latest prices on the stock exchange. She scooped the rice up with her chopsticks, holding the bowl close to her mouth, then suddenly stopped, cocking her head to listen, her eyes growing alert again. The announcer had come to the sports news. The eminent banker and community leader, Mr. Chen Hsiaolai had just acquired Mr. J. Denton's champion pony and was expected to be the most successful owner this season.

She scooped the rice up more slowly, eating with less relish. Which ponies would she bet on now? She couldn't bet on Denton's anymore, now they belonged to Pockmark Chen. She sighed and shook her head. Nobody had ever said what the ransom money was, yet everyone knew it was a million dollars. No wonder master had sold his pony. She sighed again and belched under her breath.

Out of the corner of her eye she saw a figure passing

the window. She glanced up at the doorway. The light darkened. It was her husband.

Her heart checked, then beat faster. He looked cautiously round the kitchen before he stepped inside. She got up slowly, wiping her lips with the back of her hand. "How long are you here for?" she asked, looking at his patched, fading shirt.

The sharp lines running from his nostrils down past his lips seemed to deepen as he spoke. "I'm living in the old city now. I'll be there quite some time. Don't tell anyone you've seen me."

She nodded slowly. "The others are on holiday. It's their day off."

"I know," he muttered impatiently, glancing from her bowl to the rice pan on the stove. "That's why I came."

"Have you eaten?" she asked, turning to get a bowl for him.

"What's all this about Yin-hong running away to join the Green Triangle?" he demanded harshly. "What's he been up to? And that boy being kidnapped?"

"I'm afraid he had a hand in the kidnapping," she said turning back. "Master thinks so, too, I can tell..."

70

When Denton suggested hiring bodyguards, Su-mei shook her head firmly. "You've paid Pock-mark Chen," she said. "You've given him face. It's like protection money. If you don't offend him again, we'll be all right. He keeps his word." Her eyes narrowed and her voice hardened momentarily. "If you'd listened to me earlier, Michael wouldn't have lost his finger."

That momentary hardening of her voice seemed to be the symptom of something deeper in her that had also hardened. She turned away from him in bed, she avoided even his touch, there were more and more moments when she was constrained with him, as if she would have preferred to be alone. We've become tense because of the strain, Denton thought. We must all have another holiday. We deserve it.

But on the holiday, again in Japan, there was the same constraint. When they were with the children, they forgot it, but when they were alone in the hotel room, in the ship's cabin, it would steal over them once more, as if there were some fissure between them, narrow yet deep, which each hesitated to cross. They came back unchanged.

"I don't feel like it," she said in English, turning her face away one night when he put his hand on her breast and tried to kiss her.

"Why not?"

She shrugged and pouted, almost like a little girl. "Don't know. I just don't."

They lay gazing up at the ceiling, side by side yet separate. "Something's happening to us," he said with an effort at last, acknowledging it for the first time. "Ever since this business with Michael."

A tug whooped in the harbour, answered by the deep vibrant blast of a ship's siren. Su-mei didn't reply, and after some time he thought she'd fallen asleep. Then, as his own lids were growing heavy, he heard her sigh. "*Why* did you keep going to the police?" she asked with a quiet vehemence. "Why didn't you *listen* to me? *Why?*"

He lay still, with a cold weight on his chest. She'll never forget that, he thought hopelessly. It'll always be there. He had no answer to give her. He pretended to be asleep himself.

The opera company collapsed. They couldn't get the audiences any more. "They don't want Shaohing opera these days," Su-mei said, then shrugged. "My voice was going anyway."

Sometimes, when the children were restless in the cooler autumn days, he would take them out in the car, all except Lily, who was too busy preparing for her examinations at school—she was to go to St. Johns University afterwards, to study medicine. They would drive far out into the countryside, as he used to drive with Su-mei. And just as he used to meet columns of starving peasants then, trudging wretchedly along towards the city, so now they met refugees from war as well as famine. But now there were more of them, thousands more. Mile after mile they plodded on, towards the golden city where they hoped to be safe and fed, to find work, and even wealth, under the protection of the foreign devils. But what would the city do for them? he thought, as even the children's chatter died at the sight of so much misery. With every thousand that came, wages went lower. He'd heard Jacob say so time and again. Soon, no matter how many new sweat shops opened, there would be no more work. There would be a great ant heap of beggars living in rat-infested slums. How long would they stand it? And all the time Chiang Kai-shek's armies moved closer and the foreign powers brought in more troops to guard what they held. If Chaing attacked them, the refugees who'd trudged hundreds of miles to the illusion of food and safety would be slaughtered between the two armies.

He would tell Lau to turn round then and they would travel silently, guiltily, back. The children were almost as awed as he was. He couldn't prevent them seeing the occasional corpses lying by the road, often hidden beneath squirming packs of ravenous half-wild dogs.

Every week he would try a different route—north, south and west—in the hope there would be no worn, straggling columns of marchers. But wherever they went, sooner or later they met them.

Jacob had moved all his capital to New York and was applying for an Argentine passport. "They're easiest to get," he said. His old Russian one had been useless since the revolution, "and shameful before it." Only his cotton mill kept him in Shanghai. "Transfer your funds and leave," he advised Denton. "If everything blows over you can come back." Denton thought of his shares, still at the price he bought them for, or lower. He'd paid Jacob and Wei back by selling gold. He'd be poor if he left Shanghai now. He held on, and held on to Wei's assurance that there'd be no war. But his confidence was weakening. Suppose there was a war, suppose they were all killed.

"It will have been a pity wasting a million dollars saving Michael's life if we're all going to be killed anyway," he said one evening to Su-mei.

"You think it was wasted?"

"You know what I mean."

She tossed her head. 'Nobody's going to get killed except a few soldiers, for the sake of appearances," she said coldly, after a pause.

He felt the fissure opening between them, and at the same time marvelled at her calm, chill poise.

That night was the first time since their marriage that he went out deliberately to avoid her. He left the car at home and took a rickshaw, just as he used to when he was married to Mary-Ellen. The coolie pulled him along Maloo first, where the sing-song girls went dashing past from one party to another, bodyguards running along beside their brilliant rickshaws. The girls' pert, pretty faces were lit up by lamps that shone on them from hidden recesses in the rickshaws' ornate canopies. Outside each restaurant where the girls stopped to enter, beggars clustered with lustreless eyes, more than Denton had ever seen before.

He had the coolie pull him into Chapei next, past the settlement boundary, guarded by British soldiers now, as it had been after the revolution of 1911. Many of the old, festering canals had been filled in, only to make space for more tenements, more hovels. Girls were still being sold as slaves, lining up docilely when purchasers appeared, stern-faced women with calculating eyes and tight, pursed lips. And the brothels flourished, too, of course, their bright doors alluringly open, while the greasy smell of opium drifted down from upper floors, whatever the law might be. He left the rickshaw and walked up and down some of the streets, half-ashamed, tantalising himself with the thrill of adventureous desire again; then on an impulse he took another rickshaw all the way to Little Moscow, and got off at the first nightclub. White Russian hostesses were languidly dancing with staid Chinese businessmen in neat dark suits. The businessmen had a wondering look of triumphant pleasure gleaming in their eyes, as though they could scarcely believe they'd got their arms at last round the white women who'd been unattainable for so long.

"Want some company, sir?" the Russian head waiter bowed by his ear in the dimly-lit corner where he sat. But he shook his head, paid, and went on to the next cabaret and the next, drinking a double whisky in each, watching the girls, Chinese and Russian, with a distant lust, afraid of what he might do if he went too close.

He returned home half-drunk, climbed the stairs to each child's bedroom and inspected their sleeping faces. Michael's damaged hand lay on the pillow beside his head, as if he was nursing it still. His mouth twitched slightly in his sleep. On top of the wardrobe Denton could see the dark shadow of the new violin they'd bought him the day after the rest of his finger had been amputated. "It is possible, it is possible," his teacher kept assuring him. Michael had tried it a few times and then climbed on a

540

chair to put it away in its case up there. He never touched it again, but he wouldn't have it moved.

It was then, as he was about to leave, that he first heard the distant rumble of gunfire, a subdued thunder that made the windows rattle. He glanced at the children, but they didn't stir.

It wasn't until he opened his own bedroom door that he smelt the opium. The pipe was on its side by the lamp. Su-mei lay on the bed half-dressed, breathing slowly, her head pillowed on her arm. He spoke to her, but she didn't answer. She didn't move when he covered her with the bedclothes, nor when the gunfire rumbled again, nor when he raised her lids and saw her entranced eyes. I'm drunk, he thought as he lay down beside her, and you're drugging yourself with opium. Each of us separately. What's happening to us?

71

Although they played together at home, Michael had little to do with Alec at school. Alec was in a higher class because he was three months older, which counted for a year by the school's class allocation system, and he had many friends, most of whom were English or American. But Michael looked quite Chinese, which put many white children off, and besides he was solitary and withdrawn like his father, wary of others. It was over a term before he made a friend in his class, and even then it was the other boy who made the first approach. "What's your first name, Denton?" Grusenberg had asked in the playground once, where they were both outsiders watching the others play.

"Michael." Michael had hesitated, surveying the long, pale, freckled face with watchful grey eyes, then decided to go on. "What's yours?"

"Yuri." Grusenberg's eyes dwelt on Michael's for some time. "Your name's English, isn't it? You look Chinese." He spoke reflectively, as if considering a puzzle rather than preparing to taunt him with "*Chink*" as the others did.

"My mother's Chinese," Michael said, half-defiantly. Grusenberg took this in without comment, and Michael felt encouraged to go on. "Yuri's not an English name," he said.

"No, it's Russian. My father's Russian."

"You don't look Russian." Actually Michael wasn't sure about that, but Grusenberg seemed to accept it.

"My mother's American." He paused, glanced round the shrieking, yelling playground, then leant closer to Michael. "My real name's Borodin, not Grusenberg. Grusenberg's my mother's name. I can speak Russian. Can you speak Chinese? I was born there, in Moscow. It snows a lot. You get tons of it."

The bell rang for the end of break.

That was before the kidnap. When Michael returned to school, always trying to hide his hand, despite the brief fame and popularity it gave him, Grusenberg remained his only friend. It was Grusenberg he told about the long days and nights of his imprisonment, the quilt and the barred windows and the two men, while to the others he merely shrugged, or muttered some offhand remark—"It was all right. It wasn't too bad"—which quickly killed off interest. It was to Grusenberg alone that he confided his nightmare, the one that kept coming back, of the dreamy-eyed kidnapper with the tuft of straggly hair on his face casually cutting his fingers off one after another, whistling through his teeth all the time, until his hands became bleeding fingerless stumps. And then the other kidnapper, the big one, would hand him his violin and tell him to play. He would always wake up at the moment when he tried frantically to clamp the bow between both hands and the violin slipped from under his arm and smashed on the floor. But the funny thing was, it was the big one who'd actually cut his finger off, the dreamy-eyed one had only helped to hold him down. Often for fear of having that nightmare he wouldn't let himself fall asleep at night. He would lie awake with a softly pulsing heart, listening to Alec's snuffling breathing, listening to the creaking of the stairs, while his eyes glanced incessantly round the room, probing every shadow.

Grusenberg listened seriously. Like Michael he rarely smiled. He agreed it was funny that it was the dreamy-eyed one who cut his fingers off in the dream. They considered that silently for a time. Then, "My father was sentenced to death once," he said thoughtfully, gazing away across the playground. "By the White Russians. I wonder if he has nightmares."

Michael was puzzled. He thought it was always the *White* Russians who were sentenced to death by the *Reds*. But he didn't want to make a fool of himself asking Grusenberg if he really meant what he'd said. After all, he ought to know.

"If we went looking for buildings with drainpipes and electric wires hanging down, we might find the place they kept you in," Grusenberg suggested.

"Yes..." Michael said doubtfully. The idea scared him, and he was glad Grusenberg never mentioned it again. In any case, their friendship was confined to school—they never met outside it, never invited each other to their homes, were seldom asked to the birthday parties of other boys. They merely waited for each other before school started, walked together round the playground till the bell rang, and met in the breaks, eating their snacks side by side. It was with Grusenberg that Michael first became unself-conscious about his injured hand, holding his sandwich with it, instead of keeping it clenched behind his back or deep in his pocket.

After school too, Michael would walk to the gates with Grusenberg, where the children waited for their chauffeur-driven cars to pick them up. Grusenberg's car was a large black Oldsmobile, driven by a stern-faced Chinese. It was always waiting there for him, never late. Michael would nod goodbye as it drove away, then go to join Alec, who would be lounging against the wall with his friends. Alec was always a little impatient and distant to Michael then, until they were alone in the car and he could talk naturally to him without risking sneers and digs from the others.

72

Su-mei gazed through the car's windows at the almost deserted, lamplit streets. "The wireless said the northern troop' are moving out." She spoke in English, so that Lau wouldn't understand, and yet Denton caught a slight lifting and tensing of his head, as though he was listening anyway.

"There are still a lot of them outside the city," he said.

She shrugged. "They're going," she declared. "The wireless says so."

They were approaching the British barrier at Garden Bridge. Lau turned on the interior light, and the sentry, peering at Denton's white face inside, waved them through. Denton saw his shoulder flash. *Coldstream Guards.* A faint little shiver of pride ran through him, the last vestige of his youthful patriotism.

"They say General Sun's gone already," Su-mei went on. "With his harem."

"Who say?"

She shrugged. "People. Everyone."

"Well his armoured train was still here this morning, anyway. I saw it at the North Station."

Her hand lay on the seat beside him. He looked down at it, small and still smooth, her fingers wearing the rings he'd given her over the years. He lifted his own hand, hesitated, then placed it over hers. "Don't smoke opium by yourself," he murmured quietly. It was the first time he'd alluded to that night a few weeks ago—when he woke the next morning she'd cleared things away and behaved as though nothing had happened; it was he who had the thick head.

Su-mei's brows arched faintly. "Who else is there to smoke it with?" she asked softly.

Me he wanted to say. And yet he didn't say it. The car drove slowly over the bridge, behind a barrow and two rickshaws. "I always feel a bit worried now, leaving the children at home," he said, to cover the silence between them.

She shook her head, the tear-shaped silver earrings that he'd given her over twenty years before quivering and gleaming. "No one would dare touch them, now *he's* had something to do with it." She avoided saying Pock-mark Chen's name. "So long as we don't offend him, it will be all right."

"You make it sound as though he owns us."

Her lips tightened. "Doesn't he?"

He looked away, smarting as if she'd slapped his face.

They were approaching the Japanese barrier at Hongkew now. Again Lau turned the interior light on and they were waved through. There was something more menacing about the sentries there. Perhaps it was that, unlike the British, they had fixed bayonets on their rifles.

544

A fragment of conversation floated into Denton's mind—
"It's the Japs I'm worried about." He recalled the accent and
the rich genial tone clearly, but it was some time before he
could place the speaker. Nixon, that was it, the chairman
of the Bank, at some meeting or dinner. That was in the
days when Pock-mark Chen wouldn't have dared touch
him. Denton thought again how far he'd slipped.

A little further on, a Chinese man was walking past
two Japanese marines. The man was smoking a cigarette.
He ducked his head nervously as he passed them, stepping submissively out of their way, but they stopped him at
bayonet point and began shouting at him, words which
clearly he didn't understand. One of them pulled the
cigarette out of his mouth and slapped his face repeatedly.
Denton felt Su-mei's hand move under his, but neither of
them spoke. As the car drove past, the marine was still
slapping the man's face and shouting at him. He was a
middle-aged man, wearing glasses. The glasses slid off his
face, hung crookedly a moment from one ear, then fell to
the ground. The man winced at every blow, but he made
no sound, his arms dangling by his sides. People on a
passing tram stared down in silence just as Su-mei and he
stared in silence from the car window. Then they were
past.

They didn't speak again, until they reached Jacob's
drive. But Denton's hand had tightened round Su-mei's,
which had curled into a little fist. Then, as Lau held the
door open for her, "Why were they doing that?" she asked
with a bite in her voice.

"It's an offence to their emperor to smoke in front of
someone wearing a uniform. The uniform represents the
emperor, apparently."

"You believe that?"

"*I* don't, *they* do."

She tossed her head in scorn.

As they were climbing the steps to the porch, "Who
else is going to be here?" she asked discontentedly, as if
her resentment of the Japanese had spilled over onto
Jacob.

"I don't know. Why?"

"I don't like coming here, that's all. Jacob always look'
at me as if I was a tart."

He'd never heard her use "tart" before. He smiled.
"Jacob looks at every woman under sixty like that. Be-

sides," he went on as she shrugged contemptuously, "we must meet *some* people. We can't go on talking to each other for ever, we'll have nothing left to say soon."

"Already," she said as the smiling houseboy opened the door and Sarah came down the hall towards them.

Sarah's greeting had an exaggerated, almost hysterical warmth, as though she was trying to convince herself as much as them that she was pleased to see them. Her face was painted and powdered like a woman's half her age, though nothing concealed the cracks and pouches round her eyes and chin. Her hair had been bobbed in the latest style and dyed in a gingery red. She jangled with her gold bracelets and beads as she ushered them towards the living-room with flustered, hen-like flappings of her arms and hands. They heard Jacob's voice drifting out into the hall.

"... greatest threat to the world is communism," he was asserting loudly, not stopping even when his eyes smiled a welcome at them. "If communism comes to China, it will take you two hundred years to get over it. Look at Russia."

Sitting round him—he'd naturally and probably unconsciously placed himself in the middle of the room— were Wei, Philip Wei and his wife, another Chinese businessman, an Indian with his wife, Jacob's wizened father-in-law, and Janet Pulham of all people, in a shapeless grey dress with the packing creases still in it. Denton wondered what the Weis were doing there. Jacob introduced Denton and Su-mei quickly, obviously anxious to get on with his discourse. "What happened in Canton? Riots in the city. Communists openly inciting people to attack foreigners. What happened in Hankow? Nanking? No sooner do the communists arrive than the riots start. All very nice. Kill the foreigners, like in the Boxer times. Like the cossacks killing the Jews in Russia. But what are they going to eat?"

He turned suddenly towards Philip, who was talking in a low voice to the other Chinese behind Jacob's back. "In Nanking a hawker sells some oranges to an Englishman. Nobody else can afford to buy them, so what should he do? Starve? But no, the communists in the KMT have said no selling to foreigners. Anti-foreign boycott. So somebody sees him. Result? The Englishman has his head shaved and gets paraded round the streets in a cangue, and the hawker gets strung up by the thumbs and beaten to death. And that my friend is communism—either starve or be killed! If it happens in Shanghai, China will be put back a hundred years—two hundred!"

Janet Pulham turned to Denton. "Lucky you're here tonight, I was thinking of asking you for another donation. I've asked several people here already, and now it's your turn."

Denton wondered how many of the people she'd asked had agreed.

"And who d'you think I got a donation from last week?" she went on, burrowing inside her large black handbag that was almost as capacious as the baby bag she used to carry. "Chen Hsiao-lai—Pock-mark Chen. I know he's supposed to be an awful rogue," she pulled a man's handkerchief out of the bag and blew her nose loudly on it, "but I just went and saw him in his office, and he gave me a cheque right away. D'you know him at all?"

"Slightly," Denton said. "He proved to be quite useful when my son was kidnapped."

"Oh, yes, all those lines to the Shanghai underworld," she said briskly, as though they were as innocent as lines on the London underground. "I was away when all that happened, visiting our mission in Ningpo. You got him back all right in the end, didn't you?" She made it sound as ordinary as the recovery of an old wallet.

"Yes," Denton sipped his whisky "Minus a finger."

"You see, I don't believe a lot of these stories about Chen and people like that," she went on crisply, as though she hadn't heard Denton, or perhaps thought fingers were nothing to complain about. "There's good in everyone Can I rely on you for a cheque? We're building an extension to Jerusalem House." She shook her drab grey hair back from her still bright, pale blue eyes and smiled when Denton nodded. "And how is Lily? I'm still praying for her you know, she was a great help to us at one time."

"She is very busy now," Su-mei said brittly. "She has no time."

"All the time there is, I'm sure," Janet Pulham rejoined cheerfully.

Jacob gripped Denton's arm. "How is Michael?" he asked, his warm brown eyes peering into Denton's.

"OK." The truth was, he didn't know how Michael was. His eyes were a wall Denton never surmounted. "Physically OK, anyway—What are all these people doing

547

here tonight?" he went on swiftly, to deflect any more questions. "Most of them don't seem your type at all."

Jacob rubbed his hands together, his eyes gleaming. "Business, business," he whispered. "I'm fixing up a deal to supply the Weis with cotton."

"A month or two ago you were telling me to get out of Shanghai."

"If Wei wants to do business, he knows the international settlement's all right." Jacob laughed at his own cunning, or Wei's. "He doesn't like me, but I make the lowest bids."

"Surely Janet Pulham isn't in on the deal?"

"Who? Oh her," he said in a scathing tone. "Sarah picked her up. She wants to start a home for Jewish orphans and that Pulham woman's supposed to give her advice. Well, it gives Sarah something to do..." He turned to the Indian businessman, whose wife kept her head demurely covered with her sari.

Sarah was trying to conduct a conversation between her deaf old father, whose sharp, deep-set eyes glinted with beady dissatisfaction, and Wei, who answered every question with a politely smiling monosyllable. She looked at Denton imploringly. Denton went and sat between Sarah and Wei. Sarah lapsed gratefully into loud streams of Yiddish with her father, becoming suddenly animated and expressive.

Wei cleared his throat. "Shall we go and admire Mr. Ephraim's garden?" Without waiting for an answer he pushed himself out the depths of his chair, with difficulty for all his spareness, and went to the veranda windows, which had been closed against the cold night air.

They stood silently side by side, looking out over Jacob's long lawn and shrubs to the empty darkness of Szechuen Road. Wei started speaking slowly in Shanghainese, without turning to look at Denton, as though he needed to keep his eyes on the dark to keep his thoughts clear. "I would like to explain about Chen—Pock-mark Chen. You probably think it was he who had Michael kidnapped. But I know for a fact it wasn't. You see I went to see him as soon as I heard about it..."

Denton glanced at him. Wei was still frowning out at the dark, speaking in a voice that age had made tremulous. A column of soldiers appeared, marching up the road, driving pigs and poultry along with them. "He immediately gave orders to find out about it. It was a surprise to him too, you see..." His cheek puckered into a wry little smile. "He has more important things to do than kidnap children. After all he is one of the most powerful men in China now. It was he who stopped them from harming Michael when you called in the police."

"Stopped them?" Denton held up his little finger.

Wei shook his head with another wry smile. "You know that was nothing compared to what they might have done."

"So I owe Michael's life to him?"

Wei nodded. "Of course he expected you to pay the price."

"Yes," Denton sipped his whisky, held it in his mouth, swallowed. "That's more or less what Su-mei thought had happened," he said slowly.

Wei's glass glinted as he shot a brief, inquiring glance at Denton. "Yes, she would be bound to know," he murmured almost to himself.

They stood silent for some minutes, gazing out at the road. It was filling up now with more and more marching troops. Some horses went past, pulling a field gun, then carts drawn by mules. Then the slow, plodding infantry filled the road again. A horn sounded imperiously in the distance, growing gradually louder. Soon the headlamps appeared, moving along the trudging columns like angry glaring eyes, casting a flickering light over the figures of men, carts and animals. Long shadows wheeled across Jacob's peaceful lawn, the shadows of the trees lining the road as the headlamps passed them. For a moment Denton recalled the long shadows of the oak trees and the cricketers on the playing field of the English public school two years ago. Soon they would all be going to school in England, Jenny, Alec, Michael.

Then Jacob called out behind them, "What's all that commotion out there on the road?"

"It is the northern troop' retreating," Wei said, turning his head. "Chiang Kai-shek will be here in a day or two."

"Do you really think he won't try to take over the international settlements?" Denton asked quietly in Shanghainese. "I'm holding a lot of shares."

"Positive."

Nearly everyone had come to the veranda now, peering through the windows at the untidy retreating columns.

"Listen!" Philip exclaimed, holding up his hand. "Gunfire!"

It wasn't the low thunder of artillery that they'd been hearing on and off for several weeks now, but the sharp rattle of machine guns and rifles. Yet the plodding northern troops seemed indifferent to the noise, as if the fighting, wherever it was, couldn't concern them. Their faces, briefly illuminated by the headlights, never looked back. They marched stolidly on, driving their pigs and poultry before them.

"I'm so frightened when I hear gunfire," said the Indian woman, in a low, thrilling voice, actually rather excited.

The comrades had posted her on the roof above the British check-point almost opposite the North Station. Lily felt self-conscious at first calling them "comrades," especially Kwok-choi whom she'd known before he went to Nan Yang University last year. But they all insisted, so she'd gradually grown used to it. Then the older, sterner, men from Nanking had filtered into the city, and taken over the students' meetings; "comrade" seemed just the right term for them. They were practical, impersonal men, impatient and rough-tongued—she would never have dreamed of calling any of them by their personal names. Kwok-choi had been excited and proud at being made a cell leader and going to meetings with those people— *comrades* who were high up in the party.

"*If more than twenty foreign soldiers come up to the barricade,*" he'd said importantly that morning, "*or if tanks come, you dial this number and say what you see.*" And the comrade from Nanking who was with Kwok-choi had made her repeat it three times as if she was a child before they left. She'd felt it was a bit like playing a game—or she would have done but for that unsmiling comrade from Nanking and her memories of the Louza Street massacre.

From the roof where she was standing she could see down into the station on one side and along Honan Road into the international settlement on the other. A crowd of refugees had milled round the check-point all afternoon, waiting to be let in to the sanctuary of the settlement.

When the shooting began, the children started crying and the women clamoured like geese. At first the British soldiers hadn't taken much notice, but then as the Great

Wall steamed into the station, they'd taken up positions behind their sandbags and barbed wire, hurrying the refugees through quickly with only a cursory glance at their bundles. Lily's heart had begun to thump unsteadily.

The main entrance to the station was empty. The shooting was all going on in the marshalling yards. Lily could see the Great Wall slowly lumbering up and down like a rhinoceros, while bullets and home-made bombs exploded against its massive but torn and dented armour plating. Further on, beyond the signalling box, she could see where the rails had been pulled up, blocking the train's escape. As it jolted and shunted to and fro in its trap, the little metal shutters in the carriages would open and flashes of gunfire spurt out as the White Russians fired into the overturned waggons and signal boxes where the comrades were shooting from. What was Kwok-choi doing down there? She didn't know, she wasn't allowed to know, so that if the northerners captured her, she couldn't give anything away, not even if they tortured her. The strange thing was that she hadn't been as frightened as she'd expected since she'd been able to see what was going on. There was just this irregular thudding of her heart. Backwards and forwards the train rumbled, bullets clanging on its metal flanks while occasional shouts sounded nearby and the air split with the crack of rifle fire. Sometimes she saw a dark figure that had been running across the yards suddenly fall and lie so very still. But most of the time the firing was sporadic, sudden bursts punctuating long silences in which the ungainly train moved uneasily backwards and forwards on the little stretch of track left to it, as if it were sniffing for a way of escape.

It was worse in Louza Street, Lily thought with tentative relief. I won't panic if it stays like this, I won't run away. Her heart was still thumping of course, but everything was under control. She felt she'd won the battle up there against her fear, whatever happened down at the station.

But then there was a sudden loud explosion in the station, a great deep blast that slammed against her ears. She looked back, startled. A river of flame and smoke was lapping along the side of the Great Wall's long, round boiler. At the same time there was a flurry of shooting from the train, and then in the dark she saw the figures of men running from the signal boxes and overturned wag-

551

gons towards the Great Wall, while the Great Wall's shutters opened and long continuous volleys exploded from them. The men running towards the train staggered and wilted. They seemed to hesitate and hang there, like a wave before it falls, then the next second they'd broken and were running back for shelter, leaving several dark figures lying on the ground. And in the sudden lull as the firing stopped on both sides—a lull that seemed unnaturally still and quiet—she thought she could hear screams and shouts. She began to feel afraid, really afraid, that same paralysing fear that she'd felt outside the Louza Street police station.

The soldiers below had changed too. She saw them standing close to the barricade now, handling their rifles quietly and more tensely. The refugees went on clamouring, their voices rising higher, wailing with fear.

She remembered to look back along the road. No, no more soldiers coming. Her lips had gone dry and that wild drumming in her ears and wrists was coming again, the drumming she remembered feeling outside the Louza Street police station, as if her blood was stampeding in terror through her whole body. She tried to breathe deeply and calmly, to repress the mounting frenzy of her nerves and muscles that urged her to run away and yet left her too weak to move. She stared at the station again, with its name in Chinese and English still brightly illuminated, as if everything inside was normal and you could go and buy a ticket to Peking if you liked. And as her glance shifted along the gleaming tracks towards the Great Wall, that was silent and stationary now, as if wondering where the next attack was coming from, the train's boiler suddenly burst. There was an even louder explosion than before, a great lump of metal soared into the air, and a hissing cloud of steam enveloped the engine. Then, as the steam cleared, she saw that a long slit had been ripped along the bottom of the boiler, and the wheels had come off the rails. Smoke and flames flickered underneath the whole length of the engine. A low hissing came from the boiler, like a slaughtered animal's dying breath.

For half a minute there was a stunned silence, as if everyone was awed by the death of the engine, then the doors of the train swung open and men jumped down, running crazily in different directions like ants running frantically from a trampled ant-hill. At the same time the firing from the overturned goods waggons and signal boxes started again, and one by one the little ant-like figures fell to the ground, some writhing and kicking, others lying absolutely still. Some must have got away though—she saw them dashing suddenly straight out of the station entrance, for all the world as if they were merely running to catch a bus, except that there were no buses and their faces—she could see them clearly now—were contorted and staring-eyed. They were making for the barricade below her, she realised, for the safety of the international settlement, and she found herself urging them on, willing them to get there before they were caught, as if she was on their side.

But a mob of people closed in on them from the side of the station, howling and waving bamboo poles, knives and cargo hooks. The mob set on them, pulled them down and butchered them in a yelling frenzy of beating, stabbing and hacking. The one nearest her broke loose for a moment, blood running down his face and staggered wildly on towards the British barricade. She heard the soldiers calling to him, encouraging him, he had only twenty yards or so to go, and she herself was silently willing him on too. But several men leapt on him again and he went down with a scream as their arms flailed him with knives and hooks. She turned away, screwing her eyes shut, her whole body shuddering uncontrollably. Her face was twisted as though she was crying, but she knew her eyes were dry and tearless. It's just shock, she kept trying to tell herself, it's just shock, but still she went on shuddering. She crouched down against the wall, covering her face with her hands.

After a while, as she grew calmer, she heard footsteps on the stairs behind her. She spun round terrified, almost expecting to see one of the White Russians charging to avenge himself on her. But the footsteps were light and swift, it was Kwok-choi, his eyes glittering with excitement and pride. "I got one! I got a Russian myself!" he shouted exultantly. "Come on, it's the police station in Chapei now. It's all over here!"

She found that after all she could move, although her whole body was numb and her legs trembled as she walked.

Jenny, Alec and Michael were sitting with the servants in the kitchen, listening to the news of the fighting on the old, crackling wireless. The English channel had carried staid, neutral announcements about the fighting and reminders about the curfew in the international settlement, but the Chinese station Ah King had tuned in to was giving an excited commentary on the destruction of the Great Wall and the attacks on Chinese police stations on Chapei and Nantao. *"Groups of workers have taken over!"* the announcer declared. *"Shanghai is being liberated! It will be the turn of the foreign settlements next!"*

"Groups of workers indeed!" Ah Leng repeated cynically. "Communist bandits more likely." She glanced round at them knowingly. "If they get past the foreign devil soldiers, we'll all be killed."

"Rubbish," Ah King said. "If you don't know what you're talking about, why don't you shut up?"

Ah Leng bridled. The old hostility between them was always ready to revive. "If Chiang Kai-shek comes," she declared solemnly, "and beats the foreign soldiers, he'll kill all the foreign devils, man woman and child."

"Well he won't beat the foreign soldiers," Alec said bravely.

"Huh!"

Jenny laughed, uncertain how much to believe. Ah Leng was always trying to scare you with her stories of ghosts and bandits and things. But then Michael *had* been kidnapped...She picked up the cat and stroked it on her lap, a vague uneasiness in her stomach. "What would they do to Lily and Michael? And tai-tai? They're not foreign devils."

"Any Chinese woman living with a foreign devil gets thrown in the river in a pig basket," Ah Leng asserted. "That's what they did in Hankow and Nanking. And their children with them. I heard it in the market."

Ah King scowled at her, while Ah Man shovelled in his rice in his usual abstracted fashion. Cheong put his bowl in the sink and went out silently into the garden.

"What a thing to say," Ah Sam said, massaging her cramped fingers. "In front of the children, too."

"Well, it's true!" And yet she was grinning, as though she didn't really believe it.

"Ah, Man, why don't you get another bird?" Alec asked.

Ah Man put his bowl down and burped. "No more
554

birds," he said absently. He gazed across the kitchen with unseeing eyes, then stirred and folded the paper on the table in front of him. 'No more birds for me."

Ah King twiddled the knob to find another station, watching the magic green tuning eye open and close as she passed from channel to channel. Voices twittered and faded through the speaker, music blared and instantaneously died. She settled on an advertisement for the Wing On department store.

"I went there on Sunday," Ah Sam said, still massaging her swollen knuckles. "To Wing On. They had a sale. Everything reduced."

"They make you pay to go in," Ah Man muttered, frowning down at the paper. "Before you buy anything."

"You get it back if you buy."

"Yes, but suppose they don't have what you want?" He turned to the racing page and began studying it carefully, pushing out his underlip.

Ah Sam shrugged. "I saw Mr. Ephraim there, buying shirts. With all his money, he buys shirts at the sales!"

"Why not?" Ah Leng said. "No point in wasting it."

"He saves money on the trams too," Alec said.

"Trams? He doesn't go by tram, a rich man like him!"

"He does! I heard him tell master. He always has the right change in coppers, so the conductors can't cheat him. And he gets off one stop early to save fares."

"Go on!" Jenny said incredulously.

"He does! I heard him say it."

"Well, why shouldn't he?" Ah Leng asked. "I do too."

"And keep the money tai-tai gives you for rickshaws," Ah King muttered.

The front door slammed shut with a noise that set the windows rattling. Ah King, nearest the hall, pushed back her chair and looked out. "Only Lily," she said. "She'll knock the house down next."

"All that studying," Ah Leng said understandingly. "It makes her tired."

"She's tired, so she slams the door," Ah Man murmured, marking his paper with the stubby pencil he always kept in his pocket. "What's she going to do when she isn't tired?"

Opera music was following the Wing On advertisement, gongs clashing, a man's nasal, almost whining voice. Suddenly Michael reached out his damaged hand and switched the wireless off.

"Aiya, what'd you do that for?" Ah Leng shouted. "Turn it back on!"

"Shh! Listen!" Michael had cocked his head to the door. "She's crying."

Lily was leaning against the wall by the front door, shuddering and sobbing hysterically. As they crowded round her, they saw she was dishevelled and bleeding from a cut on her face. She had dropped a bundle of dirty old clothes on the floor.

"She's been raped!" Ah Leng screamed. "She's been raped!"

But Lily shook her head, almost laughing at her through her tears, as though rape was a trivial thing compared with what she'd suffered. She pushed through them, ignoring all their questions, and climbed the stairs, her shoulders still shuddering. Ah Leng hung fluttering round her, interrogating, blaming, examining and crying herself.

The bundle of clothes lay by the door, dark sticky bloodstains on them.

"She's been raped," Ah Sam declared confidently. "That's her blood."

"Shut up, wooden-head," Ah King snapped. "What would you know about rape?—Jenny, telephone master at Mr. Ephraim's."

But Michael was dialling the number already, watching the stump of his little finger with a strange indifferent detachment, as though it belonged to someone else.

By the time Denton and Su-mei had got back from the Ephraims', the car nudging its way slowly against the thick sluggish stream of the retreating northerners, Lily had washed, cleaned her wound and got into bed. Her quivering spasms slowly ceased and she'd sunk into an empty despairing calm when Su-mei pushed the door open. She shook her head to all Su-mei's questions, as if she only half-heard them, and wouldn't look at her mother, staring with long vacant eyes out of the unshuttered window. Su-mei grew angry, yanked the bed-clothes off and examined her body mercilessly. Lily went rigid and pale. "*I am not a sing-song girl sleeping with men for money,*" she said coldly, pulling her night dress down and jerking the bedclothes up to her chin again. Su-mei slapped her once, hard. Her ring cut Lily's lip, just below the cut she had already.

It was Denton, her stranger-father, whom she could never talk to, whom she always felt uneasy with, of whose English blood in her veins she now felt ashamed—it was him she eventually told what had happened. When Su-mei had left the room, her lips compressed, her eyes tight with fury, Denton stayed behind, almost apologetically. He was holding the bundle of clothes she'd dropped downstairs. "Shall we have these washed, or throw them away?" he asked with a rueful smile, as if he too understood defeat and cowardice and disillusionment. And then, quite suddenly, without answering his question, her eyes on the bloodstained clothes in his hand, she began telling him about the Great Wall and the White Russians and Kwok-choi, who'd been hit in the fighting at the Chinese police station on Kwong Fon Road. She spoke in English and Chinese, slipping from one to the other, sometimes in the same sentence, without even noticing it. All the time her father sat on the bed, not even looking at her, gazing with attentive, slightly narrowed eyes out of the window.

"Kwok-choi?" he repeated. "Who's he?"

Her voice shook treacherously. "A student at Nan Yang. It was through him I joined the party. He took me to some meetings. He was the leader of our cell."

"Was?" Even then he didn't look at her. His brows merely rose faintly as he stared unseeingly out of the window, the pupils dark and empty as though they were focussed inward on the images of what she told him.

"The police wouldn't give in," she said in a low, toneless voice. "some people set fire to the building. And when the police started running out through the smoke, they...they just killed them. Especially the ones from Nanking, they did most of the killing. And then Kwok-choi got hit by a bullet somehow. In the stomach. He started screaming. He wouldn't stop screaming. Someone had a look at him, he said they couldn't do anything. And I just ran away." She put her hand up to her face. "I don't know how I got this cut. It's not deep." She shivered suddenly. 'I was trying to hold him up, the blood went all over my clothes—I changed in the garden before I came in. But I didn't know what to do with the clothes. I suppose you should throw them away. It's not my blood, it's his. Nobody saw me changing," she added with sudden

557

girlish modesty, thinking of her mother's suspicion. Her father's lips twitched into a wry smile.

He stood up and went to the window, dropping the clothes by the door. The sky glowed over the city in the north-west. In the street below there was no movement, no noise, and for a moment he wondered why. Then he remembered the curfew. "There are fires over there in Chapei," he said thoughtfully. 'I suppose they're still at it." He rubbed his chin with the back of his hand. The bristles scraped against his skin. 'It's lucky you ran away."

She watched him inquiringly from the bed, but he didn't go on at once. he switched off the light first, as if afraid they might be seen, though seen by whom she couldn't think. The comrades wouldn't come after her, they'd be too busy with their killing. Probably they'd just forget her, write her off as a useless failure. And the Chinese police, or the northern soldiers—they certainly wouldn't be coming for her. They were all dead, or dying, or gone.

"They'll all be killed in a few days," her father went on sombrely at last. "Your communist friends. Wei told me tonight—not for the first time. Chiang Kai-shek's through with them. Pock-mark Chen's people will finish them off. I'm afraid you joined the losing side."

"Killed?" She shook her head unbelievingly. Those men from Nanking were so tough and grim. "There must be ten thousand of them," she protested.

Denton shrugged. "Pock-mark Chen has at least five times that many. They've walked into a trap..." He came and stood beside her, rubbing his chin thoughtfully again. "Does anyone else know you've joined the party?"

"Lily isn't going to school today," their father told them at breakfast the next morning.

"What about her exams?" Michael asked.

"What?" He'd been staring absently across the room at the veranda doors. "There aren't any today." he lifted the newspaper, shook it straight and started reading it, his brows drawn close together.

"What happened?" Jenny asked. "Did she get raped?"

"What do you know about...things like that, Jenny?" When he lowered the paper they saw he was blushing. He raised it again quickly. "Of course not, she simply got

558

caught in a bit of a mob, that's all. On the way back from the library."

"What were all those old clothes she brought in with her?" Alec asked suspiciously. "They'd got blood on them."

"Masses of it," Jenny added.

"Oh she just found them," Denton said unconvincingly. "Get on with your ovaltine Alec, you'll be late."

"I bet she was raped," Alec whispered in the back of the car, nudging Jenny with his elbow and sniggering. "That's why dad went all red. Tied up and raped."

"Shh!" she nudged him back, glancing theatrically at Michael. "Not in front of the children." She examined her face in the driving mirror, wondering if her freckles would ever go away.

Jenny got off at the Girls School, and the car took Alec and Michael on through the check-point to the Boys. There was an armoured car standing by the barricade, its gun pointing down the road towards Chapei. Michael got out after Alec, hitching his satchel onto his shoulder. A column of smoke rose slowly from the direction of the North Station, thick and black against the crisp pale blue of the cloudless sky.

"Come on, Chink," one of the monitors chivvied him as he stood looking at the smoke. "No hanging around outside today. Your Chink pals are up to something over there."

Michael walked on slowly, reluctantly almost, to the playground. He was afraid Grusenberg might not be there, and he wanted to put off the moment of sinking disappointment as long as possible. He'd obscurely expected it, somehow, ever since they passed the barricade. He was right, there was no Grusenberg. He could tell at a glance, because he wasn't in the usual place by the wall. Michael went forlornly up to it and waited, telling himself Grusenberg might still come. But when the bell rang, he still hadn't come. He'd never missed a day's school till then.

Just before break, when Mr. Smith was giving out the Latin homework, the monitor who'd called Michael "Chink" rapped on the door and brought in a note. Mr. Smith read it through to himself with a frown, while a murmur of excitement sounded indistinctly round the class. "Listen," Mr. Smith said, raising his voice. "School is being cancelled after break. Your parents are being asked to arrange for you to be picked up. No boy is to leave school by himself, is that understood?" His voice, a weak tenor, squeaked, and he reddened as they all tittered, even the monitor. "Quiet! You must all wait till you're picked up. Listen to the wireless for announcements about school tomorrow."

"What's happened, sir?"

"Has Chiang Kai-shek come?"

"Is it a war, sir?"

"No, no," he waved his hand, flapping the flimsy typed notice. "Just some trouble in the Chinese city, but it might make it difficult for you to get home later. Don't forget, listen to the wireless about school tomorrow."

In the playground, while the others played or shouted wild speculations at each other, Michael sat alone, where he used to sit and talk with Grusenberg.

"My father says its the communists attacking!"

"Mine says it's Chiang Kai-shek!"

"Bet it's the northerners coming back!"

"Did you see the destroyers in the harbour? Three of them, came last night!"

Michael sat with his hands clasped round his bare knees, the good hand over the bad one, a forlorn feeling like a lump swelling in his throat. He felt sure Grusenberg would never come back.

Scattered shots sounded like whip snaps from Chapei and Hongkew as Lau drove them back toward the international settlement. Sometimes there were prolonged ragged volleys, followed by a few single shots. The children gazed out of the windows, which Lau insisted on keeping closed as if they were bullet-proof.

"They wouldn't shoot at us," Alec protested. "We're British."

But Lau only shook his head. "Tai-tai said keep the windows closed. If you open them, I'll tell her."

"What's going on anyway?" Alec wound his window up again unwillingly. "What's going on, Ah Lau?" He spoke with a lordly air to compensate for his surrender. "Who's fighting who?"

Lau shrugged. "Pock-mark Chen and the reds, they say."

"Why? I thought they were both against the northerners?"

Lau shrugged once more, rasping some phlegm up into his throat and spitting out of the window, conscientiously winding the glass up again afterwards. "They don't tell *me* what they're fighting about," he answered at last, slowing down as he approached the British barricade.

Ah King was restless all that day, nervous and irritable, working slowly and apathetically. She was peevish even to her relatives Ah Sam and Ah Man, and she scolded the children angrily at lunch for keeping on at Lily about what had happened the previous night. Lily ignored them though, picking at her food silently, her face pale. In the afternoon, Ah King went to her room and lay on her bed, disregarding the pile of ironing in the kitchen. She stared up with set eyes at the ceiling, grimy with the smoke of the joss sticks she burnt every day. At about five o'clock she got up and started the ironing at last.

"What's the matter, aren't you well?" Denton asked her.

"Of course I'm well," she muttered. "All this shooting makes me tired though."

He gazed at her sceptically.

"If Lily's off her food, that means she's pregnant," he heard Jenny whispering to Alec as he opened the living-room door. They were sitting together on the sofa. Michael looked up at him from the floor, where he was poring over the newspaper. "What does 'agitators' mean?" he asked.

"Where's Lily?"

"Gone up stairs. What does 'agitators' mean?"

"People who stir up trouble. Why?"

"It just says it here, that's all." Michael read on silently to himself. *"Mr. Borodin is well-known as a communist agitator, and his sudden departure to his native Russia will sadden no one who has China's true interests at heart..."* He thought of Grusenberg's pale narrow face.

Denton stood uncertainly, snapping his fingers. In the distance there was a sudden flurry of shots. A police car went speeding down the Bund, its bell clanging. Alec and Jenny ran to the veranda. Michael glanced round, then looked back at the paper, frowning as he read.

Again some scattered shots sounded, nearer this time. Was Pock-mark Chen's army assassinating communists inside the international settlement as well as in the Chinese city? He went to the veranda himself, feeling a sudden lurch of unquiet in his stomach. What about Lily? He heard Michael following. A police car was travelling north down the Bund, while another car, a large American saloon, was going south. They passed each other and the driver of the American car waved. Soon afterwards the American car slid to a stop by the kerb and four Chinese men jumped out. They ran into the Public Gardens.

"I thought Chinese weren't allowed in there?" Alec asked.

Almost as he spoke there came the sound of several revolver shots behind the azaleas. They sounded just like firecrackers, yet they were sinister. The children watched with suddenly troubled eyes. The American car swung round across the road to face the other way.

"It's a Buick," Alec said, unnaturally quiet. "Are they detectives?"

He wanted to be told this was not murder, it was cops and robbers. "They might be..." Denton lied after a pause.

Then the four Chinese came back. They weren't running now, but walking, sauntering almost, across the inviolable foreign devils' grass. They climbed nonchalantly into the waiting car. The doors slammed and it drove off.

"What were they doing?" Jenny asked uncertainly.

"I don't know, perhaps they were detectives chasing someone," Denton prevaricated. And yet he felt they all secretly knew and were shaken that he accepted it, that he did nothing about it. "Come along, it's getting cold out here now."

Su-mei sat at the dressing-table, smoothing cream into her face. She glanced up at him in the mirror. "What was all that noise?"

He sat down on the bed heavily. "Pock-mark Chen's men, hunting communists," he said slowly, gazing at the carpet between his feet. "In the Public Gardens."

She paused, a dab of soft white cream on her fingertip. "What d'you mean, hunting communists?" She frowned at him as if she suspected some trick. "In the Public Gardens? How d'you know?"

"I saw them. I heard the shots."

She shrugged. "A gang fight."

"The gang fight now is between the communists and

562

Pock-mark Chen. The police aren't doing anything to stop him, right outside our door. Suppose they found out about Lily?"

She had wiped a streak of the cream onto her cheek, but now she stopped and turned round to look at him. "Are you serious?"

She believed him now. Her eyes had widened with the realisation of what it might mean. "What are we going to do?"

"I don't know—stick to this story we've told the children. And tell her to stick to it too. And keep her in for a while. I'll go and talk to her. You'd better not come, the two of you will only get across each other again..."

As he went up the stairs to Lily's room, he began to feel his fears were unreal. It was unthinkable that this house where he'd lived for twenty years, where he knew every stair and every ledge, where his own hands had worn the banister smooth, could suddenly be invaded by gunmen searching for a seventeen-year-old girl. Unthinkable! He slapped the rail, determined to reassure himself.

Lily sat at her desk, her books spread out in front of her, for all her father knew she might have been studying all afternoon, yesterday's horrors wiped clean from her mind. She sat still and demure while her father talked, her veiled eyes gazing idly down at *Chemistry For Higher Certificate Students*. It was a secondhand copy, bought from the school bookshop. The previous owner, Emily Kwan, had written Chinese translations of the technical words in the margin. She half-listened to her father, half-read the characters, while all the time she felt a smooth, hard core of resolution forming inside her. Her long, almost black hair was plaited in a queue again and hung down to her waist. When she shook her head or nodded obediently, the end twitched against her back, and she thought of the twitching hands of the Russian she'd seen die yesterday, of the spasmodic heaves of Kwok-choi's chest—while he panted and wheezed frothy blood from his mouth, outside the burning police station. She thought of the blood welling out over her blouse and trousers. It was only yesterday, yet it seemed as though it belonged to a different kind of time altogether.

She nodded and shook her head, but only half-listened. All the time he was talking she could feel that core of

563

resolution growing harder and colder inside her. She'd flinched, she'd run away, she'd let them down yesterday, she'd betrayed her ideals—but she'd make up for it. Next time she'd make up for it, whenever, wherever the next time was. She'd make herself think of the blood wet and warm on her hands, she'd imagine it every day, she'd remind herself of it if she ever forgot, and in the end it wouldn't horrify her any more. She'd be able to accept it, to see it, to touch it, even if it was her own blood, without flinching. She fingered the cut on her face, tracing the rough crust of the scab with her finger. She felt the mark made by her mother's ring on her lip.

"You've got to give these ideas up," her father was saying almost apologetically, as if he knew really that he had no right to make such demands. "What China needs is doctors and engineers, not revolutionaries."

She nodded silently, dutifully. Her glance strayed over the characters for *titration, molarity,* and *saturation.* Idly she followed each stroke as if she were building the character up herself, while in her head she saw the blood throbbing out of Kwok-choi's stomach, bubbling out of his lips. See, already she could think of it without shuddering. She'd have to change her name eventually of course, go back to using her mother's family name, something that was truly Chinese. Otherwise they'd always suspect her loyalty, especially after she'd run away like that...

She shut her ears to the sharp, loud barks of pistol fire, as she shut them to her father's words. *University of London Higher Certificate Examination,* Emily Kwan had written in copperplate script at the bottom of the page.

After midnight the firing seemed to die down, to move off into the distance. The English station on the wireless had scarcely mentioned the battle with the communists. "There have been disturbances in the Chinese suburbs," the announcer had said urbanely "but, apart from a few isolated incidents, the international settlement and the French settlement have been calm and peaceful. General Chiang-Kai-shek's forces are now within a few miles of the city and it is expected that the situation will return to normality shortly."

The Chinese station that Ah King had listened to the previous night was off the air. The servants had gone to their rooms straight after dinner, unsettled both by the

564

fighting and by Ah King's oppressive sullenness. Denton went out through the empty kitchen into the garden, for the first time that day. The night was clear and calm, glittering with stars, indifferent to the troubles of Shanghai or anywhere else. He watched a meteor shoot briefly across the dark, and sniffed the breeze that blew off the river, bearing the smell of smoke and oil, and, mingled with them, the scent of the watered earth and leaves of the garden. He thought of Chiang Kai-shek with his smooth young face and cold diamond eyes. With the communists out of the way, he'd be able to strike a deal with the foreigners, offering them security—for a while at least—in return for a greater share of the spoils. How else would he pay the armies? He'd make a sensible Chinese bargain, squeezing the settlements, but not squeezing them to death. He still needed them. Shanghai would survive. So, for all the corpses that would be lying in backstreets in Chapei and Nantao and Paoshan tonight, once the new government took over, everything would go on just the same as before. In China everything came back to the same in the end. The actors changed, but it was always the same drama.

I've become a cynic, he thought as he turned back to the house. Then he stopped with a sudden catching of his breath. Two men were outlined against the yellow light of the open kitchen doorway, one tall and square, the other slight. For a moment he couldn't tell whether they were looking out at him, or into the room. Oh god, he thought while his limbs seemed to melt, they've come for Lily. Then he saw Ah King's shape appear in the doorway. The men pushed her in and closed the door. The light went off.

He hurried down the path with his heart throbbing, while confused images of what might be happening behind the door galloped through his mind. He saw Ah King lying on the floor, clubbed, knifed. He saw the men running up the stairs shouting, he saw them creeping up stealthily. He saw Lily screaming. He saw her with blood leaking out of her breast. For a second he paused at the door, afraid to open it, then he forced himself to turn the handle. The light switch was just inside. He pushed the door suddenly open and flicked the switch on.

The two men were still with Ah King. They swung round and he saw startled fear in their eyes. Then he recognized the big one—Ah King's husband. Denton sighed with astonished, incredulous relief. His taut nerves slackened and he felt himself shaking. He glanced at the other man. He was small and wiry, with thick black brows which nearly met above his nose. They all stared at each other for several still seconds. Then Denton closed the door and took a deep breath.

"So you're back again," he said unsteadily to Ah King's husband. Except that he was thinner and his eyes looked red and exhausted, his face was unchanged. Still the same grim expression.

He nodded dourly without speaking, glancing from Ah King to the other man, then back to Ah King. Then Ah King spoke; her face was worn and heavy-lidded, as though she was ill. "Let them stay, master," she said in a dull voice. "Pock-mark Chen's men are after them."

So that's what you are! Denton suddenly realised, gazing back at her husband. That's why you've always been so mysterious. "Stay?" he repeated uncertainly. "Stay here?" Images flashed through his mind again, too quick for words—the men here in the kitchen, Pock-mark Chen's men arriving in a black car, shots, Lily, shots...

"If you would be kind enough to let us stay here for one night," the slight man said in courteous, but accented Shanghainese, "we would be most grateful. Naturally, we would repay you for your trouble. Tomorrow, early, we will be leaving by boat." His eyes gauged Denton's expression while he spoke. *"Parlez-vous français?"* he added, judging from Denton's bewilderment that he hadn't understood a word. "English?"

"No, Shanghainese is fine," Denton said unevenly in Shanghainese.

The man bowed faintly. "I was born in Chekiang, I'm afraid my Shanghainese is not perfect." He gave an apologetic shrug.

"No, it's very good," Denton said mechanically, with an uneasy certainty that this friendly courtesy was also cunning. "Better than mine of course."

"You see we are no more friends of Mr. Pock-mark Chen than I believe you are..." With the ironic emphasis he gave to the *"Mr."*, he also looked directly into Denton's eyes, as if to let him understand they were well-informed about his relations with Pock-mark Chen, all the way back perhaps to his quarrel over Su-mei. "As you know, he

566

doesn't treat people he dislikes very well. In short, he's anxious to kill us. If his people find us they *will* kill us. Possibly they will kill your daughter too." His bushy brows twitched slightly and he smiled, an icily charming smile that seemed to be printed across his face and then instantly erased.

Denton felt as though the floor had just rocked. His heart was pumping wildly again. "What's my daughter got to do with it?" he asked, putting on a show of amazed ignorance, although he knew it couldn't take them in. It was an instinctive protective gesture, like lunging to keep his balance when he was already falling.

The man merely lowered his lids, as if to say *There's no need to pretend, we won't even mention it.* "If you're ... unable to let us stay, we shan't be able to get far from here. They're looking for us all round this part of the city. If they find us near your home, they may suspect, or..." his eyes held Denton's unblinkingly, driving his words deeper into his brain. "Or they may try to get it out of us." The same cold smile slid over his face again, "It is really safer for everyone if we stay out of sight here until morning."

"And suppose they catch you tomorrow morning when you leave?" Denton tried to keep the tremors out of his voice.

He shook his head. "They won't be looking tomorrow." Denton noticed the fatigue and defeat on his face now, the drawn, greyish cheeks, the deep lines of weariness spreading from the corners of his eyes and mouth. "Your police have given them until tomorrow morning only. At present they have *carte blanche*"—he pronounced the words in French, so that at first Denton didn't recognise them. "It is like the hunting season in Europe," he added, this time without a smile.

Ah King's husband had been watching and listening intently. Denton turned to him. "Every time you come you bring trouble," he said.

The slight man bowed, understanding that Denton had agreed, however unwillingly. "By seven o'clock we shall be gone." He printed that chill, fleeting smile across his face once more. "Perhaps one day I may be able to be of service to you in my turn. Now I think it would be better if we turned off the light. I am sorry your wife no longer appears on the stage, by the way. I used to enjoy her performances."

"What are you going to tell the others?" Denton asked

Ah King, taking in that last remark at the same time. Was there nothing this man didn't know about him?

But it was the slight man who answered, raising his shoulders in an almost Gallic shrug. "Her husband has brought a friend with him, that's all," he said. "We will all sleep in her room."

'I'll be in the study," Denton said to Ah King as her husband flicked the light switch off. "Don't answer the door if anyone comes. It's better if I go."

He checked that all the doors were locked and bolted, the shutters fastened, then climbed up the stairs, his heart gradually slowing, but still loud and heavy. Su-mei wasn't in the bedroom. He went on up towards Lily's room. By the time he reached her door, he'd decided he wouldn't tell either of them what had happened. The fewer people who knew about it the better.

Su-mei was with Lily, brushing her hair in reconciliation. The mark from her ring where she'd slapped her had left her lip bruised and swollen, just below the line of the cut on her cheek. Denton thought the cut was so clean it must have been done by glass or a knife. Lily kept fingering her lip while Su-mei pulled gently at her hair. It was almost as though she was doing it to remind her mother of how much she'd hurt her.

"What are you looking like that for?" Su-mei asked, pausing with the brush in her hand. "What's the matter?"

"Was I?" he looked away quickly. "I didn't know..." He got up to look out of the window. "It seems to have all quieted down by now."

He stayed awake all night in the unlighted study, gazing out of the window. Although there was a curfew, and only soldiers or policemen should have been about, several times he saw large dark saloon cars cruising down the Bund, crawling along the kerb, turning, then crawling back again as if on patrol. Near dawn, one of them stopped, and two men with torches got out, walking again into the Public Gardens. He watched the torches swinging up and down and from side to side through the trees, like lanterns at the Moon Festival. This time there was no shooting and eventually they returned to the car, talking loudly, laughing.

Soon after dawn, as the sky slowly opened and a thin grey light disclosed the shapes of the trees and shrubs, a police truck drew up beside the Gardens entrance. Two men in dark overalls took out a stretcher and followed a policeman along the path. They disappeared behind the azaleas. A few minutes later they came back, carrying a body. The sun's rim was just rising over the river in the east now, touching the tips of the ships' masts and stacks with a faint, hesitant pink. For a second Denton saw the upturned face of the motionless figure on the stretcher, then the men slid the stretcher into the dark back of the truck and slammed the doors. A tug hooted on the river as the truck rattled away.

Gradually life thickened on the Bund—barrows, rickshaws, trucks, pole-carrying coolies trotting to the morning markets, the first trams. He opened the window. With the cold air came in the hubbub of talking and calling, the indignant squeals of pigs and anxious honking of geese, the growing whirr and clatter of engines. He looked down as the kitchen door was stealthily opened below. Ah King's husband and his slight companion slipped away under the bauhinia trees towards the street. In a moment they were gone, absorbed by the morning tide flooding into the city.

73

Denton sat in a corner seat, watching the crowded tables, his hand absently toying with the whisky glass. The December sun had abandoned the street outside, and through the windows he could see an old beggar woman shuffling amongst the deserted pavement tables, picking cigarette stubs out of ash-trays and dropping them into a blue canvas pouch she had tied round her waist. It reminded him for a moment of Janet Pulham with her baby bag. He drank, glanced at his watch, put the glass down. He was glad she was late, he needed the whisky to numb him before she arrived. On the next table three Chinese in neat western suits, young and sleek-looking, were drinking wine with two white Russian girls. Although the twilight chill was already creeping into the room, the girls' coats still hung over the backs of their chairs, and they sat there in short summer frocks displaying their bare white arms and bare white legs. In the middle of their table, as on every other table, two paper flags had been set, the French tricolour and the red and blue of the Kuo Min Tang. And the menu cards were embellished with smudged pictures of Generalissimo Chiang Kai-shek and Miss Mei-ling Soong, beneath the words *Wedding Day Suggestions* in English and French. Denton looked away, raising his glass again, as one of the Russian girls glanced over her shoulder and eyed him with a lingering, assessing look. The last of the whisky rolled round his mouth like a little burning ball of mercury. He swallowed and beckoned the waiter to bring him another. He was beginning to feel it behind his eyes now, that faint heaviness and warmth, bringing a lazy carelessness and indifference with it.

"Sorry I'm late," Suddenly Mary-Ellen stood there beside him, pulling out a chair.

The same fluffy fair hair, a little darker and stiffer now, the same frank blue eyes. Her face not so full though, her skin coarser, more deeply lined. But her body was just as heavy.

She was scrutinising him too, with an ironic, quizzical light in her eyes. "The traffic's terrible with this wedding. I got stuck in a jam outside the Majestic. Saw Chiang and the bride though, driving away. Pretty, in a doll-like way— your taste, I guess. Surprised you didn't go to the reception. Weren't you asked? I'd have thought you were still just about important enough for that?"

"Wei did offer to get us an invitation as a matter of fact."

"'Us' meaning you and your sing-song girl I suppose?" she grinned placidly. "Not you and me?"

"What d'you think?" He paused while she ordered a gin and vermouth from the waiter who was refilling his glass. "But I didn't feel like going."

"Oh? Mei-long Soong was at Wellesley you know, class of seventeen. So we're both alumnae. She's going to make Chiang become a Christian, so they say. A rice Christian, I guess."

"A dollar Christian, I would have thought."

"Why didn't you want to go? I guess Wei's one of the big men round Chiang now?"

He nodded. "I didn't want to see Pock-mark Chen receiving homage from all the arse-lickers in Shanghai."

She raised her brows on mock distaste. "You never used to use such coarse language with me. Where on earth did you pick it up? In fact you were kind of prim."

"I've improved, then?"

570

She shrugged. "I'd have thought you'd lived here long enough to be able to stomach that kind of thing by now, anyway. Or have you got something special against him?"

Denton shook his head. Mary-Ellen had been in Peking when the business with Michael happened—she knew no more about it than what she might have read in the papers at the time, and what Jenny and Alec might have told her on their irregular visits afterwards—if she'd bothered to ask. "I think it's disgusting, that's all," he muttered.

"Sounds like sour grapes to me," she said blithely. "You always wanted to be number one, didn't you, on the municipal council and all that? If you ask me, you're sorry you threw it all up for that sing-song girl."

"Do I refer to your...your friend as a junk shop dealer?"

"Well she's not."

"And Su-mei isn't a sing-song girl either."

"She was once."

"Well she's not now, and she wasn't when I married her."

"OK, OK," she raised her hands to calm him. "Sorry—I didn't know you were so touchy."

"Anyway, it's years and years since I was interested in politics," he said, swallowing his irritation. "I haven't got any ambitions in that direction now." He ignored her raised eyebrow and waited while the waiter poured the vermouth into her glass, sending transparent, bead-like bubbles travelling up to the rising surface. "Well, what did you want to talk to me about?"

She sipped her drink, pursing her lips as she swallowed, as though considering the best way to approach him. Then she looked straight at him with a faint opaque cloud beneath the candid surface of her eyes. "Helen's offered me her share in the gallery. We're splitting up, as a matter of fact. She's going back to Peking."

"I see." He glanced away at the next table again, feeling a mild, crowing pleasure at the thought of Helen's leaving her. How strange, he thought gazing at the Chinese man's fingers stroking the Russian girl's arm. Strange that I should still feel that little spiteful twinge after all these years.

"It's a hundred thousand dollars," Mary-Ellen was saying with contrived casualness. "With goodwill and everything. I wondered whether you might lend me the money?"

"I take it the bank won't?"

She shrugged and pouted at the same time. "They would at fifteen per cent. It makes it a lot more expensive. I'll pay you back in five years. It's a good business. Really. There's no risk..."

He gazed down at his whisky, tilting the nearly empty tumbler. Yes, he was numb, that haze of peaceful indifference heavy behind his eyes. "Are you going to run it all by yourself?" he asked slowly, almost drawling. "Or...?"

The opaqueness clouded her eyes again, and then she smiled almost sheepishly. "Well, there is someone else, a White Russian actually. But she hasn't got any money."

So it was she who was leaving Helen, not Helen her. His mild sense of triumph turned sour. She always came out on top.

"I can show you all the accounts," Mary-Ellen said. "It's a paying business. You can spare the money, can't you? Don't be mean."

"The ransom for Michael was a million dollars," he said sharply. "Not that I suppose that's of much interest to you."

"The papers said you didn't pay a ransom!"

"Well I did. In a roundabout way."

"Well you're not exactly a pauper anyway, are you?" She seemed to check herself, then went on more sympathetically, as if she thought that might be more persuasive. "I did think of calling you when I heard about it, but there wasn't anything I could do. How is he now? All right?"

"Yes, fine—I suppose your alimony is enough to keep you in reasonable comfort?" he went on acidly, before she could ask any more about Michael. "The two of you, that is? You came in for a fair bit of money when your parents died, didn't you?"

She shook her head slowly and wonderingly, her blue eyes quite frank again and curious. "You *are* bitter, aren't you? What's the matter, hasn't it worked out?"

"I'm not bitter, I just prefer it when you don't make your voice all oily with bogus sympathy."

"Now you're being prim again—"

"And I don't know what you mean by its not working out," the words seemed to tumble on before he'd thought them, "but if you mean my marriage with Sú-mei, in the

572

first place it's no concern of yours, and in the second place, it's worked out very well thank you."

"It sounds as though it has," she drawled in her old needling way.

He stared past her coldly for some seconds. The beggar woman had shuffled away outside. A waiter was collapsing the large canvas parasols and setting the chairs upside down on the tables. When Denton looked back, she was smiling imperturbably. "I guess I've picked the wrong day to ask you then?" she said with a resigned little shrug as their eyes met.

He gulped the last of the whisky down and shook his head violently as it burned his throat. "It's the way you ask that gets me down. You just assume I'll give it, don't you?"

"I thought just now you were saying you didn't like displays of bogus sympathy?"

"That doesn't mean you've got the right to think I'll give it to you just because you ask." He stared briefly into her eyes and was met by that wide, candid, half-mocking expression. He'd never seen anything resembling shame or self-reproach there, he thought, and he never would.

"Lend," she said pleasantly. "Not give."

"What's the difference in your case?"

"If you give it, you start off knowing you won't get it back," she drawled. "Whereas if you lend it, you don't find out till later."

He smiled in spite of himself, then leant back, closing his eyes. The whisky was warming his chest, spreading its paralysing consolation throughout his body. He let his anger go with a shrug. "All right then, I'll send you a cheque. As it happens I've done quite well on the stock exchange recently."

"Don't you want to make an agreement and all that?"

"Not after what you've just said," he waved his hand. "Besides, I don't suppose Su-mei'd be pleased to find out I'd put money on such a poor risk as you're likely to be."

"Keeps her eye on you, does she? What do you get up to?"

"Let's just say she takes more interest in my affairs than you ever did. In fact she's probably got a better eye for investments than I have." He glanced at the two Russian girls as they got up to leave with the Chinese men.

"Still got a roving eye, I see," Mary-Ellen murmured.

"Not at all, I was just watching."

573

"That's what I said."

"I presume neither of those girls is the woman you're thinking of, er, collaborating with."

"They're your type, not mine."

He shrugged, raising his hand for the bill. "Have you heard from Jenny recently?"

"No. Have you?"

"No. Not for more than a month. Of course, her spelling's so bad, perhaps the post office can't work out the address..." Suddenly he found himself confiding in her, things that he'd never told Su-mei. It must be the whisky, he thought, as the words ran on. But he didn't seem able to hold them back. "It's strange, when Alec and Michael go next year, the house will be almost empty. There won't be any point in being here then. Perhaps I ought to leave too. Go back to England as a retired gentleman..." He smiled wryly. "Except that no one would believe I was."

"Retired?"

"A gentleman."

She laughed mockingly. "You used to have more life in you ten years ago."

"We all did ten years ago."

"You'll never go back. Neither of us will. We're rooted here now."

"If that's the case, I'm not sure the soil suits me as much as it used to..."

74

Denton gave up his Wei agency. He'd lost all appetite for business, and he didn't need the money. Wei seemed relieved when Denton told him—the agency hadn't been doing well for years. Philip Wei had one of his Chinese American friends appointed instead.

So Denton had more time to spend now. Or to kill. He took to walking about the city. Lily had started medicine at St. Johns, Jenny was at school in England, Alec and Michael would soon follow, and Su-mei and he were still estranged—it seemed she could never forgive him for calling in the police when Michael was kidnapped. The house was growing still and empty, the image of his life.

He wandered aimlessly, in bookstores, antique shops, out in the country. When he saw people he knew, he avoided them, and he sensed they were avoiding him. He would come back dissatisfied, to a house as still and empty as he left it. In the long hours of the evening he would listen to his records or force himself to try to read, but music began to pall, and his programme of self-education had long ago collapsed—even his appetite for novels was failing. Often he would find himself daydreaming over the page, and the daydreams would be pale and fleeting things, vanishing from his mind as soon as he woke. He drank more whisky, and kept a bottle in the study. Often, when he went to bed with blurry eyes, he would see the opium pipe on the floor and smell the cloying scent, while Su-mei would lie asleep in the bed, asleep and drugged. They never smoked together any more. Sometimes he dreamt he was walking down a long flight of steps that grew steeper and darker the further he went. With every step he went faster, but he couldn't hold himself back. Whenever he tried to stop or turn round, something nudged him on and he had to go further down, faster and faster, until he missed a step and fell. Then utter blackness hurtled past his head.

He came back early one January evening to find Su-mei sprawled on the floor in the bedroom, the pipe still in her hand, the lamp still burning. The room, the stairs, the whole house was thick with the smell. He blew out the lamp and lifted her onto the bed. Her lids fluttered, but she didn't wake. They were bluish, he noticed. And there were bluish shadows under her eyes. He felt himself sag where he stood, as though he'd suddenly grown old.

He couldn't face her, he couldn't bear to see her eyes when she came round, he couldn't bear to sit in frozen silence with her later at the dinner table. He turned and went out again.

Cheong paused in the garden, leaning on his hoe. Denton nodded, walked a few yards along the Bund, then hailed a rickshaw.

"Where to, master?" He was a middle-aged coolie, his face weathered and lined, with a squint in one eye.

Denton didn't know. Then a moment later he did. He gave the address of the house in *rue* Molière, where he'd first seen Jacob Ephraim and Pock-mark Chen. The coolie

575

nodded and set off, swinging the rickshaw dangerously round against the oncoming traffic. Denton leant back, buttoning his jacket against the bleak wind blowing off the river. "*Take a concubine*," she'd said peevishly the other night when he'd tried once more to touch her, and once more she'd turned away. At the time it had seemed just a fit of temper. But now the words came back to him, as a taunt she really meant. Well, he'd go one better than that. He'd take a whore.

The house had hardly changed. The shutters were still green, the door was still open, a man still sat on a bamboo chair on the wooden porch. Perhaps the paint had been touched up, but the same path of cracked, uneven stones led up to it, with tufts of coarse-bladed grass half-heartedly struggling to live between them. He hadn't thought of those stones since the last time he'd trodden them, that night when he'd gone there before Lily was born. It came back to him vividly now, the whole scene. He'd walked out on Su-mei then too because she wouldn't even let him touch her; but when he'd gone inside, he'd suddenly lost his nerve, or felt ashamed. He remembered the man with the toothpick, the gas lamp in the hall, the rich smell of opium, the old, spindle-legged coolie who'd taken him there and back. This time he wouldn't leave.

"M'sieu'?" He was an old man. Perhaps he was the same one as before. But he didn't have a toothpick.

"A girl," Denton said in English. He glanced past the man at the wooden stairs and dark, polished balustrade leading up from the hall. Yes, it was still lit by gas. The stairs were covered with a beige, patterned carpet, neither new nor old, neither rich nor tawdry. He wondered whether that had been there before. It might have been a boarding house.

"I got new one for you," the old man was saying. "Tonight just start. Very youn'. Special for you."

Denton shrugged. "All right." He changed to Shanghainese. "Let me see her."

"Ah you speak Chinese!" The man smiled. "Very good, very good." He stood up, catching the rustling newspaper as it slid off his knees, and led him inside, calling quietly up the stairs. "This girl's very pretty, you'll like her. You've been living in Shanghai a long time?"

"Quite long." He sniffed. Yes, there was the smell of opium too.

The man smiled again, the friendly smile that you sometimes met in a hawker. As if he too were selling something wholesome and innocent.

Denton glanced up at the shadowy walls and the dim light from the gas lamp. Suddenly he recalled Su-mei as a young girl, watching the flame, enthralled as she played with the gas lamp in his room in the Customs Officer's Club. But the memory didn't weaken his desire. It merely made him momentarily sad, like a passing thought of distant childhood.

A woman appeared at the top of the stairs in a long silver cheong-sam. She was almost portly, middle-aged, but her face extravagantly painted and her nails scarlet. "*Bonsoir m'sieu*," she smiled winsomely and glanced with a raised, plucked brow at the man.

"Yuriko," the man said.

"Ah, Yuriko," she repeated, in a tone that seemed to compliment Denton on his choice. "Yuriko."

"I want to see her first."

"I'm sure you'll like her," she smiled again. "Your Chinese is very good. This way please."

As though I was ordering a meal, Denton thought, but the thrill quickened in his stomach as he followed her up the carpeted stairs.

She half-turned at the top, where a large cut-glass chandelier threw a dim light over the landing. "Of course she's a little more expensive," she smiled. "She's very pretty."

An old amah in a white jacket was taking fresh towels and sheets from a closet. She scarcely glanced at the two of them as they passed. Denton heard girl's voices chattering along the corridor. "How much?" he asked.

The woman paused at a heavy brown door, taking a keyring out of the silver reticule she was carrying. "Only fifty dollars for two hours." She fitted a key into the lock and turned it. "Why not stay all night? Only two hundred dollars." She swung the door open and gestured him in.

"I'd better see her first."

"I'll go and get her. I'm sure you'll like her."

He looked round the room. There was a dressing table with an oval mirror, a large dark wardrobe, and a wash basin. The walls were painted white, and framed prints hung on them—nineteenth century scenes of country towns and sailing ships, not women. It was how he

577

imagined a provincial French boarding house might look. Yes, there was something reassuringly ordinary about the place. He could see why Jacob had kept recommending it all those years ago. It wasn't tawdry or plush. It took away the sense of sin—not that that had ever bothered Jacob—and replaced it with a feeling of guiltless, decent pleasure. He touched the bed, patting it as if it were a dog. The sheets were fresh and starchy. Just like a boarding house.

He heard footsteps and turned around.

"This is Miss Yuriko," the woman said ceremoniously. "Isn't she pretty?"

The girl was young and dainty. She was dressed in a kimono and those Japanese sandals that made women walk with a swaying shuffle almost as though their feet were bound. Her hair was done in the Japanese way too, with a large comb in it. There were faint pink circles of rouge on each cheek, but the rest of her face was pale. She glanced up at him almost shyly and smiled without speaking.

"Wouldn't you like to stay all night with her?" the woman coaxed him. "She's very affectionate."

"I thought this was her first time?" Denton asked drily.

"Ah..." Her eyes clouded with vagueness. "She's very young, that's right..." she said evasively. "Wouldn't you like to stay the night?"

"I'll think about it."

"See how you get on, all right," the woman smiled equably.

The amah came in with a half-bottle of wine and a carafe of water on a tray. She set the tray down on the table by the bed, and turned the sheets back. Just like a boarding-house.

Yuriko followed the two women to the door, murmured something then closed it. "Like some wine?" she asked, going to the table. Her voice had a faint accent, as if she really was Japanese. And yet she looked more Chinese to him.

"All right." He watched her pour it. "What about you?"

She shook her head, pouring herself some water. "It makes me ill." She held the glass out to him with both hands. He brushed her fingers with his as he took it. The desire stirred again.

"What about opium?" he asked.

578

"Opium?"

"I thought I smelt it when I came in."

"You want to smoke opium?"

"No, I just wondered if that made you ill, too."

"Ah, just wondered," she repeated absently. She went to the other side of the bed, sat down with her back half-turned to him, and took out her comb.

He sipped the wine. "Are you really Japanese?"

"Chinese. I can speak Japanese though. My parents live in Yokohama. I was born there." She laid the comb down on the table and began drawing out her hairpins. "So they say I'm Japanese."

"What do they do—your parents?"

"Restaurant."

"Why did you come here?" he gestured round the room, meaning *to this life.*

She paused, her hands at her hair, as if she hadn't asked herself that before. Then she shrugged. "Money," she said.

He nodded and drank some more wine. "And how long have you been here?"

"About three months." She shook her hair free. It fell loose down to her waist. Then she started undoing her kimono. The formalities were over.

He finished the wine and walked round to stand in front of her. She glanced up at him, the kimono half off her shoulders.

"Your skin is very pale," he said.

"I keep out of the sun." She wriggled her shoulders till one sleeve slipped down and he could see her small full breast. "You like me?" she asked, looking up at him almost demurely.

He eased the other sleeve off her shoulder. "So far," he said. She stood up and the kimono slithered down onto the floor. She had slim, boyish hips. Her thigh, he noticed, had a little brown mole on it. She unfastened his jacket and leant against him. Her head came up to his chest. He held it there and let his cheek rest on her hair while her fingers picked at his shirt buttons. Her hair smelt fresh, as though she'd just washed it.

"Goodnight sir," the man called from his bamboo chair as Denton left and walked down the cracked stones of the path.

There were three rickshaws waiting outside, the coolies huddling in their cabs against the cutting wind that still blew off the river. They were smoking wide, hand-rolled cigarettes which glowed more brightly as they inhaled, lighting up their dark, creased faces.

"Rickshaw?" Denton called.

One of the coolies climbed slowly out of his cab. He was bowed and grey-haired. "Where to?" he coughed, dragging the last smoke and warmth out of his cigarette before throwing the flattened, sodden butt away.

"The Bund. Near Garden Bridge."

"A long way," he said sullenly. "One dollar."

Denton shrugged his agreement and climbed in. The other coolies laughed at the old man's luck. "A woman makes them generous," one of them grunted to the other, and they both chuckled again. The old man coughed and spat.

Denton leant back under the canopy, sheltering against the wind, his eyes tired with that heavy-lidded contented fullness that he hadn't felt for months—a fullness that he knew would gradually turn to sadness as the spell wore off and his mind dropped back into its old worn grooves. But still, for now that fullness was enough. So he leant back, listening to the soothing slap-slap of the coolie's sandals, to the steady ticking of the rickshaw's wheels. I'd almost forgotten what a woman could do, he thought, recalling the girl's lips and tongue caressing him, the black, fringed curtain of her hair sweeping over his face. Even if it was only for money.

The coolie kept hawking and coughing every few steps. He slowed to a walk as the cough hacked deeper in his chest. His gaunt shoulders began to heave as though he couldn't get his breath. Denton watched his rounded, shaking back uneasily. "Just stop and wait a minute," he said.

The man stopped, still coughing, put down the shafts with a little jolt and leant against the lamppost, spluttering and wheezing. His face had turned a dull purplish red beneath the leathery skin and his eyes bulged with the prolonged racking of his lungs. Denton stepped out of the rickshaw and stood uneasily beside him while he shuddered with each new paroxysm.

He heard the unhurried tread of hobnailed boots and glanced round. A Sikh policeman was approaching. He

580

surveyed Denton, then the coolie, who was at last beginning to catch his breath, sighing and spitting as the coughing eased. At least he hadn't been coughing blood, Denton thought with relief. He couldn't be too bad.

"All right sir?" the Sikh asked Denton in English.

"He just had a coughing fit. Seems to be getting over it now..."

The coolie squatted down, gasping and spitting, holding his head in his hands. The Sikh nudged him with his boot. The toe cap gleamed like an anthracite mirror in the lamplight. "Hey, you," he nudged him again, speaking in Shanghainese now. "What's the matter?"

The coolie shook his head wearily, heaving for breath still, and wiped some clinging spittle off his lips with the back of his hand.

"You getting too old for rickshaw pulling?" the Sikh asked accusingly, as if age was some sort of offence. "Can't you see you're keeping the gentleman waiting?"

"It doesn't matter," Denton said. "I can wait."

"Got far to go, have you?" the Sikh continued, throwing Denton a respectful but firm glance, as if to say, Leave it to me, I know their little tricks. "You mustn't work if you're ill. You can't take people where they want to go."

The coolie straightened up and stepped between the shafts without answering. Still breathing heavily, he was staring down at the ground, as though steeling himself to bend and grasp the handles.

"I think he's all right now," Denton said.

But the Sikh ignored him this time, planting himself, legs apart, in front of the coolie. "Hey you," he tapped him warningly on his thin, panting chest with his thick forefinger. "I'm talking to you! Don't you go pulling rickshaws if you're not fit. Understand? Suppose you fall down and cause an accident?" He felt for his breast pocket, still gazing at the coolie severely, took out his notebook and slowly, ostentatiously, jotted down the rickshaw's licence number. "How old are you?"

The man shrugged sullenly. "Forty-eight, fifty...I don't know."

"You're getting past it then, aren't you?"

Denton felt a little weight suddenly fall on his chest. He was forty-six himself.

The policeman stepped back, glancing at Denton again

with an expression at once respectful and patronising. "All right, sir."

"Take it easy," Denton said as he stepped in. "There's no hurry."

The man moved off at a walking pace, muttering to himself between breaths, clearing his throat and bringing up gobbets of phlegm which he spat fiercely onto the ground, as though he hated them. "Don't pull rickshaws if you're not fit!" Denton heard him grunt sarcastically. "What does he expect me to eat? Dog-shit?"

Denton stopped him a hundred yards or so from the house. He took out a ten dollar note and offered it to the man. The man shook his head. "No change," he muttered. Even now he was breathing heavily.

"Keep it. Buy yourself some medicine."

He took it ungraciously, tucked it into his belt and turned the shafts slowly round.

As Denton walked towards the house, he heard the man coughing again behind him, that long hacking cough from deep in his lungs. "I should have given him a hundred dollars," he thought ashamedly. "I've just spent that much on that girl." He looked back, but the man was plodding away now, his head sunk between his shoulders. He walked slowly up the steps to the door, past the ragged poinsettias.

As he went in, he heard the kitchen door open. It was Lily, carrying a steaming cup. Her winter coat hung open from her shoulders, reminding him for a second of the kimono hanging from the girl's naked shoulders a few hours earlier. They must be about the same age, he thought detachedly.

"Hello, Lily," he said. "Have you just come in? You're late."

She looked at him with faintly narrowed eyes. "You're late too," she answered in Chinese.

Although their voices were casual, there was an edgy undertone to their words, as though each was accusing the other.

He persisted in English. "What've you been doing?"

"Nothing much," she said obstinately in Chinese. She sipped from the cup, then went upstairs with it. "There was a meeting at St. Johns."

"Not a political meeting?"

She turned. "You know they're not allowed," she said calmly, still in Chinese.

"Have you forgotten how to speak English?" The edgy undertone poked through at last.

"Not yet." She turned and went on, balancing the cup carefully. "I'm trying though."

He let her go, swallowing his irritation. She could be good-looking, he thought, if she didn't insist on being plain. And so damned earnest. If she was playing politics again...He thought of the Kuo Min Tang police, the rumours of how they tortured suspects. He didn't doubt them. Roasting them in the fires of railway engines, for instance.

The light was on in his study. As he opened the door he heard Lily's step on the next landing. Su-mei was sitting at the desk, which was covered with files and accounts. She glanced up at him a moment, then bent over the papers again without speaking.

He leant back against the door. He didn't want to go too close to her, she might smell the other woman. He'd have a shower first.

"Do you realise nearly all our money's still in property? We ought to sell half of it and invest in shares, or buy gold."

"Gold's high now," he said uninterestedly.

"D'you know how much rent we're getting from these houses in Yangtzepoo Road? Why not sell them for a start?"

He shrugged. "See what you'd get for them." He watched her fingering through the documents, a light, alert frown on her forehead.

She glanced round at him again, a little longer this time. "Who was that you were talking to on the stairs?"

"Lily."

"Lily? Coming in at this hour?"

"It's only eleven and she's nineteen." He held back from telling her his suspicions. He didn't want her running upstairs to question Lily or plead with her. Not with Lily in her present steely mood. Su-mei's lips tightened but she didn't answer. "I told them to keep some food warm for you," she said evenly, after a few seconds.

"Did you enjoy your afternoon opium?" he asked.

She glanced at him sharply. "How did you know I'd been smoking?"

"I came back this evening and found you on the floor. Why are you smoking so much? *Too* much?"

She looked away. "I do it to forget."

"Forget what?"

"Things you'll never remember."

He sighed. "When I saw you like that, I had to go out again."

She started closing the files one by one on the desk. Then she laid her hands on the last one and turned her head away to gaze out of the window. "To a woman?" she asked quietly. Then, when he didn't answer, "I saw it in your eyes the minute you came in."

There was no reproach in her voice, only a tone of wondering sadness, as if she was thinking Well, then, that's that. "Isn't that what you wanted me to do?" he excused himself with a stab of bitterness. "You told me to take a concubine!"

He saw her lips move as she swallowed, still gazing away out of the window. "At my age," she said slowly and desolately, 'I suppose that is the thing."

"You're not old," he said with sudden gentleness and remorse. "That's not why, you know it isn't."

"Forty-one," she lifted her brows. "Would you call that young?"

If only she'd lose her temper, shout, scream, cry, hit him! But there was nothing. Only this deadly calm.

"But please don't sleep in my bed tonight," she added quietly, still gazing out of the window. Even that she said without a flick of scorn.

75

"In here," Alec said, pulling the drawer further out. "Behind all those letters and things." He held up the heavy brocade cloth that hung down over the front of the chest so that Michael could see better.

Michael reached in. The letters were all addressed to his father. They were fastened with several rubber bands, most of them perished and melted in the heat of past summers. "What *are* all these letters?" he asked, fingering the torn yellow envelopes. "Look they've got American stamps on." He hardly noticed his missing finger now.

"They're from my mother," Alec said in a superior tone. "Nothing to do with you. The thing's right at the back. She wrote those letters years and years ago, before they were married."

"Have you read them?"

"Some of them. The writing's hard."

Michael reached further back. There were piles of soft white cloths, musty still from the humid heat of summer.

"I can't find anything," he said.

"Further across." Alec knelt down beside him. "Got it." He drew the thing out carefully. "There, what d'you think *that* is?"

Michael frowned down at the thing, which Alec was holding gingerly in both hands. It was like an old-fashioned car horn made out of glass, with a red rubber globe at the end. The rubber there too was cracked and perished. Michael squeezed the globe, softly at first, then harder. But there was no sound.

"I've tried that," Alec said. "It doesn't work."

They looked at the trumpet end, turned it over and shook it gently. There was a little glass bulb beneath the stem which was stained an old, greyish white inside.

"I bet it's old," Michael said.

"Let's ask Ah King."

"Suppose it's something secret?"

"Who cares?"

Alec led the way downstairs to the kitchen, holding the thing behind his back as they passed the dining room, where their father sat over his coffee reading the paper. Ah Sam was washing up the breakfast dishes in the sink. Ah King was sorting laundry, laying it in different piles on the ironing board. Ah Man sat on the kitchen step, where the morning sun had just reached, smoking a cigarette and turning his face up to the sun like a dog asking to be stroked. The cat lay beside him, washing its ginger fur.

"What's this, Ah King?" Alec asked, holding the thing out in his hand.

She frowned down at it. "Where did you find that?"

"What is it?"

"In the chest of drawers on the landing," Michael said.

She flapped a towel in their faces then tucked it under her chin to fold it in two. "That's your mother's

585

thing, Alec," she said, snapping the towel taut as it fell doubled between her hands. "To take the milk out. When the baby doesn't want it."

Alec stared at her uncomprehendingly. "Take the milk out?" he repeated blankly.

"Yes, milk out, mother's milk!" She took it from him as Ah Sam turned from the sink with a sigh to watch. "Like this." She pressed the trumpet through her tunic against her breast and squeezed the globe. As she slowly let the globe go, the thing seemed to cling to her a moment, then she caught it as it fell off. "When you squeeze here," she said, doing it again, "Milk comes out here, goes into the glass. Next time there's more for baby. See there?" She tapped the bulb. "Old milk in there, from your mother. All dried up. Very old."

Alec frowned sceptically. Jenny had never told him about that.

"You put it back now," Ah King said, giving the thing back to him.

"What's it called?"

Ah Man moved slightly to one side as Ah Leng came in from the market. "It's called a milk squeezer," he murmured without turning his head.

Ah Leng's basket was overflowing. She dumped it on the floor with a sigh, taking out bamboo shoots, white-stalked bean flowers, dark green Chinese spinach, fish with wet shiny scales and still-glistening round eyes. The cat rubbed against her leg, its tail up, purring. "I saw some communists being driven to the execution ground," she said, stroking the fish scales critically, as if not quite sure after all they were that morning's catch. "Two lorries full of them."

Ah King, drawing another towel out of the laundry basket, paused before folding it. "Where were they from?" she asked casually.

"No idea." She nudged the cat away with her foot. "Somewhere in the south, the fish man said."

Alec was trying to make the milk-squeezer stick to his own chest through his pullover, like Ah King had.

"Look at him!" Ah Leng exclaimed, pointing a finger sticky with blood and scales. "Thinks he's a woman!"

Alec started playing up to them, pretending to milk one breast then the other. But while the other laughed,

586

Ah King scowled. "Go on Alec, put it back or I'll tell master. Quick! Go on!"

Cheong craned his head round the door. His mild eyes blinked at Ah King. "Letter for you," he said, holding the cheap envelope out carefully, as though he was afraid it might break if he dropped it.

"For me? A letter for me?"

"Postman gave it to me outside." He pointed to the characters on the envelope with his earth-stained finger. "This is your name, he said."

Ah King handed the envelope to Ah Man. "Is this my name?" she asked suspiciously.

Ah Man turned his head an inch or two and frowned down at the letter for some time, moving his lips as he made out the characters. "Looks like it," he said at last. "Want me to read it?"

"And have you missing out half because you couldn't understand it?" She plucked the envelope out of his hand. "Or making it up, more likely." Ah Man shrugged, closing his eyes and shifting his face back to the sun again. "I'll go to the letter writer," Ah King said. "They can read what's really there. Now will you two put that thing back, whatever it's called, before I tell master?"

"It's called a milk-squeezer," Ah Man repeated absently.

Alec hid it behind his back again as they passed the dining room. Their father glanced up, turning a page of the newspaper, then looked down.

"Do you think Chinese women use them as well?" Michael asked uncertainly as he pulled the drawer open again.

"No. They're a different shape."

Michael fingered the bundled letters again as he reached into the drawer. The large, careless writing in fading brown ink, written before he was born, gave him a feeling of quiet wonder, as if he was handling the dried bones of a dead person. He thought of the bones which the peasants kept in pots on the hill-sides for years before they buried them. He'd come back by himself and look at those letters again, one day.

Ah King hurried to the street of the letter writers. The old man had moved his table away from the wall into the sunlight. He was sitting on his stool arranging his ink, pens and brushes. He glanced up at her shrewdly over his steel-framed glasses as she sat down opposite him. "You're early." He rubbed his stubbly grey beard with the palm of his hand. "Something important to say? Shall we use the brush this time, or the pen? Important news deserves to be well-written, and I can see your news is important, so that means the brush." He took up a brush, as if that at least was settled, and started to prepare the ink.

"Wait a minute, wait a minute," Ah King protested, dragging the letter out of her tunic. "Can you read this first, please?" Her normally gruff voice had taken on a hesitant, pleading tone. Learning always overawed her.

The old man laid down his brush and smoothed out the envelope, which had got crumpled in Ah King's pocket. She had already slit it open, but he examined the address and the postmark carefully, pursing his lips judiciously. "This comes from Hong Kong," he pronounced as he drew the letter out. "One of your family?"

Ah King nodded. She leant forward to listen, her eyes switching from the old man's face to the characters on the cheap, flimsy paper as he read. The letter was only a few lines long.

> I have arrived here after a long journey. I am well. There is some work for me to do here, so I shall stay for some months. Send a money order for one hundred dollars to me at this address, as I need it to buy clothes and tools. My friend is no longer with me but he is also well. Do not trouble with Yin-hong any more. He is not worth it, as I hear. I hope you are well. Your husband.

He looked at her over his glasses again, laying the letter down on the table.

"Is that all?"

"Did you expect me to leave something out?"

She shook her head apologetically, folding the letter and sliding it back slowly into the envelope. Then she pulled it out again. "Did it say when he wrote it?"

He shook his head. "No date. Show me the envelope and I'll tell you when it was posted." He took the envelope and pored over the post-mark. "Four days ago," he concluded, looking up again. "Very quick. Now what about your answer? Brush or pen?"

"Pen," she murmured, but it was hardly necessary. With a resigned sigh he was already putting the brush away and selecting a pen. He smoothed out a sheet of paper, dipped the fine, sharp nib into the ink and looked up at her expectantly. "Well?" he held the pen ready over the page.

She was gazing down at her letter, frowning as she recalled it. "I will do what you say," she dictated self-consciously.

He smiled indulgently. "What about greetings? Thank you for your precious letter? I have read of your doings with great interest? Something about your husband's health, your children? Don't you think he wants to know?"

"Yes, yes, all right," she folded and unfolded her letter nervously in her fingers. "Thank you for your precious letter. Start like that."

"Thank you for your..." the old man said as the characters flew together under his scratching nib. "How about treasured letter? Isn't that better?"

By the time he'd finished coaxing and cajoling her, Ah King's brief sentence was embedded in a page and a half of flowery, submissive courtesy. He frowned at the awkwardness when she wanted to add two more sentences of her own. "May I know what you have heard about Yin-hong? I have no news of him at all." But he wrote them without comment.

She paid him twenty coppers more for reading her husband's letter as well as writing her own. As she was getting up to leave, she glanced round casually. "So it only takes four days from Hong Kong?"

The old man nodded, dropping the money into his pocket. "But it may take longer from here to there, going the other way."

"Longer?"

"Maybe. But there's no hurry, is there? He said he'd be there for months."

"Yes, that's right," she said absently. "So he did." She glanced up and down the street. A barber was cutting a man's hair across the road. "Did they bring the communist bandits this way?"

He grunted again, rearranging his pens and paper fastidiously. "They'll all be dead by now, I should think." When the pens were all lined up, he opened a newspaper he'd had folded on his lap all the time.

"I suppose they'd be ones they caught a long time ago?" she speculated tentatively.

The old man spread the paper out on the table without looking up. "More than four days ago, anyway," he said, settling his glasses more firmly on his nose and beginning to read.

Lily would get up early, eat a Chinese breakfast, and leave for the university before either Denton or Su-mei had come down. But one morning Denton too rose early and met her as she was leaving, her books under her arm.

"Going to the university?" he asked in Shanghainese. "I'll give you a lift."

"It's all right, I can take the bus."

"I'm going that way," he insisted. "Besides, I want to ask you something."

She gave him a suspicious, defensive glance, then shrugged resignedly.

When she got into the car, she leant back in the corner, her face smoothly immobile. As though she'd wrapped an invisible veil round herself.

"Go down Avenue Edward VII," Denton told Lau, "then along Jessfield Road to St. Johns."

"That's a long way round," Lily said expressionlessly.

"I wanted to show you where I used to live."

"You've shown me before. You've shown all of us."

"Well, perhaps I wanted to show myself," he said. "As a reminder." He didn't want to admit he'd chosen the long way to give them more time to talk. Besides, he did want to see the old place again. The past was becoming more important to him, now that he felt he had less future.

But he didn't speak for some time, wondering how best to lift that forbidding veil she'd draped round herself. He gazed out of his window at the trees blossoming in the heavy, moist spring air, while Lily stared silently out of hers at the crowded river, on which the sun was shining with a mild, caressing warmth.

"This is like the summer in England," he said at last.

She shrugged lightly to show her ignorance, or perhaps her indifference.

They were passing the Shanghai Club now. He nodded up at the colonnade on the first floor and smiled wrily. "I was thrown out of there, you know, once," he said in English.

"Thrown out?" she glanced at him with a sudden
590

gleam of interest. She even slipped into English herself, realising that he didn't want Lau to understand.

"Expelled. Not physically hurled out of the building."

"Why?"

"For leaving my first wife and taking your mother to live with me. I knew they would, of course, when I did it..." He smiled again, savouring the grudging look of respect she threw him. "Why, didn't you think I had it in me? D'you mind if we speak English for a bit, by the way? I know you don't like to, but..." he nodded faintly at Lau's head.

The wary veil floated over her face again. She looked at him watchfully.

"You remember that promise you made...?" he began.

"Which promise?"

He ignored the stiffening of her voice, like hackles rising. "When the communists were massacred, before Chiang Kai-shek marched in."

"Oh, that was years ago," she said dismissively, as if nobody would remember a promise as old as that, let alone feel bound by it.

He glanced across at her. She was holding the strap, gazing out now at the grinding trams and rickshaws along Avenue Edward VII, her eyes half-closed against the sun. Not *holding* the strap exactly—her wrist was resting in the loop of the leather and drooping down with unconscious elegance. "But you do remember it, though?" he persisted.

She shrugged. "What about it?"

And this was the girl who'd been so shy and obedient until she was sixteen!

"You haven't kept it, have you?"

"Haven't I?"

"You know you haven't. You're always coming in at odd hours, trying not to be seen. Or sneaking out, for that matter. I've noticed it quite a lot recently."

"Spying on me?"

"Worried about you, that's all. I would imagine the Kuo Min Tang's intelligence service is pretty good. And you know what happens to people they catch. Even students. Or if you don't, you ought to." She began to speak, but he overrode her. "I'm not trying to stop you, I realise that wouldn't be any use. You're nearly twenty now. And I haven't told your mother"—he saw her cheeks tighten at that—"I just hope you'll be careful, that's all."

"There isn't any risk in what I'm doing," she said coldly. She lifted her hand out of the strap to wipe away a strand of hair that had somehow escaped and blown over her eyes, then slipped it back with the same unconscious grace.

"What is it exactly that you're doing, then?"

Her lips compressed. She looked away out of the window. "Look, there's Sarah Ephraim," she said. "Haunting the jewellers as usual..."

Denton glanced past her. Sarah was just leaving one jeweller's, and about to walk into another next door. Her face, despite its heavy make-up, looked haggard, almost desperate.

"I'd rather die than end up like that," Lily said witheringly.

"Perhaps she would have once, too."

She glanced at him swiftly a second, trying to understand, then dropped her eyes. She was too young to have thought of complexities like that before.

They stopped at the crossroads. Two trams went clanking past, followed by a crowd of rickshaws and wheelbarrows.

"What *is* it that you're doing, Lily?" he asked again as the traffic policeman waved them on.

"Something better than buying another bit of jewellery every day," she said, but with the sting drawn from her voice.

"Such as?"

She said nothing, looking away out of the window with almost a sneer on her lips. It was more cutting than any outburst of words would have been, more arrogant, more unjust. "You wouldn't understand," she said at last.

"Well, I can guess, anyway."

They sat silent for some time, watching the street. Then she turned to look at him abruptly as if she'd suddenly made a decision, turned her whole body on the seat as the car swung round onto Jessfield Road. "They say you made all your money with opium," she said accusingly.

"Do they?" He felt his mind groping behind the screen of words he threw up. "We'll be passing my old place in a minute or two. It's one of the older houses, remember. There weren't so many houses here then of course..."

"Is it true?" she insisted coolly.

Very well, if she must know. He sighed and settled back in the seat. "*Who* says that?" he asked.

"People. The people I work with, other people. Your own servants for instance."

"Yes, well it's true in a way..." he gazed unseeingly ahead at the barrows and rickshaws, the buses, cars and trucks. "I had quite a lot of money from other things, but then I lost most of it in the war... I was nearly bankrupt. And then I got the chance of buying this opium cheap just when the price was about to climb, so I did..." For a moment his eyes seemed to see Mason in that shabby house with the Chinese woman. "That's how I saved myself, and I actually became richer in the end. So you could say it's true, yes." He felt her eyes were hardening against him, although he didn't look at her. "In those days there was nothing illegal about opium dealing of course," he added defensively. "It was just a commodity like any other..."

"You knew what opium did to people?"

"I knew what it did to addicts. But you didn't have to be an addict if you smoked. I smoked, your mother smoked. We didn't become addicts." (He wondered suddenly whether Su-mei wasn't becoming one now, then pushed the idea out of his mind.) "You wouldn't prohibit alcohol just because some people became alcoholics, would you?" But he thought perhaps she would.

"Some people! It was half the country."

"We didn't have figures like that at our fingertips then," he said drily. "I wonder where you got them from? There's the house," he nodded suddenly, leaning forward to see the lawn and veranda through the trees. It all looked trim and well-cared for still.

"Did you trick Pock-mark Chen out of the opium?" Lily asked inquisitorially, hardly troubling to glance at the house. "Is it true he had something to do with Michael's kidnapping—that's how he got his own back?"

Denton's cheeks flushed. He frowned at her. "Do they say that as well? How interesting I must be. Do they ever talk about anything else?"

"They say you used to be on the progressive side in the council," she said, as if summing up the evidence for and against him. "But now you've given up. They say

593

you're afraid of Pock-mark Chen, too." Obviously the weight of the evidence was against him.

"Well if I was afraid of him," he murmured, "I wouldn't be the only one." Then, after a pause, he went on. "It's true I gave up—true in a way. I gave up whatever influence I might have had in this city when I married your mother. I did it deliberately. I thought it was worth it. But it's a long story, and rather complicated—why are those people so interested in me?"

"They're not. It's just that I have to convince them I'm not like you," she said dispassionately. "Otherwise they won't trust me. It's bad enough being half-English." She leant forward and spoke to Lau in Shanghainese. "Stop anywhere along here please."

"We're not there yet," Denton said. "There's half a mile before—"

"I'd rather not arrive in a Rolls-Royce." The car drew up at the entrance to Jessfield Park. She got out and looked at him reproachfully through the open window. "I couldn't kow-tow to Pock-mark Chen," she said. "Not even to save my life."

"What about to save someone else's?"

She didn't reply. It was as though she hadn't heard, as though his words had bounced off her forehead.

"If you're not careful," he called after her, "you'll end up an intolerant prig!"

He watched her cross the road and walk quickly away towards the university drive. There were several groups of students chatting as they walked along in the same direction. Many of the girls looked smart and rich. Lily walked past them all without a glance.

He leant back, gazing numbly out, till the car passed the tenement on Bubbling Well Road where he'd first lived after leaving the customs. It was shabbier, dirtier, more teeming than ever now. Huts had been added onto the roof, the old verandas covered with plywood and glass to make extra rooms. The woodwork was split and warped, the grimy plaster pitted and flaking. I should have shown her this, he thought. She might have understood a bit then. He thought of her hand drooping gracefully down from the loop of the strap. The curve of her wrist was like Su-mei's. Could she really just reject what her body had so clearly inherited in favour of sexless comradeship with humourless idealists? He was sure that was what they were.

76

"Who is giving out the prize' this year?" Su-mei asked as they stepped out of the car and walked towards the school hall.

"Someone from the municipal council," Denton answered. "Walker, his name is. He once rode my pony at the races. When he was a griffin." He took a programme from a monitor with fair wavy hair and a ruddy face glowing with perspiration.

Su-mei slipped back into Shanghainese as they passed through the double doors into the crowded hall. "Don't you wish you were in his place now? You might have been, except for me."

"That's all past now," he said curtly. "I never think about it." He glanced up at the Union Jack hanging on the stage behind the long table with the prizes on it. "The only thing I wish now..." He hesitated as they sat down in two empty seats near the back.

"What?"

"I wish I knew what to do with the rest of my life."

He felt her looking at him uncomprehendingly. He handed her the programme. She scarcely glanced at it. She was scanning the rows of boys crammed onto benches facing the parents, just below the stage.

"There's Michael," she said. "There's Alec. Why aren't they sitting together?"

"Because they're in different forms, I suppose."

There was something about her silence which said, If they'd been in the same form, still they wouldn't be sitting together.

The piano started playing and the boys stood up with an echoing coughing and shuffling of feet. The parents' murmuring sank away as they all craned to see their own children.

The boys' voices rose beneath the slowly turning fans that hung down squeaking faintly from the raftered, sloping ceiling. They were singing the school song. The headmaster and all the teachers were wearing their gowns,

595

some with the bright silk hoods of their university degrees. I might have been one of them, Denton thought detachedly, if father hadn't had to stop working. The boys' voices took him back to the church at Enfield when he'd sung in the choir, searching for Emily's smiling, downturned face in the congregation.

He glanced sideways at Su-mei. He knew from the light in her eyes that she was watching Michael. Probably she was laying plans for him, to make him into a taipan, overcoming the stigma of his mixed birth by means of wealth and power. It gave her something to live for. But she'd lose it in the end. It couldn't last. Nothing did.

The boys sat down and the headmaster began speaking in a weak, bleating voice, hardly rising above the squeaking of the fans. The man next to Denton breathed heavily, as though he was dozing.

Denton studied Walker's face on the stage. Sitting on the headmaster's right, he was gazing up at him with an assumed air of attentiveness that only the vacant eyes belied. He must have had plenty of practice in that pose at council meetings. Denton wouldn't have recognized him as the young griffin from Jardine's who'd ridden his horse and thanked him so politely all those years ago when he was still married to Mary-Ellen. He'd grown heavy-jowled and pompous-looking, the boyish diffidence replaced by flushed self-satisfaction.

It was no surprise, when he stood up to award the prizes, that his voice sounded creamily complacent. Michael had the class prize as the best all-round student, Alec a prize for verse-speaking. Walker smiled genially at each of them, as he did at every boy with scrubbed sheepish face that climbed the platform to the applause mainly of his parents.

After the prize-giving, there were refreshments in the playground. Denton and Su-mei stood awkwardly by themselves. As self-conscious as the boys on the platform, Denton thought wryly. They knew few of the other parents, and although the scandal of his divorce and remarriage had long been forgotten, it was still enough that he had a Chinese wife for an uneasy ostracism to take place, as though they carried some harmful germ. They felt it every year. But as they were about to go, Walker left the headmaster and approached them, smiling genially.

"Mr. Denton!" he greeted them heartily. "Mrs. Denton. A long time since we met."

"I don't think you've ever met *this* Mrs. Denton," Denton said coolly.

"No," he smiled unperturbed. "I believe you're right. Glad to have the pleasure at last. Proud of your two boys, I expect?" He turned to Denton as soon as he could. "You know some of us think it's an awful pity you're no longer involved in public affairs. We really need someone with your experience back on the council. Have you ever thought of re-entering that sphere?"

"I hardly thought I was acceptable in it."

"Oh . . ." Walker shook his head and gave a disclaiming laugh as he glanced at Su-mei and back again. "I know things were a bit . . . er sticky at one time, but times have changed a lot since then, haven't they? In this day and age I mean . . . After all, we've got fully-fledged Chinese members on the council now. Your old associate's son, Philip Wei for instance."

"We're even allowing them into the Public Gardens as well," Denton added expressionlessly.

"Yes, well . . ." Walker looked momentarily fazed, then recovered. "That's right, times are changing . . . To tell the truth," he leant closer again, lowering his voice, "we really need people who know how to deal with the Chinese, know what I mean? And who better than you?"

"I even married one of the blighters after all, eh?" Denton said sardonically. He almost repented when he saw the embarrassed consternation on Walker's face—*he'd* never done them any harm that Denton knew of. Except that he'd been one of that group when Green insulted him in the Shanghai club bar.

"Does that mean you won't consider it?" Walker asked, still flustered.

"I'm afraid so. Excuse us, we have to be going."

"There was no need to humiliate him," Su-mei murmured as they walked towards their car. "He might have been useful one day."

"I've been waiting to say that for ten years. I couldn't let the opportunity slip."

Michael and Alec were already in the car, talking to Lau, showing him their prizes.

"I wouldn't have thought I mattered enough to you any more for you to worry about all that now."

"What?" Michael asked. "Worry about what?"

"Nothing. Let's have another look at your prize."

77

Denton got out by the main entrance to the university and sent Lau home with the car. "I'll get a taxi back," he said as Lau glanced at him in surprise. He didn't want the car to be noticed, as Lily was so sensitive about it. The autumn sun was setting, filtering thick golden beams through the leaves of the trees. There was a light breeze. A few dead leaves fell off the branches and fluttered down onto the ground. Near the main building, a banner had been tied across the road. *St. Johns University Annuel Debating Championship*. He followed the pointers to the lecture theatre. Knots of students had formed on the steps, talking and laughing, while others were threading their way between them into the hall. Denton paused. Wei's car had just arrived and Wei was being helped up the steps by Philip, accompanied by a number of respectful students. Philip's glance met Denton's.

"So you have come to hear Lily speak?" he asked as Denton approached.

"Yes. What about you? What are you doing here?"

Philip glanced at his father, who used a thick, rubber-tipped stick to walk with nowadays. "One of my sons is speaking too," Wei said in a voice that seemed to tremble in his throat. "Unfortunately on the other side."

Second wife's son, Denton realised. He must be about the same age as Lily. He let his eyes stray over Wei's face. His skin seemed to have wrinkled still more, all that tautness gone that had preserved it for so many years. His lips moved as if he was nibbling them. But his eyes, behind the round walls of his lenses, were still sharp.

"We're going up to the front," Philip said, taking his father's arm while the escort of students waited. "Father's a bit deaf now."

"Oh. I'm going to sit at the back. Lily doesn't know I'm coming and I don't want to put her off."

Denton climbed up to the gallery and sat down beside a pillar at the back. A banner with the same words hung over the stage. Again *Annual* was spelt *Annuel*. The four speakers were already seated at their tables, two each side of the chairman. Lily was the only girl. She still did her hair in that same severe style and flaunted her disdain of fashion by wearing the same simple, ill-fitting kind of skirt and blouse she'd worn ever since she'd left school. He recognised Wei's son at once, by the sly yet genial look on his face, a look which the father seemed to have lost in passing it on to his son.

Lily was scanning the hall now, and Denton leant back so that she wouldn't see him. She smiled at someone below him, softening her eyes. That must be a boyfriend, he thought, her cheeks were blushing faintly. Despite all her stern attempts to brush any laxity out of her hair, a strand had struggled free in front of her ear, and hung down in a wispy curl against her cheek. She looked away, scanning the hall again, the smile still hovering round her lips. He leant further back behind the pillar.

Two students next to him were discussing the speakers in loud, superior tones. "Lily Kwan is always trying to prove she's really Chinese," the one nearest him said. The other laughed and said something he couldn't quite hear, ending with the English words "not much fun, ah?" then they were suddenly quiet, glancing sidelong at him and each other. Of course, Denton thought. She would be known by her mother's name, not by mine. The thought hurt.

The chairman stood up, a tall, stooping student with thick-lensed horn-rimmed glasses. "Friends and fellow-students," he began in an earnest, over-articulated voice. "Welcome to this year's debating championship finals..."

Denton closed his eyes as the voice went lengthily, tediously, on, introducing the two teams and the judges, rehearsing all the rules.

His eyes opened with a start when he heard Wei's name mentioned. "We want to thank Mr. Wei heartily," the chairman declared in that same earnest, over-articulated voice, curiously expressionless for all the trouble he took with it "for donating us with the prize for this year's annual debate."

Another patter of applause. Philip Wei looked around smiling, but his father's head didn't move.

At last the chairman got to the motion. He picked up a slip of paper and read out, blinking behind his glasses, "The motion is that Japan will be involved in the next world war before America." He licked his lips. "I will now call upon Miss Lily Kwan to propose the motion."

Denton's hands clenched lightly. After all, he realised with surprise, he was nervous for Lily.

"Japan is undemocratic, militaristic and expansionist," Lily began swiftly and tensely almost before the chairman had sat down. "All these are ingredients for war. The real question is not whether Japan will be involved in the next world war before America, but when she will *start* it..."

Denton leant back again, his fingers unclenching. Lily spoke fluently and sharply. He'd been afraid she might dry up, but she was all right. There was no humour, no wit, no flexibility; though she slowed her pace as she settled down. But she spoke powerfully, with a cold, clear marshalling of arguments, like a lawyer demonstrating a clear-cut case. It was steely. Whether or not she was right, her conviction itself was convincing. He thought of his own speeches at the council meetings years ago. He'd never had that gift of certitude, that chilly assurance. It was a politician's speech, the sort you could make only if you'd rid your mind of doubts and questions. And it was aggressive. If there were Japanese spies there, or even Kuo Min Tang spies, they couldn't doubt her enmity to Japan. And the Kuo Min Tang were trying to appease the Japs, to give themselves time to finish off the communists in the north. Could anyone doubt she was really a sympathiser with the communists?

He began to feel afraid for her. She was too reckless. And when she sat down, he could tell by the hush that followed before the applause that most of the audience thought so too. Here and there were pockets of enthusiasm, but the bulk of the audience was quiet and disturbed. People looked at each other uncomfortably and whispered. After all, several students had disappeared soon after Chiang Kai-shek arrived in Shanghai. And several had died in Pock-mark Chen's massacre. In the end they only wanted to be left in peace. Like him, he supposed.

The students next to him were talking to each other in low voices. One of them chuckled derisively. Denton watched Lily's face. It was still tense but he saw her glance at the same spot in the hall as before, and her eyes softened and smiled. He felt still more afraid for her; she was vulnerable.

The Weis, he noticed, didn't clap at all.

It was Wei's son who was to speak against her. Like his father, he was slightly built. He had the same shrewd eyes, but unlike either his father or Lily, his voice was pliant and calm; he was relaxed. Lily had made a speech, but young Wei's casual posture seemed to announce he was merely going to talk to them in a chummy way and together they'd get to the bottom of this whole mysterious business. They'd see just how much of what this warlike lady—he referred to her with a smiling bow as "My warlike friend"—how much of what she said was true. He spoke English with the same facility as Lily, though with a slight American accent. So Japan was militaristic, the warlike lady declared (she actually seemed to *want* a war!), but didn't she know the British fleet was larger than Japan's? Didn't she know, or had she some reason for forgetting— and here he called her for the only time by her English name—had Miss *Denton* some reason for forgetting that Japan was a developing Asian power, while Britain was one of the original imperialist western powers that had plundered China in the last century? What could have led Miss *Denton* to forget that, he wondered? Was *Denton* perhaps an English name?

Lily flushed and the audience chuckled. She bit her lower lip and blinked, then her face grew pale and intent again and she picked up her pencil to jot down a note.

Denton glanced across at the judges, one Chinese, one American. They were smiling appreciatively. He could feel young Wei winning them over as he went along, winning the whole audience over, with his witty, roundabout speech.

As he sat down to an immediate, warm round of applause, Denton looked at Lily again. She was whispering to her seconder, her hand almost over his ear. He was nodding, eyes vacant behind his glasses, as he tried to take in what she said.

Neither of the seconders' speeches were as good as the first two. They spoke English less fluently, they hesitated and groped for words, they failed to deal with their opponents' arguments either head on or by evasion. The audience began to get restless. Voices murmured in the hall, seats creaked, shoes shuffled. They wanted the main speakers again.

At last their turn came to make their concluding speeches. Lily stood up slowly, her face pale and intent.

"Mr. Wei asks whether I have some reason for forgetting that Britain was acting imperialistically in China before Japan. The answer is that I haven't forgotten. But our question, as he so rightly said, is about the present and the future, not the past..." She turned to gaze at the Weis, father and Philip, who were sitting in the place of honour in the front row. "*I* ask, has Mr. Wei some reason for forgetting the role that Japan is now playing in China and is clearly going to play tomorrow—the last and worst imperialist power of them all?"

There was a stunned, embarrassed hush in the hall. Both Weis were well-known to support the policy of appeasing Japan. And Wei was a venerable figure in Shanghai, one of the Kuo Min Tang's most respected counsellors. Lily's accusing stare and accusing words had overstepped the mark. She was deliberately insulting Wei, and he was giving the prize. Denton thought of the Kuo Min Tang spies carrying her words back, and of the Weis' loss of face. Old Wei, he noticed, sat rigid in his seat, but he could see Philip's face darkening right down to his neck as he turned to glare at Lily. Denton felt a spurt of fear for her.

While young Wei was replying, ignoring her taunt, or, rather, drawing attention to it by declaring he would ignore it, a student in a white shirt and simple blue trousers slipped past the front rows to hand up a slip of paper to Lily's seconder, who handed it wordlessly to Lily. People began to turn from young Wei to watch her as she read it with an intent frown. Wei's voice faded as he too glanced at her, and for a moment he faltered. Before he could recover, Lily started up. "Mr. Chairman," she declared, but looking out over the hall. "I have just been given a copy of a message broadcast an hour ago by Peking Radio. Japanese forces have attacked Mukden and are advancing towards the province of Jehol. Chinese forces, taken by surprise, are resisting valiantly."

There was a hush as she handed the message to the chairman, a hush of shock and fear. As if they'd been watching a stage murder, and had just realised that one of the actors really had killed the other.

Then voices began shouting from the hall, from just those places where her support had been before. "Death to Japan!" they chanted rhythmically, standing up in solid groups. "Death to Japan!" Their feet stamped in time. Lily and her seconder were chanting with them on the stage. Young Wei and the chairman, the two judges as well, sat there helplessly with confused, sheepish smiles on their faces.

It was all planned, Denton realised. The whole thing had been staged. They'd known all along they were going to bring that message in. They must have had advance warning of a broadcast before it had reached Shanghai. For some reason he recalled that urbane communist he'd sheltered with Ah King's husband that night in twenty-seven. Chou En-lai he was called. He'd seen a photo of him later in the paper.

People in the gallery had started shouting as well. He couldn't tell whether they'd been planted there or were joining in spontaneously. The noise swelled and filled the hall, though half the audience or more were silent. Denton looked down at Wei. He was sitting, still beside Philip, his head bowed dejectedly, while Philip kept glancing anxiously over his shoulder as if he expected to be attacked. Then Wei's bodyguards appeared and escorted them out through the side door by which the message had been brought in. And while they shuffled out, all those standing groups of students were staring at them accusingly, hurling their slogans like stones.

"Did you see your father was there?" one of them said to Lily as they walked down the dingy alley towards the food stall at the bottom. Paraffin lamps hissed and flared in the darkness. Farther on they saw the blue sparks fizzing from a tram wire.

"My father? Where?"

"In the gallery. By one of the pillars."

She shook her head, making the little pigtails fly that gave her such a girlish look, and frowned. They didn't mention her father again.

The open drains gurgled on each side of the alley as grey, soapy water swilled down them, carrying dirt and refuse along with it. There was the usual smell of in-grained grime. The key-cutters and cobblers glanced up from their stools as the serious-faced, yet elated, young students passed with their teacher. "Hey, what's this we hear about the Japs up in the north?" The lone seal-carver called to the teacher.

"Yes, it's true," Pak-kay paused. "The war's started.

It'll be in Shanghai next. General Tsai's army's just outside the city."

"Tsai? Which one's that?"

"Nineteenth Route Army. The one that beat the warlords."

"Flat-nose Tsai? The one from Canton?"

"Right."

The seal-carver shook his grey head and bent over his seals again, muttering dubiously.

Lily took the bamboo stool next to Pak-kay. The others left it for her as if they tacitly acknowledged it was her place. They ordered tea and soup. She felt suddenly limp with exhaustion, resting her face in her hands as she watched the barefoot old man pouring tea from a charcoal-blackened kettle and ladling soup out into the bowls.

"Tired?" Pak-kay asked.

She nodded and smiled. "It went all right, though, didn't it?"

"Perfectly."

The others were talking about the demonstration too. He leaned towards her as he sipped his tea. "When I gave my first lecture, I couldn't sleep the whole night before. Now..." he shrugged. "You get used to it."

The stall-owner was collecting the dirty bowls from the other tables. He put them into a bucket of greasy water, sloshed them about, and started wiping them with a wet cloth. He was bending down, and Lily could see a scar on his calf, a large patch of angry, reddish skin. A burn mark, she told herself, proud of her medical knowledge.

Pak-kay touched her arm. He lowered his voice, signalling the others with his brows to lean closer. "There's going to be a big Boycott Japanese Goods Campaign," he said, fingering his beard. "There'll be a lot of work to do in the next few days. Meet at the usual place tomorrow evening, seven o'clock."

As they nodded and leaned back again, it seemed to Lily that their heads were like the petals of some great clumsy flower closing and opening. What a silly idea, she upbraided herself, glancing at the old man's scarred leg again. Then quite suddenly she folded her arms on the table and laid her head on them, closing her eyes.

She heard the fat sizzling in the pans as the old man went on cooking. She smelt the acrid smell of burning grease, she heard the others scraping back their stools and

604

muttering goodbye. When she opened her eyes again, Pak-kay was the only one left.

"Come to my place," he said. "You can rest there."

As she got up, his arm brushed the back of her hand, but he didn't apologise or move away. Instead he let his arm stay touching her for two or three seconds. And she left hers. Their eyes met. They smiled. They walked on down the alley without speaking. The sour smells and running drainwater seemed to fade into a pleasant haze.

Pak-kay stopped a rickshaw on Brenan Road, and when he got in beside her, his leg rested against hers. "After the revolution, there'll be no more rickshaws," he said in English. "And normally I never take one. But today's an exception."

The air fanned their faces as the coolie padded along, the cool night air of autumn larded with petrol fumes and dust. "I'm giving up my job," Pak-kay went on abruptly, gazing with narrowed eyes past the coolie's bobbing head. "They want me to edit a paper." His leg was still touching hers, as if he hadn't noticed.

"Does that mean you're leaving Shanghai?" she asked, unable to keep the disappointment out of her voice.

He smiled reassuringly. "No, here in the international settlement. It's safer here than anywhere else in China at the moment." His American-English accent sounded so strange sometimes, coming from that dark, bearded Chinese face. "Not that the KMT will touch us now. We'll both be fighting the Japs now."

"A party paper?" she asked tentatively.

He shook his head and turned to smile down at her where she lolled against the canopy. "That would be a mistake. It'll be an anti-Japanese paper, that's all. The party will stay in the background." He stroked his beard, then took her hand in his. "You could help. We've been looking at some of those pieces you wrote. You write quite well."

78

Yin-hong strolled into the kitchen and sat down on a chair at the table, tilting it back on its legs. Only Ah Man was there, kneading dough, his forearms dusty with flour. In the corner, the wireless was announcing the runners for the main race, through storms of blurry crackle. Ah Man glanced at Yin-hong, then looked down at his pastry again. It was as though he'd merely noticed a fly or a lizard.

Yin-hong let the chair fall forwards, the legs grating on the tiled floor. He picked a crumb of pastry up on the tip of his forefinger and licked it off. "Surprised to see me again?"

"Disappointed."

Yin-hong sniffed and swallowed "Where is everyone?" he asked. "I see the big-wigs are all out."

"You wouldn't've come if they weren't, would you?"

Yin-hong shrugged. "Makes no difference to me."

Ah Man cocked his head to the wireless and listened attentively to the odds. Then he turned back to the pastry. "Funny how you never arrive when they're in, though, isn't it? Quite a coincidence, eh?"

Yin-hong sniffed again, hawked, looked round the kitchen, then went to the door. Gathering the phlegm into his mouth, he worked his cheeks and spat stylishly into the garden. "What about the rest of them?" he asked, returning to his chair.

Ah Man rubbed the flour off his hands, went to the wireless and turned the volume up. The commentator's voice grew tenser as the horses went under starter's orders. He walked back to the table and put his hands into the pastry again. "Working for their living. If you know what that means."

"Wouldn't suit me." Yin-hong slid a cigarette packet out of his breast pocket. "Where's my mother in particular?"

Ah Man rested both doughy hands on the table again, turning his head to the wireless as an excited roar and the high-pitched shout of the commentator announced the start of the race. "Upstairs," he said. "Laundry."

Yin-hong lit his cigarette, dropping the match negligently on the floor. He tilted his chair back again and looked up at Ah Man knowingly. "If you've got money on Black Devil you're going to lose," he remarked casually.

Ah Man's eyes swivelled slowly from the wireless to Yin-hong, regarded him vacantly, then swivelled back to the wireless as the commentator's voice rose to a prolonged shriek.

"It won't win, take it from me," Yin-hong assured him calmly. "It's been fixed."

The commentator yelled deliriously above the wild roar of the crowd, then, like a clock unwinding, slowly calmed as he announced the winners' names. Ah Man's face stiffened, his lips pressed together. He lifted the dough with a sigh and began kneading again.

"What did I tell you?" Yin-hong said. He raised one shoulder resignedly. "You should have listened to me."

Ah Man gazed at home again between the dark pouches of his lids. He stared into Yin-hong's eyes for several seconds, while Yin-hong stared challengingly back at him. Then he returned to his kneading. "You on opium?" he asked uninterestedly.

Yin-hong let his lids slowly, scornfully, droop for answer.

Already the commentator was reading out the runners for the next race. Yin-hong glanced round the kitchen, letting the smoke waft up over his face again. Nothing had changed, the room was just the same, and the daily routine was the same too—Ah Man cooking, the others at the market or cleaning the house. For a brief second or two he felt a childish yearning to belong there again, as the boy he'd been when he ran away. Studying on the corner of the table, for instance, with his rice to come and none of that uncertain fear he lived with now. But then the weakness passed. He hardened his eyes and drew deeply on his cigarette, hearing the tobacco rustle as it burned, feeling its warmth between his fingers.

"Come for money, I suppose?" Ah Man muttered, grimacing as he squeezed and thumped the dough.

Yin-hong leant his head back and blew the smoke up towards the ceiling without answering. He heard his mother's steps in the hall.

"What I wonder," Ah Man grunted, folding and refolding the dough, "is why a good lad like my son had to go and get himself shot while a shit like you stays alive."

Yin-hong's eyes narrowed faintly, while his nostrils flared. He drew in a mouthful of smoke, pursed his lips and blew it out in a long funnel over Ah Man's face. Then he reached forward and tapped the ash off his cigarette into the dough. It lay there, a little grey powdery smudge on the pasty white.

"Yin-hong!" Ah King exclaimed, coming into the kitch-

607

en with an empty laundry basket. "I told you not to come here!"

"Well I have come, haven't I?" Yin-hong hadn't even glanced at her. He put his cigarette slowly between his lips and inhaled again, gazing all the time up at Ah Man.

"What d'you want? Master will be back soon." She put the basket down nervously, then paused, gazing apprehensively from one to the other. "What's going on here?"

Ah Man was wiping the dough carefully off his hands. He took a spoon and scooped the dough round the ash away, dropping it in the sink. When he turned back to the table, he had the meat cleaver in his hand. He laid it down on the table beside the pastry bowl. Ah King remembered the night he'd gone berserk, the night his son had been killed. Ah Man turned to her, ignoring Yin-hong, "I was just saying," he said in a voice that was measured and pleasant, except for the little quiver in it, "That what I can't understand is why they didn't shoot this little shit instead of my son." He laid his fingers lightly on the cleaver handle.

"I wouldn't try anything if I was you," Yin-hong said unevenly. "I've got friends outside..." he let himself be pulled away by Ah King, sneering at the same time. She tugged him into her room, but he reached across and switched the wireless off defiantly as he went in.

She shut the door. "I told you never to come here!" she hissed fiercely. "What d'you want now?"

"I need a bit of money," he said sullenly, sitting on her wooden bed, its bare boards covered with a thin rush mat. "A hundred dollars."

She stood considering him grimly. "What for?"

He couldn't meet the accusing glare in her eyes, so he looked down at the mat, picking at its frayed edge, remembering its smell of old straw. "I can get it other ways if you like," he shrugged. "If you don't want to give it to me."

The wireless had been switched on again. They heard the commentator's voice rising in its shrill crescendo.

"What d'you want it for?" she insisted.

Another shrug. "I need it." He drew on the last of his cigarette and flicked the stub out of the barred little window beside the bed.

Her eyes were still scrutinising his down-turned face with a hard, interrogatory stare. "I haven't got a hundred, anyway," she said slowly.

"Fifty?" He glanced up.

"What are you going to do with it?"

"If you want me to steal it, I can do that too," he said in a surly, aggrieved voice.

She stood there in front of him undecided, twisting her green jade ring round and round on her finger. This time he met her gaze. Her face was leaner than he remembered it, her jaw and cheek-bones seemed harder and more prominent.

"I'll pay you back," he said, still in an injured tone, as if she ought to have known that in any case.

Her eyes flickered unbelievingly. "Well, this is the last time," she sighed at last.

He watched her unlock the little cupboard where she kept all her things—her spare clothes and sandals, a black umbrella, a few bottles of Chinese medicine, and the old biscuit tin in which she kept a yellowing photograph of Jonathan together with her money. Outside, the commentator's voice had shrieked to its climax and was now recovering exhaustedly.

"So what's been happening here?" he asked, only a little less sullenly. "Michael and Alec gone away to school?"

She glanced sharply at him over her shoulder, sliding the biscuit tin back onto the shelf. "What d'you want to know about them for?"

"All right, all right," he raised his hands deprecatingly, an innocent whine creeping into his voice. "So I won't ask. There's no need to look at me like that, I've told you a hundred times I had nothing to do with that kidnapping business. Would I come here if I had?"

She slapped the folded bills into his hand. "Yes, they're in England," she said gruffly. "This is the last time, all right? If your father knew, he'd kill me."

Yin-hong suddenly grinned, a boy again. "He'd kill me too."

One morning when the first frost of the year gripped the city under a bright, hard sky, Ah Sam didn't get up. Her leg and arm felt numb, she said. Ah King tried some of her pungent-smelling poultices, Su-mei told her to rest.

"She's had a stroke," Lily said when she came back late as usual in the evening. "She should see a doctor."

Ah Sam refused at first, then agreed to a Chinese herbalist. The herbalist came in his long blue gown and his skull-cap, took her pulse, examined her eyes, prescribed some concoction to be drunk morning and night.

"This is ridiculous," Denton said. "He didn't even look at her arm or leg."

"Why should he?" Su-mei had still never been to a western doctor herself, although she allowed the children to go and had never objected to Lily's studying medicine. "Ah Sam told him they were numb, he was looking in her eyes to find out why."

Lily's lip curled faintly. "That's the kind of witchcraft that's keeping China back in the middle ages," she said, quietly so that Su-mei didn't hear.

Denton insisted on calling McEwan.

Ah Sam looked at him fearfully when he told her the western doctor was coming, not daring to refuse. "I'll stay with you when the doctor comes," Lily promised. But Ah Sam preferred Ah King. Her worn, crooked knuckles on the quilt were like the smooth, hard handles of Chinese walking sticks.

Glancing round her small, bare room, Denton noticed four or five dolls lying on the unpainted table. They were western dolls, fair-haired, rosy-cheeked, blue-eyed. "She buys them at Wing On," Ah King said in a low voice. "Because she never had a baby."

He dropped his eyes as if he'd been prying, and went out into the kitchen. Su-mei was there, telling Ah King what to buy at the market. Denton went to the window and stood looking out. A Japanese warship was steaming slowly upstream, the red sun bold as blood on the white field of its flag. He sensed how chill the wind must be that was snapping the flag out straight above the choppy brown water. The image of Ah Sam's dolls lay on his mind.

The door bell rang. He waited, listening to the curt tones of McEwan's voice coming down the hall. Su-mei showed him Ah Sam's room. She stood with Ah King at the foot of the bed while McEwan lifted Ah Sam's hand and took her pulse.

"Sorry I'm a wee bit late," he muttered tersely. "All these anti-Japanese demonstrations clogging the streets." He sat down unceremoniously on the wooden bed, breathing heavily. "What happened exactly?"

"I'll be in the dining room," Denton said through the open doorway.

"Now can she move her leg?" McEwan was asking, with that irascible edge to his voice that suggested you'd only got yourself to blame if you fell ill or were even dying.

Su-mei followed Denton. He waited for her in the hall and they went on together. He didn't speak at first, constrained by that reticence, like a stone on his chest, that had lain there ever since he'd been going to other women. *"We have a true Chinese marriage,"* Su-mei had said wryly once as they sat at the dinner table with spaces of silence between them. *"Except that you haven't asked me to approve your choice of concubine."*

"I suppose McEwan still reeks of whisky?" he said at last at the dining room door.

"Didn't you smell it?"

He shook his head.

She was going on towards the stairs. "Because you drink so much yourself these days."

He glanced after her, smarting from the truth. He put two tumblers down on the sideboard with an indignant little thump, and half-filled each with whisky. Well what if he did drink too much? He slumped down and crossed his legs, staring out at the river through the closed veranda doors. The Japanese warship was letting its anchor down now. He saw the chain smoke as it poured through the vents in the bow. It reminded him of how he'd seen his first anchor chain thirty years before when he was leaving England for Shanghai.

McEwan's heavy shoes clumped down the hall before Denton had drunk half his whisky. He took his tumbler silently, sat opposite Denton and stretched out his legs. "Aye, it's a stroke all right." He sipped the whisky, held it on his tongue a moment, then swallowed. "She's fortunate it's no affected her much. But you're no likely to get a lot more work out of her."

"That's not the point," Denton began sharply.

"I didn't say it was."

Denton glanced at McEwan's face, the lines gouged like trenches into his hectically flushed cheeks. He let go. "How serious is it?" he asked.

"Och, she should be able to get about all right for a while yet. She can move her leg, though I dare say she'll be dragging it a wee bit. The arm's not bad and her speech isn't affected. I'd keep her in bed for a while yet, she must have rest." He stroked his bushy white moustache that had reminded Denton of the philosopher Nietzsche

611

ever since Jacob Ephraim had given him a copy of *Beyond Good and Evil* with a photograph of the author in the front, looking as shaggily ill-tempered as McEwan.

"She had a herbalist first," he said. "He just looked at her and gave her some tea of some sort or other."

"Exactly what I did," McEwan said testily. "Except I didn't think of the tea."

Denton had expected him to be as scornful of the herbalist as Lily had been. "So there's nothing that either of you can do?" he asked, chastened.

"Nothing whatsoever," McEwan said. "Except charge ye for our services." He sounded grimly satisfied. "Well I'll be going." Placing his tumbler down on the sideboard, he glanced at Denton suspiciously. "Since when have you taken to drinking whisky at this hour of the day?"

"Well *I* don't drink it at breakfast time, at least," Denton replied, nettled.

"Pist, man, I'm used to it. It's when ye change your habits that ye want to look out. I've been drinking the same amount for thirty years now. But it looks to me as though you've started increasing your daily dose somewhat. That's a different story altogether."

Denton shrugged, accompanying him silently towards the porch.

"I'll look in tomorrow," McEwan said. "Make sure she rests, she'll need a few days before she tries to get about again."

"Doesn't all this illness and death that you see ever depress you?" Denton asked suddenly.

"Ye get used to anything. Mark you," he added as he went down the steps, where Cheong was silently watering the poinsettias. "Ye'll find doctors as a class are more prone to suicide than other professions. Ask any actuary. Insurance companies don't like us. Ye can make what ye like of that." He gave a sardonic laugh. "About the same time tomorrow, all right? Plenty of rest, no excitement."

As he drove away Denton noticed a coolie with a barrow who had been waiting behind McEwan's old black car. "What does *he* want?" he asked Cheong.

Cheong's mild eyes looked up from the poinsettias' leaves, that were just beginning to be pricked with red. "Eldest daughter brought him," he said apprehensively, as if he were somehow to blame.

The coolie, leaning against the barrow, gazed back at

Denton morosely. "When's she coming, then?" he called out. "She said she'd only be a minute."

But while he was speaking Denton could already hear Lily's footsteps in the hall behind him. She was carrying two suitcases. "What did McEwan say?" she asked.

Denton stared at her. "Where on earth are you going?"

She hesitated, then walked on down the steps. "I've left my address upstairs on my desk," she said in an unsteady, defiant voice. "I'm moving out for the time being, sharing a flat with someone." She handed the cases to the coolie, who had wheeled his barrow across to the foot of the steps.

He had an image of a cold wind rushing down empty corridors, sweeping her with it out of the house. "Moving out? Where? Why?"

"I've left the address upstairs."

"You can't just walk out like that." It sounded hollow—he knew already that she could, she would. "What about your mother?"

"It's all in the note upstairs, I've explained in the note." She was speaking hurriedly, glancing back up the steps into the hall. "I don't want her to make a scene." She looked at him, at once defiantly and pleadingly. "Don't try to stop me, you know you can't."

The coolie was watching them interestedly now. So was Cheong, but with anxiety shining in his eyes. Both were following their words, although they were speaking English. Denton felt a scene was developing already on the steps. He flinched at the thought of Su-mei joining it.

"Of course I won't try to stop you," he said stiffly. "It's just a bit sudden, isn't it? Why the rush?"

"Yes, well it's all in the note," she said, blushing as she ran down the steps. "I'll phone tomorrow, all right?" She waved goodbye with a hasty flicker of her hand. "I'll come and see Ah Sam soon."

But not us, Denton thought.

The coolie looked disappointed at the tame ending to the drama. He gestured her to cling onto the barrow beside the cases.

"No, it's all right, I'll walk," she said over-brightly. "It's not far. Just past Garden Bridge."

The coolie sighed and muttered peevishly, rearranging the cases to balance the barrow. Denton watched her walking away down the drive beside him. At the road, as they turned towards Garden Bridge, she turned and waved again, a slow, unhurried wave this time, as if now that she felt sure she'd really got away, she could afford to bid a more graceful farewell. There was something final about it. She was saying goodbye not only to him, but to Su-mei, the servants, the house, her whole childhood and youth. He remembered the softening of her eyes when he'd been watching her at that debate a couple of months ago. She must be going to him, whoever he was. What was he like, this man who'd calmly taken her away without even showing his face? He felt a surge of jealousy and loss. Soon there would be only Su-mei and himself left. Again he had that image of a cold wind blowing down long empty corridors.

Cheong was gazing after her too, water dripping unheeded from the dented spout of the watering can. He glanced back at Denton with troubled eyes.

"You're spilling the water," Denton said curtly. He'd never spoken like that to Cheong before, and he felt immediately ashamed as Cheong dropped his glance with a start and turned back to the flowers. Denton stood there still, gazing at the traffic hustling and rattling along the Bund, trying to think of something that would draw the sting from what he'd said. But all he could think of was Lily being absorbed into that flood of traffic, of himself being suddenly older, as though she'd taken some of the life out of him as she walked away. He didn't move until he heard Su-mei calling him agitatedly from upstairs.

"Yes, I know, I know all about it," he said soothingly as she hurried down the stairs towards him. He glanced at his face in the hall mirror. There were only a few streaks of grey in his hair after all, and the lines looked no deeper than before in his face.

"It's all right, Su-mei, it's all right," he raised his voice slowly and calmly over her alarmed, indignant exclamations. "I've just spoken to her, it's all right."

79

Moseivitsch played with the Shanghai Symphony Orchestra in the Town Hall. Su-mei wouldn't go—"I don't understand western music and anyway I can't stand the piano"

—so Denton went alone. It was the Emperor Concerto. He knew it well, there was a time when he listened to it every week on his gramophone. But this time he wasn't affected. Not even the slow movement touched him—and he could remember when the crackling record that he had of it could hold him so still that it almost seemed as if the world had stopped turning. But that was years ago. Now for the first time he heard it live, and he couldn't listen. Every few bars, his mind kept straying.

"It was the coughing and rustling," he explained to Jacob afterwards in the Palace Hotel, where much of the audience was drinking and talking, the women glittering with jewels. "And the faces. I couldn't get them out of my mind."

"It was the orchestra," Jacob declared, pouring some vodka. "They're nearly all White Russians. Brilliant soloists—can't play together. What else would you expect from a lot of Russians?" He swallowed, then fixed Denton with a bright, suspicious eye. "What's all this I hear about Lily? Going round organising Japanese boycotts and such-like what-nots!"

Denton gazed down at his glass, frowning lightly. "She's moved on since that. Or moved out, rather."

"What d'you mean, moved out?"

"Gone to live with someone—an American Chinese who used to teach at St. Johns. He's editing an anti-Japanese paper now. I'm calling on them tomorrow evening. Su-mei refused to go."

Jacob's eyes widened in amazed condemnation. "You haven't let your daughter go to live with a man?" he expostulated. "Not married? How could you?"

He shrugged. "In the first place, I can't very well stop her except by locking her up. And in the second I don't really see why I should. She's twenty-one next month, after all."

"What? You would allow your own daughter to be...to be somebody's mistress without doing anything to prevent it? You, her father? My daughters would never dare such a thing. I would throw them out of the house!"

"Wouldn't that have roughly the same effect as letting her walk out on her own?" Denton smiled. "All she's doing is living with her lover, as her mother did with me. Perhaps she's going to marry him, I don't know. But if you

615

think of most marriages would you honestly advise her to?"

"I am very happily married," Jacob said with chilly dignity, "all things considered. But a wife is one thing and a mistress is quite another. *My* daughters will become wives, not mistresses. I'm astonished you allow Lily to debase herself like this. Who is this man, anyway? Have you inquired? No, of course not! Either an adventurer after her money or someone out for a good time who will throw her over in a few months like...like..."

"Like you would if you were in his place?"

"Like a used glove," Jacob said, deflated but stubborn.

While he was talking, Denton had recalled the image of Sarah as he'd last seen her, wretchedness hanging round her like a shroud, as she wandered aimlessly from one jeweller's to another. He didn't answer Jacob for some time, thinking of Sarah, of Jacob's blindness to her, his inconsistency, his warmth, his generosity, his meanness, of the crazy furrow he ploughed through life, oblivious of the good as well as the harm he scattered round him as he went. "The man in question," he said reflectively at last, "is one of the leaders of the anti-Japanese campaign. I suppose I'll know more about him tomorrow."

It was Lily who opened the door. She looked at him with narrowed, withdrawn eyes—that self-concealing veil again.

"Am I early?" he asked. His voice was awkward; he didn't know how to speak to her, now she was more a woman than a daughter.

"No, no..." she unhooked the door-chain and let him in. "Only a little. It doesn't matter at all." Her hair was no longer in those stiff little pigtails that made her look so schoolgirlish, but hung loose down her back. Of course, the man must have done that for her, it must have been him that made the clenched flower open.

"You've changed your hair," he said as she led him along a narrow hall into a light, airy room, its bare walls painted white. The cool evening sunlight slid through the slats of the bamboo blinds that took the place of curtains.

She put her hand up and touched her hair with a smile as if she'd forgotten all about it. "Yes, Pak-kay likes it better this way." The softness that he'd first seen in the lecture hall at St. John's had come into her eyes again, fading swiftly as she let the wary veil float down over her once more.

"Who is it?" a deep voice called in Chinese from another room, opening off the main one.

Lily gestured to him to sit down. "It's my father," she called out, in a voice as awkward as Denton's. "Come and meet him."

There was a silence and Denton, going to the blinds to prise open the slats and peer out, visualised the man's eyes widening in annoyance or even apprehension. The apartment was in one of the newer blocks, and Denton could look down onto the flat, dirty roofs of the old buildings below. Further away, the river gleamed between the solid banks and hongs of the Bund. The sun had lost its warmth. He could sense the hard cold in the sky. "You can see our house from here," he said.

"Yes," the voice answered just behind him, in English now. "It sure is a good view."

Denton turned, startled. He had the uncomfortable sense that the man had been secretly studying him for some time while he looked through the blinds.

"I'm Pak-kay Lee," the man said. He held out his hand. "Glad to meet you, Mr. Denton."

He was tall for a Chinese. Denton judged that without his unusual beard and moustache, which made him look like one of the old martial heroes, he would look under thirty. As it was, he looked older. His handshake was firm and strong—Denton could tell from that alone that he'd been brought up abroad. And there was something abrupt and direct about his manner, not formal and supple like a true Chinese. "Yes, how d'you do?" Denton said circumspectly, sitting down in the rattan chair the man offered him. "Would you prefer to talk in Chinese by the way? I know Lily always does—or did," he added with a wry smile.

"As you like," the man shrugged, still speaking in English. "If you don't mind my American accent, as so many Britishers do."

Denton bristled slightly. The man's tone was offhand and arrogant, as though he was really saying that he didn't give a damn what Denton thought of his accent, or of anything else for that matter.

"I'll make some tea," Lily said, in English too.

617

"Or something stronger?" Pak-kay raised his heavy brows at Denton inquiringly.

"Tea will be fine."

He watched her walk out. The floor was covered with rush mats and she was barefoot, as was Pak-kay, making no sound. Her loosened hair lifted faintly and floated out behind her, Denton glanced round the room. It was only half-furnished—a few rattan chairs and cushions placed anywhere, and a low table, covered with papers, against the wall. When he looked back he found Pak-kay's eyes scrutinising him frankly.

"You've lived in Shanghai a long time, Mr. Denton?"

"Quite long, yes. Tell me, what is your English name? Patrick, did Lily say? Is Patrick the English version of Pak-kay?"

"Kind of. Pak-kay, Patrick, yes." He shrugged. "It was the nearest they could get. They took me to the States when I was six months old. I guess I didn't have much say in what they'd decided to call me."

Their eyes fenced with each other as they chatted, Pak-kay's blunt and overbearing, Denton's probing and cautious. I'm really more Chinese than he is, Denton thought fleetingly, and he's more foreign devil than I am. After some minutes, when Lily had brought the tea in, Denton asked Pak-kay what had brought him back to China.

Lily, sitting next to Pak-kay smiled at that, as though the question could only be asked by someone ignorant and naive. She glanced at him expectantly.

"To make it free," Pak-kay said simply, opening his hands. "Free of colonialism, exploitation, feudalism, corruption, superstition..."

"In short, just about everything?"

"Well there's plenty to get rid of, and that's for sure."

"All by yourself?"

"No," his voice grew more wary. "With others. Like Lily. People who don't want to squeeze a fortune out of the place and then get out." He stared a moment into Denton's eyes with a defiant, challenging glare.

Denton sipped his tea, glancing at Lily. She was still gazing admiringly at Pak-kay. For god's sake! he thought. The tea was a strong one, the kind that old men would take before visiting their young concubines. "And you're starting with this anti-Japanese boycott?" he asked, making an effort.

"That's not where we're starting, but we are doing that right now, yes." He glanced towards the other room. "And the paper. That's part of it of course, too."

Denton nodded noncommittally. He'd begun to realise why he was fencing with Pak-kay, fencing with him now in front of Lily. It was because he'd taken her away from him and slept with her. He wouldn't have cared a jot about him except for that, but because of that they were enemies. He realised it obscurely, yet it didn't change anything. He still wanted to defeat him, to pierce his self-confidence, to lessen him in Lily's eyes. And perhaps Pak-kay for his part wanted to humiliate him too, to break whatever ties might tenuously still bind her to him, or to her family.

"Lily writes quite well," Pak-kay was saying in a calmly patronising tone. "She's helping with some of the articles. I guess you don't read Chinese?"

Denton sipped his tea. "I can usually manage a newspaper," he murmured ironically. "Of course your style is probably much too sophisticated for me ..."

"Not at all. We try to make things as simple as possible." He didn't deny that a sophisticated style might be beyond Denton's grasp.

"In that case even I might be able to understand."

Pak-kay put his cup down and reached for the table behind him. He couldn't quite touch it. Lily jumped up eagerly and took a newspaper from it, giving it to Pak-kay. Her eagerness pricked Denton like a needle. It was as though she wanted to throw her admiration of Pak-kay, her subjection to him, in her father's face. She wouldn't even hand him the paper herself. It must come through Pak-kay's hands.

Pak-kay glanced at the first page, turned to the inside and passed it, ready folded, across to Denton. "This is by Lily," he said.

Denton sipped his tea again, the tea that fortified old men, and scanned the article. It was like her English speech in the debate, plain, clear and accusatory, rehearsing Japan's crimes against China, with facts, dates and explanations.

"Yes, I can understand this," he said, lowering the paper. "It's very clear. Like your speech at that debate.

Incidentally"—he glanced from Lily to Pak-kay—"I've often wondered about that message that was brought in, you know, about the Japanese invasion of the northern provinces. Was that stage-managed? Did you know already, before the debate began?"

Pak-kay nodded complacently. "We knew in the morning. In fact we jumped the gun. Peking didn't announce it till the evening, but we had our own sources of information."

Denton sipped again, reflectively.

"You don't approve?"

Denton shrugged. "It was good theatre." He thought of all those young faces shining with blind idealism. "But I don't like seeing people manipulated like that. I don't like seeing people shouting slogans. They look mindless to me."

Pak-kay smiled almost pityingly. "We call that mobilising the masses," he said.

"No doubt you do." He raised the paper again, thinking of that black beard on Lily's breast. "Mobilising the masses," he repeated musingly. "People shouting slogans sound like a regiment of parrots to me."

"Always the cynic," Lily said. And yet there was some fondness in her tone, as though she thought there was something endearing about his persistence in error, like a child who couldn't know any better, and was harmless anyway.

"I would have thought the cynicism lay in manipulating people like that," he answered tartly. "Is there anything by you here too, Pak-kay?" It was the first time he'd addressed him by name, and it made him uneasy, suggesting an intimacy he didn't feel.

"The editorial. Page three."

Denton turned the page and read. Lily's article had at least contained facts and dates but the editorial seemed to be pure rhetoric and abuse. The Japanese were vilified to a man as a nation of monstrous, barbarian murderers, intent on nothing but pillage and rape, against whom the great masses of the Chinese people were now uniting in patriotic outrage. Already the Japanese dwarfs in Shanghai were cowering before the solid front of the Chinese boycott of their goods. Soon they would slink away like rats, back to their holes in Japan . . . And any Chinese who broke the boycott, who sold as much as a cup of rice to a

Japanese, or gave him even a friendly word, deserved to be shot as a traitor and running dog...

He laid the paper down on the floor. They were both watching him expectantly. "Powerful stuff..." he said, rubbing his chin with his finger and thumb.

Pak-kay waited.

"Only I read a report in another paper a day or two ago," Denton went on. "I don't know whether you saw it—about a mob attacking a couple of Japanese school-children in Hongkew? No? Well, I don't suppose it would appeal to your paper. Anyway, a Chinese shopkeeper let the children into his shop, and managed to bolt the door against the mob until the police arrived. I was just wondering whether you'd think that shopkeeper was a traitor? He ought to have been shot for saving a couple of kids?"

"There are always innocent victims in war," Pak-kay said levelly.

"It looks as though some of them might be laid at your door." Denton felt a surge of almost joyful anger as he spoke—the joy of having a good reason to dislike Pak-kay, a reason that wasn't that instinctive personal one.

"Don't you realise what the Japs are doing in Manchuria?" Pak-kay asked. "All over northern China?"

Their eyes clashed angrily. Denton thought again of that coarse black beard straggling across Lily's breast. "A boycott is one thing," he said curtly, "lynching's another."

"I never advocated lynching in that editorial."

Denton stood up. "You came damn close to it." He dropped the paper behind him on the chair.

Pak-kay and Lily stood up too. "Pity you don't like it," Pak-kay smiled ironically. He was calm again at once. "I was hoping we might get a contribution out of you, for the paper."

"I'm afraid I could only support a more responsible kind of journalism," Denton said, drooping his lids. He turned to Lily. He'd hoped to see some doubts now in her eyes, some wavering. But the self-concealing veil still hung over her face. He smiled ruefully. "Thanks for the tea."

"Please don't mention it," she said coolly. Her voice was like a door closing. "How is everyone? Ah Sam?"

"All right." He was walking down the long corridor to the front door. "Your mother still..."

"She hasn't got over it yet?"

621

"No, not really." He turned to Pak-kay, who was following them. "It was...interesting meeting you," he said.

"Sure. Sorry we couldn't agree about everything."

"Or anything," Denton murmured.

He turned back to Lily. "As a matter of fact, Jacob Ephraim was almost more shocked that you'd moved out than your mother was. I saw him yesterday."

"Shocked? Why should he be shocked?"

He smiled at her surprise, which had a touch of pleased vanity in it. "Well, he thinks that daughters should never leave home unless they're properly married."

"He can't think that about *everyone's* daughter," she said severely. "Otherwise where would he get his whores from?"

Denton flinched inwardly. He'd never heard her say "whore" before, and she said it with such a cold, condemning emphasis. And she glanced at him as he said it. "Yes, well Jacob's full of contradictions," he said as she lifted the chain off the door. "Like most of us."

80

Denton dropped his pen with a sigh and leant back from the desk. He found it harder and harder to write to his children in England now; each letter seemed a repetition of the last. He could scarcely visualise them clearly any more, and when he did, he saw them as they were before they left Shanghai, as if they hadn't grown and changed in the years of their absence. They were strangers to each other now, they would be constrained when they met again, their eyes would slide shyly past each other while they groped for words to span the gaps that had opened between them. He recalled how old and alien his mother had seemed when he first returned to England. Would his own children look on him with that little shock, that shiver running through their bodies, when they saw Su-mei and him waiting on the quay, and all the years caught up with them in one crumpled instant?

He glanced down at the unfinished letter to Jenny, sighed again and pushed back his chair, reaching out to switch the wireless on. He felt she'd ceased to be his the day she left for boarding school with her pale, tearful face and her brand new trunk and brand new cases. He was writing to a memory.

The wireless was tuned to a Chinese station. He twiddled the knob through a choked gurgle of voices and music to the English language service. "In Shanghai," the announcer's voice came through with sudden clarity. "Mayor Wu has replied to the Japanese Consul-General's demands of January 21st, following the death of a Japanese citizen in a disorder in Chapei. He has declared his acceptance of the demands made by the Consul-General. A number of foreign consuls and Mr. J. B. Walker, chairman of the International Settlement's municipal council, have expressed their relief and appreciation of what they called Mayor Wu's statesmanlike attitude..."

Denton switched off, watching the luminous green tuning eye fade and vanish. So despite all Pak-kay Lee's efforts, it looked as thought the Chinese weren't going to fight the Japs in Shanghai. He hadn't got his united front after all. He felt a small triumphant glow of pleasure at Pak-kay's failure, but then he realised that if the KMT really were going to make a deal with the Japs, the communists would be in trouble again. And that meant Lily. It soured the taste of his triumph.

He went downstairs out into the garden. It was a cold, dreary day, the grey clouds piling over the city like fold after fold of thick rumpled blankets, oppressive and heavy. It was nearly evening; the sun must be setting, but he couldn't tell where it was—the sky was the same dull grey wherever he looked. Those rare, sunless winter days with their raw, wet chill reminded him of England, and at the same time reminded him of his own distance from it, not just in space but in spirit too. If ever he went back there, he'd be an exile; it would be foreign to him—more foreign even than when he last returned. And yet he was an exile in Shanghai too.

He wandered down to the wooden seat he'd bought when he first moved in. He hadn't sat in it for a long time, not since Alec and Michael had left for England. Really, he'd begun not to *know* the garden any more. He sat down, hands in pockets, his legs stretched out in front of him. The air was moist and raw. He could see his breath steaming when he breathed out. Cheong was raking the dead leaves off the grass behind him, a regular tearing, scratchy sound, like someone combing wiry hair. As Denton glanced round the garden, he noticed something metallic and red, half-buried in the earth under the hedge. He got up and moved it with his toe. It was a toy car—a lead model of a London bus. He remembered it at once. It used to belong to Jonathan. And then Alec and Michael had played with it. He picked it up and tried the wheels. They wouldn't move, they were clogged with dirt. He started picking the earth away with his finger nail. Suddenly it seemed important to free the wheels, to make them turn.

Ah King came down the path behind him to take down the still-wet laundry.

He turned to show her the little bus. "Remember this?" he said. "It used to be Jonathan's."

Her cheeks puckered sourly. "No good now. Better throw it away."

"There's nothing wrong with it. It just needs to be cleaned and oiled."

She snorted, flapping a wet towel irritably. "Are you going to have more children to play with it?"

"It used to belong to Jonathan," he repeated. *Wasn't that reason enough?* He'd got one of the front wheels free and it turned stiffly as he rolled it along his thumb.

"Jonathan's dead," she muttered roughly. "Who wants it now?"

He glanced up at her, frowning. Her voice was gruff and sullen, with none of its usual underlying warmth. "What's wrong with you today?" he asked.

She tightened her lips, puckering her cheek again, as she stooped to lift the laundry basket. "On the wireless," she said grimly. "Didn't you hear? They've given in to the Japanese again. Always giving in, never fighting."

"Perhaps they're trying to gain time," he was picking at the earth round the next wheel now. "They know they aren't strong enough yet."

"Gain time?" She twitched her head scornfully. "They're making a deal! Just like before, like the warlords. They don't care so long as they can make a deal." She turned to go, then looked back at him, scowling. "Like you, you don't care either, these days."

"What?"

"You don't care! Mending toys, chasing women—Always giving in, giving in!"

"Ah King!"

624

"You don't care any more. You don't care about anything!"

"Shut up!"

"You want me to leave, I'll leave." She swung round and strode off, still muttering surlily. "I don't mind, just tell me and I'll leave tonight."

He watched her all the way to the kitchen, conscious of Cheong gaping at her as she passed.

"Stupid bitch!" he muttered under his breath. He shrugged elaborately for Cheong's benefit, then went on picking at the earth round the bus's wheels. But he couldn't keep her words out of his mind, they kept coming back to gnaw at him. *You don't care, always giving in.* At last he stopped and dropped the bus down beside him. It slipped between two of the bars and wedged there, just beneath the arm. After trying to wriggle it out, he pushed it resentfully further in until it stuck fast, punishing it for his own deficiencies, his own dissatisfaction. Well what if I have given in? he thought sullenly. What's it to do with her?

The wan light was draining out of the sky. It was getting cold. He got up, slapping the arm of the seat angrily. Lamps shone from the dark shapes of the ships in the harbour, lights beamed from the cars and lorries on the Bund. He went inside. Ah King was ironing, Ah Man cooking dinner, Ah Sam sweeping the floor, her right foot dragging slightly, Ah Leng stacking plates on a tray. None of them looked up. He might as well have been a shadow. As he walked down the path, he'd heard them talking loudly and excitedly. But they stopped as soon as he came in. The kitchen prickled with silence, he sensed the quills pointing at him as he passed. He paused at the door and looked back. Somehow he had to overcome that silence, to face them down. But he couldn't think what to say. He felt stiff and awkward in their presence, an intruder. "Is tai-tai back yet?" he asked at last.

"Not yet," Ah Leng said after a pause, without looking up from the tray.

That night he was more than usually broody at dinner, drinking half a bottle of wine but only picking at his food—he couldn't even have said what the meal was once Ah King, still surly, had taken his plate away.

"What's wrong with her?" Su-mei asked in her distant

voice from her distant place that was nevertheless beside him.

"She's like you," he said, fingering the stem of his glass. "Thinks I don't care any more. Thinks I've given up."

"Haven't you?" Su-mei asked in a small voice.

He shrugged. "I suppose so, yes."

She waited while Ah King brought the coffee in. Then, as the door closed, "You're so down, aren't you?" she said sadly.

Before he could answer—before he'd really taken it in—the night suddenly shattered with the sound of gunfire. For an instant Denton could make out distinctly the steady clatter of machine guns, the sharp separate reports of rifles, the tremendous reverberating roar of mortar shells. Then everything was a confused barrage of noise.

"Where is it?" she asked as they hurried to the window.

"Where the Japs are. And Flat-nose Tsai's army. They must be fighting after all. We can see better from the study."

They went upstairs. Looking out, they could see sudden flashes from explosions over towards Chapei, and the shallow arcs of tracer bullets streaming like fireworks.

Su-mei touched his arm and pointed down. All the servants were on the front steps, watching too. Ah King was muttering in hushed tones, the others silently listening.

PART FOUR

The soldier lay panting quick, shallow breaths, his face grey in the grey light of dawn, cold pearls of sweat starting on his forehead. His young, scared eyes pleaded cloudedly with Lily as she leant over him. His tunic was dirty and bloodstained, but at first she couldn't see where the new blood was coming from. Overcoming the sense of horror that she still felt whenever she touched the wounded, she gingerly loosened his tunic. Then she saw it, the fresh new blood streaming gaily down his sleeve. It wasn't trickling, like the cuts and injuries she'd seen so far—they hadn't let her deal with the bad cases yet—it was flowing freely like water from a tap. An artery, she realised.

There was a sudden burst of firing nearby, in the next alley perhaps. She felt a gust of panic. All the Chinese soldiers had gone now from the rubble-strewn street. They must have left before dawn while she dozed with her head on a sandbag, too exhausted to hear their shuffling feet, the grate of rifles and ammunition boxes being dragged away, the whispers and groans. Why hadn't they told her? Why hadn't they woken her? They must have just forgotten her in the dark. And now she wasn't even sure *where* she was, they have moved about so much in the night, from street to street, from house to house. She clenched her fists against the panic leaping up inside her. The soldier's eyes still pleaded with her dumbly, like a sick dog's.

Then, in the strengthening light, she heard children's voices singing, singing a hymn. And instantly she knew where she was. Although so many of the houses had been smashed and burnt in the fighting, she knew that down there on the right, only a hundred yards or so, Miss Pulham's Jerusalem House must stand, protected by its vast Union Jack and the white flag that looked like a sheet, hanging side by side from the upper windows, protected from both Chinese and Japanese soldiers.

If she could only get him there before the Japanese

came. She looked back at the man. The pallor of his face, the bruised, bluish colour of his lips became more ghastly as the light grew. Fear jumped up inside her again as she heard another volley of shots. Yes, they were near. And the children's voices seemed to waver in their singing, as if they too were turning in panic at the sound of the firing. The soldier's eyes watched her all the time from the depths of his pain, holding her own eyes with the unspoken fear that she was going to leave him there. If the Japanese found them, they'd bayonet them both. She bent close to his face again. It smelled of sour vomit. "I'm going to pull you up the street," she whispered to him, as if the Japanese might be listening for their voices. His eyelids slowly drooped and she realised that even if he'd heard her, he probably hadn't understood—those soldiers were nearly all Cantonese who couldn't understand Shangainese. Cautiously she stepped out into the road a little. Yes, there the flags were, hanging limply down from that same upper floor. It wasn't a hundred yards; it was less than fifty yards away. The children's voices rose again in another verse of the hymn. She could hear the harmonium groaning beneath them.

She bent down, took the soldier by his bare ankles and pulled. Immediately his eyes opened in startled pain and he screamed aloud, his voice thick and gurgling as if blood was choking him. But his scream only increased her own panic and she gripped his ankles all the tighter, almost running backwards. He was quite light. It was like pulling a sack of rice. His head bumped over the rubble, lurching in every dent and crevice she dragged him through, and a thin, interrupted trail of dark red blood smeared the ground behind him. But he didn't scream any more. He didn't even moan. Probably he'd fainted. She felt him growing heavier. His ankles slipped in the sweat of her palms, but she only gripped him tighter and dragged on. Her back prickled. For all she knew she might be going towards the Japanese. But she dared not look round or stop.

The children's voices sounded closer now. The words of the hymn went silently through her mind as, gritting her teeth, she pulled him along the last few yards.

> *There is a green hill far away*
> *Without a city wall...*

629

She let the soldier's feet drop and turned to the door. As she did so, she saw, with a throb of terror, something moving across the street. But it was only a dog slinking amongst the rubble. The dog was sleek and fat; she knew why.

The children must have been watching her—before she could even knock, she heard them calling out frightenedly. The harmonium wheezed on a few more notes then hesitantly stopped as well. Lily banged on the door and called out in English. "Miss Pulham? Miss Pulham? I've got a wounded man here. Quick, open up please!"

The shutters were all closed. On the door someone had painted *British Citizen* in crude Chinese characters, *Only Children Here.*

A shutter opened upstairs. Lily looked up between the union jack and the white flag. Miss Pulham's face peered down. Her hair was completely grey now, a lank, lifeless grey, hanging down each side of her round, sunburned cheeks. She gazed at Lily blankly.

"Miss Pulham it's me, Lily Denton! Please let me in, I've got a wounded man here, and the Japanese are coming!"

Miss Pulham peered down still, shaking her head faintly as if she couldn't understand what Lily was saying.

"Don't you remember me? Lily Denton? Please let us in, he needs help!"

At last her pale eyes seemed to glimmer. "Lily Denton," she said.

"Yes, can we come in?"

"Oh no, dear, I'm afraid not." A queer look came over her face, at once genial and distant, as though she was gazing at Lily without seeing her. "I can't take soldiers in, this house is neutral. Only children dear, nobody else."

"But he's badly wounded! Please!"

"Only children," she said firmly. "Try somewhere else." The shutter closed with a bang. Inside children's voices rose, anxious, whimpering, crying.

Lily banged on the door again with both fists. "Miss Pulham, we'll be killed out here! You've got to let us in! Please!" There was no answer, only the wailing of the children.

She turned away at last. It was no use. She'd have to

630

try and hide him somewhere in the ruins. But first, better stop the bleeding. She started pulling his tunic off, roughly and quickly, no longer squeamish, only afraid. The soldier's eyes rolled up and closed again in a faint. Her fingers tugged clumsily at his sleeve.

Then she saw the wound. It must have been shrapnel, tearing a gaping hole in his arm, up by the shoulder. Yes, it was an artery, she could see the blood welling out in feeble pulses, as though the heart was simply getting tired of all that futile pumping. She recalled the sallow-skinned little Portuguese instructor's voice in the St. John's Ambulance Brigade Hall last year, at the first aid course she'd taken—in the university she'd learnt all about medicine but not how to bandage a wound. "If nothing else is available, put your fist in the wound. That gives you time to think." She clenched her fist, brought it near the hole, closed her eyes and shoved it in. It felt like warm, oozy mud. She swallowed down a shudder of revulsion and pushed harder till she felt the bone against her knuckle. Then she made herself look, shivering. Her fist was stuck in his arm like a bung in a barrel. Blood seeped out round it, but more slowly now. His eyes were open again. They seemed to regard her with distant amazement from behind the film of pain that covered them. She stared back at her hand, wondering through her fear and horror whether she'd ever be able to separate it from him again. I must find a bandage, she thought. There was his tunic. If she rolled it up into a ball, she could stuff it instead of her fist into the hole. And tie it there with something. All at once she seemed to know what to do. She scrunched up the tunic bit by bit with her left hand while she kept her right hand shoved tight into the wound. She realised she was gritting her teeth, her lips were pressed tight together. She was going to save him, she began to think, she was going to save him.

Suddenly the door bolts scraped behind her. The door opened a foot and Miss Pulham looked cautiously out. She put a towel and a jug of water on the step. "There, that's all I can do, dear," she said breathlessly, as if she'd been running up and down the stairs. Her pale eyes still had that genial yet disconnected gleam in them, as if she saw Lily and yet didn't see her at all. "We only take children here, no adults, I'm afraid."

"Miss Pulham!"

"Sorry dear, only children."

The door shut and the bolts grated home. Numbly Lily dropped the tunic, took the towel and pulled her hand away with a squelchy sound, pressing the towel in its place. She bunched the towel up tightly in the wound, wiping the blood off her hand at the same time, then closed the man's arm over it and tied it to his side with his torn tunic sleeves. She worked calmly again now, although everything trembled inside her. I will save him whatever happens she kept thinking. When she was finished she stood up. Her blouse was spattered with blood, there was blood on her hand right up to her wrist.

She must hide him quickly in the rubble. Just a drink of water and then...She knelt down with the jug in one hand and raised his head with the other. The water simply splashed over his face as though it were a rock. He didn't swallow a drop. She looked at his eyes. They were slowly hardening. The pleading look, the pain, the glimmer of life had all gone. He was staring stiffly up at the sky now, his eyeballs motionless and opaque.

So I haven't saved you after all, she thought, lowering his head. It was all wasted. Then, as she put the jug down by the soldier's head she heard voices. Her stomach curdled. There they were at the end of the road, a group of Japanese marines coming down the road towards her. They were moving carefully, in single file, some on each side of the street, hunched and crouching. For a second she stared at the foremost marine, who was staring at her. Then she turned and fled, hearing them shout behind her. At the same time, from the shuttered windows of Jerusalem House, the children's voices rose in another hymn, unsteady and fearful. She saw the cement on the littered road chip up beside her and heard the loud whip-cracks of rifles firing. As she dodged behind a shattered wall, she was strangely conscious of her feet running, her breath panting, her heart pounding, all with a kind of paralysed detachment like a sleeper at his own nightmare.

There were voices in front of her too, high-pitched voices shouting out orders. With a silent scream that seemed to send a wind of fear rushing past her ears, she doubled back, crouching behind the ruins, hunting desperately for somewhere to hide. There was a dark gap under a fallen wall, hardly more than a foot wide. She flung herself at it and wriggled underneath, as far in as

632

she could. Lying there panting, sobbing, she tried to lie still, her eyes staring wildly at the gap through which she expected any second to see a peering Japanese face with a bayonet beside it.

At first she could still hear the children singing and the voices of the Japanese. She must have doubled back almost as far as Jerusalem House. Then there came a stillness almost more dreadful than the shouting and the shots. Her skin prickled. She felt certain the Japanese were nearby, waiting, holding their breath perhaps and gazing at the block of masonry she imagined concealed her, nudging each other and grinning. They were *there*, she could feel the tension of their presence like a charge in the air.

Far away there was more firing. But she knew *they* were near. She had to bite her knuckle to prevent herself from screaming out loud. In her mind she could hear herself shrieking and see the long glittering bayonets lunging into her a moment later.

Then she heard the voices again. She'd been right, they *were* very close, perhaps the other side of the wall. They seemed to be discussing something coolly, unconcerned, laughing even. After a few minutes they moved away. She began to cherish a tiny, wan flame of hope. If they moved on, she might be able to get away. Not in the daylight, but later on when it was dark again.

Then she heard a sudden shout, and simultaneously the splintering crash of breaking wood. After that there was a mad, terrible confusion of noise. She heard the Japanese shouting, the children screaming, and once, above the others, Miss Pulham protesting. "How dare you!" in a voice of shocked outrage. Then the children's screams became suddenly wilder, piercing terrified shrieks. The Japanese voices shouted louder, there were rifle shots, more shrieks, more shots, then, gradually, only occasional moans. She lay there trembling, listening to the moans and whimpers, the last straggling shots, the unhurried shouting of the Japanese up and down the street, calling to each other. Even when there was no more noise she was still trembling, but it wasn't fear now, she had passed through fear to a cold shivering horror. She knew what must be there on the street.

At some time during the long stillness that followed, she licked the sweat off her lips. At some time a dog began

633

sniffing at the wall, but then she heard its claws clicking on the cement as it moved away. A sharp stone was digging into her hip, but she didn't move. Quite swiftly, without warning, she fell asleep, started awake, forgot where she was for a second, forgot what had happened, shuddered as she remembered, then just as swiftly fell asleep again.

There was rifle and machine gun fire somewhere far away, and the deeper explosions of grenades. She stretched cautiously and moved her limbs one by one, felt under her hips and pushed the stone away. Her movements made little rustling noises, and she paused anxiously after each one, but there was no answering sound. She knew the Japanese had gone now, with that same mysterious intuition with which she'd known before that they were there.

When she wriggled slowly, inch by inch, out of the hole, and looked about her, there was nothing but an eager snuffling sound, which it took her some time to realise was the greedy sniffing of a dog. It was late afternoon now. Her body was stiff and numb. She crawled forward until she could see the road.

She'd been right, she had come back nearly as far as Jerusalem House. The bronze, sloping sun was slanting its light into it, through the broken, hanging shutters and the shattered door. Without surprise she saw the small inert humps of the children's bodies scattered along the road, and the larger humps of the Chinese soldier's body and Miss Pulham's. Nearest her, only a few yards away, a little girl of about ten with short hair lay on her back, her face screwed up in an astonished grimace of pain. Her dress had been torn off, her legs were spread lasciviously apart, and a slashing wound, black with flies, ran from her navel to her breast bone. Her stomach sagged open like a split sack. The same dog that Lily had seen in the morning trotted away from another body nearby as she made a horrified gesture with her hand. Its nose dropped and it began snuffling round a corpse further away, its ears cocked though, its eyes warily watching her. She looked away with a shudder of horror. The dogs would eat them whatever she did. Or if not the dogs, the rats.

She looked up at the house. The Union Jack had been half burnt. Its charred remnants still hung down from the upper window. The white flag had gone. Broken glass glinted on the ground outside, amongst hymn books and prayer books, smashed pictures, plates and cups, bedding and clothes. Something had been scrawled in chalk on the broken door. *Punished for helping Imperial Japanese Forces' enemies*, the characters read. She gazed at the door which was leaning like a hanged man from its topmost hinge. I caused this, she thought. If I hadn't brought him here, they'd have been left alone.

82

As soon as he undressed he knew he wouldn't be able to do anything. Yuriko lay smiling on the bed, her hair hanging down over the edge almost to the floor. But he felt detached, uninterested, as if he'd got nothing but air between his legs. He kissed and bit her, licked her nipples, her throat, he let her hands fondle him, but it was all no use. That observant self he always carried in his head watched with aloofness, with an almost puzzled distaste, as though his antics were novel, weird and ugly. He gave up at last and lay still beside her. She watched him warily from beneath her slanted, heavy lids, as if afraid he was going to blame her. He turned his head away, staring dully at the wall with its prints of nineteenth century scenes that he couldn't imagine seeing anywhere in Shanghai except here in *rue* Molière.

"Don't I please you any more?" she asked in a small voice.

"No, it's not that," he shrugged. "Talk to me."

"Talk?" She laughed incredulously. "What about?"

"Anything."

She lay silent for some time. He started counting the prints. There were six.

"I can hear the guns, can't you?" she said at last.

He nodded. Chapei was a couple of miles from Frenchtown, but you could hear the guns all right. He gazed at her breasts, at her slim waist and long slender legs—perhaps too slender—at her ankles and small feet. Why was he suddenly dead to her? Were his powers failing? He thought of Jacob and the slow collapse of his face. Was it happening to him too? A pulse throbbed in his temple. He looked in the oval mirror on the dressing table, and saw an anxious-eyed, greying man with lines in his cheeks, lying beside a very young girl.

She sat up and rested her chin on her knees. Her straight black hair fell forward round her face. She began wriggling her toes, gazing down at them absently.

He watched her still in the mirror. The throbbing in his temple was growing stronger. He regarded himself again. He could hardly believe that lined face was his.

She flung her hair back over her shoulders. "Want me to give you a massage?"

He lay down prone and closed his eyes. She sat astride him, beating his shoulders gently with her fists, kneading the muscles. She began to breathe more heavily as she pushed and thumped and kneaded. "You know if you took heroin," she panted, "That would make you stronger in bed. Have you ever tried it?"

"I used to smoke opium."

"Want me to get some opium next time?"

"I don't know." He remembered the pipe and the lamp and smoking with Su-mei. "I'll think about it."

"I can get some good stuff in Hongkew."

"Can you?"

She turned round to face his feet and began kneading his ankles. "Want me to get you some?"

"I'll let you know." He raised his head to listen to the guns again. Feeling him move, she glanced round at him, raising her brows.

"Chapei must be a ruin now," he said.

"Who's winning?"

"Nobody."

She began sweeping her hands up his body, from his legs to his shoulders. "Put your head down flat," she commanded. "I suppose they'll build it all up again, afterwards."

"What about the people?"

"Huh?"

"The Japs have killed thirty thousand people."

"In war, everyone kills," she panted. "Are they worse than anyone else?"

"Yes."

"In that case," she said, lying down beside him again, "perhaps I should change my name?"

* * *

636

When they were dressing, she stood in front of the mirror, fixing a large pin in her hair with a gesture that reminded him of Su-mei when she was young. She paused, glancing round at him. "You aren't going to come again, are you?"

"Why do you say that?"

"Because you gave me such a big present."

He looked down at his fingers buttoning his shirt. One button, then another, then another. "No," he said at last. "I suppose not."

"Because of what happened today?"

"I don't know. Well—"

"Well what?"

He came and stood beside her at the mirror, eyeing the creases in his forehead, the slanting lines in his cheeks, the tired lids. Then he gazed at her face, firm and smooth, as it would be for years, provided she didn't take too much opium. "Nothing," he said, watching her head turn on the young stalk of her neck as she adjusted the pin. The throbbing in his temple was thudding right through his head now.

She caught his glance and smiled.

"I'll be fifty next birthday," he said.

Lily laid her head down on her arms and listened to her watch ticking by her ear. At eleven o'clock she would start moving, she thought. She'd start moving west towards the front line. All her fear and horror seemed to have gone now, as if she'd only got so much, and once that was spent there couldn't be any more. Or was it just that she was so tired? Her eyelids drooped, then started open again. There had been a faint squeak near her head. It was a rat, scurrying past her in the dusk, its dark button eye shiny and timid. Her eyes closed again. Perhaps it had thought she was dead too, like the others. It was large and fat.

On his way back from Frenchtown, Denton stopped to watch the refugees crowding through the checkpoint manned by French police. The police searched them perfunctorily for arms, prodded their bundles and let them through. There were hundreds of them at that little barrier alone, men, women and children, waiting as patiently as cattle. Behind them black smoke hung over Chapei, machine guns hammered, there was the crump of mortar

637

bombs and grenades. Some of the refugees were bandaged, some had shocked, staring eyes.

They were camping on the pavements, in the alleys, along the river, even on doorsteps. Some were begging, some were scrounging, most had given up. Denton avoided their hopeless, apathetic gaze. What could he do? There were too many of them, and too many more to come. In China numbers swamped everything.

In his wallet lay a stiff little blue evacuation card, issued the day before by the British Consulate. It guaranteed British subjects a place on a British ship in case of emergency. There wasn't one for Su-mei. He thought of the silver necklace he'd given Yuriko. On an impulse he went into a jeweller's and bought some gold earrings for Su-mei. He couldn't have said why. Was it because he'd finished with Yuriko? He gave all his change to beggars and didn't have enough to pay the taxi when he got home.

He gave Su-mei her present after dinner, laying it on the arm of her chair.

"Gold," she said with a little smile. "When I was young it was silver. I suppose you give silver to your concubine now?"

"I have no concubine." He took the earrings from her and fastened them on her ears. "I wish we could talk like we used to," he said sadly.

She shook her head with another rueful, but determined, smile. "One day we'll talk," she murmured, going to the mirror to examine the earrings. "Not now."

"Why not?"

She was turning her head from side to side. "Because when you put these on you didn't feel anything. Except pity."

He turned away with a sigh. Of course it was true, what she said. Except that he'd felt self-pity as well. A Kiangsi vase stood by the veranda doors, one of the relics of Mary-Ellen. It was almost the only thing she'd left him, as though she'd wanted to leave just one reminder. He drew his finger slowly round the rim. "Well, it doesn't matter," he said resignedly. "It's amazing we even think it's worth mentioning, with all these people dying and killing each other all round us."

"People have been dying and killing each other all

round us all our lives," she said quietly. "Why should it make a difference now?"

He went out onto the veranda and leant over the balustrade, gazing unhappily down at the darkened garden. A pale oblong of light from the room stretched out across it, giving the lawn a wan grey colour. Whenever he tried to approach her, she cut him off. And yet he sensed she didn't want to.

"What was that?" he heard her ask behind him.

"What was what?"

She had come out onto the veranda. "That noise, someone calling."

Then he heard it as well, the cry he used to hear often in the old Chinese city. *"Shang hei tze! Yau ma shang hei tze!"* It was a youngish man with three children, outside the Public Gardens, which had become a temporary refugee camp. His wife followed behind him with a baby strapped to her back. "Children! Children for sale!"

The next morning at breakfast, a large headline on the front page of the *Morning Post* met his eye. He read about the death of Miss Pulham, who, the Japanese authorities said, had been aiding and abetting the Chinese. The British consul was requesting more information.

He handed the paper wordlessly across to Su-mei.

"I suppose the children were helping the Chinese too," she said acidly after she'd read it.

Denton laid down his spoon and gazed absently across the room. He thought of Janet Pulham leaning over him when he was sprawled on the ground vomiting with cholera. He thought of her baby bag and Lily. He thought of his evacuation card, still snug in his wallet. "I think you ought to get a British passport, Su-mei," he said.

83

Jenny sat on the boat deck writing a post-card, the last she would write from the *Empress of Asia*. She looked up often, glancing at the sunlight sparkling on the sea, glancing at the white-hot haze of the sky between the lifeboat davits, glancing most of all along the freshly-scrubbed deck towards the bridge, where every few minutes the second officer appeared, strolled to the very end of the bridge, then after scanning the horizon, smiled secretly at her as he strolled back.

She lay back in the deck chair when she'd finished, and closed her eyes. The sunlight was warm on her lids, the humid, salty breeze just strong enough to cool her face. The deck quivered faintly with the throbbing of the engines and the waves hissed along the sides, scarcely rocking the boat at all. She didn't realise that she was smiling, remembering how the second officer, called Alan, had put his hand inside her blouse last night, and how she'd nearly given in only she'd wondered whether Robert, the Jardine's man, wasn't nicer really and you ought to do it first with someone you really liked. Not that she didn't like Alan, she just wasn't absolutely sure which one she liked best...

A shadow fell over her face. She opened her eyes. The second officer stood in front of her. "You've dropped your card, Miss Denton," he said bowing gallantly as he handed it to her. His eyes stayed on hers longer than they should have done, smiling teasingly.

"Oh thank you—Why aren't you on the bridge? Isn't anyone driving the ship?"

He laughed. "Just finished my watch. We'll be there in a couple of hours."

"I suppose you'll be too busy to have any shore leave?" she asked casually.

"As a matter of fact I will be having some. If you'd care to give me your phone number, I might perhaps show you one or two of those little places I mentioned?"

"We're in the book. Look it up and give me a ring. You know we're one of the oldest families in Shanghai— English families, I mean," she added with a proud little smile, pushing Su-mei and Lily and Michael out of her mind. "So we've got a very short number—easy to remember."

The sparkling blue water became suddenly muddy as they came to the Yangtze estuary. It was a distinct line in the sea, as though it had been painted browny-yellow from then on. She stood looking out over the rail at the hazy coastline, purplish on the horizon. She stood by herself, where Robert could easily see her and come and join her.

And the joy of it was she was just outside the second officer's cabin as well. She smiled warmly when Robert did come up to her at last, his fair hair neatly parted, his skin ruddy and fresh. If only he'd be a bit more forward, she'd probably like him more than the ship's officer.

"Whereabouts exactly on the Bund did you say your house was?" he asked.

"Goodness I can hardly remember now," she laughed. "It's so long since I saw it. It overlooks the Public Gardens. But we won't see it for a long time, we've got to go all the way up the river first."

Then as the green fields and the junks with their ribbed, drab sails glided silently past, her memories began to stir. It was like unrolling one of the those old scrolls her mother kept—as you unfurled it, you realised you'd seen it all before. You never knew what was coming next, but when it was there, it was all familiar to you. The bends in the river, slowly opening onto views of bright green rice fields, the little villages sheltering under the trees, the temples with their curving roofs, the wet, grey, water buffaloes patiently standing or plodding—she seemed to remember them all as they passed before her eyes. There was the ruined fort at Woosung, with the customs post which her father had so often pointed out to her. And the Point Gardens, with people picnicking and waving to the boats as she used to do. Why, she even remembered being there with Jonathan and Ah King once, when she couldn't have been more than five or six at the most. Then, as first the docks, with all the rigid arms of the cranes, then the tall, glittering white buildings of the Bund came into view, she felt a sudden, treacherous sadness filling her. They'd look so changed and old, she thought, when she saw them again, her father and Su-mei and everyone, while every-thing else, all the buildings and the harbour and the countryside hadn't changed at all. Why must people get old? She forgot the second officer, and she forgot Robert standing beside her, until he asked uncertainly, pointing at the wharves along Hongkew, flat, scruffy and shimmering with heat above their tin roofs, "Is that the Bund?"

"No, no," she laughed. "The Bund's up there, past those warships. This is just the wharves and the godowns. The Bund is rather grand." Her arm touched his shoulder as she pointed and she let it lie there a second before she moved. "Now you *will* give me a ring when you're settled in, won't you?" she said. "I expect there's quite a lot of places I could show you if you're a bit lost. And I can still speak the lingo fairly well."

Half a mile further on she saw the house again, the long sloping garden and the wooden seat at the bottom. For some reason she didn't point it out to Robert after all.

But they weren't so changed after all, she thought, as she saw them standing in the customs hall, her father, Su-mei and Lau. She needn't have been so worried. Her father's hair had more grey in it, and the lines in his face were deeper than she remembered, but really he was scarcely changed at all. And Su-mei and Lau—well, they never changed, Chinese always seemed to look the same for years and years. Su-mei was wearing a long, green, silk cheong-sam with short sleeves. Jenny wondered if she'd be able to wear a dress like that. It only seemed to suit Chinese women really. She waved and smiled as she walked towards them.

"Hello everyone," she said coolly. "Gosh it's hot."

After a second's hesitation, her father kissed her and hugged her. Su-mei just brushed her cheek and shook both hands in a restrained way. Lau grinned sheepishly and took her bag.

"The trunks are coming," she said in Shanghainese, and laughed. "That's the first time I've spoken Chinese for six years."

"Very good," Lau nodded encouragingly, grinning now.

They stood embarrassed, awkward, waiting for the porter.

"I thought the place would be all battered about after all that fighting between the Japs and the Chinese?" Jenny said, her voice a little strained.

"It is knocked about over in Chapei. You can't see much from the river."

"It was exciting reading about somewhere you know. I s'pose it's all over now?"

"For the time being, anyway. They patched up a truce—business as usual." Her father spoke jerkily, with a sardonic little smile. "More than usual in fact."

They laughed uncomfortably and looked about them, avoiding each other's eyes, shifting their feet.

"How's Lily?" she asked Su-mei brightly. "What was all that about being in the battle?"

Su-mei flicked her an inquiring little glance before she answered. "She's all right," she said in English still. "She works on a paper."

"She's not living at home now, of course," her father added.

"Where does she live then?"

"Near Frenchtown." He hesitated, glancing at Su-mei, then went on. "She has this boyfriend, he's the editor of the paper. It's very political and anti-Japanese... She lives in his flat."

"With him," Su-mei said precisely half-closing her slanted lids.

"Really? Lily?" Jenny's voice soared in amazement. "Not Lily? Living in sin?"

Her father looked relieved, as though he'd been afraid she'd be shocked. "They don't believe in marriage," he said, then smiled. "Or sin."

"Lily?" was all she could say. "I can't believe it!"

"Without marriage how can she be safe?" Su-mei asked. "He can leave her any time."

"Still, it means she can leave him too, doesn't it? Fancy her being so modern!"

"Modern?" Su-mei repeated. "Maybe. But it will all end bad."

"But you and..." She couldn't say Daddy. "But you two lived together before you were married, didn't you?" She looked at them mischievously. "And that didn't end badly did it?"

"Here comes your porter," Denton said quickly. "Is this all your luggage?"

When they were in the car, Jenny looked out at the big new buildings along the Bund, not bothering yet though to ask what they were. There was still the reassuring comfort of all the old ones, the Shanghai Club, the Banks, Jardine's...

"I met someone who's going to join Jardine's on the boat," she announced casually. "He's probably going to give me a ring. And one of the ship's officers is too."

Her father smiled absently. "I was just thinking, you're almost the same age now that I was when I first came to Shanghai..." He glanced across at Su-mei, with a little wistful glimmer in his eye. And suddenly he did seem to

643

have aged. Not in his face, but in the regretful tone of his words, and in that sad glimmer in his eye, like the far-off lights she'd sometimes seen at sea.

84

"The typhoon's coming this way, the wireless says." Su-mei looked up from her breakfast tea as he came into the dining room in his dressing gown. "I hope it won't spoil your birthday."

"Why should it? I quite like typhoons." He glanced over the envelopes beside his plate. All birthday cards.

"I've arranged dinner in Lahière's. I don't want them to close because of the weather."

"Dinner at Lahière's? Who's coming?"

"Jenny, Lily and Pak-kay. The Ephraims."

He glanced up surprised from the envelope he was slitting with his knife, an envelope with an English stamp on it, addressed in Michael's precise, round hand. "Lily and Pak-kay?" he exclaimed. "Have you made it up at last?"

"It doesn't mean I approve. But it is your fiftieth birthday. I've arranged for something afterwards too. A surprise. That's why I'm worried about the typhoon."

He raised his brows and smiled wrily. "What have I done to deserve all this?"

"It's your fiftieth birthday," she said. "One of the most important birthdays."

"Perhaps we should have asked Wei? I haven't seen him for ages, but..."

"I did ask him. He said he wasn't well."

Denton nodded, sliding Michael's card out of the envelope. "It would be tricky in any case, I suppose, if Lily and Pak-kay were there. He can hardly have forgotten that debate. And he's even closer to the Japs now."

She got up and switched the fan on faster. The air fluttered the envelope flaps as he opened them one by one. He glanced out through the veranda doors at the harbour. Little white-tipped waves were stirring the sullen brown water, rocking the junks and sampans already. The first rolling clouds were just appearing over Pootung, and the leaves in the garden had begun to rustle and stir apprehensively, like old ladies pulling their shawls about them. He poured some coffee and opened the next envelope. Su-mei leant forward, resting her chin on her delicate fist. It was a card from Jenny. There had been cards from everyone, even Lily. The last envelope must be from Su-mei. He recognized her brush strokes. She'd written the Chinese version of his name.

When he opened the envelope, he frowned in puzzlement. It wasn't a card. It was a certificate of registration from the Race Club. Su-mei and he were named as joint owners of a chestnut China two-year-old named Just Deeds.

"What on earth's this?"

"My main present."

"You want to start racing again?"

"I paid a lot for it. I want you to race it against Pock-mark Chen's horses." Her voice had suddenly become alert and lively. Her eyes gleamed. "I want everyone to see you beating him."

"Race against Pock-mark Chen? What on earth d'you mean?" He dropped the certificate on the table, then, as it fluttered away under the fan, slapped his knife on top of it. "Haven't we had enough to do with him? After all these years, to..." He raised his hands and let them drop helplessly. "I never want to even hear his name again, let alone play petty games with him."

"This isn't games, this is serious!"

"Racing? Serious?"

"Of course it is! D'you want to live in his shadow the rest of your life."

"I ignore him."

"You live in his shadow, and everyone knows it. He's humiliated you. People smile when they see you, they say he's the one that had to bow down to Pock-mark Chen. They pity you. Don't you realise what it's doing to you? What it's done already?"

He looked away. Her eyes reminded him of Lily's. He gazed out at the warships in the harbour, their flags fluttering stiffly in the rising wind. "It hasn't done anything to me," he protested uncomfortably.

"No, it's taken away your pride. You've given up. You don't respect yourself any more."

"Of course I do. Or if I don't, it's not because of him."

"Because of what, then?"

He looked down at the certificate, puckering his cheek, and prevaricated. "I suppose I've known myself too long to have much self-respect left." Before she could take him up on that he asked quickly, "How much did it cost?"

"I bought it with my own money."

"I thought it all went on opium?"

"I don't smoke much any more."

"No, that's true. You don't." He hadn't realised till then.

"Say you'll do it," she said, as if it was his last chance.

"But I don't like horse-racing—besides it's all changed now. They have professional jockeys and trainers and everything."

"Never mind. Show everyone you can beat him."

"I'll think about it," he said grudgingly, gazing out at the warships again—a dark grey American destroyer and a light grey British gunboat. They were both straining against the current and the wind, their anchor hawsers taut. "Thank you, anyway, Su-mei," he added. "It certainly is a surprise." All the same, he thought, it's a crazy idea. I'll have to talk her out of it somehow.

Then the servants came in to congratulate him.

He was withdrawn all day. Not even Jenny's present of some new gramophone records, specially brought in her trunk from England, nor Lily's unexpected gift of a volume of stories by Lu Xün, a new Chinese writer, could break through the wall of his abstraction for long. He leafed through the books and played one of the records but when the record ended he didn't notice, gazing heedlessly out of the window, while the needle scratched and bumped, scratched and bumped round the centre of the disc. In the evening, after his third whisky, he spoke to Su-mei about the horse again.

"But you must see, Su-mei, this idea's absolutely crazy."

"You just think about it," she said, not pleading, but as if confident he would come round.

The Ephraims, Lily and Pak-kay were to meet them at the restaurant. When Su-mei, Jenny and Denton drove through the overcast streets towards Frenchtown, the winds were at last getting up, and the air stirred continually with the advancing pressure of the storm. Shop signs hanging over the street creaked as they swung, many shops were shuttered

646

and barred, the few rickshaw coolies still about had turned their cabs to the wind and were huddling inside, while sporadic gusts of rain spattered down on their taut canvas hoods. The trams and buses were still running, crowded with pale blurs of faces behind their rain-splashed windows, but there were few cars. Wheelbarrows were stacked against the walls in every alley, bamboo scaffolding poles quivered, and torn awnings flapped with a sharp cracking noise. Looking out at the growing violence of the air, Denton began to feel more buoyant. "I love storms," he murmured, almost to himself.

"Just imagine, I haven't seen a typhoon for six years," Jenny answered. She was wearing a blue silk cheong-sam that Su-mei's tailor had made for her, the slit reaching audaciously up her thigh. But still she wasn't sure it suited her as much as it did Chinese women, and she kept wondering whether she should have put her hair up like Su-mei did.

Jacob and Sarah were already sitting at the table with Pak-kay and Lily. Sarah's face sagged in woebegone pouches. Her eyes had a harassed expression, nervously switching from side to side as though she was constantly on the lookout for some sudden attack. She kept fingering the strings of pearls round her loose-skinned neck. Does Jacob really not realise how unhappy she must be? Denton wondered. But then the thought was followed by another— Suppose he looks at Su-mei and wonders just the same about me? He glanced covertly at Su-mei. No, there was no wretchedness engraved on *her* face or peering through *her* eyes. Only that impervious bland composure. And her skin was almost as smooth as ever.

"You are completely wrong to oppose the Japanese in Shanghai," Jacob was declaring with patronising geniality, his face almost as wrinkled as Sarah's, but quickened with exuberant life. "If you'd succeeded in throwing them out, a third of the population of Shanghai would have been out of a job for the rest of their lives."

"We need the Japanese like we need the plague," Pak-kay said curtly.

"Can't we be more peaceful, tonight of all nights?" Sarah pleaded, looking at Denton. And they all hesitated, taken aback more by the fact that she'd spoken at all in her sad, lost voice, than by what she said.

But the argument smouldered on throughout the

dinner. Denton, drinking the red wine steadily, listened and watched, while some remoter part of his mind pondered Su-mei's obsession with Pock-mark Chen.

"How is business?" Su-mei asked Jacob, when there was a lull, in the manner of a polite hostess stifling a yawn.

"Never been better! Never been better!" He'd never asked a question merely to make conversation, so he never recognised one when it was put to him. He threw himself into an energetic, voluble lecture on cotton, silk and speculation in silver, his eyes glinting round at them all enthusiastically. "But silver is the thing now, you should get into silver," he proclaimed. Taking a dollar out of his pocket, he rang it expertly on the table to show it was genuine. "Sell this here," he said, holding it up between his finger and thumb, "one U.S. dollar. Sell in New York, one dollar thirty." He flicked it up and caught it as it fell spinning down. "I'm exporting silver, as much as I can."

"I guess you're not interested in what all that silver exporting is doing to China's economy?" Pak-kay suggested in the same level tone as before.

"Of course I am! We sell silver, we buy dollars. With our dollars we employ more workers in our factories, we make Shanghai richer and Shanghai makes China richer—"

"Oh look, there's someone I met on the boat over there," Jenny exclaimed. She'd been glancing round boredly for several minutes now. "The one who was going to work for Jardine's." She waved gaily, managing to stretch out her leg so that Robert would see the long slit of her cheong-sam. She sensed Lily glancing scornfully at her, and that obscurely pleased her. But Robert's smile of recognition faded swiftly, and with an embarrassed nod he turned back, blushing, to the two other men at his table, who were studying her covertly.

Suddenly she thought she understood why Robert hadn't rung at all in the month since they'd landed. It was that Chinese thing, Su-mei and Lily and Michael. Probably it was part of the Jardine's Mess gossip. *Something funny there,* she imagined them warning Robert. *"Old Denton married his Chinese mistress. Nobody knows them now. I'd keep clear if I were you."* Her lips tightened resentfully against Robert, and against Su-mei too, and her children who were spoiling things for her. Feeling Lily's disapproving gaze still on her, she turned and faced her. "Don't you find it difficult in Shanghai, being Eurasian?" she asked bluntly.

Lily was resting her chin on the back of her curved hand, meeting Jenny's eyes with a half-lidded stare of her own. *A Chinese stare*, Jenny thought. "I did find it hard for a time," she said coldly at last. "Until I decided I was Chinese."

"Ah my dear," Sarah leant towards Lily suddenly, speaking shyly, with a moist film over her sad eyes. "They'll never accept you." She spoke so quietly that no one but Lily seemed to hear. "Whatever you do, they'll never accept you." It was two thousand years of Jewish history speaking.

"I am Chinese," Lily replied as quietly to her, her eyelids lowering faintly, as if to close the discussion once and for all.

No you're not, Denton thought. Sitting next to Lily, he glanced at her with detached remorse—he had made her, he was responsible for her existence, he was to blame for her stiff idealism and all that she would suffer. Even though he hadn't meant it. Sarah was right. You'll try so hard, but they'll never accept you, Lily. Not the Chinese, not the foreign devils. You'll always be in between.

She looked up suddenly as though he'd spoken aloud. "How is your paper going these days?" he asked quickly, before her direct, questioning eyes could probe too far into his.

Her lips turned down at the corners. It was a smile—a wry smile, but still a smile. "We're running out of money."

"Again," Pak-kay added.

"Still campaigning for a united front?" he glanced ironically at Pak-kay now, who was scratching his chin through his beard.

"We're concentrating on the Jap atrocities in Hongkew and Chapei at present. And what they're doing there now. Did you know they're turning the whole place into a great big opium and gambling den? Pock-mark Chen's in it of course. He sat on the fence during the fighting and now the Japs have given him the opium contract."

"Pock-mark Chen?" Jacob's grey brows corrugated his forehead in disbelief. "He's Chiang Kai-shek's blood brother."

"And how d'you know all this?" Denton asked gently. "Did they announce it on the wireless?"

"They might just as well have done. We have our sources."

Su-mei had scarcely spoken throughout the meal. But now she asked with quiet interest. "And what are you doing about all this in your paper?"

"So far we've been concentrating on the Japanese. If we can keep going, we'll start on Pock-mark Chen too. If he's discredited, Chiang might have to drop him."

"Have you thought what Pock-mark Chen might do about seeing himself attacked in your paper?" Denton asked sharply. He glanced at Lily. "Or doesn't that worry you?"

Pak-kay smiled complacently, "We keep inside the Foreign Settlements, and we have...friends looking out for us. Besides, I've got an American passport and Lily's is British. That's a help. They don't want to create a diplomatic incident."

"And I thought you were both Chinese!" Jacob laughed delightedly. "I thought you were both Chinese! You're quite right to hedge your bets, though. Meddle in Chinese politics by all means, but don't get a Chinese passport, eh? That's taking things too far! Look at me—I haven't got a passport at all! Even Argentina wouldn't give me one!"

"My passport's merely a tactical convenience," Pak-kay said in his humourless harsh voice. "It's a useful document, that's all."

"Like a marriage certificate," Su-mei mentioned icily.

"Can't we be more peaceful?" Sarah pleaded, raising her veiny hand like a flag of truce. "It *is* John's birthday dinner."

Out of the corner of her eye, Jenny saw Robert and his friends leaving their table. Robert glanced across at her, but she turned her head away and raised her shoulder disdainfully. She despised him, she never wanted to hear his name again, let alone see him. And at the same time she hated Su-mei and Lily, and even her father, for putting her in this awful position.

They had finished their coffee. Su-mei signalled to the waiter. "Now there is a surprise," she said impassively. "We are going to the Ta Wu Tai for some Peking Opera. Mei Lan-fan is performing. I've got the best seats in the house."

"Ach, you know I can't stand Peking Opera," Jacob groaned theatrically.

Ta Wu Tai was the theatre Su-mei used to perform in. Su-mei was looking at Denton. They were both remembering.

The theatre was crowded and noisy despite the approaching typhoon. When they arrived, the drab scenery of the understudies was being replaced by Mei Lan-fan's magnificent backdrops, and his own musicians were taking over from the others. The audience was changing too. The servants who'd been sent to keep seats were shuffling out as the ushers led their masters and mistresses in. Meanwhile the music and singing continued casually, with nobody listening.

Denton leant across to Jenny, taking his hot, scented towel from the attendant and wiping his face and hands with it. "I remember when women weren't allowed in here," he said. "In the auditorium, I mean. They had to sit upstairs in the balcony."

She patted her hands on her towel sulkily. Ah King used to take Alec and her to the street theatres sometimes, and all she remembered now was the weird noises and slow-motion gestures of the actors. So boring, and they might have gone to a nightclub instead! But she took the hot green tea and the saucer of melon seeds the attendant offered her. Those she'd always loved.

Now the stage was empty, the musicians idly tuning and twanging their instruments. The last seats were being filled, and the raucous talking and shouting sank to an expectant murmur. Denton bit a melon seed and glanced along the row of seats. Sarah's lids were drooping with fatigue. Beside her, Jacob himself looked uncharacteristically weary, his eyes for once dull and uninterested. Further on, Pak-kay and Lily sat at the end of the row, expectation shining on their faces a shade too intensely, announcing a shade too self-consciously their determination to appreciate China's greatest actor. He knew Lily liked opera—she'd grown up with it. But did Pak-kay? Denton doubted it.

They were sitting in the back row of the most expensive seats, with a wide aisle separating them from the cheaper seats behind them. An usher sauntered self-importantly along the aisle and asked for their tickets. When Su-mei gave them to him, he examined them briefly then shook his head. "Upstairs, balcony," he said tersely. "Not here."

Su-mei took the tickets back from him. She leant towards Denton and they checked them together against the seat numbers. "No, these are the right seats," he said.

"Balcony," the usher muttered stonily, shaking his head. "These seats are reserved."

"I don't care whether they're reserved or not," Denton said curtly. "We paid for these seats and we're staying here." He turned back to the stage, folding his arms.

"Balcony," the usher repeated behind him, rapping imperiously on the back of his seat.

"Shut up, will you?"

Su-mei laid a warning hand on his knee and nodded to the right. Half a dozen or so men stood in a group at the end of the row. At first in the dim light he couldn't make out who they were. Then, as the group opened slightly, he recognised the gross bulk of Pock-mark Chen. Beside him stood a small, bespectacled Japanese with a scrubby moustache. Although he wasn't moving, there was something martial and pompous about the way the Japanese held himself, something that seemed ridiculous in a man of his size, like a bantam cock parading amongst a herd of buffalo.

While the group waited, gazing at them, the theatre manager scurried up to Denton and Su-mei and spoke to them in a hurried, flustered whisper. "Very sorry mistake," he began in English. "I give best seat upstair', more better."

Denton turned back to stare stolidly at the empty stage, sensing faces turning towards them and voices hushing. "I prefer it here," he said loudly in Shanghainese.

Jenny stared haughtily at the men bunched at the end of the row. They were wearing those wide-lapelled double-breasted suits you saw in American gangster films, and their faces had that stony look about them. She smiled contemptuously, but the hard unwinking return she got made her suddenly uneasy. No Chinese had ever looked at her like that before.

The manager was growing more flustered, pleading and cajoling with Su-mei, whom he knew from her singing days, glancing anxiously back at Pock-mark Chen who stood monumentally waiting, betraying his impatience only by the occasional flicker of his eyelids over his bulging eyes. At last Chen shook his head with a surprisingly light and darting movement and waddled along the row, flanked by two of his bodyguards. He laid his hand on the back of Denton's seat. Glancing down at it, his neck prickling, Denton noticed how strangely small it was, pale and hairless as a woman's.

"I am sorry Mister Denton," the instantly familiar voice wheezed in English. "You sit in my seat."

Denton twisted slowly round and looked into the smooth moon face with its cold, protruding eyes and short, scanty brows. "Your seat?" he repeated. "But we have tickets for all these seats."

Pock-mark Chen's eyes didn't move from Denton's. "There are plenty seat' in upstair'," he said, his voice as threaded with catarrh as ever. "The official will refund the payment," he glanced at the manager indifferently. "It is his mistaken selling." He paused expectantly. When Denton obstinately didn't respond, he started again in the same monotonous catarrhal wheeze. "How is your daughter?" His eyes swivelled momentarily towards Lily and Pak-kay, while his face remained turned towards Denton. "She is interest' in political thing' I think? That can be danger'." He spoke with pleasant menace. "I hope you are careful to her?"

Lily and Pak-kay sat rigidly where they were, but Su-mei abruptly stood up, letting her seat clatter behind her. In the tense hush that enveloped them the sudden noise was as startling as a gunshot. "Let's go," she said loudly in Shanghainese. "The performance is ruined now anyway."

"There are plenty seat' upstair'," Pock-mark Chen repeated tonelessly, yet with a courteous little bow to Su-mei.

"Come on," Su-mei muttered. "I don't want to stay now anyway." She moved past him. After a long second's hesitation, Denton stood up and followed her out, his cheeks stiff and burning. Amongst the bodyguards at the end of the row he came face to face with Yin-hong, taller and heavier now, but undoubtedly the same Yin-hong. Yin-hong's eyes flickered then stared away past him. The Japanese gazed at him with an insolently curious interest, then unaccountably bowed, chin on chest in the formal Japanese style, as if Denton had just done him a great favour.

He followed Su-mei along the aisle, feeling a thousand eyes gazing at his retreating back. He heard Lily's voice behind him, unsteady but clear. She and Pak-kay had sat in their seats till the last moment, leaving only with sullen, grudging reluctance. "How many Chinese women and children did you butcher in Chapei, Colonel Saito?" she asked the Japanese in English. For a few seconds the little man blinked up at her—he was a few inches shorter than Lily. Then he slapped her face, twice. Not hard but stingingly, as if she'd been an impertinent child. Pak-kay stiffened, his eyes flared, but the bodyguards, Yin-hong amongst them, moved threateningly round him and Lily tugged his sleeve. "They're not worth it," she said, in Shanghainese this time, and turned away. Pak-kay followed her with a humiliated scowl while the Japanese strutted along the row to join Pock-mark Chen. Denton saw the faces nearby staring at Lily. Nobody was sneering. They only gaped, stunned, cowed, or ashamed. The bodyguards, muttering amongst themselves, sauntered along the row to take the rest of the emptied seats.

Pak-kay and Lily walked past him, gazing rigidly ahead as if they hadn't seen him there. But then Pak-kay half-turned his head. "See what I mean about Pock-mark Chen?" he grated quietly. "Believe me now?"

Denton turned to follow them. As they went out past the gawping attendants, as if at a signal, the music started for Mei Lan-fan.

"Disgraceful! Unheard of!" Jacob exclaimed in the lobby. "Ask for your money back! You should call the police." Yet there was something subdued about his indignation. He seemed almost crestfallen when he met Pak-kay's eye, while Pak-kay looked grimly triumphant.

"To hell with the money." Denton trod through the litter of orange skin and melon peels, out onto the street. Lau was dozing in the car, his hat over his eyes. "Su-mei, why did you get up? We should've just sat there."

"He made a threat," she said simply. "Didn't you hear?" She got into the car before him. He noticed her hand was quivering.

"And yet this morning you wanted me to race against him?" he whispered accusingly.

"Because that's not dangerous," she hissed back. Her eyes glittered. "Can't you see? It's the same thing with

654

racing, only not dangerous. D'you want Lily kidnapped too?"

Jacob said he would take Sarah home and called goodbye hastily, bundling her into a taxi as the wind whipped round them, fluttering her dress against her body to make her seem more forlorn than ever. "Write to the newspaper!" he was calling out as he climbed in after her. "Report it to the police! Blatant intimidation, I'll be a witness!"

Pak-kay and Lily came with them in the car. Quite suddenly the rain began, heavy blinding sheets cascading over the roof and dragging on the wipers. The trams and buses had stopped running, the streets were dark and empty except for the wind-driven curtains of rain.

None of them spoke until they were nearly home. Then Jenny took out a cigarette and lit it with the lighter in the car. "Those people are absolute barbarians!" she said in a high, indignant voice that nevertheless sounded small and hollow in the brooding silence that received it. She felt she'd said something inadequate, that there were dimensions to the whole thing which she didn't understand. She tossed her head irritably. "Who was that beastly little Jap, anyway?"

"Saito," Lily said, gazing with raised, reflective brows out at the trees bending and swaying along the Bund. "In charge of Japanese Security." She stroked her cheeks gently with her fingertips, first one side then the other.

"Did he hurt you?" Jenny asked. "You could sue him for assault. If he'd touched *me* I'd have slapped him back."

"It didn't hurt," Lily answered almost impatiently, as if Jenny was disturbing her with superficial chatter.

Denton was staring out of the window too, his face set and rigid. Sheet after driven sheet of rain went over them, white in the headlights, then black as night, sending thick layers of water streaming blindly across the windscreen. "It's enough to make me think of supporting your paper," he said to Pak-kay, his voice unsteady and thick, as though he had to drag the words by brute force out of his chest. "Just to get even with that bastard."

The whites of Pak-kay's eyes gleamed faintly in the dark. He was stroking the end of his beard with rapid little movements of his finger and thumb.

The shutters had been closed on all the windows, the pot plants placed against the shelter of the walls. Ah King

655

and Ah Leng came out with umbrellas, but their clothes were all soaked by the time they'd hurried up the steps to the front door. "You'd better stay the night," Denton said to Pak-kay and Lily, looking not at them, but at Su-mei, who said nothing, only briefly lowering her lids. "Would you like a drink?"

"No, thanks," Pak-kay said. "Perhaps we could talk about the paper in the morning? If you're serious."

"I'm always serious. That's my trouble. The question is whether I'll have changed my mind. Ask Ah King to arrange a room for you, Lily. For you both," he added, glancing again at Su-mei. "Goodnight."

He went up to the study and sat in the dark, opening the shutter slats to watch the glistening leaves of the bauhinias waving and streaming outside like the banners of some tumultuous army. Pock-mark Chen's moon face and cold bulging eyes, the little Japanese slapping Lily's cheeks, and Yin-hong's evasive stare all tumbled behind his eyes, as if his thoughts too were being tossed about by the rising winds.

Su-mei was lying on her back when he went to bed, gazing up at the ceiling. One of the shutters was rattling. He tightened the bar across it. He lay down beside her, pillowing his head on his clasped hands. He felt closer to her than he had for months—or even years. But he didn't know quite why, yet. A gust of wind battered the shutters. As it shouted away, they listened together to the stinging hiss of the rain rushing over the windows. "That horse," he said slowly. "What did you call it?"

"Just Deeds."

He nodded, then heaved himself onto his side to face her, sighing in the air that the closed windows had made stifling and musty. "Perhaps you're right," he murmured after a time.

"About the horse?"

"Yes. It would be nice to beat that bastard."

She turned and laid her hand tentatively on his shoulder. That too was the first time in months or years. "You can't imagine how much he deserves it," she murmured. "Shall we have some opium?"

Then he thought he understood why he felt closer to her. It was because he hadn't given up after all.

85

The horses thudded past, steam snorting from their nostrils, turf chips flying up behind their hooves. The dawn sunlight glinted on the windows of the clubhouse across the track. Denton looked back at the orange globe of the sun, barred with clouds, rising beyond the dark shapes of the towers along the Bund.

"Well, what do you think of your horse now?" Su-mei asked. She was leaning on the white wooden rail, watching the horses as the mafoos led them back to the stables. A warm coat hung over her shoulders against the October chill. When she spoke, her breath steamed in the air, just like the horses'. "What d'you think of him then?"

He shrugged. "It's what Solnikov thinks that matters."

They walked towards the clubhouse, where ten years ago Su-mei wouldn't have been allowed in. The grey-haired Russian trainer was drinking his lemon tea, his hands clasped round the steaming glass. He shrugged too when Su-mei asked him, eyeing them both with melancholy brown eyes. "A good horse, he moves well," he conceded doubtfully. "But I can't say how good yet."

"Does he have any chance of winning the Stewards' Cup?" Denton asked as Solnikov sipped his tea.

"Ah, Mr. Denton," he shrugged again, sucking in the frayed edge of his moustache. "Every horse has some chance. Suppose all the others go lame?"

"Are you sure he knows what he's doing?" Denton asked Su-mei as they walked back across the turf, waiting for another string of horses to canter past. "He doesn't seem very sure of himself."

"They say he's the best."

"Who do?"

"Well, he had most winners last season."

As they walked on towards the gate, a European in a cap and raincoat, who'd been watching the horses through binoculars, came towards them, smiling familiarly, showing uneven yellowish teeth beneath a shaggy, grey, nicotine-stained moustache. "Who's this?" Denton murmured, gazing unsurely at the tall, heavy, yet somehow sagging figure.

"Long time no see," the man said, half withdrawing his hand from his pocket, then pushing it uncertainly in again. His voice was hearty and at the same time hollow, as if he couldn't quite fill it with conviction.

"Mason?" Denton asked. "You're not Mason are you?" He stared at the purple-veined cheeks, the dark pouches beneath the bloodshot eyes.

"What, have I changed that much? And I knew you at once. Both of you. Mark you, I thought you might be here watching your nag." His hand did leave his pocket now, and he brushed his moustache upwards in that old gesture with the back of his knuckle. "Back with number one lady again, I see," he said in a voice that was at once ingratiating and sneering. "I'd heard about it of course. Don't look much the worse for wear, either of you, if I might say so."

"What are you doing here?" Denton asked curtly.

"Didn't expect to see me again, eh?" Mason kept glancing suggestively from Denton to Su-mei.

"I wouldn't have thought this was the healthiest place for you to be in."

"After that opium business?" He laughed, more confidently now. "No, it wasn't for a time, I can assure you. I was in Japan for ten years. Yokohama. Had a little bar there. You know, for the sailors. Then I made my peace with..." he cocked his head sideways and winked, "with you-know-who. I was able to be a bit useful to him, matter of fact. You know, connections with sailors and so on, always comes in handy, doesn't it, never know when it's needed, eh? I'm quite well in with the Japs too, now, over, in Little Tokyo. That helps."

Su-mei was buttoning her coat. She glanced at Denton and raised her brow, nodding towards the gate.

"Now I'm the racing tipster for the *Daily News* as a matter of fact," Mason went on quickly, his voice like a hand on the sleeve. "Horses and dogs. Of course I do one or two other little jobs as well. That's why I thought I might see you around here sooner or later. Heard you had to sell your other horse." A trace of the old sneer slid into his voice. "Didn't fall on hard times, did you, by any chance? Not Mr. Denton, the municipal councillor?"

"I'm sure you know all about that," Denton said coldly.

"Yes, well, heard a few rumours, I can't deny," Mason

658

grinned knowingly. "Still, you're doing all right again now, eh?"

Su-mei had began to move away. She hadn't even acknowledged Mason yet, let alone spoken to him. His eyes followed her, narrowing slightly. "Though you're not so high and mighty as you used to be now, are you?" he sneered openly now. Then he glanced back at Denton. "I hear you've gone into journalism too, in a way?"

"Do you?"

"The *Shanghai Star*?" Mason winked as though it were a pornographic journal. "I hear you've got an interest in that?"

"You seem to hear a lot of things."

Mason chuckled, brushing his moustache up again with that characteristic gesture. "I make it my business to pick things up. Ever go to the canidrome, by the way? In Frenchtown? You might see me there. Can't remember if you were much of a betting man. I'm one of the starters."

"As well as being one of the tipsters for the *Daily News*?"

"That's right," Mason grinned innocently. "Nothing wrong with that, is there?"

"I wouldn't know." He turned away with a brief nod, then glanced back. "Isn't the canidrome largely owned by...by you-know-who?"

Mason winked again, letting the bluish lid slide very slowly down over his eye. "If you can't beat 'em, join 'em, eh?" he chuckled.

The outrageous insults to his imperial majesty, the emperor of Japan, Denton read, *which daily appear in some of the more scurrilous Chinese newspapers, must stand in a special category of infamy.*

"What are you snorting at?" Jenny asked as she buttered her toast. "Anything about the Paper Hunt Club Ball?"

"Anything about what?"

"Never mind, I'll look later."

"You'd better hurry, I'm leaving in five minutes."

Jenny bit off a piece of toast, dabbing the dry little crumbs off her lips with her napkin. She was thinking of Robert. He was all right after all, she decided. She really did believe him now about that evening in Lahière's. After all, he was very shy. She'd practically had to invite him to kiss her last night, although once he'd got going...Not like Alan of course, but all the same. Yes, she really did believe he didn't mind about Su-mei and all that side of her family.

The car turned out of the drive. Jenny glanced at the road, teeming with barrows, rickshaws and lorries. The sun was hot by now, although it was autumn; everyone was frowning against the glare, and the coolies' backs were slippery with sweat. "Are you going to see your paper again today?" she asked.

"It's not exactly mine," he said as he nodded. "I've only got a half-share. But I'm thinking of buying the others out."

"Whatever for? I thought you'd lost all interest in business, you told me?"

"This isn't business, it's politics." He glanced away out of the window, holding the strap by his middle finger. "If I buy out the left-wing groups, I might be able to rein in young Pak-kay—"

"Isn't he *awful?*"

"In some ways he is, yes." Denton considered a moment. "In all ways but one, in fact."

They watched the trams clanging down Maloo, grinding and jolting over the points, the hawkers pushing their carts along the gutters, the rickshaws running in and out among the clumsy wheelbarrows, and the people spilling off the narrow pavements, shoppers, beggars, musicians, clerks and messengers.

She looked back at her father. "When are you going to race Just Deeds?"

"When I'm sure he'll win."

"Just Deeds," she repeated. "Why did you pick that name? Was it just for your initials?"

"Su-mei picked it." He smiled to himself.

The car slowed. The traffic had been halted at Tibet Road for a column of Japanese troops. "Look," Denton said drily. "The conquering heroes."

The troops marched past four abreast, led by an officer on a white horse, their bayonets glittering in the sun. The Chinese on the pavements, in the buses and trams, watched in fascinated grim silence. Two or three Japanese bowed reverently as the rows of soldiers passed them one after the other.

Lau shook his head and sighed loudly as the last of the column passed. Suddenly he leant his head out of the window and spat—a thing he'd never done in Denton's presence before. Jenny glanced at her father, but he was gazing straight ahead as if he hadn't noticed.

The car started smoothly forward. They were all three silent as the traffic slowly uncramped itself. The street filled up with noise again, the ordinary raucous voices of hawkers, beggars, and coolies, of bargaining and gossip. They glanced up Tibet Road as the car crossed the junction. Traffic had been halted all the way along the sides of the road while the soldiers marched up the middle. "They look so cocky," Jenny said uneasily. She thought of that Jap who'd slapped Lily's face. "Cocky and nasty."

"Thank god they're not big as well."

"They shouldn't be allowed in the international settlement!"

"Unfortunately, they've got as much right here as our troops have," Denton answered. "Or as little. And there are a lot more of them than there are of ours."

The green turf of the race club opened out suddenly on their left, with old men in white flannels and straw hats clustering on the bowling green beside it.

"I wonder what...mother will look like now?" Jenny asked. She said *mother* with a little hesitating qualm, as if the word didn't really fit.

"I haven't seen her for over a year now," Denton shrugged. "You know she's living with another...friend now, not Helen Bolton?"

"Oh, it's all right," she giggled at his delicacy. "I know what her friends are. I *have* been to boarding school after all. Isn't it awful having a lesbian for a mother, though?"

"It was worse having one for a wife."

She got out as the car drew up outside the gallery. Denton leant back in the corner. "Sure you'll be all right getting back?"

"Honestly, you'd think I was still a child!"

In many things, the things that mattered, Denton thought, she was.

Lau drove the car carefully down the narrow, dirty alley. One-room factories, garages, dark, greasy metal-work shops, crowded each other along the pavement. Outside one black, dingy store, a man was sawing through a long metal pipe with a hacksaw. Next to him, almost back to back, another was hammering sheets of zinc into the round shapes of buckets. Further along, an old woman squatted against a wall, smoking a water pipe and watching from half-lidded eyes as a young boy of twelve or so tinkered in the gutter with the insides of an old wireless. Dogs and cats prowled amongst the refuse, or lay, chins on paws, silently watching the gleaming car go past.

"Go down to the end," Denton said. "Turn right." He hadn't taken the car there before. It made him uneasy, to show his wealth amongst so much poverty. Yet what could he do?

The car had to mount the pavement on the other side as it swung round the corner into an even narrower alley, a cul-de-sac.

"Last one on the left." Denton gazed along the grimy walls at the few faded shop signs hanging down like the dejected banners of a forgotten army. What could he do? Perhaps keeping the paper going was all. If only he could make it more reasonable.

"Police," Lau said.

Denton looked ahead. A police car stood outside the newspaper office and a small crowd gawped in a semi-circle round it.

"All right, stop here." He got out and walked towards the office with the same sickening lurch of apprehension that he remembered feeling when he saw the police cars outside the house the day Michael was kidnapped. And with the same absurd detachment he was aware of the movement of his legs, the stepping of his feet. A pungent tang of urine rose above the smell of grease and dirt in the gutter—he noticed that too.

The windows of the office had been smashed. Two Chinese constables stood by the police car, stolidly survey-ing the jagged splinters. Inside, by the press, Pak-kay and Lily were talking to a European inspector. Lolly Kwai of all people appeared in the doorway, dressed in plain clothes, glancing suspiciously up and down the street while he scolded the constables.

"When I was in the force, I'd have got here from Louza Street station in two minutes," he complained. "Why did it take you half an hour? Lose your way, did you?"

"What's happened?" Denton asked, relief blowing like

662

a cool wind through him that Lily hadn't been hurt. "And what are you doing here, Lolly?"

"Mister Denton!" Lolly exclaimed in English. "See what these naughty people are doing. Please go inside."

Denton walked in. The press and the floor were covered with ice-blue splinters of glass. Pak-kay seemed elated with anger, as though no other emotion would ever satisfy him as much.

"A bomb blew the windows in," he said. "No other damage."

"Will you come to the police station and make a statement," the inspector said after glancing uncertainly at Denton a moment. His tone was peremptory rather than inviting. But his pale blue eyes, shifting from Pak-kay to Denton and back again, were weak and uncertain.

"I've got work to do here," Pak-kay declared sourly. "Can't I make the statement here?"

The inspector hesitated, his face flushed at the obstinate impertinence of this American-speaking Chinese with his strange antique beard. Denton saw he was going to bluster.

"It would be a great help if the editor could make his statement here, inspector," he said smoothly. "We have to get the paper out you see. I'm one of the proprietors, by the way—Denton." He offered his hand. "Inspector . . . ?"

"Robinson," the inspector said, shaking hands. He sighed, putting on a look of exasperation. "Very well then," he spoke with a flat suburban London accent. "As a special concession to you sir."

Pak-kay led him into the office, a room just large enough for the shabby green metal desk and two folding chairs it contained.

"What happened?" Denton asked Lily.

Lily shrugged, gesturing towards Lolly. "It was like this when we arrived."

"Yes, Mister Denton," Lolly said in English again. "Did you know I am not in police force any more? I work with Pak-kay and Lily now."

Denton's eyes stirred faintly. *With Pak-kay and Lily.* Not even *for* them, he thought. *With* them.

"Guarding the office," Lolly went on, beaming. "This morning I go to eat rice at the stall down the road. Suddenly bang! I see naughty people running. No time

663

for shooting." He shook his head regretfully. "Next time I kill. No damage is fortunate."

Lily interrupted him, in Shanghainese. "You'd better make a statement too."

"All right, all right," he patted Lily reassuringly on the shoulder. "I know what to do, I was a policeman myself once."

When he'd gone, Denton looked at Lily. "What would have happened if you'd been here?"

"They wouldn't have dared if we'd been here," she answered with a shrug. "Just a few thugs trying to warn us off. We'll have to keep a better watch in future." She frowned severely, "Lolly shouldn't have gone off like that, leaving the place unguarded. He knew how many threats we've had."

"I didn't know you'd had threats?"

"Only triad thugs," she said with a little flick of her shoulders.

"She's asleep," the Russian woman said, her lips tightening inflexibly. She was nursing a smoky Siamese cat on her lap, stroking it rhythmically from head to tail.

"I'll go up and wait, then," Jenny said.

The woman shook her head with its short fair hair. "Better you come back later." She got up from the carved blackwood chair, holding the cat against her breast, and stood at the bottom of the stairs as if to bar her way.

"But I arranged to come at nine!"

"Never wakes up before ten," the woman said. "Better you come back."

Jenny eyed the woman dubiously. She was tall and determined-looking. She went on stroking the cat and Jenny could see the cat's body rippling under her hand while it purred loudly and slowly swished its tail. "I'll wait here," she said defiantly. "It's twenty past nine anyway."

Turning her back, she began negligently looking at the statues and vases on a table by the wall. There was one of those naked ivory women with her hand over her groin that Chinese doctors used. Jenny leant nearer, trying to see under the protecting hand. How life-like were they, really? They wouldn't be much use if they weren't. She picked the statue up and examined it casually, turning it over. Not very life-like she decided. She stroked the smooth surface thoughtfully.

"You like it?" the Russian woman asked behind her.

"Yes, it's quite nice."

"Want to buy?"

"No, I don't think so, thanks. I'm just looking really."

"If you don't want to buy, don't touch."

Jenny flushed. "Are you the owner of this gallery?" she asked pointedly. The woman didn't answer, gazing down at the cat, so Jenny deliberately fingered the statue again before putting it back. She sauntered further along the narrow aisle between the close-packed desks, tables and chests. The place smelt of mould and cats, and there was a thick layer of dust over everything. At half-past nine I'm going up, Jenny thought. I'll just walk straight up the stairs before she can say a thing. The woman was reading some magazine now, holding it above the cat. Every now and then she glanced up suspiciously at Jenny, then slowly lowered her eyes again, frowning as she read. Jenny stopped to look at the tall lacquered screen with Chinese figures on it. Then she heard her mother's voice.

"Sonia?" she was calling down the stairs. "Sonia?"

"Your daughter's here," Sonia answered, licking her finger as she turned the page. "Shall I send her up?"

"Jenny? Already?"

Jenny saw her mother's bare feet and pale heavy calves descending the stairs, then the frayed hem of her nightgown. "Hello mother," she called, going to the foot of the stairs. "Your friend made me wait down here."

Her mother's face gazed down at her, sleep still staining her blue eyes. God, how old she looks, Jenny thought with a shock as she noticed the bluish pouches under her mother's lids, the wrinkles in her face, the drab, wiry hair that gathered in knotty curls round her head.

"Hello Jenny," her mother said, scratching absently under her arm. "Come on up. How are you?"

Jenny followed her up the stairs. The room seemed just the same as last time she saw it—vases, scrolls, plates and bowls standing on the tables, on the chests, on the floor. Jenny wondered if she'd actually sold anything in the past six years.

Her mother went into the bedroom, "Come in," she called. "Talk to me while I dress. Have you had breakfast? I've got to be in Hongkew at half-past ten. There's a Japanese dealer with some netsuke I want to see."

"Yes, I've had breakfast," Jenny said, glancing at the double bed with its grubby, rumpled sheets.

Her mother slipped her white, flabby arms out of her nightgown and pulled a bright, flowery dress over her head. "So you've met Sonia?" She glanced round. "Sit down. Sit on the bed, we're cramped for chairs in here."

Jenny sat at the foot. It was a soggy mattress that sank beneath her with a tired squeal of the springs. "She wasn't very friendly, Sonia," she said.

"Oh, she's terribly jealous," her mother said casually. "Worse than Helen used to be."

Jenny glanced round the room. It was just as untidy as the rest of the place. Clothes seemed to lie just anywhere, where they'd been taken off, Jenny supposed. On the square table that stood by the head of the bed she noticed a hypodermic syringe lying on a saucer. "Has someone been ill?"

"Ill?" Her mother turned round, taking a brush from the dressing-table. "Oh, that. No, that's just..." she paused, a sheepish look on her face. "That's nothing really. I must have left it there sometime...Now tell me all about yourself and I'll make some coffee." She began dragging the brush through her tight, stiff curls.

But Jenny found it hard to tell her mother anything. She would begin talking about school or her friends, only to realise that she wasn't listening. Her abstracted blue eyes would betray her with their vacancy as she ladled coffee powder into her cup or searched for milk or abruptly called down to Sonia, who apparently refused to come upstairs while Jenny was there. "Yes, dear, I'm listening," she would say when Jenny paused. But then, a minute later, her eyes would start at the end of a sentence and she would say: "What was that? I missed that."

Jenny asked her about the gallery. "Oh business isn't bad," her mother answered carelessly, "but you never have enough money, do you?" Eventually they sat there in silence, Jenny tense and awkward, her mother absently clasping her cup in both hands and gazing unseeingly out of the barred window, above which a rattan blind hung down, slanting tipsily.

"I'd better be going," Jenny said at last, "if you've got to be in Hongkew..."

Her mother's eyes drifted back and filled as if she were seeing her for the first time. "Why not come along with me?" she suggested with sudden briskness. "I can drop you on the way back afterwards. It won't take long."

Sonia was sitting in the same chair when they came down, still reading her magazine. Her mother bent over her and whispered something, but Sonia only frowned and shook her head irritably. Her mother shrugged and led Jenny out.

"She's terribly jealous," she said again on the kerb, her voice lazy and indulgent. "Let's take a taxi. I sold my car years ago."

When they came to the Japanese barrier on Chekiang Road, the driver refused to take them any further. "No can do," he said dourly, shaking his head.

"But I told you I wantee catchee Hongkew," her mother protested. "No can leave this side."

The driver pointed to the Japanese sentries searching everyone who passed. "No can do," he kept saying obstinately.

Jenny spoke to him in Shanghainese, but he wouldn't budge. "You pay me up to here," he said. "I'm not going in there. If they don't like your looks they beat you up. It's all right for you, you're foreign devils."

"Oh, never mind," her mother said impatiently, trying to follow the driver's words. "Let's walk, it's only half a mile from here anyway. Just before Boone Road. Have you got any change? But don't give him a tip, will you?"

Jenny paid. The driver took the money silently and drove away.

"Yes, I'm really hard up these days," her mother confided. "You might mention that to your father. I'd sell up and go back to the States, but for Sonia. She can't get a visa, you see. No passport..." Her steps slowed and for a moment she looked directly at Jenny. "I couldn't go and leave her behind. I couldn't." Jenny saw something blindly determined in her mother's eyes. She looked away uncomfortably.

There were several Chinese waiting docilely at the barrier while the sentries inspected their baskets one by one. Jenny noticed how all the Chinese bowed to the soldiers. "Look at them all kow-towing like that!" she said scornfully. "No wonder the Japs walk all over them."

"Oh, it's nothing much really," her mother answered indifferently. "It's just a form of greeting really. A salute, I guess."

"They won't catch me doing it!"

Her mother glanced at her curiously. "Haven't you been across to Hongkew since you came back then?"

"Not on foot."

"Everyone does it."

Her mother did lower her head to the sentry as she passed through the barbed-wire barrier. And when Jenny passed, she too involuntarily dipped her head. Despite his shortness—he was two or three inches shorter than herself—the sentry seemed to compel a token nod just by staring at her under the peak of his cap with his hard, brown eyes. She walked on beside her mother, angry with herself and humiliated, the soldier's blank young face sharp behind her eyes. For fifty yards or so she hardly noticed where they were going. It reminded her of Lily being slapped by that Jap colonel—but then Lily was only half-white.

"Any idea what you're going to do with yourself?" her mother's voice jolted her out of her shamed brooding.

"What? No, not yet, really ... I'm just sort of looking round now. I thought I might try to get a job on the radio—you know, announcing and things. But I haven't really thought about it much, yet. Daddy—*father*—wants me to do something of course."

"Why should you?" her mother smiled. "I'm sure you don't need the money. But he always was one for work," she added disparagingly, beginning to walk more slowly, tiring already. Well with all that fat, Jenny thought, she would be. "When he stopped having to work, he didn't know what to do with himself."

Jenny stiffened, as she always used to when her mother spoke against her father. It made her feel so embarrassed. And he never said a word against her! Well, hardly.

"That's when he started his little tricks," she was saying, giving Jenny a meaning look. "I suppose he still gets up to them?"

"Tricks?" Jenny repeated blankly. "Is it far now?"

"Sing-song girls," her mother said. "Cheap little whores. I can't believe he doesn't still go chasing after them. That's how he met that Su-mei woman. Not that it bothered me of course." She was short of breath now and stopped for a rest. "It was his taste I minded. He never had any taste, not in women, not in anything else."

Not even when he married you? Jenny demanded in her thoughts. She glanced away up the street, which she suddenly realised was full of Japanese, not Chinese, and thought of the tall fair Russian woman stroking the cat. She thought of them in bed together. And then there was that syringe—well, she knew what they did with that!

"At least the people I choose have taste," her mother said, going on up the street again. "They have a bit of culture. Sonia writes poetry for instance—That's the shop, the one on the corner over there, on Boone Road."

Jenny sat idly in the shop while the smiling fat Japanese bowed her mother round the showcases.

"Come and see, Jenny. This is really good," her mother called. But Jenny obstinately refused, staring out of the window at the Japanese women swaying past on their clopping getai as if they had bound feet, while the Japanese police and soldiers marched up and down, forcing the few Chinese coolies on the street to step deferentially aside and bow their heads. "I thought Hongkew was part of the international settlement," she said tartly. "Why are there only Japanese police here?"

The fat Japanese came and stood beside her. "Many Chinese bad men," he explained smilingly. "Throw bomb, kill Japan woman and child. Therefore much police."

Her mother haggled half-heartedly with the Japanese, but obviously she couldn't afford his price. They walked back to the barrier and again, with an inner shrinking of her courage that she despised herself for, Jenny lowered her head as she passed the sentry. Her mother stopped a taxi, but instead of dropping Jenny off first, as she'd suggested earlier, she had it drive back to the shop, letting Jenny take it on from there. "Have you got enough money on you?" she asked perfunctorily, without troubling to open her bag.

"Yes, it's all right," Jenny nodded distantly.

"And do mention how hard up I am to your father, won't you?" She waved goodbye. "Can't even afford a taxi, tell him."

"Mother kept saying how hard up she was," Jenny told her father later. "She seemed to think you might be able to do something about it."

Denton was looking out over the lights along the Bund and in the harbour. He did that every evening after dinner, as another man might smoke a cigar. "I love this view," he said.

"Mother seems to be short of cash—"

"Yes, I heard the first time," he answered shortly. "I just didn't want to think about it. That Russian woman is bleeding her white." He gazed up and down the river, as if he was expecting some long-awaited ship to arrive. "I suppose the shop's a failure?"

"It didn't exactly look as though they were doing a roaring trade."

He smiled ruefully, thinking of the hundred thousand he'd given her. He'd never had a cent back. She'd probably even forgotten she'd ever had it by now.

"I think they take drugs, too," Jenny said tentatively. "Perhaps that's where the money goes."

"Drugs?"

"There was a syringe on the bedside table. A hypodermic, I mean."

He let his eyes rest on hers reflectively a moment, then looked away at the lights and the night again. "Well I'm damned," was all he said, slowly and reflectively. "Well I'm damned."

"Does that shock you?"

"Shock me? No." He smiled ruefully again, thinking of the opium things he'd kept hidden from Mary-Ellen all through the early years of their marriage. "Somehow I never expected that of her, though, that's all. She didn't seem the type."

"Is it true Su-mei was a sing-song girl once?" she heard herself ask suddenly, as if the words had come out of their own accord. "I think that's fantastic. They're all so incredibly pretty."

His eyes flickered towards her, but he didn't turn his head away from the river. "No, she was always an actress," he said evenly at last.

86

"So glad you could come after all," Walker said. His voice was richly amiable, but tentative, as though ready to change its tune at once if it failed to please.

Denton glanced round at the dark panelled woodwork of the bar. "Place doesn't seem to have changed much since they threw me out," he remarked. "I wondered whether the doorman would let me in, as a matter of fact."

"Oh really," Walker laughed deprecatingly. "Those days are long past now, you know. Times have changed, even in the club. What'll you have to drink?—Ah, there the others are," he nodded towards the door. "You know John Roberts of course?"

"As a matter of fact I haven't had that honour."

A trio of grey-haired, fair-skinned, ruddy-cheeked men were approaching, exuding conviviality and self-satisfaction. He recognised Nixon and Gilbert at once. The short, plump, younger man in the middle he knew only from newspaper photographs—Sir John Roberts, the British consul. "I'll have a whisky and soda please."

"You don't look a day older," Nixon smiled. "Good to see you again." He stooped slightly and had deep pouches under his eyes. Otherwise he seemed unchanged.

"I thought you'd left China for good?"

"I had," Nixon nodded. "Went to Japan after I retired officially from the bank. Getting a bit unpleasant there now, though. So here I am again. Got back last month—You know Sir John Roberts?"

"From the papers, yes."

"Ah," the plump consul shook his head with a surprisingly firm grip, gazing searchingly up into his eyes. "And I've been reading *your* newspaper, Mr. Denton," he said. "Which has told me something about you, though not perhaps as directly."

"The editor will be gratified to learn that he's read in the British consulate," Denton smiled bleakly. He turned to Gilbert, who shook his hand wordlessly, but with a wry smile that seemed to express inarticulate regret for the ostracism of the past fifteen years. It wasn't my fault, his brown eyes seemed to be pleading, I didn't have anything to do with it. The sun-tanned skin still corrugated on his bald head when he raised his brows, but the surrounding hair had gone grey.

"Well, shall we have a drink?" Walker suggested as they stood hesitating a moment, eyeing each other cautiously—sniffing like dogs, Denton thought.

"And what's the circulation of your paper now?" the consul turned to Denton after he'd ordered a Bristol Cream. "It seems to have been rising somewhat since you bought out those left-wing groups?" His grey eyes probed Denton's frankly while an amused smile formed on his rosy lips. "Not that that seems to have altered the editorial policy much," he added in an ironically pained tone.

"It's about a hundred and twenty thousand now. We're thinking of doing an English language edition shortly. Just weekly at first."

"With the same editorial policy?"

"Yes."

"Ah." He gazed down at his glass reflectively.

"Sticky today," Nixon said.

"It always is in August," Gilbert's pleasant tenor chimed in.

Nixon moved round to Denton while the others talked about the weather. "How's your wife?" he asked with an uncertain smile.

"Which one?"

Nixon's smile broadened, dimpling his fine-veined cheeks, which despite their wrinkles, were still smooth and soft. "How many have you got?"

"Well I've got a different one now from the one I had when you left Shanghai."

"Oh I knew about that," he laughed richly. "Created quite a scandal, what? So my own wife told me after one of her trips back here—you know I never came back until last month."

"I remember seeing your wife once or twice, soon after it all happened." Denton swallowed some whisky. "Unfortunately she didn't seem to be able to see me though. Not even from three feet away."

Nixon nodded, unsurprised. "She's dead now, of course," he said, rubbing his chin reflectively.

"Oh I'm sorry." Denton said hastily. "I didn't know."

Nixon shook his head. "Long time ago now. Seven years." He narrowed his eyes, gazing at his glass as though surveying the long tunnel of years through which they'd travelled together. "She was a narrow-minded, cross-grained woman," he said detachedly. "Hell to live with...But the thing was, our daughter was killed in the Boxer business in Peking. A stray bullet. She was only four. Rather soured her, what?"

"I didn't know," Denton said again, feeling the firm ground neatly removed from under his feet.

"No . . . She didn't like to talk about it. It was our only child."

He rubbed his chin ruminatively, then looked up with a sudden smile. "I'm in the newspaper world myself now, you know. Director of the *North China Daily News*, as from September. Though what they want with an old codger of seventy-three I really don't know . . ."

"Shall we go in?" Walker suggested. "I've booked one of the private rooms."

Denton looked round the bar again as he put his glass down. They were standing at the head, where he used to stand twenty years before, a few feet away from the taipans of Jardine's and Swire, who were now throwing sidelong glances at them, circumspect and inquiring. At the lower end, a bunch of fresh-faced griffins were laughing, with that braying chortle peculiar to young Englishmen who'd been to public schools. In the corner by the window he thought he saw Green's head, half-turned away, as if even after all those years he couldn't bear to look at someone who'd let the side down so treacherously.

"Thank you Mr. Denton," the barman said.

Denton started. The barman's face wasn't at all familiar. "You know my name?" he asked.

"Oh yes, Mr. Denton," he replied gravely. "Long time no see. You been away?"

"No—Well, yes, I suppose I have really."

"Long time away," the barman said.

"Yes. Fifteen years."

The others were waiting for him. He followed them to the door.

They talked desultorily about China and Japan during the meal, speculating about the truce between the communists and the nationalists, and their united front against the Japanese. Denton said little. He listened and waited, guessing why they'd asked him.

At last the port and brandy came, the cigars were lit and Nixon got his pipe going. The consul turned to Denton, while the others, as if on cue, paused to listen.

The consul's lips pursed into a rosy smile. "I wonder if I might put a certain view of Anglo-Japanese relations to you, Mr. Denton? A view which happens to be His Majesty's government's view, and therefore"—he smiled again—"one I am officially bound to endorse?"

Denton cocked his head.

"The view is that Japan, after a period of militaristic expansion—aggression, even—is now willing, as her ambassador in London recently put it, to return to the path of international co-operation." He rolled the brandy in his glass and sniffed it appreciatively. "It is in Britain's interest to encourage this new attitude, particularly now that Mr. Hitler is making all those war-like noises in Germany—we would not like to have a hostile Japan in the east whilst we were possibly engaged with a hostile Germany in the west. So the government wishes to avoid any provocation of the Japanese—"

"Ah," Denton put his coffee cup down with a little chink and straightened in his chair.

"Which is I'm afraid how your paper is regarded by the Japanese consul. A very nice man, by the way. Have you met him? No? Well, perhaps in the circumstances..." he smiled discreetly. "Not only does your paper call for a united front against Japanese aggression—which of course I fully understand, though I can't exactly agree with it—but it also refers to the Japanese as dwarfish barbarians and vandals. It describes the emperor, if I recall correctly, as an insignificant nincompoop at the beck and call of a crew of military adventurers who are hand in glove with the well-known gangster who rules the Shanghai underworld. We need hardly speculate who is meant by *that*."

Denton smiled. "You have a good memory."

The consul shook his head. "It's been brought to my attention so many times by the Japanese consul that I'm afraid the words have worn grooves in my brain. I keep explaining that I have no power to interfere, but you can imagine how the Japanese look at it, can't you? While the paper was in Chinese hands, they didn't take much notice. But when they found out you owned it—it didn't take them long, by the way—you, a former councillor with er...Chinese connections shall we say?—well, they began to suspect all sorts of intrigues and conspiracies. I'm afraid if you do bring out an English-language edition, that will only confirm their suspicions..."

"In other words, you want me to lay off the Japs and start supporting them?" Denton asked bluntly.

The consul raised his pale, hairless hands almost in horror. "That would be beyond my wildest dreams," he protested. "But I wonder whether you could see your way to er, shall we say, moderate the tone?"

Denton toyed with his coffee spoon, frowning down at it. "And if I think this view that you mention—the British government's view—is wrong?"

"Believe me, Mr. Denton," the consul said, this time not smiling at all, "In the next few years Britain is going to need every ally it can get."

Denton sipped his brandy, and wished he'd ordered whisky. He twisted the stem of the glass round and back between his finger and thumb.

"Of course the whole business community agrees with the government," Walker said.

"Of course," Denton repeated drily. "You may not know," he continued slowly, gazing at the brandy balloon twisting backwards and forwards in his hand, backwards and forwards. "But when I took over the paper, I did intend to... moderate the tone, as you put it. I still intend to if I can. But I can hardly suppress the facts."

"Are you sure they really are facts?" Nixon asked, tapping his pipe out into the ashtray.

"Pretty sure. Aren't you?"

Nixon paused, then shrugged, scraping out the ash from the charred bowl of his pipe. "Wonder if *anyone* really knows, what?" he murmured.

"I think we all know about the torture, the abductions, the executions, don't we? We all know Pock-mark Chen has a big share in the opium trade through that Japanese company. And in the brothels of course. We know Chinese coolies are forced to work for next to nothing and they have to take their pay in notes that are only accepted in Japanese stores. Does anyone seriously doubt that?"

"Perhaps it isn't a question of whether it's true or not," Gilbert said mildly, "But whether it's appropriate to say it just now." He coughed and cleared his throat apologetically. "In view of the government's policy, I mean."

"That depends on whether the policy's right. I happen to think it's wrong." Or do I? he thought.

"Forgive my saying so," the consul purred, his lids sleekly lowered as he gazed down at his manicured finger drumming on the table cloth, "but it might perhaps be wondered whether you really had such very strong feelings about, er, opium or prostitution? Whether you were entitled to express them so... so vividly, as the *Shanghai*

Star does?" He glanced up suddenly, his eyes unexpectedly mordant. "People who live in glasshouses, you know?"

"Might it?" Denton felt himself flushing. "I've never run opium dens or brothels."

"Oh of course you've never *run* them," the consul said deprecatingly. "But I'm only thinking of what people on the other side *might* say if things got nasty," he hinted with his little purse-lipped smile. "They do have their own scandal sheets, after all."

Denton gazed down silently, his cheeks stiff and hot. He imagined what they could say about him and Su-mei, the one-time sing-song girl. About their use of opium, perhaps about the deal he made with Mason. About his visits to *rue* Molière and the other places—they'd be bound to know. About Mary-Ellen probably, and how he'd abandoned her, as it would be made to seem. He imagined Jenny and Michael and Alex reading it in the papers, wondering how much was true.

"I do hope at any rate that you'll give the matter a little thought," the consul was saying blandly. "It may be worth considering, you know."

"Oh, I'm willing to consider anything," Denton said, still gazing at his glass. "Within reason, that is."

He took a rickshaw to the new office of the *Shanghai Star*. As he passed Garden Bridge, he saw a widening flood of Chinese pressing over. The coolie slowed his steps. Women, children, old men, loaded with baskets and shoulder poles, pushing high-stacked barrows and trolleys, driving dogs, ducks, chickens and even pigs. They hurried over, and they hurried in silence. It was a silence that was disturbing. Only fear could make them all so quiet.

"Go down Ningpo Road," Denton said. "You'll never get through that lot."

"Longer way master. You pay more?"

"All right." Denton gazed at the vacant, anxious eyes, the shuffling gait, the paltry possessions clutched like treasures.

"What do they want?" the coolie muttered.

Denton had seen them before, many times. He'd seen them when the coolie was only a boy playing in the muddy pool of some village with the dogs and pigs. "There must be some trouble in Chapei or Hongkew," he said. "How long have you been in the city?"

"Not long. About half a year." He swung the rickshaw round.

When they reached the office, while Denton was feeling for some cash to pay the coolie, Lolly Kwai came out of the door, grinning excitedly. He pushed past the guard who was standing on the pavement, nursing a loaded shotgun.

"They've shot two Japanese sailors out at Hung Jao," he called out. "Spying on the airfield. Now there'll be some fighting at last."

Denton paid the coolie and went inside.

"Heard the news?" Pak-kay asked, looking up from his desk with glowing eyes. "That'll get things going. This time it'll be war in Shanghai. Chiang will have to fight now. The Japs will force him. It's either fight or surrender."

87

"I can't see what all the fuss is about," Jenny declared, leaning back for Ah King to take her plate. "They'll just fire a few shots at each other to save face, and then go back home, won't they? Isn't that how they fight out here?"

"You seem to be absorbing too much of the Jardine's mess gossip," Denton said behind the paper.

"Well isn't it?" She poured herself some coffee.

A car horn tooted in the drive, discreetly but insistently.

"God, is it half-past two already?" Jenny jumped up, went to the window, waved and came back to the table, gulping her coffee down standing up.

The horn tooted again, a little louder.

"Ask him if he couldn't change his mating call, could you?" Denton muttered. "It's getting a bit monotonous."

On the edge of his mind Denton heard the car's engine throbbing away, while he read through the editorial again.

However bitterly Japanese aggression may be resented, it can hardly be denied that its extension would be encouraged rather than stayed by physical resistance from the Central Government, and would be accompanied by such

677

complete destruction of China's resources that all hopes of national reconstruction might have to be indefinitely postponed.

"This paper might just as well be published by the British consulate," he said, glancing up at Su-mei.

Her eyes were abstracted, full of her own thoughts. "What?" she asked, dragging herself back to him. "Why?"

He read the sentence out to her.

"But it's true isn't it?"

"In that case the *Shanghai Star* is wrong."

"Of course the *Shanghai Star* is wrong. You've let yourself be carried away by Pak-kay. He's pulled you in too far."

"Maybe."

"Your coffee's getting cold," she said after a minute. Then, in the same matter-of-fact voice, "Ah Sam wants to leave."

"Leave? For good? Why?"

Su-mei shrugged. "She says she's not up to it any more, with her bad leg. That stroke has weakened her. It's true she can't do much any more."

"What would she do if she stopped working?"

"Go back to her village. We could still send her money."

"Yes..." He was remembering her red, sore hands with the inflamed knuckles the first time he saw her, when Ah King brought her to him. And now she wanted to go. Thirty years, give or take. It was more than many people's lives. "Where is she?" he asked. "I suppose we ought to talk to her."

"Gone shopping. I gave her the afternoon off."

Ah Sam limped up to the turnstile at Wing On Department Store and put her ten cents in. "Any bargains today?" she greeted the doorman as she eased her hips through the narrow passage.

He put his head on one side, his eyes watching the turnstiles superciliously as if customers on Sales days were beneath his notice. "Third floor, dolls," he muttered, scarcely parting his lips. "Twenty per cent."

Ah Sam nodded politely. "Thanks, I'll have a look," she said. "See if I like any of them."

678

"Worth it at the normal price," the doorman said, shaking the turnstile change in his hands. "Bargain today."

I suppose your sister's one of the salesgirls with ten per cent commission, Ah Sam thought. But she ducked her head politely again and walked painfully off towards the stairs, secretly thrilled. She hadn't bought a doll for months and months.

On the first floor landing she took a rest, glancing through the window at the big gleaming block of the Palace Hotel and the slowly thinning banks of clouds over the river. Now there were hardly any ships in the harbour, she noticed, except for those Japanese barbarians. All the rest must have moved out because of the new trouble. She made a face at the battleship *Idzumo*, bristling with guns, its Rising Sun flag flying stiffly on the breeze.

Jenny lay on her back by the side of the pool. Robert, lying on his front a few feet away, his chin on his folded arms, was watching her through half-closed lids. She gazed up between her lashes at the patch of blue that was slowly widening in the sky, the sun tinting the edges of the parting clouds a misty yellow and white. The water was still trickling down her face and shoulders, warm and soothing. Her lids closed. She listened to the splash-splash of someone swimming.

"It's nice it's so empty," Robert said.

"Because of the weather."

"And the political situation," he said importantly. "A lot of people have got the wind up."

Jenny shrugged. "All the better for us."

"Mm. What about coming to the dinner dance tonight?"

She half-opened her eyes. "Here?"

"Yes. What about it?"

She turned her head to look at him. He was leaning on his elbow now, his fair hair, darkened by the water, falling untidily over his forehead. He had freckles on his arms and a little hair, glistening with water drops, growing in the middle of his chest. When he smiled, as he was smiling now, his cheeks dimpled. And his eyes were a sort of hazel colour, flecked with yellow. Really rather nice eyes.

"All right," she said. She rolled over onto her front, her face towards him, and wriggled her shoulder till the strap slipped off, smiling provocatively. His eyes stared at

679

her shoulder. She wondered how far she'd let him go tonight.

Slowly her eyes closed and she dozed in the heavy warm air. She could feel the sun piercing through the clouds, warming her back deliciously.

The clock chimed four. The plop of rackets striking tennis balls filtered gently through the soft warm layers of her drowsiness. And somehow she knew he was watching her all the time.

"The Japanese consul stated this morning that he had so far received no reply to his country's demand for a withdrawal of all Chinese forces from the demilitarised zone," the announcer said. Denton turned the volume higher and glanced out of the window at the Japanese warships moored close to Hongkew. He could see the marines disembarking from them, being ferried across the smooth brown river in low, flat landing craft. "The consuls of Britain, France and America have sent an urgent appeal for restraint to Japan..."

The phone rang. He switched the radio off before he lifted the receiver. "The Eighty-Eighth Division are arriving at the North Station," Pak-kay's voice declared triumphantly in his ear. "They're putting up barricades. There can't be any going back now."

"Where's Lily?"

"Asleep. She was up all night. You see you were right to back us."

"The Japs are disembarking in Hongkew. I can see them from here."

"The Eighty-Eighth will push them into the river. They've got German advisers."

Denton glanced down at the black mouth piece of the phone, misty from his breath. "Very comforting," he said.

"Besides, they won't attack the International Settlement," Pak-kay added with a flick of scorn. "If that's what you're worried about."

"Who won't?"

"The Japanese. They've got enough on their hands as it is."

"Hm. What about the Chinese?"

"The foreign settlements will be preserved," Pak-kay's voice pronounced oracularly. "For the time being."

"Very comforting," Denton said again. He heard the

doorbell ring downstairs. "Ask Lily to phone when she wakes up, would you?"

A minute later Su-mei opened the study door. The caller was Philip Wei, dressed in a dark suit and carrying a leather briefcase. He sat down with only a perfunctory greeting, his eyes tense behind the thick lenses of his glasses.

"How is your father?" Denton asked formally in Chinese.

"Not very well," Philip answered brusquely in English. "He can't get about much now." He snapped open the briefcase and took out a folded newspaper. As he began speaking, nervously and jerkily, Denton saw it was the *Shanghai Star*. Su-mei left the room to order tea.

"How much longer are you going to support this scandal sheet?" Philip asked abruptly, speaking in English still, as though Chinese was unsuitable for such bluntness.

"What's the trouble?"

He slapped the page with the back of his fingers, "These constant attacks on the Japanese!" His voice was shaking with the effort to control it. "Don't you realise how difficult it's making things?"

"Difficult for whom?"

Philip opened his hands. "Nobody wants to fight in Shanghai. The war is up in the north. The Japanese don't want it, and nor does Chiang. But here's your paper—" he slapped it again distastefully with the back of his fingers "—inflaming hatred against the Japanese, inciting to war..." He stuttered inarticulately, flushed with indignation. "I've just come from a meeting of the council. The Japanese members raised it again. They said it was violating the neutrality of the international settlement."

Denton glanced away from his face, more agitated than he'd ever seen it before. "They're just using that as a pretext," he said. "Whatever's going to happen has already been decided. It's started anyway," he nodded at the window. "You can see the Japanese marines coming ashore from here. And the Eighty-Eighth Division is arriving at the North Station to meet them."

Ah Leng brought in a pot of tea. Su-mei followed. She poured them each a cup, then sat by the window looking out, as if, although she had a right to hear it, she had no wish to take part in their conversation.

"China's economy depends on Shanghai," Philip said,

681

as though he hadn't heard. "If that goes, China will be ruined."

"And the Wei companies as well?"

Philip was sipping his tea. He put the cup down, his hand trembling so much that the tea spilt. "I think I ought to warn you that Pock-mark Chen, as you insist on calling him, is getting upset by your paper." He licked his lips, his eyes now unblinking and steady on Denton's. "My father's done his best to protect you, but he can't do any more."

Out of the corner of his eye Denton saw Su-mei's head lift and turn a fraction towards them.

Ah Sam felt shy and overawed in front of the salesgirl. Before coming out she'd changed from her white amah's tunic to her best black one, the one she'd paid three dollars for at the night market before the last new year's holiday. She'd hardly ever worn it except on holidays and it still looked quite new, but now for the first time she began to wonder whether it was really so nice after all. At least, the salesgirl wasn't impressed. She'd just placed the doll down on the counter in front of Ah Sam with a snooty glance down her fine little nose, turning to a foreign woman as she did so and saying something warningly about not touching the goods. As if Ah Sam's hands weren't as clean as the salesgirl's, even if they were raw and swollen. Or the foreign woman's for that matter.

The foreign woman was wearing one of those indecent dresses that showed her shoulders and half her bosom. She reached past Ah Sam to pick up another doll lying on the counter and Ah Sam's nose wrinkled as she smelt the sweat beneath her strong sweet perfume. She tried to remember if master's first wife had smelt like that too, but then, gazing absently at the doll, she was suddenly taken by its prettiness, by the round blue eyes and dark long lashes. Did the eyes close when you laid it down? She glanced uneasily at the salesgirl. "Yes madam," she was saying in English as good as tai-tai's, "Cash or account?"

Well if the foreign woman could touch the dolls with her sweaty hands, why shouldn't he? The salesgirl was writing the bill. Ah Sam reached out and gingerly laid the doll down on the counter. The eyes didn't close. She felt a little tug of disappointment in her chest.

"Don't touch the goods with your great big paws," the

salesgirl said sharply. "I've told you once already. If you want to handle them, you'd better buy."

Ah Sam snatched her hands away meekly as the salesgirl sat the doll upright again a few inches further back on the counter. The salesgirl went on writing the foreign woman's bill, one plucked eyebrow raised in disdainful exasperation.

Ah Sam's hands hung guiltily down by her sides. She gazed at the salesgirl's delicate and nimble fingers. "I will buy it," she said defiantly, pushing aside her knowledge that she didn't really like it so much now that she knew the eyes didn't close.

The salesgirl tore off the bill and took a hundred dollar note from the foreign woman, putting the doll back on the shelf as she went to the cash register at the end of the counter.

"Miss?" Ah Sam called diffidently, timid again now after her little outburst. "I will buy it. Twenty per cent off, is it?"

"Wait a minute, can't you?" the salesgirl said haughtily, without even turning her head. "Can't you see I'm busy?"

Something was tickling her mouth. Jenny twitched her lips and nose, drifting off to sleep again. But the tickling returned. A fly crawling over her skin. She brushed her face with her hand, frowning. A second or two later it had landed on her shoulder. She wriggled irritably. But now it seemed to be crawling under her costume. An ant? She opened her eyes and felt behind her. It was Robert, with a straw, one of those long ones; he was kneeling beside her, slipping it down the back of her costume. Her eyes were level with his red trunks and she could see his thing was getting big. She snatched the straw away and put it between her teeth, pointing it at the bulge in his trunks while she stared at it hard. Robert blushed and lay down on his front.

"Don't squash it," she murmured.

"What?"

"You heard."

He blushed more deeply.

"What about getting me some lemon juice to go with this straw?"

When they'd drunk and swum again—she could swim

every stroke better than he could—they went to change. "You'll have to get me home by six, so I can get my glad rags on for this evening," she said as they sauntered towards the changing rooms. "All right," he answered. "Though I don't see why you can't go in the things you came in, they look so fetching." It was the first compliment she remembered him paying her.

Ah Sam watched the salesgirl count the money, then, with a supercilious sniff, nudge the parcel across to her. She took it without a word and pushed her way slowly through the crowds in the children's clothes department, where there were more reductions. Mothers had brought their children in and were slapping them to stand still while they measured skirts and jackets against them. There was a crowd at the head of the stairs too. She decided to wait a minute and went to the window to look out at the harbour again.

Nothing but those Japanese barbarians' grey warships and the blue sky opening above them as the fleecy clouds slowly drifted away. In the distance, she saw several dark specks against the fresh deep blue, flying like birds straight towards the harbour.

Then, quite suddenly, without any warning, there was smoke and flame spurting from all the Japanese ships, and little puffs of black smoke bursting in the blue near the flying things. They were planes she realised, Chinese planes. They came straight on through the bursting shells, and soon they were so close she could see the markings on their wings. She caught her breath in delight as she saw little black eggs drop out of the first plane and, a second or two later, great gouts of water splashing up beside the *Idzumo*. The guns hammered incessantly back into the sky and the window shook with the noise while the little black mushrooms of smoke blossomed harmlessly all round the planes. The planes were roaring towards the Bund now, climbing and turning and she sensed they were banking to return to the *Idzumo*. By now the crowd was all round her, children and parents, pointing excitedly as the planes soared overhead, their engines clattering wildly only a hundred or so feet above the store. None of them understood the meaning of the shrill, swooping shriek that followed as the invisible bombs wobbled down through the sticky air towards them.

"Protect me?" Denton repeated, glancing out of the window at the aeroplanes droning lazily towards them, high in the sky. "What do you mean?"

"Surely you realise there'd have been much more trouble for your whole family if my father hadn't been protecting you? Pock-mark Chen, as you call him, has held off for my father's sake—"

"I thought *everyone* called him Pock-mark Chen?"

"—But he can't do any more. We have certain...arrangements with Pock-mark—with Mr. Chen. We can't risk them any further. I guess you don't need telling how awkward he can make things for you."

The droning of the planes had been growing louder all the time Philip was speaking, but it wasn't till Denton heard the sudden clamour of gunfire and the distant thump of bursting shells that he looked away at the Bund again. Then all three of them hurried to the open window. Orange flashes leapt from the gun turrets of the Japanese warships and the upward-pointing muzzles spurted out little puffs of grey smoke; the deep roar of the firing following a second later so that the flashes at first didn't seem real.

"Well it's started," Denton said heavily as he watched the planes, five or six flying in a straggling line, dip down through the bursting shells towards the *Idzumo*. Little black dots tumbled down from the planes like pebbles tossed off a cliff. They landed in the river, straddling the battleship, sending up great fountains of yellowish water with thick muddy hearts and silvery white edges. Below in the garden, all the servants had come out to watch. Detachedly, Denton noticed Ah Man's hands were covered with flour. And traffic was stopping along the Bund. Cars, lorries, taxis, even buses and trams had halted while the passengers leaned out of the windows to watch. They treat it like a firework display, Denton thought. In the Public Gardens, some Volunteers looked up from their two squat armoured cars.

"This is the worst thing that could have happened." Philip groaned, in Chinese now. "The worst possible thing."

The planes soared up over the *Idzumo* and flew towards the Bund, banking and climbing. "They're going to have another go," Denton said. Then they heard the bombs falling. Instinctively they ducked away from the window. When the explosions came, the glass splintered and smashed with a splitting, tinkling noise as the force of the blast rushed past like a sudden typhoon. Then it was over and the planes were droning steadily away, as peacefully as if they'd merely been out for a pleasure jaunt.

When they looked out again, the river was calm, the *Idzumo* unscathed, its flag still flying, the other warships all undamaged. On the ground below them there were splinters of glass. The servants had gone in. On the Bund people were still watching the disappearing planes. It had only taken a minute.

"Where did they hit?" Philip asked unsteadily.

"Further down the Bund," Su-mei said. She went to the phone. "I'll ring Lily."

"I'd better see if the servants are all right," Denton said suddenly.

They were all speaking in hushed voices.

The servants had shut all the broken windows and closed the shutters downstairs. No one was hurt except Ah King, who had a cut in her cheek. "Never mind," she said gruffly. "I only hope they come back and kill those Japanese dwarfs."

"They won't come back today," Lau muttered. "It was just a warning, that's all. Just to show them."

"Show them? Show them what?" Ah King splashed her cheek in the sink. The water ran pink with blood and she looked at it in wonder. "Show them their heads chopped off, that's all they understand."

Su-mei came in. "No reply," she said tersely. "There are ambulances and fire engines going down the road. Lots of them."

They all paused to listen to the urgent clanging of the fire engines' bells. First one, then another, then a third and a fourth.

"Lau, get the car out," Denton said. "We'd better go and see."

Su-mei's face had that pale tautness, which it had when Michael was kidnapped, as though beneath the skin all the muscles were pulling together. "Where's Philip?" Denton asked as they got in to the car. He'd forgotten all about him.

Su-mei shrugged. "Gone, I suppose. His car's not here."

They drove along towards Maloo. A grey cloud of smoke, heavy and thick with dust, hung over the road, obscuring the buildings. Policemen and Volunteers stood in the middle of the road, turning back the traffic while fire engines and ambulances nudged their way past heaps of rubble into the swirling smoke.

"We'd better get out and walk," Denton said. "It looks as if the Palace Hotel's been hit."

Leaving the car at the side of the road, they walked quickly towards the smoke. Quite suddenly the smoke cleared for a moment and they saw the twisted girders and broken concrete towers of the Palace Hotel. Denton saw a figure hanging half out of a window, on a wall that seemed to be standing without any support. Then with a crack the wall collapsed as though the bottom had been jerked away by some giant, and the twitching figure, the window, the whole thing was gone in a new cloud of smoke and dust.

As they hurried nearer, they could hear the shouts of rescue workers and the screams of the injured. An open truck drove past them. At first Denton thought it was loaded with meat. Then he realised they were the limbs and torsos of bodies torn apart by the bombs, dressed, half-dressed and naked. He stopped, feeling giddy and sick. "They wouldn't have been here," he said irresolutely.

"Who?"

"Lily or Jenny."

"We don't know where they might have been," she said tautly.

Another lorry drove past with mutilated limbs and bodies piled inside it. He imagined someone trying to fit the limbs to the bodies.

They went on.

Jenny had just left the changing rooms when the bombs fell. Robert, waiting in the bar, went out onto the veranda with all the others, the White Russian women in their alluring dresses, the French civil servants and their peevish wives, the ferret-eyed businessmen, even the waiters and barmen. Jenny found him there, watching the pall of smoke slowly rising and growing over the Bund.

"Chinese planes," he said, as she pushed her way to him through the gesticulating, speculating crowd. "Seems they were trying to bomb the Japs' warships. I think we'd better go."

"Where's the smoke coming from? Is that where they hit?" Jenny's heart skipped. "It's near our house, isn't it?"

"I can't see exactly. I think it's further south."

"South? Which way is south?"

"Nearer us," he said reassuringly. "I'm afraid we'll probably have to call this evening off, Jenny. I'll be wanted for the Volunteers if the balloon's gone up."

Oh blast this evening, Jenny thought agitatedly. If only they haven't gone and bombed our house. In her mind she saw a smoking heap of debris on top of which lay her father and her old teddy bear, both equally broken and dead.

"Let's go," Robert said.

"You can't go up there, sir," the English inspector said. "It's a charnel house."

"We're looking for relatives." Denton kept walking.

"It isn't very pretty," he warned, glancing at Su-mei. "A direct hit. Palace Hotel and Wing On."

"Ah Sam was going to Wing On," Su-mei said quietly.

"Why did they bomb *them*?" Denton exclaimed. "What for?"

"Accident." The inspector turned to halt a rickshaw coolie who was trying to squeeze past the barrier. "Can't aim straight, that's their bloody trouble." He started shouting at the coolie, swearing in broken Shanghainese.

They walked on towards the wrecked buildings. Firemen, policemen and municipal workers were combing the rubble, lifting away great slabs of broken concrete and peering into holes, from which sometimes muffled moans and screams came out. The rubble seemed to cover quite a small part of the street, and for a moment Denton wondered how there could be so many dead and injured from so little wreckage. But then he remembered the height of the building—six floors, eight floors, he wasn't sure how many—they'd all collapsed into those piles of rubble, and every floor might have a hundred people on it. So this is war, he thought dazedly. It seemed strange that he'd lived all his life up till then without ever really seeing it.

"Over there," Su-mei said. She was pointing to the pavement further down the road. Bodies were being laid out there, the dead and the injured all together, while doctors and nurses went down the rows checking for life or death. The dead were being dragged onto one side while ambulances took away the wounded. A large lorry had its tailboard down, and coolies were throwing in the limbs and bodies of those who were too mutilated to be identified. It was the throwing that turned Denton's stomach. They did it so casually, as if they were handling pigs' carcasses from the slaughterhouse.

Su-mei had gone on to the rows of the dead who could still be recognised. Mangled, bruised, and still bleeding, they were at least all in one piece. She was treading carefully amongst them, her arms folded about her despite the heat, as if to keep herself aloof from them, uncontaminated. He joined her, gazing numbly down at those strangers' faces stilled in their last expressions—racked, surprised, perplexed and terrified. Here and there a white face appeared amongst the Chinese ones. One, a girl about Jenny's age, but with dark hair, seemed unmarked, as though she were merely sleeping. But when he looked more closely, he saw dark red blood seeping from a gash in the back of her head, seeping down through her hair. Beside her lay a shrivelled old Chinese man with toothless gums, one temple crushed to give his face a crumpled, leering expression. Denton stared down at the two faces while the groans of the injured and the scraping of picks and shovels sounded in his ears.

"Look," Su-mei said quietly, a few feet away.

It was Ah Sam. She too lay almost as if she were asleep, except that her head was at an impossible angle, one ear nearly touching her shoulder. Her clothes were torn and dirty, covered with a pale grey dust that was also in her hair and over her face. The swollen fingers of her right hand grasped a headless doll with a frilly dress on; there was still wrapping paper round it. Gazing at Ah Sam's face, perversely lolling on her shoulder, Denton felt he had to take it between his hands and set it straight—yet at the same time he shuddered at the thought of touching her.

Then he heard another plane droning overhead. The scraping of picks and shovels ceased as everyone paused to look up at the sky that was clear and serene now. Only the moans of the injured continued unchanged.

* * *

689

"We'd better go down here," Robert said. "Avoid the jam." He turned left into Kiu Kiang Road. "Could you see where the damage was?"

"It was up on Maloo," she said with relief. "That's well clear of our house, isn't it?"

"Yes. About half a mile at least." He glanced at her, the yellow flecks in the hazel eyes. Golden flecks, she thought, not yellow. He was smiling comfortingly. "You were worried, weren't you?"

"Weren't you?"

"Just a bit. Seems all quiet now, though. I expect it's all over."

Jenny relaxed into her relief as if into a warm bath. She leant back and let her hand trail over the red coachwork of the Morgan. "I felt sick," she admitted. "Absolutely sick."

He looked sideways at her, smiling. He was about to say something, then frowned, glancing up at the sky. "What's that?"

"What?"

He cocked his head, slowing down so that the engine's growly noise faded to a putter. "Sounds like another plane."

Jenny looked all round, above the race track, over the Great World amusement park, over the river behind them. Then she saw it, a plane flying straight towards them, as if chasing them down the road.

"Stop!" she shouted in a voice that was somehow strangled and paralysed. "It's coming up behind us!"

The plane was already over them by the time he'd stopped. Robert looked up while Jenny ducked down, shuddering, below the dashboard. Shuddering, and yet at the same time feeling ridiculous and embarrassed for cowering away like that when really nothing was happening.

Robert laid his hand reassuringly on her bare shoulder. "It's all right, it's gone," he said.

But before she could move, there was a tremendous bang, like a thunderclap overhead, and then a second one immediately after. She heard the air screeching with bits of shrapnel and the crack of buildings breaking like snapped bones, followed by the enormous cascading rumble of collapsing masonry. She heard the thud of things smashing against the car. Then it was quiet. In the stunned silence that followed she could hear her heart thumping wildly, and the calm, indifferent putter of the idling engine. Robert's hand was still on her shoulder.

When she straightened up, there was the tinkling sound of glass falling onto the floor of the car, and Robert's hand slipped heavily off her. The windscreen had vanished, except for a few lonely, jagged pieces sticking out from the frame. Robert sat with his head back, as if still looking up at the sky. But he wasn't looking at all. His face was slashed and covered in blood, and a long sliver of glass was sticking out of his left eye like the blade of a knife.

They'd gone past every corpse and then past all the injured, and afterwards they'd met Everett coming across the road to speak to them. "We can't be sure we'll get everyone out," he'd said, "There's no way of accounting for everyone." His cap, beneath which his hair had gone white, had silver braid on the peak, and he carried a little black baton. Assistant Commissioner of Police now. "Those other bombs fell on the refugee camp at the New World," he saluted with his baton as he turned back to his car. "I'm afraid the casualties will be worse there." Then Su-mei and he had decided in quiet level voices to go home and phone Lily and the paper and the French Club, instead of waiting for more bodies to be dug out of the debris.

They came upon another pile of dismembered bodies waiting to be carried away. A tarpaulin had been thrown over them, but a European with a camera was calling to a couple of coolies to pull the tarpaulin away. It was Mason. As Su-mei and Denton walked past, he turned and waved.

"No one you know here, I hope?" he asked in a phlegmy but jaunty voice, an aging echo of his younger tone. "Just taking a few press photos."

"Yes?" Denton said without stopping. He imagined Mason gloating over the photos as once he'd gloated over pictures of decapitated pirates.

"Chinese atrocities, get the idea? For the Japanese press. Pays well, too." He grinned, brushing up the bristles of his greying moustache in that gesture by which Denton would always remember him. "Told you I was a bit of a journalist, didn't I?" he called after them. "Seem to work more for the other side, though, eh?"

They heard him shouting at the coolies to lift the tarpaulin further back.

As soon as they got home, Su-mei phoned Lily. She'd just woken up, having slept through the bombs. She was in a hurry, on her way to the paper. There'd been a few shots at the Yokohama Bridge, but no real fighting yet.

The line to the French Club was out of order, but the operator said no bombs had fallen in Frenchtown.

Ah King brought in some tea. She had a lotion over the cut in her face, a herbal lotion smelling vaguely of leaves and flowers and oil. Su-mei looked meaningly at Denton.

"Ah King," he said quietly. "Ah Sam was where the bomb fell. At Wing On."

Ah King stared at him, straightening up from the tray.

"She's dead. We saw her."

"Dead?" She looked at Su-mei, then back at Denton.

"We will pay for the funeral," Su-mei said.

Ah King's face stiffened. "Thank you master," she said, and went out.

Denton gazed at the door that Ah King had closed quietly behind her. "When Jonathan died she was beside herself. And now—"

"She was responsible for Jonathan," Su-mei said quietly. "She wasn't for Ah Sam. I'll go and talk to her about the funeral."

The door closed again. Denton looked down at the jasmine blossom floating in his tea. They talked about Ah Sam's death as though it had been no more than walking through a door, he thought, both Su-mei and Ah King. But then that was just what it was. Ah Sam had been with him for thirty years and then walked out through a door, that was all. In another thirty years they'd all have passed through the same door. What else was there to say? It wasn't as if they were young any more.

When the doorbell rang, the noise startled him like an alarm ringing in the middle of the night. Yet it was only half an hour later and he was sitting in the same chair. Jenny stumbled in, her face streaked with dust and grit, her lips quivering. At first she couldn't speak, heaving unsteadily for breath, then the words came out in spasmodic bursts. It was some time before he realised she was telling him Robert was dead.

Her body was rigid and trembling. When he sat her

692

down in a chair, though, it seemed to let go, slackening into great shuddering sobs. As he sat beside her, watching and helplessly waiting, he thought When I saw that man beheaded on my first day in Shanghai, I must have felt like she does now. So she must go through this too.

And while he was thinking, he heard the distant clatter of machine guns and rifles, the solid crump of exploding shells, over in Chapei and Hongkew.

Sarah Ephraim had gone to Wing On that Saturday afternoon too, to the jewellery department on the ground floor. The rest of the building collapsed on top of it and her body was never found. The firemen couldn't get to the bottom of the pile.

"I never thought I'd miss her so much," Jacob said a few weeks later. His face, wrinkled and folded, with deep shadowy pouches under his eyes, seemed to have fallen in, as though the scaffolding of bones that held it up had given away. "Believe it or not, I haven't looked at another woman since she died. I just don't feel like it."

The Chinese fought the Japanese all over again through the streets of Shanghai, round the thinly guarded perimeters of the international settlements. This time there was heavy artillery, there were more planes, and more troops. Refugees crammed the settlements, there were more outbreaks of cholera; when he looked across the barricades where the fighting had been fiercest, Denton could see the bodies, Chinese and Japanese, blackening in the sun.

Evacuation cards were issued again, and this time Su-mei got one too. She had become a British subject. But neither of them would leave, not yet. "We haven't raced our horse yet," Su-mei smiled over the opium pipe, which they smoked together again now. "How can we possibly leave?" The thud and crash of shells no longer disturbed them—it was just like thunder.

"But you ought to leave," Nixon said once, when they met in the street. "Given your political views and that scandal sheet you own, what?" Like Gilbert, he never bore a grudge, and treated their differences in the public school spirit, as though it was all a game of cricket.

"Do you remember how you used to worry about the Japanese taking over?" Denton asked him. "And now your superior scandal sheet is doing its utmost to support them?"

"Ah well," Nixon puffed genially on his pipe. "If you can't beat them, join them, eh?" He was another Mason, only with fine manners.

Jenny found a job in the radio station, and wore a little brooch with its call-sign—RU OK. So far she'd only given the weather reports. Denton was stunned the first time he heard her voice on the wireless. It sounded just like Mary-Ellen's of twenty years before, except that Cheltenham had replaced New England. She went to parties, nightclubs and dances as if the world outside the Bund was a thousand miles away, not a thousand yards. Two months after Robert's death, she met a lieutenant in the Seaforth Highlanders. Denton wished she was less of a child; he wished Lily was more of one.

He spent much of his time now in the *Shanghai Star* office, arguing with Pak-kay about his editorial direction and setting up the English language edition, which soon came out daily, not once a week. Su-mei looked after their money, placing it more and more in New York and London. She had a better head for it than him. "It's because you're Chinese," he said one night, watching the flashes of the Chinese guns in Pootung. "The craftiest people in business alive."

"No," she said with a little smile, at once sad and mocking. "Because my parents had to sell me when they were starving."

The Chinese shells arched overhead and burst somewhere behind the Japanese lines in Hongkew. It came to Denton at that moment that despite the war and the danger, he was happy. "I wouldn't have believed it possible," he murmured half-aloud.

Su-mei glanced at him, but didn't ask him what he meant. As if she already understood.

How long can it last? he wondered.

Then, one day, they woke to a silence that seemed eerie. The guns were still. Chapei was burning again, covered with dense black smoke. Behind the smoke, the Chinese had fallen back twelve miles.

"A new era of reconstruction and reconciliation," the *North China Morning Post* proclaimed. Pak-kay announced the retreat on an inside page, leaving the front to shout out Japanese atrocities. He called it a tactical redeployment.

88

The boat moved slowly nearer the quayside, its propellors churning the brown water into a scummy froth. Ropes snaked out and the waiting coolies heaved the hawsers over the bollards.

"Can't see them, can you?" Alec said, gazing along the quay. "Remember Big Ching, Michael?"

Michael nodded silently beside him, glancing up at the clock tower over the customs building. It was five to eight. The sun was fierce already. It will strike before we see them, he told himself.

"I say, wouldn't it be awful if war broke out in Europe and we were stuck here?" Alec said suddenly.

"Why?"

"Well, it'd probably be all over by the time we got back to join up."

"*I* wouldn't join up," Michael said, as if he'd made his mind up about that long ago. "I'm not—"

"Look, there they are," Alec cut in. "Over there by the gate."

They both gazed in silence at the little group that was silently gazing back at them. As if both sides were trying to adjust their minds to the uneasy strangers they saw before them.

"Who's that with them?" Alec spoke first, strangely reluctant to mention his father's grey hair, feeling it would be somehow disloyal to do so. "Ah King, is it? Or Ah Leng? I've forgotten what they look like."

"Ah King," Michael waved self-consciously in answer to his mother's raised hand. He waved with his good hand, the other, with its missing finger, unnecessarily gripping the rail as though the ship were still rolling in the China Sea.

Big Ching struck eight.

As soon as the ship had tied up, narrow gangways were put out fore and aft, and coolies carrying shoulder poles loped up along them. Before the passengers' gangway with its canvas awning had been secured, the coolies were already returning, their poles swinging with their

695

loads, chanting that rhythmical chant that had lain embedded in Michael's and Alec's memories for the whole six years of their absence.

"Now I know we're back," Alec exclaimed. "I can even smell it."

"I think we're almost the only ones getting off," Michael said. "I suppose a lot of people think Shanghai's dangerous now."

"Why should they? The war's miles away, isn't it?"

There was no room for Ah King in the car. "Maskee," she muttered gruffly in pidgin. "Never mind, I catchee taxi bime by, longside luggage."

"Taxi? No rickshaw?" Alec asked in Shanghainese.

"Eh, you've not forgotten Chinese?" Her gruffness thawed. "No, I'll watch the luggage in the taxi." She grinned, "Nowadays everyone's a thief. How big you are! I bet your bed's too small now." She fingered the little triangular scar in her cheek as she looked up at him.

Alec sat next to Jenny in front, while the other sat in the back. "I say, are you still a virgin?" he whispered in her ear.

"Alec, really!"

"I thought not," he said aloud.

"Thought what?" his father asked.

"Thought Jenny hadn't got a boyfriend," he declared innocently.

There was a sudden silence.

"Well how was the trip?" Denton asked hastily, but Su-mei had already started. "She had one," she said with that quiet matter-of-factness that was both chilling and refreshing to Denton. "He was killed in an air raid. Didn't your father write about it?"

Alec glanced remorsefully at Jenny. "I didn't realise he was your boyfriend," he apologised lamely.

"Oh long time ago now," she said lightly. "I've got another one now. Did you know I'm an announcer on the wireless?" She showed him her brooch. "We've got to call on mother this evening, by the way," she went on quickly, as if anxious to avoid questions. "It's her only free evening, she said. You must see Just Deeds too, he's an absolute champion..."

* * *

696

After lunch they drove to see Lily and Pak-kay at the newspaper. Hawkers squatted in the shade beside their stalls, trams clanged and jolted as crowded as ever, and shop signs still hung out over the road, red and gold.

"Nothing's changed at all," Alec said.

"There are more beggars," Michael said. "And more soldiers."

"And more refugees," Denton added.

Michael had hardly spoken since he'd arrived, not even to Su-mei. But his eyes had been watchful—withdrawn, slipping away from questioning glances, but observing and absorbing, as if he drew everything he saw inside him and contemplated it there.

"We also have police protection now," Denton added. "For what it's worth."

"Police protection? Whatever for?" Alec glanced at Michael as though he might be kidnapped again right before their eyes.

Denton nodded out of the rear window. "See that car following us? The Morris? Plain-clothes police. The paper's had a few threats, so they give us an escort. Pak-kay and Lily have their own bodyguard." He spoke so offhandedly that Alec wondered at first whether he was joking. But certainly the Morris was following twenty yards behind them, round every corner. And when he saw the two guards with shotguns outside the newspaper office, he was convinced. As Michael got out, he glanced involuntarily over his shoulder at the Morris drawing up a few yards away. A long forgotten image had floated up like a bubble of air to the surface of his mind, the image of a car door opening and hands grabbing his shoulders.

"Pleased to meet two products of the English ruling class's educational system." Pak-kay greeted them ironically. His voice had grown harsher in the past few months, and his eyes glowed more feverishly. There had been two more bomb attacks on the newspaper, and, though they hadn't done much damage, the tension was showing in the tautness of his face.

Alec smiled unperturbed. "Is that beard real, or do you glue it on in the mornings?" It was Michael who seemed to resent Pak-kay's irony; he stiffened and his eyes hardened faintly as he turned questioningly to Lily, as if expecting a jibe from her too. But she only put her hands on his arms and smiled as if to reassure him. She seemed calmer than Pak-kay, Michael thought. Not so jumpy.

697

Pak-kay took Denton into his office. Lolly sat in the corner of the tiny room, a shotgun at his feet, drinking tea. "So your sons are back?" Lolly said, peering past him through the half-open door. "I'm still angry we never caught those kidnappers." He stood up, cocking his head to examine Michael's oblivious face, as though he still hoped somehow to find some clue there.

"Here, you'd better see this," Pak-kay said brusquely. He handed Denton a cutting from a Chinese newspaper. Denton read it carefully while Lolly sat down again, sucking up his tea.

This white declaimer of anti-Japanese filth lives with a whore, having abandoned his American wife and children. Even the worst nationalists of his countrymen cannot forgive him that. He is also known to have conducted underhand double-dealings, blatantly cheating Chinese businessmen earlier in his career as an exploiter of Asian people. Still earlier he was employed in the Chinese customs service, but dismissed because of suspicions of bribery and malpractice. It is this shameless monster, shunned even by his own compatriots, who now dares to hurl scandalous abuse and filthy lies against our Japanese fellow-Asians, thinking himself safe in the bolt-hole of the international settlement. But Chinese and Japanese patience alike is running out. He is lifting a boulder to drop on his own feet.

"Sometimes I think there should be a law of libel in Shanghai," Denton said as he handed the cutting back.

"We could hardly print some of our own stuff if there was." Pak-kay laid the flimsy cutting carefully, like a precious specimen, down on his desk.

"Which paper does it come from?"

"The Chinese edition of the *Daily News*."

"The one Mason works for?" Denton raised his brows, gazing at the little jagged-edged slip of paper—or, rather, gazing beyond it to the early days when Mason and he had that precarious friendly-hostile relationship in the customs service. "So that's who they get their dirt from," he said.

"Well, it means we're getting to them," Pak-kay said. "I guess it's a kind of compliment that they write that kind of stuff. After all, we're the only paper in the settlement that dares run an anti-Japanese line right now."

Denton sighed. "And what good has it done?"

The door opened wider before Pak-kay could answer, and Alec put his head round the edge. "Is this where the editorials are written? I say, is that really true, what Lily's been telling us? About the Japs running opium dens in Hongkew and so on?"

Pak-kay looked at him witheringly, stroking his wild, antique beard. "Yes it's really true, old fruit," he said putting on a fancy English accent. "The Japs aren't allowed to buy it, only the Chinamen. And the police drive round in the morning and throw the dead addicts in the river. It's the cheapest way of getting rid of the blighters. After all, there are plenty more Chinamen where they came from, what?"

"Actually we call you chaps Chinks," Alec said sweetly, quite unruffled. "Not Chinamen."

Michael had come in while Pak-kay was talking. He listened attentively, yet Denton couldn't have said what he thought until he spoke. His wary brown eyes were like dark shields raised to protect his thoughts. But then, "Can you prove all that?" he said to Pak-kay.

"She lives with this Russian woman," Jenny said. "It's weird, they take drugs."

"Honestly?" Alec's eyes gleamed. "How'd you know?"

"They have hypodermics lying about the place."

"Gosh." He leant back against the brass frame of the rickshaw. "What a mother we've got. A lesbian drug addict. Which one of them plays the man, by the way, her or the Russian woman?"

"How would I know? I haven't seen them at it. Sonia's her name. She's supposed to be a poet."

"Oh, you can tell just by looking at them," he said knowingly. He gazed across at the night market, where the oil lamps were just being lit and the peddlers were noisily setting up their stalls. The sultry, petrol-fumed air moved past his face like a thick warm curtain as the coolie padded along in the shafts, his head bobbing up and down as he ran. "This is the first rickshaw ride I've had in six years. Imagine that."

Alec told the coolie to stop a minute outside the old temple on Bubbling Well road. A cluster of beggars squatting on the steps swarmed round them as he led Jenny through the grimy side entrance beside the locked main doors. At once the hubbub of traffic and hawkers' cries was muffled, and they stood in dim, musty silence. "What's this in aid of?" Jenny asked. "Along here," Alec said. The dense, warm air seemed to smother his voice. He led her past the garish statues of three gods, past an old bell caked in dust, and across a brick courtyard to the life-size effigy of a mandarin. It stood on a little altar which was covered with an embroidered cloth, its worn, frayed threads grey with the ash of smouldering joss sticks.

"Remember this?" Alec asked while a legless beggar pulled himself towards them on his hands, dragging his stumps, covered with old leather patches, behind him.

Jenny shook her head, wrinkling her nose at the smell of centuries of grime, which the scent of the joss sticks only made more greasy. "Never been here in my life," she declared. "And never want to come again, either."

"Yes you have. Ah King brought us once. Don't you remember?"

"Never."

"When Michael was kidnapped. She came to pray for good luck."

Jenny shook her head, frowning.

"Well I remember, anyway. See that tablet?"

Jenny glanced at the tall red tablet with dull gold characters, veiled with cobwebs.

"She told us what it says. The lord ten thousand times ten thousand times ten thousand years."

"She can't read!" Jenny thought she'd caught him out.

"Well someone must've told her. I rememember when we said the Lord's Prayer in school, for years afterwards I used to think they meant this chappie here." He gazed up at the mandarin with his once-brightly painted clothes, pink cheeks and long black moustache and beard. "Looks a bit like old Pak-kay, doesn't he?"

A young woman lit a joss stick in front of the effigy and bowed three times, shaking her clasped hands in front of her forehead. The heavy, perfumed smoke curled slowly upwards in flat spirals past the mandarin's blandly smiling face.

"Wonder who he was?" Alec said. "I expect Michael would know."

"This smoke's making my eyes water."

The legless beggar was plucking Alec's trousers, gently but insistently, as a young child might. "War wound," he kept whining. "No brothers or sisters, no mother or father. War wound, can't work. No brothers or sisters..."

Alec pulled out some coppers and dropped them with a clatter in the beggar's tin. "Come on, let's get out before we're mobbed by the rest of them."

The coolie was folding the rickshaw's canopy down, surrounded by a silent, watchful ring of beggars—women, old men and children.

"Got any change?" Alec asked as they stepped in over the lowered shafts. "I used all mine up on that legless wonder."

Jenny searched in her handbag as the coolie started forward again. The beggars followed, touching the rickshaw with their hands without slowing it, as if it were a sacred carriage. At last she found some cash and dropped the coins scrupulously one by one into the waiting palms.

They had to ring the bell several times before the light went on above their heads. Jenny peered through the window. "She's always got the same stuff here," she muttered. "I don't believe she ever sells a thing. No wonder she's hard up."

Mary-Ellen came down the stairs, a large vague figure in the dim light at the back of the shop. She squeezed her way past the tables and chests, frowning perplexedly at the door. She was wearing an evening dress and was heavily made-up. "Oh god," Jenny moaned, "she's forgotten we were coming. I knew we should have phoned first."

Mary-Ellen stared at them through the glass, then unlocked the door. "Is it today?" she exclaimed. "I can't possibly today, we're going out. Hello Alec, you look all right. Had a good trip? I'd hardly have known you." Her eyes were dilated and glistening. She spoke in a loud, elated voice. "It's the literary society tonight, I can't possibly miss it. Sonia's reading a poem..." At the same time she let them in and squeezed her way back up the stairs, leading the way.

After Jenny's description, Alec was surprised by her appearance. He'd expected her to look just terrible, but really she didn't look too bad at all. Her hair wasn't even grey like their father's, though she might have bleached it, he supposed. And with all that lipstick and jewellery and stuff, she certainly didn't look as decrepit as Jenny had made out. Fat of course, but then she always had been. He caught Jenny's eye and nodded at his mother, raising his brows approvingly.

"Wait till you see her without her war-paint on," Jenny whispered.

"I'll tell you what," Mary-Ellen said, panting slightly at the top of the stairs. "You could come along to the meeting with us. Then we can all have a drink afterwards. How about that? Because I couldn't possibly miss Sonia's poem."

Jenny rolled her eyes open-mouthed at Alec. He spread his hands helplessly and shrugged. "Lovely," Jenny said.

Sonia sat on the sofa in black silk trousers and a tight-fitting jacket. She was leaning over a notebook on her lap, smoking a thin black cigar.

"Alec, this is Sonia," Mary-Ellen said. Sonia raised her hand without looking up. "Don't speak to her now," Mary-Ellen whispered. "She's going through her poem. We've got to be there in half an hour. Come and talk to me in the bedroom."

A white-haired old man with warm brown eyes and hanging, sallow cheeks approached Jenny as they went in, his face creasing into a slack-mouthed smile.

"Hello, Jacob," Jenny said. "This is Alec, remember?"

"Is Michael here too?" Jacob said, pushing out his moist underlip. "Your father should have sent you to America." He walked beside them with a slight limp, as though he'd hurt his foot, and set them down on a sofa near the open window, patting Jenny's hand. Mary-Ellen and Sonia had gone immediately to the two empty chairs near the table, on which several plates of cake stood. Mary-Ellen surreptitiously broke off a piece of fruit cake and slipped it into her mouth while Sonia lit another black cigar, dropping the match on the table cloth, and frowned down intently over her notebook.

"Have you been in Shanghai long?" a slight, bald man with half-moon glasses on the tip of his nose asked Alec, leaning across from the adjoining chair. He spoke in a thin plaintive voice, wiping his hands on his handkerchief. "Oh, Mary-Ellen's son? Come to hear Sonia perform, I suppose? My wife's performing too, the lady in the blue dress over there. Harris is the name."

While Jenny chatted with Jacob, who was still patting

her hand, Alec glanced round the room, half-listening to Mr. Harris, whose voice droned on beside him, interrupted by frequent little sniffs. The hostess, Mrs. Dalton, who'd met them when the houseboy led them in, was an American, with large brass rings in her ears. They gave her a gypsy look, which she accentuated with a red shawl tied round her waist. But where was Mr. Dalton? Probably slipped off to the American Club, knowing what to expect if he stayed at home.

"...And then I moved to the rating and valuation department," Harris droned on, wiping his hands incessantly on his handkerchief. "Been there six years now..."

There were about twenty people altogether, mostly middle-aged women like his mother, except for three Chinese girls sitting together in a corner by the door, talking amongst each other in giggling, behind-the-hand whispers. They were rather pretty, especially the one in the middle, slightly taller, who'd glanced once or twice in his direction whilst smiling abstractedly at the others' whisperings. He risked a smile as their eyes met. The girl looked straight through him, not even troubling to glance away.

"Now those three Chinese girls," Harris sniffed, passing his clammy palm carefully over the dark strands of hair plastered across his bald head. "They've been to college in America. Come here every week and never say a word. You wonder why they bother. Unless it's just to hear some proper English..."

The gypsy-like Mrs. Dalton stood by the table and clapped her hands. The heavy bracelets on her wrists jangled. "I'm pleased to see some new faces here tonight," her eyes glowed at Jenny and Alec. "As well as the familiar ones of course. And tonight we're very lucky as we've got two authors to hear, a short story writer and a lady poet."

"Just a poet," Sonia said loudly. "You don't call Shakespeare a man poet."

"Yes, well a poet," Mrs. Dalton corrected herself, her earrings quivering as she shook her head. "And first Mrs. Harris with her story, which is set here in Shanghai, entitled *Coming Home*."

"*Going Home*, actually," Mrs. Harris said mildly, clearing her throat. "It is Going, not Coming. As you'll see that's rather important."

Mr. Harris murmured plaintively and sniffed, while

Mrs. Dalton, by now a little flustered, said *"Going Home,"* and sat down.

"She was in Shanghai again after so many years," Mrs. Harris read in a high tremulous voice, as thin and plaintive as her husband's. "She was in Shanghai to marry her fiancé before they both left for the old country. Yes, after so many years, she had specially asked for this favour on the way home from Japan..."

Alec's eyes strayed round the room. It was hot, he'd forgotten how hot it could be in the Shanghai summer and he began to feel sleepy. The large ceiling fan in the centre of the room was turning gently, but he was too far away to feel its draught. And the air outside the open window was as still as death. He blew his breath up over his face and glanced round at the three Chinese girls. They were sitting erect, hands folded in their laps, attentive smiles on their lips. The one in the middle let her eyes slowly turn in his direction, and then expressionlessly turn back, as though she hadn't seen him, or else hadn't cared for what she saw. He shrugged and moved his head a little lower on the back of the sofa, closing his eyes to concentrate on Mrs. Harris's thin trembly voice...

He was awakened by Jenny stealthily kicking his ankle. He blinked his eyes and gazed up at the ceiling. A little green lizard hung motionless by the corner, occasionally jerking its head to one side or the other, as if it were trying to catch what Mrs. Harris was saying.

There was a moment of silence when she finished, then Mr. Harris clapped his limp, moist hands and the others joined in tepidly, stirring, murmuring and clearing their throats.

"In my opinion," Mr. Harris declared, his eyes moist above his half-moon glasses, "that was Literature." He spoke in the same plaintive tone, but with a faint edge now, as if he expected Alec to contradict him.

"Jolly good," Alec said politely. "I could tell it had style."

Then Mrs. Dalton had started speaking again. "Well that was a very moving story, I'm sure you'll all agree. And very relevant too, which I always think is so important. Maybe one of our Chinese lady members might like to contribute something one day on the subject of er...of intermarriage and so on?"

The three Chinese girls gazed blankly at her as if

they hadn't understood, then smiled and whispered to each other behind their hands.

"Well, one day maybe, we'll look forward to that," Mrs. Dalton said brightly. "And now," she shook her head, sending the earrings flying, "we're going to hear a poem by a lady—I mean a poet—who had her first work published in Russia before the revolution when she was still in her teens. Miss Sonia Raimon . . . Raimonskikorsi."

"Raimonskikorski," said Sonia sharply. She leant forward on her chair, holding her notebook up with both hands like a singer holding a score. Between two fingers of her right hand her black cigar protruded, the dark grey smoke streaming away under the fan.

"*Old Age,*" she announced in a hard, keening voice, then cleared her throat, glancing imperiously round the room till they were all still and attentive. At last she declaimed in high, keening tones.

> "*What is this? Whiskers on a woman?*
> *Who could love*
> *A face like that?*
> *Her voice is as low as a man's,*
> *The enchantment of youth*
> *Forgotten. Forgotten.*
> *Her lovers.*
> *Her long fair hair is white now,*
> *Unclean and scanty.*
> *Her teeth are rotten and fall*
> *Out.*
> *She smells from her mouth, she*
> *Breaks wind incontinently . . .*"

The cigar burnt down to her fingers. She let it drop onto the carpet without a pause. Mrs. Dalton flinched and half-rose, then subsided again as Sonia glared at her over the top of her notebook. Mary-Ellen put out her foot and ground the glowing butt into the pile. It looked like a Tientsin carpet, Alec thought.

When she'd finished, Sonia sat rigid with eyes closed for several seconds, then slowly lowered her notebook as though coming round from a trance.

Nobody spoke. There were only a few uneasy throat-clearings and secret sidelong glances. An amah brought in tea and placed it on the table; the quiet thump of each pot sounded through the room. Then, in the seats near Sonia, instigated by Mary-Ellen, polite murmurs of inarticulate appreciation rose; a few hands clapped.

"Bravo," said Alec loudly. "Jolly good."

Amongst the bewildered, dutiful expressions of praise, which Mr. Harris joined in only with a few wordless ahems and sniffs, Mrs. Dalton stood up again.

"Well, I can tell how powerful that poem was by the way we all were like speechless when it finished. It absolutely took my breath away, and I'm sure everyone here was as moved as I was—"

"I don't agree," Jacob interrupted. "I think it was exaggerated and lacked form."

"Exaggerated?" Sonia asked in menacingly purring tone.

"Yes. I think you said something about no more lovers in old age."

"Forgotten her lovers," Sonia chanted softly, taking out another cigar.

"Yes, it is the same thing."

"Not at all, the form is different," Sonia let her eyes droop disdainfully. "Since you are interested in form..."

"But now I'm talking about the content. And that is exaggerated and false."

Sonia, lighting her cigar, said something sibilant in Russian, dropping the match and grinding it with her heel. Mrs. Dalton flinched again.

Jacob answered back, his eyes sparkling with the joy of combat.

They bandied Russian insults across the room, their voices growing louder and higher. After one exchange, Sonia pursed her lips, her eyes glittering, as though she was going to spit at Jacob. But then she swallowed abruptly and merely hissed out a stream of incomprehensible invective.

"Now let's all have some cakes and tea," Mrs. Dalton called out desperately, her brass earrings quivering. "Then we can discuss afterwards. Over by the table please, everybody help yourselves! Cakes and tea! Cakes and tea!"

Alec glanced round at the Chinese girls as they got up, leaving Sonia and Jacob to their quarrel. The girls were whispering behind their hands once more, giggling and laughing. He tried smiling at the tall one again, but again her gaze slid through him. He joined Jenny and the others at the table. Jacob and Sonia were shouting at each other across the room, neither of them moving, as if to do so might be interpreted as surrender.

"There you are," Mary-Ellen said delightedly as she broke off another piece of cake. "I told you she was a poet. None of your father's women could do anything like that, could they? There's only one thing they could do."

"It was very good." Jenny said with an effort, while Alec mumbled indistinct agreement through a mouthful of cake.

Mary-Ellen turned to him. "So what are you going to do now, Alec? Go to college?"

"Oh I don't know," Alec answered nonchalantly. "I'm not really bright enough. Michael's got an exhibition to Oxford, he's the clever one."

"Talking of Michael," Mary-Ellen's cheeks bulged as she munched her cake. "That short story reminded me of him: Wonder what he'd've thought of it? Staying in Shanghai all his days, eh?"

"Well he's supposed to be going to Oxford next year," Alec repeated languidly. "So it might be me that ends his days here."

The three Chinese girls came to the table and took plates and cups. Alec, standing near the teapot, swiftly raised it and poured for them. "Thank you," "Thank you," "Thank you," each of them said in a high tinkling voice without looking at him. Then they trooped back to their seats. "I say, who are those girls?" he asked Jenny.

"Oh, they're the Three Sisters," Mary-Ellen answered casually. "That's what Sonia calls them." Again she hardly troubled to lower her voice. "The tall one's Philip Wei's daughter, but the other two aren't really her sisters. I don't know who they are. Well, I'd better go and rescue Sonia before she starts fighting with Jacob, I suppose."

"Did you notice how loud her voice was all the time?" Jenny asked in the rickshaw on the way home. "It's the effect of the drugs."

"Is it?" Alec was watching a sing-song girl's rickshaw racing past them to some party, her face gleaming brightly from the light under the canopy. It was after midnight, but the streets were still crowded. Hawkers were selling melon slices, lychees and mangoes, the tea and cooked food stalls were swarming with noisy, shouting customers, and the clang of cymbals, the weird nasal voices of the opera singers, floated across from the stage in the night market. "Isn't it fantastic to be back!" he exclaimed. "And Shanghai hasn't really changed at all."

"Wait till you see Hongkew," Jenny said. "See what the Japs have done to that."

"Is it really true white people have to bow to Jap sentries? Won't catch me doing that!"

"That's exactly what I said," she answered caustically. "You just wait till you see them, though." And even while she was speaking, an olive green truck full of armed, helmeted Japanese soldiers raced down the middle of the road towards Garden Bridge. Its headlights were full on, and its horn blared continuously. The rickshaw coolie pulled anxiously into the gutter as the truck passed; so did everything in its way, even lorries and buses.

When they got home, Alec nudged Jenny, nodding at the car parked outside the drive on the other side of the road. "Is that our police guard? I bet they're asleep."

But as they walked into the drive after paying the rickshaw, he saw the two dim shapes in the car stir behind the windscreen. "Just like a film," he said happily.

Su-mei was talking to Michael in the living room, leaning towards him urgently, as if she was trying to convince him.

"But I want to study history," they heard him say in Chinese as they came in. He stopped and looked up at them, the blank shields sliding down over his eyes that had seemed excited, and even rebellious, while he was speaking.

Su-mei glanced round, then leant slowly back. "How was your mother?" she asked, without much interest.

"It's OK," Jenny said blithely. "You two carry on quarrelling. We'll go upstairs."

Their father was standing in his shirt-sleeves in the study, lighting a fragment of a mosquito coil.

"Mosquito coils," Alec sniffed. "I'd forgotten what they smelt like."

Denton held up the match and blew it slowly out, watching the flame first sway back from his breath, then reluctantly give up and die. He stooped to place the coil in its stand on the floor, straightening up with a little sigh. "Well, had a good time? How was your mother?"

"A bit strange, actually. She took us to a literary club

meeting and Sonia read a poem." Jenny laughed. "It was really awful, all sorts of arty people there. And Jacob Ephraim."

"Philip Wei's daughter was there too," Alec said. "She wasn't arty. She thought it was a joke."

"How do you know? She never said a word."

"She was laughing all the time. All three of them were."

"You must've been watching pretty closely," Jenny gave him a long look.

Their father scarcely seemed to have heard. He sat down, rubbing his chin, gazing abstractedly across the room at the wireless by the bookshelves.

"What about you?" Alec asked him. "What's been going on here?"

"Nothing much," his father said, still gazing thoughtfully across the room. "Things have been going on in Europe, though. Germany's just invaded Poland. It was on the news."

His mother argued and pleaded with him time and again, but Michael was obstinate. "All right, study history at Oxford," she said, "but you can't become a historian, a teacher. You're going to get a quarter of a million dollars when you're twenty-one, you've got to use it to make yourself richer."

"Richer? Why should I be richer than that?"

"Because you're a half-breed," she said bluntly. "They'll never accept you unless you're rich, richer than they are."

"Who won't?"

"Everyone—the Chinese and the foreign devils. Who else is there? What did they call you in school? Did they accept you in England?" she asked him mercilessly. "D'you think the Chinese will accept you unless you're rich? We're as bad as the foreign devils. Look at Lily. She goes crawling to them, please forget I'm a half-breed, let me be Chinese. But I tell you this, they won't forget. When the time comes, they'll throw her out." Her eyes hazed for a moment and she fingered her earring thoughtfully. "One of you has got to be rich," she said with a kind of sad certainty. "You're going to need it."

She never spoke of his future in his father's presence, as though she was afraid he wouldn't support her. So one

709

morning Michael appealed to him obliquely. "Mother keeps saying I ought to go into business after Oxford," he said warily, his tone suggesting he was uncertain and undecided himself.

"Business?" Denton looked up from his book amazed. "I thought you wanted to be a historian? Why should you go into business?"

Michael shrugged as if he didn't know why.

Denton shook his head slowly, gazing out of the window at the Bund with its solid temples of commerce that had drawn the wealth of China down into their vaults—and he too had had his share. "Well, all I can say is this, Michael," he smiled ruefully. "I made a lot of money here, by being shrewd I suppose, and by having good luck. But I never liked business—I just did it to survive. I never gave a damn about it once I was well enough off." He glanced at Michael almost shyly. "Business is what you do when you *need* money, not when you've got it."

And Michael had listened and said nothing, thinking of his Eurasian blood, of Su-mei's words, of the taunts in his early years in school, when he'd learnt to answer to Chink as to his own name. He listened and nodded, and then asked his father how the paper was going now, as though the question of his future had only fluttered briefly into his mind and had already slipped out of it.

I never know what he thinks, Denton thought wryly as he told him about the paper. And I never will. He watched Michael's eyes, neither Chinese nor European, clouding with layers upon layers of secret thought.

Michael walked to Kelly and Walsh that afternoon, to ask whether they'd got Burkhardt's *Renaissance* for him yet. There was no sign now of the bombs that had destroyed the Palace Hotel and Wing On. He walked past the tomb of Sarah Ephraim—rebuilt and open again, though almost empty now because of the war—without even noticing it. He did no more than glance at the new Wing On store, where Ah Sam had been killed while he was entering the sixth form. He did notice however how empty the counters were behind the thick plate glass. The war in Europe had sucked away many of the wealthy Europeans, and the encircling Japanese had squeezed out many of the rich Chinese. The shop was so empty, they no longer needed to charge for admission. The salesgirls yawned and did their nails. Only the moneyless refugees were increasing, flowing into the foreign devil's city for shelter as they had in the time of the Taipings and the Boxers and the warlords. The refugees had a pathetic, almost superstitious belief in the foreign devils' protection, but the foreign devils themselves had not. Their wives and children were sailing to Australia and America, the hongs' messes were almost empty as the young men went back to the war and trade dwindled. Only old men remained, and those who couldn't get out, the White Russians and the Jews. They dined in their lonely clubs and drank in empty cafés. They went to the races and the deserted nightclubs, they invited each other to their homes, they watched the solitary battalion of British troops bravely showing the flag, they drilled with the Volunteers. They remembered the battle of thirty-seven, the battle of thirty-two, the communists' uprising of twenty-seven and Chiang Kai-shek's sudden massacre of them, the butchery of Pock-mark Chen. Some of them even remembered the Boxers. They read their papers, which said the war in Europe was a phoney war and would soon be over, and they waited, as they'd waited so many times before, for the troubles to blow over, for things to settle down.

He'd reached Kelly and Walsh. As he went in, he wondered whether this time they'd wait in vain. His father didn't think so—at least, he was staying on. But then he was so committed to that paper. Alec was waiting for a passage to England and the war, though. And he himself? He just hoped the war would be over by next year, so that he'd be able to go to Oxford. He had nothing to do with that war. Nor with the war in China. He didn't belong to any side, it was true.

No, the spectacled assistant, who looked like a student himself, told him. They hadn't got the Burkhardt in yet. With a cool glance at Michael's face he switched to Chinese. "All our orders are months late because of the war in Europe. There aren't any ships. It's probably in the Public Library, though."

"I've tried there, it's missing." Michael started browsing amongst the shelves. The books were stacked anyhow, as far as he could see, without reference to subject, author or title. He found a novel by Aldous Huxley next to a short history of Tibet. Perhaps somewhere in that maze they had a Burkhardt all the time? He ran his eye along the shelves.

There was hardly anyone else there, only a few middle-aged European women flicking through six month old copies of *Woman's Own* and *Ladies' Home Journal*. Michael pulled out an old guide book to Shanghai, and turned the pages slowly, gazing at the faded photographs of temples and guild-houses, of women with bound feet blinking dazedly at the camera, of opium divans from which vacant-eyed Chinese stared out unseeingly, of Manchu bannermen with long-barrelled rifles and lances.

"How much is this?" he heard an Englishwoman ask behind him. He turned to another photograph. *In the Native City*, the caption said. The sky was white, the trees were grey, the canal running under an arched bridge was white, the houses with pagoda roofs were grey. He imag-ined the glaring sunlight that had defeated the photogra-pher, turning everything into a dazzling haze.

A finger tapped him smartly on the shoulder. "I asked how much this is," the same voice said curtly. "Didn't you hear?"

He started round. The woman was lean and shrunk-en, with shrivelled brown skin, her grey hair tightly permed. Her lips were painted an incongruous bright young red. She was holding out a magazine, shaking it impatiently in front of his face. "How-much-is-this?" she repeated with exaggerated distinctness. "How much catchee?"

"I haven't the faintest idea. Why don't you ask one of the assistants?"

The woman stared at him a second in disbelief, then tossed her head. "Well where *are* the assistants then?" she demanded irritably as she turned away.

It wasn't till she'd gone that Michael realised he was trembling faintly with resentment. He walked out of the shop and wandered through the flower market and the silk alley, along the narrow lanes where tailors bent over their machines with tired eyes in dark little rooms open to the street, and where children scuffled in the gutters filled with stagnant, oily water. Suddenly he was in Frenchtown, crossing the Avenue Edward VII before he realised where he was. Only two streets away was the old city, which the Japanese controlled now. He could see the French Annamite soldiers at one barrier and the round dark helmets of the Japanese sentries a hundred yards further on. Something made him keep on walking towards the barriers, as though they were a challenge he had to meet. He followed a coolie who was wheeling some piglets in rattan baskets along in his barrow.

The Annamites waved them through. Michael watched the coolie bow to the Japanese sentry as he offered him his permit with both hands. The sentry examined the permit, walked slowly round the coolie and his barrow, handed the permit back and nodded the coolie on. As the barrow lurched forward, the sentry leant forward and heaved one of the baskets off, letting it tumble on the ground beside the barbed wire. The other soldiers behind the sandbag emplacement laughed. The piglet had let out a grunt as it hit the ground, but now it lay still and silent, staring straight ahead with its round little eyes, as though indifferent whether it was a Japanese or Chinese knife that slit its throat. The coolie lunged on, sweating, without as much as a murmur or a glance at the soldier. It was as though he hadn't noticed. But he had.

Perhaps something showed in Michael's face, some flicker in his eye or stiffening of his cheek. He bowed to the sentry and held out his permit, but the Japanese slapped it out of his hand. "You think I can read upside down?" he shouted in broken Chinese. "Show it the right way round, you dolt!"

Michael picked up his permit and held it out again, his heart suddenly thumping with the realisation that he'd put himself in their power. He held it out deferentially with both hands, his head bowed so that he could see no higher than the sentry's belt. As he waited, he saw the muzzle of the soldier's rifle slowly passing beneath his face till it touched his chest. He gazed down with a fiercely hammering heart at the round, bluish metal, the black, sharp wedge of the foresight, the brown Japanese hand round the wooden stock.

"Take off your shirt."

"Pardon?" Michael glanced up uncertainly.

The soldier was smiling tightly. There was a little blackhead on his chin, which was greasy with sweat. "Shirt!" he repeated, giving a little jab with the rifle.

Michael's fingers trembled as he unbuttoned his shirt. He held it out with both hands. Behind he could hear footsteps shuffling, the docile tread of coolies. He imag-

713

ined their dull, lustreless eyes watching his humiliation, only grateful it wasn't them.

The sentry fished the shirt out of his hands with the muzzle of his rifle and felt inside the pockets. There were only a few dollar notes. He replaced them with a contemptuous sniff and slowly lowered the barrel till the shirt slid off onto the stone flags of the old road. "Trousers," he said, quietly at first. "Trousers!"

Michael heard the other guards snigger behind the sandbags. He dropped his trousers and waited abjectly. He could feel his legs weak and unsteady as he gazed wretchedly down at the crumpled cloth round his ankles, and he thought with relief I'm going to faint, I won't know any more. But he didn't faint. He just stood there, pathetic and ridiculous.

The sentry laughed, not the polite little giggle he'd heard from Japanese before, but a round, hearty guffaw, high-spirited and cheerful. Michael remembered the laughter of the changing rooms and the dormitories at school— *"Let's see what you've got Chink! Come on, drop 'em!"*—merry, bullying, English laughter. The Japanese prodded his trouser pockets with the rifle, stepped a pace forward, standing on the shirt, then slowly raised the muzzle along his calf, his knee, his thigh, up between his legs. He lifted the barrel a little, then released it, lifted and released. The other guards were shouting with laughter along with him, *"Let's see what you've got, Chink!"* echoed in Michael's head, and the chortles of half-broken voices.

He looked up hesitantly. The sentry's face was crinkled with laughter too, his eyes almost closed. He lowered the rifle again and gestured Michael to dress. Michael shoved his shirt unbuttoned inside his waistband and bowed. He hurried on, his belt undone, holding his trousers up with both hands. Behind him the hooting guards were calling to each other. He didn't dare look back. He didn't even stop to dress properly until he'd turned into the square of the sedan chairs—there were no chairs there now, only a few shabby rickshaws. The squatting coolies watched him incuriously, smoking their wide cigarettes in the shade of the decaying wall. When he was ready and the thudding inside his chest had calmed, he turned and walked on. He wouldn't think about it, not yet. He'd just let it settle in his mind until the thoughts eventually rose of their own accord. But now he wouldn't think about it. He walked on slowly, his mind blank and empty.

He wandered down the narrow alleys with their worn, uneven flagstones, along the ivory-workers' street, into the street of singing birds. Many of the shops were closed, but a few bamboo cages hung unhooded in the May sunlight for the birds to preen themselves. They cocked their jerky, beady-eyed heads at him and twittered a few broken little phrases, as if they'd lost the heart to open their throats fully and sing at length. At the end of the street, so narrow he could touch both walls if he spread his arms, was the restaurant he remembered from his childhood excursions with Ah Leng, the one where deer were kept in cages outside for a customer to choose them for some banquet. And there were two deer there now in the same cages, one each side of the door. And the same smell of cooking, the same sizzle and splutter of hot fat. Only most of the customers were gone; there were no more than a dozen sitting at the tables, picking their teeth or sipping tea. Michael remembered the raucous shouting and laughter there used to be there. A waiter pushed some bamboo leaves into the deer's cages. The deer sniffed and munched, their mild shiny eyes following Michael as he passed Only tell us how long we've got, they seemed to be pleading. That's all we ask.

He walked on over the zig-zag bridges to the Woo Sing Ding tea-house. But it was closed, the doors barred, the windows covered with ill-fitting shutters. Only an old man with matted grey hair and bare feet, blackened with grime, was there, lying asleep on the steps like a stray dog. This is China. Michael thought. A million places like this. He walked on, past the City Temple, down the streets of the idols. Some woodcarvers were carving an over-life-size statue of Kwang Ti out on the street. It must have been too big for their shop. He walked on.

Suddenly, when he left the old city and entered Nantao, everything changed. Here was the new China, the China of Japanese Co-prosperity. A new-fangled pedicab was competing with a rickshaw for a couple of suited businessmen, one Chinese, the other Japanese, who were politely urging each other, with many bows and smiles, to make the choice for both of them. Japanese cars honked along the road, Japanese signs hung above the shops, and neat,

715

precise women in kimonos fingered the cloths the Chinese salesmen unfurled for them.

Michael went across to a stall and asked for some tea. When he offered a dollar, the hawker shook his head. "Only Japanese money," he said.

"I haven't got any."

The hawker's eyes slid to left and right under his half-closed lids. "All right, two dollars," he muttered.

"Two dollars for a glass of tea!"

The hawker shrugged for answer and edged the glass away from him. "I have to use that money in the foreign settlement," he muttered again. "It's no use here. It's not easy going across there and back. Not worth my while unless you give me a couple of dollars."

Michael reluctantly passed the coins across. The hawker covered them immediately with his hand and slid them off the ledge into his pocket, looking steadfastly away from Michael as he did so. Michael gazed up and down the street as he sipped the tea.

"Want to change some money?" the hawker murmured behind him.

Michael shook his head. He watched a black American car, gleaming and large, coming down the street, honking impatiently at two rickshaws running abreast in front of it.

"Chase the dragon?" the hawker's metallic voice coaxed.

"What?" Michael turned round now, frowning puzzledly.

The man's eyes slid off his and looked up the street. He made a gesture with his closed fist as though he were smoking a pipe, then another with his fingers as though puffing on a cigarette. "Opium," he said, barely opening his lips. "Can't use dollars here. You've got to buy it with yen. How much d'you want? I'll give you a good rate."

Michael shook his head, turning back to the street again. The black American car was just passing now. For a moment he saw Philip Wei's face in the back. He was smiling as he talked to the man beside him, a Japanese with steel-rimmed glasses that gleamed flatly as he turned towards Philip. Philip was leaning back against the headrest, comfortable and relaxed.

"What d'you come here for if you don't want opium?" the metallic voice muttered peevishly behind him. "It's the cheapest you can get."

*   *   *

716

It was dark when he returned home. He'd walked up and down the streets of Nantao for hours, watching everything with grave, silent fascination. Gangs of coolies heaving bricks for a Japanese barracks, a Japanese soldiers' brothel, with a guard outside, Chinese puppet policemen directing the traffic and patrolling in pairs, swaggering in a ragged imitation of their Japanese masters. He came on a shabby but brightly lit building with *Amusement Palace* in gold characters on a red board over the entrance. A Japanese notice hung on the wall by the door. He couldn't make it out and asked a puppet policeman what it said.

"Out of bounds to Japanese Forces," he answered condescendingly, without troubling to look.

"Why?" Michael asked innocently.

The policeman shrugged. He looked no older than Michael, probably a peasant from somewhere, proud of his uniform and the face it gave him. "The Japanese have their own places," he answered vaguely.

From the bare, neon-lit entrance arch the greasy, clogging smell of opium drifted out, but there was no sound of amusement, no music or laughter. The place was grim and silent. Michael strolled on, and watched from a rice shop across the road, listening to the rice clicking drily as the assistants dug their trowels into the pearly, shifting heaps behind him. The men who went into the amusement palace were all coolies, not young ones but lean and old, with drawn cheeks and red-rimmed eyes. Some of them went in rolling their sleeves up, and came out a few seconds later rolling them down. After a few steps they started staggering and collapsed against the walls or on the pavement. It was some time before he realised they'd been buying heroin injections.

He made his way back towards Frenchtown eventually, scrupulously bowing and stepping into the gutter whenever he met Japanese soldiers. He crossed at a barrier nearer the river. It was manned by sailors who waved him through wordlessly when he bowed and presented his permit.

Alec was just leaving in his khaki Volunteers uniform when Michael arrived. "How do I look? Pretty smart, eh?"

"One of your puttees is longer than the other."

Alec frowned down disbelievingly, then bent over to adjust them. "You ought to've joined you know," he said, straightening up. "It's quite fun, really."

717

"I've been over in Nantao," Michael said, as if that explained his failure to volunteer.

"Watching the little brown dwarfs, eh? What did you think of them?"

"Perhaps Pak-kay was right—"

But Alec was already clattering down the steps in his boots, the metal heels ringing on the stones. "Can't stop now, I'm late."

His father was in the study, listening to a record, gazing at the revolving black disc as though it was the orchestra itself. "This record's pretty scratched by now," he said as he got up to lift the needle off. "I suppose I ought to get a new one. But it's one of the first I ever got, I don't want to throw it away..."

Michael had meant to tell him about Nantao, but there was something abstracted and pensive about his father's eyes; as if he was going through the years of his past like the pages of an old photograph album, turning them one by one.

"I used to sing in the choir," Denton said ruminatively, then paused, listening, glancing at the window.

Then Michael heard it too, the grinding sound of heavy engines passing regularly, one after the other along the Bund.

They looked out. British army trucks were driving in a long column, pulling trailers behind them. Ah King, carrying laundry down from the bedrooms, peered out of the window beside them. She shook her head dourly.

"Where are they going?" Michael asked.

His father pointed to a solitary ship anchored off the French Bund. Barges and lighters were ferrying the trucks to the ship's sides. Derricks slowly hoisted them aboard under the bluish white intensity of arc lamps flaring from the masts.

"Now the foreign devil soldiers are leaving us," Ah King muttered sourly. "Who's to keep the Japanese out now?"

"I suppose we'll just have to do it ourselves," Denton said ironically.

Soon after midnight Jenny came in with pale cheeks. "They're leaving in the morning," she said. "They're all on board already." She couldn't repeat there and then in front of all of them what the Seaforth's lieutenant had said as he kissed her goodbye by the side of the godown that smelt of damp gunny sacks. *"Tell your people to get out while they can."*

She told her father next morning when they were alone at breakfast, but he only smiled. "No point in panicking. Six months from now the war may be over and they'll send the troops back. Besides I want to race Just Deeds in the Stewards' Cup."

It was as if he just couldn't believe in the danger, or even was deliberately courting it. Like that absurd Pak-kay of Lily's, whom she detested, always trying to prove something.

89

All the stands were full. The crowd pressed right up to the rails, waiting restlessly, shouting, talking, jostling for a better view.

"Amazing how many people there are here, considering," Jenny said, gazing down from the Dentons' box.

"Considering what?" Alec asked.

"Well considering all the people that have been evacuated and so on..."

He leaned out to survey the crowds. "They're all Chinese," he said, sipping his wine. "No shortage of *them* here."

"Here they come," Michael said. "I suppose they'll be starting soon."

They looked down at their father, Su-mei and Jacob Ephraim making their way through the members' enclosure towards them.

"Is there any more wine, Ah Man?" Alec asked, holding his glass out without turning his head. He heard the wine poured and steered his glass back to his lips. "Look, there are the Weis, too."

Their father was the tallest. His hair was completely grey now, receding at the temples, and his face even at that distance looked gaunt and lined. Yet otherwise, in his body and his movements, he'd hardly changed. Jacob walked with that slight limping gait that he'd had for some time now, carrying his white-haired head with an aggressive forward thrust. Su-mei, on Denton's other side, seemed

719

to have aged the least. She walked with the same light step, and was as slim and erect as ever, her hair still black. She was wearing a red cheongsam just like the one she wore when they met Jenny off the boat four years before. It was only perhaps the set of her face, something almost regal, that showed, at that distance, she was not a young woman. They met the Weis, and paused to speak to them. Old Wei was being guided along by Philip on one side and Philip's tall daughter on the other, each supporting one of his frail arms.

"There's that girl again," Alec said.

Michael looked at the girl. She was watching her frail grandfather with detached protectiveness, as if he were a bird with a broken wing. "What's her name?" he asked.

They shrugged. Nobody knew.

The two groups separated coolly. "Not very pally, are they?" Jenny said. "I don't think you've got much chance with that girl, Alec. Especially as she's probably kept under lock and key, while you loaf around the nightclubs getting tipsy when you've finished parading with the Volunteers."

"It's not my fault if I can't get away to fight for king and country."

"It's the tipsiness they'd object to more. Why don't you try your luck, Michael? You're half-Chinese at least."

"Michael?" Alec laughed. "Know what they used to call him at school?"

"Chink," Michael said. He was still watching the girl, I want to know her, he thought quite simply and distinctly. It was a discovery, not a decision.

"No, later on, in the sixth? Chink the monk."

"There's Pock-mark Chen," Jenny said. "Look the Weis are going to his box."

"And look at those Japs with them," Alec whistled. "They're really in with the Nips now, aren't they? In that case I certainly don't have a chance."

They gazed at Chen's massive moon-shaped face. He was flanked on each side by a dapper, alert Japanese, one with a little moustache, the other cleanshaven. Michael recognized the cleanshaven one. It was the man he'd seen in Philip Wei's car in Nantao.

"Isn't that one with the moustache the one who slapped Lily's face?" Jenny asked.

"How would we know? We weren't here," Alec answered. "Besides they all look the same anyway, don't they?"

After a great deal of bowing, the Weis sat down on Chen's right and Philip immediately began talking to the cleanshaven Japanese. On Chen's left were two young girls, richly dressed, with rouged cheeks, arched brows and full, sulky lips. Around them, above and below, the bodyguards sat, dressed in suits with wide shoulders. Michael stared at one of them, frowning. Could it be him? he wondered. Could it be the one who cut off my finger? He sipped his wine, glancing at his damaged hand, then looked back at the man. The man moved; Michael couldn't see him properly now. Besides, it was all so long ago. His eye strayed to the Wei girl. The people round her were all talking, but she merely looked out over the crowd. She seemed separate, like him.

"Just in time," Jenny called out as her father, Su-mei and Jacob entered the box. "They'll be off any minute now. They're under starter's orders, look." She made room for Jacob, who leaned on both elbows beside her, his moist underlip pouting slightly.

"Tell me when they start," he said morosely. "I can't see from here."

"Don't worry, you'll hear."

Ah Man just had time to fill all the glasses, and then the start was greeted by a huge excited roar. Everyone leant forward, even Jacob who could only see the finishing post. Ah Man slipped off his black cloth slippers and stood on a chair, shading his eyes with his hand. Denton stood beside Su-mei, both of them tense and silent as they watched the horses round the first bend. All round them, in the stands, in the boxes, and most of all down by the track, the excited murmuring was rising, a muffled, drawn-out wave of sound, growing slowly louder and louder. Just Deeds was lying third, with Pock-mark Chen's grey second. They, and the black in front, were gradually drawing away from the rest of the field. At the start of the second bend, Chen's grey began to move up outside the black. Urgent yells of encouragement sounded over the rising roar of the crowd. Just Deeds was still lying by the rail in third place. Denton watched the turf flying up behind the horses' hooves. He licked his lips. They grey was going ahead, his jockey using the whip, while the black seemed to be tiring. He glanced apprehensively sideways at Su-mei. Her face was set.

It was the same order when they turned into the

straight, but Just Deeds was going up slowly on the black, still hugging the rail. The grey had moved a length ahead.

"He's got to do it now," Alec muttered. "He's leaving it too late."

Denton's hand clenched. He glanced at Su-mei again. Her lips had tightened. Alec was right, Just Deeds was leaving it too late. He was boxed in with the black on his side and the grey in front. The grey was a length and a half ahead now, and Just Deeds was scarcely gaining on the black at all. His nose was only just edging up past the hind quarters.

Michael looked away at Pock-mark Chen. His cropped, dark head had turned slightly as the horses passed beneath him and Michael saw the tightest of smiles just moving the corner of his mouth. Below, in the stands, the crowd was growing frenzied, shouting and urging wildly.

"Come on Just Deeds," Alec growled tensely. "Come on!"

Only two hundred yards to go. Just Deeds moved slowly up into second place, his tail just clear of the black's nose. But there was still a clear length between him and the grey. The crowd's roar was immense, fifty thousand raucous, yelling throats stretched wide with hope or despair. Another fifty yards, and Just Deeds had closed the gap. Fifty more, and his nose was by the grey's shoulder. The grey's jockey whipped furiously. They were neck and neck. For the first time in his life, Michael heard Ah Man shout, a high-pitched wordless scream of encouragement that turned to exultation and triumph as Just Deeds moved into the lead, passing the post a head in front of the grey.

Denton looked at Su-mei as he felt his fingers uncurling and the tightness in his nerves slowly loosening. The only expression was in her eyes, those slanting lids lowered, while a quick, dark movement of the pupils flickered in the narrow slits they left. She smiled at him. He put his hand over hers. He became aware of Ah Man, standing on the chair, both hands clasped above his head, his eyes wide and dancing.

It was several seconds before Ah Man mastered himself, while they all smiled and laughed at him—all except Jacob. Then he stepped down, putting his servant's personality on again with his slippers. "Shall I open the champagne now, master, or after you've led the horse in?" His voice was shaking.

"Afterwards," Su-mei said firmly.

"How much did you bet on him?" Jenny asked.

"One thousand dollars, seven to one," he said happily. "You listen to them cheering when master leads the horse in. Everyone wanted him to beat Pock-mark Chen." He glanced up at Su-mei as he spoke, as if only she would understand why.

"You're very quiet, Jacob," Alec said.

He was still leaning over the box, gazing with his dim eyes at the finishing post, his jaw thrust sullenly forward. "I backed the wrong horse," he said grimly. "The only time in my life I bet on a horse, and I back the wrong one."

"Why on earth didn't you back Just Deeds?" Jenny demanded accusingly.

"I never thought Pock-mark Chen would let you win," he muttered, shaking his head gloomily. "I was sure he'd have had it fixed."

"You should have asked me," Su-mei said, as cold as steel. "He doesn't cheat when he gambles."

The applause from the paddock swelled up as she spoke, louder than usual, as Ah Man had predicted. It seemed to gather force like a wave gathering water, spreading out into the stands and over the track. Only the block round Pock-mark Chen remained silent, and he himself sat motionless, holding his race-card up to his face as if he were studying it intently—but the last race had been run. Michael looked at Philip Wei's daughter. She was gazing down at the crowd with the same detached air with which she'd held her grandfather's arm earlier.

Denton brought Solnikov back with him. Jacob perked up, speaking Russian to the sad-eyed trainer, who even after two glasses of champagne was still shaking his head disapprovingly. "He left it too late," he kept saying lugubriously, as if they'd lost instead of won. "After all I told him, he still left it too late."

"We're going to eat Sichuan food tonight," Denton said. "Come and join us."

"Sichuan food?" Solnikov's mild eyes looked alarmed. "Excuse me, Mr. Denton, too spicy, too hot. Such food is bad for my stomach. No, I go home to my cats better." He sucked the ends of his unkempt grey moustache into his mouth, as if to capture any last drop of champagne that might be clinging there, but refused another glass, folding his pale hands apologetically over his delicate little paunch.

Pak-kay and Lily joined them at the restaurant. Lily's stomach was beginning to swell, and despite his distaste for bourgeois institutions, Pak-kay had married her, for the sake of his unborn child. There'd been nothing to prevent him showing his disapproval of the sport of kings and taipans, though, and he'd refused brusquely when Denton invited them to the races.

"We won," Alec called out as they came in. "We won and everyone cheered because we beat Pock-mark Chen. Even horse-racing can have a political significance, you see?"

Lily looked pale and tired, mauve circles under her eyes. And she could have been a beauty like Su-mei, Denton thought, only half-listening to Alec's and Jenny's account of the race.

"I wish I could have seen it," Lily said simply.

"You *were* invited," he answered.

She glanced sharply across at Pak-kay, raising her brows, but said nothing.

"We had more important things to do," he declared irritably. "This Nazi conference they're holding here—we're covering that."

Denton watched him combing his beard with his stubby fingers, frowning impatiently. Yet he seemed to be avoiding Lily's eyes. You didn't tell her about the invitation, Denton accused him silently. You didn't tell her, did you?

Jacob, mellow now from his first glass of vodka, laid his hand on Lily's arm. "Just as well you didn't go," he assured her. "The excitement might have given you a miscarriage. I never let Sarah so much as lift the samovar when she was pregnant. And she never had one miscarriage even though her womb was tilted wrongly. They said she might have one just from sneezing too hard." He lifted an empty glass. "See, her womb was like that. It should have been like *this*, but it was like *that*. It made birth easier but she was always liable to have a miscarriage."

"Really Jacob, Lily knows all about that kind of thing, no need to go into it in such detail," Jenny protested, "She *was* a medical student after all."

"Isn't that Nazi conference being held in the Park Hotel?" Alec asked. "I saw a swastika in one of the windows yesterday. I don't know why they allow it."

"The international settlement is neutral," Michael said.

"It was the same in the first war—" Denton began.

"Yes, you British made a mistake there," Pak-kay interrupted. "You should have made it a colony like jolly old Hong Kong, what?" He reached for a piece of ginger with his chopsticks and smacked his lips as he ate it. "Then you could have bunged the jolly old nasties out!"

"There's nothing quite so tedious as constant repetition of a flat joke," Alec remarked gently.

"Yes, you'd do far better spending your energy trying to persuade your own country to join the war," Jenny added. "Instead of sneering at someone else's all the time."

"My country *is* in the war," Pak-kay said calmly. "It was in before yours."

"I mean America."

"I know you do." Again he smacked his lips as he munched. "But China's my country. I turned my American passport in last week."

They stared at him. He smiled, enjoying the effect.

"You did what?" Denton asked.

"Turned my passport in. I'm pure Chinese now."

"That was just about the stupidest thing you could possibly have done," Denton said, anger flooding into his voice. He stared at Pak-kay's complacent brown eyes and his moist red lips moving in the black thatch of his beard, and wondered remotely how Lily could bear to let him kiss her. "So long as you were an American citizen the Japs had to be careful with you. Now they can do what they like." He caught Lily's eye turning anxiously towards Pak-kay and felt resentful that she could be so blind to his absurd, dangerous posturing. "Or haven't you noticed how differently the Japs treat foreign devils and Chinese?"

"Sure I've noticed," Pak-kay said nonchalantly, reaching for another piece of ginger. "That's why I did it."

Jacob slapped his empty glass down on the table. "Mr. Pak-kay, you're out of this world," he laughed delightedly. "You're a political masochist! That's right, my boy, join in the suffering. And next time you see the Japs shooting some Chinese, why don't you line up with them and ask them to shoot you too? Show them your brand new Chinese passport!" He poured more vodka into his glass, shaking his head and chuckling. "Out of this world, out of this world! And last time we met you were using your American passport as a shield!"

The waiter brought the first dish, of diced chicken, and they all paused while he poured tea into their cups. Denton's anger seethed quietly. "Just when the British troops have been withdrawn," he said as the waiter left, "and when the Japs are stepping up their attacks on the paper—that's the moment you choose to make yourself most vulnerable! What d'you want to be—a martyr?"

Pak-kay was breaking a piece off the chicken. He lifted it with his chopsticks and placed it in Lily's bowl. It was the first mark of affection Denton have ever seen him give her. "We'll be all right in the international settlement," Pak-kay shrugged. "What good would a few hundred British soldiers have done against twenty thousand Japs anyway? Or do you think one white man is worth a hundred yellow ones?"

"Japs are brown, actually," Alec murmured. "It's the Chinese who are supposed to be yellow."

Su-mei spoke for the first time, smiling deceptively. "You must know that Chinese opponent' of the Japs some-time' disappear even in the international settlement," she said quietly. "Now you are Chinese, maybe you will disappear." The smile slid off her face. "I don't care whether you live or die, but what's going to happen to Lily if you are kill'? She carries your child."

Pak-kay's dark brows rose faintly, but before he could answer, "I've applied for Chinese citizenship too," Lily said. "Only it takes longer because I'm ..."

"Because you're a half-breed like me," Michael finished for her.

They ate quickly and glumly after that, almost in silence. Pak-kay and Lily left immediately the last dish was finished. The others followed soon after. They waited on the pavement for the car, wrapping their coats about them in the chill of the November night.

"Should think there might be a frost tonight," Alec murmured to nobody in particular, stamping his feet. The others only glanced at him with an abstracted stirring of the eyes, then looked silently away.

As the car drew up by the kerb, they heard a burst of singing from the Park Hotel opposite. They looked up.

The windows of the ballroom had been opened, and groups of men stood at them singing and waving their arms. Their voices were hoarse and boisterous. Everyone on the street looked up, rickshaw coolies, beggars, the traffic policeman on his high pedestal at the cross-roads, the hawkers and their customers.

"What are they singing?" Jenny asked.

"The Horst Wessel song," Jacob said uneasily. "One of the Nazi songs." He gazed up at the windows, blinking in his effort to see clearly. The men were still singing, but now they were throwing leaflets out of the windows as well, handful after handful like giant confetti. The leaflets snowed down to the street and people reached to catch them, smiling curiously and laughing. Alec picked up one that landed in the gutter at his feet.

"What does it say?" Jacob asked anxiously, peering over his shoulder.

"It's in German—oh no, the other side's in English. Hold on a minute." Alec held it up to the lamplight and read it aloud. *"The following is a list of Jewish businesses in Shanghai with which all Aryans are hereby required to have no further dealings."*

Jacob snatched the leaflet out of his hands and took it into the restaurant entrance, squinting in the light as he read the message himself. He turned to the other side and read the German as well.

They watched him stuff the leaflet into his pocket and join them at the car. Three Japanese officers were marching up the steps to the hotel as they drove away, and the leaflets were still falling. Jacob pulled the crumpled paper out of his pocket and stared down at it again, although it was too dark to read.

"Is your name there?" Denton asked softly.

Jacob nodded. "It was signed by Henschel," he said. "Remember Henschel?"

"Henschel? Yes, I remember him." Denton thought of Henschel with his spiky blond moustache blandly commenting on the execution of those bandits in Soochow, and years later sparring with Nixon in the Municipal Council.

"Apparently he's with the German embassy in Tokyo now."

Jacob was silent all the way back to the new flat he'd bought in Tibet Road, overlooking the race course. But then, as the car drew up, he snorted. "Pah, all I'll have to do is pay a bit of money to get my name off the list. These Germans aren't like the Russians, they're civilised people after all..."

Lau opened the door and he climbed stiffly out, shoving the leaflet back in his pocket as he turned to wave goodbye.

90

"What's your name?" she asked casually as she unbuttoned her dress.

"John," Michael said.

"Your real name?" She glanced up at him, smiling. "Everyone says they're John."

He began loosening his shirt, starting with the bottom button. "Michael," he said grudgingly.

She bent down to undo her sandals. "What are you? Eurasian?"

"Yes."

"You look more Chinese."

"Yes I know."

"You give me the money now?" she asked, stepping out of her sandals.

He felt in his pocket. He'd put the notes there ready. She counted the bills and put them carefully into her bag. Then, with a shrug of her shoulders she slipped her dress off and folded it neatly, laying it over the chair beside the bag. Michael's fingers moved up to the next button.

She kept her back to him while she took off her underwear and laid that neatly too on the chair. Then she stepped to the bed, lifted the sheet and slipped beneath it so quickly that he scarcely saw her heavy, swinging breasts before they were covered again. It was almost as though she was shy. "There's a chair behind you," she said, plumping the pillow and spreading out her fair hair. "For your clothes." He turned away as he took his trousers off, folding them meticulously before laying them on the chair on top of his shirt.

"Too much light?" she asked matter-of-factly. "The switch is by the door."

He walked self-consciously to the door and pushed the brass switch up. When it clicked, the harsh light from the ceiling vanished and there was only the soft pink lamp by the bed.

"That's better, isn't it?" she said encouragingly. "Come on, John."

"Michael," he said, as he wobbled on one foot to pull off his sock.

She threw back the sheet as he came to the bed. Her breasts didn't seem as large, now she was lying down. The nipples looked like giant moles though, he thought. He sat down beside her, gazing down at her white skin.

"Are we different from Chinese girls?" she asked, raising her hand to stroke his chest. "Russian men have hair there." Her hand reached up to brush his chin. "Do you have to shave? Chinese don't, do they? Not often, anyway..." Her fingers walked teasingly down his chest, down to his belly, down to his groin. He sucked in his breath. "Got a bit of hair there, though, haven't you, eh?" she smiled. He lay down beside her. She took his hand and placed it over her breast.

He heaved himself on top of her, kissing her mouth, her breasts. Soon he thrust himself into her, raising his body on his hands to gaze down at her face. She seemed unaffected. She was looking away, eyes half-closed, as though bored by the whole business now she'd got it going. Every now and then, though, she gave little sighs and moans of simulated pleasure.

When he was finished he fell on her shoulder and lay there panting and sweating, half-asleep. He heard her breathing in his ear, light and soft. The pink light from the lamp shone through his lids, and he fumbled for the switch without opening his eyes. She raised her hand to help him, but he clutched her and held her still.

"All right, all right," she murmured, and let him grope until he found the switch and turned it off. He laid his hand back on the pillow and tangled her hair in his fingers. This is what you wanted, he told himself, to have a white woman underneath you like this.

She stirred beneath him, as if she'd heard. Her skin was as slippery with sweat as his. He tugged her hair and she lay still again.

"Move over," she muttered. "I can hardly breathe."

He shifted slightly, so that he lay only half on her. She

stretched and sighed. His lips were pressed against her breast. This is what you wanted, he told himself again. How does it feel now you've got it?

It felt tired and empty.

Presently her fingers began running lightly up and down his back. They slithered up the side of his body, along his arm, touched the back of his hand. She stopped. "What happened to your finger?" she asked.

"Someone cut it off."

She sniffed disbelievingly. "What happened really?"

"If you don't believe me..." he shrugged heavily, drowsily.

He stopped the rickshaw at the side of the house and went in through the garden. The police car that was usually parked near the drive wasn't there. How easy it would be to throw a bomb now, he thought. Or kidnap someone even. The hair prickled faintly at the back of his neck and he couldn't prevent himself from glancing round at the grey shapes of the trees and bushes, while the image of that greasy quilt over his head flitted ghost-like through his mind. Then he noticed someone sitting on the old garden seat, a cigarette glowing brightly in his mouth. A spurt of alarm started through him before he realised it was Alec. Alec raised his hand languidly as he approached, shifting along the seat to make room for him.

"Hello Michael," he murmured lazily. "Where've you been? Not out on the razzle-dazzle, surely?" He was in his Volunteers uniform. He'd taken off his cap and loosened his shirt to the waist, pulling it open to get some air onto his chest, but it was useless, the air was as hot and moist as his skin. "Bloody hot night," he said. "Not a breath of wind." He leant back, blowing a long jet of smoke up towards the glistening stars, whose light seemed to come through a watery mist. "Just come off duty," he yawned. "Guarding the telephone exchange while you make whoopee." He yawned again, slapping the rifle barrel leaning against his knee.

They sat looking out over the Bund. There were several Japanese warships moored in the river off Hongkew. Further upstream, almost opposite the house, a British gunboat and an American frigate lay close together, as if huddling for safety from the Japanese. Between them and the Japanese ships, the river gleamed dully in the starlight, like tarnished silver.

"Have you got a cigarette?" Michael asked.

"Thought you didn't smoke?"

"I didn't."

Alec glanced at him quizzically as he flicked the carton with his thumb and tapped a cigarette up for Michael to take. "What have you been up to then?"

Michael shook his head, as if to say Nothing special. He lit his cigarette from the end of Alec's. "Just roaming round a bit," he said at last.

"Come off it," Alec nudged his elbow. But when Michael shook his head again, he didn't press him. He leant back instead to search for the plane whose loudly throbbing engine they could hear overhead. "I suppose it would take every bit of half an hour for the Japs to take this place if they wanted to," he mused. "And yours truly would be quite likely to cop it in the first five minutes...Oh well." He shrugged fatalistically. "What are you going to do about going to Oxford?"

Michael shook his head. He was smoking in short, quick puffs as if he wanted to burn the cigarette up as fast as he could. "The way the war's going in Europe, there may not be any Oxford left by October. Now that France has given in."

Alec chuckled. "Oxford's got a better chance of surviving than Shanghai has, if you ask me." He drummed with his fingers on the wooden stock of his rifle. "You'd have a rough time of it if the Japs took over here you know. They don't treat the Chinese all that gently. Not like the Europeans."

"I've noticed."

"Not that you're Chinese exactly, but you know what I mean..."

"I'd look like a Chink to a Jap?"

"Exactly." Alec chuckled again. "You bloody half-caste."

Michael drew on the last of the cigarette until it burnt his fingers. "That might be an advantage if you were trying to get away," he said slowly. "Looking Chinese."

Alec's eyes widened. "That's true. I'd never thought of that." He blew out several smoke rings, watching them slowly widen and disperse. "So you'll go up to Oxford after the war, then?"

"If it's still there. What about you?"

Alec shrugged. "Father keeps asking me that, but the trouble is I can't think of anything I really want to do, except enjoy myself. And that doesn't exactly sound like a career, I'm afraid...Talking of enjoying myself, though," he lowered his voice confidentially, "there's a smashing little bar girl at the St. George's. I've been thinking of buying her out and, you know, having a go. You can get them on a sort of permanent basis too—I mean you're their only one, kind of thing. But you have to set them up in a room somewhere, and that comes pretty expensive of course...Still, she's a real smasher, you ought to see her."

Michael smiled, thinking of the white Russian girl.

"I say, what on earth's that?" Alec pulled at something wedged between the bars of the seat. He lit a match. "Well I'm damned, it's that old bus. Remember how we used to fight over it? Wonder how it got there?"

They gazed at the bus by the flickering light of the match. Michael ran his finger over it thoughtfully. "I always thought buses would be different in England," he said.

"How?"

"I don't know exactly..."

"Well they *are* different. They're about ten years younger, not like these old boneshakers out here."

"No, I meant the people as well. I thought they'd all be rich. I couldn't imagine there were poor people there—poor white people. I imagined the buses would be like first class railway carriages with only rich people in them."

The match burnt down and Alec dropped it. "Actually, what I'd really like to do in life is to be a drummer in a jazz band." He stretched and yawned, then stood up shouldering his rifle. "Ah well, I suppose that's not much of a career either. Coming?"

They walked together towards the kitchen door. It was like when they were younger, Michael thought, before they went to school in England and they used to play together in the garden. "Actually I had a girl tonight," he blurted out impulsively. "A White Russian girl."

Alec stopped and glanced at him suspiciously. "What d'you mean, 'had'?"

"*Had.*"

"Go on!" Alec stared at him doubtfully, then his face slowly creased into a congratulatory grin. "Honestly? I never thought you'd got it in you, you sly devil."

"Chink the monk," Michael said with a rare smile.

"Broken your vow, eh?" Alec said, taking out his key. "What was she like?" They heard the front door bell ring inside.

"What time is it?" Denton asked, frowning.

"Ten past two." Su-mei was propped on her elbow, listening.

Again the bell sounded downstairs, a long, insistent ring. They looked questioningly at each other.

"Michael hadn't come in when we went to bed," she said.

"Nor had Alec." He got up and slipped on his dressing gown. "Probably one of them's just locked himself out." His gown brushed the mosquito coil smouldering by the bed and knocked it over as he walked past. Despite his reassuring words, he felt an anxious tremor in his legs.

"Don't open the door," Su-mei called after him in an urgent whisper. "Look through the spy-hole first."

He padded down the stairs in his bare feet, hearing Su-mei behind him. It's bound to be Alec or Michael, he told himself, and yet there was still that faint tremor in his legs. And his heart was beating faster.

The kitchen light went on as he reached the hall. Alec and Michael appeared in the doorway; behind them Ah Man, blinking the sleep out of his eyes.

"Was that you ringing the bell?" Denton demanded irritably, yet at the same time relieved.

But the bell rang again, startlingly loud, just by their heads.

"We just came in the back way," Alec said.

Denton turned back to the hall. Michael followed him. Alec's eyes lit up. He slipped out through the kitchen door again. Nobody noticed.

"Look through the spy-hole first," Su-mei whispered urgently once more.

Denton put his eye to the hole. He could make out the dark shape of a man standing looking at the door. Stealthily Denton reached for the switch and flicked on the light. For one second he was looking at a Chinese in a blue shirt, carrying a parcel of some sort, gazing at the door as if he could see straight through it into Denton's eyes. The magnifying glass in the peep-hole distorted his face, giving it a bulbous appearance, but Denton knew it

733

at once. It was Chan. The next second he was gone, dropping the parcel in the porch.

"See anything?" Alec whispered.

Denton gestured him to keep quiet. His pulse was thudding in his ears, and he felt a tightness in his chest. "It was Chan," he said slowly. "Our old driver. He dropped a parcel and ran off."

"Don't open," Su-mei warned. "It might be a bomb. What's happened to that police guard?"

"They weren't there when I came home," Michael said.

Denton heard Ah Man muttering, then Ah King's gruff, sleepy voice. "Chan, master?"

"Yes." He was still looking at the parcel that lay on the porch, so near the first step that it looked as though it might roll off. Then he began drawing the bolts. They were squeaky and stiff.

"Don't, it might be a bomb," Su-mei warned again.

But Denton knew it couldn't be a bomb, from the casual way Chan had carried it, from the way he'd dropped it, from the dull, soft thud it had made when it landed.

"Better switch the light off," Michael said.

"Don't open, call the police," Denton heard Su-mei pleading.

"Shh!" He switched off the light and waited till his eyes were used to the dark again, staring all the time through the spy-hole. The parcel lay there still, a dark shadow by the plants that stood peacefully in the porch. Nothing moved in the dark. He heard the far-off wail of a ship's siren. "What's going on?" Jenny's voice sounded sleepily from the stairs, instantly shushed by the others. He turned the key and opened the door a crack. Still nothing happened. He opened it a little wider, so that he could see the parcel clearly. "Switch on the light, someone," he muttered.

Michael pressed the switch. The porch filled with light, making the dark beyond it blacker. Denton was momentarily dazzled. Then he saw.

The parcel was loosely wrapped in brown paper, which had partly unfolded and opened. He could see something dark, like the bristles of a brush, protruding through the wrapping. Cautiously he opened the door wider, so that they could all see. "It looks like brushes or something," he said perplexedly.

"Don't touch," Su-mei said, but Ah King suddenly

734

pushed past him and bent down, pulling the brown paper away. Then she recoiled with a gasp.

They could all see now. It was Pak-kay's head. His neck was towards the door, with a clean white edge of a bone showing clearly through the mess of bloody flesh. His mouth was distorted in a fixed grimace of pain. His eyes were bulging, as if the blow that severed his neck had nearly started them out of their sockets. Little drops of sweat still stood out on his forehead. The beard he'd been so fond of fingering was untouched, jutting up towards them all, and for a second, as Denton turned away with nausea in his throat, he visualised the executioner's hand carefully moving the beard out of the way before he struck.

Ah King was muttering inarticulately, the others still staring in horror. Some echo of those executions he'd seen in the early days came back to Denton, a roaring in his ears like the exultant roar of the crowd.

Suddenly there were two shots near the bottom of the drive, one high, one deep. The night seemed to crack open.

"The police?" Michael said.

But then they heard Alec's voice calling.

"Over here! For god's sake over here!"

Michael got there first. Alec was leaning against a tree, trembling, his rifle shaking in his hand. A few yards away on the grass a man lay face up, blood welling out over his blue shirt.

"Is he dead?" Alec asked shakily. "He started it, he shot at me first."

Then Michael noticed the pistol lying in the moonlight beside the man's head. His father was there now, kneeling beside the body. Michael went closer and stared at the face. There was a scar on the side of the temple.

"Yes he's dead," his father said unsteadily. "It's Chan."

"It's the man who cut my finger off," Michael heard himself saying.

91

Denton shrugged on his overcoat and stood in front of the mirror as he buttoned it. Su-mei watched from the dining-room door. She was carrying Lily's son in her arms, patting his back. All that Denton could see of him was the scanty fuzz of black hair that barely covered the top of his head above the quilt Ah Leng had wrapped him in. Denton glanced back into the mirror, at the drooping skin under his eyes, the stern lines scored in his cheeks, the loose fold beneath his chin.

"You look at yourself these days more than a young girl would," Su-mei said mildly, but with a hint of re-proof.

"A young girl looks to see how beautiful she is," he leant closer to the glass, examining his eyes. "I'm merely watching the process of decay."

"Growing older isn't decaying."

"What is it then?"

She joined him before the mirror without answering, turning the baby round to the glass. There were little milky bubbles on his lips. His eyes, grave and yet vacant, seemed to be the same shade of brown as Pak-kay's. But the rest of his face was Lily's. The child gazed solemnly at his own reflection. Denton glanced at Su-mei. Her eyes met his, and she touched her cheek lightly with one hand. "Now you're looking for decay in me," she smiled sadly.

The baby started gurgling and flapping his arms. "Ah Leng," Su-mei called. She handed the bundle back. Ah Leng carried it into the kitchen, jogging it on her arm and cooing.

Denton turned away to the door. He'd heard the car drawing up outside. "Isn't it time we heard from Michael?" he asked.

"It's a roundabout way for letters to come." She followed him to the door. "Don't you want a hat? It'll be cold in the wind."

"The decay hasn't reached my head yet." His lips twitched into a wry self-mocking smile. He went down the steps, avoiding the spot where Pak-kay's head had lain, and got into the car.

Shanghai International Settlement Ratepayers' Annual General Meeting, November 17th 1941, the notice proclaimed outside the racecourse. The Chinese constable saluted him as he went inside. He made his way towards the grandstand, which was half-full with muffled and overcoated ratepayers, the last of the rich of Shanghai. They were sitting by nationalities now, the British and Americans in one group, with a sprinkling of Scandinavians and Chinese amongst them. A smaller group of Japanese sat apart from them, drilled into their seats as if on parade. They all seemed to be wearing the same long dark coats. Like a flock of vultures, Denton thought. Between the Japanese and the British and Americans sat the smallest group, Germans and Italians, uncomfortably wedged between the white men who were now their enemies and the Asiatic allies whom strictly they regarded as racially inferior.

As Denton climbed the steps, British and American voices called out to him, and then some hands began to clap. The clapping grew louder. Soon they were all clapping, and he had to stand still and acknowledge the applause with an awkward bow and smile. The Germans and Japanese sat still and grim. He'd become a prophet with honour at last. Pak-kay's assassination, and the bombing of the newspaper office the following day, in which Lolly Kwai had been killed, had happened just at the time when people were beginning to realise Japan couldn't be bought off. Their minds had changed, they had stiffened against the Japanese at last, and now openly sided with the Chinese. But it was all too late of course, much too late.

He saw Jacob waving his agenda paper and sat down beside him as the clapping faded. "Fame at last," Jacob said delightedly. "You could go back on the Council now."

Opposite them, on the race track itself, a platform had been put up. The members of the Municipal Council, also in national groups, sat facing the meeting. Walker, portly and complacent as ever, smiled at him genially from the platform. There was an empty chair between him and the two Japanese members, who sat upright and tense, with a worried yet courteous expression in their eyes.

Jacob gripped his arm with the old enthusiasm, al-

737

most the old strength. "I've found a girl," he whispered. "Wonderful—A Cantonese from Macau. Nineteen years old, you must see her. I'm thinking of starting another family." His eyes, which had been dull and faded for so long after Sarah's death, had recovered their old brilliance. "Eugenically it's perfectly all right. I've been studying the journals. It doesn't matter how old the father is, it's the mother's age that matters—well, look at Abraham, still begetting children when he was eighty. But no woman should have a child after she's thirty." His grip tightened under the excitement of his new theory. "Fifteen to thirty, that's the best breeding time. Fifteen to thirty."

"How long have you known this girl?" Denton asked, glancing at the platform. The Chinese members of the Council had arrived, and were formally greeting the others. Philip Wei, fatter and more self-important than ever, bowed especially to the Japanese, who both rose immediately and bowed back. "Where did you meet her?"

"I got her through an agency two weeks ago."

"You mean you bought her?"

"Certainly not!" Jacob relaxed his grip, looking offendedly away over the race course. "I paid the woman—the agency—a fee, that's all." He thrust his underlip out sulkily and lifted his agenda papers.

A heavy hand fell on Denton's shoulder, and they both looked round.

It was McEwan. "Ye didn't expect to see me here?" the doctor greeted him dourly, his cheeks flushed beneath his silver hair. "Is there room for a wee one beside ye?" He clambered over the back of the bench with surprising agility and sat down by Denton. "It's the first of these meetings I've ever attended," he announced in a haze of whisky-laden breath. "Not that I didn't qualify before, but I didn't care to come."

"Well it may be the last you'll ever attend, too." Denton said.

"Pish man, Shanghai'll go on for ever." McEwan unfolded his agenda papers and began studying them. "Or was it me ye were thinking of? Because I'm good for a few more years too. I've only come to vote against the Japanese of course. I hear your children have abandoned the fort after that wee episode with that young man, what was his name?"

"Pak-kay? Hardly a *wee* episode, I should have thought."

738

The chairman was calling the meeting to order in a weak, reedy voice. He was a Swiss, the only nationality acceptable to everyone.

"Michael's gone to Chungking," Denton murmured, "but Alec's staying. And so is Lily, for the time being at least. Jenny's leaving tonight."

"Where to?"

"The States. She got the last seat on the plane." He glanced up at the cloudless sky as if he expected to see the plane suddenly appear. The sun was slowly warming the chilled air. There had been frost in the night. "She's been offered some sort of job in a radio station in New York."

McEwan's eyes, sharp despite the filmy layer of moisture that seemed to lie over them, flickered impatiently, as if to brush aside such a feeble reason for leaving. He turned to the platform with an expression of aggressive intentness.

Denton looked down at his agenda paper. Hayashi's motion was first, and Denton smiled wrily as he read it. *Proposal to meet the Council's deficit by raising a loan and to instruct the Council to devise a different system of tax revenue.* Could anything have been drier? Yet that was what divided them by nation and politics. Because it was proposed by a Japanese, the Japanese would all vote for it, and because the Japanese would all vote for it, the British and Americans would all vote against it. And since the British and Americans were the majority of the ratepayers, the motion would be defeated. What a farce. They'd come to defeat the Japanese symbolically, because they couldn't in reality. What an absurd gesture, he thought. And yet he'd come too, to take part in it. So had McEwan and Jacob. While Hayashi read his speech in halting English, nervously adjusting his glasses after every sentence, Denton thought of another symbolic gesture, the gesture that hundreds of Chinese had made at Pak-kay's funeral. They'd paraded silently behind the hearse, all the way to the cemetery, without flags or placards, but simply as if they were relatives, so that the Japanese couldn't label it an anti-Japanese demonstration. Lily had walked first among the mourners, ahead of the family; and then the students had suddenly appeared, quiet and orderly, to follow them along the street. As soon as the funeral was over, they'd vanished back into the alleys and lanes. He could hear that slow, silent shuffling of their feet even now. Perhaps there was something to gestures after all. There'd been something to *that* one anyway. People had stopped in the street to watch. The police had held up the traffic. Everyone had known what it meant.

That was six months ago now, almost to the day. The paper had stopped publishing—nobody could be found to take on Pak-kay's job—so the Japanese, or Pock-mark Chen, had succeeded in that. But Pak-kay had become a martyr. His story had been in all the papers of free China. Perhaps in the long run he would be the winner after all. Was that what he'd intended all the time?

Hayashi finished speaking. The Japanese broke into loud, disciplined applause. One of the British councillors rose to reply. Denton half-listened. What would happen if the Japanese marched in? Lily would leave. She had "friends," she said. But what about the rest of them? What about the child?

Jacob leaned towards him and whispered loudly, "I met Mary-Ellen the other day. She's still with that Russian poet. Business is terrible, she said."

"Yes, I know."

Jacob looked at him inquiringly.

"She keeps asking me for loans. Or what she calls loans. I suppose there aren't many customers for Chinese antiques now. Not that she ever seemed to find many customers before..."

Voices rose in agreement and hands clapped all round them as the councillor finished. Hearty voices, British and American, rich and well-fed still. Did they believe they'd be there next year and the year after? Well, that was how Shanghai had survived in the past, by such outrageous confidence.

The chairman put the motion. Although the Germans and Italians voted, sheepishly, with the Japanese, the others were stronger. There had never been any doubt.

"The motion is lost," the chairman declared in his weak voice, examining the agenda paper for the next item. While he did so, Hayashi appeared again, walking from the Japanese group towards the platform. He climbed the steps and confronted the councillor who'd spoken against his motion. Denton saw Hayashi's lips moving. The councillor shook his head impatiently and turned away. Hayashi reached into the pocket of his long, floppy overcoat, pulled out a pistol and fired twice. The councillor staggered back but didn't fall, looking down at his arm in amazement. Hayashi stood still, a wisp of smoke trailing from the gun in his hand. Everyone was stunned for a moment, as if it were only a play and the actors had frozen, forgetting their lines. Then someone behind Denton shouted "You Jap bastards!" and, turning round, Denton saw a heavily-built, bald Englishman stalk into the Japanese seats and start flailing with his fists. For a moment the Japanese, even those who were hit, stared at him as if he were a madman, then several of them started hitting back. Britons and Americans ran to help him, yelling and shouting. Soon nearly everyone was fighting in the stands while the men on the platform, even Hayashi, watched in stunned surprise.

"Gentlemen, please!" the chairman appealed feebly in one of the sudden lulls in all the shouting while the inept punching and wrestling went on like a schoolboys' scrap. Meanwhile a police inspector appeared and took Hayashi by the arm, leading him unresistingly away.

A few people in the stands sat in their places gazing straight ahead, their detached, supercilious expressions declaring they'd have nothing to do with such brawling. But they were gradually drawn in as men from the other side ran up and attacked them. Denton watched an elderly Japanese with a fine, immobile face who sat with folded arms, an indifferent smile on his face, while all around him people were striking out wildly. Then a European punched him in the back, and with a sudden howl, as if he'd only been waiting for the chance, the Japanese jumped up and struck back. Then Jacob jumped up too. Someone had called out "Jewish swine!" from an ungainly scrum of Britons and Germans in the aisle nearby. "Jacob, don't be an idiot!" Denton called out, but Jacob was already limping round the mêlée, cuffing and punching. Someone grabbed him from behind, threw him down and started kicking him. With a sudden shout, which was as much embarrassed as angry, Denton went to his rescue. But McEwan was already there, pulling the man off. Then a Japanese slapped Denton's face and suddenly real anger spurted up in him. Denton caught him by the neck and got his hands round his throat. He heard himself screaming at the man, digging his fingers into his flesh as he tried to throttle him, while the man clawed at his arms and tried to kick him in the groin. All round him the taunting tribal yells went up amongst all the grunting and shouting, until suddenly, at the sound of several police whistles, the two sides gradually drew apart, as if at the end of a match, glaring at each other and panting. Slowly, as the police approached, they returned to their seats, muttering threats and challenges.

"My rib's broken," Jacob moaned, clutching his side.

McEwan examined him cursorily, pushing his hands under Jacob's jacket. "Only a bruise or two, I should think," he said, breathing heavily. "I'll look at you properly afterwards, but ye'll have to pay."

The chairman, in a high, wavering voice, declared the meeting adjourned.

As the stand emptied, the two sides leaving by different gates, Walker strolled across to Denton. "I should say we were getting the better of them, wouldn't you?" he smiled proudly, like a middle-aged schoolboy. "I must say you were right about the Japs. Force is the only language they understand." He smacked his fist into his palm.

"Pity we haven't got any then, isn't it?" Denton said. "It'll make communication difficult."

When he reached home, Denton saw Jenny's suitcases waiting by the door.

"The plane's leaving early," she said unsteadily. "The Japs are closing the airport tonight. No more foreign planes. I was afraid you wouldn't be back in time to say goodbye."

Her face was as pale and tearful as when she left to go go to school in England.

In the evening, when Alec should have been on duty with the Volunteers, he came back early, throwing his cap on the sideboard. Denton and Su-mei looked up from their dinner.

"We've been stood down," Alec said flatly, pulling out a chair. "Ah Man, can you bring a plate please for me?" he called out in Chinese.

"What do you mean, stood down," Su-mei asked laying down her chopsticks.

He stretched his legs out under the table. "Finished. Packed up. Sent home. Apparently the Japs object to us. They say it's provocative or something. Adjutant says we couldn't fight them anyway." He started drawing on the

742

tablecloth with the chopsticks Ah Man had brought him. "So no heroic resistance, no death or glory...Well, I can spend more time in the nightclubs, there's always that consolation."

Shooting Chan had left no mark on him, after the first few days. "It was him or me," he'd say with a shrug. In the nightclubs he'd become a hero. The bar-girl he liked treated him with awe.

Denton glanced across at Su-mei, and found her eyes looking evenly at him. "Looks as though it won't be long now, if they really mean to walk in. We'd better do something about Lily and the child," he said. It was strange to be talking about it so definitely. Talking like that seemed to make it more certain the worst would happen, to hasten the day. When Michael left, it had only been to travel. He was going to come back, unless something happened.

"Lily will look after her herself," Su-mei said calmly.

"You should leave too. They'll treat us more kindly than you."

She shook her head. "After you poured all that money into the *Shanghai Star*?" she asked ironically. "If anyone should get away, it's you."

"But I don't want to," he said, without really knowing why.

92

Lily leant back against the seat and raised her face to the sky, closing her eyes. The December sun shone warm and comforting through the veined veil of her lids. Pak-kay was gurgling beside her on the grass, trying to climb up the wooden legs of the seat. She'd laid her physiology book down on her lap, meaning to memorise what she'd just read, but her mind slipped away into emptiness. She felt her hair stirring faintly in the breeze from the river and heard Pak-kay panting as he pulled himself triumphantly upright. Her lips lost their stern expression and her brow cleared. To Cheong, approaching with his rake over his shoulder, she looked quite young again. He stood looking at them both a moment, then coughed.

She heard him through the drifts of sleep that were piling over her, and opened her eyes.

"There's a man come," he said apologetically. "He's got a message for you, he says." He nodded down the garden. A man in a coolie's shirt and trousers, with rope sandals on his feet, stood looking at her patiently.

"A message? All right."

Cheong signalled and the man approached, waiting for Cheong to leave before he spoke. "I've come from Wong," he said, fumbling with a piece of paper that he took out of his pocket. "They didn't say anything about a kid, though." He held the letter out to her deferentially, with both hands. They were real coolie's hands, she noticed, rough-skinned and dark.

She took the paper. As she unfolded it, the book slid off her lap. The man stooped quickly to pick it up. "Put it on the seat," she said carelessly; then, ashamed of her authoritative tone, "Thanks, comrade," she added self-consciously. *Come and drink tea at the usual place*, the characters said, *Between nine and nine-thirty tonight*.

The coolie watched her reading, glancing from the characters to her face, then down to the characters again. "They didn't say anything about a kid," he said again.

"It's all right." She looked down at Pak-kay, who was sitting on the grass now, sucking his thumb and regarding the man intently. "It's all right, I've made arrangements." She felt her heart thudding gently against the wall of her chest. Not faster, but louder, stronger.

"I've got to take the paper back," the man said. "Can you remember what it says?"

"Yes, yes, it's all right."

"So will you sign to say you've read it?"

She scribbled her name with the pencil. Not her real name, but the name she was known by. He bowed deferentially again as she offered the paper back politely with both hands. All this formality, she thought. When will we get rid of it?

"Well that's all then." He stepped back, glancing once more at the baby as he slipped the paper back into his pocket. "I'll be off, all right?"

"Thank you, comrade," she said again, less self-consciously this time.

He cleared his throat hesitantly as he left as if he was afraid she might be annoyed by the sound. She watched him pass Cheong, pause at the drive and look each way before walking off. And that's all there is to it, she thought. Will I ever see Pak-kay again?

Pak-kay was reaching for the little toy bus wedged between the bars of the seat. She watched his soft, pale fingers curling round it and tugging. He gave a little whimper of vexation when it wouldn't move and looked pleadingly up at her. She watched him for some seconds, while the thought went slowly deeper and deeper into her mind. Will I ever see Pak-kay again? She felt sure she'd be killed somewhere, somehow, before the war was over. She felt she was looking at him from far away already, as if through the wrong end of a telescope.

At last, "Come on, then," she said, and gathered him up. He squirmed and cried, kicking his legs and waving his arms in anger at having to leave the little bus. His face grew red with fury and tears filled his eyes, flooding the lids till they ran over. "I'll find you something else," she promised, bending to pick up her book. "I'll find you something else inside."

His fists beat her shoulder helplessly as she carried him down the garden. Cheong looked up from his raking, with a half-amused, half-troubled light in his eyes.

"She won't come back," Su-mei said definitely. "I know she won't."

They stood looking down at the sleeping child. He lay flat on his back, his head on one side, pouting slightly in his sleep. His tiny curled fist, with pink, shell-like nails, gripped the edge of the blanket.

"Of course she'll come back," Denton murmured, without conviction. He led the way out of the room and waited till she'd gently closed the door before he spoke again. "But it means they must know the Japs are planning something. Let's send Pak-kay off tomorrow—I wish she hadn't given him that name. But I suppose it was inevitable."

"I'll tell Ah Leng to get ready," she nodded. "Don't you wish we'd all got away now?"

"I don't know." He turned away towards the study. "Too late to bother now, anyway."

She watched him all the way up the stairs. He shut the door, switched on the electric heater, and went to the window. The lights of the sole British gunboat, the *Petrel*, shone forlornly in the dark, casting faint reflections on the black, fast-moving waters of the river. A stiff wind was blowing, whipping up little waves. The waves looked as though they were racing down to escape into the sea. He imagined the *Petrel* tugging at its anchor, anxious to escape too. Switching on the desk lamp, he fingered through his records in the teak cabinet he'd had made for them by that opium-smoking carpenter, he couldn't recall how many years ago. He found the record he was looking for—Selections from the Messiah. Laying it carefully over the spindle, he fixed a new needle and switched the gramophone on. He sat down at the desk to listen, turning off the lamp and gazing out of the window at the night again. The stars glittered icily over Pootung. He thought how cold it must be up in space, how cold and lonely. Where would Lily be by now?

Lily waited for the Japanese patrol to pass, pressing back against the side of the house. There were three of them, talking quietly, one of them occasionally humming fragments of some tune. When they were level with her, they stopped and one of them giggled. She held her breath, her eyes straining at the darkness. Her heart thumped softly. They seemed to be quiet for several seconds, then she heard a matchbox rattle, the scrape and flare of a match. The voices started chatting quietly again and they moved on. She saw the bright red glow of a cigarette.

Her nerves let go and she slowly breathed out. Peering round the corner, she saw that the alley was empty now. She measured the distance to the godown. The door would be unbarred. She waited another second then ran across. The door swung open. She stepped inside and closed it quietly, forcing herself to move slowly and carefully. The hinges were silent, they must have been oiled. She eased the bar across inch by inch and waited, breathing quickly. There was no light at all. The whole place smelt of moist sacking. There would be rats there, she told herself. She mustn't jump if she heard a little rustling noise.

As her eyes grew used to the dark, she saw a shadow move from the wall a few feet away. She tensed. It was Wong. He moved quickly to her side and gripped her arm, laying his finger on her lips. "Japs next door," he whispered in her ear. "Follow me." His breath was warm and smelt of garlic. She turned her head away instinctively, but nodded at the same time.

Su-mei came in and waited by the door for the record to finish. "Would you like a pipe of opium?"

"Opium?" They hadn't smoked since before Pak-kay was killed. "Any special reason?" he smiled.

"Well, it's nearly Christmas, and we may not get another chance for..."

"For ever," he said. He glanced out at the *Petrel* and imagined the sailors having Christmas dinner with rum in three days' time. It was so vivid, his image; he could see the paper chains, the cotton wool blobs of snow glued to the mirror, the commander going round filling the sailors' mugs with rum. Did they really do things like that? Even in wartime? He didn't know. In all those years he'd lived there on the Bund watching the ships come and go, he'd never been on a warship. "What a lot of things we miss in life," he murmured, turning back to Su-mei. "All right, let's have a pipe, shall we?"

"I'll get it ready," she said.

Su-mei was kneading the pellets over the lamp when he came down to the bedroom. She had undressed and loosened her hair. It fell forward round her cheeks as she knelt in her nightdress, her eyes gleaming in the flame.

He undressed too and put on his dressing gown.

"It's ready," she said.

He lay down facing her, and she handed him the pipe. The warm, rich, sweet smell permeated the room. He put the stem between his lips and inhaled.

After the second pipe, the old serenity began to take hold of him, the old drifting contemplation. He gazed at the black outlines of the branches outside the window against the paleness of the sky, and it seemed as if he could see each little twig separately, vivid and sharp. It seemed as if he could see each star close to, as if his head were up there in the spaces between them. He seemed to be traveling amongst them, or they rushing past him, at tremendous speed, as though he were caught up in the tail of a comet. And yet they were still, fixed beyond the window, and never changed.

He looked at Su-mei. She was lying with her head on her arm, which itself lay crooked on her hard pillow. He gazed at the white of her arm disappearing into her loose sleeve, at her throat rising from the opening of her nightdress. He reached out to touch her arm, and it was a surprise to see how near she was. "Why did you turn away from me all those years ago?" he heard himself ask, not sadly or with rancour, but as if it was a question about some distant age.

She seemed to have been waiting for his question. Perhaps she'd even meant him to ask it. "Because I hated you," she said, smiling at the past. "I hated you because of what happened to Michael. I blamed you for it. And then..." she hesitated, closing her eyes.

"Then what?" he asked drowsily.

"Then, you never knew, but I went to Pock-mark Chen as well. Wei told me it was what he was waiting for, after you paid the money. When nothing happened."

"Pock-mark Chen?" he repeated slowly. How brilliant the stars were, rushing past his eyes, how sharp and still the little twigs on the branches.

"It wasn't money he wanted from me."

He turned to look at her again. Perhaps this was all a dream, a trance. Her lids were raised and he was looking straight into the dark circles of her pupils, looking through them, he felt, into her mind. No it was really happening.

"And I hated you for that too. Because you couldn't tell. You never even suspected..."

He lay gazing into or through her eyes for some time, he'd no idea how long. Whatever had happened, it had all passed now. For some reason the fact that Wei had known all along lodged in his mind, though, as if that was the important thing.

"Do you know why he's called Pock-mark although his face is clear? The marks are on his body."

For a long time Denton seemed to see Pock-mark Chen's body in front of his eyes, vast and flabby, pitted all over with smallpox scars. "Why are you telling me now?" he asked at last.

"There may not be another chance." She let her eyes close. "He promised he wouldn't do anything to any of us again, though. And he kept his word. They do keep their word, the triads."

"He had Pak-kay's head chopped off."

"He wasn't one of us. Besides, that was the Japanese as much as him."

* * *

748

Denton didn't know if he'd been dreaming or not. It was still dark when he woke up, his hand was still on her arm, and she was still asleep. Her hair lay half over her cheek. He lifted it away and kissed her. Her eyes opened and she turned her mouth to his.

"So that's why you wanted me to race against him?" he murmured later.

"It's all past," she whispered drowsily. "And he kept his word."

93

At first he thought it was thunder. But then immediately after the crash that awakened him, there came the repeated roar of shell-fire and the yammer of machine guns.

Su-mei had sat bolt-upright, her startled eyes still misted with sleep. "It's started," she said. The room was grey with the comfortless light of dawn.

"Why does everything bad that happens to us start when we're asleep?" he complained, trying to make a joke of it. But fear went on fingering him inside.

They slipped out of bed and went to the window. Between the branches they saw orange and yellow flashes from the *Petrel*'s guns. Fiery red tracer bullets streamed away towards the hull of a Japanese destroyer two or three hundred yards away. It was the destroyer's heavy guns that made the thundering roar as they replied. A great spout of water went up by the *Petrel*'s bows, falling in a misty spray all over her. The *Petrel*'s guns went on firing madly.

"It's hopeless," Denton muttered. He thought of the coloured paper chains and the cotton wool snowflakes he'd imagined last night. He saw the mirror splintering, the snowflakes drifting off, the paper chains broken and scattered amongst the wreckage.

The baby began wailing next door. Su-mei slipped on her nightdress and went out. At the same moment there was a flash of light amidships on the *Petrel*, leaping up into the sky like a reverse stroke of lightning. The sound of the explosion followed at once, making the air shudder. For an instant he thought the ship must have survived, it looked unchanged. But its guns were suddenly all silent.

Then he saw its back was broken. Flames and smoke were shooting along the decks and between a crack amidships that had opened vertically down the hull. He saw a body jump or fall into the water. In only a few seconds the ship was sinking, the bows and stern pointing up despairingly into the sky like drowning hands as the water poured in through the crack and dragged it down. The Japanese had stopped firing.

The door opened and he turned. It was Alec in his pyjamas. Alec stared at his father's naked body, then glanced swiftly away. "What on earth's happened?" he asked.

"It's started." Denton reached for his dressing gown. "They've just sunk the *Petrel*. They must be taking over." He saw Alec's eyes switch from the opium pipe on the floor to the window and the sinking *Petrel*. He saw his nose wrinkle at the stale sweet greasy smell of the opium. He tied the cord of his gown and knelt down silently to gather the pipe and lamp together. "Could you go and see what the servants are up to?" he said in a voice that he was struggling to make calm. "We might as well have breakfast before they come."

He waited till Alec had gone, then he put the opium things back in the bottom drawer of the wardrobe.

Su-mei came in as he was pushing the drawer shut. "Ah Leng's leaving with the baby at once," she said. "I've told the others to go too. It won't do them any good to be here when the Japs come."

He made a wry face. "I've just asked Alec to get them to make some breakfast! Is nothing sacred?" He tried to smile, but found that he was only twitching his lips.

"I'll put some coffee on," she said, coming and leaning against him. "Don't you want to see Pak-kay off first, though?"

He held her to him. It was he that was trembling, not she. He thought of Japanese soldiers finding her in her nightdress, throwing her on the bed..."We'd better get dressed," he said. He wished they'd all got out like Jenny and Michael. He wished it more than anything in the world now.

She rested against him a second longer.

"It doesn't matter now, what happened before," he said. "When Michael was kidnapped."

Her head nodded faintly, then she moved away. "We'd better hurry," she said calmly.

But in fact they had hours to wait.

"Soldiers," Su-mei said from the window.

Alec and Denton went to look. The Japanese were marching along the Bund in full battle dress. The long bayonets fixed to their rifles glinted in the sun above their round, grey-green helmets. An officer stalked along at the head of the column. He was wearing a Samurai sword, which he had to hold up with his hand, to prevent the scabbard dragging along the ground. He looked immensely, arrogantly, proud; but holding the scabbard had upset his rhythm, and his legs were flinging up out of step with the troops following him. It made him after all seen absurd and ridiculous.

"Poor old bandy-legs," Alec scoffed. "The only one in step. Well, I suppose we'll be interned now," he added wistfully. He wished now he'd made that arrangement with the girl at the St. George's. He could have had some fun before this happened. That's my trouble, he thought resignedly. I never get down to things like Michael does. It seemed to him in a moment of rueful self-illumination that he'd still never get down to things even when the war was over. He went back to his coffee.

The soldiers passed. For several hours the three of them sat quietly on the veranda, watching the river. There had been frost in the night, but now the sun warmed them. Denton watched the frost thawing on the grass as the sun rose higher. A Japanese naval launch was moored by the wreck of the *Petrel*. The *Petrel*'s mast, miraculously unbroken, slanted out a few feet above the running water, like a cross leaning over a grave. Like the cross over Jonathan's grave.

Denton listened to the wireless, turning from one station to another. "They've attacked the American fleet at Pearl Harbor," he told them when he came back to the veranda. "And a lot of other places as well."

"Oh well, they won't last long then, will they?" Alec said. "Perhaps they won't even bother to intern us, they must have their hands full with so many other things."

Denton didn't answer. He went to the garage and got the watering-can out. The road outside was empty and silent. Everyone must be waiting. There hadn't even been any Japanese soldiers since that first column. He filled the can and watered the plants on the porch. The poinsettias were blooming, the petals deep crimson. The only sound was of the water hissing into the earth. He looked at the spot where Pak-kay's head had lain. Then he looked out along the deserted drive to the deserted road. The absence, the silence was like the pause before a leopard springs, he thought. He took the watering-can back, locked the garage, and went through the house, bolting all the shutters room by room. Alec glanced at him inquiringly, lighting a cigarette.

"I don't want people to get in if we have to leave the place," Denton said. And the moment he said it, he realised how futile his precautions would be. If they wanted to get in, all they had to do was force one shutter. Nothing could be simpler. But he went on pulling them shut and bolting them just the same.

Then they heard a car drawing up outside. Alec could tell it was Japanese by the sound of the engine. The wheels scrunched the gravel. The doors slammed, footsteps sounded in the porch.

"I'll go," Denton said when the bell rang. There seemed to be a void in his stomach. Three Japanese in dark suits and hats stood at the door.

"Kempetai," one of them said. "Police." They pushed him aside and shut the door as if they thought he might try to escape. "Denton?" the same man asked.

"Yes?"

He took a photograph out of his breast pocket and compared Denton's face with it suspiciously. The other two looked in over his shoulder.

Su-mei and Alec came out of the dining-room.

"Chinese go," the one with the photograph said, pointing at Su-mei. "English intern."

"What?" Alec asked.

They ignored him. Taking Denton with them, they went from room to room, of the house, pasting paper strips with some official seal on them across the windows and doors. In the study, they talked undecidedly amongst themselves a minute, then put the seals on the drawers of his desk and filing cabinet as well. I suppose that means they're honest, Denton thought. Honest and stupid. They told Denton and Alec to take one suitcase of clothes each with them and watched them pack.

Su-mei had closed the shutters in the living room. They sealed them as well. "Chinese go," the man with the photograph said again.

"Where are you taking them?" she asked, eyes lowered submissively.

"Intern! Intern!" the man said impatiently. He gestured them out of the house and sealed the front door too.

Outside on the Bund, a long, straggling column of foreign devils were walking along, escorted by armed Japanese soldiers. Each person carried a suitcase. The same policeman tapped Alec's shoulder and pointed to the column. "Go," he said. "Intern."

"What about him?" Alec nodded at his father.

The policeman slapped his face.

"Go on," Denton said. "I expect they're going to question me first."

They opened the car door and Denton got in. They sat one on each side of him. It's like a gangster film, he thought. Alec had already joined the column when the car swung out of the drive. Looking back, Denton glimpsed Su-mei standing by the porch, watching the car. I didn't even say goodbye, he realised suddenly. And then they were in the road.

The column of foreign devils straggled along for several hundred yards. There was something strange about them, and at first Denton couldn't think what it was. Then he knew. He'd never seen foreign devils carrying their own luggage in Shanghai before. No wonder the few Chinese, standing timidly amongst the trees in the Public Garden, gaped. The balloon has burst, he thought, the magic balloon. He watched the trudging, dejected procession numbly, wondering at how few of their faces he recognized. Near Garden Bridge, he saw a bald, burly Englishman kneeling to fasten his suitcase. A soldier shouted at him, gesturing him to move on. The man shook his head indignantly, pointing to his case. The soldier kicked him, sending him sprawling. The man scrambled up, gathering his case in both hands, and rejoined the column, holding it clumsily in front of him. His face had turned pale, and he was blinking back tears of shock and humiliation. It was the Englishman who'd started the fighting at the Ratepayers' Meeting. The balloon has burst, Denton kept thinking, the magic balloon has burst.

The car passed over the bridge into Hongkew. Almost the last person he saw in the procession was Mary-Ellen. She was carrying a bulging basket case, her hips moving stiffly under a shapeless grey dress. She was by herself.

The car drove on through Little Tokyo. Paper Japanese flags hung in nearly every shop window. The Japanese on the streets looked excited and happy, as if they were going to a party. The car stopped outside a building which still had its English name engraved in the stone lintel. *Bridge House Apartments 1929.* A uniformed Japanese policeman stood outside.

"Out," the one who spoke English said. "Interrogation."

94

Ah Leng pushed the last grains of rice into the baby's mouth and spread the carrying sling out on the grass while he munched it. She sat him in it, hoisted him onto her back and bent forward, balancing him while she tied the tapes. Straightening up with a sigh, she jogged him into place. His legs straddled her waist and his head lay heavy against her shoulder.

"All right, then," she murmured. "Not far now." She started walking again, leaning forward slightly against the weight of the child, scanning the empty fields ahead. There was a scraggy line of trees on the horizon, like a dark fringe laid on the cold, fading blue of the sky. Once they reached there, it could only be another couple of hours to the village. She glanced around at the dull red globe of the sun sinking in the west behind a dusty veil of cloud. It would be well after dark when they got there. Pak-kay had begun to suck his thumb. She could hear the soft, moist cheeping sound behind her. The fields on either side of the rutted mud road were unploughed, unplanted. It had been like that all the way. There was no one left to work them. She trudged on doggedly. Already the air was getting cold.

It was long after nightfall when she reached the village. There was only one light showing, a lamp on the old wooden bridge that led over the stream into the Tang family's fields. She saw the outline of a Japanese soldier, momentarily moving against the yellowish flare of the lamp. Japanese voices talked and laughed from the little temple that stood beside the bridge, marking the boundary of the Tang's fields. She hesitated, then went on uneasily.

The soldier was a young fellow with a faint moustache. He glanced at her with amusement as she bowed and showed her pass. "What have you got there, granny?" he called out in Chinese. "Smuggling weapons for the bandits?"

"My nephew, sir," she answered respectfully, bowing again. She didn't know whether he was going to turn nasty or not. "Only a little child."

The soldier stepped forward and lifted the blanket covering Pak-kay's head. She stood still, gazing straight ahead like some dumb animal waiting patiently for the command to go.

The Japanese clicked his tongue and patted the baby's cheek. "Sleepy, eh?" he said quietly.

Ah Leng allowed her eyes to glance briefly at him. He was smiling at the child. "You speak such good Chinese, sir," she murmured deferentially.

"Oh, I was born in Shanghai," he answered, folding the blanket round Pak-kay's head again. "Went back to join the army in thirty-six." He nodded her on and strolled back to the parapet of the bridge, stretching and yawning.

The dogs started barking as she made her way over the frozen ground. At least they were working the fields here, she noticed, growing things. There'd be something to eat. She pushed open the door to her brother's stone hut. "It's me," she whispered as the dog jumped growling. She heard people stirring on the floor round the ashes of the fire, and saw the dim shapes move.

They put another piece of wood on the fire and poked amongst the embers till at last it caught.

"What are you going to do with him?" her brother asked, frowning at the baby as she told her story. "Suppose the Japanese find out who he is?" He glanced expressively at the door as if he expected the soldiers to rush in at any moment.

"He looks Chinese and he's got a Chinese name," she said, placing the child down on the mat by the fire. His eyes opened briefly in his sleep, then closed again when

755

he saw her face bending over him. "How could they find out?"

"Doesn't look Chinese to me." He rubbed the grey stubble on his chin, which glinted like metal splinters in the firelight. "And how can we feed him, anyway?"

But then Ah Leng's nine-year-old grandniece picked Pak-kay up and carried him round the smoky room, jigging him in her arms till his eyes opened dazedly, and he gazed round in apprehension, searching for Ah Leng again. Just as his face began to crumple and he heaved in his breath to cry, Ah Leng took him from the girl. Pak-kay gave a snuffling whimper and closed his eyes once more.

Somehow the girl's action seemed to have settled the matter, as if she'd performed some adoption ritual. Ah Leng's brother was silent.

"After the war they'll give us a lot of money," Ah Leng said, to clinch it. "And I've got silver here too, sewn in the blanket."

"After the war!" her brother muttered scornfully. But his eyes brightened. He felt along the blanket hem with his calloused, grimy fingers till he found the little bumps where the silver coins were hidden.

I must make my mind blank, Denton thought, I mustn't think. The guard prodded him along with his club, round the corner and down some stairs. It seemed strange that they hadn't made him leave his suitcase somewhere, that he'd had to carry it to the office where they'd questioned him, and now he was carrying it again, he didn't know where. But he mustn't think, he must make his mind blank.

They'd questioned him in broken English first, then, when they realised he could speak it, in fluent Chinese.

"Did you write this insult to the Emperor of Japan?"

"I wrote nothing. I was only the proprietor of the paper."

"Did you authorise it to be written?"

"I did not interfere with the editor."

"But you approved what he wrote?"

"I agreed that Japan was..." he hesitated, "was acting mistakenly in China. I didn't always approve of the way the editor's views were expressed."

"Did you know the editor was a member of the communist party?"

"I never asked."

"Did you *know*?"

"I thought he was sympathetic. I didn't know whether he was a member." Well that's my first downright lie, he thought, watching them write his answer down. Will they be able to catch me?

They wrote everything laboriously down, their questions and his answers. When he thought they'd finished, they began asking exactly the same questions all over again, checking his answers against their notes. It took hours.

"At least they haven't beaten me yet," he thought with relief—with gratitude, even. Perhaps they wouldn't be so bad.

The guard muttered something as they came to a metal door in the wall. "In here," he said in a strangely accented Chinese that Denton could hardly understand. He shoved Denton in and slammed the door.

The cell was crowded. People were so close pressed that he couldn't move or turn without bumping into someone. They glanced at him with dull abstracted eyes, as if, apart from their fears for themselves, they had no further interest in the world. Some were standing, others sitting on suitcases or cardboard boxes tied with string, or cloth-wrapped bundles. There was a barred window high up in the corner, through which a cold draught of air was blowing. The cell seemed about fifteen feet square. Denton thought there must be fifty prisoners there.

He leant back against the door, looking round at the silent faces, which had now turned away. They were all men. They all seemed to be Chinese. But then, in the far corner, he saw a grey-haired European. It was Everett. Denton didn't recognized him without his police uniform, until Everett twitched his brows at him in a ruefully jocular greeting and beckoned him over. Denton edged his way towards him. People pressed back to let him pass, then filled up the space behind him. How would they all manage to lie down if they had to sleep there? The acrid smell of urine caught his nose as he nudged his way between two silent, lethargic men who were gazing blankly past him. He saw a couple of buckets against the wall, someone urinating into one of them while another waited his turn just behind.

"I suppose you're here because of that paper you ran?" Everett muttered.

"Yes. What about you?"

Everett shrugged. "I've been running the political department for the past couple of years."

Denton squeezed back against the wall beside Everett, put his case down and sat on it. Everett too leant back against the wall, letting himself slowly subside till he was squatting on his own case, a thick brown leather one. He rubbed his eyes with the heel of his thumb. "Wonder how long they're going to keep us here?" Glancing up at the abstracted faces round them, he leant close to Denton's ear. "Wouldn't care to be in some of these chaps' shoes," he whispered. "I know their records." He turned the corners of his mouth down and made a slitting motion with the flat of his hand across his throat. "Commies," he muttered. "Like your late son-in-law." His eyes flickered uncertainly a moment, as if he'd just realised he might have been tactless to mention Pak-kay, but then he went on reassuringly, "We knew you weren't a commie of course. I'll tell them that if it's any help."

Denton nodded vaguely. He wondered what Everett would say about the Chinese who were commies, if the Japs asked him about them. But suddenly he was too tired to take the thought up. A heavy weariness kept dragging his lids down. No matter how often he blinked them open, the weight returned. All he wanted to do was sleep. It was late afternoon now. They'd been questioning him all day and he'd had nothing to eat or drink. His lids closed once more and he felt himself drifting off, but Everett's voice woke him almost at once.

"Try to keep away from the rest of them as much as you can," he advised. "Lice, typhus. It's always been the problem in the prisons out here. Not that you can keep much of a distance, but still . . ."

They both looked up as the grill in the door was scraped open and the guard's face peered through. "Tsang!" he shouted in that distorted accent.

A stooping, middle-aged Chinese who'd been sitting on the floor, rose uncertainly, eyebrows questioningly raised towards the grill.

"Yes, you! Tsang!" the guard bawled.

The little Chinese shuffled obediently forward, careful not to tread on people's cases or feet, yet at the same time giving an impression of obsequious haste. The door opened, he stepped out with a respectful, timid bow, then the door clanged shut again and the plate scraped back over the grill.

"Commie," Everett whispered with a knowing, doleful look. "The guard's Korean. They're a nasty lot, too."

It hardly seemed half an hour before the door was opened again. As every head anxiously turned, the little Chinese was shoved inside. His face was bleeding and lumpy. He collapsed at once onto the floor like a half-filled sack of rice. The men nearby shrank away, as if he were contaminated, glancing down at him almost with disgust.

"They'll be watching to see who his friends are," Everett murmured out of the side of his mouth. "We used to do the same."

"Mr. Chen is too busy to see you today," the secretary's voice said coolly. "He says will you please write to him and he will see what can be done about it."

Su-mei gazed at the telephone dial as she listened, at the silvery ring with its little finger holes, and the shiny black bakelite beneath it. "Could I have an appointment next week, perhaps?" she pleaded.

"I'm afraid Mr. Chen has too many engagements next week." There was a little conclusive click in Su-mei's ear. She put the receiver down slowly, still gazing at the silvery ring.

I must not think about it, he kept telling himself all through the night. He counted and recounted the prisoners. There were thirty-two. He counted the cracks in the wall, the number of coughs in one minute, the number of times he heard someone whispering. As it turned out, there *was* just room for everyone to lie down, although some did not. He lay down himself, wedged between Everett on one side and a Chinese on the other, and pillowed his head on his suitcase. Remembering Everett's warning about lice, he shrunk away from the Chinese. Everett had made sure he had the wall on his other side. The draught from the window became a freezing blade cutting into him, and, however tired he was, he was too cold to sleep. He wished he'd packed another pullover. Occasionally he dozed.

"The worst thing about this is having to answer calls of nature in public." Everett grumbled as he stepped over a supine body back to his place beside Denton. "Those buckets need emptying, too."

A few minutes later, the little Chinese who'd been beaten began moaning quietly. Not ordinary moans of pain, but animal-like sounds, reminding Denton of the repeated bellowing of cattle waiting to be slaughtered. There was a space of two or three bodies round the man. No one had wanted to lie down near him—they preferred to sit against the wall all night, or even stand. Now the man's body began to twitch in the space, arms and legs jerking in spasmodic little convulsions while the hoarse, wordless groans sounded monotonously from his mouth, as though they'd been dragged up from deep inside his chest. Heads lifted and turned to watch the helpless dance his body was making, but still nobody tried to help. Denton stared at the man with a dull sense of shame. He knew he too wouldn't go near him.

The noise had been going on for ten or fifteen minutes when the plate was drawn back over the grill and a narrow cone of torchlight played over the close-packed bodies in the cell. Raised heads subsided and eyes closed as if they'd been sleeping all through the man's agony. Soon the beam found the man and stayed on his rigid, open mouth and staring eyes. Then the beam was cut off, and the plate slid over the grill again. After the time the moaning grew weaker and the convulsions diminished to occasional twitches. Denton's eyes closed. He pulled his jacket up over his head and dozed, woke, dozed and woke again, until the dim cheerless light of dawn seeped through the window.

The Chinese was dead now. His mouth was still open as though he were about to give one last despairing groan, but his eyes were fixed in a blank upward stare.

The door opened before the light had strengthened and a guard shouted for the buckets to be emptied. Two men carried the buckets outside and returned a few seconds later with them empty. There was some more shouting, then a guard came in, took a look at the dead Chinese, grabbed him by the ankles, and dragged him out of the cell. The man's clothes made a swishing sound over the stone floor like sand being poured from a lorry, and his head, swollen and bloody from its beating, jolted dully over every bump. Another guard took his belongings, an old basket suitcase tied together with string.

The door was slammed shut again. Two orderly silent queues formed behind each bucket. I won't think about it. Denton told himself as he returned to his place. But he noticed blood where the man had been lying—his eyes were drawn to the spot. He sat down on his suitcase again.

"I wonder if they'll let us shave?" Everett asked.

Two large iron woks of soupy rice were pushed in later. There was nothing to eat with. They reached in with their hands and stuffed the rice into their mouths. At first reluctant to shove and grab, when Denton saw the rice disappearing, he scooped two soggy handfuls out for himself. It was the worst rice, with little pieces of grit in it.

For the first time Everett began to sound less calm. "They can scarcely expect us to keep body and soul together on that," he muttered apprehensively.

Denton wasn't questioned again that day. Everett was summoned though, and came back an hour later, looking relieved. "They just wanted information about political suspects," he whispered. "I told them you weren't a commie." He glanced round the cell guardedly. "Some of these chap's 'll be for the high jump though."

"Did the Japs want to know about them?" Denton asked.

Everett nodded. "I tried not to give too much away," he murmured defensively. "But I couldn't very well say I didn't know anything, could I?"

Several Chinese were called out. Most of them didn't come back. Some more prisoners were shoved in. Their eyes slipped over each other's faces mutely, without expression.

In the evening some buckets of water were put in and they were told to wash themselves. The water was a rusty colour and smelt of oil. They splashed their faces with it. Afterwards two brooms and an old dustpan were handed in. Each man swept his space, brushing the dirt towards the door. The man nearest the door swept the little piles of dust into the dustpan and handed it with the brooms to the guard.

Two more woks of rice soup appeared.

Old Wei's voice was quavery and his eyes flickered apprehensively at her as she sat down. His hands, resting on the arms of the blackwood chair, were veined and knobbly, loose-skinned as though the flesh had all wasted between them. Third wife sat beside him, his only surviving wife, a stern woman of forty-five now with a harsh mouth that seemed to reflect the grim struggle she'd waged against the other two wives in the years before they died.

"I have little influence with the Japanese," he said drily and deliberately, seeming to pick his words one by one from some inner dictionary. "I don't know many of them. Just a few business contacts that Philip and I have developed." His eyes blinked waterily above the glasses that rested half-way down his nose. "I know nothing about the police, the Kempetai. Except it isn't good to cross them," he added with a wintry smile.

"Perhaps one of your friends might know where they're keeping him? I'm sure your business contacts are very important people?"

Wei lifted his hand deprecatingly, "Not very important at all. Only ordinary businessmen." One of his lids was drooping slightly, hooding his eyes.

"Perhaps Mr. Chen can help?" Third wife suggested, her lips hardly parting as she spoke. Old Wei nodded encouragingly.

"Mr. Chen is too busy to see me." Su-mei glanced back at Wei as she spoke and saw his eyes dull with disappointment. The hope of fobbing her off had been extinguished. "John always had a great respect for you as his teacher," she insisted gently. "Even though he came to support the other side."

"I haven't forgotten he was my student," Wei answered sharply, for all the trembling in his voice. "Or my business associate. But he didn't take my advice. Was that respect?"

She looked down, fingering the jade bracelet on her wrist. "One more time," she pleaded. "None of this would have happened except that you arranged for me to meet him that first time, in the floating restaurant. He would have gone back to England."

"I suppose you were paid for it?" Third wife inquired sarcastically.

Su-mei didn't answer, still looking down at her bracelet. An amah brought in tea and poured it in silence. They watched the light golden liquid gently gurgling into the fine porcelain cups. A jasmine flower fell out of the spout into Wei's cup. The amah left the room, shuffling her cloth shoes on the floor as if she had bound feet. Wei cleared his throat and sighed resignedly as the door closed. "I'll see what I can do," he murmured quaveringly at last. He held his cup in both hands and raised it precariously to his mouth.

When they'd been there eleven days (Everett punctiliously scratched a line on the wall each morning when he woke up), the guard called out Denton's name.

He'd been interrogated three times so far, each time hearing the same questions repeated, having his answers checked against their written record. He went to the door, expecting to be taken along the corridors and up the stairs to the same little office. But the guard merely handed him an opened parcel of food. He guessed that much had been pilfered on its way to him, but some at least remained—fruit and bread and a slab of bean curd. It must have come from Su-mei, he realised. So she was all right so far. He wondered how she'd found out where he was. It was hard to share the food with Everett—they'd had nothing but that rice gruel to eat so far and his belly ached with a dull hunger night and day.

Within another week or two there were food parcels for several of the other prisoners too. Most of them shared with the prisoners next to them. Denton always shared with Everett, who never got one. "I should have got married. Especially a Chinese wife," Everett said. "She'd have come in useful now." He was questioned every day, "but quite politely," he told Denton in a satisfied, even grateful, tone.

More prisoners were taken out and never returned. The rest were able to lie down without touching. The stone floor was cold and they shivered at night, but already they were too weak to stand up for long.

95

I mustn't think about it, I must close my mind up to survive. Denton thought the same words every day, sitting or lying in the cell, while the weather grew slowly warmer outside, and the smell of sweat hung on the dank air as strong as the pungent fumes from the ever-full buckets.

One day Everett was told to bring his suitcase out; he never came back. Denton hadn't the will to go on scratching the days and months on the wall. The regulation of time no longer seemed important. He became more passive and hollow-eyed, sitting for hour after hour on his suitcase, gazing at the wall opposite. Sometimes his mind was a grey-white blank, at other times scenes from his life would drift across it. Mary-Ellen, skating along the frozen river in America, his father sitting in the old torn leather chair with the horse-hair stuffing, his first meeting with Su-mei, Jonathan's dying of cholera...Scene after scene passed before his eyes without order or significance, as if to tell him that his whole life had been insignificant, an incoherent jumble of events without pattern or reason. But then sometimes a different thought would come. I'm only here because of the newspaper, it would occur to him. Because I stood up for something at last. And then the insignificance, the emptiness, seemed to be gone for a moment, as though his feet, sinking in water, had touched solid ground.

More prisoners were taken for questioning and never came back. Then the guard, swinging his bamboo club, would stand in the open doorway demanding the prisoner's case or bundle of clothes. Some of those who did come back were bruised and bleeding, others untouched and humbly relieved. Three more men died. They all died at night, as if wanting to slip away unobserved. One died of no apparent cause. He was simply stiff and cold in the morning. Two others died after beatings, although others, who looked worse when they stumbled back into the cell, recovered in a day or two.

Denton was the only European now. The Chinese occasionally whispered to each other, but they never talked to him. They merely glanced with a kind of awe at the long grey beard that had grown down to his chest. Sometimes he was left for what seemed weeks without being questioned, then he would be taken, half-dragged now, to the same office on the first floor, two or three days running, while questions he'd answered months before were repeated yet again and his answers meticulously checked. Then they would forget him again. One day, he thought, they'd forget him altogether and he'd die in the cell of old age. The thought was almost comforting. The slow tide of his memories ebbed and flowed on the blank shores of his mind. For much of the day he stared at the same dark patch on the wall opposite, focussing on it till his mind became empty and he was aware only of the patch and the shallow movement of his chest as he breathed. *I must close my mind up to survive* he told himself, almost unconsciously now. He focussed on the dark patch, but he never looked more closely to find out what it was.

His food parcels still came, two or three times a week. He thought of Su-mei's hands folding the paper and tying the string, a string which was always undone when the parcel arrived. He could visualise the jade bracelet on her wrist, but somehow he couldn't see her hands, her fingers. There the pictures always blurred.

Now that Everett was gone, he shared the food with a young Chinese who was next to him. The Chinese smiled and said thank you, but they never spoke apart from that. Most of those who got parcels shared them, but some didn't. Watched silently by their neighbours, they gobbled the food on their laps with quick, nervous motions, glancing guiltily round as though they were afraid it might be snatched away from them. But the others merely watched with that apathetic, unaccusing stare with which he recalled the beggars and refugees used to watch the rich driving past on Maloo or the Bund.

One afternoon, it must have been full summer, they heard a typhoon blowing outside. The window high up in the wall was slammed shut, but water trickled steadily in round the edges and the walls of the building shuddered from the force of the wind—they could hear it screaming round the corners, rushing down corridors, hurling distant doors shut with violent, echoing thuds.

With the window closed, the air became more and more oppressive; the humidity and the stench made it almost impossible to breath. When the guard brought the evening rice, with a few threads of green vegetable in it, he wrinkled his nose, grunted and slammed the door again. A few prisoners got up to eat, but most lay in a weak, listless stupor where they were. Then suddenly the window was opened outside, and a cool blast of wind and rain surged through the opening. When the storm had passed, the cell was six inches deep in water. Some prisoners stood up, holding their cases or bundles, their feet slithering on the greasy floor. Others, the weaker, sat where they were, watching lethargically as the water swirled round them. Outside, cataracts of water rushed through the gutters.

The floodwater slowly seeped out into the corridor. It wasn't until the next morning that they were given rags instead of the usual brooms to wipe up the slime.

It was soon after that typhoon, when the clothes in his case were still wet and mouldy, that Denton was called again by the guard. He walked unsteadily to the door. The guard shoved him back with a jab of his club. "Case!" he ordered, imitating the action of lifting a case. "Case!"

Denton dragged the case out into the corridor. They led him up to the ground floor and out into the street. He was dizzy and panting by the time he reached the door. The sunlight hurt his eyes. It was the first time he'd seen it since he'd been imprisoned. A truck was waiting with the tailboard down. He was too weak either to lift his case or to climb in himself. The two guards heaved him in and he sprawled beside a soldier sitting in the back with a rifle. His case followed. The tailboard was slammed shut.

"Where to?" he asked the soldier as the truck moved off.

The soldier merely narrowed his eyes a fraction, as if the question annoyed him.

Denton clung onto the rattling side of the truck, watching the streets of Hongkew pass in the incandescent, blinding sunlight. The streets seemed nearly empty, except for soldiers, police and a few Japanese civilians. Where were the Chinese? For a moment he glimpsed the river between two tall, shabby grey factory buildings. It was empty too, except for a Japanese warship with rust eating into its dark grey paint along the waterline. Where were the junks, the sampans, the cargo ships? Then the truck stopped outside a brick building with barred windows. The soldier, who'd sat impassively holding his rifle, now spoke off-handedly as he unpinned the tailboard and let it drop. "Kiangwan Prison," he said in halting English, as if announcing the name of a railway station. "More better here."

What will happen to my food parcels? Denton wondered as the guard roughly helped him down and dropped the suitcase at his feet. He looked round, still dizzy, as if he might see Su-mei passing by chance and let her know where he was now. The soldier pushed him along to the entrance.

He was reunited with Everett, in a cell with only one wooden bed in it—some planks laid across two trestles. Everett had managed to shave, but his cheeks were gaunt, and they had boils growing on them in ugly mauve clusters. He glanced up from the bed without moving when Denton stumbled dazedly into the cell. "We take it in turns of sleep on the bed," he said in a slack, unsurprised voice. "Chap who was in here died the other day."

Denton lay down on the floor to rest. Even when he was lying down he felt giddy.

"Do you still get food parcels?" he heard Everett ask enviously. His voice sounded as if it came from a great distance, through a vast hazy space.

Denton nodded, his eyes closed. "I did," he murmured weakly. "But how will she know they sent me here?"

Yet after a week or ten days, the parcels began to arrive again, always opened and pilfered. There was never any message with them. He wondered whether Su-mei wrote letters and they were removed. He shared the food with Everett again. Sometimes he wondered whether they really did come from Su-mei. For all he knew they might be from someone else—Ah King for instance—and Su-mei might be dead.

"I wish I hadn't shaved," Everett said after some minutes' gloomy silence. "I suppose that's how I got these boils, when I cut myself." But he still scraped the uncorrupted areas of his face when the stubble grew too long.

He no longer bothered to count the days.

When Denton painstakingly washed himself with the bucket of water they were given a few evenings later, he found that the little toe on his left foot was numb.

Everett watched him pressing it between his finger and thumb. "You want to watch that," he said ominously. When his boils became too painful, he would set his jaw, screw up his eyes and squeeze them. A little greenish-yellow maggot of pus would pop out, and he would sigh with satisfaction, "That's got rid of that one." But there always seemed to be more boils appearing. The clusters grew larger and angrier.

Denton found a stain on the wall to focus on. He could let it hold his eyes while his mind floated off into the imagery of his life, which still continued in jumbled incoherence—his last opium pipe with Su-mei melting into

767

his first encounter with Pock-mark Chen in *rue* Molière, his first speech at the Municipal Council merging with his first months in the Customs service, when he'd been with Johnson down at the Woosung Forts, watching him swim from the muddy bank of the river. I must start at the beginning, he told himself sometimes, and go on from there. But his memory always followed some other, random order. And still it was only when he remembered the *Shanghai Star,* that had brought him there to prison, that he felt he touched something solid in his life, something about which he could think I was right, there. I was right.

It was getting cold again at night. Everett's boils spread to the back of his neck. Denton found a second toe had gone numb, the one next to the first one. It was like the numbness of his mind, he thought, of his refusal to think, to hope, even to complain. If someone pressed my brain, I wouldn't feel that either. He was never taken for questioning again. He imagined his file being mislaid in some office, perhaps accidentally burnt, so that they no longer knew why they were holding him.

Once a week they were taken out with the other prisoners to a little enclosed yard for exercise. All the prisoners were white. Denton saw faces he recognised but none he knew. Occasionally they smiled warily at him; usually they passed each other with listless eyes, beyond caring. All were emaciated, many limped. He recalled the Van Gogh picture Mary-Ellen had in one of her books, of the prisoners exercising in a walled yard, their eyes as blank and empty as the eyes of cattle.

One day, when the cold was giving way again to the warm humidity of spring. Mason appeared at exercise. He wasn't starving like they were, but fairly well-fed. At first Denton thought he must have been planted amongst them as an informer, but there was a look of such hopeless terror in his eyes that he decided Mason was a genuine prisoner after all. What had he done? How had he run foul of the Japanese whom he'd been serving for years? The questions were like dreams in his mind; they slipped vaguely away, and he didn't bother to pursue them. For all his stoutness, Mason's body seemed to sag and crumple, and he avoided Denton's eyes when they passed. One cheek was puffy and bruised, Denton noticed now. But perhaps he hadn't avoided Denton's eyes? Perhaps he no longer recognised him? The thought drifted off, dream-like, unimportant. Denton shuffled on carefully. Although the food was a bit better there, he often felt a swimming greyness before his eyes, and had to lean against the wall until a guard shoved him on. Not to collapse and be kicked—that was the whole aim of his life.

The next day was different. The prisoners were all unexpectedly summoned out to the yard again and made to stand in a square against the walls. My god, are they going to shoot us? Denton wondered in sudden panic. Then Mason was led in, his hands tied behind his back. Denton's heart slowed again. The camp commandant spoke in a harsh, nasal voice, pausing while a young bespectacled interpreter translated nervously.

"Illegal trade in currency and petrol..." the interpreter said in a failing voice while the commandant waited, standing stiffly to attention, his head slightly cocked, listening to the interpreter as if checking for mistakes. "Attempts to bribe Japanese officials...Immediate death."

At the word *death*, the commandant clicked his heels, forcing himself into a still more rigid posture, and uttered one more sentence. "All will observe for warning," the interpreter said.

The two soldiers beside Mason pushed him down onto his knees. He knelt obediently, as if hoping even at that moment that abject submission might yet get him off. His eyes were bloodshot and some inarticulate murmur dribbled from his slackened lips, gradually rising to a desperate wail as a third soldier marched up to the commandant carrying a heavy sword. The commandant half-drew the sword, tested the blade with his finger, then nodded. The soldier turned about and marched back to Mason. He drew the sword right out and handed the scabbard to the soldier behind him. Then he spread his feet and shuffled slightly, gripping the hilt with both hands and flicking his wrists testing like a golfer with his club, while he measured the distance to Mason's neck. Mason's wail had become a continuous whining appeal for mercy now. Denton made out the slobbery words "helping Japan." And yet Mason didn't try to draw back, as if he knew it was hopeless really. He knelt there with the white nape of his neck exposed, looking as though at any moment he might topple forward onto the ground.

The soldier slowly raised the sword, his eyes fixed on

Mason's neck. The commandant snapped the order out in a high voice, and with a little hiss of effort through his teeth the soldier whipped the blade down, lifting himself up on his toes as he did so. At the last moment Denton closed his eyes, and behind them he saw the sword flashing down forty years before, on his first day in Shanghai, and heard Mason's ironic, gloating laugh, echoed by the exultant howl of the crowd.

Mason was still moaning his hopeless pleas when the blade struck. Denton heard the startled grunt that cut them off, then a second later the little thump of his head striking the ground, followed by the rush of pumping blood spattering the earth.

When Denton opened his eyes, Mason's trunk had collapsed. The bound hands behind his back were still twitching, as though they hadn't realised it was too late now, it was all over. Someone near Denton was sobbing or retching. The interpreter kept licking his lips, his cheeks pale and flickering.

The executioner wiped the blood off his sword with a white cloth. Denton shut his eyes again and swallowed down the nausea that was welling up his throat. I will not think about it, he kept murmuring to himself. I will close my mind up.

The guards marched them back to their cells. Even they seemed awed, hustling them along in voices that were almost subdued.

"I suppose he couldn't resist a bit of squeeze," Everett said later, fingering the bunched pustules on his neck. "We had a bit on him in the political department of course. I always thought he'd be too slippery to get caught, though..."

Ah King squatted on the grass bank, spreading the peaches out on the ground in front of her. She tilted her wide-brimmed straw hat to keep off the sun. The coolies mending the road were stripped to the waist, their sun-burned bodies glistening with sweat. Beyond them, through the barbed wire, she watched the foreign devils in their camp. A Japanese guard, walking part inside the wire, paused to look at her. She held up a peach. "Shanghai peach? Very sweet?" she called out. The guard smiled and shrugged his shoulders, shook his head faintly, then turned and went on. One of the coolies laughed, leaning on his long-handled shovel. "Better learn some Japanese, old woman, if you want to make a sale there."

Ah King's eyes narrowed slightly. She saw Alec sauntering from one of the huts.

At midday, when they took their rest and ate the rice they'd brought with them, the coolies bought some peaches from her, haggling down to the last cent. Some of the foreign devils watched from the wire fence. Alec was among them. The sun was fierce. The coolies lay on the grass, shading their heads in their shirts. The foreign devils had left, all except Alec. Alec had his hand in pocket. He glanced round casually, then withdrew his hand. A second later a stone landed at Ah King's feet. There was a piece of paper tied around it with an old shoe-lace.

When the coolies went back to work, Ah King gathered her unsold peaches together and trudged away down the road.

It's too boring here and the grub's terrible, Su-mei read. *Intend to skip on Thursday night (no moon). Nod on Wednesday if you can put me up for one night. If not, shake your head.*

"He's crazy," she said, screwing the paper up, and then, on second thoughts, setting fire to it with a match. "This is the first place they'd look for him, even if he got this far. And where would he go after one night?"

Ah King sniffed the acrid smoke, watching the burning paper curl up and blacken on the stone floor. "He always was reckless," she said slowly, remembering. "He never thought." But she was smiling as she watched the orange flame consume the last corner of the paper. He always made her smile.

She went early on Wednesday morning, her basket of flat Shanghai peaches strapped to her back. She came back late, with more than half of them unsold.

"He wasn't there," she said grimly. "He never came."

Su-mei clenched her fists and beat her temples. "Just like him!" she muttered fiercely, "Just like him!" Ah King noticed there were one or two threads of grey in her hair now.

Everett's boils grew worse, always erupting in new places on his body. He had to give up shaving, but the bad blood, as he called it, had travelled far from his chin by then.

The swellings broke out on his back and on his legs. At first, wincing and gritting his teeth, he would keep on squeezing the angriest ones, with blistery heads, until they popped, swabbing the puss and blood with handkerchiefs or torn strips of shirt. But after a time they refused to heal; ulcers developed, little runny craters in his flesh, and he decided it would be better to leave them alone. Denton let him sleep on the bed all the time now because the floor was too painful. As the days grew warmer and more humid, the boils seemed to multiply more quickly, as if seeds that had been sown in his blood were all sprouting exuberantly in the spring. He became feverish, and left his food, even the food in Denton's parcels. Denton gave him water. His clothes were stained with the purulent discharge from the blossoming boils. He stopped talking or answering questions and lay inert on his back with closed eyes. "Doctor," Denton said to the guards. They glanced at Everett wordlessly and shrugged their shoulders. Two days later, when Denton could see drifting yellow and white clouds through the barred window above the shabby grey walls of the building opposite, Everett became delirious. He muttered thickly, isolated words and phrases—"dogs," "Picking up apples," "when the rain"—fragments perhaps of his past, like the random scenes Denton recalled himself. "Doctor," he appealed again to the guard. The guard shrugged, taking Denton off to the exercise yard alone. But when he returned, a Japanese doctor was examining Everett. Later, in the afternoon, when the sun was shafting mote-laden white beams through the window, two orderlies dumped Everett on a stretcher and took him away. Denton eyed the stains his body had left on the bed, and decided he'd still sleep on the floor. The next morning the guard took away Everett's case.

Soon after that, the toes of Denton's right foot began to go numb as well. He found it harder and harder to walk when they took him to the exercise yard. Don't think about it, he ordered himself as he staggered along. Close your mind. Images of his past still fluttered through his head. But when he remembered the *Shanghai Star,* it no longer seemed so significant to him that he'd stood up for something. It no longer felt as though he was touching solid ground. Nothing was firm any more.

And then quite soon the day came when Denton too couldn't get up. His toes had been merely pale and blood less when the numbness first affected them, but now they were beginning to turn a dark mauvish colour, as if they'd been badly bruised. They didn't hurt, but he'd grown much weaker and the numbness was spreading along the soles of his feet. It had become more and more difficult to keep his balance when he got up in the morning. He had to roll onto his side first of all, with his legs curled up into a foetal position, then force himself over onto his knees and crawl to the bed, clinging on to it and hauling himself gradually upright. Often that last effort would be too much and he would collapse onto the floor and have to start the whole business all over again.

On that morning, however, he found when he was at last upright that he couldn't walk at all. He felt he knew it before he tried, but, disregarding the presentiment, he stepped gingerly out all the same. His foot seemed incapable of holding the ground and he slid down onto the floor again, pulling a plank from the bed on top of him. None of this hurt him. The plank lay across his chest. When he tried to lift it, he couldn't. I'm as weak as a baby, he thought detachedly, gazing up remotely at the guard when he came in. I suppose this is the end. It was the guard who spoke a little English.

"Why not standing?" he demanded, slapping the palm of his hand with his club. He was the guard who blustered most but did the least. Denton had never seen him hit anyone. "Why not standing?" he demanded again.

Denton pointed to his feet. "I can't," he said weakly and closed his eyes. "Fall down." It seemed a great effort to speak.

He imagined the guard sucking in his lip, gazing uncertainly down at him, anxious above all to avoid being slapped by an officer for doing the wrong thing. But Denton was too weary now to open his eyes and look. Doctor, he thought, but it seemed too laborious to say it. They could do what they liked with him.

He heard the guard's boots scrape and the door slam shut. He lay there half-conscious, his mind straying idly between dreams and day-dreams. He was sure now he was going to die and the thought seemed, not frightening as it had been when he was young, but quite natural and ordinary. He visualised Su-mei packing food parcels that he would never get, sending them week after week, until one day she got a letter or read a notice somewhere, or perhaps was simply sent his suitcase full of mouldy clothes, and realised he was dead. And then there'd be all the business of the funeral to bother with, he thought wearily, as if it would be a bother for *him*. Or would the Japanese simply dump his body somewhere and forget about it? In a way that seemed better, only then she might not know and go on sending those parcels...

His mind floated away again into the incoherent memories of the past. He was with Jonathan in Jessfield Park, visiting his mother in Enfield, driving with Su-mei out to the hills, with all the children in the mountains in Japan...He listened to his breathing, quick and faint. He'd never heard breathing like that before. It was as though his ears were actually inside his chest, listening to the machinery of his lungs gently running down. How much longer can this go on? he wondered incuriously.

Sometime during the day he found the same doctor bending over him that had bent over Everett. He gazed indifferently up at an abstracted face, brown eyes surveying him thoughtfully under a furrowed brow, on which the cap sat crookedly, as if to emphasise how ill-suited the doctor really was to army life. Denton closed his eyes. When he opened them again, the doctor was gone.

He couldn't hear his breathing any more.

Still later he was picked up, laid on a stretcher, carried out of the prison and put on the floor of an open truck. He saw the sun, a white burning globe, behind a steamy veil of cloud that was brilliant with the light that shone through it. The truck jerked forward, he saw the wall of the prison move away, then his lids drifted down again. The road grew bumpier, jolting him through the metal floor of the truck. There were alternate patches of light and shade on his lids as trees or buildings blocked off the sunlight then released it again.

It was a long ride. He dozed in a drowsy trance, scarcely conscious of the jarring of his body. When his eyes opened again he saw peach blossoms along the road, the branches sometimes clashing against the sides of the truck. For a confused moment he thought he must be in Japan, then he dozed again until the truck stopped and the driver shouted out. A voice answered and the truck lurched forward again. He saw the slanting pole of a bamboo barrier which barbed wire covered in curling tendrils like a metallic creeper. The sky was open, free of buildings. Then as they lifted him out and laid him on another stretcher, he glimpsed the tip of a pagoda, immediately cut off by a white wooden wall. Of course, he thought, the Lung Hua Pagoda—the road to that led through the peach orchards. He remembered driving along it with the children all those hazy years ago.

"Now what's the matter with *you*?" he heard an irascible voice demand from somewhere behind his head. It was McEwan's inimitably testy Scottish accent. There was a pause and then his face, as flushed as ever, but also haggard now, with tired dark pouches under the eyes, peered down at Denton cross-temperedly. "As if we hadn't got enough trouble," he muttered, running his hands over Denton's feet.

"Where is this?" Denton muttered feebly. "What are you doing here?"

"Can ye feel anything in your foot?" McEwan asked sharply. "You're in Lung Hua internment camp and it's not much better than where you've been till now."

His eyes closed. "No, I can't feel anything."

"There's a fair bit of gangrene here," he heard McEwan grunt. "What on earth have ye been doing with yourself."

"I'm going to have to take some of your toes off," McEwan said tersely the next morning. "Maybe bits of your feet. You've got beri-beri." He was in shirt sleeves, a silvery stubble glinting in the still ruddy skin of his drawn cheeks.

"Bits of my feet?" Denton gazed up at him weakly from the wooden cot they'd put him in.

"Your toes are gangrened," McEwan said peevishly. "Ye should have made them bring you here earlier. Did ye not report sick at all?"

"You don't report sick where I've been," Denton murmured faintly. "You report dead." Suddenly he wanted to laugh. He was getting used to the idea that he wasn't going to die after all. Soon he would have to act again, to think, to decide. It seemed like a long steep hill he'd have to climb. But not yet. For the moment he could just let go. "Who else is here? Alec?"

"One or two people you'll be likely to know," McEwan grunted, frowning down at Denton's feet. "I'll be cutting your toes off this morning. It's a pity ye couldn't have been repatriated. There was a Swedish ship left only last month.

They'd have had a proper theatre there. But there ye are, you'll just have to take your chance."

"Was Alec on it? Mary-Ellen?"

McEwan was moving away. "No, they weren't on it," he said.

He was dreaming how he would change after the war, how he would fill his life for the years that were left him. But as the anaesthetic wore off and he slowly drifted up to consciousness, the dream slipped away.

"I was dreaming," he said thickly to McEwan, not yet awake enough to control his thoughts. "I was going to change my life when the war was over."

"You'll have to change your shoes too," McEwan growled. "I had to take half your feet away."

It wasn't until the next day, while he was checking the wounds, that McEwan told him about Alec and Mary-Ellen. He gave Denton a pain-killer first that made him drowsy. "Ye may as well know now, before someone else tells ye. They're both dead." He was winding the bandages himself; the only nurse, a grey-haired woman with faded blue eyes, had been up all night with a dysentery patient. "Alec had some mad plan of escape. Thought he could get out to Free China. I ask ye—" he snipped the air exasperatedly with the scissors "—Hoping to look like a blond Chinaman for a thousand miles, he must've been crazy."

"What happened?" Denton asked weakly. He listened numbly, as numbly as he'd watched Mason's beheading, thinking only that later, sometime later, he'd begin to feel what it meant. It was a secret wound, it wouldn't show on the surface yet, it would work stealthily inside him, festering invisibly.

McEwan snipped the bandage and tied it tightly, frowning as he worked. "They saw him one night as he was climbing through the wire..." he shrugged as he finished the knot. "He kept on running, and they shot him."

"Did he...Was he wounded, or...?"

"No, he was killed at once." McEwan began the other foot, turning his shoulder away from Denton as if to discourage him from asking more. Then, "Through the

776

head," he said dourly. "I saw it myself. He wouldn't have felt a thing."

Denton gazed up at the back of McEwan's head, the silver hair still thick, though long and untidy. He imagined a bullet smashing through the bone into the brain. So Alec's gone he thought with the same dull numbness, as if he were looking down a dark hole in the earth. After a long time, "When did it happen?" he asked.

"Last summer. August. You'll be able to see where he's buried later, when ye can get about." He was changing the dressing, shaking his head as he inspected the wound. "This needs cleaning out. It's going to hurt a bit. Even with that injection I gave you. We have to be sparing with drugs."

Denton's fingers gripped the side of the cot. It felt as though a knife was being pushed right through his instep. He sucked in his breath and clenched his teeth, but the pain grew worse and worse. Now it felt as if McEwan was scraping his bones with a blunt trowel. He felt he was going to scream, but his eyes simply went grey and misty and he fainted.

When he woke, he seemed to be listening inside his chest again, hearing his breath panting quickly and weakly all round him. At the same time there was a cold sweat on his forehead and the light was still grey before his eyes. He couldn't have been out for long. McEwan didn't seem even to have noticed. He was talking about Mary-Ellen now. "She was offered a place on this Swedish repatriation ship, but she wouldn't take it," he said scornfully. "Said she couldn't leave her White Russian friend behind."

"Sonia?"

"I've no idea what the lady's name was," McEwan grunted distastefully, winding the bandage on now. "She wasn't interned, that's all I could say. She appeared outside the camp once or twice but the guards shooed her off. They're still more or less free in the city, I believe, the White Russians. I told Mary-Ellen she'd die if she didn't go, but she wouldn't hear of it. She was addicted to morphine—ye knew that, I suppose? Always trying to wheedle drugs out of me, as if I'd have any to spare! She died a few days after the ship sailed, so I suppose she might have died on board anyway. She couldn't do without the drugs ye see. Or without that Russian woman apparently." He fastened the bandage with an impatient little tug of the knot. "A woman of her age!"

It was some days before Denton remembered Everett.

"Never came here," McEwan answered with a shrug.

Denton was alert enough by then to notice the whisky on McEwan's breath. A little later the same morning, he saw him drinking a clear brown liquid from a bottle which he replaced next to opaque jars of antiseptic on a wooden shelf. His eye, bloodshot and tired, met Denton's, and he looked guiltily away, stumping out of the hut with a scowl. But the next morning he was almost genial.

"So ye caught me at it yesterday," he muttered with a look that wavered between a threatening frown and a sheepish grin. "In case you're wondering how I manage it, I've got a friendly arrangement with the contractor who handles the night-soil." The frown surrendered to the grin, which settled on his face precariously, as though expecting to be dislodged at any moment by his habitual irascibility. "He's an old friend of yours—Jacob Ephraim." Turning immediately to Denton's bandages, he gave a sardonic laugh. "Now you'll have to walk like the Chinese girls used to with their bound feet," he said.

Denton couldn't remember ever seeing McEwan laugh before.

Gradually he learnt to walk with a broomstick in each hand, to hobble along the floor of the hut and back to his bed again, where he would collapse in sweaty and dizzy exhaustion, too weak at first even to lift his legs up onto the bed. But as the food was slightly better, and there was more of it, he began to strengthen. His walks became longer, he slowly recovered; but he didn't leave the hut. When he could manage with only one stick, McEwan used him as an orderly, brusquely commanding him to bring bandages, empty bedpans—there were only two—and carry the medicines that he doled out with grim, miserly thrift.

When he wasn't helping McEwan, he lay on his bed, gazing up at the wooden beams that supported the corrugated iron roof of the hut. He watched the flies idly zigzagging in the warm moist air between the beams, and the lizards darting for mosquitoes along them or clinging motionless upside down on the roof, their heads occasionally flicking from side to side as they spied a prey.

778

It was summer again. The heat through the iron roof was paralysing, and McEwan kept growling that he was going to kick him out of the hut; but Denton still lay most of the day on his bed, his will atrophied, his eyes gazing up at the unapproachable world of flies and the lizards, while memories of the past floated like white fluffy clouds across the still sky of his mind. He thought of Alec and of Mary-Ellen. He hadn't seen their graves yet; one day when he was stronger he'd go out and look at them. Now they were gone, he realised for the first time how little he'd ever known them. He couldn't even remember the night when Alec was conceived. Or the first, unsteady steps he'd taken in the garden—Denton knew he'd watched them, but there was no memory there, no image. Only dark spaces. And how he'd died exactly, where he'd run away, what he'd said before he started, whether he was joking or grim—the list was endless for just those few minutes alone; what would it be like for the whole of his life? Of his own son he knew only a few scattered glimmering points, while all the rest was dark space, unknowable. He would carry that darkness inside him for the rest of his life.

And Mary-Ellen was the same, a few sparse lights in the immensity of the dark. What weird desire and loyalty had bound her to that Russian woman? He would never understand. Even for Mary-Ellen he felt a pang now.

"I need your bed," McEwan interrupted rudely. "Got a baby to deliver. How they have the nerve to keep at it in a place like this is beyond me. They're worse than rabbits. Well, she'll have no chloroform, I've none to waste on frivolous things like that."

Denton hobbled outside in the shade of the hut, hugging the wooden wall. It was the first time he'd gone outside. The wood had once been painted white, but now it was a dirty grey colour. He could smell the heat coming off it, he could see the cracks made by rain and sun. Tomorrow I'll look for the graves, he thought. The woman started screaming inside, and he could hear McEwan's biting admonitions between the screams. For some reason the pangs of birth reminded him of Su-mei. There had been no more food parcels, but McEwan had told him, roughly, not to worry. Parcels weren't allowed; the Japs maintained that internees were properly fed and had no need of them. "Next time Jacob Ephraim comes, we'll get some news." But Jacob hadn't come all the time Denton had been in the camp—over three months.

The woman screamed again, a long series of shrieks, each louder than the last as the pangs strengthened. Denton leant against the hut. The wall was hot against his back. The sun was almost directly overhead and he shaded his eyes with his hand as he looked across the camp to the seven stories of the old pagoda. He remembered visiting it years ago, soon after the first war. Su-mei had taken him. It must have been when he was about to leave Mary-Ellen. An old man, the caretaker, had refused to let them climb up at first, mumbling that it was dangerous. But they'd given him some cash and he'd grudgingly unlocked the door to the worn stone steps. They'd climbed to the top and looked out over the peach orchards, all the way to the smoke and haze of the city. The tall white buildings of the Bund had risen above the haze, windows winking brightly in the sunlight. He'd held her hand as they climbed the last flight of narrow steps, and he remembered he hadn't let go, but gripped it tighter as they looked out. If only time could have been stilled at that moment! They could have been looking out with that slightly breathless, close contentedness for ever. He realised he was gripping the broomstick as if it were her hand.

A Japanese truck had entered the camp and was driving slowly past, jolting and clanking over the baked, rutted earth. Suddenly it stopped, lurching on its creaking springs, and a face appeared beside the Chinese driver's, peering aggressively through dark glasses. It was a white face. It was Jacob. They stared at each other, neither was quite sure.

"Hello Jacob," Denton said, as if they met like that every day.

Jacob's face disappeared. The far door opened and after a few seconds he appeared again, walking with a stick round the front of the truck. His limp had grown worse, and he was much thinner. It wasn't till Denton saw him close to that he realised how much thinner. His skin hung on him like a suit that was several sizes too big. His cheeks were grey and flabby, as if the blood no longer reached them. Denton thought fleetingly of the plants whose leaves had turned white when Cheong had left them once in the basement. But Jacob's full lips smiled as warmly as ever as he took off his glasses, uncovering deep, dark pouches, and hung them in the neck of his shirt. He gripped Denton's arm in the old way, except that his grip was no longer fierce, or even firm. His hand felt light and bony, like a sparrow's claws.

"Why have you grown a beard? It doesn't suit you," Jacob said, his eyes glimmering with warmth in their brown pupils. "I've just had dysentery. How long have you been here? What are you walking with a stick for? Two old men with sticks, eh? You're as thin as a rake too."

Denton blinked. "Su-mei?" he asked nervously. "Is she all right?"

"Su-mei? Of course she is!" Jacob shook Denton's arm with his claw-like hand, emphasising each word as though he thought he was deaf. "She's living in Frenchtown. You know the Japs didn't take it over until a few months ago because the Vichy French were neutral? She bought a lot of property there—she's as shrewd as I am, you ought to be proud of her. We're both born to survive. They took my factory of course, but I'm running the sewage disposal in all the camps—what a job for a Jew. Gets me out of the ghetto, though. I had to bribe them of course. You know they put us in a ghetto, the Jews?" He paused to examine Denton. "I don't like your beard at all. And why the stick?"

His eyes widened with sympathy when Denton told him.

"I wear the same shoes, but they're half full with old socks," Denton ended. "Just for padding. But when I get shoes made after the war—"

"I'll get you some made," Jacob interrupted, leaning closer. "I know a man. Just draw round your feet on some paper. I'll be back next month." He glanced round at a guard who was eyeing them coldly, and lowered his voice. "Have you heard the news? The allies have invaded France."

"Which allies?"

But Jacob stepped back. "Well, I must be on my way," he said loudly. "I'll see you next time I come."

"Jacob!" Denton hobbled after him. "Tell Su-mei I'm all right." Suddenly he felt tears pricking the back of his eyes. "Tell her I got the food parcels!"

The truck rattled away. Jacob leant out of the window to talk to the guard, then he was gone. Denton watched it bouncing along the road outside the barrier. He remembered that he hadn't asked about Lily or Michael. Or whether Su-mei knew about Alec. Or what had happened to Jacob's Cantonese girl, to Sonia, to the house on the Bund... His mind teemed with unasked questions. The world outside was rushing towards him again, colour, life, feeling. It's like when I got over the cholera, he thought. I shall want to do things again soon, to live again.

They heard the war was over in Europe. Then American bombers raided Shanghai. After each raid they could see smoke rising from fires in the city. There was less food, the guards grew more strict, edgy. Then, quite suddenly, one day in August they opened the barriers and told them they could all leave. "War finish," they said. And they left themselves.

The internees waited uncertainly, coming out of their huts, sitting on their cases, talking in low, uneasy voices. They weren't used to this, they seemed to be saying. They didn't know what to do with freedom. They felt it might be a trick. Then a convoy of lorries and vans, led by Jacob in the same Japanese truck, entered the camp, rumbling, squeaking, rattling and backfiring, with black smoke pouring from their exhausts. "This petrol's so bad you can't even light a fire with it," he said. "Have you heard about the bomb? The whole of Japan destroyed! Not a soul living! I wish they'd done it to the Germans."

Denton rode in the cab beside him, and Jacob told him what he'd heard of the new bomb that burnt whole cities to a cinder, and of the German gas chambers in Europe. The steady flame of his trust in German civilisation, which had survived even the Nazi leaflets fluttering down from the Park Hotel, had been put out at last. "You know they tried to persuade the Japs to build gas chambers in Shanghai?" he said. "And now they're all starving in Germany. Well, let them starve."

The truck jolted over deep pot-holes and ruts. Japanese soldiers filed along or stood dejectedly by the side of the road while the convoy rolled past them, sending clouds of dust and choking petrol fumes into their faces. "Poor fellows," Jacob said, shaking his head compassionately. "No country to go home to. Burnt to a cinder, everything destroyed."

The Chinese driver felt differently. He steered deliberately close to the Japanese, so that they had to jump into the ditches to avoid being hit. His face was still and stony; only the faint flickering of his lids expressed his feeling.

They drove into the city through Nantao. Red and blue paper Nationalist flags hung from every shop. Denton recalled the Japanese flags he'd seen in Hongkew the day he was arrested. People waved at them from the pavement, and he felt a sudden throb in his throat. He'd never seen Chinese waving to Europeans on the streets before.

Then suddenly they were on the Bund. All the buildings were there unchanged, except that they looked older and shabbier, like clothes that have been left unused for years.

The river was full of American ships, warships and supply ships, all dark grey. The sun beat down relentlessly on them, and they seemed to flatten themselves under the heat, like squat little water beetles.

"America!" Jacob declared, waving at the river. "The country of the future!" But then he sighed. "Unfortunately it has no culture."

In the hurried clandestine conversations they'd held in the camp, Denton had never asked Jacob about his Cantonese girl.

"She ran away," he answered glumly now. "After all the money I paid for her—the Agency's fee for introducing us, I mean. She ran away."

Denton clambered down from the track at the entrance to the house. Su-mei would be waiting for him, Jacob had promised. "I'll phone you tonight," Jacob said, passing his stick and case down from the cab. "If the phones are working."

He turned to face the house. A hesitant reluctance held him back, a reluctance, a fear, to take up what he'd been torn away from three years before. He was scared after all of acting and thinking again, of coming out of the shadows into the light.

He'd learned two kinds of walk—a limping stride with his stick, and a slow shuffle without it. He held his stick in one hand and the case in the other, and adopted the shuffle. It gave him more time.

Su-mei opened the door and stood on the porch. She watched him carefully climb the first step, moved to help him, then checked herself, guessing he'd want to do it by himself. "The servants haven't come back yet," she said quietly. "Ah King's looking for them. They're scattered about. I was just starting to go through the place." There was a smallness, an uncertainty, in her voice, as though she was uneasy too. Their eyes met and quickly flew away like shy birds. He stood next to her now, his stick in one hand, his case in the other. He smiled as their glances met and skimmed off once more. She was wearing a blue cheong-sam, one she'd had for years. Her skin was as smooth as ever, only faintly lined round the eyes and lips. Age had touched her with a lighter hand. He didn't notice the few grey hairs.

"You haven't changed," he said.

She smiled, lowering her head deprecatingly. "I was just going through the place," she repeated.

"All right then." He put his case down in the hall and they walked together into the living room. Half the furniture was gone, some of it was broken, pushed into a corner. There was a cigarette stubbed in an ash-tray. It made Denton feel there was an intruder still in the house, the Japanese who'd casually squashed his cigarette out there. The walls had oblong patches on them where the pictures and scrolls used to hang. The vase that Mary-Ellen had left behind still stood on its little table, coated with a fine grey film of dust, its neck laced by a spider's web. "Who lived here?" he asked, leaning on his stick.

She shrugged. "Different people. The Japanese navy were last."

"It doesn't feel as though its ours now. I suppose they took the pictures?"

"No, I had them put away." She smiled at his surprise. "The Weis helped. How d'you think I found out where you were?"

He walked into the dining room. "Is old Wei still alive, then?" The table had been pushed against the wall. Two of the chairs had broken legs, leaning against each other like two cripples embracing. A flask of *sake* stood half-empty on the sideboard.

"He's still alive," she said behind him. "Very old. They're making their peace with the government. Philip flew to Chungking yesterday."

Denton smiled wrily. "They backed the wrong side."

"I think they backed both sides. Like Pock-mark Chen." Her voice darkened slightly as she said his name.

He reached for the *sake* flask, and saw something

784

brown and furry move behind it. He recoiled. It was a small rat. The rat scuttled along towards the edge. Without thinking he hit it with his stick. The blow caught it on the neck and it died at once, its hind legs quivering in futile running motions for only a few seconds before it was still. A spot of bright red blood dropped out of its mouth onto the wood. He turned away with a faint shudder, suddenly remembering the stroke that cut off Mason's head, and Pak-kay's head on the doorstep.

"Let's have the whole place done up, Su-mei," he said. "New furniture, walls, floors, everything. Get rid of every trace of the Japs."

She was watching him seriously, as if she hadn't been listening. "Was it very bad?" she asked at last.

"In the camp?" He shook his head. "Prison wasn't too good though. I saw Mason executed." He thought of the soldier cleaning the sword with a white cloth. "Not that that was the worst," he added.

As they went up the stairs, he pushing himself up with thrusts of his stick, she said "No news of Lily yet. Michael's been doing some kind of liaison work between the British and the Nationalists in Chungking."

"I know. Jacob told me. No news of Jenny either?"

She shook her head. "Young Pak-kay is still in the village with Ah Leng. They're all right. Except he's become a village boy."

Neither of them mentioned Alec or Mary-Ellen.

The study seemed to have been left as it was. Even the seals the Kempetai had put over the drawers of the desk and filing cabinet were unbroken. But a Japanese record lay on the gramophone. The cardboard box with his own records was gone. He picked up the Japanese record and dropped it on the floor. It broke in two. "Did you get my records away too?"

She nodded. "I couldn't move the books, though."

He gazed at the shelves, grey with dust and cobwebs.

"Did you move the things from Alec's room?" he asked outside the door.

She shook her head. "We tried to warn him not to escape, but he wasn't there," she said. "He must have just gone off on his own."

He put his hand on the handle, then let it go again. He would look later, another time. "That would have been like him," he murmured.

785

It wasn't till they were in the hall again that he touched her. He took her hand and held it against his cheek. "It'll take a little time," he said slowly.

She gave that little teasing smile she used to mock him with when she was young. "Maskee," she said. "It doesn't matter."

"Let's get the place done up as soon as we can."

"All right. Shall we go to Frenchtown then? Where I've been living? It's the same house as before."

"My feet are a mess." That house, he thought, the one in *rue* Molière. The woman with the little girl.

She smiled. "We don't have to walk. We can take a rickshaw. We might even find a taxi." She bent down to open his case, then stood up, wrinkling her nose. "You can throw that away now. Everything's mouldy inside."

He shook his head. "I'll keep it till the day I die." His eyes met hers for the first time without any awkwardness. "Tell me about all this property Jacob says you've been buying. Tell me in the rickshaw."

She carried his case and he limped beside her with his stick.

96

"I've never had an American car before," Denton said, glancing out of the window at the washed and painted buildings of the Bund. "How do you like it, Pak-kay?"

The boy's wide, dark eyes gazed round the Buick uncertainly. He'd hardly ever even seen a car till a few weeks ago. "Quite good," he said cautiously. He looked wonderingly out of the window at the river again.

Lau half-turned his head. "Better than the Rolls," he said decidedly. "More silver." During the war he'd driven a truck for Jacob's night-soil operation.

"Chrome," Denton answered absently. "Not silver. I preferred the Rolls." He was watching a Chinese family clustering round the bronze lions outside the Hong Kong and Shanghai Bank. Two little girls in scarlet quilted jackets had climbed on one of the lion's backs while a boy was stroking its paws for luck, as people used to before the war. The parents stood back on the pavement, the father holding a camera to his eye while the mother clapped her hands to attract the children's attention. He supposed that was what peace meant. "If we hadn't had to wait so long for it to be delivered," he went on to Lau, "I'd have got a Rolls instead."

"What is a Rollsi?" Pak-kay asked.

Lau turned into Nanking Road. A convoy of Nationalist troops in American trucks had blocked the traffic. He cursed under his breath and turned left into Szechuen Road, then right along Kiu Kang Road. The pavements teemed there with beggars, hawkers and shoppers. The letter-writers were sitting out in the autumn sun again, their awnings and umbrellas furled. A grey-haired woman was squatting on an upturned box, having her hair done. The flower market was crowded, the flowers glistened with water which the hawkers kept throwing over them to keep them fresh.

"What is a Rollsi?" Pak-kay asked again.

"It's another kind of car. I used to have one, but it vanished in the war." He glanced at Lau. "Everything's back to normal again at last."

Lau shrugged. "Very much normal," he said with a cynical little smile Denton had never seen before. "They've taken my son off to fight the reds in the north, and everyone's on the take down here. The only change is we drive on the right hand side of the road now."

When they reached Jessfield Park, the sun was sinking into the smoky mauve haze that rose from the factory chimneys beyond the railway. It looked large and blood-red, ominous, as if some violent storm was coming. Denton limped along beside Pak-kay, out towards the refreshment room. The grass was vivid and green after the summer rains. He heard the whoop of a train's whistle, and showed Pak-kay the gap in the trees where the train would appear. "Have you ever seen a train before?" Denton asked him.

Pak-kay shook his head apprehensively, his eyes fixed on the gap. At last it came, a long black engine spouting steam, its piston rods winding the great wheels along, its tender heaped with a mountain of coal, followed by waggon after waggon, each one loaded with American guns or trucks. For the past forty years there's always been a war in China, Denton thought. I suppose Lau was right about things being normal. He watched the boy's rapt amazement at the enormous waggons, their iron wheels clunking over the rails with regular massive jolts.

At the refreshment room he ordered tea. "One of your uncles used to like watching the trains here," he told Pak-kay.

The boy frowned, thinking of the uncles he knew in the village. "Which uncle?" he asked.

"He died a long time ago, before you were born. Jonathan."

"Chong Ah Tong," the boy said, struggling with the uncouth foreign word. His hair had been cropped all over like a peasant's when Ah Leng brought him back, and it was still stiff and spiky. He held his cup clumsily in both hands and slurped up the tea, belching unself-consciously.

"You'll have to start school next year," Denton said. "You'll have to learn English."

Pak-kay was looking back over the park at some children flying kites. They had cropped hair too. Their clothes were torn and patched and they shouted shrilly, gazing upwards as they reeled and unreeled their spools of twine, playing their kites like anglers playing fish. The flimsy rice-paper triangles, stretched over springy slips of wood, soared above them, over the trees and the factory chimneys blossoming with smoke.

"Can you fly kites?" Denton asked.

The boy nodded eagerly.

Denton bought him one from the hawker by the door. Already, on the way back to the car, Pak-kay had it up in the air, walking backwards as he went, sensing the air currents with his fingers. Denton could see no trace of his English blood in him. Perhaps his hair was not quite black, but his eyes, his bones, his skin colour were all Chinese. Lily will be glad, he thought. Or would be.

He had Lau stop the car by the Bank, and took Pak-kay to stroke the lion's paws for luck. The bronze was worn and shiny there, from all the stroking, a lighter colour, golden instead of dark brown.

"Tomorrow you'll see your uncle and aunt," Denton told him as he got back into the car. "Michael and Jenny. They're coming from hundreds of miles away, for the Moon Festival."

"Is my mother coming?"

"No, not yet." Or ever, for all we know, he thought. The thought was like a weight on his chest.

"My father's dead," Pak-kay said importantly, as though that was something to be proud of.

After dinner they all went out into the garden. Cheong had put up paper lanterns for the festival. Red, yellow, orange and blue, they hung from the trees, shivering faintly in the breeze from the river. Down in the Public Gardens the lantern processions wound between the dim shapes of the shrubs and bushes. Denton stood apart, leaning on his stick. The lights reminded him of something. Was it his first moon festival with Su-mei; when he'd given her the silver earrings?

"You should have gone," Jacob's voice jarred behind him suddenly.

"Gone where?"

"To the victory celebration. People were asking where you were. You're a celebrity now."

"I didn't want to see them all fawning on Pock-mark Chen," he said curtly. "I won't go anywhere where he's a guest."

Michael joined them. They stood looking round at the lanterns in the garden.

"Nobody was fawning on Pock-mark Chen," Jacob said. "He's a great philanthropist anyway."

"I wonder how much he paid to cancel the record of his collaboration with the Japanese," Michael said in a cold, hard voice. His face had become strangely old and set for his age, as though he'd put on make-up for an older role and forgotten to take it off when the play was over. He began arguing with Jacob about Pock-mark Chen. Denton joined Jenny, Su-mei and McEwan.

"It's the first time I've ever left them," Jenny was saying to McEwan. "And I know how much we were left when we were young."

McEwan grunted, handing back the photos of Jenny's two children without comment. "Considering your mother's morals," he said, swallowing some whisky, "it may have been just as well that ye were left."

"You mean I might have turned out a lesbian?" Jenny laughed. "Well I've got two children already."

"So had your mother," McEwan answered dourly. "You're getting an American accent, too," he added with a frown. "I hope you won't be taking out American citizenship?"

789

"Why not? My husband's American, after all." Jenny turned to her father, laying her hand on his arm. "Anyway, that's why I can't stay longer. I can't leave the children with Bill's parents for ever, after all."

All that Denton knew of Bill was gleaned from a few photographs and Jenny's scrappy letters. He was a television director. Denton had never seen television. "Yes, that's all right," he said, feeling that it wasn't. "I know you were left too much yourself..."

"If you'd known the things we got up to," she laughed. "You'd blush to hear."

When she laughed, her face seemed to take on one of Mary-Ellen's expressions. Surely she wasn't going to end up looking like Mary-Ellen? She hadn't been to see Alec's grave yet, he remembered. Perhaps she didn't want to?

"Well, have ye changed your life?" McEwan asked him abruptly. He turned to Su-mei. "Ye know when people come round from anaesthetics they're at their most unguarded. Your husband here, when he came round after I'd cut his toes off, he let it be known he was going to change his life. I haven't seen much sign of it yet," he smiled sardonically. "But ye never know..."

"It was easier to change my shoes," Denton said, glancing down at his feet in embarrassment, as though McEwan's disclosure had made him seem ridiculous. "But as a matter of fact I've been thinking of starting the *Shanghai Star* again," he went on tentatively. "I'm waiting for Lily to come back, really, to see how she feels about it."

"Lily may never come back," Su-mei said in that distant voice in which she invariably spoke of Lily now, a voice that seemed to set her firmly in the past. "We haven't heard from her once in all those years."

"Well I'll wait and see about that," Denton said determinedly. He was still staring down at the club-like shape of his special shoes. "What I'd like to do is turn it into a national newspaper and sell it all over China. With an English language edition as well."

"Pish, man," McEwan said testily, drawing his brows together. "The Nationalists will never allow you to do that. Look what's happened to Shanghai since they took over. The time for all that was twenty years ago. Besides, you're too old for that kind of thing." He held his glass out to Ah Man, who was passing with a tray. "A double, please."

"I'm not as old as you are."

"Ay, but I'm leaving next year. And I can read the signs. We'll not be wanted here any longer. They'll squeeze us out now China's ruling the whole place. And a pretty mess they'll make of it—Isn't that so, Michael?" he asked as Michael and Jacob approached, still arguing.

Jacob's eyes were flashing with triumph, while Michael looked sullen, as though he'd been tricked out of victory.

"Isn't what so?" he asked unwillingly.

"Dr. McEwan says there'll be no place for us in Shanghai," Jenny said, "now we've given the foreign settlements back to them."

"Who is *us*?" Michael asked her ungraciously. "You or me?"

"Whatever you are," Jacob broke the sudden silence that followed, "Shanghai's not the place for business any more. Look at my factory—it might just as well be owned by the Japs still, for all the good it does me. Restrictions on this, licences for that, bribes here, bribes there...I'm moving to Hong Kong, Shanghai's finished."

"At your age and in your condition," McEwan grated irately, taking his whisky from Ah Man, "you should be thinking of retiring, not starting another business in Hong Kong."

"How could I retire?" Jacob gazed at him in astonishment. "There are two things I'll never give up—business and women."

McEwan's face was growing furiously red. "In your state of health it would be dangerous to have much of the first or any of the second," he rasped vehemently. "And I'm speaking as your doctor."

That night Denton woke up gasping for breath. He pushed himself up in the bed and sat upright till his breathing grew easier. It was as though something had been pushing up against his lungs, squeezing them, so that they couldn't open. When he lay down again, the same slow, steady, painless pressure returned. Within minutes he was suffocating again. He forced himself upright frantically. Again the pressure slowly relaxed and his pounding heart grew gratefully quieter as he breathed more easily. This time he waited longer. The night's silence lay like drifts of black snow over everything, over the bed and the room, over the river and the city. Far away a motor cycle stuttered; then a car passed, and he listened to its engine slowly fading away till the silence was complete and dense again. Su-mei lay sleeping peacefully, her hand lightly clasped by her cheek, frowning slightly. She wouldn't have frowned, he thought, when she was younger.

When he was convinced the fit, whatever it was, must be over, he let himself slowly down again. But once more he felt his breath getting gradually shallower and quicker, as that slow, relentless pressure squeezed his lungs. Within a few minutes he was gasping again. He forced himself up with the same helpless terror and waited desperately, clenching his hands, until once more the pressure blessedly let go.

He dared not lie down again. He got stealthily out of bed and sat in the armchair, resting his head against the wing and dozing apprehensively. When he woke, Su-mei was laying a quilt over him. Birds were chirping sleepily and the darkness was beginning to fade.

"What's the matter?" she asked. "You'll get cold."

"I couldn't sleep."

"Aren't you coming back to bed?"

"Not yet." He shivered suddenly under the quilt. "I'll stay here a bit longer."

She stood looking at him doubtfully, her glance straying down to his deformed feet peeping out under the quilt.

"Don't look at my feet like that," he said, tucking them in.

She held out her hand. "You'll feel better in bed."

He shook his head, closing his eyes to fend off any more questions. He knew that a new thing had entered his life, something that would never leave it, a quiet, gnawing fear that would lurk on the edge of his mind like a rat behind the wall of an old house.

She went back to bed, but she didn't sleep again, any more than he did. Her head was turned towards him, and she watched him secretly through her lashes.

"I'm prescribing ye some pills to take," McEwan said, putting his glasses on to write. "Three times a day after meals."

"What is it, then?" Denton asked, with an effort at jaunty carelessness. "What have I got?"

"You're heart's not as young as it was, that's all," he muttered without looking up. "Ye mustn't strain it." He scribbled his signature and tore the sheet off his pad.

792

Denton folded the prescription slowly as he got up. He wanted to know the name of his disease, how it would go on, how long he had, but at the same time he was scared of knowing, he wanted to stay ignorant, to avoid hearing his sentence. How strange that he'd been so indifferent to death in prison, and now he was afraid of it. But then in prison he'd had nothing to hope for, whereas now he had. He wanted to find Lily, to start the paper again, to help bring up Pak-kay. If he was going to die, fate should have let him die in prison when he didn't care.

"How long will I have to take these pills?" he asked, with the same assumed air of nonchalance.

"As long as ye live," McEwan said exasperatedly, glancing up over his glasses. "And you've to avoid any strain now," he went on severely. "I want to see ye again in a fortnight, we may need to adjust the dosage."

He'd ask what his disease was next time, Denton thought. There was plenty of time, he needn't know all at once.

97

Ah Man came into the kitchen carrying a long silvery fish, a rolled-up newspaper under his arm. "So many soldiers," he muttered. "They're digging trenches in all the parks." He dropped the fish on the draining-board and sat down at the table, spreading out the newspaper.

Ah Leng turned the wireless up louder. "Government forces are preparing to repel the communists," the announcer declared. "The enemy's forces will be decisively defeated..."

Pak-kay looked down at the fish. Its scales were still wet and shiny, its eyes bright and clear. He pushed his finger gently into its mouth, and felt the teeth sharp and light against his skin, like the teeth of a fine comb.

"If the communists come," Ah Leng said, switching off the wireless, "they'll throw all the foreign devils out. Or kill them."

Ah Man put on his glasses and pored over the paper while Ah Leng returned to her ironing. "I should ask Ah

King about that if I were you," he said at last as he turned the page. "She ought to know about these things."

Ah Leng spat on the iron, then thumped it down on the sheet she was pressing. "I suppose she knows when the reds will be here, then?" she asked ironically.

Ah Man shrugged. "Why don't you ask her?" He took his glasses off, folded them carefully and slipped them back into the pocket of his black cotton tunic. "*I* say the reds'll be here in two weeks. That what *I* say."

Ah Leng sniffed. "Want to bet?"

"Five dollars?"

"All right. Two weeks from today."

Ah Man smiled as he got up. He took the cleaver and started gutting the fish. "They say Pock-mark Chen's leaving," he said casually.

Ah Leng glanced up. "Who do?"

"In the market. They say he sent a whole plane-load of gold out last night, to Hong Kong. And women too."

Ah Leng's lips tightened, then she tossed her head. "They say anything in the market," she muttered disparagingly.

Pak-kay picked up the fish's severed head. "Can I give this to the cat, Ah Man?"

"No, that's for soup."

"Is Ah King's husband a communist?"

"You go and play outside," Ah Man said. "Who told you to listen in?"

"I can listen if I want to," he said loftily. "I can do what I like." But he did go outside, down to the bottom of the garden. A convoy of army lorries was driving along the Bund towards Garden Bridge. Some of them still had the old United States Army star on their doors. Pak-kay waved, but none of the soldiers in them waved back, though he was sure they saw him. They just stared at him blankly.

There were no more American ships in the harbour.

They saw Jacob off at the airport. He'd had a second stroke. It was the first, mild one that had given him his limp, but it wasn't until he had the second that McEwan told him he'd had one seven years before. One side of his face was paralysed now, and his speech was slightly slurred. His arm and leg were affected too, but he could still get about with the aid of a stick.

"You must come to Hong Kong," Jacob said in the airport lounge. The right half of his face was fixed in permanent mourning, while the other half compensated by quivering with extravagantly expressive life.

"I'm waiting for Lily," Denton said, glancing at Su-mei who, with her merciless realism, had given up waiting. All round them people were chattering nervously, gripping bulgy suitcases, thronging ticket counters and immigration desks. And in the distance they could hear once more the dull rumble of shell-fire.

"Lily is just the sort of person who wouldn't have written." Denton looked away from Jacob's lop-sided face. It reminded him of his own illness, though he still hadn't asked what exactly it was. "If we leave, we'll never find out. You don't know what it's like not to know."

Su-mei's eyelids flickered, but she didn't speak.

Jacob beckoned Denton closer. "My only regret is that I didn't have a girl last night," he muttered. "The last time in Shanghai." His good eye gleamed at Denton's startled look, while the other stayed hooded. "You think I can't any more?" He clutched Denton's arm in his, by now weak, bird-like grip. "That's what they think too, But then I surprise them."

"Your flight's being called," Su-mei said.

Jacob joined the shuffling, nudging, anxious crowd moving toward the gate.

"Michael will be there at the airport," Su-mei reminded him calmly.

"I hear the Weis aren't leaving?" Jacob asked, as he was about to pass through. His hand was trembling faintly.

"They're hoping to make another deal. Besides, old Wei's too frail to make the journey. Most of the family's in Hong Kong, though. Michael's met some of them there."

Jacob nodded, gripped Denton's arm a last time, pecked Su-mei's cheek—she turned her head away—and limped through. His good eye was watering.

"You could have let him kiss you once," Denton said. "He probably won't have another chance." He watched Jacob limping along until he turned a corner, and was gone.

"You know how I feel about him," she answered quietly. "I just couldn't let him slobber all over me. Not even now."

* * *

Denton walked cautiously down the steps from the airport building, Su-mei watchful by his side. As they neared the bottom, a large Cadillac swept to a halt and four men stepped out, fanning across the steps and glancing all round before the chauffeur opened the door. One of them was Yin-hong. Denton heard Su-mei draw in her breath.

Pock-mark Chen emerged, wearing dark glasses. He was older, but as gross as ever. He began mounting the steps, then saw them coming down. They had to meet.

"Mr. Denton," his voice wheezed, unsurprised. "so your foot are better. How is your son do in Hong Kong?" His tone was neither friendly nor hostile. It seemed to be just a bare voice, without any feeling at all. His expressionless face turned fractionally to take in Su-mei.

"You will go to Hong Kong yourself soon, I think?" his voice struggled on through the chesty entanglement of his catarrh. "The communist are come here in one week. I go myself today."

In one long second, Denton thought of his vast, pocked body on top of Su-mei's, of Michael's hand and his own maimed feet, even of Pak-kay's severed head. He felt his heart beating faster and felt his own impotence. Then he remembered how they'd fought outside the Customs Officers' Club.

Pock-mark's face was turned towards his, expectantly, the lenses of his glasses dark and blank. Denton felt his hands trembling at the thought of slapping Pock-mark's face as Lily's had been slapped in the theatre ten years before. He imagined the slap of his hand against that pale, bloated cheek.

"Remember Michael's in Hong Kong," Su-mei murmured tensely in English beside him.

He breathed in slowly and clenched his fists, then walked on without a word. The bodyguards' eyes followed them all the way to their car.

A few days later, the gold and silver in the bank of China's vaults was carried out onto lorries and driven down to the quayside. From his study window Denton watched it being loaded onto a Nationalist warship. Two more days and the communists were in the suburbs. It was exactly a week, as Pock-mark Chen had said.

There were one or two brief skirmishes, then some

gunfire by Garden Bridge as the Nationalist rearguard retreated onto the last of the ships that carried them off to Taiwan. A few hours later, people came back onto the streets to watch the soldiers of the Liberation Army take possession of the prize.

"They don't look bad," Su-mei stood by the window. "They're not bandits."

"Perhaps we'll hear from Lily now," he said.

98

"Ask him his name," the official said in Shanghainese.

"What is your name?" the interpreter asked in English.

"My name is Denton, you know that already," he answered in Shanghainese. "And I speak Chinese."

The interpreter, sitting on the left of the official, glanced from one to the other uneasily.

"Tell him to speak English," the official said, opening a file on the desk in front of him. He had short grey hair and a mole on his cheek, from which a long strand of hair sprouted, also grey.

"You must speak English," the interpreter said. He was young and wore rimless glasses. He looked embarrassed. His English had an American accent.

"Isn't that a waste of everybody's time?" Denton asked impatiently in Shanghainese.

The official was reading in the file. "Tell him we can't understand what he's saying," he said, stroking the hair on his mole.

"My name is Denton," Denton said quickly in English. "I'm trying to find my daughter. She worked for the party."

The official raised his head from the file while the interpreter translated. He looked straight past Denton's ear as though he didn't exist.

"Tell him to fill in the form," he muttered, returning to the file. "There are thousands of people looking for someone or other."

"I've filled in a form already," Denton interrupted the interpreter.

The official stopped reading to listen to the translation, then bent his head again. "In that case there's nothing more to do. We'll let him know if we find anything out." He turned a page and took out a document, reading it carefully while the interpreter translated, then passed it across the desk, "His exit permit," he said, returning to the file.

"This is your exit permit," the interpreter said.

"Exit permit? I haven't applied for an exit permit."

"Valid for three months," the official said. "If he doesn't use it he may not get another one. Tell him a lot of foreign devils aren't getting exit permits, but he's lucky, because he did one of our people a service once."

"I don't want to leave! I want to find my daughter." The image of the courtly, bushy-browed Chinese with Ah King's husband flickered through Denton's mind, the night Pock-mark Chen massacred the communists. Now he was their prime minister. "Do you know who it was I did a service to?"

"Tell him it was a party official."

"It was Chou En-lai."

The official shrugged. "Never mind who it was. That's why he's got an exit permit, tell him."

"I'll write to him."

"It would be no use." The official smiled at the idea.

"Why should I leave?"

"He doesn't have to leave. He's not being deported. But if he doesn't leave, he may not get another permit."

"I also did your people a service with the *Shanghai Star*."

"That's been considered too. That's why he's been granted permission to transfer his funds abroad as well. Tell him he's lucky."

"But I don't *want* to leave!"

"Get rid of him," the official said, closing the file. He took another one from the pile and opened that.

"What about my wife?"

"She can go too."

"But she's Chinese."

"She doesn't have to go."

"I won't go till I find out what's happened to my daughter."

"The interview is over," the official said.

It was in the old town hall, where Denton had first spoken as a municipal councillor.

"You should have let me go," Su-mei told him when he got home.

"I thought as a foreign devil they might take more notice of me." He rolled a tablet out onto the palm of his hand.

"Those days are over." she said, without pride.

He tossed the tablet into the back of his throat and gulped it down with some tea. "Perhaps they just want a bribe?"

"I'll go tomorrow."

But she came back with the same answer.

"They just don't want us to find out," she said.

99

"I can't come to the house," he said. "People would get suspicious."

Ah King glanced round her husband's office. It was a small bare room, with a large picture of Mao Tse-tung on the wall behind him. There was writing under the picture, in big red characters. And a sheaf of documents on the desk. "So you learnt to read and write," she said ruminatively, as though she'd only just realised it. "See what it's done for you."

He stirred impatiently on his chair, reaching for the glass of tea that stood half-empty on the corner of his desk. His hair had gone grey and his face was creased round the eyes and mouth. He was still tall and square-shouldered, but thinner, almost gaunt.

"What do you do here all day?" she asked. "Why can't you come to the house?"

"I'm too busy. Besides, I've just told you, it's not good for me to be seen going to a foreign devil's house."

"Busy at what?" she looked at the documents wonderingly. "What d'you do?"

"Never mind that. Important work." He put the glass down carefully in the same place and wiped his mouth with the back of his hand. "And you'll have to leave them too."

"Leave them? Leave who?"

"The foreign devils!" he said irritably. "Stop working for them."

"Why?" she stared at him amazed. "What am I going to live on? How often have you sent me money?"

"Shh! D'you want everyone to hear?" He leant forward over the desk, speaking swiftly and angrily in a low, hissing voice. "Now listen, will you, you stupid bitch? I've got enough trouble as it is explaining away a son who works for Pock-mark Chen. If my wife goes on working for foreign devils now, after liberation, I'll really be in the shit."

"Liberation!" Ah King said, as if she was going to spit.

"How d'you know they aren't spies anyway?"

"My master a spy?"

"And don't call him master! Haven't you got any pride? Those are the people that sucked China dry for a hundred years!"

"Well, they pay me good wages anyway," Ah King said flatly.

"They can afford to! It's money they've stolen from China. They've lorded it for long enough. Remember how they hit you with the shotgun pellets? I've never forgotten."

"It was an accident, wasn't it?" she muttered sullenly.

"Accident? It was part of their fun!" He leant back slowly. His habitual moroseness seemed to have turned into a stern, bitter fury. "You leave them. I'll fix you up with another job. Understand? Otherwise—"

The door opened and a man with cropped hair and a round, cheerful face peered round the edge. "Oh. Busy, eh?"

"No comrade, just finished." He sounded uneasy. "I'll be right along."

"Hurry up then. We're late already, and there are a lot to get through."

"Otherwise what?" Ah King asked coldly as the door closed.

"Otherwise I can force you to leave." He glared at Ah King for some seconds. "I can say they're exploiting you," his eyes narrowed and gleamed faintly. "I can get them in big trouble. How do we know he isn't a spy, that Denton? No, I can't have a wife who works for foreign devils!" he whispered fiercely as she opened her mouth to protest. "I'll find you another job."

*   *   *

She walked down the alley of the letter-writers. There were only two old men sitting there now, reading the paper, their awnings unfurled to shade them from the sun. One of them, sitting on his foot, his sandal on the ground beneath his stool, glanced up at her as she passed. "Haven't you got a letter for me to write, comrade?" he asked, scratching his foot.

"Who would I write letters to?" she muttered peevishly.

He blinked at her with watery eyes, then looked back at the paper with a shrug, still absently scratching his foot. "You've got a husband somewhere, haven't you?" he asked mildly. "Or a son?"

"What would you know about that?" She threw him a sour look and walked on.

The alleys were all emptier than usual and some of the little shops were closed. Not that they had anything much to sell these days, but at least they were usually open and the wireless blasting out the latest news and propaganda while the kids ate their rice.

There was a shop selling fruit though, and she stopped to buy a papaya. "Where is everyone?" she asked the woman as she paid.

"They've got one of those mass trials on. Of the Nationalist spies." She dropped the money in a tin box. "In Foochow Road."

Ah King walked on. She'd never been to a mass trial, though Ah Man had read out reports about them in the paper. At the end of the alley, she hesitated. Then, instead of turning right towards the river, she crossed the street towards Foochow Road. She was in no hurry to go back anyway, she couldn't think what she was going to tell master.

"But why d'you want to leave now?" Denton asked resentfully. "Why so suddenly?"

"It's too much work," she said gruffly, staring past him out of the window. "I'm too old. You can get someone else, someone younger."

"I don't want anyone else!" He glanced at the little white scar in her cheek from the time when the Palace Hotel was bombed. He felt she knew he was watching her and was purposely staring away out of the window, refusing to meet his eyes.

"Is anyone ill?" he asked. "One of your grandchildren?"

"Nobody's ill," she answered tonelessly. "I'm too old, that's all."

"That doesn't make sense."

She shrugged. "I'm giving one month's notice."

Denton frowned down at his special shoes. He'd never get used to that truncated shape. "I was thinking of raising your wage..." he began.

"It's not money," she said woodenly. "I have to go, that's all."

"Have to? Why?"

She pressed her lips together. "I want to."

"You said have to. You've been with me for forty years—."

"Forty-four," she muttered sourly.

He raised his hands helplessly, following her obstinate gaze out of the window. There were only a couple of cargo vessels in the harbour, berthed at what used to be the Blue Funnel wharves. Now they'd simply been given numbers. It was part of the drabness of the new regime imposed on everything.

"Forty-four, then," he said. "And from one minute to the next you suddenly decide to leave? This morning when you went out you had no thought of it. And as soon as you come back—What happened?" His bewilderment began to change to suspicion. "Has anyone been getting at you?"

Her lids flickered. She glanced at him uncertainly, then away out of the window again. "I saw my husband," she said reluctantly at last. "He's something high up, in an office. He told me I've got to leave. Otherwise he'll be in trouble, his wife working for a foreign devil..."

Denton leant back, blowing a long, sighing breath out of his mouth. "I see..." He looked away out of the window again. A dull grey gunboat was steaming up the river, an enormous red flag fluttering at its stern. "Does he remember I saved his life once?" he asked bitterly.

She shook her head. "He only remembers bad things. He remembers how your friends made fun of him once, when the shotgun pellets hit me."

It was the first time either of them had mentioned that incident, in all the years she'd been with him. "They weren't my friends," he said quickly. "They weren't my friends at all."

802

She knew that, but she shrugged. "To him they were your friends. That's all that matters. And then later this morning, on the way back from his office, I saw them holding a mass trial. They said they were Nationalist spies. And he was doing it, he was one of the ones in charge."

"Who was? Your husband?"

She nodded. "Perhaps he had to do it, perhaps it was his duty. But he was enjoying it. I could see he was enjoying it. They just shouted at these people and then they took them away and shot them. You could see the shooting if you wanted to."

He watched the wisps of dark smoke streaming from the gunboat's funnel, shredded by the breeze that was kicking up waves on the muddy water. "Would you like to leave Shanghai?" he asked suddenly. "Go to Hong Kong, where Michael is?"

She shook her head. "They'd never let me go, the wife of a party official. There's nothing I can do, I'll have to leave you. Otherwise..." she recalled her husband's words. *"I can get them in big trouble."* She turned to him with sudden urgency. "It's you who must leave Shanghai! This place isn't good for you any more!"

"Not till I've found out about Lily, Ah King. I'm the only one who believes she's still alive."

He was in the study a few days later when Su-mei came back from her weekly visit to inquire for news of Lily. The fan was stirring his hair. He was listening to the record of *Aida*, his eyes closed. The needle was worn and there were deep scratches across the grooves, but he heard what used to be there, not the rough, tinny sounds that actually came from the speaker. He opened his eyes as she closed the door.

"Any news?"

"Not of Lily." Her voice, and the way she looked at him, hinted at something else.

He got up and walked to the gramophone, wincing at the pain that he sometimes felt in his feet.

"Old Wei's dead," she said as he lifted off the arm. She spoke in a calm, remote voice. "He jumped off the roof of the Wei Building."

"What?"

"They arrested Philip apparently. And old Wei jumped off the roof."

803

"How d'you know?"

"I came past soon after. I must have just missed it, they hadn't even taken him away yet. There was a crowd of people, and some police and...His head was smashed in."

"How could he possibly have got there onto the roof?" Denton sat down slowly, thinking of Wei's head crushed like a wrinkled walnut. "He was an invalid!"

Su-mei shrugged. "Some woman said she saw it happen. One of those nosey women they put in charge of the buildings now. Someone must have helped him—Third Wife, I suppose."

Next morning, in a little corner of the *People's Daily*, there was a report of the suicide of the capitalist and Japanese collaborator Wei, whose son had recently been arrested. *To avoid interrogation himself,* the report said, *he persuaded his wife to help him jump off the roof of the building in which his notorious capitalist and counter-revolutionary schemes had been hatched. His wife is being questioned.*

"We must get out," Su-mei said, while Ah King, in her best white tunic and black trousers, cleared the breakfast table with a rigid face. "How many more warnings do you need? Can't you see it's all over?"

"We've got to find out about Lily," he answered obstinately. "Once we leave here, we'll never know. Besides, the Weis were collaborators, and mixed up with the KMT."

"If they want to get you," Su-mei said, shaking her head, "d'you think they won't be able to find an excuse?"

100

Denton took Pak-kay's hand and led him through the kitchen into the garden. Ah King was hanging up the washing. Three weeks of her notice had gone, and still she was wearing her best tunic and trousers, as though she were going to a funeral. And her face too, as she stretched up to the line, was taut and grim, unsmiling as a mute's.

"We must find an English name for you," Denton said to Pak-kay, leaning on his stick to look up at the dried,

804

twisted bauhinia pods. It was May, time for them to fall. "I suppose your mother would like Patrick..."

"Pat-rick," the boy repeated.

Denton gazed down at the grass, dappled with shadows from the leaves. "I don't care much for that name myself, though," he murmured. He walked on down the garden. Pak-kay glanced appealingly at Ah King, but she grimaced at him ferociously, her teeth clenched on three pegs, nodding him peremptorily after his grandfather. He sighed loudly and walked along behind him, following all the way to the old wooden seat.

Denton eased himself down, stretched out his legs, and laid his stick across his knees. He patted the seat beside him, and Pak-kay sat there, his hands under his knees, kicking his feet rhythmically together. The river gleamed with a dull, yellowish sheen from the morning sun. A rusty tanker was pushing its way slowly upstream, while a few junks and sampans drifted down past it, their sails flapping idly in the calm. Below Denton, in the old Public Gardens, people strolled along the paths, men and women alike wearing washed-out blue cotton clothes. A torrent of bicycles flowed down the Bund, parting to wash round the trams and bushes. The tram bells clanged uselessly against the flood.

"When you were born," Denton said slowly, "the streets used to be full of cars and lorries. And there were thousands of rickshaws too. And everyone wore bright clothes."

The boy glanced up at him expectantly.

"Of course there were lots of beggars as well..."

Pak-kay's eyes dulled. Was that all? He began to look round restlessly. Denton noticed, smiled and shrugged. "Well, never mind..." He felt for the toy bus that had stayed wedged between the bars all these years. "Here," he tugged at it. "Here's something for you to play with."

Neither of them could move it at first, but then Denton levered it out with a stick. It was rusty and dented, and the wheels wouldn't turn. Denton held it in his palm a minute before giving it to Pak-kay. "It used to belong to your uncles," he said, turning it this way and that. "They all played with it when they were children. Two of them are dead now. There's only Michael left."

Pak-kay took it politely with both hands and peered

inside the windows. It was empty. No seats, no floor, no driver. He felt let down.

"One day you'll go to London and see buses like that," his strange old grandfather said.

Pak-kay frowned, wondering whether London buses were old and rusty and had no seats. He tried to turn the wheels, pressing down hard on the roof as he pushed it along the arm of the bench. But they were jammed solid, they merely scraped along without turning.

"Mind you don't break it," his grandfather said. "Ask Ah Cheong for some oil."

Denton looked out over the Bund as Pak-kay's feet retreated up the path. It was only nine o'clock, but the sun was too hot already. He'd go inside a minute. A bauhinia pod cracked as it fell to the ground behind him. So they were falling; soon they'd all be dropping down, snapping like tiny firecrackers. He took out Michael's latest letter and read it through again. It was a stilted letter, as if he'd had to dredge his mind for things to say. Denton recalled all those dutiful letters he himself had written to his mother, getting harder and harder to write as he grew year by year more distant from her. It must be the same with Michael. They'd never be at ease with each other again. But then they hadn't been for years. It wasn't new. He'd always kept himself private and concealed, behind locked gates. Only Su-mei was allowed in. Or forced her way in. And Denton himself had been just the same. Michael was merely taking after him. If anyone ever wrote the story of my life, he thought wrily, they'd call me Denton, never John. And the same with Michael.

There was one thing Michael had written though that was spontaneous. Denton held the letter out at arm's length to read it—he was long-sighted now.

Pock-mark Chen has bought a whole stretch of property along the waterfront. He's supposed to have had a heart attack though (at last!) and nobody ever sees him. But I ran into Yin-hong in the street the other day. I wouldn't have recognised him, but he stopped me and introduced himself. He said he was in business, but didn't say what. Something shady, no doubt. He looked very flashy. You remember when I was kidnapped I thought I saw him once? Talking to him on the street I suddenly felt certain I really did see him. I think

*we were both remembering it. Oh well, I don't suppose he
could have had much to do with it, and it's a long time ago
now. You know Jacob Ephraim's married again, I expect?*

Denton folded the letter again slowly, pinching the
creases between his nails. He assumed all his mail was
opened by the secret police. He wondered what they made
of it. What would they think of the reference to Pock-
mark Chen for instance? He imagined it being noted
down meticulously in some dossier. Yes, he remembered
Michael's mentioning Yin-hong when he came back,
mentioning him shyly as if he'd been afraid he might get
into trouble. He remembered the day of his return and
the day of the kidnap. He remembered coming home to
see the police cars in the drive and the front door open.
He remembered it all, but no longer with the same intensity. It was as though he'd been a spectator at those scenes
now, not a participant. All his memories seemed to be like
that these days. They weren't vague or less detailed, but
more detached, as though he wasn't involved in them any
more. Am I taking leave of life? he wondered.

He looked down at the Public Gardens again. The
azaleas were just coming into bloom. Some PLA soldiers
were walking towards them in their drab, shapeless
uniforms. One by one they disappeared behind the
flowering bushes where the lady with the little girl had
disappeared all those years ago. Now the last one was
gone. And already the first was emerging the other side.
But the lady and the little girl with her hoop, they'd
never reappeared. A tram clanged its bell in the road
below, and he heard some more bauhinia pods cracking
behind him.

If only he could find out about Lily. He wouldn't
mind leaving Shanghai then. Su-mei was right, it was all
over. The city was dying. For better or worse, it was
dying.

And then he saw her. He saw Lily. She was wearing
the same blue tunic and trousers that they all wore now,
walking along the path where the soldiers had just gone.
She was going away from him, but he was sure it was her.
It was her walk, her hair, just lighter than black, her way
of carrying her head with that challenging lift of the chin.
She was older of course, but there was no doubt it was

her. In a few seconds she'd be behind the azaleas and he'd have lost her.

He called out to her urgently. She turned her head. Yes, it *was* her. She gazed up inquiringly, her face a little thinner, but with the same promise of beauty that had never quite been fulfilled, the same light in her eyes, at once open and severe. Now she saw him, she raised her hand, she began to smile in recognition. And as she smiled her face grew misty, her face turned slowly into the face of the woman in *rue* Molière, the woman with the little girl who had also walked in the Public Gardens.

"What was that master just said?" Ah King asked, carrying the empty clothes basket past Pak-kay.

Pak-kay shook his head. Oil dripped off the wheels onto the path, making round shiny little spots. He set the bus down and forced it along. The harder he pressed, the more the wheels began to turn, in grudging, grinding little jerks. He pressed harder still. Suddenly the bus lurched beneath his hand and one side collapsed. He held it up anxiously. The axle had snapped.

"*Mind you don't break it,*" he remembered his grandfather saying. He walked slowly, guiltily back down the path and stood in front of the old man, holding it out. "It's broken," he said contritely. "I put lots of oil on it, but it broke."

His grandfather didn't move.

"It's broken," he said more loudly.

Still he didn't move. Pak-kay regarded him silently for some seconds, then softly put the bus down on the seat beside him. Holding his breath, he tiptoed away. When he reached the bauhinia trees, he began stepping on the fallen brown pods that lay dry and twisted on the path. They cracked under his feet like dead twigs in winter. Cheong smiled under his round straw hat from the edge of the lawn, but Pak-kay didn't smile back.

"Grandfather's asleep," he announced when he reached the kitchen. "The bus broke."

Ah King was just setting some rice on to boil. "You can't even get any good rice now," she muttered irritably as she slapped the lid on the saucepan. Ah Man glanced up from the newspaper he'd spread out on the table, his glasses perched on the end of his nose.

"Where's Ah Leng?" Pak-kay said, his lip suddenly

trembling. "It wasn't my fault it broke. He won't talk to me, he's asleep with his eyes open."

Ah King paused, looked closely at Pak-kay, who was blinking back tears now, glanced at Ah Man, and hurried out, wiping her hands down her trousers. She walked more slowly as she approached Denton, treading stealthily, afraid she'd wake him if he really was asleep. She heard Ah Man muttering to Cheong behind her.

Denton had slumped down on the seat now, his eyes stilled in a look of pleased surprise.

A few weeks after the funeral, a letter arrived, addressed to Denton and Su-mei. Su-mei recognised Lily's hand at once. She took it up into the study to read. Lily was in the northeast, in Sinkiang. She'd been ill, but she was better now. She sent her love. She'd come when she could, but at present her unit couldn't spare her. She wanted to know how Pak-kay was. She'd written several times, but never had an answer—had they got her letters? As soon as she got leave, she'd come to Shanghai and take Pak-kay back with her. It was rough, but he'd get used to it...

Su-mei sat a long time in Denton's chair, gazing down at the Bund, the letter in her hand. She thought of Lily's inflexible idealism, of the primitive wastes of Sinkiang, of the years that she and Ah Leng had spent bringing up Pak-kay, during the war and after it. She thought of Denton's affection for him.

She folded the letter and put it in the envelope which held Pak-kay's birth certificate and Lily's letter of the night before the Japanese takeover, appointing Denton and Su-mei joint guardians of her son.

Three weeks later she left with Ah Leng to join Michael in Hong Kong. It was almost the last day of her exit permit. They'd renewed it once, but they said they wouldn't renew it again.

She took Pak-kay with her.

She didn't answer Lily's letter until she was safe in Hong Kong, when she told her what had happened and what she'd done.

She never heard from Lily again.

Epilogue

Years later, Michael sailed up the Whampoa in a Chinese boat, on a business trip to the People's Republic. It was his first visit since the communists took over. The warm, moist, luminous clouds of April drifted across a calm blue sky. He looked out at the city from the rail of the ship, while an armed guard watched him suspiciously in case he dared to take a photograph. The buildings were all there— the banks, the Club, the Customs House, the hotels. They all looked the same, only dowdy and drab, put to other uses, like aristocrats dispossessed and fallen on hard times. The harbour, he noticed, was silting up, and the solitary dredger didn't look as though it was going to make much difference.

Yes, he thought, gripping his brief-case as the ship tied up, the city was the same, the muddy waters, the reddish banks downstream and the green rice paddies. His father would still have known the place. But it was like a shell discarded on the beach, emptied of its life now. The passions, the greeds, the lusts, the ambitions that had burned so intensely there were all extinguished now, and the city was as cold as his father's grave. He lies in his grave and his grave lies in the grave of his city, he thought in a rare leap of poetic extravagance.

He had endless talks with officials, and dinners every evening. He scarcely had time to walk about the streets round his hotel at night—the Peace Hotel, that used to be the Cathay.

On his last day an old woman approached him outside the hotel. She had grey hair and a drawn, bony face with a little scar on the cheek, but she walked with the same upright, slightly splay-footed gait, and he knew her at once. Ah King took him to his father's grave which was next to Jonathan's, and talked in gruff apologetic tones about the house on the Bund, which was now a workers' hostel. She seemed to blame herself for that, because her husband had been in the housing department when they decided what to do with it. She apologised, too, for being unable to show him Alec's grave—not because it was too far, but because it had vanished under a new factory. Michael had to attend a farewell dinner, so they parted early in the evening. Before he left her he asked about the other servants, whom he sent money every year under the terms of his father's will. They had all gone back to their villages. Had she ever seen or heard of Lily? She shook her head. Ah King didn't mention Yin-hong, but on the steps of the hotel, which she wasn't allowed to enter, she did ask about his mother.

"She died last year," he told her, and went on hurriedly about Pak-kay, who had just finished the public school in England where Alec and he had gone, and where his own children, whose mother was the tall daughter of Philip Wei, would soon be going.

He didn't tell her how Su-mei had died. The doctors found she had cancer of the jaw, and recommended radical surgery. They talked soothingly about rebuilding her face after the operation.

"At seventy-five?" she asked witheringly. She had never trusted western medicine.

That night she swallowed all her opium. It must have been hard; it had become painful for her to swallow anything at all. She wrote a note saying that she wanted to be cremated, put on her best nightgown and went to bed.

When Ah Leng found her in the morning, her face, though drawn, was still smooth and unravaged.

ABOUT THE AUTHOR

CHRISTOPHER NEW was born in Britain and was educated there at Oxford University and then at Princeton University in the United States. Mr. New has traveled widely, spending a great deal of time in Indonesia, Europe, Russia and Asia. He currently lives in Hong Kong with his wife and three children. Mr. New is Professor of Philosophy at the University of Hong Kong.